New from Harlequin Romance
a very special six-book series by

The town of Hard Luck, Alaska, needs women!

The O'Halloran brothers, who run a bush-plane service called **Midnight Sons,** are heading a campaign to attract women to Hard Luck. ***(Location: north of the Arctic Circle. Population: 150—mostly men!)***

"Debbie Macomber's *Midnight Sons* series is a delightful romantic saga. And each book is a powerful, engaging story in its own right. Unforgettable!"
—Linda Lael Miller

TITLE IN THE MIDNIGHT SONS SERIES:

#3379 BRIDES FOR BROTHERS (available in October 1995)
#3383 THE MARRIAGE RISK (available in November 1995)
#3387 DADDY'S LITTLE HELPER (available in December 1995)
#3395 BECAUSE OF THE BABY (available in February 1996)
#3399 FALLING FOR HIM (available in March 1996)
#3404 ENDING IN MARRIAGE (available in April 1996)

DMS-1

When danger lurks in the shadows and you don't know who you can trust, you need—

Caine O'Bannion lived to serve his country, but his job description didn't include baby-sitting visiting royalty. Unless, of course, the royalty in question was a gorgeous princess named Chantal.

Shasta Masterson knew she was the perfect woman for Kane Stone. Now all she had to do was keep him alive long enough to prove it to him.

Logan McNeill was on a routine assignment—to check out the estranged wife of a suspected spy. But soon he found himself on the run, protecting the very woman he'd been sent to investigate.

Keeping watch—day and night

Relive the romance....

Three complete novels by your favorite authors!

About the Authors

JoAnn Ross—JoAnn Ross, a favorite among Harlequin readers, is best known for her versatility. This talented author has written family sagas, romantic fantasy and even glitz and glamour.JoAnn is the author of over fifty novels, and has more than eight million copies of her books in print.

Evelyn A. Crowe—Evelyn A. Crowe worked for twelve years as a media director in an advertising company before turning her hand to writing in 1983. Now her bestselling books are favorites with readers around the world. Evelyn makes her home in Houston, Texas.

Pamela Bauer—Award-winning author Pamela Bauer has gained many fans worldwide for her heartwarming stories. Pamela often takes a lighthearted approach as she explores the relationships between friends, families—and, of course, lovers. Pamela lives in Minnesota with her husband and two children.

JoANN ROSS
EVELYN A. CROWE
PAMELA BAUER

Harlequin Books

TORONTO • NEW YORK • LONDON
AMSTERDAM • PARIS • SYDNEY • HAMBURG
STOCKHOLM • ATHENS • TOKYO • MILAN
MADRID • WARSAW • BUDAPEST • AUCKLAND

HARLEQUIN BOOKS

by Request—The Bodyguard

ISBN 0-373-20117-6

This edition published by arrangement with Harlequin Books S.A.

Printed in U.S.A.

CONTENTS

He specialized in
around-the-clock surveillance.

GUARDED MOMENTS

JoAnn Ross

1

HER NAME WAS CHANTAL, from the French form of the Latin *cantus,* meaning "a song."

The very sound of it conjured up scenes of Parisian nightlife: smoky cafés, boisterous bistros and the lively music halls of Montmartre. Any woman graced with such a musical name was expected to be forever bright, beguiling and beautiful. In every respect, Princess Chantal Giraudeau de Montacroix did not disappoint.

As the celebrated love child of American film star Jessica Thorne and Prince Eduard Giraudeau, the tragically married regent of the tiny European principality of Montacroix, Chantal's birth twenty-nine years ago had made headlines. When she was five, as flower girl at her parents' formal wedding, she succeeded in capturing the heart of the world. She was, one particularly ebullient society columnist declared, the quintessential fairy-tale princess.

Through the years, she proceeded to lead a jet-set existence that brought her both scandal and fame. During her teens, she flirted with the European film industry, captivating audiences with her world-weary dark eyes and childlike pout. At twenty, she became engaged to the French director and star of her latest film; their subsequent battles fueled the columns until the inevitable breakup six months later.

Unsurprisingly, the movie, when released, was an international hit. No one seemed to care that the plot was nonexistent or that critics had unanimously panned the film. Fans flocked to the theaters in droves for an opportunity to watch the ill-fated pair's passionate love scenes. It was voyeurism, pure and simple, but as P.T. Barnum had discovered so long ago, voyeurism sold one helluva lot of tickets.

While soothing her broken heart at the French ski championships at Chamonix, Chantal fell madly and publicly in love with one of the sun-bronzed, devil-may-care Scandinavians who flocked to the Alps each winter. When the passionate romance ended with the season, Chantal drifted down to the Greek isles, where she was reported to have fallen in love with an heir to a shipping fortune, who, according to the ever-vigilant tabloids, she subsequently dumped for an Italian count.

Her highly publicized romances continued to scandalize Europe until, at the ripe old age of twenty-five, she eloped with an American race car driver who had taken the Grand Prix by storm. If the marriage came as a shock to her long-suffering parents, the subsequent announcement that Chantal was now retiring from the social whirl in order to direct all her energies toward becoming an ideal wife and mother stunned everyone who knew her. Not so surprising was her divorce two years later.

CAINE O'BANNION'S FROWN deepened to a scowl as he flipped through the various news clippings he'd been handed immediately upon entering the office. There was probably no one in the civilized world who wouldn't recognize the stunning face instantly. Just this morning it had smiled at him from a supermarket tabloid as he'd bought a jar of instant coffee and a package of frozen bagels.

"I don't understand," he said finally. "What does some jet-set princess have to do with me?"

"Patience, Caine." The man on the other side of the wide mahogany desk banged the bowl of his pipe into an ashtray to dislodge the tobacco. "Everything will become clear in the proper time."

Silence hovered over the room like a cloud. The only sign of Caine's building frustration was the flash of irritation in his gray eyes as he automatically reached into his suit jacket pocket for a cigarette; he'd quit smoking during his enforced stay in the hospital two months ago. Times were definitely changing, he considered with grim humor, when an assassination attempt could prove beneficial to a guy's health.

His gaze drifted out the window. After a bleak and particularly harsh winter, Washington's weather had suddenly turned unreasonably balmy, bringing with it the heady promise of spring. The Japanese cherry trees surrounding the Tidal Basin were in full bloom, looking like fluffy pink clouds against a clear blue sky.

But Caine's awareness was focused not on the weather or the bright blossoms. He turned back to the man who was currently jamming a fuzzy yellow wire into the briar stem of his pipe—his superior, James Sebring, Presidential Security director.

"May I say that you're certainly looking well, Caine," the director said.

"Thank you, sir. I'm feeling quite well."

"Good. I hear that you're eager to get back to work."

Caine decided that "eager" didn't begin to describe his feelings. "Let's just say I've discovered that I'm not cut out for a life of leisure."

Sebring held the pipe up, peering into the long, narrow stem as he twisted the pipe cleaner with practiced movements. "Still, you don't want to rush healing."

"I certainly wouldn't ask to be returned to active duty if I wasn't fit to perform capably, sir."

The older man raised a snowy eyebrow at Caine's atypically gritty tone. "No one is questioning your professionalism, Caine. By the way, I've been meaning to ask, how is your mother?"

Caine reminded himself that he was a patient man: all too often his career demanded that. But no one, he thought in exasperation, could draw out a conversation longer than James Sebring.

"Mom's fine, sir," he said, knowing that nothing would be gained by not playing alone. "She framed my medal and hung it on the wall next to Dad's Medal of Honor and his Purple Heart."

Caine had been eleven years old when Alan O'Bannion, a crack naval aviator, had been shot down over Vietnam. All his memories of his father, sketchy as they were, were of a strong, brave, larger-than-life man. There were times, in his rare introspective moments, that Caine wondered if he hadn't spent the twenty-two years since his father's death trying to live up to those memories. Trying to be the man Alan O'Bannion would have wanted his son to be.

"She's a lovely woman, your mother," the director said. "I was pleased to meet her at the ceremony."

Small talk. Normally Caine enjoyed an opportunity for these little one-to-one chats with his superior. But today it was driving him crazy.

"I got the feeling that little piece of bronze meant a great deal more to your mother than it does to you," Sebring said.

"I was just doing my job," Caine insisted, not for the first time since what he'd begun to think of as *the incident*. "That doesn't make me a hero."

"Try telling that to the rest of the nation." After tapping the loose tobacco down, Sebring lit it, and with a satisfied expression, leaned back in his chair and began puffing. "Although the Presidential Security manual may state that an agent is expected to step in front of a bullet meant for his commander in chief, those individuals not under such an obligation considered your behavior an extreme act of heroism."

Sebring's gaze reflected concern as he looked from Caine's impassive face to his injured shoulder. "So, how are you really feeling?" he asked again. Before Caine could answer, the director held up his hand. "The truth this time."

For one brief instant, Caine was tempted to lie. "I still get a few twinges," he admitted, "when I first get up in the morning. But after I work out, it's fine."

"I'm glad to hear that. By the way, I received the report from the attending physician at Walter Reed this morning."

Caine forced down a flare of anxiety, but outwardly he remained completely calm. "And?"

"Dr. Lansing's opinion seems to second your self-diagnosis." He brushed at the ashes that fell onto his slacks. "So, it looks as if you're back on active duty."

Believing the interview to be over, Caine rose from his chair. "Thank you, sir. I'm looking forward to accompanying the president on his upcoming trip."

"That won't be necessary."

A frown furrowed Caine's brow. Next week's economic summit had been months in the planning. "Has the Mexican conference been called off?"

"No. The president is still going to Mexico, as planned. But I'm afraid you're not."

A giant hand began to squeeze Caine's gut. For the past eighteen months he had been privileged to work on the plum presidential detail; he couldn't believe that he'd been called into his superior's office this morning to be demoted.

"I see." He remained military rigid: neck and shoulders, back, jaw.

"No, my boy," James Sebring said patiently. "I don't believe you do. Please, sit back down."

Not one to disobey an order, no matter how badly he wanted to leave the suddenly stifling confines of the office, Caine returned to his chair. This time, however, instead of sitting back comfortably, he perched on the very edge. Patience be damned.

"You asked what a European princess had to do with you," the director reminded him needlessly. "Well, I'm about to tell you. First of all, what do you know about Montacroix?"

Caine tried to recall the European history course he'd taken during his midshipman years at Annapolis. "As I recall, it's a small principality, purchased by the Giraudeau family from the French government shortly after Napoleon's disastrous Russian campaign in 1812. Principal industries are banking, tourism, with a steady growth in wine production. The per capita income is among the highest in the world, taxes among the lowest."

"Do you know that Montacroix is also one of our strongest economic allies?"

"Yes, sir," Caine answered, wondering where this little history lesson was leading.

"Then it should come as no surprise that the United States cares very much about the security of the Montacroix government."

"No surprise at all, sir." Caine glanced down at the manila folder he was still holding, curious about where the jet-setting princess came in.

"Eduard Giraudeau and his wife are also close personal friends of the president," the director continued. "As are Prince Burke and the princesses Chantal and Noel."

"I see," Caine murmured with a thoughtful frown, liking this conversation less and less. For the second time since entering the office, he wished he hadn't stopped smoking.

"You may have read about our cultural exchange program with certain foreign governments."

The words sparked an image in Caine's mind of the headline on that tabloid at the checkout stand. "Batten Down the Hatches. America Prepares for Hurricane Chantal." Hell, Caine thought darkly as comprehension dawned, after eighteen months of providing personal security for the president of the United States, he was being demoted to the role of executive baby-sitter.

"'Certain foreign governments' meaning Montacroix." Ominous storm clouds swirled in his gray eyes—a warning signal Sebring ignored.

"You always were an astute young man, Caine. As it happens, Chantal Giraudeau will be touring our country with the royal Montacroix art exhibit. My wife, who is quite an expert on such things, assures me that it's an extraordinary collection of modern European art. There are also several works by youngsters who are the beneficiaries of Chantal's favorite charity, the Rescue the Children Fund, for which she'll be seeking donations. I'm told that as a special drawing card, the exhibit also includes several works by the princess herself."

Caine wasn't surprised. The princess could probably paint like a baboon with a fistful of crayons and still get her work exhibited. Who in the hell would be brave enough to turn her down when her daddy owned not only the gallery, but the entire country, as well? "She'll be touring the country? For how long?"

"Chantal is scheduled to be here for three weeks."

"I assume she'll be accompanied by her own security force," Caine said with a studied calm he was a long way from feeling.

Sebring sighed. Caine waited.

"Chantal is a lovely young woman," the director said finally. "Unfortunately, she is also incredibly strong willed." Before he could elaborate, the disembodied voice of his secretary came over the intercom, telling him that the White House was calling. "Just one moment," he said to Caine as he picked up the receiver. "Director Sebring here.... Of course I'll hold for the president."

Caine listened as his superior assured the nation's chief executive that the princess would be well protected during her tour. Then, as the topic of conversation shifted to the president's upcoming trip to Mexico—the trip Caine would not be taking—he glanced down at clippings he held. A cover photo from *People* magazine was on the top of the pile.

The photograph had been taken during a ski trip in the Montacroix Alps. Her face, surrounded by a hood of lush Russian lynx, was undeniably exquisite, possessing high, slanted cheekbones any *Vogue* model would kill for. The color of burnt sugar, her eyes were both sultry and mischievous at the same time; the teasing smile she directed at the camera was designed to turn the most stalwart of men to putty.

She was beautiful, he admitted reluctantly, recalling the old adage about pretty is as pretty does. From what he had read about Chantal Giraudeau through the years, it was obvious that the princess's beauty was only skin-deep.

As James Sebring discussed motorcade security with the president, Caine scanned the rest of the photos. There were several shots of Princess Chantal on the beach at Monaco, scantily clad in a piece of string that would have gotten her arrested in all forty-eight of the contiguous United States, along with Hawaii and Alaska. There was another of Chantal wearing a strapless, midnight blue velvet evening gown designed to display her lush curves to advantage. Diamonds twinkled at her throat and ears, and a diamond the size of Rhode Island gleamed from the ring finger of her left hand.

There were a series of photos taken during her time on the Montacroix Olympic dressage team, seated astride a horse, a little velvet cap perched jauntily atop her sleek dark hair. It seemed this woman couldn't take a bad picture.

Of all the complimentary photographs, the one that captured his attention the longest was one of Chantal laughing merrily, her head thrown back as she frolicked through an alpine meadow, clad in a full-skirted, enticingly low-necked, flower-sprigged dress that made her look like a half-wild shepherdess. As he stared down at the photo, Caine felt a vague sexual pull. He ignored it.

"I'm sorry for the interruption," Sebring's voice cut into his thoughts. "Now, where were we?"

"I believe we were discussing the princess's strong will."

"Yes. Over the past six months, the princess has experienced an unsettling number of accidents," the director continued.

"Only last week, she drove her Ferrari into a tree on the family's estate."

"Perhaps the princess ought to try driving at something less than the speed of sound," Caine suggested dryly.

"Prince Eduard believes that the brakes had been tampered with."

"Does he have any proof?" Caine asked, his interest captured.

"Only a suspicious leak in the brake fluid line. Along with the sudden disappearance of the royal mechanic."

"While it's admittedly an interesting coincidence, it certainly doesn't prove that someone made an attempt on her life," Caine felt obliged to point out.

"There are other things."

"Such as?"

"Such as a dangerous incident of some roof tiles almost striking her on the head. And a mismarked ski trail that led her out onto a glacier. If the Swiss Olympic team hadn't been in the area, she could well have frozen to death, skied off the edge of the mountain or perished in one of the area's frequent avalanches."

He handed Caine another file. "Everything you need to know about the princess and her upcoming tour is in here. You'll have a week to acquaint yourself with the data before she arrives. To tell you the truth, after reading those documents regarding her recent series of accidents, I'm afraid I find myself agreeing with her father."

"It's natural for a father to worry about a daughter. Especially one as headstrong as the princess is reputed to be."

Sebring shook his head. "Many years ago, when I was a young agent, I had the privilege of being assigned to guard Prince Eduard during his frequent visits to this country. Although the prince is admittedly an emotional man, he is also highly intelligent and incisive. Chantal is in grave danger, Caine, even if she does refuse to accept that fact."

"Are you saying she won't be traveling with her own security?"

"That's exactly what I'm saying."

"No disrespect intended, sir," Caine argued carefully, "but if she won't even accept her own security people, what makes you think she'll accept a Presidential Security agent hovering over her all the time she's in this country?"

"Therein lies the problem," the director admitted. "Chantal would hit the roof if she discovered that her father had gone against her wishes. You're just going to have to make certain she doesn't find out who you really are."

"What?" Caine was on his feet, staring down at his superior. An order was an order. Those words that had been drilled into him first by his father, then later, during his plebe year at the academy. But dammit, some orders were just downright insane. And this one had to be the craziest of the bunch.

"As you mentioned, Princess Chantal can be an extremely headstrong young woman," Sebring said. "Her father fears that if she were to learn that she were being guarded, she'd try to slip away in order to display her independence. It's a risk the prince is not prepared to take." His blue eyes turned resolute. "Nor am I."

"So how am I going to stay close to her?" Caine asked, unreasonably frustrated. "And please don't tell me that I have to become this season's fiancé."

Sebring laughed. "Don't worry, my boy, there are limits to the sacrifices you are asked to make for your country. Chantal will be told that you're a deputy under secretary of state, assigned to make her tour more comfortable. I'm also assigning Drew Tremayne to act as her driver."

Drew was also a Presidential Security agent, and Caine's best friend. Under normal circumstances he would have looked forward to working with him on a special assignment. But babysitting? Behind his impassive features, Caine was seething. A damned flunky, he considered grimly. Subject to a spoiled brat's every whim. This assignment was beginning to make getting shot look like a cakewalk.

"So," the director said as he pushed himself out of his black leather chair, "will you accept the assignment, Caine?"

Did he have a choice? "Of course I'll accept, sir," Caine said evenly. "With pleasure."

Rubbing his hands together as if he'd never expected any other outcome, James Sebring chuckled. "You've always been a rotten liar, Caine." Throwing a friendly arm around the younger man's shoulders, he walked him to the door.

"The Montacroix ambassador will be hosting a reception for the princess the night of her arrival in this country," he said. "Although you'll ostensibly be attending as her escort, your prime responsibility is to keep her safe."

"I'm sure everything will go smoothly, sir."

Caine was damn well going to make certain it did. Maybe the princess was accustomed to throwing her weight around in Montacroix, but this was America. Here the product of years of European royal inbreeding didn't rank one iota higher than the offspring of a naval aviator from Waco, Texas, and a Back Bay debutante turned Harvard literature professor.

"Spoken like a man who hasn't met Chantal yet." Sebring chuckled again. "By the time you finish this tour, Caine, you may have earned a second medal for your mother to hang on the living room wall."

Although Caine had always thrived on challenges, the director's parting words were somewhat unsettling. As he left the building, his thoughts were not on the appealing warmth of the sun. Nor were they on the crowds of tourists chattering excitedly in a multitude of foreign tongues as they took in the plethora of monuments and government buildings.

No, Caine's thoughts—as black and stormy as they were—were all directed toward one exotic and dangerously appealing package of trouble. Trouble that was headed his way.

ACROSS THE ATLANTIC, in a century-old palace, Chantal Giraudeau was engaged in a battle royal. Although she was physically weaker than her attacker, she was no less aggressive, advancing in lightning-swift lunges, retreating just in time to avoid the cold steel of her opponent's foil. A deadly silence hung over the combatants, laced with an electric excitement that was almost palpable.

Despite his size, the man's fencing style was smooth, almost graceful, and even with his face hidden behind the wire mesh of his mask, Chantal could sense his self-confidence. A confidence, she admitted furiously, he was entitled to. He wasn't even breathing hard, while her own heart was pounding a million miles a minute. Beads of perspiration glistened above her full upper lip as he deftly parried her attack without missing a beat.

She managed to parry his riposte, trying to remember to stick to the basics. No flash. No showing off. Just simple—hopefully deceptive—plays that might lull her attacker into a false sense of security. Changing the mood, she began relying more heavily on defense; retreating, forcing him to close the gap. Slowing the pace allowed her to get a much-needed second wind.

"It isn't going to work, you know," the man chided from behind his mask.

Chantal retreated as he moved forward in a lazy, supremely confident offense. "What?"

"Attempting to throw me off by changing tactics. You forget—I know you. Perhaps better than you know yourself. You're not the type of woman to resort to purely defensive measures for very long." There was a sudden clash of metal as his blade found hers.

Damning him for being right, Chantal struggled to ignore his softly spoken words. "I hadn't realized I was so predictable," she snapped, parrying quickly, determined to prevent him from claiming victory.

He laughed at that. A deep, rich laugh, thick with an easy masculine arrogance she found even more infuriating than his accusation. "More so than you like the world to believe, *ma chère*."

Her stamina was fading. Chantal knew that if she was to win, she would have to make her move soon. Otherwise, his superior strength and speed would prove her downfall. Although it took an effort, she refused to allow him to draw her into a verbal battle, saving her energies for the field of combat.

She knew that by continuing her defensive measures, there was a chance her opponent would make a mistake. Even the most skilled fencers were capable of misjudging distance or underestimating their opponent. But this was not a man who made mistakes, nor was he apt to underestimate anyone. Especially not her; of all the men who had passed through her life, this man had remained. As he had maddeningly pointed out, he knew her well.

Putting aside her careful techniques, Chantal suddenly went on the attack, lunging toward him with a flash of gleaming steel, the tip of her foil headed toward his chest. Taken by surprise, he could not muster a defense, and the hit landed unanswered against his white jacket.

"Witch," he said, pulling off his mask in order to shoot her a mock glare.

As Chantal took off her own mask, she realized that her head was drenched. Damn. She'd have to wash her hair again before the bon voyage party at the royal gallery. "You're just angry because I finally beat you," she pointed out with a saucy grin, and at that moment she was worlds away from the pouty, sex-kitten teenager who had threatened to set European movie screens on fire.

"You cheated."

"I did not." She tossed her damp hair over her shoulder. "Admit it, Burke. I outsmarted you."

Burke Giraudeau, heir to the throne of the principality of Montacroix and Chantal's half-brother, shook his head in self-disgust. "It was my own fault," he muttered. "I never should have given you that damn challenge."

"Ah, but you did, brother dear," she said silkily, going up on her toes to brush her lips against his cheek. "I believe it's a case of being hoisted with your own petard." Her eyes were brimming with laughter. "Will it make you feel any better if I give some of the credit for my victory to my teacher?"

"Since I taught you everything you know about fencing, I suppose it might ease some of the pain."

There was something strange about Burke today, Chantal mused. He seemed distracted. Although she hated to admit it, his preoccupation had probably contributed to her victory, the first she'd ever scored against him.

"Anything to make my big brother happy."

"Anything?" he asked as he returned his foil to its place on the wall.

Chantal sighed as comprehension dawned. They'd been through this more times than she could count. "You're still insisting that I take some of Papa's security force with me to America."

Burke dragged his long fingers through his thick, dark hair. "I'm worried about you."

"So am I."

"Really?"

He looked so hopeful that Chantal experienced a twinge of guilt for teasing him. "I'm worried that I'm becoming horribly accident-prone."

"If they *were* accidents. Chantal, if those skiers hadn't been there . . ."

"But they were. And a woman could do worse than to get rescued by the entire Swiss ski team."

"You don't take anything seriously," he complained. "Here I am concerned for your safety, and all you can do is laugh at me. I'm beginning to wish the idea of this damn cultural exchange had never come up."

"But you were the one who said it would be good for me to go away."

"Perhaps I've changed my mind. If anything happens to you over there, I'd never forgive myself for convincing you to accept the president's offer."

Chantal loved Burke more than anyone in the world. Through the years he'd been her rock, her source of strength. She'd confided in Burke all her youthful hopes, as well as her fears. And it was Burke, alone, who knew her secret pain.

She crossed the room and put her hand on his arm. "But you were right, as you always are. Honestly, brother dear, as much as I adore you, there are times when it gets a little tiring to live with such a perfect person."

Burke felt the coiled tension slowly leaving his body. She'd always been able to dispel his dark, introspective moods, even as a Gypsy-eyed infant. The first time she'd reached out of the antique oak cradle and grasped his finger in her tiny but surprisingly strong fist, he'd fallen in love with her.

He would have had to have been deaf not to hear the pain edging her teasing words. Cupping her chin in his fingers, Burke lifted her gaze to his. "So it still hurts, *chérie?* Even now?"

Chantal could feel traitorous tears stinging her eyelids. Furious that she could experience such raw pain after all this time and determined not to let such destructive feelings get the best of her, she blinked them away.

Knowing she wasn't fooling her brother for a minute, Chantal nevertheless forced a smile. "Only when I laugh."

2

HER PLANE WAS LATE. Not surprising, but irritating nonetheless. Although Caine had never considered himself a superstitious man, he took the fact that he'd been forced to cool his heels at Washington National Airport for the past hour as an ominous sign. That, along with the gray hair he'd discovered this morning, did nothing to improve his mood.

"You realize," Drew Tremayne offered as they waited for the Air France jet to land, "that the way this assignment is starting out, things can only get better."

Caine thought about the file locked in his top desk drawer, the file documenting the past twenty-nine years of Chantal Giraudeau's decidedly untranquil life. "If even half the stories about the princess are true," he countered, "I'll be lucky if I haven't turned entirely gray by the end of Her Highness's royal tour."

"It would have been a lot easier on everyone if she had agreed to overt security."

Caine grunted his assent. The first time he'd read through the papers detailing the various alleged accidents, he had shrugged them off as coincidences. The second time, a familiar feeling had made the short hairs on the back of his neck stand on end. The third time through the file, he reluctantly came to share his chief executive's feelings. Someone out there was attempting to harm Montacroix's flamboyant princess.

As always, the terminal, which had once been criticized for being too large, was filled beyond capacity. Conversations in a myriad of languages filled the air. Diplomats complained about increased security measures while babies cried and children fussed, wiggling impatiently on molded plastic seats, their mothers alternately bribing them with ice cream and threatening them with corporal punishment.

Harried-looking businessmen staked claim to the banks of pay telephones along the walls and barked orders into the mouthpieces. Boisterous groups of teenagers—obviously civics classes from around the country, excited to be visiting the nation's capital—added to the din.

As Caine paced the floor, drinking bitter vending machine coffee he didn't want and watching out the window for the arrival of Chantal's flight from Paris, he realized that eighteen months of traveling with the president on Air Force One had spoiled him. The idea of spending the next three weeks in crowded terminals, crammed like sardines into the flying cattle cars that typified commercial airliners these days, was less than appealing.

THE FIRST THING Chantal did upon her arrival at Washington National Airport was to thank God the plane had landed safely. Although its downtown location was undoubtedly convenient—her tour book informed her that it was a mere three miles to the White House—she couldn't help questioning the wisdom of putting a major international airport in such a densely populated area. As they'd flown over that last bridge, she'd almost been able to see right into the commuters' cars. Still, it was a most attractive site, she decided, admiring the dark green riverbanks fringed with graceful willows.

As she stood up and prepared to leave the plane, she smiled at the bearded man seated across the aisle, one row behind her own first-class seat. He had been studying her surreptitiously for much of the overseas flight, but accustomed to such behavior, Chantal was not overly annoyed. On the contrary, she was extremely grateful that he hadn't intruded on her privacy.

After exchanging ebullient farewells with the flight crew, who professed to be unanimously thrilled to have the famous, or infamous, Princess Chantal on board, she gathered up her belongings and made her way to the cabin door.

It would have been impossible to miss her. Clad in slender black flannel pants and a black cashmere turtleneck topped by a flowing yellow gold wool cape, Chantal entered the terminal like Napoleon entering Berlin. All that was missing, Caine mused, was a uniformed honor guard and a flare of trumpets.

Drew whistled under his breath. "That is one good-looking woman."

"She also makes one helluva target," Caine complained. "I suppose it would have been too much to expect her to arrive in something a bit less flamboyant."

"That lady could make a burlap bag look good," Drew offered, standing up a little straighter.

Both men watched as Chantal strode briskly across the concourse, her dark eyes roving the terminal, inspecting then dismissing one man after another. More than one scrutinized and discarded male looked as though he'd give anything to be the person Chantal was looking for, including a summarily dismissed businessman who went so far as to move directly in front of her, as if hoping to change her mind.

Without breaking stride, Chantal flashed him an apologetic smile and edged to her right, easily making her way around him to stop directly in front of Caine.

"Mr. O'Bannion," she greeted him with a slight nod as she held out her hand. A brilliant canary yellow diamond held claim to her ring finger; a small silver band circled her pinkie. "I'm sorry my plane was late." Their hands met in a brief, cordial, businesslike greeting.

"There must be two hundred men dressed in identical gray suits in this terminal," Caine said. "How did you know which one was here to meet you?"

"The president described your scowl perfectly."

Caine was irritated to know that he'd allowed his feelings to show. "That bad, huh?"

"Not really." There was something about this man—the hardness of his gunmetal gray eyes, perhaps, or the sense of tautly leashed power surrounding him—that had Chantal feeling uncomfortably vulnerable . . . yet strangely safe at the same time. "I lied."

Caine's only response was an arched brow.

"The president didn't mention your scowl. But he did send my father your photograph along with a long letter stating all your qualifications," she explained. "I believe he wanted to assure Papa that you were a properly serious deputy under secretary of state who would prove a respectable chaperon for my tour."

"I wouldn't think a woman of your vast experience would require a chaperon, Princess."

It would have been impossible to miss the disdain on his face. Obviously, the man had already made up his mind about her, preferring gossip to fact. Well, she decided, if he was expecting the rich, spoiled princess of the tabloids, that's precisely what he'd get.

"You're quite right, Mr. O'Bannion," she said, giving him a calculating smile totally devoid of warmth. "I don't need a chaperon nearly as badly as I need someone to retrieve my luggage." She reached into her black leather clutch, extracted a stack of bright blue cardboard tags and held them out to him. "I assume that's to be your job?" she asked in a haughty tone that one of her ancestors might have used on a recalcitrant footman.

The flare of anger in Caine's eyes would have made a lesser woman flinch. Chantal held her ground, refusing to be intimidated by his blistering scrutiny.

"The limo's parked right outside in the VIP lot," he ground out as he snapped the luggage tags from her fingers. "Mr. Tremayne will be your driver while you're in this country," he said, indicating the smiling man standing beside him. "He'll get you settled in while I collect your bags."

Proper manners, drilled into Chantal by a rigid British governess who'd been with the family for two generations, were nearly her undoing. She started to thank him, then remembered that a princess—at least the type he thought her to be—need not acknowledge any effort on her behalf. "Please don't take all day," she instructed briskly. "Waiting around in limousines is such a dreadful bore."

The back-and-forth motion of his jaw indicated Caine was grinding his teeth. "I'll try not to dawdle, Your Highness."

"See that you don't."

As she walked away, Drew following on her heels, Caine could have sworn he saw an invisible crown perched atop her sleek sable head. Muttering a particularly virulent curse, he headed toward the baggage claim area, deciding that he'd take a dozen crazed would-be assassins over one snotty princess any day.

At least the driver was friendly, Chantal considered. Although his manner had been properly polite, his eyes had smiled at her in a way that almost made up for Caine O'Bannion's rudeness. Alone in the back seat of the State Department limousine, she thought about her reasons for coming to America.

Burke had been the one who insisted all she needed to lift her spirits was some time away from Montacroix. An opportunity for a new lease on life. After giving the matter serious consideration, Chantal had agreed that a change of scenery might just do her some good.

The trick had been to find a place that held no painful memories, something easier said than done. Then the letter had come inviting Montacroix to take part in a cultural exchange program.

The offer, along with an opportunity to raise much-needed funds for the world's underprivileged children, had seemed the answer to a prayer. During the six months that she'd prepared for the exhibit, selecting works from remarkably talented yet still obscure European artists, along with the appealingly primitive artwork of the children, she'd managed to go hours, sometimes even days at a time, without dwelling on the past. By the time she'd boarded the Air France jet today, she'd felt as if she were standing on the brink of a bright new life.

And then she'd run smack into Caine O'Bannion and that cold, hard look of disdain she remembered all too well. Her husband had perfected that look, wielding it with brutal efficiency. After her divorce, Chantal had thought that she'd never have to see that look directed her way again. Obviously she'd thought wrong.

"Damn," she murmured, leaning her head against the back of the glove-soft leather seat and rubbing her throbbing temples with her fingertips. "What do I do now?"

"Since your welcoming reception at the Montacroix embassy is only a few hours away and you've had a long flight, I'd suggest going straight to the hotel for a nap," a deep voice beside her offered.

Lost in introspection, Chantal had failed to notice Caine's arrival. Now, as she lowered her hands to her lap, she reminded herself that it was important—vital—that she remain calm.

"I do not take naps."

Her tilted, arrogant chin was quintessential princess, but the obvious exhaustion in her eyes and the pallor of her cheeks hinted at something soft and vulnerable lurking beneath that vivid, self-assured exterior. Telling himself that such flights of fancy must be a residual, unexpected side-effect of the pain medication they'd pumped him full of last month, Caine shrugged.

"Fine. You can spend the rest of the day hanging up all the clothes you brought with you." He thought of the numerous pieces of Louis Vuitton luggage he and Drew had finally managed to stuff into the roomy trunk of the limousine. "May I ask you a personal question?"

"I suppose that would depend on how personal."

"Did you leave any clothes back at the castle?"

If he'd been anyone else, Chantal would have laughed and confided that Burke had asked her that very same question when he'd driven her to the airport. But her brother's question had been in the vein of good-natured teasing. Caine's was heavy with scorn.

"I am here in America representing my country," she said blandly. "As Montacroix's unofficial delegate to the United States, I have a reputation to uphold."

"Excuse my ignorance, Your Highness," Caine shot back mockingly. "I hadn't realized that an entire country's international reputation depended on the size of its princess's wardrobe."

It crossed Chantal's mind that if Caine O'Bannion was typical of the country's State Department officials, America's foreign affairs were bound to be in a great deal of trouble. She couldn't remember ever meeting a more undiplomatic man.

"Don't tell me that my luggage is too heavy for you to manage?"

"Of course not. However, I *was* wondering whether you plan to lug all those cases around from town to town for the next three weeks."

"Don't be ridiculous. I have no such intention."

That, at least, was something, Caine decided. Obviously, she'd decided to pull out all the stops for the diplomatic circuit, intending to ship a lot of the stuff back home to good old Montacroix before they moved on to their next stop.

"*You're* going to lug them from town to town for the next three weeks," Chantal returned silkily, her tone schooled to annoy.

As she watched the smoldering fury rise in those hard eyes, she swallowed, all too aware of her heart hammering in her throat. Feeling defensive and hating herself for it, she turned away.

Before Caine could come up with an answer that was even remotely civil, she was pointing out the window. "Oh, the Lincoln Memorial," she exclaimed as the limousine sped past on the way to the hotel. "I read in my travel guide that on a clear day you can see Mr. Lincoln's statue in the Reflecting Pool. Is that true?"

The transformation had been so rapid, so unexpected, that Caine was forced to blink slowly to regain his equilibrium. The haughty princess was gone, and in her place was an enthusiastic young woman whose dancing dark eyes could bring even the most stalwart of men to his knees. As he struggled against an unruly tug of attraction, Caine tried to recall the last time he'd stopped to look at any of his adopted city's famed landmarks.

"If it says it in black and white, it must be true."

Chantal was leafing madly through her book while at the same time trying not to miss any of the sights passing by the tinted windows.

"So many statues. My great-grandfather adored statues—he had them built all over Montacroix. There are those detractors of my family who insist that we have more statues in Montacroix than we do citizens, but of course that's an exaggeration. Still, I have to admit that even when driving through the countryside you can't get away from my great-grandfather Leon's statues."

"The pigeons must love him."

Chantal glanced back over her shoulder, surprising him with a saucy grin. "That's the same thing Burke always says."

"Burke is your brother."

"Technically my half brother," she corrected. "His mother was Papa's first wife. Burke was only five years old when my parents fell in love. He was ten when they were finally permitted to marry. Those five years in between were definitely not easy on anyone." She exhaled a soft, rippling sigh. "Divorce is so horrible. I can't imagine what it must be like for a child, having his world turned upside down before he's old enough to comprehend what's happening."

"It sure as hell isn't easy," Caine said, thinking of his own disrupted life.

Something in his gritty tone caught her attention. Interest, along with a surprising hint of sympathy, appeared in her eyes. "Were your parents divorced?"

Caine wondered how the hell they'd gotten started in on his personal life. He was a bodyguard, nothing more. And a reluctant one at that. He had no interest in knowing anything more about Chantal Giraudeau than whatever basic facts he needed to ensure her safety. And he damn well didn't want her knowing anything about his personal life.

"My father died when I was a boy."

"Oh. I'm sorry." Chantal studied him silently. Then, reminding herself that she had no interest in this man other than whether he could effectively manage her travel arrangements, she fell silent, content to simply observe the scenery going by the tinted windows.

Unaccustomed to Washington's streets, Chantal had no way of knowing that the limousine's abrupt turn was taking them in the opposite direction from the hotel. Aware that Drew must have spotted a tail, Caine stiffened, shifted his gaze to the rearview mirror and automatically reached for the gun hidden beneath his jacket.

The tense moment passed as the yellow taxi that had appeared to be following them continued on its way down Connecticut Avenue. Drew returned to their initial route, leaving Caine to breathe a sigh of relief. Within minutes the limousine pulled up in front of the hotel.

As Chantal entered the luxurious lobby, with its gold domed ceiling and gleaming travertine marble floors, she hoped that the check-in would be achieved with the Americans' usual display of efficiency. She had no desire to remain with the obviously disapproving Caine O'Bannion any longer than was absolutely necessary.

HER SUITE WAS ROOMY, gracious and full of the small details that made a hotel a pleasure, from the authentic antique furniture to the wide, comfortable bed with goose-down pillows to the basket of imported soaps, lotions and fragrant bath salts. As she toured her spacious quarters, Chantal knew that had it not been for the silent man following her every move, she would have been very comfortable here.

"It's quite lovely," she said after returning to the living room.

She'd tossed her cape onto a chair immediately upon entering the suite, and as Caine observed the stark but obviously expensive black sweater and slacks, he decided that this was a woman who'd look good in anything. Or nothing. Try as he might, he had not been able to get the picture of her lying on the beach, her nearly nude body gleaming with oil, out of his mind.

"I'm glad you approve."

For the sake of peace, Chantal decided to ignore his clipped tone. She also decided that it was time to drop the prima donna princess act. Not only was it exhausting to behave so out of character, she had the impression that Caine was not a man to be easily fooled for long.

"You don't like me very much, do you, Mr. O'Bannion?" she asked as she attempted to untie the ribbon on the enormous cellophane-wrapped basket of fruit and cheeses on a nearby table.

Reaching into the pocket of his slacks, Caine pulled out a compact Swiss army knife and deftly dispensed with the ribbon. "I don't know you."

"True." Selecting a peach, Chantal bit into it, savoring the succulent rush of juice. "You don't know me. Nevertheless, you have formed a decidedly negative opinion regarding my character." She plucked a red Delicious apple from the basket. "Would you care for a piece of fruit?"

The way she looked right now—her dark hair in a wild tangle around her shoulders, her full lips glossy with nectar, the ripe, red fruit in her outstretched hand—enabled Caine to have a good idea how Adam must have felt when Eve showed up in the Garden of Eden with the suggestion that they try something different for dessert.

"No, thanks." Caine was trying to relate this self-possessed woman with the devil-may-care princess of the tabloids. Impossible. "You've got a busy night ahead of you. I'd better leave so you can get some rest."

Her early-morning departure, the differences in time zones, jet lag, not to mention the unsettling meeting with Caine, had all conspired to make Chantal suddenly exhausted. "I believe I will take a nap before the reception," she said. "I'm strangely tired."

"I suppose even princesses get jet lag."

She'd been a princess all her life. For the past twenty-four years, discounting those disastrous months of her marriage, she'd lived a life of luxury in the royal palace. Yet, for some reason, the way he insisted on pointing out her position was beginning to grate on her nerves.

"You do know," she said evenly, "that my mother was—and still technically is—an American citizen."

"Of course." Despite all his warnings to himself to keep his distance, Caine smiled. "I remember that no matter where my father was stationed in the world, he never missed a Jessica Thorne film. My mother always accused him of having a crush on her."

"Really." Although she couldn't begin to count the times she'd heard similar declarations, Chantal found herself responding to his sudden grin. He should smile more often, she decided. It made him look warmer. Nicer. More human.

"I can't remember the name of his favorite, but it was the one where she played a mermaid caught in the net of a fisherman in the Greek isles."

"Siren Song."

"That's it. Mom told me about one night when it popped up on the late show and Dad became so enthralled with those scenes of your mother perching atop her rock that Mom threatened to divorce him."

"Surely she wouldn't have done that?"

"Of course not. But the next night, to make up for his perceived indiscretions, he took her out dancing." Caine didn't mention that that was his father's last night stateside before his death.

"*Siren Song* was Mother's last picture. It is also my father's favorite. They met while she was filming it on Mykonos and fell in love at first sight. Rumor has it that the censors didn't know which to be more upset about—her amazingly scanty wardrobe or her heated, offscreen romance with a married prince."

Chantal smiled as she thought about the fairy-tale story of her parents' love affair. A love affair that scandalized European society for five years. "Everyone said it would never last, but they're as much in love today as they were thirty years ago. Perhaps even more." Her eyes turned dreamy. "Papa still calls her his siren. Isn't that amazing?"

Caine realized he was being given a glimpse of yet another Chantal, this one an unabashed romantic. Her open smile enticed him nearer, even as he knew he'd drown in the swirling depths of those mysterious dark eyes. She exuded sensual heat from every pore, making him want to reach out and touch her skin, to discover if it was really as warm as it looked.

"Not so amazing," he said gruffly, "if she's anything like her daughter."

As their eyes met and held, Chantal couldn't have moved if she'd wanted to. Just when she was certain that her heart had stopped beating, a sudden knock on the door shattered the expectant mood.

"That'll be the bellman with your luggage," Caine said.

Chantal wondered if his frown was due to the untimely interruption or the fact that for one suspended moment he'd allowed himself to be as drawn to her as she was to him.

She glanced down at her slender gold wristwatch, but her numbed mind was unable to decipher the Roman numerals. "I hope I still have time to send tonight's evening dress down to be pressed," she murmured, seeking something, anything, to say.

She was obviously flustered and trying not to show it. Her cheekbones were splashed with scarlet and her eyes—those amazing, sultry eyes—were still wide with an enticing blend of confusion and passion. Dragging his gaze from her exquisite face, Caine went to open the door.

"I'm sure you won't have any problem getting someone to press your gown," he said once the bellman had left with a generous tip. "After all, according to the fairy tales, whenever a princess snaps her fingers, her minions immediately scurry to do her bidding."

Well, Chantal considered, sinking onto a gold-brocade-covered Louis XIV chair, the moment, as intriguing and unsettling as it had been, had definitely passed. The old Caine O'Bannion was back. In spades.

IT WAS EARLY MORNING in Montacroix. The streets were silent save for a sleepy shopkeeper taking the shutters from his windows while his wife hosed down their section of cobblestone pavement. A fat cat, the color of old stonework, curled up on a balcony overlooking nearby Lake Losange and took a bath in the first shimmering beam of golden alpine light.

Two men—one in his mid-thirties, the other at least twice that—sat at a wrought-iron table on the balcony, talking quietly over their café au lait. "She has arrived," the younger man said.

The older man nodded. "So it begins. What security have the Americans provided?"

"None."

The older man didn't answer immediately. Instead, he appeared to be mulling over the unexpected news as he lit a cigarette. "That is a surprise."

"A pleasant one."

"Perhaps." The man exhaled a cloud of smoke, watching the slender blue column rise, then dissipate on the crisp air. "The princess is traveling all alone on this cultural tour?"

"Not exactly."

"Aha. I thought not."

"There is a man accompanying her. But he is only a minor diplomat and no threat to us."

"I wonder." The man reached down and stroked the cat's damp, newly bathed fur. In the early-morning silence, the animal's purring sounded like a small, finely tuned motor. "If this American diplomat proves to be a nuisance, he must be eliminated, as well."

"Of course. I've already made provisions for such an eventuality."

"*C'est bon.*" His lips, beneath the salt-and-pepper mustache, curved upward as he lifted his cup in a silent toast.

"This time," the younger man promised, "we will not fail."

Rigid determination hardening their dark eyes, both men's gazes moved to the island in the middle of the diamond-bright lake, where the Giraudeau palace turrets jutted above the mist-shrouded trees.

3

THE MONTACROIX AMBASSADOR'S reception for Princess Chantal was the social event of the season. While in other cities wealth might be the key to social success, in the nation's capital, political clout was what counted; tonight, all the heavy hitters were in attendance. Everyone in "The Green Book"—Washington's social register—had been eager to meet the glamorous princess.

And Chantal did not disappoint. She was, quite simply, the most beautiful woman Caine had ever seen. Eschewing the elaborate beading, sequins and chiffon flounces worn by the other women, who seemed grimly determined to outdo one another, Chantal had opted for a strapless, floor-length tube of black satin that captured the light from the crystal chandeliers and gleamed with her every movement.

She'd pulled her thick, dark hair into an elaborate twist at her nape, thus emphasizing her high cheekbones and sultry, dark eyes. An avalanche of milky pearls curved around her neck, tumbling down toward a single, flawless ruby. Enormous blood-red rubies adorned her ears, and a glowing pearl had replaced the canary yellow diamond on the ring finger of her right hand. She was, Caine noticed, still wearing the thin silver ring.

From the moment she entered the embassy, Chantal was in total control of the situation. As he watched her in the reception line, standing beside the ambassador and his wife, greeting the Washington notables with a graceful warmth that seemed inbred, Caine couldn't help wondering if there was some genetic code that made a princess a princess.

While he admired her behavior, Caine found the ease by which she slipped into a friendly yet vaguely distant regal bearing strangely inhibiting. Although he'd been surprised to discover Chantal to be such a multifaceted woman, thus far he'd been able to deal with all her varied personalities, including the one he most disliked—the pampered prima donna. But the woman he now observed possessed an intrepid self-assurance he knew went all the way to the bone. Gleaming steel wrapped in black satin—that was the princess Chantal.

He felt an unwelcome stir of desire and told himself that it was going to be a very long three weeks.

STRANGE HOW he reminded her so of Burke, Chantal mused later in the evening as she cast a surreptitious glance toward Caine. For a diplomat, he was surprisingly aloof, standing rigidly apart from the others, refraining from entering into any of the obligatory social small talk. And although he hadn't hovered over her, whenever she turned around he was somewhere nearby, watching her with a steadiness that revealed little about his thoughts.

There was nothing relaxed about this man, nothing easy. He was all intensity and intellect. Just like her brother. Chantal wondered if he also possessed Burke's patience and loyalty. And his passion. An image flashed through her mind, a patently erotic image of lovemaking with Caine that caused a quick thrill to race through her, leaving her weak.

Caine saw the color drain from her face to be replaced seconds later by a pair of red flags in her cheeks. Instantly alert, he scanned the crowded room as he deftly wove his way through the guests to her side.

"Are you all right?"

His voice was low, meant only for her ears. The light touch of his fingers on her elbow burned her skin. "Of course," she said.

"Are you sure? You looked as if you were about to pass out."

His tone reflected more than polite concern. Although she had no reason to believe that Caine possessed the gift of second sight, she also knew that it would be impossible to keep anything from him. Those unwavering eyes saw too much.

"Positive." She managed a reassuring smile. "It's been a long day. I probably should not have had so much to drink."

"You've been carrying that same glass of champagne around all night."

They were face-to-face now, their bodies nearly touching, effectively closing out the others.

"You're very observant."

"It's my job to be observant."

"Perhaps." She studied him, all frank eyes and lingering curiosity. "Yet, isn't it also a diplomat's duty to mingle at functions such as these?"

"I suppose you could include that in the job description."

"The Montacroix ambassador has spoken with everyone here tonight," Chantal observed. "I myself have exchanged greetings with representatives of countries I didn't even know existed. But you haven't said a single word to anyone."

There was no way Caine was going to tell her what his usual function at gatherings such as these was. "I'm talking to you."

"I'm the first. And only."

He shrugged. "I guess I'm just antisocial."

She gave him a long, measuring look that had Caine believing the princess was quite possibly more than just another pretty—no, stunning—face.

"Would you consider me rude if I were to suggest that if you really are antisocial, perhaps you should consider another line of work?"

"Such as?"

Chantal toyed with the silver ring on her finger as she looked up at him, carefully framing her answer. "That's difficult to say... without knowing you better," she said slowly. "But the first thing that came to mind when I saw you at the airport, then tonight, looking so stern and alert, is that you reminded me of one of my father's palace guards."

His eyes remained remote, his face expressionless. "Now that's an interesting idea. If I were to apply for the position, would I have to wear one of those striped uniforms with pantaloons and a funny plumed helmet?"

"I believe those are the Vatican guards you're referring to," Chantal said. "They're Swiss. We are far more restrained in Montacroix."

"That's a relief. I've never looked all that good in tights."

"'Tights'?" a deep, laughing voice repeated. "Whatever are you two talking about?"

Caine and Chantal turned toward the tall, distinguished-looking man who'd joined them. When they'd been introduced earlier in the evening, Chantal had recognized the name Sebring immediately and had been pleased to meet the man her father had always spoken of so highly.

"I was merely suggesting alternative career choices for Mr. O'Bannion, Mr. Sebring," Chantal answered with a smile.

"'Alternative career choices'?"

"In the event he might ever tire of the State Department."

"Oh?"

"Princess Chantal doesn't believe I have much of a future in the diplomatic corps," Caine said dryly.

"Is that a fact?" The director exchanged a look with Caine. "I do hope Caine hasn't offended you, Princess."

Chantal decided to apply a little diplomacy herself by not bringing up Caine's earlier snide remarks. "Certainly not. Mr. O'Bannion has been the soul of discretion," she said sweetly. "It is simply that he's unlike any other diplomat I've ever met."

"I remind the princess of one of her father's palace guards," Caine offered.

James Sebring's jaw began to twitch. "Is that right?"

"There is a decided resemblance," Chantal replied. "Perhaps if Mr. O'Bannion ever tires of the State Department, he could come to work for you in the Presidential Security."

"Now there's an idea," the director said with forced enthusiasm. "By the way, Princess, my wife and I were discussing the photographs of your paintings in the gallery catalog earlier this evening. She was particularly curious about the inspiration for your most recent work."

As the director deftly steered the conversation onto a safer track, Caine took the opportunity to drift back into the crowd, remaining, as always, only an arm's length from Chantal.

A palace guard, he mused. As he watched her carrying on an obviously stimulating conversation with Sebring, a senior senator from Illinois and a newly appointed Supreme Court justice, Caine wondered if Chantal had any idea how close she'd come to hitting the bull's-eye.

THERE WAS A LIGHT RAIN falling when they left the reception. For the first time since they'd entered the lofty, dignified reception hall of the embassy, Chantal allowed herself to relax. Leaning her head back against the leather seat of the limousine, she closed her eyes.

She was so silent and so still that Caine thought she'd fallen asleep until she said, "I'm famished."

"You should have eaten something at the reception."

"Impossible. Royal etiquette decrees that a princess never eats in front of her public."

"You are kidding."

"Only slightly." Opening her eyes, she met his incredulous look. "Whenever I'm on public display, especially in such a formal setting such as tonight, it's safer to refrain from eating. Think what a disaster it would be if the princess of Montacroix spilled cocktail sauce down the front of her dress. Or worse yet, someone else's gown."

"Probably change the free world as we know it today," Caine agreed dryly. "The dining room is probably closed at the hotel, but there's always room service."

"I'm not certain the room service menu has what I'm hungry for."

Her sultry scent surrounded them in the warm air of the limousine, filling his head. "Don't be ridiculous," Caine countered, reminding himself that she was merely an assignment—an assignment he didn't want. "You're a princess. The chef will undoubtedly be thrilled to whip up anything your royal little heart desires."

Since the scorn seemed to be missing from his tone this time, Chantal decided not to challenge his renewed reference to her royal status. "Do you think he'd be all that eager to grill a cheeseburger?"

"A cheeseburger?"

"With French fries. And lots of catsup. I do believe that cheeseburgers and French fries are one of the best things about America."

Her light laughter made Caine think of silver wind chimes touched by a summer breeze.

"I've tried for years to teach Bernard, our family chef, the way to grill a proper cheeseburger, but he can't seem to manage such a simple task. Although I can't prove it, I believe he refuses to learn out of spite."

"Spite?"

"I'm afraid he's not much of a fan of America," she said on a slight sigh. "Actually, as far as Bernard is concerned, Montacroix is the cradle of civilization. Anyone who is not a citizen of our small country is obviously a barbarian, guilty of all sorts of primitive behavior."

"Such as eating cheeseburgers and French fries."

Chantal nodded. "Exactly." She caught a glimpse of a blue-and-green neon sign flashing outside the limousine window. "The sign says Open 24 Hours," she exclaimed happily. "Driver, please stop here."

Drew, only slowing slightly, lifted his eyes to the rearview mirror. "Mr. O'Bannion?"

Chantal was not accustomed to having her instructions questioned. Especially not by a chauffeur. "Mr. Tremayne," she repeated firmly, in that tone Caine was beginning to recognize, "I asked you to stop."

"I'm sure you'll be able to order a cheeseburger from room service," Caine assured her, waving Drew on with his hand.

Chantal's previously merry eyes flashed with temper. "I'm going to be spending far too much time in hotel rooms as it is during this tour. I wish to eat out tonight." She lifted her chin, daring him to defy her request. "I wish to eat at that restaurant we just passed."

"You know, my grandmother O'Bannion has a saying—if wishes were horses, beggars would ride."

Chantal found herself wishing that she'd been a princess in a former century so she could banish Caine O'Bannion to the dungeons. "What does some ancient family proverb have to do with my dinner?"

"Think about it," Caine suggested. "Besides, that restaurant is nothing but a greasy spoon. The hamburger bun would undoubtedly be dripping in grease, and the coffee would taste like battery acid. We're returning to the hotel."

The dungeons were too good for this arrogant, unpleasant man, she decided. "Precisely the way I like my dinner. Now, are you going to instruct your driver to turn around, or shall I simply return after you take me back to my suite?"

Their eyes met and held; blazing amber eyes dueling with hard gray. Caine tried to remember when he'd run across such a hardheaded woman and came up blank. "Okay, Drew," he said on a frustrated burst of breath, "take the princess back to the damn diner."

Satisfied, Chantal rewarded him with a dazzling smile that didn't quite expunge his irritation but nevertheless managed to ease it a great deal. "Thank you, Mr. O'Bannion," she said. "That's very diplomatic of you."

As the limousine made an illegal U-turn in the center of the nearly deserted street, Caine didn't answer. He didn't dare.

Thirty minutes later, Caine was sitting in a red vinyl booth, looking in awe at Chantal across the scratched and nicked green Formica table. For a princess, there was certainly nothing dainty about her appetite, he considered, watching as she single-handedly made a cheeseburger, a double order of fries and a chocolate milk shake disappear. At the moment, she was debating over dessert.

"I suppose, since I'm in America, I should have the apple pie," she mused aloud. "But the chocolate cake sounds heavenly."

Where did she put it all? As he cast an appraising glance over her slender but oh so pleasingly curved figure, Caine decided that her metabolism must be locked into high gear.

"Why not order them both?"

"What a marvelous idea! I can eat the apple pie now and take the cake back to the hotel for later. Thank you, Mr. O'Bannion. That was a decision worthy of Solomon."

"Not quite, but I'll accept the compliment nevertheless. On one condition."

"Do you think the waitress would be willing to serve the pie à la mode . . . ? What condition is that?"

"You're in luck. Apple pie without vanilla ice cream is unpatriotic. And the condition is that you stop calling me Mr. O'Bannion. The name's Caine."

Chantal nodded. "Caine," she repeated slowly, as if measuring the taste and feel of it on her tongue. "Caine O'Bannion. It's a fine, strong name. I like it."

"I'll tell my mother," he said dryly. "She'll be so happy that you approve."

Chantal refrained from answering immediately, waiting while Caine gave her order to the waitress. She braced her elbows on the table and linked her fingers together, studying him judiciously. "Why do you insist on being so sarcastic," she asked quietly, "when it's not your nature?"

Caine took a sip of his coffee. He'd been wrong; it didn't taste like battery acid. Toxic waste was more appropriate. "What makes you think it's not?"

"The president has been a friend of my family since I was a child. He'd never have requested the State Department to assign you to me if he'd known how rude you'd be. Or how much you were going to dislike me."

"I don't dislike you."

"Don't you?"

"Not at all. Oh, maybe I did at first, when you pulled that little stunt in the airport, but if you want to know the truth, Princess, you're beginning to grow on me."

"Always the diplomat," she murmured.

When he stretched his long legs under the table and brushed hers, Chantal felt a tingle of something indiscernible race through her veins. What was it? Pleasure? Desire? Fear? As she met his unwavering gaze, she reminded herself that just because Caine O'Bannion was different from any man she'd ever met, didn't mean that he was special.

For someone who'd been schooled in royal discretion since birth, Chantal's face was an open book. Caine watched as the emotions washed over her delicate features in waves. When he viewed what could only be fear, he wondered what the hell he'd done to make her afraid of him. Whatever it was, he considered, he'd have to correct things before they got out of hand. Before she called the president and requested that he be replaced.

While trying to think of something to say that would ease the tension hovering over the table, Caine was saved by the waitress returning with Chantal's dessert. Putting his hand over his chipped white mug, Caine turned down the offer of a refill on the toxic waste.

"Montacroix is a constitutional monarchy, isn't it?" he asked in an apparent attempt to change the subject. In truth, he wanted to see if he could determine a reason for the attempts on the princess's life.

"That's right. Besides my father, the country is ruled by the prime minister, a four-member cabinet appointed by the prince, and an eight-member elected parliament."

"The monarchy is always represented by a prince?"

"Succession to the throne is through the male line."

Obviously no one was trying to keep Chantal from ascending the Montacroix throne. "Does that bother you?"

"Does what bother me?"

"That you'll always be merely a princess with ceremonial duties and no real power?"

Chantal laughed. "If you knew my brother, Burke, you wouldn't be asking me that question," she said. "In the first place, I'd never want all the responsibilities he's going to inherit. And in the second place, though I dearly love my country, I'm not certain I wish to spend the rest of my life in Montacroix."

So far everything they'd discussed had been in her file, but this last statement was news. "What's the matter, is Montacroix getting a little too provincial for you, after all those years of jet-setting around the world?"

Chantal ignored his gritty tone. "Not at all. I love Montacroix, but I have become more introspective as I approach my thirtieth birthday, and lately I've been thinking that since I've spent the first twenty-nine years of my life in my father's country, I should see how I adapt to my mother's homeland."

"I'm afraid there's not a lot of demand for royalty in America, Princess."

Her chin came up. "Has anyone ever told you that you're a very rude man?"

Her annoyance rolled off him as he shrugged. "If by rude you mean I'm not continually tugging my forelock in your presence, I suppose I could plead guilty."

"That's not what I'm talking about," she tossed back on a flare of temper. "I'm referring to the way that you continually insult me for something I have no control over."

They were the only customers in the diner. Realizing that she had drawn the interest of both the bored, gum-chewing waitress and the late-night fry cook, Chantal lowered her voice.

"There are those in Montacroix, even now, who cannot forgive my father for falling in love with my mother. Despite the fact that long before they'd met, the doctors had informed him that his first wife, Princess Clea, would never be sane enough to leave the sanitorium where she'd been a patient for years."

He knew the story, of course. Anyone who didn't know the story of the beautiful love child produced by Prince Eduard and international sex symbol Jessica Thorne would have had to have spent the past three decades camped out on the dark side of the moon. In fact, Caine recalled, a condemnation of the American actress had actually been written into the congressional record by a Mississippi legislator running for reelection on a morality platform.

"I knew that his wife had been hospitalized," Caine said. "I hadn't realized she'd had mental problems."

"According to my father, instability ran in her family. Her mother committed suicide in a mental institution. Princess Clea had been getting progressively worse throughout their marriage. Shortly after Burke was born, she was committed to the sanitorium, where she finally died last year."

"It must have been tough on your father."

"My governess, who was also governess to my father, once told me that life around the palace had been dreadful for a very long time. Which is why I've always been happy he was fortunate enough to receive a second chance at love, despite the fact that even as a child, I heard people whispering about my mother and their affair behind my back. When I was seven, I finally got up the nerve to ask my father what they meant when they referred to me as 'the bastard princess.'"

The sudden surge of tenderness came as a surprise to Caine. Feeling like a first-class heel for causing that haunting shadow to drift into her eyes, he reached out and took her hand in his. The compassionate caring man in him wanted to apologize, to assure her that she didn't have to tell him any of this. The professional in him recognized a possible motive for her sudden rash of "accidents."

"Who are 'they'?"

Distracted by the feel of his thumb tracing slow circles on the delicate skin of her palm, Chantal failed to comprehend Caine's question. "Pardon?"

Her skin was soft, like the underside of camellia petals. And warm. As he watched the need rise in her eyes, Caine's body responded with an answering heat. "The people who talk about you," he said, forcing himself to keep his mind on his assignment. "Who are they?"

The treacherous thumb had moved to the inside of her wrist. Chantal wondered if he could feel the hammering of her pulse. "No one."

Caine was not accustomed to having his concentration sabotaged this way. And he damn well didn't like it. Princess, hell, he decided as he fought the need to drag her out of this tacky diner and into the back seat of the limousine, where he could finally satisfy his taste for those full, dark lips. She was a witch. A siren. For the first time in his life, Caine understood his father's obsession with Jessica Thorne; like mother, like daughter.

"Someone was talking about you," he pointed out, his voice brusque as he struggled to regain control of both mind and body. "And it bothered you enough to ask your father."

It was his curt tone that brought Chantal back to earth with a bang. Fool, she chided herself. She had no doubt that Caine knew exactly what he was doing to her equilibrium and was enjoying himself immensely.

"I don't understand," she said softly, retrieving her hand with a slight tug. "Your duty, as I was led to believe, is merely to see that my upcoming tour goes smoothly. That nothing will happen to embarrass your country."

"That's about it in a nutshell."

"Then why are you so interested in me?"

Good question, Caine acknowledged silently. The pearl on her finger gleamed like white satin, making the narrow silver band beside it appear almost austere. The two pieces of jewelry were as dissimilar as the disparate personalities he'd witnessed. Who the hell was Princess Chantal Giraudeau, really? And why was the answer suddenly so important?

"You're right. My job is simply to take care of your travel arrangements and make certain that you're comfortable."

He was lying. Of that Chantal was certain. *Why* he was lying, she didn't know. "The story of my childhood is not important. I don't know why I brought it up."

"I believe you were attempting to point out that I was no better than those Montacroix citizens who harbored prejudice against an innocent child," Caine said mildly.

He might be rude, but Chantal had to admit that she liked his directness. So unlike a diplomat, she mused yet again. "You can be quite astute when you put your mind to it, Mr. O'Bannion."

"Caine."

She nodded. "Caine. And as it appears that we will be practically living in each other's pockets for the duration of this tour, you must call me Chantal."

Caine had already determined that it was going to take every ounce of his concentration during the next three weeks to keep his professional distance. He wasn't certain he wanted to dispense with yet another barrier.

"I don't know...."

"Please." Although the restraint necessary for a princess had been drilled into her from a tender age, touching came naturally to Chantal. She reached out and touched his arm, feeling the muscle harden involuntarily under her fingertips. "I really will go mad if you insist on calling me Princess for the next three weeks."

Knowing when he was licked, Caine shook his head. "Does anyone ever say no to you?"

Satisfied with having gotten her way and pleased by the reluctant smile curving his grim lips, Chantal grinned. "There are always a few brave souls who attempt it."

"And what happens to them?"

"What else?" she asked, mischief sparkling in her dark eyes. "I have them flogged."

Her throaty laughter tugged at some unseen chord deep inside Caine. "What else?" he muttered as he tossed some bills onto the table and rose to leave.

It was high time he got the princess back to her hotel room before she touched him again and made him forget his lifelong tenet of never mixing work with pleasure.

4

CAINE LAY AWAKE for a long time, staring at the ceiling and thinking about the woman sleeping in the adjoining suite. As beautiful as she'd always appeared in the various magazines, the photos didn't begin to do her justice, he mused, remembering the way her dark hair gleamed under the sparkling lights of the embassy's crystal chandelier. Her complexion possessed the smooth, fine glow usually associated with fine porcelain. And those tawny eyes . . . A man could easily drown in those eyes. That is, if he was weak or foolish enough to permit himself to get that close.

Caine had never considered himself either weak or foolish.

Although he had been assigned to the princess to protect her during her stay in America, Caine knew that if he really wanted to keep Chantal from harm, the best way to do it would be to figure out who was staging these so-called accidents. With that in mind, he gave up on sleep. Slipping into a pair of old tennis shorts and a sweatshirt, he took the manila folder out of the closet safe and began reading. . . .

The sun had just barely risen over the horizon, splitting the pearl gray sky with brilliant shafts of amethyst and gold, when Caine heard movement in the room next to his. Instantly alert, he shoved his feet into a pair of ragged sneakers and reached for his revolver.

Her door opened, then closed. Cracking his own open a fraction of an inch, Caine watched as Chantal pressed both palms against the wall of the hallway, then stretched the long, taut muscles of her calves. A moment later, she entered the elevator and was gone.

Cursing himself for not knowing about the princess's exercise habits, Caine was out the door in a flash, headed for the stairway.

Chantal smiled as she ran through the peaceful neighborhood. She knew that soon there would be noisy traffic on the street and the sidewalks would be crowded with harried pedestrians making their way to work. But now, in this early-morning light, there were only a few other people stirring. An elderly woman walked an overweight dachshund. A young man in helmet and racing pants madly pedaled his bicycle as if he were toning up for the Tour de France. A delivery truck bearing the name Martini's Fresh Fish turned up an alley to deliver seafood to a Spanish restaurant; when the driver rolled down his window and wolf-whistled, Chantal decided that some things about America were rather nice.

She'd been running about twenty minutes, checking her time on the diver's watch Burke had given her for her last birthday, when she saw him out of the corner of her eye. A man. A tall, dark-haired man who seemed to be following her.

Chantal increased her pace. Glancing sideways into a shop window, she noticed that the man, without any overt effort, speeded up, as well.

She slowed. The stranger followed suit.

Although she'd never considered herself a hysterical sort of woman, Chantal realized her heart was pounding in her ears. Deciding that discretion was the better part of valor, she turned down an alley, looking for someplace to hide.

Caine was mentally cursing a blue streak as he watched her turn into the narrow alley. Running alone on the streets of any major metropolitan city was foolhardy; taking off down alleys in this neighborhood was downright suicidal.

He'd barely entered the alley himself when Chantal suddenly stepped out from behind an enormous orange Dumpster. "It's you!"

Caine stopped dead in his tracks. "What the hell are you doing out here?" he demanded, grabbing her shoulders.

Chantal jerked free of his hold. "What does it look like?" she snapped back, as bewildered by his behavior as she was angry. "I'm running. As you undoubtedly know since you've been following me for at least three blocks."

"Following you? Princess, your paintings must really be something to see, because you have one wild imagination."

Although he tried telling himself that the only reason he hadn't spotted her was that he hadn't expected her to hide behind a trash can, such a feeble explanation didn't ease his feeling of self-disgust. If he'd been this careless two months ago, the president would be lying under an eternal flame at Arlington National Cemetery. Caine didn't know who he was angrier at: Chantal for risking her life this way or himself for not doing a proper job of protecting her.

They were nose to nose, close enough for Chantal to see the blazing fury in his eyes. Along with the anger was another emotion that she could not quite discern. She was not allowed to dwell on it, because as he glared down at her, Chantal experienced a quick flash of desire so hot, so strong that it left her stunned.

Reminding herself exactly who—and what—she was, she wrapped herself in the emotional cloak she had learned to don whenever her fellow students at her private Swiss boarding school had begun whispering behind her back.

"I suppose it is my imagination that you and I just happen to be running on the same street . . . at the same time?"

Her jaw was jutting out and her back was ramrod straight. A dangerous tempest swirled in her eyes, daring him to lie. Caine wondered if she would be as passionate in bed as she was at this moment and decided that with the right man, she just might be.

"Coincidence is a funny thing," he said with a half shrug.

"Coincidence."

Caine was beginning to wish he'd opted for the CIA instead of Presidential Security after his stint in the navy. He might have gotten killed trying to pull off a dangerous covert operation in some godforsaken country, but at least he would have learned how to come up with an acceptable cover story.

"I run every morning. This is the logical route from the hotel."

Her eyes were still stormy, but now Caine could see a growing seed of doubt in them, as well. "I suppose you could be telling the truth."

"Of course I am. Why would I lie?"

Chantal frowned as she considered his question. "Why, indeed?" she murmured.

"And now that we've had a little breather, how about I accompany you back to the hotel?"

With her long stride she easily kept up with him as they ran back the way they'd come.

As they approached the hotel, Caine noticed a nondescript brown sedan parked across the street, the face of the driver hidden by the pages of the *Washington Post* he was reading. Although he couldn't swear to it, Caine was certain that he'd seen that same car parked in the identical spot when they'd returned from the reception last night. Making a mental note of the license plate, he decided to have Drew run a check. Just in case.

THE SOARING, ANGULAR East Building of the National Gallery of Art was a dazzling example of artistic inspiration. Inside was an explosion of space and light: marble staircases, flying bridges. A vast skylight floated high overhead like a shimmering cloud, flooding the building with sunlight, creating a kaleidoscope of constantly changing colors on the pink marble floors and walls. A bright and whimsical tapestry reflecting Miró's fanciful vision of woman spilled some thirty feet down the central court's south wall.

The gallery had been designed, not as some dark and formal place where visitors would be intimidated, but as intimate rooms where one was invited to absorb the art.

After all the effort she'd put into the Modern Images of Europe exhibit, Chantal had been gratified to see that the works had attracted a crowd of both Washingtonians and tourists.

"It appears that you're a hit, Princess," Caine observed as they sat over sandwiches and coffee in one of the gallery's cafés. Although it had taken some coaxing, he'd finally managed to pry Chantal away from a clutch of adoring art fans who seemed to be every bit as fascinated by this real-life princess as they were by the paintings she'd brought to this country with her.

"They're marvelous works," she said, beginning to relax for the first time since she'd entered the building. "More than capable of attracting crowds even without my participation. And, of course, the children's artwork always receives rave reviews."

"You can't deny you're an added draw."

"Now you sound like my father. He was the one who insisted that I come to America after learning about the cultural exchange program. He said that as the family's resident artist, it was only proper that I represent Montacroix."

Caine wondered what Chantal would say if she knew that the real reason for her father wanting her to come to America was to get her out of harm's way. Away from whoever it was who was threatening her life.

"I suppose this is where I tell you that I'm impressed by your own paintings." Although what little Caine knew of painting came from an art history class he'd taken in his plebe year at Annapolis, even he could tell that Chantal possessed an enormous gift.

There were three of her works exhibited, the first two abstracts done in primary colors that were so vivid, so filled with joie de vivre that it would have been impossible to keep from smiling while viewing them. The third, however, was the one that the director's wife had obviously been inquiring about at the reception a couple of nights ago. It was as different from the others as night from day.

"Thank you."

"May I ask a question?"

"Of course."

"Why did you paint that third painting?"

Chantal had known all along that it had been a mistake to include that particular painting in the exhibition. But Noel had insisted that by allowing others to view the painting Chantal had done immediately after her separation from her husband, she would finally succeed in exorcising the man as well as the disastrous experience from her life. When Chantal had continued to waver, Burke stepped in, agreeing with Noel, and soon Chantal found herself relenting under the velvet steamroller of her sister and brother's united front.

"Why does any artist paint anything?" she asked with a careless shrug, turning to gaze out the window over the vast green expanse of the Mall. A young man clad in jeans and a Washington Redskins T-shirt was tossing a Frisbee to his Irish setter. But Chantal was only vaguely aware of the dog and his owner as she sought to soothe the panic that had suddenly begun to pound in her head. "It was simply a creative impulse. Nothing more."

"It must have been a pretty grim impulse." The beautiful but cold and stark winter landscape, done in shades of gray and black, double matted in white and framed in cool, polished aluminum, lacked the vivid colors that made the first two paintings such a delight to view.

For not the first time, Chantal wondered what it was about Caine that had her telling the truth when a polite little lie would do. "It was."

"You know," he suggested mildly, "if you're not prepared to talk about it, perhaps you should pull that particular painting from the exhibit."

His tone was so calm, so damn self-assured. Chantal waited for the annoyance, vaguely surprised when it didn't come. "Noel and Burke talked me into it. They said it would do me good."

Caine found it interesting that anyone could talk this woman into doing anything. "And?"

She glanced down at her watch. It was fashioned of antique gold pounded wafer thin. "Really, Caine, I believe it's time I returned to the exhibit."

Recognizing the emotional barriers she was erecting between them, Caine realized he had two choices: he could either skirt them or charge right through. Although he'd always considered himself a proponent of the direct approach, he decided that perhaps in this case, diplomacy might achieve the desired results.

"Anything you say, Your Highness," he agreed easily.

Chantal searched his impassive face, looking for a sign of humor at her expense. Finding none, she rose from the table and started toward the door.

She'd dressed in a bolero jacket and slim-skirted dress of scarlet silk that had made her stand out in a room of pretty spring pastels. But as Caine followed her out of the café, watching the pleated peplum skirt sway with the smooth movement of her hips, he decided that Drew was right—the princess could probably wear a burlap bag and still be the sexiest, most desirable woman he'd ever seen.

He spent the next few hours suffering that now-familiar pull of sexual attraction that occurred whenever Chantal was near and trying to forget that puzzles—all kinds—had always fascinated him.

LATE THAT AFTERNOON Drew informed him that the brown sedan had been a rental. The papers had been signed by a Max Leutwiler, an officer of Crédit Suisse in Geneva.

"So the car's clean," Caine mused.

"Seems to be," Drew agreed.

Although he could think of no reason why a Swiss banker would want to harm Chantal, a little voice in the back of Caine's mind was telling him that something about the situation didn't quite ring true. "Let's run a check on this Leutwiler guy," he said.

Drew had worked with Caine long enough to trust his friend's instincts. "I'll get on it right away."

That evening, as they left for a dinner at the White House, Caine looked for the car. When it wasn't there, he told himself that he should have been relieved. But he wasn't.

LATER THAT NIGHT, across the street from the hotel, two men—one blond and bearded, the other dark and clean shaven—sat in the rented sedan, watching Chantal's window as they drank coffee from plastic foam cups.

"Her lights just went out."

"And O'Bannion has not left the hotel. Again." The gravelly voice was thick with scorn.

"Perhaps he's acting as a bodyguard."

"Don't be naive. In the first place, there's been no sign that anyone suspects that the bastard princess's recent incidents have been anything more than a rash of unfortunate accidents. And in the second place, when I telephoned the State Department this afternoon and asked to speak to Mr. O'Bannion, I was told that he's currently on assignment." The dark-haired man cracked open a window and lit a cigarette. "Diplomats make poor bodyguards."

Although the days were growing warmer, the nights were still tinged with the chill of winter. The bearded man turned his coat collar up around his ears and hunched lower in his seat as the cold came whistling through the open window. "Do you think they are having an affair?"

The other man uttered a sound of sheer disgust. "What do you think?"

"I think that I would like to trade places with O'Bannion, for just one night."

"Don't get any ideas. You are not being paid to spice up your sex life."

"So what's wrong with mixing a little pleasure with business? So long as I get the job done?"

"It's not in the plan."

"Hey, you're the boss," the bearded man said. "Forget I mentioned it." As he returned his attention to Chantal's darkened window, his teeth gleamed in the darkness. "Soon," he murmured under his breath.

"Soon," his companion agreed, flipping his cigarette out the window. The tip gleamed in a sparkling red arc for an instant before being doused in a puddle.

CAINE WAS SIFTING through Chantal's file, searching for some clue he'd overlooked, when the strident ringing of the telephone shattered the predawn silence.

"O'Bannion."

"Caine," James Sebring said without preamble, "you and Chantal have company."

Instantly alert, Caine reached for the shoulder holster he'd put on the end table immediately upon entering the room. "What kind of company?"

"All we know is that a man called the State Department late this afternoon, asking for you."

"And?"

"The receptionist confirmed that you were on assignment."

"That satisfied him?"

"For now." There was a moment's hesitation. "Caine, be careful. I wouldn't want your mother receiving a posthumous medal for you in another rose garden ceremony."

"That makes two of us," Caine agreed. "Don't worry, sir. If it looks as if Drew and I can't handle this alone, I'll request additional help."

"You do that," the director answered promptly. Once he considered a problem taken care of, he was able to put it behind him and get on with other matters. For a man responsible for the safety of the president and vice president, their families, former presidents, their wives and children, major presidential and vice presidential candidates, not to mention visiting heads of state and distinguished foreign visitors, such an attitude was imperative. "By the way, how are you and Chantal getting along?"

"She's an interesting woman," Caine hedged.

"'Interesting.'" The director chortled. "That's one word for her, I suppose, although not the one I would have used. Has she thrown you any curveballs yet?"

"None that I can't handle, sir."

"Just hang in there and keep swinging," he advised.

"Yes, sir."

"You'll be certain to keep me informed about anything suspicious, won't you, Caine?"

"That goes without saying, sir."

"Good. Good. And meanwhile, Prince Eduard's men are working to uncover something in Montacroix, but so far, they keep running into dead ends. Damn, if we could just come up with a motive, we might know where to start looking."

"Have they spoken with her former husband?"

"Of course. He's currently in Africa, preparing for some Saharan road race. From what I'm told, the scoundrel is too busy romancing the ladies to worry about killing his ex-wife. What time do you leave for New York?"

"Ten-thirty."

"Call me when you land. We're still trying to trace that call to the State Department. Perhaps we'll have some luck."

Caine agreed, said goodbye, then hung up. Then he returned to the file, looking for the single clue that would ensure Chantal's safety.

DURING THE NEXT TEN DAYS, as the exhibit moved from Washington to New York, Chantal and Caine fell into an easy routine. She insisted on beginning each day with a morning run, so he always stopped by her hotel room door shortly before seven, prepared to accompany her through the nearby neighborhood.

Although Chantal steadfastly refused to believe her father and brother's assertion that she was in any danger, she couldn't deny that after her initial fright that first morning, she found Caine's company vaguely reassuring. Not to mention that the sight of his strong legs clad in a well-worn pair of white shorts, hard thigh muscles flexing with each stride, was more stimulating than a dozen cups of coffee.

Following the invigorating exercise, they'd go their separate ways again, meeting an hour later for their drive to the museum, where Chantal would spend yet another exhausting day holding court over the Montacroix exhibition. As he watched her standing hour after hour on those ridiculously high heels, ever smiling, Caine decided that being a princess might just be a tougher job than he'd first believed.

During those long days when he remained nearby, watching over her like a Praetorian guard, Caine attempted to unravel the mystery of Chantal's potential assassins. While he had not been at all surprised to learn that there actually was a Max Leutwiler working at Crédit Suisse, neither had it come as any revelation that the good banker was still in Geneva, where he'd been every day for the past three months. Obviously, the car parked outside Chantal's hotel had been rented by an imposter.

But who was he? And where was he? And when was he going to make his move?

Those questions tormented Caine every hour of the day and into the night, when over dinner in some out-of-the-way place—Chantal, to his surprise, consistently eschewed all the "in" restaurants—he'd carefully pump her for information about her life in Montacroix, trying to find something that might provide a clue.

"I believe it's going well, all things considered, don't you think?" she asked on their last night in New York. After a somewhat heated discussion over whether Tex-Mex qualified as authentic Hispanic fare—Caine insisted it didn't, while Chantal's ubiquitous tour book recommended it highly—they'd settled on a cozy Mexican restaurant in the heart of the theater district.

"Better than well. If you pull in a third as many people in the rest of the cities, you can consider your tour a smashing success."

"Please," she murmured, rolling her eyes toward the ceiling, "let's not talk about the upcoming travels."

"You sound tired."

"I am, a bit."

"It's no wonder, considering the grueling hours you've been putting in. Personally I'm surprised that your lips haven't frozen into that royal smile."

"You mean they haven't?" Chantal asked with mock surprise.

"Not yet. You know, I really am impressed."

"Oh?"

"You're not at all what I expected," Caine admitted.

"Ah, yes. That pleasure-seeking princess of the tabloids."

Although Caine would never consider himself guilty of stereotyping, he couldn't deny that he always felt more comfortable when he could categorize people. In a way, his work encouraged such a habit; on more than one occasion, he'd utilized the FBI's assassin profile to uncover some potentially dangerous crackpot.

"I knew they were probably exaggerating," he said on a half shrug, "yet—"

"Where there's smoke, surely there must be fire," Chantal finished for him.

Caine was uncomfortable, which was a distracting feeling for him. He was accustomed to being in control of both mind and body. Yet lately, his mind—both waking and sleeping—had been filled with thoughts of Chantal. And if that wasn't bad enough, he thought as her tongue gathered in a few of the salt crystals garnishing the rim of her glass, desire kept slamming into him.

"Tell me about your marriage," he said, struggling to turn the conversation back to his mission.

He'd already determined that the male ascendancy rule kept her from being a threat to anyone not wanting a Giraudeau on the throne. And his confidential report gathered by intelligence sources in Montacroix had stated that although a few old-timers resented her mother's affair with the prince, everyone in the country appeared genuinely fond of their headstrong, glamorous princess.

It was then Caine had thought of her race car driving husband. What if he was the dangerous type who refused to let go?

His reference to her ill-fated marriage coming as a complete surprise, Chantal paused in the act of tugging a cheese-covered chip from a mountain of nachos. "Why on earth would you want to know about that?"

"You're the one who doesn't want me to think you're the princess in the papers," he pointed out. "I'm just attempting to separate fact from fiction."

"My marriage was a mistake."

"So are fifty percent of the ones in this country. But they don't receive nearly so many headlines."

"Why do I have the feeling that there's more to your question than mere curiosity?"

"Beats me."

She'd managed to extricate the chip and took a bite, eyeing Caine thoughtfully as she chewed. "All right, among other things, Greg Masterson was a pathological liar. In the beginning, I was too infatuated with him to notice the warning signs. Later, I developed sort of a built-in radar, like those—what do they call them—those instruments that sense earthquakes."

"Seismographs."

Chantal nodded. "That's it. I possess a very accurate internal seismograph, Caine. And at this moment its needle is going off the chart."

"That's ridiculous."

"Is it?"

"All right," Caine hedged, wondering exactly how to squirm out of this one. "It's more of a half-truth. Sort of a white lie."

During his childhood years, first his father, then later the nuns at Saint Gregory's Catholic School, had punished him severely every time he'd attempted to tell a lie. Being a bright kid who caught on fast, Caine had decided that it was easier and a great deal less painful to stick to the truth. The outcome of such youthful lessons was that Caine was a lousy liar. Yet in the past ten days, he'd probably been forced to tell more falsehoods than he had in his entire thirty-three years.

"'A white lie,'" Chantal repeated, her tone inviting elaboration.

"I was just trying to figure out what kind of damn fool would let you get away," he said, surprised to discover as he heard the words leave his lips that there was more truth to the quickly thought up explanation than he had intended.

His tone, gruff with the desire he'd been trying to conceal, gave the proper veracity to his words. As she stared across the table at him, Chantal felt that same draining weakness she'd experienced too many times to count.

"That's a very nice thing to say," she managed, her own voice husky as she struggled to clear it.

"It's the truth."

Chantal would have found his words far more encouraging if he hadn't looked so angry. "So you are attracted to me. I'd wondered."

Caine knew it would be futile to lie. "What man wouldn't be?" he returned with forced casualness. "You're beautiful, intelligent, albeit a bit stubborn—"

"I prefer tenacious," Chantal murmured.

"Stubborn," Caine insisted. "Hardheaded. Like a Missouri mule."

"A Missouri mule?" she inquired, allowing herself to be sidetracked by a reference she didn't understand. "This is a new American expression to me. Why not a Washington mule? A Kansas mule? Or even a Montacroix mule?"

"Hey, it's just a saying, okay? I don't have any idea where it came from."

"Perhaps they raise a great many mules in the state of Missouri," Chantal suggested helpfully.

"Perhaps that's it. The point I was making, before I was interrupted—" Caine was cut off by the arrival of the waiter with their main course.

"You were saying?" Chantal asked once they were alone again.

"I was just attempting to explain that any man would be attracted to a woman like you," he said gruffly.

"But some men would not be happy about it. You are not happy about it."

He put down his fork to meet her strangely vulnerable gaze. "Look, Chantal, it's nothing personal."

"It's not?"

Damn, she definitely wasn't making this easy for him. "Of course it's not. Whatever I feel for you—"

"And I for you," she interjected quietly.

"Whatever we feel, the fact remains that we live in two different worlds. You're a princess, for crying out loud, and I'm just a, uh, deputy under secretary of state."

Her dark eyes displayed hurt. "I did not realize that Americans believed in class distinctions."

"We don't, but—"

"Yet," she continued gravely, her eyes not leaving his, "you are willing to turn your back on whatever is happening between us because of artificial barriers."

"They're not artificial," he insisted.

How could she not see that they came from different worlds? Different universes. His days consisted of long, often boring work, and although traveling with the president of the United States had its moments, his life was far removed from the glitter and wealthy circles a princess moved in. He lived in a comfortable, two-bedroom apartment in one of the city's more eclectic neighborhoods; she resided in a palace. He made a decent living; her jewels alone were worth more than the entire treasuries of most Third World nations.

"Your food's getting cold," he pointed out, looking at her untouched plate of enchiladas, tacos, rice and refried beans.

"I'm suddenly no longer hungry."

"Now that's a first."

"As you so succinctly pointed out," Chantal said, "I'm full of surprises." Rising from the table, she marched out of the restaurant, leaving Caine to follow.

The ride back to the hotel was a silent one. A short, intermittent rain had begun during their dinner, and the only sound in the limousine was the swish-swish of the wipers as they brushed the water off the windshield.

"Aren't you at all curious?" she asked finally.

"Curious?"

They'd stopped at a red light. Chantal's head was turned away, her gaze directed toward the rain-washed sidewalk where a man and woman were kissing under the protection of a wide black umbrella. As she watched the tender lovers so oblivious to the outside world, Chantal felt a sharp stab of envy like nothing she'd ever known.

"I've been wondering for days what it would be like to kiss you," she said. Her soft voice was little more than a whisper but easily heard in the intimate confines of the limousine.

"I suppose it's a natural enough curiosity."

"Then you have also wondered?"

Caine shrugged. "Of course. You're a remarkably enticing woman, Princess. Any man would be tempted to kiss you."

"Yet you're not a man to easily succumb to temptation, are you, Caine?"

"No. I'm not."

He was an absolute paragon of restraint. Chantal found herself admiring Caine even though his rigid self-control was driving her crazy. She sighed softly. "Then I'm afraid we have a slight problem."

"What's that?"

"Unlike you, I've always believed in following my instincts. And to tell the truth, I'm not certain I can get through another night without knowing."

As the light turned green and the car started through the intersection, she leaned toward Caine, her eyes gleaming with sensual intent.

5

MUTTERING A SOFT OATH, Caine succumbed to the inevitable as Chantal brushed her lips lightly against his, tasting, testing.

She had thought she'd known what Caine's kiss would be like, but as he drew her closer, she realized that even her most vivid fantasy paled in the face of reality.

It wasn't that his mouth was harsh or impatient. To her surprise, he made no attempt to rush them into quick intimacy. When the tip of his tongue circled her parted lips, she sighed. When his teeth nibbled enticingly at her lower lip, she trembled. And when he slipped his tongue between her lips to touch hers, she sighed again and shuddered.

Chantal had grown up in the lap of wealth and privilege. Never had she known need. Until now. As every tingling nerve ending in her body became focused on her mouth, on the sheer glory Caine was capable of bringing to a mere kiss, Chantal, for the first time in her life, experienced true hunger.

"Well? Is your curiosity satisfied?" he asked, nibbling gently on her earlobe.

"Oh, not yet." Her hands went to either side of his face, drawing his lips back to hers. "More."

"Anything you say, Your Highness," he said against her mouth. He'd tried to resist her and failed. Now the only thing to do was to accept this for what it was—an exceptional, once-in-a-lifetime experience—then get on with his life.

A longing slowly built up inside Chantal as Caine kissed her with a patience that made her bones melt. His lips plucked at hers, tenderly, teasingly, before skimming up her face, leaving sparks on every inch of heated skin: the crest of her cheekbones, her eyelids, her temples, her chin. When his treacherous mouth loitered at the base of her throat, she heard a slow, drugged moan of pleasure and realized that it had escaped her own tingling lips.

Clouds covered her mind as he murmured to her, quiet, enticing words that thrilled her as she felt them being formed against her mouth. Degree by glorious degree he deepened the kiss until what had once been soft and gentle grew more demanding.

It was torture. Ecstasy. It was torment. Bliss. The rainy world outside the limousine tilted, then slowly slipped away as Chantal's attention centered solely on Caine's sinfully talented lips. It was as if he meant to kiss her endlessly, and as her avid mouth clung to his, Chantal prayed he'd never stop.

He'd thought he was safe. What harm could there be in a simple kiss? All right, Caine allowed, so it wasn't a simple kiss, but hadn't he realized that would be the case? There hadn't been anything simple about the Princess Chantal yet, so why should he have expected this to be any different? As he felt her skin heating to his touch, felt her warm, soft lips move hungrily, almost desperately against his, he felt himself slowly, inexorably sinking into quicksand.

He'd kissed other women before. More than he could count. But as he kissed Chantal, all those other faces and names blurred into an indistinct, distant memory. He'd wanted other women before, but as an outrageous need to strip off her clothing and taste every fragrant inch of warm, satiny skin—to absorb her—raced through him, Caine knew that no other woman had ever made him burn this way. No other woman had ever made him weak.

Whether he wanted to admit it or not, the princess was like no woman he'd ever met. And that, Caine acknowledged grimly, was precisely what made her so dangerous.

When he realized that they were pulling up in front of the hotel, Caine allowed himself one more lingering kiss, savoring the sweet taste of her lips. That was it, he vowed. That was as far as he could go without getting in over his head.

"I'll see you to your room."

"Yes." Her wide, passion-laced eyes met his, handing him a gilt-edged invitation he was determined to ignore.

As much as he warned himself not to touch her, Caine's hand rested on her back as they rode up in the elevator. Her white cashmere coat was soft; Caine suspected that her skin would be softer.

"Amazing," she murmured, luxuriating in the possessive touch of Caine's hand against her back.

He was a strong man. She'd seen his strength each morning as they ran, witnessed the play of rigid muscles, the power of his long, sinewy legs. But she'd suspected that he could be gentle, as well. And the exquisite tenderness of his kiss had been proof of that. Strength and tenderness—an irresistible combination for any woman, but especially for Chantal. She had waited her entire life for such a man.

He twined his fingers in her hair, tempted to press his lips against the gleaming, dark strands. "What's amazing?" The hell with it, he decided, giving in to temptation. There were still fifteen floors to go; plenty of time to regain his willpower.

Chantal sighed with pleasure as his warm breath fanned her temple. "I was exhausted earlier, yet now..." Her voice drifted off, her dark eyes enticed, her slightly parted lips seduced. "You must be a magician."

Standing close to her as he was, Caine could not avoid meeting her gaze. Thoughts—all of them erotic, each of them dangerous—raced through his mind. Images of hot, humid nights, cool jazz and steamy sex. Of laughing, lazy sex in flower-strewn meadows, while the summer sun smiled benevolently overhead. Lying beside her in a mountain cabin, in front of a crackling fire, her naked flesh gleaming with the reflected orange glow of the firelight as they created a storm that made the blizzard outside pale in comparison.

Princess Chantal was temptation incarnate. A temptation he was finding more and more difficult to resist.

"Not a magician," he said, backing off slightly and shoving his hands into his pockets. "Just a man."

The passion was still there. She could feel it surrounding them, pulsing beneath her skin, like a thousand live wires. But now there was something else, as well. Something she reluctantly acknowledged as she watched the shield close over his smoky gray eyes. "A man determined to resist my feminine charms."

Caine read the hurt in her eyes and realized what a challenge it must have been for her to pull off that casual, teasing tone. "Chantal—" He reached for her, but she backed away, shaking her head.

"No," she insisted in a voice that wavered only at the edges. "Don't make things worse by apologizing, Caine." She gave him a smile—a brave, trembling smile that tore at something deep inside him. "I've always been impulsive. It's one of my more unattractive traits—"

"I doubt that there's anything unattractive about you."

At the moment, when she was struggling to hang on to one last shred of dignity, Chantal did not welcome his kindness. "Please," she said, pressing her fingers against his lips, "don't say anything. Not until I finish."

Caine nodded.

Drawing in a deep breath that was meant to calm but didn't, Chantal tried again. "Despite what you've read of my alleged romantic escapades, the truth is that I've never been very good at relationships," she began quietly. "Something—or someone—always seems to get in the way."

She thought of the various individuals she'd given her heart to, only to learn the hard way that too many men received an ego boost from attracting—then subsequently dumping—a princess. Even those not attracted by her title had found her wealth irresistible, courting her by day even as they spent their nights with beautiful, sexually hedonistic women who were not foolish enough to expect love or commitment in return.

Perhaps, she considered, it was she who was wrong. Perhaps it was not that the men in her life had promised too little, but that she had expected too much.

"What I'm attempting to say," she continued falteringly, "is that if you walk away from me tonight, I'll live. It won't be the first time a man has rejected me, and I doubt that it will be the last. But—" she took a deep breath "—if you are at all tempted to seize the moment, so to speak, I would not send you away."

As he watched the vivid color bloom in her cheeks, Caine realized that the princess, who had displayed amazing composure under some very trying conditions, was more than a little embarrassed by this intimate conversation.

"I can't think of anything I'd rather do than make love to you," he said honestly.

"But...?"

"I thought I had explained all that."

"The part about us coming from different worlds."

The elevator door opened onto her floor, and although Caine was tempted to ride down to the parking garage and back up again all night long if that's what it took to get this settled, he didn't trust himself to be alone in such a confined space with a woman whose very scent drove him to distraction.

"Exactly." Putting his hand under her elbow, he guided her out into the hallway.

Chantal was quiet as they walked the short distance to her door. She was not in the habit of offering herself to a man, and although Caine's rejection stung, she wasn't about to let him see he had the capacity to hurt her.

Relieved when she appeared willing to allow the matter to drop, Caine escorted her into the room as he did every night, his swift, surreptitious gaze sweeping the suite. The day before their arrival, he'd arranged for her doors and windows to be wired to an alarm system that sounded both in his room and in the manager's office downstairs. If anyone had broken in during their absence, he or Drew would have been informed of the fact by the desk clerk. But it still didn't hurt to double-check.

"I'll want to run in the morning, before the flight," she said, shrugging out of her coat. The snowy cashmere fell unheeded onto the plush carpeting.

"You really do look tired," he said, noticing for the first time the pale blue shadows under her eyes. He picked the coat up and tossed it over the arm of a nearby chair, noting as he did so that it carried her scent. "Perhaps you should sleep in."

She kicked off her high heels as she headed for the bedroom. "All I need is a good night's sleep. I have no intention of foregoing my run tomorrow. If you're not here, I'll simply go alone." Her back was to him, and as she pulled down the zipper of her black silk dress, Caine was treated to a generous expanse of creamy flesh.

Biting down a surge of desire so strong that it was all he could do not to toss her onto that king-size bed, Caine opted to leave now, while he still could. "Hey, Princess."

"Yes?" She turned in the bedroom doorway.

"Anyone ever tell you that there are times a guy might just mistake you for a Missouri mule?"

Fluttering her dark lashes, Chantal gave him a saucy, impertinent Gypsy's smile. "Only one man. But since I have reason to question his judgment, I choose not to believe him. *Au revoir*, Caine. I will see you in the morning. Early." Flashing yet another smile even more tantalizing than the first, she shut the bedroom door between them.

As he entered the room he shared with Drew, it crossed Caine's mind that she wasn't the only one questioning his judgment. How many men would have turned down what the princess was offering this evening?

"DON'T SAY A WORD," he warned as he encountered Drew's knowing grin. An instant before that heated kiss, it had occurred to Caine the partition was open and Drew could see them in the rearview mirror. But then her lips had touched his and coherent thought had fled his mind. "Not one single word."

"About what?" Drew asked with feigned innocence.

Caine was about to reply when the telephone rang. "Yeah," he answered abruptly, not bothering to conceal his irritation.

"Mr. Caine O'Bannion?" The hesitant feminine voice, faint, as though coming over long-distance lines, caught him by surprise. Besides the hotel manager, only two people—Director Sebring and the president—knew he was staying at this hotel.

"Sorry, wrong number," he said.

"Mr. O'Bannion, please don't hang up. This is Noel Giraudeau. Chantal's sister."

"Chantal?"

"Oh, please, let us not waste time with foolish games. Not when Chantal is in such grave danger." Her voice was calm, but Caine could detect an undercurrent of fear.

"Look, Princess—"

"Please, call me Noel," she interjected.

"The thing is, I have no idea who or what you're talking about. Besides which, I'm a little busy right now. If you really want to talk, I'll have to get back to you, okay?"

"But . . ." Her voice drifted off. "I see," she said thoughtfully. "That is very clever, Mr. O'Bannion. I should have realized that you would want to confirm that I am who I say I am before talking with me. Papa says the president assured him that you're exemplary at your job."

Instinct, along with the mention of the president, told Caine that this woman was exactly who she said she was. Experience kept him cautious.

"I'll call you when I have more time to talk."

"Of course," she agreed smoothly. "I'll be waiting for your call, Mr. O'Bannion."

Caine hung up, exchanged a look with Drew as he counted to ten, then dialed the private number he'd been given upon accepting this assignment.

Noel Giraudeau answered on the first ring. "You're very prompt, and cautious. You've no idea how that eases my mind, Mr. O'Bannion."

Her voice was a great deal like her sister's, but more restrained, more soothing. From the file photos, Caine had deduced that pretty, ice blond Noel was cool to Chantal's hot.

"I'm glad to hear that," he said sincerely. "Is that what you were calling for? To check me out?"

"Gracious, no." She sounded flustered. "You come highly recommended. I wouldn't think—"

"Then why did you call?"

"To beg you to stop Chantal from going to Philadelphia tomorrow morning."

"You of all people must know that it's difficult to get your sister to do anything she doesn't want to do," Caine pointed out. "And of all the cities on the tour, she's looking forward to Philadelphia the most."

He didn't bother to add his irritation about her sudden, last-minute decision this afternoon to stay at the home of an old friend. The hotel they'd booked was secured; he and Drew had seen to that. Her friend's house, on the other hand, was an unknown quantity. And that alone made it dangerous.

"I am aware of that, Mr. O'Bannion. But you must stop her just the same."

"No disrespect intended, Princess, but why?"

"Because they are going to make another attempt on her life!" This time she didn't try to conceal the fear that had a grip on her throat. "In Philadelphia. And Mr. O'Bannion, I'm terrified that this time they'll succeed."

She'd definitely captured his interest. Caine took a pad of paper from the desk drawer, a silver pen from his pocket. "Okay," he said in a calm, authoritative voice, "why don't you calm down and start at the beginning."

6

"SO TELL ME, Princess," Caine said, "what makes you believe your sister's in danger?"

"If she weren't in danger," Noel Giraudeau replied calmly over the long-distance telephone lines, "you wouldn't be sleeping in the next room. By the way, Mr. O'Bannion, do you carry a gun?"

Caine wondered if she was one of those people who thought that the bad guys obediently put down their weapons the moment you flashed your ID. "It goes with the territory, Princess. Now about your sister—"

"Have you ever had to shoot anyone with that gun?"

"Princess—"

"Noel," she reminded him. "And I'd really like to know, Mr. O'Bannion."

If he'd had any questions about this woman's identity in the beginning, Caine no longer harbored a single doubt. Her tone of voice was vastly familiar—her quiet self-assurance brooked no argument. It was an order. Softly spoken but couched in stone. Deciding that he'd only draw the conversation out longer by refusing to answer, Caine considered that if one princess was proving troublesome, two were a royal pain in the neck.

"The maniac who tried to kill the president didn't walk away."

There was a short, significant silence as Noel considered his words. "Good," she said finally. "I'm glad to know that you've been tested." Her tone became grave. "Because someone may die before all this is over, Mr. O'Bannion. And I don't want it to be my sister."

"If you want me to protect her, perhaps you'd better fill me in on what you know," he suggested with more patience than he was currently feeling.

"Of course. But first, what do you know about my grandfather?"

"Not a thing."

"I thought not. The summer of his twenty-first year, Phillipe Giraudeau, my grandfather, went on holiday in Arles after his graduation from Cambridge. The trip was a gift from his father."

"I see," Caine murmured, wondering just how long this little family saga was going to drag on.

"It was during this holiday that he fell instantly and passionately in love with a Gypsy flamenco dancer. Unfortunately, his father, Prince Leon, did not feel a flamenco dancer was an appropriate wife for the future regent of Montacroix."

"I suppose that's not so surprising."

"I suppose not," Noel agreed. "What my great-grandfather hadn't counted on was Phillipe marrying Katia in Spain without his blessing. Great-grandfather Leon was furious. He threatened to disinherit Phillipe."

It crossed Caine's mind that Phillipe may have been the first Giraudeau to have taken what his family considered a highly unsuitable bride, but as Chantal's own father had proved, he was not to be the last.

"Which, of course, he couldn't do because of the male line of ascendancy," he said.

"That's right. So you have studied our country's history, after all."

"A bit. And as delightful a love story as this is, Noel, I still can't see what it has to do with Chantal."

"I'm getting to that," she replied with equanimity. "Of course, once my father was born, Great-grandfather Leon welcomed the young couple back with open arms. So Montacroix's future was assured and Leon stepped down, allowing Phillipe to take his rightful place on the throne, an act that caused not a little dissension."

"Oh?"

"You see, my Grandmother Katia had been born with the gift of second sight. This caused some of her detractors to accuse her of being a witch. Her husband and children, however, learned to trust in her uncanny intuition."

Comprehension slowly dawned. "Intuition that has been passed down to her granddaughter."

"The president assured my father that you were very bright, Mr. O'Bannion. I do hope that you also believe—even a little—

in clairvoyance." Her tone rose a little at the end, turning her softly spoken statement into a question.

Although he would be the last person to describe himself as a fanciful man, through the years certain inexplicable incidents had led Caine to believe that there were forces in the universe that science had not yet begun to explain.

Like the woman who walked into the Washington, D.C., police station five years ago claiming to have information concerning the kidnapping of a prominent British diplomat's two-year-old boy. The case had driven the cops crazy for years; there'd been no clues and every lead they had managed to uncover had resulted in yet another dead end.

Yet Margaret Reed, who'd only moved to the city a month prior to her visit to the department, and who alleged never to have heard about the kidnapping had described the child in startlingly accurate detail. She'd also given them a description of the kidnapper—a former pediatrics nurse at D.C. General Hospital—and an address of a red brick house where they could be found.

The woman was unable to name the city, and it seemed that every city and town in America possessed an Oak Street, so it took a while to locate the house. But five days later, Phoenix police, responding to a request from the Washington department, called to say they'd found the now seven-year-old child watching television inside a red brick house that was identical in every way to the one Mrs. Reed had described.

If that hadn't made Caine a believer, his own experience would have. In the predawn hours of the day of the assassination attempt against the president, he'd awakened in a cold sweat, a nightmare still reverberating in his head. The face of the man holding the gun was still vivid in his mind's eye as he reported for work. And later, when he saw that same unforgettable face in the crowd lining the sidewalk outside the hotel where the president was to speak, Caine didn't hesitate to push the president out of the way even as he pulled his own revolver. As he lay in Walter Reed hospital, waiting impatiently for his wound to heal, Caine realized that his early-morning dream had prevented the country from suffering a horribly painful tragedy.

"I like to think of myself as open-minded," he answered finally.

"You've no idea how happy I am to hear that," she said. "I had a dream last night, Mr. O'Bannion. A dream about Chantal. She was lying in the dark, surrounded by clouds of thick, dark smoke. I could hear her calling out to me, and I tried to save her, but a wall of flames kept me from reaching her."

Her words, spoken with a quiet intensity, had the effect of making the hair on his arms stand on end. "How do you know it was Philadelphia?"

"Because, over her cries and the roar of the flames, I could hear a bell tolling. That's how I found her in the first place, you see, by following the sound of the bell."

"The Liberty Bell."

"I saw it, famous crack and all." This time her softly modulated voice trembled a bit at the edges. "Chantal must not go to Philadelphia, Mr. O'Bannion. You must stop her."

Once again Caine considered exactly how difficult it was to talk Chantal out of anything. "I'll do my best."

Her relief was evident. "Thank you, Mr. O'Bannion. We all are very grateful to you."

As he replaced the receiver on its cradle, it crossed Caine's mind that the family would have a lot more to be thankful for if Chantal returned safe and sound to Montacroix eleven days from now.

Reminding himself that he had a busy day ahead, he attempted to get some sleep, but instead he kept staring at the ceiling, seeing Chantal's exquisite face, surrounded by flames, in the plaster swirls overhead.

CHANTAL HAD ALWAYS slept well in hotel rooms. This trip, however, was proving different. She tossed and turned, finding sleep to be elusive as the past ten days with Caine kept running through her mind over and over, like scenes from an all-night movie.

She couldn't stop thinking about him. At first light, during their early-morning runs, she'd noticed how their strides were so perfectly matched and couldn't help wondering if everything between them would be such a close and perfect fit.

During the long and wearying days, as she extolled the genius of the various artists represented in the exhibit, she'd make the mistake of glancing across the room and her gaze would collide with his—steady and watchful. Invariably, their eyes would hold, and in that suspended moment there would be a flash of heat so brilliant, so warm, that she was amazed they hadn't set the museum on fire from spontaneous combustion.

After that initial argument over where she would be eating her evening meal, he'd done his best to guide her to some wonderfully authentic ethnic restaurants, but although she was certain that the food was every bit as delicious as promised, she hadn't tasted a bite. All her attention had been riveted on Caine, on the smallest of details, like the lines fanning outward from his eyes, or the cleft splitting his chin, or the way his long, dark fingers curved around the handle of his coffee cup.

Afterward, driving back to the hotel in the limousine, Chantal would sit beside him, drinking in a dark, masculine scent that owed nothing to shaving lotions or expensive colognes but was his alone, and wonder what his lips would taste like on hers. How those strong, capable hands would feel on her body....

Damn, she thought, sitting up to punch the plump goosedown pillow into a more acceptable shape, he had no right to take over her mind this way. She still couldn't believe the rash way she'd thrown herself at the man. Now that the seductive moment had passed, Chantal could admit to being grateful that he'd rejected her. Making love with Caine would have created problems she was not prepared to deal with.

If it had merely been a physical attraction, Chantal would have had no trouble handling it; she had, after all, been practicing self-denial for most of her life without any great difficulty. She'd simply thrown her passions into her work, experimenting with new styles, new textures, playing with pen and ink, chalk, flirting with misty, dreamy watercolors for a time before finally returning to her first love—oils.

Before coming to America, her mind had been filled with new ideas, and had it not been for this tour, she probably would have locked herself in her studio, working feverishly around the clock, ignoring her family's insistence that she stop to eat, until all her visions were safely captured on canvas. That was the way she worked. Unrepentantly impulsive, she'd always painted in mad dashes as inspiration struck.

Logical Burke, on the other hand, would mull over a problem for as long as it took, looking at all sides before acting. And

Noel, despite her amazing gift of clairvoyance and her romantic streak, was as practical and unfrivolous as a Montacroix farm wife.

The truth was, Caine O'Bannion frightened Chantal. If she wasn't careful, she knew, she could fall head over heels in love with him. And that, she reminded herself, picking up her sketch pad as she abandoned trying to sleep, was not something she would permit to happen.

Ten minutes later, she was putting the final touches on a sketch of the man she could not get out of her mind.

IN A RENTED ROOM directly across from the hotel, Chantal's would-be assassins were forced to bide their time, as they had been doing since her arrival in the country twelve days earlier.

"This waiting is beginning to get on my nerves," the bearded man complained.

The other man looked up from his crossword puzzle. "Patience, Karl." He frowned as he tried to think of an eight-letter word for revenge. "By this time tomorrow, our mission will be accomplished."

"What makes you think we can pry her loose from O'Bannion?"

"By changing her plans at the last minute and deciding to stay with her friend in Philadelphia, the princess has taken care of that little matter for us.... Of course! Vendetta." He smiled as he filled in the blanks.

Satisfied, he rose from the table, poured some schnapps into a pair of glasses and handed one to the man whose gaze was directed at Chantal's darkened window. "To Philadelphia," he said, raising his glass in a toast.

"To Philadelphia."

AFTER A SLEEPLESS NIGHT, and his early-morning run with the princess, Caine sat in the coffee shop of the hotel, drinking a five-dollar cup of coffee and plotting strategy with Drew Tremayne.

"You sound as if you're taking the sister's premonition seriously," Drew said, plucking a fresh cinnamon roll from the silver basket between them.

There weren't many men in whom Caine would have confided his fears. After having worked with Drew for six years, he was one of a select few. Caine would trust his friend with his life, as indeed he did every time they went on an assignment together.

"I can't afford not to," he said, cringing as Drew stirred a second spoonful of sugar into his coffee, tasted, then added one more for good measure. "I'm amazed you have any teeth left."

"Never had a cavity. According to my daddy, all us Tremaynes are born with strong teeth and bones, quick minds and incredible good looks."

"Don't forget modesty."

He grinned. "That, too," he said, digging into a bowl of cereal.

"I can't believe I actually know someone who eats colored cereal with miniature marshmallows for breakfast."

"Beats the hell out of those nuts and twigs you eat."

"You and the princess would get along great."

"Think so?"

"Yeah, she never met a food she didn't like, either."

"You know," Drew murmured, "I'm really beginning to like that lady." He licked the bun's white frosting off his fingers. "Are you going to eat that blueberry muffin?"

"The two of you are definitely a match made in heaven," Caine muttered, pushing the basket across the table. "Think of all the gooey pastries you could get the royal baker to whip up."

"The idea is sounding better and better," Drew said, plucking the muffin from its bed of white damask. "Unfortunately, I'm afraid I'd strike out before I even got up to bat. The lady is far too busy mooning over you to even notice me."

"That's ridiculous."

Drew stopped in the act of buttering the fragrant, hot muffin. "What is it about Chantal that bothers you, Caine? The fact that she's ridiculously rich or breathtakingly beautiful? And, besides being sexy as hell, is genuinely nice?"

It was certainly not the first time he and Drew had discussed the opposite sex. As a matter of fact, women usually finished in the top three categories of conversation, right up there with work and the Redskins. But something about Chantal—about his reaction to her—had Caine feeling strangely unsettled.

"What bothers me is the fact that she's the most intransigent, impossible woman I've ever met. And much as I'd love to stay here and watch you create havoc with your cholesterol, I'd better get upstairs before she takes it into her fool head to leave without me," Caine grumbled as he stood up.

"She's a mite headstrong, all right," Drew agreed easily with a slow drawl that was the result of seven generations of Tennessee ancestors. "But some men prefer a challenge." Repressed laughter glinted in his eyes as he looked at Caine. "Seems to me I remember you being one of those men."

"The princess is a helluva lot more than a challenge," Caine growled as he signed the check. "She's an ulcer just waiting to happen."

"You could always 'fess up. Hell, Caine, she's an intelligent lady. If she heard all the facts, she just might be a little more cooperative."

"There's nothing I'd love better than to drop all this damn pretense. Unfortunately, that decision isn't mine to make."

"So, I guess all we can do for the time being is stick close and wait for this guy, whoever he is, to make his move. You realize, of course, that when she does find out how we've lied to her, the princess is going to be madder than a wet hen."

Drew wasn't saying anything Caine hadn't already considered. It had crossed his mind more than once that when Chantal did ultimately discover his deception, she wouldn't want anything further to do with him.

As unappealing as that idea was, Caine didn't dwell on it. For now, all his thoughts had to be directed toward keeping her safe. But as he left the restaurant, he realized that sometime between their initial clash at the airport and last night's heated kiss, he had crossed the line between professionalism and his escalating obsession for a woman who was light-years beyond his reach.

7

The Philadelphia Museum of Art crowned Fairmont Hill like a massive, resplendent, misplaced Greco-Roman temple. Although it wasn't as dazzling as Washington's National Gallery of Art, Chantal felt that the facade of the beautifully proportioned building seemed to promise something extraordinarily wonderful waiting within. A promise the museum definitely lived up to, she discovered.

She spent the better part of her first day in the city with the curator on the second floor of the museum, supervising the final touches on the exhibit. If she was at all intimidated by the idea of her works being hung in close proximity to works by Poussin, Rubens, or Cézanne, Chantal did not dwell on it. For too many years she'd puttered around at her art, longing to work up the nerve to paint seriously but always afraid that she'd never produce anything that came close to the art of Picasso. Or Matisse. Or any of the other artists who'd come before her.

Finally, it had been her mother's statement about how she'd had to learn not to compare herself with other performers—everyone had a unique gift to offer—that finally gave Chantal the courage to try. Although that had been only five years ago, it seemed she could not remember a life without her art. Heaven knew, it had certainly gotten her through some tough times these past couple of years.

She was relieved at how fast the work on the exhibit progressed. The paintings, having been sent on ahead, had arrived the day before, and fortunately, the museum employees were well prepared; each of the accompanying white cardboard cards had been printed with careful accuracy, the walls had been painted a soft ivory in order to better display the paintings, and complementary lighting had been installed. Although she'd never considered herself a superstitious woman, Chantal decided to take the fact that everything was turning out to be absolutely, amazingly perfect as a propitious omen.

"Can you believe how smoothly everything went?" she exclaimed happily to Caine as they walked back out to the waiting car.

When she had first expressed surprise that they would be having the same driver throughout the tour, Caine had mumbled some vague explanation about security clearances. Although she hadn't really understood, she rather liked the idea of Drew Tremayne traveling with them. Not only was his presence making it more difficult for her to succumb to temptation with Caine, she was beginning to genuinely like the man.

Although he probably hadn't said more than a dozen words to her, there were times, especially when she and Caine were arguing about something, that Chantal would glance up into the rearview mirror and see Drew smiling back at her. His easy, good-natured grin did wonders to soothe her temper whenever Caine began behaving like an ogre, which seemed to happen every time she decided to scrap the carefully planned itinerary and take off somewhere on the spur of the moment. Spontaneity, she had decided, was definitely not Caine O'Bannion's strong suit.

"It wasn't as bad as I expected it to be," Caine admitted gruffly. His eyes, ever alert behind his dark glasses, scanned the grounds, looking for . . . what? he wondered.

He'd been distant all day. Chantal found herself missing his dry humor and reluctant smiles, even the way he had of issuing orders like some Far Eastern potentate. She couldn't help wondering if his behavior was due to what had happened between them last night, but not wanting to reopen such a potentially dangerous subject, she opted not to push.

The view from the top of the hill was breathtaking. Chantal paused, looking out over the broad sweep of Benjamin Franklin Parkway as it disappeared into the lush greenery at Fairmount Park. Sunset gilded the serpentine Schuylkill River as scullers' oaks cut smoothly through its waters; in the distance she could see the Victorian wedding-cake facade of City Hall. Flat-roofed row houses spread outward in crisp geometric formation for miles and miles.

"I wish we had time to visit the park," she murmured, her gaze drifting over the acres of trees that were wearing their bright spring coats of kelly green. Pink-and-white hyacinths, sunshine yellow daffodils and azaleas added enticing splashes of color. "I'd give anything to kick my shoes off and run across all that grass."

"That doesn't sound like very royal behavior to me."

"Perhaps not." If he was trying to annoy her, he was right on target, but Chantal was feeling too good to respond in kind. "But it certainly sounds like fun." Exhaling a slight sigh, she glanced down at her watch and continued walking toward the car. "I suppose we'd better be going."

"We should if you want to change clothes before your friend's dinner party," Caine agreed. "Speaking of which—"

"I'm not going to give in on this one, Caine," Chantal insisted, holding up her hand to stop his protest. "There is no reason why I should stay at a hotel when Blair Sherwood has a perfectly fine guest room. She was my best friend during our boarding school days together in Lucerne. We haven't seen each other for years. We'll probably be up all night talking."

Caine had several very good reasons why she should be staying at a hotel instead of this old girlfriend's house. And every one of them had to do with Chantal's safety. All day long he'd been tempted just to tell her the truth—everything, beginning with the president's request that he protect her to her sister's late-night phone call. Unfortunately, an order was an order. He wondered if the president realized just how badly he'd tied Caine's hands.

"People change," he said, opening the car door for her.

"Now there's a pithy phrase. Remind me to write that one down." The smile she gave him as she slid across the seat took the edge off her words.

"What I was trying to point out," he continued, "was that perhaps you and this Sherwood woman won't have anything in common any longer. Perhaps you'll run out of things to talk about before you finish the soup course. Worse yet, maybe you'll hate each other. Or there's always the possibility that she'll be so jealous of your position she'll make your visit miserable."

"I believe I'll risk it."

"You are a princess, don't forget."

Chantal reminded herself that temper took more energy than she was prepared to summon right now. "How could I? When you are so kind as to keep pointing it out." There was a sound somewhere between a cough and a laugh from the front seat. When Chantal met Drew's eyes in the rearview mirror, he flashed her yet another of his encouraging grins. "Besides, I was also a princess years ago, and it certainly didn't get in the way of our friendship then."

"People change."

"So you said."

Having reached a stalemate, both fell silent as the limousine inched along in the rush-hour traffic on the parkway. Chantal wondered once again what it was that had Caine so cross.

Caine knew he'd been behaving abominably. He also knew that Chantal was puzzled by what she perceived to be his gruff, inattentive attitude. How could he explain that all his senses were on red alert, watching for something, anything that might harm her? He'd actually begun to wonder if clairvoyance were contagious.

"I still don't know why you had to change your plans at the last minute," he said for what had to be the umpteenth time that day. "Why can't you get your girl talk over with, then return to the hotel?"

"And have Drew stay up all night waiting for my call?"

"It's his job."

"Whatever you may think of pampered royalty, my parents taught me to be considerate of others."

Caine wondered what Chantal would say if she knew that instead of making Drew's life easier, she was complicating it. Because unless he could get her to change her mind before dinner was over, he and Drew were going to be spending the night parked across the street from the Sherwood house. Caine could only hope that such surveillance would be enough to prevent Noel's unsettling dream from becoming a reality.

CAINE DECIDED that Blair Sherwood's gray stone Germantown mansion was a tribute to both great wealth and even greater taste. The facade of the house was actually rather plain, befitting the simplicity endorsed by its original Quaker owners. But once inside, a visitor was greeted by a vast checkerboard floor of Valley Forge marble leading to a gracefully curving stairway.

Blair Sherwood was an attractive, self-assured young matron who, as Chantal had predicted, appeared not a whit intimidated by the idea of having a princess as a houseguest. After greeting Chantal with a hug, she proceeded to lead them on a grand tour of the recently refurbished house, chatting gaily as she pointed out the hundreds of authentic colonial implements.

"It took David three years to collect those pipes," she said, pointing out the inlaid Federal pipe rack filled with long clay meerschaums. "We spent every weekend cruising the antique shops and flea markets."

"Flea markets?" Chantal asked with amusement. She couldn't picture the teenage girl who'd arrived at school with an entire closet of haute couture haggling over prices at a flea market.

"I know, I know," Blair agreed on a throaty laugh. "This from the girl who was always afraid of chipping her manicure. But really, Chantal, Philadelphia is just one big attic filled with heirlooms. You've no idea the treasures you can find in a flea market."

She pointed out an intricate chessboard stand, hinged so it could fit against the wall. "I bought that from a young couple who had inherited her grandmother's home and were cleaning out the basement. You'd never believe what I paid for it."

Her smile reminded Caine of the cat who'd just dined on a particularly succulent canary. All that was missing were the bright yellow feathers sticking out of her mouth. "It was such a steal we made a deal for everything they had. David rented a truck and we came home with enough castoffs to finish the library and the dining room."

"You and David have made a wonderful home," Chantal murmured as she ran her fingers over the design of a delftware bowl filled with fresh flowers.

She couldn't help wondering what it would be like to spend weekends with the man you loved searching for those unique little things that somehow managed to make a house a home. Greg hadn't wanted a home of their own; whenever she'd broached the subject, he'd insisted that his Grand Prix racing schedule made buying a house a ridiculous waste of time. She found it difficult to believe, looking at her schoolgirl friend, that Blair was now the mother of three children—a pair of six-year-old twin daughters and a three-month-old baby boy.

Chantal had been surprised by the stab of envy she'd felt upon seeing Blair's children. Greg hadn't wanted children. A fact he'd made painfully clear after she'd excitedly announced her pregnancy two months after their wedding. When she'd miscarried four months later, her husband had not bothered to hide his relief.

"Lord knows it's been a chore," Blair said on a long-suffering sigh that Chantal knew was feigned. "And the upstairs still needs a lot of work. In fact, the reason I didn't ask you to stay sooner was that I wasn't certain we'd be able to get at least one guest room finished in time."

She glanced over at Caine. "I'm sorry that I can't invite you to stay here as well, Mr. O'Bannion, but I'd never relegate a guest to sleeping in a room filled with cans of paint and turpentine, not to mention all the sawdust and rolls of wallpaper."

"I wouldn't mind," Caine immediately assured her.

"Nonsense. You'll be much more comfortable at the hotel," she insisted. "But I do insist that you come back for dinner tonight."

"It must be exciting," Chantal said. "Working on such a long-term project."

"'Long-term' is the definitive description," Blair said. "But now that it's finally beginning to come together, I think it's been worthwhile. And of course Karen and Kathy adore living in such a rambling old place. With all the hidden rooms and secret passages, it's tailor-made for playing hide-and-seek."

Karen and Kathy were the twins. They were attractive, polite and, Blair had assured Chantal, exceedingly bright. Nearly perfect, if you could overlook their penchant for pets. The house currently boasted six cats, five being newly born kittens for whom Blair, displaying her usual brisk efficiency, had already located homes.

"Secret passages?" Caine asked, instantly alert.

"This house was built by Quakers," Blair explained. "It was one of the stops on the Underground Railroad during the Civil War. Consequently, there are several hidden hallways behind the walls. They are so cleverly secreted that we were in the house six months before we discovered them all. Later we learned that the blueprints of the house were on file at the historical society."

As she proceeded to relate an amusing story about discovering the twins hiding in the whispering closet adjoining the parlor, eavesdropping on their parents' late-night conversations, Caine considered the added risks involved in Chantal spending the night in a house riddled with secret passages.

"In fact," Blair finished on a lilt of laughter, "Stormy had her kittens in the wall behind our bedroom. We hadn't even known she was pregnant until we heard mewings behind our headboard."

Chantal shared in the laughter, noticing that Caine was frowning as he looked around the room. His hands were shoved into his pockets, but she could tell that he was clenching and unclenching his fists. "Caine?"

He realized that both women were looking at him with interest. "Sorry," he said, "I was thinking of something."

"You must forgive me, Mr. O'Bannion," Blair said, "for chattering away when you must have better things to do than listen to my silly domestic dramas."

She linked her hand through his arm, leading him out of the book-paneled library toward the foyer. "Chantal and I have so much to talk about, and all of it would undoubtedly bore you to tears. So, I'll let you get back to your hotel. You will come to dinner, won't you? I promise that it will be an interesting crowd. And something you might especially enjoy for a change—there won't be a single politician in the bunch."

As he allowed himself to be directed toward the front door, Caine decided that the woman was a velvet bulldozer. Less direct than Chantal, perhaps, but every bit as tenacious when it came to getting her own way. If she wanted Chantal to spend the night in her home and Chantal wanted to stay there as well, Caine didn't know how he was going to change either woman's mind. Not and keep his promise to the president.

"Of course I'll come," he said. "Thank you for inviting me."

"Well, goodness, it's not that often that we have both a princess and an under secretary of state as dinner guests."

"Deputy under secretary."

She patted his arm reassuringly. "Don't worry. If you're half as efficient as Chantal claims, you'll undoubtedly be earning a promotion any day."

Mumbling something that could have been a vague agreement or a farewell, Caine left the house, feeling uncomfortably impotent when the bulbous Georgian door closed behind him.

"ALL RIGHT," Blair said, turning to Chantal once they were alone, "let's go upstairs. You can tell me all about the hunk while you're unpacking."

"'The hunk'?" Chantal asked, surprised to discover yet another Americanism she was not familiar with.

"That sexy diplomat who just left. The one who can't take his eyes off you."

"Oh, Caine," Chantal smiled. Hunk. It suited him, she decided. "He's been assigned to make the tour run more smoothly and, I suspect, to keep the outrageous, jet-setting princess from embarrassing either her own country or the United States."

"You are much more than an assignment, darling. The way those magnificent gray eyes were eating you up, if you'd been a chocolate bar, you'd have been a goner."

As her friend's words hit a little too close to home, Chantal felt color flood into her cheeks. "Which reminds me, I'd like to visit Hershey before leaving Pennsylvania." Chantal found the idea of a whole town fixated on chocolate absolutely irresistible.

"Don't try to change the subject," Blair said as they climbed the curving stairway to the second floor. "Here we are," she said brightly, circumventing a trio of five-gallon paint cans stacked up in the narrow hallway as she opened the door to the most ornately decorated of the bedrooms. "The Princess Suite, as David has dubbed it."

As she entered the decorous but inviting room, Chantal felt a pang of something indiscernible. Not envy, not jealousy, but something else. Regret for her own lost opportunities? Perhaps.

"It's lovely," she murmured, going over to the Palladian windows and looking out at the backyard gardens, where daffodils and tulips vied for the most colorful, while lush green ivy climbed the stone walls of the house. A lilac bush was in bloom beside a gazebo, its flowers a riotous display of brilliant purple. A slate roof slanted down over a flagstone terrace. "And your view is wonderful."

"David brought those garden seats home from an auction last month," Blair said, pointing out the Oriental seats that resembled brightly painted ceramic drums. "To tell the truth, they're a little gaudy for my taste, but it was obvious that he was in love with them, so I decided, what the hell." She smiled. "I think they're beginning to grow on me. The past couple of weeks I've found I can actually look at them without cringing."

"You must love David a great deal," Chantal murmured. Although she'd only met him twice, the first time at Blair's wedding, then once again at her own, she remembered a tall, lanky man with receding hairline and gentle eyes reminiscent of an Amish farmer.

"I adore him. Some days more than others, but there's not a day that goes by that I don't thank my lucky stars that I broke my leg on that miserable Swiss ski run just as David was schussing by."

"That's nice," Chantal murmured. "Not that you broke your leg, of course, but that you're still in love. After all these years."

"That's what love is all about."

"Is it?" Chantal sank down onto the four-poster. "I thought I was in love with Greg."

"That was infatuation."

Of course it was, Chantal agreed silently. With the twenty-twenty vision of hindsight, she could see that now. But how did one know when it was happening? "How did you know that your feelings for David were the real thing, and not infatuation?" she asked softly, tracing the pattern on the star-of-Bethlehem quilt with her fingernail.

"I suppose it helped that he saw me at my worst," Blair said thoughtfully. "Whining and crying and acting like a real ninny. And even that didn't turn him off."

Chantal compared that with Greg, who, after his initial relief, had found her miscarriage so distasteful that he'd taken off for a gambling holiday in Monaco with his friends. "So, the trick is to break a leg?"

"Or come down with the flu. If a man can survive the galloping crud, he'll stick around for anything. Even morning sickness." The laughter faded from Blair's eyes as she saw that Chantal was deadly serious. "Caine O'Bannion looks like a sticker," she offered. "Probably make a good husband . . . for a woman looking to get married."

"Well, that's definitely not me."

"Pooh, don't be ridiculous. All women, whether they admit it or not, want to get married."

"Now who's being ridiculous?" Shaking her head with good-natured frustration, Chantal stood up and began unpacking her suitcase. "I happen to know several women who are single and quite content. They lead active, varied social lives, have interesting careers and manage to succeed very well without a live-in man."

"All right, point taken," Blair reluctantly agreed. "But we weren't talking about those women. We were talking about you."

"I've been married," Chantal reminded her friend as she put her lingerie away in a scented, lined drawer of the mahogany serpentine chest.

"You were married to the wrong man, so it doesn't count."

"Of course it counts."

"Not really. You weren't even married in the church."

"Mama and Papa wouldn't allow it. They were certain it wouldn't work." Chantal opened the closet. All the hangers were covered with plump, scented quilting. How she wished she had even the teeniest bit of Blair's extraordinary flair for detail. "Unfortunately, they were right."

"So, since the church doesn't consider that you were married, you must not have been," Blair continued to argue. "Or have you become so stubborn you're willing to argue with the Pope?"

"I certainly wouldn't be the first woman to try," Chantal murmured. "Besides, church wedding or not, the divorce still hurt, Blair. A lot."

Although Chantal's back was turned as she hung up her clothing, it would have been impossible to miss the pain in her voice. "Of course it did, honey," Blair answered quickly. "Hey," she said, seeming to change the subject, "did I mention that I saw you on television in the last Olympics? I thought for sure that you were going to sweep the course."

"So did I, until that damn water hazard. Unfortunately, landing unceremoniously on your derriere in the middle of a pond doesn't win you a medal."

Blair was busily lining up Chantal's crystal perfume bottles atop a Queen Anne dresser. "I thought you landed with a certain élan. But as unhappy as I was for you, do you know what I was thinking?"

"What?"

"About that time in Lucerne, when we were both taking those damn dressage lessons and you flew over the top of your horse when he came to that sudden stop in front of the brick wall. Remember?"

"How could I forget? I was in bed for a week with a concussion." Chantal turned, brushing her hair off her forehead. "I still have the scar."

Blair lifted the frosted-glass lid of one amethyst-hued bottle and took an appreciative sniff. The scent was expensive and obviously uniquely blended for its wearer. "Then you also undoubtedly recall that the first day the doctor let you out of bed, you went right back out and rode the course again. Perfectly."

Chantal got Blair's point. Loud and clear. "Getting back on a horse is a great deal different from getting remarried."

"Is it?" Glancing at her watch, Blair put down the perfume bottle and turned to leave the room. "I've got to go before Jason begins screaming for his dinner," she said. "But do me a favor and think about what I've said. You're too young to be so jaded, darling."

"I'm not at all jaded," Chantal said with astonishment.

"Aren't you? What do *you* call a twenty-nine-year-old woman who's sworn off marriage?"

"I didn't say I've sworn off it. I only said I'm not ready to think about remarrying anyone."

Blair looked unconvinced. "Relationships are difficult enough without setting up artificial barriers."

How strange to hear her own words to Caine tossed back in her face. "You don't have to tell me that they're difficult. That's one of the reasons I'm not ready for any kind of relationship right now."

"How about an affair? Do you think you could handle that?"

Chantal thought about Caine. About the way she felt when he looked at her. About the way his gaze could melt the ice she hadn't even been aware had grown inside her. "I don't know," she murmured. "I'll think about it."

"You do that," Blair said, nodding her satisfaction. From the other side of the house both women heard the strident demands of the Sherwood family's youngest. "I've got to go play mommy," Blair said. "Why don't you take a long bubble bath before dinner?"

"That sounds heavenly."

"Good." Impulsively, Blair reached out and threw her arms around Chantal. "I'm so happy to see you."

As she returned the hug, Chantal caught the faint scent of milk emanating from Blair's skin and decided that the warm, sweet fragrance moved her more than any of the expensive perfumes currently laying claim to the top of the dresser.

"Not nearly as happy as I am to see you," she answered truthfully. The years between them fell away, and for a brief, shining moment, Chantal felt like the laughing, carefree, oh-so-naive girl she'd once been.

8

THE PHILADELPHIANS SELECTED for the honor of meeting Princess Chantal Giraudeau de Montacroix were unmistakably Main Line. As he diligently worked his way through the ambitiously French dinner, Caine had difficulty deciding which backs were straighter—those belonging to the chairs or the guests. They were not the type of people normally considered potential murderers, but experience had taught Caine that he could take nothing for granted.

Over a superb terrine of duck with Armagnac and green peppercorns, he exchanged a few words with a stiff-necked dermatologist whose unique solution to the city's homeless problem was to simply give the people bus tickets to Florida.

"It's warmer there," the physician explained earnestly. "They'll be able to camp out on the beaches for free."

Several replies raced through Caine's mind, each more caustic than the last. Deciding that nothing would be gained by embarrassing either Chantal, Blair, who he'd determined was a nice woman, or David Sherwood, whose devotion to his wife was obvious, Caine mumbled something into his glass as he took a long swallow of wine. All the while he kept a surreptitious eye on Chantal, every muscle in his body tensed, prepared for immediate action.

At the head of the table, seated in the place of honor, the princess was engaged in what appeared to be a stimulating conversation with the man on her right—an elderly, balding professor emeritus of the University of Pennsylvania. Knowing that she'd undoubtedly appear just as fascinated listening to the drivel the dermatologist was spouting, Caine found himself once again impressed by her chameleonlike ability to adapt instantly to her surroundings.

She'd chosen a plum silk evening suit, the deep neckline of the beaded jacket allowing an enticing glimpse of the top of her breasts. At first Caine considered that her perfumed flesh gleaming in the candlelight reminded him of marble, but he quickly corrected himself. Marble was too cold. Too hard. Amethysts glowed warmly at her earlobes; hammered gold gleamed at her wrists. Her hands fluttered as she talked, like small birds; her slender fingers were unadorned, save for that ever-present silver ring.

He was enjoying watching her when he suddenly felt a hand on his thigh. Caine immediately turned his attention to the sleek blond woman seated beside him. "You're certainly quiet," she said.

"I was enjoying the meal. Mrs. Sherwood certainly has a knack for planning a menu, doesn't she?" he asked politely, seeking an impersonal opening gambit.

"Blair attended the École de Cuisine la Varenne in Paris," replied the woman, who'd been introduced earlier as Elizabeth Bancroft. Cutting into a small bacon-and-onion tart with her right hand, she scored an enticing trail up his leg beneath the snowy damask tablecloth with her left.

"But that's our Blair," Elizabeth continued, "always working at self-improvement. At least this is better than the Japanese cooking course she took last year. As much as I absolutely adore Blair, I simply had to draw the line at raw fish. And let me tell you, I wasn't alone."

"You sound as if you know her well," Caine managed as the server took away his plate and replaced it with the next course. As the treacherous hand inched upward, he vowed to stop it before it reached its destination. The only problem was, he wasn't certain that Chantal would approve of him dumping the thin slices of salmon wrapped around a sybaritic filling of onions, cream and salmon roe into the woman's Dior-clad lap.

When the bearded blond waiter—clad in the requisite black tie—appeared beside Elizabeth, the hand abandoned its quest, causing Caine to breathe a deep sigh of relief. "We're close friends. In fact, she's been a guest at my last three weddings."

"Really?" If Caine had needed additional proof that this lady was perhaps not as stiffly Main Line as the other guests, the reference to her multiple marriages was it.

"I didn't know her the first two times," Elizabeth explained casually. "So tell me, Mr. O'Bannion, what do you think of our fair city?"

The hand was back. The muscles of his leg clenched under her exploring touch. "I've always enjoyed Philadelphia."

"Oh?" The politely interested expression on her face belied the fact that her fingers beneath the tablecloth were becoming dangerously intimate. "Are you from New England?"

"My mother's family lives in Boston. I spent most of my childhood there." Deciding he had nothing to lose, Caine covered the hand with his own and gently returned it to Elizabeth Bancroft's lap. Her expression didn't alter.

"Lovely city, Boston," she agreed with a brief nod. "Although it does have a tendency to blow its own horn a bit, don't you think?" Her smile was ever so slightly condescending. "We Philadelphians prefer to think of our city as one of the best-kept secrets in the world."

Caine was more than a little relieved when for the remainder of the meal the conversation consisted of a treatise on Philadelphia's illustrious past. Over medallions of lamb on a bed of parsley served with truffles and Madeira cream sauce, buttered scallions and accompanied by a watercress, tomato and basil salad, Elizabeth lectured Caine practically nonstop. Although he hoped that he managed to appear at least moderately interested, he was aware of her words only on the most distant of levels as he watched the others watching Chantal.

"That's very interesting," he said when the waiter arrived once again to clear away their plates. At the opposite end of the long table, Blair was announcing that dessert would be served in the front parlor. "You have a remarkable knowledge of the area. If you're ever looking for work, you could probably get a job in the history department at Penn."

"But that's precisely what I do," she informed him as she took a sip of the robust ruby red Pinot Noir wine. Beneath the cover of the tablecloth, the hand returned, more provocative than ever. "I'm a professor there. In fact, I received tenure last year." She gave him a smile loaded with feminine invitation. "And now that I've done my civic duty and filled you in on all our city has to offer, why don't we skip dessert and I'll take you on a more personal tour?"

"Look," he said quietly, for her ears only. "I'm flattered by your interest, really I am. But you see, I'm kind of spoken for."

"Oh really?" She arched a blond brow. "Are you engaged?"

"No, but—"

Living with someone?"

"No."

A knowing smile quirked at the corners of her mouth. "Pinned? Going steady?"

"Not exactly." He was beginning to feel like a fool. Why the hell did he have to explain anything to a woman he'd met only an hour ago?

"Don't tell me you're gay."

"No, not that, either."

"Thank heavens," the woman breathed with relief. "That would have been a terrible waste."

"Excuse me," Chantal's familiar voice interrupted as she stopped beside his chair on the way out of the room. "I hate to interrupt what appears to be a fascinating conversation, but if you don't mind, Caine, I need to speak to you in the library. It's about tomorrow's exhibition."

Pushing the Chippendale chair back from the table, he rose instantly. "Don't worry about a thing. After all, it's my job to see that things run smoothly." He managed a look of feigned regret as he turned back toward Elizabeth. "Perhaps I'll see you later."

"Perhaps." Her gaze was shrewd as her eyes moved back and forth between Caine and Chantal. "Then again, perhaps not. At any rate, it was a pleasure meeting you, Mr. O'Bannion. And Princess, I do hope that your tour is a smashing success."

A strange tension lingered in the air. Unable to decode it, Chantal wished fleetingly that her sister was here. With her remarkable clairvoyance, Noel always proved adept at reading people's emotions. "Thank you."

"You're welcome. Oh, Mr. O'Bannion," Elizabeth called out as the pair began to leave the wainscoted dining room.

Caine half turned. "Yes?"

This time Elizabeth Bancroft's emerald eyes were dancing with undisguised humor. "Good luck."

WHILE CHANTEL PROCEEDED to charm the assembled gathering of Main Line Philadelphians, the dark-haired man sat alone in his luxurious suite on the twenty-fifth floor of the Palace Hotel, staring at a picture of the princess on her wedding day. Clad in a frothy confection of lace, satin and seed pearls, a tiara of diamonds perched atop her gleaming dark hair, she appeared to be a princess from a fairy tale. All that was missing were the glass slippers.

She was smiling into the camera lens, and as the man's eyes settled on those full, rosy lips, he was momentarily distracted to realize that he could recall their taste even now. Not only their taste, but their softness, as well. And the sweet scent of her hair, the petallike silkiness of her skin, the inviting, dark depths of her eyes. Such vivid memories came as a startling surprise after all this time.

Then again, perhaps such whispers from the past were not so unusual, he decided, rising from the chair to resume his pacing. After all, Chantal had always been a remarkably memorable woman. In a way, he almost regretted what he was about to do. She was so breathtakingly beautiful; how could any mere mortal destroy such exquisite perfection? But just as he began to vacillate, other more painful memories managed to make themselves heard in the heated turmoil of his mind, and a single truth stood out like a shining beacon.

The Princess Chantal Giraudeau de Montacroix must die.

"WHY DID THAT Bancroft woman wish you good luck?" Chantal asked as they entered the library.

Caine shrugged. "She was undoubtedly referring to the tour."

"I suppose that's why she was stripping you with her eyes all during dinner?"

Caine could feel the heat beginning to rise at the back of his neck. "Don't be ridiculous."

"She was," Chantal insisted. "Fortunately for you, it was obvious that you were resisting her feminine ploys."

"If she had made a pass at me, I certainly would have resisted," Caine hedged. "Now, what's the problem?" Wondering if she had seen something or someone that may have triggered some internal alarm, he was considering saying the hell with orders and admitting everything when her next words caught him off guard.

"I need you to tell me a joke."

"A what?"

"A joke. Please, Caine, I've just been through one of the more agonizingly boring meals of my life. I need a little levity if I'm to survive dessert."

"You looked as if you were having a great time."

"I have been taught to appear fascinated by the most inane conversations, and if I do say so myself, I perform my duty very well. Now, however, I need some assistance to get through the next hour."

Caine searched his mind, finding it a complete blank.

"Caine," Chantal protested, "I'm counting on you."

"I'm working on it. Just give me a minute, okay?" He remembered a story the guys at the gym had been laughing about the last time he'd worked out there. Not only was the joke inappropriate for mixed company, it was definitely not princess material. Suddenly he recalled a joke his eight-year-old nephew, Danny, had told him a few weeks ago.

"Okay. What's round and purple and conquered the world?"

Chantal was silent a moment as she considered his question. "I don't know," she said finally. "What is round and purple and conquered the world?"

"Alexander the Grape."

"That's a terrible joke."

"If it's so bad, why are you laughing?"

"I don't want to hurt your feelings. I am, after all, a very compassionate woman."

"Sorry, but I'm going to have to argue with you about that one, Princess."

"I don't know what you're talking about."

Unable to resist touching her another moment, Caine brushed his knuckles along her cheekbones. "Don't you?" His voice was rough with an unmistakable desire that thrilled her. "Are you saying that you don't realize that you've been driving me crazy? That all I can think about is you? How right you feel in my arms, the soft, sweet taste of your lips, the way a single look from you, or a mere touch, can make me feel as if I'm sinking into quicksand?" His lips skimmed the path his hands had warned. "Dammit, what is it about you?"

Chantal tried to ignore the restless anger she heard in his tone, concentrating instead on his words. Words that so closely echoed her own tumultuous feelings. "I don't know," she whispered, "but whatever it is, I feel the same way about you."

Unable to resist the hidden appeal, Caine leaned closer, watching as Chantal's lips—those soft, incredible lips he'd tasted over and over again in his memory—trembled apart. It happened slowly. So slowly, so gradually, that either could have backed away. Chantal watched, fascinated as his mouth lowered to hers.

It was just as it had been the first time. His lips were gentle, persuasive, causing a stream of pure pleasure to flow through her. Meltingly soft and caressingly delicate, the kiss created a shimmering, hypnotizing cloud that settled over her mind.

After a long moment, he eased back. "You've no idea how much I've needed this." Caine framed her uplifted face with his hands, his thumbs brushing her cheeks.

"Yes, I do." Her arms wrapped possessively around him, the gesture fitting her body more closely to his. "Because I was going mad during dinner."

His hands moved against her back, palms tracing lazy circles up and down her spine, soothing gestures that excited rather than calmed. "Don't feel like the Lone Ranger," he muttered against her lips.

As she moved invitingly against him, her slender body was a contradiction of strength and delicacy that had him yearning to rip off her plum silk dinner suit and take her here, now, atop the burl walnut partner's desk Blair Sherwood had expressed such pride in. Lord, how he wanted her!

Chantal's breath shuddered out as he kissed her from one corner of her mouth to the other, which was almost Caine's undoing. For a man accustomed to maintaining control, he was finding what Chantal could do to both his mind and his body equally intriguing and disconcerting.

It was too easy to forget that she wasn't the woman for him when her lips were clinging so avidly to his. The feel of her softly yielding curves against his body drove all logic and intellect from his mind. Needs welled up inside of him, but even as his blood began to burn, Caine managed to ease her away.

"We'd better get back to the others before they send out a search party."

Chantal was breathless. She was trembling from desire, but something told her that merely making love to Caine wouldn't be enough. She wanted more. She wanted . . . what? It was impossible to sort out her tumbled thoughts while her head was still spinning.

"I suppose that would be a good idea," she said. With hands that were not as steady as she would have liked, she reached into her beaded evening bag and pulled out a jeweled tube of lipstick and a slender gold compact.

"Wait." Caine's eyes didn't leave hers as he caught her hand, stopping the creamy plum lipstick on its way to her mouth. Although this time his kiss lasted no longer than a heartbeat, it was no less devastating. "If you were my woman," he said, tracing her softly parted lips with a fingertip, "you'd have to give up that stuff."

"Oh, really?" she said archly as she gathered her wits about her.

Now that he'd discovered the fires lurking beneath the frosty regal exterior, Caine found himself beginning to enjoy her princess routine. "Really." Smiling, he lifted her hand to his lips and kissed her fingers one at a time, rewarded by her faint tremor of arousal. "Because I'd plant one on you every time those ridiculously seductive lips got within puckering range."

"'Plant one'?"

"Like this."

Chantal's blood swam as his lips captured hers for one more brief, fiery moment. "Oh." Pressing her finger against her tingling mouth, she imagined that she could still feel the heat, even now. Opening the compact, she frowned as she studied her swollen lips in the mirror. "Blair is a darling," she said, managing a reasonably casual tone as she struggled for composure, "but she's such an incorrigible gossip. By tomorrow, everyone in Philadelphia will believe that we're lovers."

As much as he wanted her, Caine wasn't wild about being included in the long list of Chantal's various lovers. "Does that bother you?"

"Only that it's not true." Repairing the damage as much as possible, Chantal closed the compact with a click. "I believe we're expected in the parlor for Blair's famous petits fours," she said, denying him an opportunity to respond. In truth, she was not certain that her self-esteem could handle another one of Caine's polite rebuffs.

Watching her struggle to regain her composure, Caine admitted to himself that making love with Chantal Giraudeau would be easy. But falling in love with her would be, as his grandmother O'Bannion would have so shrewdly pointed out, a completely different kettle of fish.

THE HOUSE WAS DARK. Quiet. The distant rumble of thunder echoed on the horizon. Chantal lay in bed, inhaling the faint scent of lilacs in the air as she tried to untangle her feelings for Caine O'Bannion.

She hadn't been with a man—hadn't wanted to be with a man—since the day she'd finally thrown in the towel and walked out on Greg. After the devastating years she'd spent trying to survive the sham of her marriage and the pain of the inevitable divorce, Chantal had encased her heart in a thick block of ice. It was safer that way, she'd assured herself, and she'd been right.

Then she had come to America and met a man who possessed his own personal blowtorch.

There'd be no sleeping tonight. Pushing the covers aside, Chantal rose from the bed and padded barefoot to the window. She'd just started to push the draperies aside when she heard the soft, plaintive cries of a kitten coming from somewhere behind the wall. Remembering what Blair had said about secret passages, Chantal began to run her fingers over the floral wallpaper, searching for an entrance. Nothing. Not even a ripple in the smoothly applied paper. The kitten's cries increased.

It had to be here somewhere, Chantal thought, turning on the bedside lamp. Wooden angels sounding trumpets were carved on the fireplace mantel, and as Chantal traced the lines of their gowns with her fingertips, there was a slight grinding sound and the back of the fireplace slid open. "A walk-in fireplace," she murmured. "How ingenious." Ducking her head, she entered the secret doorway.

"Here, kitty," she whispered, not wanting to wake up the other members of the house at this late hour. "Come here, kitty."

The secret passage was as dark as midnight and as cold as a witch's heart. Chantal shivered and had just about made up her mind to go back for her robe and a light when she heard the frantic mewing again. "Here, baby," she called out softly as she turned a corner that took her farther away from the light and comfort of her bedroom. "Come to Chantal. Here, kitty."

Without warning, she felt something come up behind her. Something too large, too solid to be a mere kitten. When a strong hand clamped over her mouth, forcing a scream back into her throat, she began to struggle, kicking backward with her bare feet, hitting out wildly with her hands. Her fingernails scraped a bloody path down the side of her assailant's face, and she felt his hold on her ease as he spewed off a string of harsh, guttural curses.

Just when Chantal thought she might actually have a chance to escape, something rigid came crashing down on her head. A flash of lightning exploded behind her eyes. Then everything went black.

9

CAINE WAS HUDDLED in the front seat of the car across the street, watching the Sherwood house.

"I hate this," he muttered.

"I don't know what you're complaining about," Drew said. "At least you were invited to dinner while your long-suffering partner was reduced to eating take-out burgers and fries."

"Anything fancier than a fast-food taco would be wasted on you," Caine countered, cringing as his partner tore open a bag of chocolate-covered raisins.

"True enough," Drew agreed with resolute good humor. "But I do thank you kindly for the petits fours."

Caine wondered if the cleaner would be able to get the chocolate frosting out of his suit-jacket pocket. "Anything for a pal. Damn, it's cold tonight." The temperature was making his shoulder ache; he rubbed it.

Drew noticed Caine's gesture. "Why don't you go back to the hotel? I don't mind pulling a little extra duty."

"I'm staying."

"Suit yourself." Drew poured them both a cup of coffee from the thermos he kept in the back seat. "Got it bad, huh?"

Caine didn't answer immediately as he took a tentative sip of the steaming, too-sweet drink. He should have known that Drew would pour half the sugar bowl into the thermos. "She's different from what I expected."

"Different good, or different bad?"

Caine considered the question. That Chantal was even more beautiful than she appeared in photos definitely lined up on the plus side of the ledger. That she was genuinely nicer and more intelligent than he'd thought were other pluses. What she was doing to his mind, however, was something he hadn't counted on. Caine decided that the unsettling feelings he'd been experiencing lately definitely belonged on the negative side. But he wasn't able to come up with any other minuses to balance out his ledger.

"Just different. You should have heard her during cocktails. The princess played that crowd like a faith healer at a tent revival. Hell, she probably collected more for her Rescue the Children Fund in ten minutes than you and I make in a year."

"Sounds as if the lady's got a future selling water purifiers if she ever decides to get out of the princess business."

"It's not a business. If you're royalty, you're royalty for life."

"And that's what's bothering you, isn't it? That when all this is over, she'll still be a princess. While you're a glorified civil servant."

"Our worlds are light-years apart."

"Did I ever tell you about my granddaddy Billy Joe Tremayne?" Drew asked, popping a handful of raisins into his mouth.

"The one who did time for shooting that federal revenuer he caught nosing around his still?"

"Nah. That was my uncle Buster Joe Tremayne. And he didn't exactly shoot him. He just winged his hat a little."

"Pumped it full of buckshot, if I remember the story correctly."

"Better the guy's hat than his head. Besides, according to the story, it was a bowler. Can you imagine what kind of blamed fool would wear a bowler in the back Tennessee hills? The way I figure it, the guy deserved what he got.

"Anyway, Billy Joe fell in love with the daughter of a family the Tremaynes had been feuding with all the way back to the Civil War. But my grandpappy could recognize quality when he saw it, and when Fayrene Drummond came home on Easter vacation from that fancy Ivy League college up north, he knew she was the girl for him. When they eloped, both families hit the roof. But nine months later, when Fayrene gave birth to my daddy, the whole thing just kinda blew over."

He held the cellophane bag out to Caine, who reached in and absently took a handful of raisins. Caine wasn't at all hungry after that enormous dinner, but stakeouts were so damn boring. "I assume there's a point to this little saga."

"Of course. The point being that every family, royalty or not, has its little differences. Differences that can eventually be overcome. Besides, you don't even know whether or not Chantal's family would object to the princess marrying a commoner."

Caine practically choked on a chocolate-covered raisin. "Who said anything about marriage?"

"A guy could do worse.... You know, life gets real humorous sometimes."

Caine tried to think of one humorous aspect of this situation and came up blank. "How's that?"

"I've been watching the two of you circle each other like a pair of my daddy's old hound dogs. Neither of you look all that dumb, yet if someone doesn't make a move pretty soon, the princess will be back home walking the floors in Montacroix, and you'll be snapping my head off in Washington. Hell, Caine, you can't deny that you're downright smitten with her."

"'Smitten'? What outdated Victorian dictionary did you get that from?" Caine muttered even as he secretly admitted the word fit perfectly.

Who wouldn't be smitten with Chantal Giraudeau? During the long, lonely nights, when he was all too aware that she was asleep on the other side of the door, he'd even fantasized about her settling down with him. But the idea of a princess marrying a guy like him was worthy of the Brothers Grimm or Hans Christian Andersen: a nice fantasy, but a fairy tale all the same.

"All right, so I'm attracted to her, okay? She's like no other woman I've ever known, and I'd love nothing more than to get out of this car right now, go up to her bedroom and ravish her until we're too exhausted and too satiated to move. Now that I've said it, will you just shut up and eat your damn chocolate-covered raisins?"

"Sure. But Caine?"

"Yeah?"

"Don't wait too long." He grinned. "She just might find out what a jerk you really are."

The night was silent; the street empty. Next door a dog began to bark and was immediately called back inside the house.

"Damn," Drew said suddenly.

Caine's own oath was just as short but harsher as he caught sight of the flickering orange light that had just appeared in Chantal's bedroom window. "Get on the horn and call the fire department," he said, throwing open the car door. "And the police. I'll get everyone out."

As he took off across the deserted street, Noel Giraudeau's nightmare flashed through Caine's mind.

THE FLASHING LIGHTS lit up the night sky. Outside, on their front lawn, surrounded by hoses, David and Blair Sherwood gathered their children around them and watched in stunned disbelief as the fire fighters worked to save their beloved house. The curious had gathered on the sidewalk across the street, watching as the flames began to lick greedily at the roof.

Inside, Drew and Caine fought their way past the powerful streams of water being sprayed from the fire trucks as they tried to find Chantal.

"Dammit!" Caine shouted, his eyes stinging from the wall of smoke as he made his way up the still-intact stairs. "What kind of woman spends a fortune on antiques but won't put out fifteen bucks for a smoke alarm?"

Drew pulled off his soaked leather jacket and put it over his head. "How about a woman who doesn't want the fire detected?"

"No way. If Blair Sherwood had anything to do with this, she would have arranged to have her kids spend the night somewhere else." The smoke was becoming heavier. The floor was growing hot beneath their feet. "Besides, you didn't see her showing off this place today. She'd just as soon cut her own wrists as torch it."

They'd reached Chantal's room. Smoke burned Caine's lungs and he began to cough. The fire had obviously begun here; the four poster was afire and flames were ravenously devouring the curtains. But Chantal was nowhere to be seen.

"She must be in the passageway," Caine said, pointing toward the fireplace. "Blair said that's the way in."

Caine and Drew exchanged a look. Both men knew that if they were trapped behind the walls when the roof collapsed it would be the end for all of them.

"Let's go," Drew said.

On the other side of the wall, Caine could feel the heat and hear the roar of the fire as it ravaged the house. The narrow passageway was starting to fill with smoke, making their flashlights almost useless. As he crawled along, feeling in front of him, he found himself making deal after deal with God.

If he could only find Chantal, he'd never sneak another cigarette again. If she was still alive, he'd call his mother once a week, whether he had anything to say or not. If he could get her out of here safely, he'd give ten percent of his salary to Chantal's beloved Rescue the Children Fund every month for the rest of his life. He might even, he promised rashly as he heard the sound of the flames whipping across the roof, try going back to church.

He was trying to think up yet another bargaining chip when his hand suddenly came across something furry. The calico kitten, terrified by the events of the night, reacted instinctively, clawing a ragged path down the back of Caine's hand. He stopped in midcurse as he bumped into a seemingly boneless bundle of silk.

"I found her," he called out to Drew, who was following closely behind.

"Is she . . . ?"

Directing the beam of his flashlight onto her face, Caine pressed his fingers against the side of her neck. "She's alive," he said, relief rushing over him.

Drew came up beside Caine and shone his own light over her, lingering on the blood staining the shoulder of her sea green silk nightgown. "Looks like somebody bashed her a good one," he said, brushing her hair back and exposing a deep gash behind her ear.

"I'm going to find who did this," Caine vowed. His cold, quiet tone was more deadly than the loudest shout. "And when I do, I'm going to kill him."

"Why don't we get your lady out of here. Then we can worry about catching the bad guys." He ran his hands quickly, professionally over her body. "I don't think she's got any broken bones. Let's see if we can bring her to."

Caine lifted her up, cradling her in his arms. Beyond the walls the sound of the fire grew louder. Outside, the lonely wail of sirens continued to rent the air as even more fire engines arrived to fight the blaze.

"Chantal." His fingers moved over her face, stroking, gentling, comforting. "Come on, sweetheart, you've got to help us get you out of here."

Chantal opened her eyes and saw Caine, illuminated by Drew's flashlight. Even as confused as she was, she knew that she'd never, as long as she lived, forget the look on his face. There was fear there. And concern. And something else. Something so remarkable, she knew she'd have to think about it later.

"Caine?" Struggling to sit up, she began to cough. "What are you doing here? What's happening?"

"That's what we'd all like to know, Princess," Drew said. "But right now, we need to get you out of here."

She dragged her hands through her hair, struggling to understand. "I'm bleeding," she said in disbelief as her fingers encountered something warm and sticky at the back of her head.

"You're going to be all right," Caine assured her. "Do you think you're up to crawling out of here?"

"Crawl?"

"The house is on fire. The air is fresher close to the floor."

"Fire?" Her head was whirling and she felt as if an elephant was sitting on her chest. She coughed again. Once. Twice. Violently. "Oh, my God! Blair! And the children!"

"They're safe," Caine said as a sound like a freight train roared overhead. The fire was obviously spreading quickly through the attic, and they couldn't afford to waste any more time or oxygen. "Come on," he said, putting his arm around her. "This place isn't going to last much longer."

They were crawling back the way they'd come when a set of sharp claws suddenly clenched at his back. "Stupid cat," he muttered, doing nothing to dislodge the frightened kitten clinging to his shirt.

"The kitten," Chantal said. "I remember now. He was crying. He sounded frightened so I came in here to rescue him when suddenly someone came up behind me." Dizziness nearly overcame her; she stopped momentarily to let it pass. "I don't know who it was."

"We can talk about that later," Caine said grimly. "Right now you need to save your breath."

They reached the bedroom and were nearly all the way down the hallway when they heard a giant whoosh. The three of them watched in silent awe as a vast column of flames rose up to engulf the curving staircase, greedily eating away the ornately carved banister.

"So much for taking the easy way out," Drew said.

"We're going to have to jump," Caine agreed.

Chantal stared at them. "Jump? From the second story?" Her eyes were tearing from the soot in the air; her lungs were screaming for just one pure, clean breath. There was nothing she wanted more than to get out of this inferno, but surely there was some other way.

"It's our best chance, Chantal," Drew said.

"The only one," Caine said. "Come on, Princess, where's your spirit of adventure? Just hold on to my shirt. If we get separated in all this smoke, I might never be able to find you again."

Chantal couldn't believe the way both men remained so calm. So in control. "I suppose it's time I confess my single failing," she said, struggling to keep her voice steady.

She was spectacular, Caine thought. Any other woman would be screaming her head off about now. Chantal was obviously royal all the way to her fingertips. "What failing is that?"

"I'm afraid of heights."

"You are kidding."

"I wish I were."

Caine thought about her admission for only a moment. "No problem. We'll just try one of the back bedrooms," he decided. "With any luck, the terrace roof will still be intact."

Slowly, inch by inch, they made their way back down the hallway. As they passed Chantal's bedroom once again, the glass in the Palladian window exploded out onto the lawn.

It was only a bad dream, Chantal thought. A nightmare. Soon she'd wake up and find herself safe and sound in bed. Then, in just a few minutes she'd be running with Caine through the streets of Philadelphia, garnering energy for the busy day ahead.

Unfortunately, this was no dream. The flames rapidly engulfing the house were all too real. Her eyes were tearing violently from the soot and the smoke, and her lungs felt as if she'd swallowed a chestful of burning coals.

"Here we go," Drew said, leading the trio into what Chantal remembered to be the master bedroom. The heat had peeled the ivory silk paper off the walls, a layer of soot had settled onto the top of the gilded Duncan Phyfe dressing table and flames had begun licking at the colorful postage-stamp quilt covering a

Sheraton field bed. "Hey, we're in luck—this room has a balcony."

The glass in the French doors had been blown out earlier. Caine crawled onto the balcony, the others close behind. "Okay," he said as he helped Chantal to her feet, "all we have to do now is jump down onto that terrace rooftop."

It was less than eight feet. Eight feet between a chance to live and the probability of dying in this inferno that only hours before had been Blair Sherwood's pride and joy. "I can do it," she said. "But we have to take the kitten."

Caine was one step ahead of her. Peeling the terrified feline off his back, he unbuttoned his shirt and stuck the cat inside. "The little troublemaker is all taken care of. Ready?"

The fire had caught on to one of the bedposts and was licking at the acorn finial. Chantal knew it would only be a matter of moments before the entire room was engulfed in flames.

"Caine?"

"Yeah?" Beneath the studied calm in his voice, she could detect an edge of impatience.

"Will you hold my hand?"

"You've got yourself a deal." Caine's strong, capable hand closed reassuringly over hers. "We'll go on the count of three, okay?"

Chantal nodded.

"One."

She took a deep breath.

"Two."

She bit her lip as the rooftop below appeared to swim.

"Three."

Closing her eyes so tightly that stars appeared behind her lids, Chantal clung to Caine's hand with all her might and stepped off into space.

10

SHE WAS SO PALE. Caine stood beside the gurney, holding her hand, trying not to think how close he'd come to losing her.

"I must look a fright," Chantal complained, combing her fingers ineffectually through her wet and matted hair. Behind her ear was a row of precisely sewn stitches.

Her hair smelled of smoke. Soot ringed her red-veined eyes and was smeared across her cheeks. Her bottom lip was split where she'd put her teeth through it earlier.

"You look beautiful," he said, brushing his thumb over her knuckles. The pearl-tinted fingernails of her left hand were ragged and torn.

Her laugh turned into a violent cough. "Liar," she said when she could finally speak.

As he lifted her fingers to his lips, Caine's gaze did not leave her face. "I thought I'd lost you."

His expression, along with the unmasked emotion in his eyes, made her heart clench, then begin beating all the faster. Chantal knew that the time was fast approaching when they'd have to talk about what was happening between them. But not now. And not here, in this bustling hospital emergency room, where they could be interrupted at any minute.

"Caine?"

"Yeah?"

"There's something I probably should have told you earlier."

"What?"

"My father and brother have thought for several months that someone is trying to kill me. In the beginning, I believed they were merely overreacting to a few random accidents."

"And now?"

"And now I'm afraid they may be right."

It was better to get it out in the open, Caine thought. Better for her. Better for him. He'd been frustrated by having to keep his identity a secret. So why was he suddenly so reluctant to admit to the truth?

"I think that's a good bet. And since you brought it up, I suppose I'd better warn you that the police are waiting outside to talk to you." Only by flashing his Presidential Security ID had he managed to keep them at bay this long. The president, upon receiving Drew's phone call, had dispatched a team of FBI investigators who were also currently cooling their heels in the hospital's waiting room.

She shook her head, grimacing slightly as giant boulders rolled around inside. "I don't want to talk to the police."

"Would you rather give the guy another shot at you?"

His harsh tone grated, but Chantal could read the honest concern in his eyes and decided against responding in kind.

"I'd rather just get away from here. From all this," she said quietly, waving her hand around the room. The green curtain around them was drawn, but there was no mistaking the hurried, competent activity going on in the emergency room.

In the cubicle beside them, doctors and nurses worked valiantly in a futile attempt to revive a middle-aged man's heart. Across the room the teenage victim of a gang fight had a gaping knife wound that was being attended by an emergency room intern who didn't look old enough to shave.

The world hadn't stopped spinning just because she'd almost died, Chantal realized with a small jolt of surprise. Life went on, as it always had. "Please, Caine, take me to the hotel."

"Dammit, Chantal, this is serious."

"I know. And I promise that after some sleep, I'll be much more clearheaded and able to answer all their questions in more detail."

She had a point, Caine conceded reluctantly. He'd questioned her in the ambulance on the way to the hospital, and her story had remained exactly the same: she'd followed the kitten into the hidden passage, was grabbed from behind by an unknown assailant, fought him off as best she could, and that's where all memory ceased until she woke to find the passageway filled with smoke and Caine and Drew bending over her. But still, every moment they waited, the bastard could be farther away.

Chantal reached up and put her palm on his unsmiling face. "I promise to cooperate. Once I get some sleep."

He couldn't remember ever vacillating like this. Part of Caine wanted nothing more than to take Chantal as far away from this place as possible. He wanted to escape with her to some balmy tropical island, where they'd pass the time lounging on sun-drenched beaches, sipping Mai Tais and making love.

As appealing as that idea was, Caine's professional side argued that he shouldn't be wasting time; that he should be trying to track down whoever was responsible for that wicked gash at the back of her head. Whoever it was had already tried to kill her more than once and would undoubtedly try again.

Caine covered her hand with his. "I'll try to stall them. But you're going to have to talk to them later today."

"After some sleep," she agreed. "And a shower."

Giving in, as he'd always known he would, Caine left the curtained cubicle, shaking his head in frustration to Drew, who'd just finished making the necessary telephone call to Chantal's family.

"They're coming over on the Concorde," he said.

"All of them?" Facing the entire royal family after such a devastating failure was something Caine was not at all eager to do.

"I can't imagine keeping any of the O'Bannions away if it had been Tara who'd been hurt."

"Point taken," Caine agreed, thinking of how his family had rallied around his sister during her recent divorce. "Look, do me a favour and stay with her, will you? I've got to take care of the police and those feds."

"Sure thing. And Caine?"

"Yeah?"

"This wasn't your fault, you know."

Caine's face was grim as he turned to leave the room. "Wasn't it?"

When Drew entered the cubicle, Chantal greeted him with a faint smile. "I think Caine's mad at me."

"Not at you. He's mad at himself."

She arched an eyebrow, surprised that a facial gesture could hurt. "Why? He saved my life. You both did."

Drew shrugged. "Caine's not an easy man to get along with all the time. As much as he expects from the people around him, he's always demanded even more from himself. He thinks he should have been able to protect you from whoever did this."

"That's ridiculous. Caine is a diplomat, not a bodyguard."

Drew wasn't about to touch that one. The truth was going to come out; it was better that Caine be the one to tell her. "Hey," he said instead, "I brought you a present." Reaching into his pocket, he pulled out a familiar yellow cellophane bag.

A light brightened in her red-rimmed eyes. "Chocolate-covered peanuts," she said on a pleased little laugh. "Drew Tremayne, I think I love you."

A little in love with her himself, Drew grinned in response.

"Sounds as if you two are having a good time," Caine observed as he returned.

"Look what Drew brought me," Chantal said, holding up the bag of candy.

Taking one look at the pleasure in her eyes, Caine vowed to buy out the hospital's candy machine at the first opportunity. "Just what you need after a shock—a sugar jolt. I got you sprung from here and bought some time before you have to talk to the police."

"Thank you." Her expression turned serious. "For everything."

"Come on, Princess," Drew said, stepping in with a good-natured grin. "Let's blow this joint."

As they walked out the door, Chantal took a deep breath of brisk, predawn spring air. Everything was going to be all right. She was going to be all right.

IT COULD HAVE BEEN minutes. Hours. Or days. The room was dark, bathed in shadows when she finally awoke in a luxuriously appointed hotel suite. Looking around, she saw Caine seated in a chair beside the bed.

"What time is it?" she asked groggily.

"About nine in the morning."

"But it's so dark."

"Blackout drapes."

Of course. She should have realized. Sitting up, she pushed her tumbled hair away from her face and turned on the bedside lamp. "You should have wakened me," she protested. "The exhibit—"

"Is managing well enough without you at the moment. You'll be glad to know that yesterday's crowds broke the museum's opening-day record."

"Yesterday's?" She struggled to concentrate. "What day is this?"

"Friday."

"But the dinner at Blair's was on Wednesday night."

"Bull's-eye."

"Then I've been sleeping for more than twenty-four hours?"

"Twenty-eight, give or take a few minutes. Those pain pills the doctor gave you turned out to be doozies. When you were still dead to the world last evening I gave him a call, and he assured me that they affect some people that way and the best thing to do would be to let you sleep it off."

"Pain pills?" That explained why her head felt as if it were wrapped in cotton batting. "But I never take pills of any kind. Not even aspirin."

"This was a special circumstance. In case it's slipped your mind, Princess, someone tried to kill you."

Remarkably, she had forgotten. Slumping back onto the pillow, Chantal pressed her fingertips against her throbbing temples. "I thought it was a dream."

Caine left the chair to sit on the edge of her bed. He lifted her hair off her neck. "These stitches are no dream. They're damn real. Just like the fire. And the faulty brake line on your Ferrari. And the roof tiles that almost hit you on the head last month. And let's not forget the way the ski trail was mismarked to lead you out onto that glacier."

Stunned, Chantal stared at him. "How do you know about those things?" When he didn't immediately answer, all the little pieces of Caine O'Bannion that she had not been able to fit into a workable whole began slipping into place.

"You're not really a diplomat, are you, Caine?"

"I work for the government."

"But not the State Department."

"No. Not state."

"What then? FBI? CIA?"

"I work in the Treasury Department."

"Doing what?"

It was now or never. "I'm a Presidential Security agent. My superior assigned me to accompany you on this tour because of what he and the president and your father perceived to be attempts against your life. I was supposed to protect you."

Stunned though she was, Chantal could still detect the self-reproach in his gritty tone. She'd have to deal with the fact that he'd lied to her later, when she'd had time to sort things out. At the moment she only knew that she hated him feeling responsible for her own stupidity.

If she'd only listened to her father, to Burke. But if she had, then she would have brought her own security force to America and she and Caine would never have met. Timing, she mused, was indeed everything.

"If you work for the president, you must be very good at your job."

"I used to think I was."

She knew she should be furious at his deception, but for some strange reason, which she'd also think about later, she could not work up the proper amount of injured pride. "Caine," she said softly, "you saved my life. Why, if you and Drew hadn't found me—"

Caine cut her off. "It never should have come to that. Especially since I had received a warning about the fire before we even left New York."

"Noel." It was not a question.

"Noel," Caine agreed grimly. "How did you guess?"

Chantal shrugged. "She has this knack. When we were children, it drove me crazy. As we grew older, I learned to listen to her." *Except once,* Chantal added silently. *I ignored all her warnings about marrying Greg.*

"She told me about a dream she'd had. About you lying in the dark, near death. She'd seen it all. The fire, the smoke." Caine dragged his hand over his face. "Dammit, I should have listened."

How could she be angry with him when he was so unrelentingly furious with himself? "What could you have done?"

"I don't know. Forced you to stay here at the hotel, I suppose, where you'd have been safe."

"But then you'd have had to tell me who—and what—you were. And I suspect you'd already given your word not to do that."

He took her hand in his. "Believe me, it certainly wasn't my first choice. Unfortunately, your father felt that since you refused to admit that your life was in danger, you'd reject any bodyguard assigned to you."

Chantal considered his statement. "Papa may have been right. I'm afraid I can be a little headstrong from time to time."

Despite the seriousness of the conversation, a half smile quirked at the corners of his mouth. "'A little'?"

"Perhaps a bit more than a little," she admitted. "Enough so that I may have indeed refused a bodyguard on principle. But that was before I met you." Her dark eyes grew wide and clouded with need as she gazed at his face. "May I ask a personal question?"

Caine willed himself to stay calm. All his life, even as a child, people had described him as a rock—unemotional, unmovable. Despite his mother's assurances that she was quite capable of taking care of them, he'd felt an unbearable need to take on the role of the man of the house after his father's death. He'd been head altar boy at Saint Gregory's, high school senior-class president, Eagle Scout, valedictorian, and to no one's surprise, had followed in his father's footsteps by going on to be cited for his sterling leadership qualities at the U.S. Naval Academy.

Even his Presidential Security assignment was a plum position, the result of hard work and an unwavering attention to duty. He'd never been a man with doubts; he'd always known who he was and exactly where he was going. He was, quite simply, a man used to charting his own course.

Until a breathtakingly beautiful princess had stormed into his life like a hurricane. During these past days with Chantal, Caine had felt hopelessly adrift, as if he'd been cast onto a dark, uncharted sea, forced to navigate by instinct alone. He was a long, long way from the controlled individual he'd always thought himself to be, and he wasn't sure he liked it. Not one damn bit.

"You're entitled to one question, I suppose. Considering all the lies I've told you."

She touched a hand to his cheek. "Were you going to tell me who you were before you made love to me?"

He wanted her so very badly. And the situation was so very tempting. Caine hesitated, duty warring with desire, honor with need. Inexplicably drawn by a power more intense than anything he'd ever known, he cursed softly as he lowered his mouth to hers.

"I could never have kept the deception up," he said against her lips. She tasted moist and sweet. "Not this way."

"I'm glad." Chantal linked the fingers of both hands around his neck. "Make love with me, Caine. Prove to me that I'm still alive."

He needed no second invitation. As he slipped the narrow straps of her nightgown off her shoulders, her skin felt like liquid satin to his touch. She'd taken a shower immediately upon arriving at the hotel, and now, as his lips skimmed over the warming flesh that he had denied himself for too many days, Caine thought he could detect the lingering aroma of the gardenia bath talc the management had generously supplied. Her luxuriously soft breasts filled to fit his hands with such perfection that it crossed his mind that they might have been created specifically for him.

"We shouldn't be doing this."

She pressed her finger against his frowning lips. "This is no time to be analytical."

One final scrap of reason tried to make itself heard in the heated turmoil of his brain. "This is crazy," he said, his words a gentle breeze against Chantal's mouth.

"I know." A golden glow infused her body as he ran his tongue around her lips. She had to touch him, to experience his body as he was experiencing hers. With hands that trembled slightly, Chantal unbuttoned his shirt. "That's what's so wonderful about it. Please let's be crazy, Caine. Let's be crazy together."

Her hands fretted over his chest; her fingers tangled in the softly matted dark hair. He was taut, tense, hard as a rock. Bending her head, she pressed her lips against him, exulting in the dark, masculine taste of his flesh. Needs tore at her—wild, wanton cravings that only he could satisfy. A lingering sense of danger, fueled by desires too long ignored, created a greed she was stunned to discover she possessed.

When her fingers trailed down his rib cage, lingering over his stomach before slipping beneath the waistband of his jeans,

Caine decided that if this was madness, sanity was highly overrated. Passions that had been building for days threatened to consume him; the memory of how he'd felt when he'd thought he'd lost her made him ache.

"Chantal." It was only her name, but never had she heard it sound so sweet. "Chantal . . . Chantal." He said it over and over again, a lush litany of wonder.

A ruthless, ripe hunger consumed them both. Chantal heard the sound of silk tearing and welcomed it. Caine's own clothing disintegrated as if blown away by a fierce desert whirlwind. The crisp sheets beneath them became a heated tangle; the cool air grew hot and steamy.

If this was insanity, Chantal welcomed it with open arms. Her hands, like her lips, refused to remain still as they roved over his body, never lingering in any one place as they teased and tormented. In turn, Caine was relentless, nipping and licking and sucking, as if he wanted to leave no part of her body untouched, unclaimed.

He'd intended to treat her like a lady. Like a princess. But she'd bewitched him from the beginning, and now he finally succumbed to her with a primitive kind of desperation he'd never known before.

Chantal wrapped her legs around him and drew him into her, thinking that having him inside of her was more than she'd ever want. Or need.

"Chantal." His breath fanned the hammering pulse in her throat. "Open your eyes, sweetheart. I want to watch you go over the edge."

Unable to deny him anything, Chantal did as he asked. Her eyes were full of restless pleasure as he began to move, slowly at first, then deeper and faster, taking her places she'd never known. She arched against him, agile and demanding, moaning softly as she reached her peak. But Caine was relentless, and incredibly the need built again, higher, hotter, until her body went wild, matching the power and speed of his.

Caine watched her eyes darken to molten amber as she gave herself to him totally. And when she peaked again, he allowed himself to follow.

"I REALIZE this will sound terribly trivial to a man," she murmured, wrapped in Caine's arms, "but I'm relieved that I let you talk me into taking only the clothes and jewels I planned to wear in Philadelphia to Blair's house. I would have hated to have had to replace everything on such short notice."

"Speaking of jewels, they're going to be sifting through the ashes, but I wouldn't hold out a lot of hope for those amethysts."

"They're insured. Fortunately, I never take this one off."

Caine took hold of her hand, toying with the slender silver ring. "I've been wondering about this."

"Burke gave it to me. On my parents' wedding day. The day we legally became brother and sister."

"Your brother sounds like a nice man."

"The nicest." Subject closed, Chantal smiled at him. "Have I told you that I love your body?"

She was remarkable. Other than the faint shadows under her eyes and the row of stitching at the back of her head, there were no signs that she'd been on the brink of death. "I don't believe the subject's come up."

"I do." She pressed her lips against his chest. "Every morning when we're out running, it's all I can do not to drag you into the nearest alley and have my wicked way with you."

He tangled her hair in his hand, pulling her mouth to his. As he drank from the honeyed sweetness of her lips, Caine wondered if he'd ever get enough of her. "It's a good thing you managed to resist the temptation. The police are an unromantic bunch. They tend to frown on public displays of lust."

"I suppose your superior might also disapprove of such behavior," she said, slipping lower to continue her tantalizing assault down his body. How she loved his dark, musky scent!

"Probably fire me on the spot." Her tongue plunged wetly into his navel, and Caine drew in a sharp breath.

"Then you'd have no choice but to come to Montacroix and be a royal guard."

Alarms sounded in his head. "Chantal. . . ."

She'd pushed too far. Burke had always chided her on her impatience. Damn, she thought, struggling to ease the tenseness from Caine's body with hands and lips, when would she learn to curb her natural impulsiveness?

"I was only joking," she soothed, not quite truthfully. Actually, the idea, which she honestly hadn't thought of until this moment, sounded wonderful.

Caine observed her carefully, looking for some hint of a prevarication. What they'd shared was special. Unique. But unfortunately, it hadn't changed a thing.

Dear Lord, she really was in danger, Chantal realized suddenly. She was in danger of falling in love with Caine. Perhaps she already had. If that was the case, he could hurt her now. He could tear her heart to ribbons, and this time she might not recover.

"Honestly, Caine, I don't expect a lifetime commitment from you. I'm entirely willing to accept a short-term relationship. A no-strings affair that will last only as long as I'm in your country."

Even as she heard the words leave her lips, Chantal knew they were a lie. She wanted more from him, a great deal more. But afraid of frightening Caine away, she tried to make herself believe that she would be satisfied with whatever he was willing, or able, to give.

Just when he'd come to believe that Chantal was not the fall-in-bed-at-the-drop-of-a-hat princess of the supermarket tabloids, she did a 180-degree turnaround and invited him to enter into a one-night—or in this case, eight-night—stand. It was such a rapid reversal that Caine felt as if he should ask the real princess to please stand up.

"No strings," he repeated dubiously, running his hand down her side from her shoulder to her thigh. Her skin was warm and soft, and she trembled under his light touch.

Her heart was drumming. Her blood warmed. Would he always be able to affect her this way? With a single touch? A mere look? "No strings," she said.

Caine's hand settled on her hip, his fingers molding to the slender bone as he remained silent for a long, thoughtful moment. Experience had taught him that nothing in life came totally unencumbered. "Is that really what you want?"

"Isn't it enough?"

Caine tried to accept her answer for what it was: a declaration that the only future he and Chantal had together was a brief, fiery affair that would last just as long as her time in the States.

Wasn't that exactly what he'd wanted? So why did he suddenly find the idea strangely distasteful?

"Do you honestly believe that it's enough?"

Because she wasn't entirely sure of the nature of her own needs, Chantal could not understand his. "Really, Caine," she protested on a forced laugh, "must you take everything so seriously?"

"I take you seriously." With fingers that were heartbreakingly gentle, he brushed her hair back from her forehead, wondering what childhood adventure had resulted in that thin scar over her eye and wishing he'd been there to prevent it. "I wish I didn't. But I can't help it."

Even as she warned herself against setting herself up to be hurt again, Chantal felt a tiny seed of hope taking root in her heart. A hope that would make her vulnerable. Dependent. All the things she'd sworn she'd never be again.

"Is that so bad?"

"I don't know," Caine said on a long breath. "I just don't know." He shaped her shoulders with his palms. Just looking at her made him want. Touching her made him ache.

Chantal didn't resist as he drew her into his arms. As their mouths met, they went together to a shimmering, glowing place where there was no need for answers.

11

CHANTAL WAS IN THE SHOWER when the phone rang. "O'Bannion," Caine answered it.

"Hey, Caine," Drew said without preamble, "I just thought you might want to know that I'm with the Giraudeau family now. Their plane has landed a little ahead of schedule, and we should be arriving at the hotel in thirty minutes or so."

Thirty minutes. Hardly time to take care of one last item of business, let alone try to explain to Chantal why he was going to leave her. Well, Caine considered, it had been nice while it lasted. But it was time to return to reality.

"Thanks. Could you do me one more favor?"

"Sure."

"Stay with them until my replacement arrives."

There was a long pause on the other end of the line. "Be glad to," Drew said finally.

"Thanks."

Hanging up the receiver, Caine dragged his hand wearily over his face. Chantal was still in the shower; he could hear her singing over the sound of the water running. Part of him wanted to join her under the streaming warm water, to make love to her one last time. Another more responsible part of him cautioned against it.

Picking up the phone again, he placed a long-distance call to Washington.

"Believe me, Caine," James Sebring said after listening to Caine's request, "the fact that Chantal found out about your little deception and didn't throw a tantrum makes me even more convinced that you're the perfect man for the job. The princess has never taken well to authority figures. Her agreeing to remain under your protection proves that you've a talent for handling her."

That was definitely one way of putting it, Caine decided grimly. "Sir, you don't understand," he tried again. "Things aren't as simple as they were."

"Now that you are no longer having to pretend to be someone you're not, I would think things would be a great deal less complicated," the director countered.

"No disrespect intended, sir, but there is nothing uncomplicated about Chantal." Perhaps it was the way he'd said her name—a softening of his tone, a lingering over the musical sound. Whatever it was, the director's next words gave Caine the impression that he'd revealed far more than he'd intended.

"Do you know," Sebring said slowly, thoughtfully, "I seem to recall Chantal's father, Prince Eduard, saying much the same thing about her mother thirty years ago."

"I don't believe you understand, sir," Caine protested.

"On the contrary, I believe I understand all too well." There was another long pause. "I appreciate your dilemma, Caine. I also know that you're an honorable man and will do the right thing. Including keeping the princess safe."

He decided to try one last time. "I believe I could be more effective tracking down her assailant." As he'd sat beside her all those long, lonely hours, watching her sleep, Caine had decided to find the man who'd done this to Chantal, to ask for a personal leave of absence in order to get the job done.

"That's not your duty, Caine," the director said firmly.

"I want this man, sir."

"So do we all."

"If you'd only assign someone else to the princess—"

"While you're an exemplary agent, I'm ordering you to leave the detective work to the FBI. Is that clear?"

Caine had worked at the agency long enough to realize when arguing would be futile. "As a bell, sir."

Chantal was still humming when she exited the bathroom, a fluffy peach bath towel wrapped around her. As she heard Caine requesting to be relieved of his duty, a dark, spreading pain started in the pit of her stomach. He couldn't want to leave her. Not after all they'd shared. Some men might take whatever a woman was offering, then vanish. But not Caine. Please, not Caine, she begged, pressing her hand against her left breast, where the hurt threatened to take root.

He'd no sooner hung up when Caine heard a slight sound behind him. Turning, he viewed a frighteningly ashen Chantal standing in the doorway. "Are you all right?" he asked, hurrying to her side. "Is it your head?"

With a calm that belied the turmoil battering away inside her, Chantal met his concerned gaze with a level one of her own. "My head is fine."

"You're too pale."

"Honestly, Caine, I'm fine."

The heat that had been practically emanating from her earlier was gone, and she'd cloaked herself in a sheet of ice. Strange, Caine considered, he would not have thought Chantal had it in her to be cold.

"You're angry with me."

Afraid of her tumultuous emotions, Chantal wrapped her arms around herself in an unconscious gesture of self-protection. "I am not."

He put his fingers under her stubborn chin and tilted her head up. "Yes, you are. And I'll be damned if I know why."

"You're imagining things, Caine. Just let it be."

Tempted to shake her, Caine grasped hold of her arms. "No. Not until I get a straight answer."

"You were arranging for a replacement," she said, jerking free. "Tell me, Caine, did you also expect this replacement to share my bed? Is that one of the perks of being an executive bodyguard?"

He'd hurt her. Badly, it seemed. Caine wondered if he could do anything right where this woman was concerned.

"Chantal, listen to me." He put his arms around her, holding her when she tried to resist. "What we've shared the past few days is very important to me. Not just the lovemaking, although that was definitely a highlight, but all of it. Even the arguments. And to tell you the truth, although I'm not at all sure how I feel about what's happening between us, I could never take it—or you—lightly."

His hands moving up and down her back cajoled as his lips against her temple soothed and excited at the same time. "You were going to leave me," she murmured into the hard line of his shoulder.

"I was going to explain later, after I made the arrangements."

"For your replacement. So you could go back to Washington."

"I wasn't going back to Washington."

She tilted her head back, studying him gravely. "You weren't?"

"No. I wanted to track the man down who did this to you. To make him pay."

A host of emotions coursed through her, thrilling and terrifying at the same time. She reached up and traced the ridged line of his jaw. "I hadn't realized a professional could feel the need for revenge."

"That's pretty much what Director Sebring said when I asked for a change of assignment." What Caine hadn't told the director was that while he was crawling through all that smoke, he'd realized that the need to protect Chantal had stopped being professional long ago.

"Does that mean he refused?"

"Turned me down flat."

"Then you're staying with me? Until the end of the tour in Los Angeles?"

Conflict raged in him. He wanted to leave now, while his heart and his life were intact. At the same time he wanted to lock the door, take Chantal to bed and spend the rest of his life making wild, passionate love to her. *Go. Stay.* The words reverberated inside his brain until he thought he'd go mad.

"Until Los Angeles," he agreed, lowering his head. When his lips touched hers, ambivalence disintegrated. "Now, if you don't get some clothes on, Princess, I'm going to forget that your parents will be here in less than half an hour."

Her family. How could she have forgotten that Caine had told her they were flying to America? "I suppose I should warn you."

"Warn me about what?"

"My father is a very perceptive man. If he suspects that there is more than business between us, I'm afraid you may be in for a parental grilling."

"Don't worry about it. I was a Seal before I joined Presidential Security."

"A seal? Like the sea animal?"

"The navy's special forces. They trained us to survive torture techniques, so I can probably handle whatever your father might think up."

Chantal sighed. "It is obvious that you do not know my father."

THE FIRST THING Prince Eduard Giraudeau did upon entering Chantal's suite was to embrace his daughter in a huge bear hug. Then he turned toward Caine, his hands on his hips, a dark glower on his face. "You're O'Bannion."

Caine would have had to have been deaf not to hear the accusation in Chantal's father's tone. "I am," he replied.

"Both your president and James Sebring assured me that you would protect my daughter."

"Papa, Caine saved my life," Chantal protested. "He and Mr. Tremayne risked their own lives to get me out of Blair's house before the flames completely gutted it."

Eduard harrumphed. "If he'd been doing his job properly, you never would have gotten yourself in such a fix in the first place," he insisted, not taking his fierce eyes from Caine's.

"You're not telling me anything I haven't told myself a million times since it's happened, Your Highness," Caine said.

Easing the awkward moment, Burke stepped forward. "I believe introductions are in order. I'm Chantal's brother, Burke. This is our mother, and I believe you've spoken with Noel."

As he stood face-to-face with Burke Giraudeau, Caine felt as if he were being thoroughly summed up. The younger prince had a lean, intelligent face and dark eyes that looked as if they never missed a thing. After shaking hands with Chantal's brother, Caine turned toward Jessica. "I've always admired your work, Mrs. Giraudeau. I wish we were meeting under any other circumstances."

Jessica smiled. "Why, thank you, Mr. O'Bannion, although I wouldn't think you'd be old enough to remember any of my movies."

"His father was in love with you for years," Chantal offered.

"Really." Her pleasure was obvious. "I'd love to meet him. Perhaps, when all this is over, if your mother wouldn't mind."

If anyone else had made such an offer, he would have thought it to be nothing but an attempt at polite conversation during a difficult time. But Jessica seemed sincere. A nice woman, he decided. And even more beautiful than she'd appeared to be on the late show. "My father died several years ago. But I appreciate the offer. Your films gave him a great deal of enjoyment."

Caine turned to Noel. "Princess," he greeted her, nodding. He observed the two sisters standing together; they were a study in contrasts. Chantal's dark, sultry looks brought to mind rich Gypsy laughter and blazing campfires. Noel's silvery blond hair and bluish violet eyes reminded him of a cool alpine stream rushing through flower-strewn meadows.

Noel's smile, in its own way, proved every bit as devastating as her sister's. "Please," she said, extending her hand. Her unlacquered nails had been buffed to a glossy sheen. "I thought we'd already settled on Noel."

As their fingers touched, Caine realized from the look in Noel's eyes that she intuitively knew that he and Chantal had been intimate. Caine's own gaze instantly became shuttered.

Noel's glance was sympathetic as she looked over at her sister.

"You needn't have come all this way," Chantal told her family as she took a seat. "As you can see, I'm quite well."

Jessica Giraudeau poured a cup of tea from the pot that had been delivered by room service immediately after their arrival in Chantal's suite. A superb arranger, Jessica had used the cellular telephone in the limousine to order a light meal on their way to the hotel from the airport.

"You're as lovely as ever, darling," she agreed, holding the cup out to her daughter. "But when one has a shock, one needs family close by."

As she took the proffered cup, Chantal thought of all the other times her mother had come to her rescue with a steaming cup of tea. To Jessica, tea was a magic elixir, soothing everything from a headache to a broken heart. "You are all wonderful."

A slight frown furrowed the smooth line of Jessica's brow as she watched Chantal stir a second spoonful of sugar into her tea, but she held her tongue. "It was all I could do to keep your father from hijacking the airplane in his hurry to cross the Atlantic."

"They had no business holding the flight up like that," Eduard complained. "I explained the importance of our mission, but the imbeciles refused to listen." Volatile, outspoken, the prince radiated a lingering frustration that had Chantal sympathizing with the Air France flight crew.

"They listened, Papa," Noel corrected mildly.

"Then why did they refuse to take off?"

"Perhaps the fact that the airport was engulfed in a cloud of fog had something to do with it," Burke said dryly. He was perched on the arm of Chantal's chair. "How are you, really, little one?" he asked, brushing her hair away to examine her stitches.

"I'm fine. Really," she insisted as he gave her one of the long, probing looks that had always been her undoing. "Better than fine."

"When we find the monster who did this," Eduard said, "I will insist that the legislature bring back the guillotine." He narrowed his eyes in warning to anyone who might want to argue the point. Understanding that he was still afraid and loath to show it, everyone remained silent.

"And now that we have dispensed with the social amenities, Mr. O'Bannion," the prince said, turning back to Caine, "would you care to tell us exactly how you plan to protect my daughter during the remainder of her time in your country?"

"Actually, I've been trying to convince your daughter that she should cancel the rest of the tour. But she's proven rather immovable on the subject."

"Chantal has always known her own mind," Eduard said with the air of a man who might constantly fret over his daughter's intransigence but refused to hear a word of criticism from anyone else.

"Tenacity is one thing," Caine said. "Pigheadedness quite another."

"'Pigheaded'?" Chantal said on a furious gasp.

"Just calling them like I see them, Princess."

It took a major effort, but Chantal resisted stamping her foot. "I am not pigheaded. And don't call me Princess."

The impending fireworks were obvious, as was the electricity arching between them. Seeing the blazing fury in her daughter's eyes, Jessica stood up and put her hand on her husband's arm. "Darling, I am suddenly so tired I can barely stand. I'm afraid that jet lag has caught up with me. Would you mind escorting me to our room? Perhaps later we can all get together and discuss Chantal's plans."

"But you never have jet lag." He pressed the back of his hand against her forehead, checking for fever. "Perhaps you've taken ill."

"I'm merely tired," she assured him. "I'll be fine after a rest. Perhaps you'd care to join me."

Eduard looked back and forth between Caine and his wife, as if struggling to make a decision.

"You can speak with Mr. O'Bannion later, darling," Jessica suggested adroitly. "When you're not behaving like a hysterical father."

"Why shouldn't I be?" he grumbled. "That's what I am. But you have a point, as always, my dear. I will allow you to cajole me into behaving in a more civilized fashion."

"Thank you, Papa," Chantal said.

He drew her into his arms, pressing his lips against her hair.

"I love you, *chérie,*" he said gruffly, his deep voice wavering. His dark eyes were suspiciously wet.

Chantal's own eyes were none too dry as she put her arms around her father, allowing his solid bulk to comfort her. "And I love you. All of you," she said on what was nearly a whisper as her loving gaze took in her mother and brother and sister.

Caine watched, strangely moved by the scene. He'd been attracted to Chantal from the beginning, but even as he'd begun to admit his feelings to himself, he'd tried to concentrate on her fire, her smoldering sex appeal. Now, as he watched her with her family, saw her in the role of daughter, sister, he had an inkling of another Chantal. A strong, loving woman who, oddly enough, reminded him a bit of his mother.

"I really am sorry I hurt you," Caine said once they were alone again.

"You needn't apologize, Caine. I overreacted."

Caine reached out and twisted a few glossy, dark strands of her hair around his fingers. "I should have realized how you'd take my leaving right after we'd made love."

"It wasn't your fault. Actually, it was more of a knee jerk reaction dating back to my ill-fated, highly publicized marriage." Her smile, as she looked up at him, wobbled ever so slightly. "Greg had a habit of disappearing."

To his surprise, Caine felt a jolt of something that uncomfortably resembled jealousy at the mention of her former husband.

"I suppose that's not so surprising for a Grand Prix driver." He wondered if Chantal had objected to her husband's traveling in order to earn his own living. Had she honestly expected him to remain in the palace like some royal lapdog? "The racing circuit covers most of the world."

"I wouldn't have minded the racing. It was his extra-curricular activities I found hurtful."

"The guy played around?" What kind of idiot would stray when he had this sexy, passionate woman waiting for him at home?

Appearing suddenly uncomfortable, Chantal crossed the room, where she stood looking out the window. Her suite had a breathtaking view of the Logan Circle gardens, but she was not seeing the brilliant flowers. Instead, her vision was directed at a scene several years and many miles away.

"The first time was on our honeymoon. Greg was scheduled to race in the Monaco Grand Prix the following week, so we'd rented a villa in Eze. A small Riviera village between Monaco and Beaulieu," she explained at his questioning look. "It's a lovely, quiet, intimate little place, perched high on a hill, with cobbled streets and medieval houses topped with dusty red-tiled roofs, all removed from the hustle and bustle of the social hubs like Saint-Tropez and Monte Carlo."

"Sounds like a great spot for a honeymoon," he said, coming up to stand beside her.

"That's what I thought. Until I returned from the market, where I'd bought the most luscious fresh strawberries I'd planned to dip in melted chocolate. Greg had teased me about not being able to cook, so I'd bought a cookbook and had decided to begin with the desserts."

"Knowing you, that makes perfect sense," he agreed, kissing her because it had been much too long.

"Mmm," she murmured happily as her lips clung lingeringly to his. "I do so love the way you kiss, Caine."

"You're not so bad, yourself, Princess. So, while you were out at the market, practicing to be a dutiful little housewife, your husband was home boinking the maid."

"She was not a maid but a singer from the cabaret we'd visited the night before," Chantal corrected. "But yes, he was indeed—" the unfamiliar but easily understandable colloquialism slipped her mind "—whatever it was you said."

"You should have kicked the bastard out on the spot."

"I'd just taken my marriage vows three days earlier."

He took her icy hand in his, his thumb brushing lightly across her knuckles. "So had he," Caine reminded her, choking back a very strong urge to curse the man Chantal had married. "Don't they have women's liberation in Montacroix?"

"Of course, but when you grow up with parents who love each other the way mine do, you develop some very strong ideas about what a marriage should be. And one of those ideas is that you shouldn't run away the first time things get a little rough."

"Another rule of thumb is that you don't screw around on your spouse."

"I know." She gave a long sigh that rippled through her. "But in a way, you see, it was my fault."

"I find that difficult to believe."

"Not only couldn't I cook, but I wasn't very good at the physical part of marriage, either," she admitted with a low, strained voice he had to struggle to hear. There, she'd said it. Hearing the words out loud didn't make them less painful, she discovered.

Caine stared disbelievingly. "You are kidding."

"Not at all." She could feel the color rising in her cheeks. "I was a virgin when I married Greg."

"Did he know that?"

"Of course. Oh, I'd dated other men before him, although not nearly as many as those horrible tabloid newspapers alleged. I'd even been engaged briefly once, and during my teens I'd had a wild crush on Burke's cousin, Stephan Devouassoux. But I had been taught that lovemaking was something special, to be shared with that one person you wanted to spend your life with, and although such a belief always seemed natural to me, my virginity did tend to scare more than one man away."

"Their loss."

Chantal smiled. "Thank you."

He shrugged. "It's the truth. But Greg was different?"

"He said he admired the fact that I had such high standards, that I had, as he put it, saved myself for marriage. You've no idea how happy those words made me. I thought, finally, after all those years, I'd found someone who shared my feelings."

A slight frown crossed her face. "Burke tried to talk me out of the wedding. He said that Greg was the kind of man who would view an untouched bride as the ultimate challenge. That once I was no longer a virgin, his passions would cool and he'd be back to his hedonistic life-style."

"Sounds as if your brother hit the nail on the head."

"Greg did have other women. But only because I couldn't please him."

Caine felt a blaze of anger. "Yeah," he said, kissing her furrowed brow, then her temple, "you're a real bust in the sack, Princess. That's why I can hardly move."

"It was good, wasn't it?" she murmured wonderingly.

"*We* were good," he corrected, trailing a lazy finger down her face. "You and I. Together."

She sighed as his lips skimmed over the trail his finger had blazed. "Together." It was happening again, she thought wonderingly as she felt her bones melting.

Need. Hunger. Want. Her body seemed to respond instinctively to his, warming at the touch of his hands, softening at the feel of his lips.

Forever, Caine mused as fresh desire rippled through him. He could make love to this woman forever. He was prepared to do precisely that when the phone began to ring.

"Ignore it," she murmured, her hands combing through his dark hair.

"I can't. It might be important." With a low oath, he reached over and picked up the receiver. "O'Bannion.... Yes, sir. She's right here." He handed the phone to Chantal. "It's your father."

"Hello, Papa," she said, exchanging a look of regret with Caine. "Of course I can be ready in half an hour.... Yes, I'll tell him.... Papa, don't you dare do any such thing.... Papa, I'm warning you.... Damn," she muttered. "He hung up."

"Problem?"

"I'm afraid so." Her expression was gravely apologetic. "Papa insists that you join us for dinner."

"I'd like that," he surprised her by saying.

"Really?"

"Really. Perhaps before this evening is over, between the two of us we can convince you to cancel this damn tour."

"You know I can't do that. The children are depending on me."

"The children don't expect you to set yourself up as a target," Caine shot back. "What I should do is simply refuse to let you leave this room until we catch the guy who's trying to kill you."

Chantal tossed her head. "You'd have to tie me down first. And you'd never do that."

"Want to bet? I've got a set of handcuffs in my room that are probably just your size."

"You're a bully, Caine O'Bannion."

"That's one way of looking at it. Personally, I prefer to think of it as doing my job, but I suppose you're entitled to your own opinion."

"I know you. You aren't serious about those handcuffs."

"We could put it to the test, if you'd like."

She studied him for a full ten seconds. Finally, a slight smile began to tease the corners of her lips. "Did anyone ever tell you that you are incredibly sexy when you start throwing your weight around?"

"All the time," he lied deftly. "How about you? Did anyone ever tell *you* that you're enough to drive the average man to drink?"

Her gaze met his in a softly challenging way. "But you're not the average man, are you Caine?"

He took a moment to answer, struggling against the sensual invitation he read in her dark eyes. "I like to think I'm not," he agreed, his casual tone taking a Herculean effort. "Now, if you think you can manage to stay out of trouble for five minutes, I want to change into a suit before dinner."

As he reached the doorway of the bedroom, Caine turned. "Whatever you do, don't open this door to anyone," he instructed, trying to conceal how desperate he was to keep her safe.

As he quickly changed out of his jeans into a charcoal gray business suit, Caine wished once again that he could take a more active part in the investigation surrounding the fire that had come so close to taking Chantal's life.

From the moment she'd been deliberately lured into the secret passage and struck, there'd no longer been any question that someone was willing to go to extraordinary lengths in order to arrange her death. But who? And why?

Caine could only hope that they found the answers before her would-be killer struck again.

THE DARK-HAIRED MAN swore at the television screen as he watched Chantal give a brief statement to the throng of avid reporters gathered in the porte cochere of her hotel. That the authorities were calling the fire an unfortunate accident was not surprising; an act of attempted murder would create an international incident, something the governments of both Montacroix and the United States would want to avoid at all cost. The investigation would be done surreptitiously.

As he watched the princess and studied the grim-faced man in the gray suit standing beside her, the man cursed himself for not realizing from the beginning that her escort was a great deal more than a mere lower-echelon diplomatic drone.

Pointing the remote control toward the television, the man vowed that after Chantal, Caine O'Bannion would be the next to die.

12

"ALONE AT LAST," Chantal said with a sigh of relief as she and Caine returned to her suite later that evening. "I truly love my family, but it was becoming quite exhausting having them hover over me like a clutch of anxious mother ducks."

"Hens."

"Whatever. I thought I'd die when Papa announced that he was joining us for the remainder of the tour. Thank goodness you were able to change his mind and convince him to return to Montacroix."

"I only pointed out that his presence would make my job more difficult."

"It was the way you did it." Chantal looked at him with undisguised admiration. "For a moment there, I was almost able to believe you were the diplomat you originally professed to be. Papa is not the easiest of men."

"It's obvious that he and the rest of your family love you. It's also obvious that they're worried sick about you continuing this tour."

She kicked off her high heels and sank down onto the couch. "Please don't start in on that again."

"In on what? Would you like a drink?"

"Brandy would be nice," she agreed. "And you know very well what you're doing. You're trying to make me feel guilty about causing them concern."

As he poured brandy into a pair of balloon glasses on the bar, Caine glanced over at her curiously. "Would it work?"

"No."

"I didn't think so," he said, crossing the room and handing her one of the glasses. "But it was worth a shot." He sat down beside her, sipping the brandy, enjoying one of the few peaceful moments they'd managed to share during the past fourteen days.

"I like your family. They're not what I would have figured them to be."

"And how had you thought of them? As a group of pompous, autocratic, self-important, wealthy snobs?"

Caine shrugged. The description hit too close to home for comfort. "I haven't had much of an opportunity to mingle with royalty."

"We're people, just like everyone else."

"Now that's where you're wrong, sweetheart," he murmured, running a hand down her hair, remembering how the long, dark strands had felt draped across his chest. "Because you are not like anyone else."

His eyes, as they settled on her face, were as intense and dark gray as a storm-tossed sea. Chantal took a deep breath and exhaled quickly. "I'm afraid," she whispered through lips that had gone uncomfortably dry.

"You should be. Someone's been trying to kill you."

She shook her head. "Not of him. Of us."

Caine managed a grim smile. "You're not alone there, Princess."

"Caine." It was only his name, but it spoke volumes. "What's going to happen? To us?"

What indeed? Caine wondered. In the beginning, he'd tried to tell himself that his attraction to Chantal was purely physical. And although he'd wanted to keep their relationship strictly professional he had assumed that if the opportunity ever arose to act on what was obviously a mutual attraction, his desire would be satisfied, his hunger satiated. It had been a logical assumption, based on past experiences. And Caine was nothing if not a logical man.

But something had gone wrong. Because instead of easing his need for her, their lovemaking had only served to make him more greedy. Somehow, when he wasn't looking, he'd crossed the line between want and need.

"Now you sound like your father."

His feigned humor didn't fool her for a moment. He was as disconcerted by all this as she was, Chantal realized. And why not? That he hadn't wanted this assignment in the first place was obvious; that he hadn't wanted to become emotionally involved with her, even more so.

Patience had never been Chantal's strong suit, yet every instinct she possessed told her that nothing would be settled by forcing the issue. They both needed time to think, to reassess the changes in their relationship. She only wished they could do so without the additional stress of the tour, and of that man, whoever he was, wherever he was, trying so hard to kill her.

"Actually, you were quite fortunate," she said. "Every time Papa opened his mouth to interrogate you, the others came riding to the rescue like the heroes in all your American Westerns."

"Noel makes a rather interesting Clint Eastwood."

"Wasn't she amazing?" Chantal asked, warming to the subject of her sister. "I had no idea she could be so forceful. Imagine her interrupting Papa like that! Again and again. She had him so frustrated, I worried that he'd explode before we finished dessert."

"Still waters . . ." he murmured. "I got the distinct impression that you two are more alike than you seem at first glance."

Chantal looked up at him with renewed interest. "Really? Most people don't see any resemblance at all."

"You don't look anything alike," he conceded, "although you're both stunningly beautiful. But I was talking about what's inside—those iron-strong wills you both share."

His perception pleased her. She'd made the mistake of falling in love with a shallow man once before; she was glad that Caine was a man who took nothing at face value. "In her own calm way, Noel can wear away a stone."

"Yet she couldn't change your mind."

She heard the aggravation in his tone and knew that his grievance was shared by her family. "I'm not going to let him win," she said in a firm, quiet voice. "I'm not going to begin living in fear just because some crazy person out there doesn't like me."

Her fingers curved around his upper arm, and her expression was intense as she tried to make him understand. "Don't you see? Like it or not, I'm a public person, and if I allow this man to send me scurrying back to the safety of Montacroix, I'll never be free of him. I'll have to spend the rest of my life hiding out in the palace, surrounded by armed guards."

Fear for her safety, plus something that was beginning to feel more and more like love with each passing day, made his words rash. "Not the rest of your life, dammit. Just until we catch the guy."

"And when you do, then what?"

"Then you can resume your tour."

"But what if I receive yet another threat? What would you have me do then?"

Even as he knew where this conversation was leading, that in her own single-minded way, she made sense, he still didn't like the idea of her setting herself up as a target for some madman.

"Don't you understand? I care about you."

The turbulent emotions she saw swirling in his eyes nearly took her breath away. "Don't worry about me. I'm under the protection of the president's personal bodyguard."

"A fat lot of good that did you the other night," he said grumpily. He'd known all along that he wasn't going to change her mind, but he never would have forgiven himself for not trying.

"Please, let's not think about that tonight," she coaxed prettily, her eyes amber pools of need as she took his empty glass and placed it on the table in front of them along with her own. "Or tomorrow." She reached up, freeing him from his red silk tie. "Let's pretend there's only now. Only this one perfect night together."

There were plans he'd intended to discuss with her, cautionary changes in her itinerary that would help ensure her safety, but as she manipulated the buttons of his white dress shirt, releasing one after another until she was able to press her hands against his bare chest, Caine lost the ability to concentrate.

"Tonight you're mine," he said in a low, deep voice rough with emotion.

"Yours." She gasped in surprise as he pulled her down onto the plush carpeting, but then she wrapped her arms around his neck and clung, eager to go anywhere he wanted to take her. "All yours."

CAINE WOKE FIRST, which allowed him the pleasure of watching Chantal sleep. Her lips were curved in a softly satisfied smile, which made him wonder if she was dreaming of the love-filled night they'd shared. A shaft of morning sunlight streamed into the room through a slit in the heavy draperies, illuminating the exquisite planes and hollows of her face.

Although his body was sated, his mind was not. How was it, Caine asked himself, that each time he made love to Chantal only made him want her more? What had begun as normal male desire was rapidly escalating to something that more and more resembled obsession.

Murmuring low, inarticulate sounds of pleasure, she turned toward him, her blissful sigh unmistakable as she pressed her body against his. Imbued with an uncharacteristic feeling of tenderness, Caine touched his lips to her sleek, dark head, content to lie quietly with her in his arms.

"What time is it?" Chantal murmured groggily into his shoulder. She tightened her arms around him, fitting her slender frame even more closely to his.

"Time to get up." He lifted her hair and pressed a kiss against her neck.

"Mmmph." She burrowed deeper, reminding him of a fox settling into its den. "I'd rather stay here. All day. With you."

"We have a plane to catch, remember?" In no real hurry to move himself, Caine idly played with her hair, sifting the dark strands through his fingers like grains of sand.

"We can always make a later one."

"We're due in Milwaukee at noon."

Unwilling to return to the real world quite yet, Chantal rolled over and straddled him, moving in such a way that the friction between their bodies seemed to create sparks in the early-morning light.

"How much time do we have, exactly?"

Caine's fingers dug into her hips as he lifted her up and settled her over him. "Enough," he said as their bodies merged and their minds entangled.

THE PHONE CALL came as they shared a hurried breakfast in the suite. They were due at the airport in a little more than an hour.

"That was Drew," Caine said as he returned to the room service table.

"Oh?" Chantal looked up from buttering her sweet roll. "Please tell me that our flight's been canceled. That we have nothing to do but spend the rest of the day in bed, where I can have my wicked way with you."

Caine shook his head with good-natured disbelief as he sipped his coffee. "Lord, lady, you are insatiable. Don't you ever get enough?"

"Of you?" She gathered the scattered crumbs from the roll into her palms. "Never. I'm afraid you've ruined me for any other man, Caine," she said cheerfully as she brushed the crumbs onto her gold-rimmed plate. "Years from now, when I'm a little old silver-haired lady, sitting in my rocking chair in some retirement home for aged royalty, I'll still be lusting after your magnificent body."

Caine felt a stab of guilt at Chantal's reference to the future. He had always been forthright with the women he'd become involved with; his romantic relationships were based solely on shared interests and mutual physical pleasure. Then Chantal had come into his life, and he'd started contemplating a future with her even when he knew one could never exist.

"Well, I'm sorry to disappoint you, but he was calling about business. He has a line on your assailant."

"Really? Who is it? Does he know?"

He put his napkin down and leaned back in the chair. "Unfortunately not. What the FBI guys did uncover was how he managed to get into the house in the first place."

"How?"

"As one of the waiters."

"But I thought you told me you and Drew had checked out the caterers before we arrived in Philadelphia."

"We had. Unfortunately, several employees called in sick with the flu that day, so there were a lot of last-minute changes. Enough that no one realized one of the waiters had been paid a substantial amount of money to disappear."

"How does Drew know that?"

"The FBI caught the guy boarding a plane to Jamaica. With a hundred thousand dollars in cash."

"Someone paid all that money just to take his place?"

"Seems so." Caine's expression was grim. "The bureau is sending a police artist to the airport so we can help them work up a composite of the counterfeit waiter."

Chantal vaguely recalled a tall blond man with a neatly trimmed beard. A man who had seemed oddly familiar at the time, but intent on raising funds for her charity, she hadn't fully focused on him.

"Caine, one of the waiters was on the plane from France with me."

Every atom in his body went on red alert. Finally, something to go on. "Are you sure?"

"Positive. He kept staring at me through the entire flight."

"Why the hell didn't you tell me that in the first place?"

"Because at the time it didn't mean anything. I am quite accustomed to men's appreciative glances."

"Too bad you can't tell the difference between honest masculine lust and murderous intent."

It took an effort, but Chantal assured herself that Caine's gritty tone was solely due to concern for her safety. "You may find this difficult to believe, but accepting the idea that someone actually wanted to kill me was extremely difficult," she said quietly.

Caine knew he was being hard on her, but he couldn't help himself. If she'd only call off this damn tour . . . and what? Return to Montacroix? Was that what he really wanted?

"Well, hopefully once we get an accurate sketch, we'll be able to get a line on the guy."

The idea of all that money kept reverberating around in her head. "Caine?" Her cheeks were paler than they should have been, her dark eyes shadowed with an unmistakable dread.

"Yeah?" He took her hand in his across the table.

"Whoever he is, he's very serious, isn't he?"

Dead serious, Caine thought grimly. "Yeah," he said instead, "I think he is."

"But why didn't he just poison my dinner? Wouldn't that have been easier?"

"It also would have been too fast. There would have been no way to poison you and get out without drawing suspicion to himself."

"How did he know about the secret passages?"

"That's an easy one. Remember Blair telling us that her home had been designated a historical landmark and that the blueprints are on file at the historical society?"

"Vaguely."

"Although only members and scholars are admitted to the archives, one of the volunteers recalls a telephone repairman recently working in the room where the prints were filed."

Chantal fell silent for a long time, absently tracing circles on the crisp white linen tablecloth. "Surely this is not the work of a single man?"

"We don't think so."

"I don't understand. Why would anyone conspire to kill me?"

"I don't know." His fingers tightened on Chantal's. "But I swear, Chantal, that we're going to find these guys. And when we do, they're going to pay."

She didn't want to think about it. It had to be a mistake, some bizarre practical joke gone berserk. But as she watched determination harden Caine's eyes to cold, gray steel, Chantal knew that this was incredibly, terrifyingly real.

ALTHOUGH CHANTAL had been to America several times, her visits had been confined to the coasts: New York, Los Angeles, with an occasional trip to Palm Springs and Palm Beach. Now, as she and Caine traveled across the vast country, she was discovering a myriad of surprises.

Milwaukee, which had always brought to mind beer and babushkas, proved to be a surprisingly cosmopolitan city, boasting an encyclopedic art museum containing collections ranging from ancient Egyptian to modern American. She was proud to have her own work displayed in such august company and pleased when the city proved more than a little generous when it came to contributing to her charity.

It was while she was in Milwaukee that Chantal received a jolt back to the past in the form of a telephone call from someone who had, for a brief time, been the most important man in her life.

Stephan Devouassoux was technically Burke's cousin, not hers, but he'd always seemed like a member of the family. Except for those turbulent teenage years when she'd had a raging crush on the tall, handsome Cambridge student.

"Stephan," she said delightedly, "how on earth did you track me down?" After the fire, her hotels had been changed and the new locations kept a closely guarded secret.

"I finally managed to convince Burke to give me your itinerary. Honestly, Chantal, his behavior reminded me of a mother bear guarding her cub."

"Burke's been worried about me."

"And rightfully so, which is why his overprotective attitude failed to insult me. How are you, *chérie?* Ever since I read about that terrible accident in Philadelphia, I've been worried sick." His voice over the long-distance wires possessed the same deep, velvety warmth that had succeeded in melting her youthful heart.

"I'm fine."

"Are you certain?"

"Positive." When Caine, seated in a chair across the room, scowled a warning, Chantal remembered that the official story was that the fire had been an accident. What no one but a select group of insiders knew was that the various empty gasoline cans discovered in the rubble had served as mute proof to the contrary.

"But you were hospitalized."

"Only for observation."

There was a pause. "Well, I shall be relieved to see for myself that you did, indeed, escape that horrible fire unharmed."

"See for yourself?" A smile claimed her face. "Don't tell me that you're in Milwaukee."

"Correct country, wrong state. I'm in Los Angeles and I have purchased a ticket for your exhibit."

"That's wonderful! But I thought you were living in Paris."

"I was until two years ago. I was approached by a group of individuals while attending the Cannes Film Festival. They were seeking funding to form an independent production company in Los Angeles, and since Paris had become boring, predictable, I decided to give California a try."

"And is California less predictable and boring?"

He laughed heartily. "What do you think?"

"I think, Stephan dear, that California would suit you perfectly. You always were the most flamboyant member of the family."

"Heaven knows I've done my best. But we all know that ever since your fifth birthday, I've come in a distant second to the most beautiful princess in the world."

She laughed at that, as she was supposed to. When Caine narrowed his eyes at the soft, musical sound, Chantal felt a surge of feminine power at the idea that he could become jealous.

Caine pointed down at his watch. "If we don't get going," he whispered, "we're going to miss the opening pitch."

Although he hated the idea of allowing her to mingle with the public, when Chantal decreed that she couldn't begin to understand his country until she had experienced America's national pastime, Caine had relented, agreeing to take her to a night baseball game.

Chantal nodded her acquiescence. "Stephan, I'm afraid I must run. But it was wonderful to hear from you, and I can't wait to see you in Los Angeles."

"On the contrary, *ma chère,*" Stephan countered with that old-world gallantry she had once found so irresistible, "it is I who will be waiting with bated breath to see you. *Au revoir,* Chantal."

"*Au revoir,* Stephan," she said softly. She was still smiling as she hung up the phone.

"Stephan. That's the cousin, right?" Caine asked. "The one you thought you were in love with."

"It was a crush, nothing more."

"Did I hear you say you were meeting with him in L.A.?"

"He's coming to the gallery," she confirmed.

"Why?"

"Obviously to see me. We were once very close."

Caine arched a brow. "Exactly how close?"

"Are you jealous?"

"Of course not," Caine countered, not quite truthfully. As a matter of fact, he hadn't liked the way her expression had softened while she was talking to this alleged cousin. "Now, if you're ready, Drew has the car waiting downstairs."

As they took the elevator to the lobby, Caine decided to check out this Devouassoux character. It was only a hunch, but Caine had learned long ago to trust his instincts. Besides, if he was going to suddenly have a rival for Chantal's affections, he wanted to know what he was up against.

IN YET ANOTHER COMPROMISE, Chantal had reluctantly agreed to watch the baseball game from a private, glassed-in box at

County Stadium, which precluded her mingling with the fans as she would have liked. There she discovered to her delight that beer and bratwurst were de rigueur in this town that still reflected a rich German heritage.

Chantal had always considered herself an intelligent woman. Even so, the game taking place on the diamond of bright green grass remained a mystery. Deciding that the smartest thing to do was simply groan and cheer along with the crowd, she found herself enjoying the evening immensely. Despite the fact that besides Caine and Drew, she'd been accompanied by a detail of blue-suited, unsmiling FBI agents.

"I'm sorry for the fans that their team didn't win tonight," she said later as Drew drove them back to the hotel. "And although I understand their disappointment, I find it difficult to believe the umpire was actually blind."

Plucking a peanut from the red-and-white striped bag she'd bought at the game, she cracked the shell and popped the meats into her mouth. As she crunched her expression was one Caine would have expected to see from a woman sampling imported caviar.

"He wasn't, was he?" she asked hesitantly. "I mean, surely that isn't possible."

"Of course he wasn't. And don't worry about the fans. If there wasn't at least one questionable call per game, they wouldn't have anything to talk about until the next one. It keeps interest up."

"Oh." Chantal pondered that for a time, deciding that it made sense. "Caine?" she said at length.

"Yeah?"

"May I ask you a question?"

"Sure."

"Have you ever been married?"

"No."

"Why not?"

From the way he dragged his hand through his hair, Chantal decided that it was not his favorite subject. "When I was in the navy, my work consisted of doing the kind of covert stuff that can end up being dangerous. I didn't think it fair to ask a woman to share that risk."

"And later?"

He shrugged. "Same story."

"But surely there are other navy men and Presidential Security agents who are married?"

"Sure, but they didn't grow up without a father. Having been that route, I swore never to inflict it on my own kids."

From his gritty tone, Chantal knew enough not to argue. "Have you ever thought about having a family?"

"Hasn't everyone?"

"What would it be like?"

He glanced down at her, half irritated, half amused. "What is this? I feel like I'm getting the third degree."

"You know about my marriage," she protested softly, understanding his tone, if not the exact meaning of his words. "I was just curious how you felt."

Caine linked his fingers behind his head and leaned back, considering her question. It had been so many years since he'd allowed himself to think about marriage that an answer didn't come immediately to mind.

"Marriage," he mused aloud. "Let's see. First of all, I'd live in the country."

"Not the city?"

"The city's no place to bring up kids."

"Then you do want children?"

He looked over at her sharply. "I thought this was a hypothetical question."

"It is," she said quickly. "So, if you were to get married, which you do not intend to do, you would want a home in the country with children."

"And a dog for the kids. None of those fancy little fuzzy toy things that spend all their time in dog beauty parlors. A real dog—an Irish setter or a golden retriever. Maybe a German shepherd."

"It sounds as if you'd need a very large house."

At the mention of houses, Chantal experienced a stab of guilt at the thought of Blair's lovely home. Fortunately, only the upstairs had suffered extensive damage, and with the help of the original blueprints, Blair and David intended to restore the house to its original glory. Chantal had talked to her friend only this morning, and although Blair had waxed enthusiastic about having a new project to embark on, she could not disguise the sadness in her voice. Immediately upon hanging up, Chantal had telephoned Burke in Montacroix, asking him to arrange for an unlimited line of credit with a prominent Philadelphia antique dealer.

"It should be roomy," Caine agreed. "Although nothing like what you're accustomed to. And it'd be white, with a wide front porch for watching your neighbors, rose bushes in the front yard and a big tree in the back for a swing."

"And what of your wife? What would she do with her days while you are out being a hero?"

He considered her question for a long moment. "She could work outside the home," he decided. "So long as it didn't interfere with her family duties."

"Family duties? Cooking, cleaning?"

"Hell, no, we'd all pitch in with that household stuff. No, I was talking about the important part of a marriage. Loving me. And letting me love her."

Chantal drew in a breath. "It sounds wonderful."

Caine laughed, obviously embarrassed that he'd permitted a rare glimpse of his innermost thoughts. "It's not bad," he agreed. "For a hypothetical."

"For a hypothetical," she agreed quietly.

"One more thing."

"Yes?"

"It'd be a decided plus if she could darn my socks."

"I think it's a good thing you aren't really looking for a wife, Caine. That sort of thing went out with covered wagons."

"What are you talking about? I'll have you know, my mother used to darn my socks."

"Then why don't you simply send your holey socks to your mother?"

He grinned. "She gave it up the summer I turned twelve. I seem to recall her saying something about having always hated the job and me being old enough to take care of my own clothes."

Chantal laughed. "Your mother sounds like a very wise woman."

"The best," Caine agreed.

A comfortable silence settled over them.

"I had a wonderful time tonight, even if I couldn't understand all the logistics of the play," Chantal said after a time. "Thank you for taking me."

It had begun to rain the bottom of the eighth inning, the moisture cooling the evening temperatures. The woodsy scent of oakmoss and sandalwood bloomed enticingly in the warmth of the car heater. Had it not been for Drew sitting in the front seat, Caine would have taken her into his arms and satisfied the hunger that had been escalating more and more with each succeeding inning.

Instead, he tugged lightly on the ends of her dark hair. "It was my pleasure," he said simply, meaning every word.

DENVER ALSO PROVED a city of contrasts. Having always thought of Colorado as a state consisting solely of rugged, snowcapped mountains, Chantal was surprised to discover that the mile-high city appeared to be situated on land as flat as a tabletop. To the east, rolling plains that seemed to go on forever gave the city an aura of isolation. To the west, the Rocky Mountains gave the city its mystery and brought to mind the gold and silver mining camps that had contributed to Denver's wealth.

She found the city's pioneer legacy strongly evident at the Museum of Western Art, which among action classics by Charles Russell and Frederic Remington, boasted pieces from the famed Taos school. For those who might tire of so many horses, the Denver Art Museum, where Chantal's exhibit was displayed, boasted one of the best contemporary collections in the United States.

"This is an amazing country," she said over a buffalo steak dinner at a restaurant founded by one of Buffalo Bill's scouts. She'd just finished making certain that the paintings were properly recrated and on their way to the state of Washington, where they would be on exhibit at the Seattle Art Museum Pavilion.

"I've always thought so," Caine agreed.

"It's so large. And the diversity is dizzying." She glanced around the dining room. An astonishing herd of animal trophies—bison, elk, caribou, moose—gazed unblinkingly down from the wall.

"I imagine Montacroix is more homogeneous."

"Vastly so. But, of course, it's a very small principality. And most of its citizens share the same roots." She grew pensive, pushing her home fried potatoes around on her plate. "Some people might find such similarity comforting."

"While you, on the other hand, find it stifling," Caine guessed.

"A bit," Chantal admitted on a soft little sigh. "Although I don't want you to think that I don't love my country. It's just that lately, as I've begun to expand my painting, I've also found myself wishing for more . . ." She paused, seeking the proper English word for her feeling. "Space."

"Elbowroom."

"Excuse me?"

"Have you ever heard of Davy Crockett?"

"Of course. He is an old American hero, is he not? The man who wore the cap made from raccoon skins?"

"That's him. Anyway, old Davy wasn't much for civilization. Professing the need for elbowroom, he kept moving farther and father into the Tennessee wilds."

"Elbowroom," Chantal murmured, pondering the term for a long, drawn-out moment. "I like it," she decided. "And you're right, that's exactly how I feel." She gave him a warm, appreciative glance. "Perhaps it is my American half who feels the need for this elbowroom."

"Perhaps. But it's the Montacroix princess who'll return home after the tour."

His words of warning had the effect of tossing cold water on what had been a vastly enjoyable day. The people of Denver had expressed appreciation of the works she'd brought to America with her, and she'd raised a great deal of money for the children, which was, of course, the important thing, she reminded herself.

"Are you angry with me?" she asked.

"Of course not."

"You seem cross."

"I was just worrying about making it through the next few days without any additional surprises," he said, not quite truthfully. "If I was short with you, I apologize. It doesn't have anything to do with us." His abrupt tone signaled that he considered the matter closed.

Well, at least he was admitting that there was an *us*, Chantal mused on the way back to yet another hotel. Although she'd been booked into the largest suites in the finest hotels in each city, they'd begun to blur together in her mind. Only those hours she spent making love with Caine in the king-size beds stood out in riveting detail.

She'd given the matter a great deal of thought, trying to discern why it was that her days, no matter how long or wearying, were brighter with Caine in them, why her heart sang at the mere sight of him and her bones melted at his touch. Why was it that the sound of his laughter, which came more easily with each passing day, possessed the power to thrill her all the way to her toes? And how was it possible to feel more intimacy sharing a box of over-salted popcorn with Caine at a baseball game than she'd ever felt sharing a bed with Greg?

The answer, when it had finally come, in a plane thirty thousand feet over Manhattan, Kansas, had been as simple as it had been frightening. She was in love with him. And although she'd vowed after her marriage that she would never again risk her heart, she knew that there was no point in fighting it. She loved Caine. And she wanted to spend the rest of her life with him.

"I'm becoming quite spoiled," she murmured once they were alone in her room. She was no longer inhibited by the fact that Drew occupied the room next to hers, while in the room across the hall two FBI men kept a watchful vigil.

"Oh?" He didn't resist as she pulled his tie from around his neck and tossed it onto a nearby chair. "In what way?"

Chantal pushed his jacket off his shoulders. "I'm discovering that I can't imagine a life without my own private bodyguard." She was gradually learning not to be disturbed by the shoulder holster and gun he wore constantly outside of the hotel rooms.

Caine shrugged out of the leather holster. He wanted to warn her that she'd better start facing reality, that their time together was rapidly coming to a close. But when she gently nudged him onto the turned-down bed and began divesting him of shoes and socks, he decided that once in a while it didn't hurt to simply relax and go with the flow.

"And here we were all sure that you'd balk at the idea of a bodyguard."

For a woman who'd worried about not knowing how to please a man, Chantal had all the instincts of a first-class courtesan, Caine mused. He couldn't remember the last time a woman had massaged his feet. In fact, now that he thought of it, no one ever had.

"You should have given me more credit." Tugging his shirt free of his slacks, she proceeded to undress him with tantalizing slowness. "I know a good thing when I see it." Between each freed button, she pressed her lips against his newly bared skin. "Or taste it."

His shoulders were wide, strong, able to carry heavy burdens. His arms were subtly muscled, offering comfort and protection, as well as passion. His hands were broad, his fingers long and lean and capable of discovering flash points on her body she'd never known existed.

Once she'd freed him of his shirt, her clever fingers moved to the waistband of his navy slacks.

"What do you think you're doing?"

Her smile as she slid the slacks down his legs was positively beguiling. "Why, I'm seducing you, Caine," she murmured, tossing the slacks carelessly onto the chair. They slid to the floor; neither Chantal nor Caine noticed. She ran a ruby-tinted fingernail up the inside of his thigh. "Is it working?"

"You tell me." His arousal, straining against his white cotton briefs, was impossible to ignore. Chantal brushed tantalizing fingers over him, pleased by his resultant tremor.

Stepping away from the bed, she pulled her dress over her head, letting it fall into an emerald silk puddle at her feet. Her lacy ivory bra was next, followed in turn by a pair of lace-banded, thigh-high silk stockings and her shoes. She hitched her thumbs into the top of her outrageously skimpy underpants and slid them slowly down over her hips, never taking her seductive gaze from Caine's face.

The rising passion in her eyes tore at his self-control; needs pounded inside him. "You realize that in the old days you could have been burned at the stake for being a witch," he said, his voice unnaturally husky.

"Don't be silly." Her smile was lascivious as she knelt beside him on the mattress and brushed her lips against his. "They never burned witches in Denver."

Her hands as they traced the contours of his body caused his blood to swim. When she pulled away the briefs in order to lightly brush that part of him aching for her touch, Caine had to grit his teeth. "Sure of that, are you?"

"My tour book mentioned nothing of such practices."

Bending over him, she rained a trail of wet kisses down his chest to his taut, hard stomach, and when her lips grazed his hipbone, Chantal heard Caine's desperate voice call out to her. But she was too fascinated with her quest, too intent on exploring this heady sense of feminine power she'd discovered, to reply.

Her hands fluttered over him like delicate birds, never still as they explored, relishing the hard, lean lines that were so different from her own soft, swelling curves. Her lips pressed lingeringly, warming his flesh, heating his blood, even as she caused her own fires to burn higher.

"Lord, Chantal," Caine muttered as her tongue stroked the straining sinews of his thighs. He reached for her, but she evaded his grasp.

"Too soon," she said as her avid mouth tasted his warm, moist flesh.

Passion flowed over them as she continued to torment and tease. It was an exercise in both devastating pain and dazzling pleasure. Caine wanted Chantal to keep touching him forever; he never wanted her lips to stop skimming over his aching, throbbing body. He wanted to take her now, quickly, before he completely lost his mind. The heat was unbearable; it was exhilarating. Every ragged breath he took was an agony of effort.

Seizing her shoulders, Caine pressed her back against the mattress and surged into her with an intense blaze of passion. Chantal shuddered when he first filled her, then, wrapping her legs around him, she lifted her hips, meeting him thrust for thrust.

Reality dimmed, sanity shattered. When she cried out his name, Caine's body shuddered with release, and he knew that he would remember this moment always.

13

SEATTLE, WASHINGTON'S Emerald City, gleamed like a jewel beside the quiet waters of Puget Sound. In the distance, the glacier-covered Mount Rainier rose through the morning fog, looking for all the world like a giant upside-down ice-cream cone.

"It's all the water that gives the city its mysterious blue glow," Chantal said, leafing through her guide book in the hotel suite. From the luxurious corner room in the high-rise tower, she possessed a dazzling view of the waterfront.

"Fascinating."

"The city is cradled by two mountain ranges—the Olympic to the west, the Cascade to the east."

"I'll try to keep that in mind," he said absently.

Caine was not in the most gregarious of moods. Not only had thoughts of Chantal kept him from sleeping, but when he had finally drifted off early this morning, he'd had a strange, surrealistic dream about the two of them starring in a colorized remake of that swashbuckling classic, *Captain Blood*.

And if that wasn't enough, Noel had called again, warning him not to let her sister go near the beach. Ever since their arrival in Seattle yesterday morning, he had worried that Puget Sound might contain the beach in question. Unfortunately, Noel's image had been frustratingly unspecific.

"The San Juan Archipelago consists of more than 170 islands scattered across Puget Sound, offering sailing, kayaking, fishing, beachcombing and bicycle riding. That last would be fun, don't you think? It's too bad we aren't going to be staying in the city longer."

"Yeah, too bad."

"But perhaps we could go to dinner on the pier after tonight's mayoral reception. Unless you'd rather hire a boat and go out into the sound and attempt to catch the killer shark that has been terrorizing the city."

"Whatever you want." It took a moment for Chantal's words to sink in. "'Killer shark'? What are you talking about?"

Crossing the room, she sat down on his lap. "You haven't been listening to a word I've said."

"Of course I have."

Chantal had a choice. She could challenge that outrageous statement or accept his word at face value, even knowing that he was not being entirely truthful. They'd been getting along so well lately, she decided against entering into an argument.

"It is a lovely city," she murmured. Turning her gaze away from his carefully guarded face, she looked out the window. The sound was filled with white sails fluttering in the wind. How she'd love to be down there with them—with Caine—sharing a chilled bottle of champagne, the sunlit afternoon and the fresh sea breeze.

"Agreed." He brushed his fingertips down the front of her crimson blouse. The silk was soft, but Caine knew her skin was softer. "I'm sorry if I wasn't paying strict attention."

Chantal had already discovered that Caine was not a man to apologize easily. Or often. "You have a lot on your mind."

Wasn't that the truth? In the beginning, the three weeks had seemed an eternity Caine was forced to endure. Now, as their time together came to a close, the days seemed to have sprouted wings. If only they had more time. . . .

For what? he asked himself. What difference would a few days make? Would she suddenly stop being a princess? Would he win the lottery? Inherit a million dollars from some reclusive, eccentric relative he'd never known he had? Besides, although he didn't want to admit it, the chasm between him and Chantal had little to do with money. Although it would take some getting used to, he could probably live with a rich wife, even if she was a princess. What he couldn't—wouldn't—do, even for her, was change who he was. What he was.

"You're worried," she said quietly.

"What, me worry?"

He was smiling, but Chantal could see the seeds of concern in his eyes. "It's going to be all right. *I'm* going to be all right," she said. He'd retreated behind those emotional barricades she'd reluctantly come to accept even as she felt her own need to breach them. "After all," she added, allowing her hand to brush through his hair, "I have a hero watching out for me."

"Drew never should have told you about that," Caine muttered grumpily.

"You wouldn't tell me how you'd injured your shoulder," Chantal reminded him. She had wondered about the angry red scar from the beginning, but when she'd asked him about it, she'd received such an abrupt dismissal that she hadn't dared bring it up again. "He's your friend. I think he wanted me to know how dedicated you are to your job. So I could understand that it's only your rigid professionalism that sometimes has you acting like Captain Bligh."

He lifted a dark brow. "'Captain Bligh'?"

She pressed her hand against his cheek. "You have been known to be a bit bossy."

"'Bossy'? Me?"

"Well, you can't deny that you're always issuing orders."

"Orders you always refuse to obey," he reminded her.

"Not always. Actually, I was thinking just this morning how good we were getting at compromising."

"'Compromising'." That was not Caine's favorite word. To him it meant giving in, something he'd been doing with increasing frequency lately. He'd tried to tell himself that he had no choice, that if he laid down the law too hard, Chantal would just go off in another more dangerous direction. But to be perfectly honest, Caine had to admit that he was simply finding it more and more difficult to deny this woman anything.

"You remember how to compromise, don't you, Caine? I give a little." She leaned forward and kissed him. "You give a little." Her lips plucked enticingly at his grimly set ones. "And after a while we're both compromised."

Her low gurgle of sensual laughter caused desire to ripple beneath his skin. "You're incorrigible."

"And you love it," she countered, linking her fingers behind his neck. Their lips met and clung. "Caine?"

"Mmm?"

"You were a sailor, weren't you? Before you joined Presidential Security."

"I was in the navy. But I wasn't the kind of sailor you see in those old World War II movies."

"Oh." She seemed momentarily disappointed. "But do you like to sail?"

"Sure. Why?"

"Although Montacroix is a landlocked country, we do have a lovely lake—Lake Losange, or Diamond Lake," she translated for him. "When I was just a little girl, Burke taught me to sail on it. Perhaps, when all this is over, you can visit Montacroix and go sailing with me."

Caine struggled not to give in to the pull of Chantal's velvet eyes. "I don't know if that would be such a good idea."

He'd withdrawn again. Although she lacked her sister's psychic gifts, Chantal was intuitive enough to realize that the stone wall Caine kept erecting between them had been a lifetime in the making. She was foolish to believe she could have permanently breached those parapets in three short weeks. But tenacity, and her newly found love, made her want to keep trying.

"When the tour ends in Los Angeles two days from now, your assignment will be successfully completed."

"Let's hope 'successful' is the operative word."

"You would not permit it to be anything less," she said, striving to keep a light tone. "Then, when it is over, you will return to Washington and I will go home to Montacroix."

"That's the plan."

Chantal took a deep breath, garnering courage to ask the next question. "We won't ever see each other again, will we, Caine?"

Caine knew he'd had no business getting mixed up with Chantal. Despite what she'd said about only wanting a short-term affair, he'd come to know her well enough to realize that despite her flamboyant public image, she was a warm, loving, happily-ever-after kind of woman. And as sophisticated as she appeared decked out in gleaming satins and sparkling diamonds, he could also envision her in a pair of brief white shorts and a cotton shirt, her dark hair blowing in the breeze, laughing with easy delight as she taught her children how to sail before the wind on Lake Losange. She deserved a man who could give her a stable, loving home, a family. Unfortunately, he was not that man.

"I don't see how it could be any other way, Chantal," he said at length, not wanting to give her any false hope.

"I see." It took a concerted effort to keep the tremors from her voice.

"We both knew this was a transitory affair," Caine pointed out.

As she read the finality in his eyes, Chantal slid off his lap with a sigh. "Of course, you're right," she said, staring unseeingly out the window at the scene that only moments before had provided such pleasure. "I hadn't realized that inviting you to Montacroix for a platonic visit would breach our agreement."

"There wouldn't be anything platonic about it," Caine argued. "We both know what would happen...what always happens."

"Would that be so bad?"

Caine gripped the arms of the chair to keep himself from going to her. "It would only complicate things even more."

"And you're a man who doesn't like complications," she murmured, more to herself than to him. "Is that all I've been to you, Caine?" she asked, turning around to face him. "A complication? A screwdriver thrown into the perfectly tuned machinery of your life?"

"Monkey wrench," he muttered.

"What?"

"It's a monkey wrench, not a screwdriver, and surely you realize that you mean a helluva lot more to me than that."

She'd known from the beginning that Caine was a man capable of restraining his emotions, of holding them back from himself and others. He was a difficult man to know, and an even more difficult man to love, but she'd fallen in love with him anyway. And heaven help her, she couldn't stop just because he was breaking her heart.

"Obviously not enough."

Unable to resist the silent appeal in her eyes, Caine pushed himself out of the chair and went over to her. "Look, Chantal, you're a terrific woman. The way you make me feel is probably illegal in at least a dozen states, and I'd love nothing more than to spend the rest of my life making mad, passionate love to you."

The idea sounded wonderful to Chantal. "But . . . ?"

"But the truth of the matter is that I'm enough of a realist to know that such a fantasy would never work. We're two different people, Chantal."

"Actually, I think we have a great deal in common," she felt obliged to point out. "We're both single-minded, cautious in our relationships with other people, extremely loyal to our friends and family..."

"That's not what I'm talking about."

She arched a sable brow. "Oh?"

"Our life-styles are too different."

"If you mean because I live in a palace and you live in an apartment, that could be altered."

He narrowed his eyes. "I couldn't move to Montacroix. I have my own life here in the States, my work. I would never live off a woman."

"I don't believe I asked you to," she snapped. Taking a deep breath that was meant to calm but didn't, she added, "I was suggesting the other alternative."

Caine realized she was striking back because she was hurting, and he didn't blame her. Still, he couldn't even begin to take her suggestion seriously.

"That you move into my apartment? With me?"

His look was frankly incredulous and, Chantal was forced to admit, none too inviting.

"Forget I mentioned it," she said, turning away from his piercing gray eyes. "It was a foolishly romantic suggestion, obviously brought on by jet lag, too much stress and not enough sleep." Marching into the adjoining bedroom, she slammed the door behind her with enough force to cause the Matisse print on the wall to tilt.

Dragging his hands through his hair, Caine told himself it was going to be a very long two days.

THE MAN WAS DRINKING champagne out of a crystal flute as he stood at the window and stared out over the sparkling, sun-gilded water. At first he'd been furious when his carefully conceived plan had failed in Philadelphia. Now, however, he realized that he'd been wrong to assign Karl to the job.

Fate had decreed that he be the one to kill the princess. And that's precisely what he was going to do.

Tomorrow.

Here, in Los Angeles.

CHANTAL HAD ALWAYS ENJOYED everything about Los Angeles. The brilliant, almost intoxicating sunshine, the golden beaches, the lushness of Beverly Hills, the quirky individualism of Venice, the nostalgic, neon glitz of West Hollywood, the glass high rises looming above Century City like monolithic sculptures, the palm trees—all of it made her feel as though fairy tales could come true.

This time, however, the sun-drenched city did little to lift her spirits. Although her exhibit drew thousands to the J. P. Getty Museum in Malibu, and she managed to raise unprecedented funds for her favorite charity, Chantal couldn't shake the depression that had settled over her.

It was all her fault, she told herself as she smiled her dazzling smile and exchanged cheek kisses with a famous actress who had enthralled three generations of moviegoers. Caine had been totally honest with her; he'd warned her up front that he was not promising a future.

But she'd been foolish enough to think that she could change his feelings about commitment. Chantal berated herself even as she laughed at the punch line of a talk-show host's joke. She'd mistakenly believed that love conquered all. There was the real joke.

And on top of everything else, having learned his lesson concerning Noel's premonitions, Caine had canceled Chantal's excursion to Catalina Island. Needless to say, she had not been pleased.

"Better watch out," a deep voice murmured in her ear, "or your face will freeze into that scowl."

Spinning around, Chantal's face lit up in the first honest smile she'd given anyone in the past forty-eight hours. "Stephan," she said delightedly, embracing him, "I'm so glad to see you!"

"Not as happy as I am to see you," he said, his teeth a brilliant flash of white as he grinned down at her.

"It was so good of you to come."

"Personal reasons aside, you don't think I'd miss an opportunity to donate to those orphans of yours?"

"They're not all orphans," Chantal corrected. "But thank you. Every little bit helps."

Reaching into the breast pocket of his Saville Row suit, he pulled out a piece of folded paper. "Then let me add my little bit."

"Gracious," she said, her eyes widening as she stared in shock at the amount of the check. "Stephan, have you gone mad?"

He chuckled, running his knuckles down her cheek. A few feet away, as Caine watched the intimate gesture with narrowed eyes, jealousy twisted his gut.

"Of course I have not gone mad," Stephan Devouassoux answered with mock indignation. "Fortunately, *ma chère,* since moving to California, business has more than surpassed my expectations. Enough so that I can share the wealth with the loveliest woman I know."

She tucked the check into her beaded bag. "You are an angel."

"And you look like an angel." He plucked a pair of champagne glasses from the tray of a passing waiter and handed her one. "Have you ever thought of returning to films?"

"As much as I enjoyed my acting days, I was much younger then," she said. "I've become a more solitary person than the acting profession permits. Painting suits me, Stephan. I enjoy it. And I'm good at it."

He laughed, raising his glass to her in a toast. "I've always appreciated a lady who knows her worth. You know, Chantal, seeing you here today, I realize that I should have kept closer tabs on my cousin's baby sister. You've grown into quite a delectable woman, *chérie.*"

As Caine watched the man's eyes practically stripping away Chantal's slender black dress, he decided that the time had come to put in an appearance.

"Is everything all right?" he asked, coming up beside her.

She tilted her chin in a way that reminded him of that haughty princess who'd handed him her luggage tags a mere three weeks ago. Had it only been three short weeks? It seemed like a lifetime.

"Everything is fine," she said frostily.

When she didn't look inclined to introduce him to the guy in the obviously tailor-made suit, Caine decided to take the bull by the horns. "The name's O'Bannion."

"Devouassoux," Stephan returned, looking curiously from Caine's closed face to Chantal's equally unreadable one and back again. "Stephan Devouassoux."

The name rang an instantaneous bell. "You're the cousin."

"*Oui,* I am Prince Burke Giraudeau's cousin," Stephan answered, his eyes revealing his surprise. "His mother, Princess Clea, was my aunt." He glanced over at Chantal. "Your friend seems to know a great deal about our family."

"He's not a friend. He's my hired bodyguard," she said, her tone heavily laced with sarcasm.

"A bodyguard?" Stephan's aristocratic features revealed concern as he took her hand in his. "Don't tell me that you are in danger, *ma petite?*"

Although Stephan's touch no longer stirred her blood as it had when she was young, Chantal couldn't deny that Caine's blistering glare was more than a little satisfying. In no hurry to retrieve her hand when it was causing Caine such obvious distress, she smiled up at her brother's cousin. "Mr. O'Bannion seems to think so," she said. "Although his judgment has been known to be impaired."

Although she'd coated herself in enough ice to cover Jupiter, the anger in Chantal's tone was unmistakable. "It's suddenly so crowded in here," she said, slanting Stephan her warmest, most feminine smile. "Why don't we take a nice stroll in the gardens?"

Turning her back on Caine, she led Stephan toward the French doors at the end of the room. Incensed by her cool dismissal, Caine held his tongue and followed.

"Your Mr. O'Bannion is quite intimidating," Stephan said once they were outside. The bright green hedges lining the walks were neatly trimmed; sunlight sparkled invitingly on the water in the long, rectangular pool.

"He is not *my* Mr. O'Bannion," she said with more intensity than she'd intended. "And he can be quite pleasant if you catch him in the right mood."

"When is that? Once an aeon?" Stephan glanced nervously over his shoulder to where Caine stood between a pair of tall white pillars, back rigid, arms folded across his chest. In deference to the bright sun, he was wearing a pair of dark glasses, but it was obvious that his gaze was fixed unerringly on Chantal. "At least you are well protected," he decided. "I can't imagine anyone trying to harm you with that man hulking in the background. I take it he's always with you."

"Day and night." Except for the past two nights, when he'd slept on the couch outside her bedroom door, she silently added. At least he was supposed to be sleeping; listening to him pace the floor had provided Chantal with a small amount of selfish pleasure. It was gratifying to know that he wasn't getting any more rest than she was, lying in a lonely bed, wondering what had possessed her to fall in love with a man who was incapable of returning that love.

The thought of his rejection tore at her heart like a rusty knife. Blinking back the traitorous tears stinging her lids, she reached into her bag. "Damn, damn, damn."

"What's wrong?" Stephan asked, instantly concerned.

"I'm out of candy."

He threw back his head and laughed. "Is that all?"

Chantal glanced over at Caine, thinking how he'd taken to carrying the snacks in his pockets. Perhaps he had some now. But her pride was a hard, fierce thing; she'd die before ever asking him for anything again.

"It's not funny," she complained.

"Of course it's not." A small smile tugged at the corners of his lips. "So why don't we leave and go to a supermarket? I'll buy you a jumbo-size bag."

"I can't leave without Caine's permission."

He clucked his tongue, eyeing her with renewed interest. "This is definitely not the Chantal Giraudeau I've always known and loved. The young, devil-may-care princess who drove her family to distraction on more than one occasion. It's obvious that this O'Bannion fellow has domesticated you, love."

"That's ridiculous. I'm the same as ever."

"Are you?"

No, she could have answered, she wasn't the same at all. She'd had her heart broken into a thousand pieces, and there had been times during the past forty-eight hours that she wasn't really certain she wanted to keep on living.

"Of course."

"Prove it by ditching that Saint Bernard over there. The way you managed to shake your governess that New Year's Eve so many years ago."

She'd been fifteen, madly in love with twenty-year-old Stephan, or so she'd thought at the time, and desperate to see the New Year in with him. Unfortunately, her parents, as well as her governess, had other ideas, but Chantal had managed to get around their objections by climbing down the tree whose branches overhung her bedroom balcony.

The dare lay there between them, waiting for her to pick it up. "All right," she agreed, tilting her chin with renewed determination.

Stephan was right; she'd allowed Caine to domesticate her, to turn her into a weak, lovesick shadow of her former self. She was a survivor, she reminded herself now. A princess. Who was he to tell her what to do, where to go and with whom?

"I'll meet you out by the parking lot in five minutes."

"That's my girl." He bent his head and pressed his smiling lips against hers. "Five minutes."

Jealousy clawing at his insides, Caine caught her arm as she walked by him on the way back into the museum alone. "Where are you going?"

She jerked free of his hold. "None of your business."

"Now there's where you're wrong. Because in case you've forgotten, Princess, you just happen to be my business."

Her temper flared. "How could I forget when you keep throwing it up in my face? And now that you've brought it up yet again, I believe this is where I tell you that I'm sick and tired of being an assignment to an ill-tempered, coldhearted man who is afraid to get close to anyone. And who is afraid to let anyone get close to him."

The words hurt more than he would have thought possible. "Tough."

There was no getting through to him. She'd tried everything she knew, even permitting Stephan to kiss her. She couldn't believe that Caine didn't love her; she'd seen it in his eyes too many times, felt it in his tender touch. But he steadfastly continued to deny his feelings, perhaps even to himself.

Taking a deep breath, Chantal looked up at him, her resolutely dry eyes hardened to a metallic sheen. "I thought you were a hero, Caine. But I was wrong. You're a coward."

This time when she pulled away from him, Caine didn't stop her. Instead, he simply followed her through the throng of people to the private ladies' lounge, where he stood guard outside the door, ignoring the interested glances from the women entering and exiting. It appeared she was going to sulk for quite some time, he determined, after she'd been in the room for several minutes. That was okay with him; he was prepared to wait all night.

Chantal had seen the window earlier. Now, upon closer examination, she realized it was a good deal higher and several inches narrower than she remembered. After waiting for the room to empty, she dragged a velvet-covered stool from the vanity to stand on. When her high heels made her footing too treacherous, she kicked them off, but without the added height, she had to jump several times before getting hold of the windowsill. She pulled herself up and through the narrow opening.

Success! She landed on the grass in her stocking feet. Then, ignoring the curious glances of passersby, she hurried to the parking lot, where she found Stephan waiting for her.

"Caine is very intelligent," she warned, glancing nervously over her shoulder. "I don't think we have much time."

"I've got the car right here," he said, putting his arm around her waist and leading her to a sleek black Ferrari. The car's engine was running loudly, sounding as if it would much prefer to be operating at top speed instead of idling here, waiting for its owner.

"Let's go, *chérie,*" he said, opening the door for her. "It's high time you found out exactly how much fun the City of Angels can be."

As he drove off with a roar of the engine, Chantal experienced an unexpected stab of guilt at playing such a dirty trick on Caine. But he deserved it, she reminded herself. And besides, it wasn't as if she had run off with a stranger. She'd known Stephan all her life. He was family.

After five minutes had passed and there was no sign of Chantal, Caine decided the time had come to have this out. Marching into the gilt and mirrored lounge, he cursed when he found it deserted. The only thing left of the princess was a pair of ridiculously high-heeled Italian shoes.

"WHERE ARE WE GOING?" Chantal asked as she bit off a piece from her chocolate bar. They'd stopped at a convenience market down the coast road from the Malibu museum.

"I thought I'd show you my house. It's just up the coast."

"Oh, you live on the ocean? How wonderful," Chantal said, leaning back in the seat and enjoying the feel of the wind whipping her hair through the car's sunroof. Coming from a landlocked country, she'd always found the sea especially exhilarating. "I envy you."

He shrugged as he pulled off the road and headed down a long, curving road. "It's just a house. Nothing like what you're used to." They stopped in front of a set of blazing white walls. Stephan pressed a code into his car's security console, and the gates opened, permitting entrance. A few hundred yards down the curving roadway, another gate appeared.

"You certainly have a great deal of security," she said, thinking that even her father's palace wasn't so elaborately guarded.

"All the better to protect gorgeous princesses who might drop by for a visit," he said with a grin that had once possessed the power to melt her heart. At the moment it only served as an uncomfortable reminder of how she'd let Stephan goad her into pulling a dirty trick on a man who, personal feelings aside, had only wanted to protect her.

"Perhaps I should return to the museum," she said. "Caine will be worried."

"If you're truly concerned, it'd be faster to call him from the house. We're almost there."

They tore around one last turn before pulling up a curving flagstone driveway, stopping in front of a six-car garage. Chantal stared, entranced.

Viewing the stone, old-world manor house, situated in a dreamlike setting among cypress and pine trees and a eucalyptus grove, was like going back in time to the elegance and grace of the turn of the century. There were chimneys everywhere and formal gardens with flowing fountains. Giant marble sculptures flanked the massive front doors.

"It's not at all the home I would have expected you to own," she said as she entered the two-story, Italian-tiled entry.

"Oh? And what were you expecting?"

She shrugged as her wondering eyes took in the museum-quality sixteenth-century tapestry chair, the Sèvres cachepots that held superb arrangements of freshly cut hothouse flowers, and a large, gilt-framed painting she recognized as Picasso's *Harlequin with a Glass.*

"I don't know. Something sleek and modern. All redwood and windows, I suppose," she murmured. "But this . . ." Her voice drifted off as she tried to recall what Stephan's house reminded her of. "Why, it reminds me of the palace on Lake Losange," she said as recognition dawned.

"That's very clever of you, Chantal," Stephan said, leading her into a vast formal salon. The enormous crystal chandelier sent sparkling rainbows winking over the Empire furniture and silk-draped walls covered with priceless paintings. A pair of fencing foils hung on one wall, their hilts adorned with precious jewels. "I had the architect design a facsimile of the palace, although unfortunately, with California property values being what they are, I was forced to decrease the scale."

His hand rested lightly on her back, and he was smiling down at her. Yet there was an edge to his voice she had never heard before. A hint of restrained anger that caused a frisson of fear to skim up her spine.

"I think I'd better call Caine now."

"Why don't we have a drink first." He walked over to where a bottle of champagne was chilling in a silver bucket.

"I'd rather call Caine." The sickly sweet smell of lilies in a Tiffany Favrile glass vase was beginning to make her head ache.

There was a slight pop as he pulled the cork from the bottle. As she watched, he poured the golden effervescent wine into a pair of thin-stemmed, tulip-shaped glasses.

"I'm afraid that's impossible, *ma chère,*" he said, holding one of the glasses toward her.

She heard a sound behind her and whipped around, hoping against hope that it was Caine; that she hadn't outsmarted him, after all. That he'd come to rescue her once again. When she came face-to-face with the bearded blond man she remembered all too well from Philadelphia, her blood turned cold.

"You," she whispered.

Reaching out with a gloved hand, the man traced her lips with his thumb. "So, Princess," he murmured, trailing his treacherous hand slowly down her throat, "we meet again."

14

"YOU LOOK a tad nervous, *ma chère*," Stephan said politely. "Are we making you uncomfortable?"

Chantal swallowed, knowing that the horrible man could feel her fear under his fingertips. "What do you think?"

He shook his head. "And here I'd always thought of myself as a superb host. Speaking of manners, may I introduce my good friend, Karl. After his little failure in Philadelphia, he's been looking forward to meeting you again. Haven't you Karl?"

"Yeah."

The man's cold blue eyes gleamed as he intimately regarded her body; his blatant perusal made her flesh crawl. His narrow face still bore the angry red scratches inflicted by her fingernails when she had struggled to fight him off.

"I don't understand," Chantal protested. "Why are you doing this, Stephan?"

He smiled at her over the rim of his champagne glass, but his eyes held no warmth. "You are an intelligent woman, Chantal. Surely you can figure it out."

"You're the one behind all my accidents?"

"I can't claim credit for them all," Stephan said. "Only the fire." He shook his head. "Personally, I felt that was the most ingenious plan of all. It would have succeeded, too, had it not been for your lover."

A violence she never would have suspected was in Stephan seemed very close to the surface. Chantal tried to concentrate on what Drew had said about Caine. His dedication to duty, his professionalism. His unwillingness to fail at any assigned task. *Oh, please, Caine,* she thought as she struggled to get hold of her whirling thoughts, *please come*. Quickly.

"What makes you think Caine is my lover?" she asked, stalling for time.

"What do you take us for, Chantal? Fools? It is obvious to anyone with eyes that O'Bannion has been sleeping with you from the beginning. Karl has become quite jealous, in fact. Haven't you, Karl?"

As his fingers trailed slowly across her shoulder blades, the blond man uttered a guttural grunt Chantal took to be an affirmative response.

"I'm quite fond of Karl," Stephan confirmed conversationally. "Despite the fact that he has one unpleasant little quirk."

"'Quirk'?"

"Idiosyncrasy," he translated the unfamiliar word. "He enjoys inflicting pain upon women."

Chantal found the implacable cruelty in Stephan's eyes every bit as disturbing as Karl's alleged perversity. "Why do you want to hurt me, Stephan?" she asked quietly. "What have I ever done to you?"

"What have you done? Why, nothing, *chérie*."

"I don't understand." She backed away from the silent Karl, relieved when he remained where he was, watching her with unblinking reptilian eyes.

Stephan reached into a desk drawer and pulled out a pack of long, dark brown cigarettes. "You know that my Aunt Clea died six months ago," he said as he lit one of the cigarettes with a thin gold lighter.

Burke's mother. "Of course. Although I'd never met her, I was sorry to hear she'd died. At the time, the news seemed to hit Burke very hard."

"She committed suicide. Hung herself with her bed sheets."

"How horrible!" Chantal wondered fleetingly if her brother had been told the truth and decided that he hadn't. She and Burke shared everything; he would not have kept such disturbing news to himself.

Stephan exhaled slowly, eyeing her through a veil of thick blue smoke. "Her father was the one who discovered her, during his monthly visit to the sanitorium. Did you know that he never stopped visiting her? For thirty-five years he made that unhappy trek from Montacroix to Switzerland in order to visit the beloved daughter your father had locked away so he would be free to marry his American slut."

"That's not the way it happened," she protested. "Clea was mentally ill. She'd been in the sanitorium for nearly five years when Papa met my mother."

"She was unhappy," he corrected. "And who wouldn't be? Living with a man who continually degraded her by sleeping with other women. By bringing his filthy whores into the place."

"My father did no such thing!"

"Of course he did. Which is why my aunt had no choice but to end his worthless life."

"She tried to kill him?"

"He deserved it. Unfortunately, she failed and as a result was locked away so the truth could never get out."

"She was insane," Chantal repeated firmly.

"She was wronged!" Stephan roared, jabbing the cigarette into a crystal ashtray. Reaching into the drawer again, he pulled out a pistol and pointed it at her. "Eduard Giraudeau made my aunt suffer for years. He has made her family suffer. He is responsible for the death of an innocent, lovely woman. And now Clea's grieving father wants the bastard Giraudeau to know exactly how it feels to lose a daughter."

She remembered her father telling her that Clea's own mother had committed suicide in a mental institution, that insanity ran in the family. A fact that was all too apparent as Stephan approached her, undisguised malice glittering in his eyes.

"How can you talk this way? We have always been such good friends, Stephan." She put her hand out, schooling her voice to a calm, reassuring tone. "More than friends. When I was a young girl, I loved you madly." Perhaps "madly" wasn't the proper word, under the circumstances, she decided. "Wildly."

He shook his head. "You say you love me. But you sleep with O'Bannion."

Stall, her fevered mind cried out, seizing the slim thread of opportunity. "I didn't realize that you still cared for me." Taking a chance, she reached over to put a supplicating hand on his arm. "Had I known you wanted me, Stephan, I never would have wasted my time with Caine."

She'd no sooner said his name when, as if conjured out of thin air by wishful thinking, Chantal caught a glimpse of Caine standing in the shadows of the foyer. He'd come. As she'd known all along he would.

"Dear, dear Stephan," she murmured, her voice half honey, half smoke, "don't you know that a woman never forgets her first love?" She was grateful for her youthful acting experience as she watched Stephan's eyes momentarily glaze over. He was obviously not immune to her gently stroking fingers. "Please, darling. Send Karl away so that we can be alone, just the two of us."

The spell snapped as quickly as it had been spun. "You're attempting to take my mind off what I must do," Stephan said. Although his eyes had cleared somewhat, Chantal could still see the madness glittering in their swirling depths. "You are no better than your mother, using your body to gain favors."

"That's not what I was doing," she protested.

"Of course it was. And it will not work. But don't worry, Princess," he said, caressing her cheek with the cold blue steel muzzle of the gun. "Karl and I will make certain that your last few hours are enjoyable."

The idea of either man touching Chantal made Caine's mind explode with fury. He wanted to kill them both, here and now, but unfortunately, Chantal was in the way. As if she'd read his mind, Chantal suddenly appeared to faint, folding bonelessly to the floor.

"What the hell?" Stephan burst out.

As the two men bent over her, Caine rushed into the room, bringing his revolver down toward the base of Stephan's skull. It might have been instinct, or perhaps he'd felt the faint whoosh of air, but Stephan ducked and rolled out of the way. Caine's blow connected with his shoulder, however, and the force dislodged the pistol, sending it skittering across the black marble flooring.

As Stephan reached for the gun, Chantal came alive. Jumping up and grabbing the gilded foil from the wall, she pointed it toward him. "Don't you dare move, Stephan," she warned softly, "or I'll kill you."

Not to be left out, Karl had pulled his own snub-nosed revolver and was pointing it at Caine.

"It appears that we have ourselves a standoff, O'Bannion," Stephan observed. "Even if you do manage to shoot Karl before he gets you, I'll still have Chantal."

"Brave words from an unarmed man," Caine said, watching both men carefully.

"You forget, I know Chantal. You wouldn't hurt a fly, would you, *ma chère?*" He glanced over at his pistol, just out of reach. "We have a treat for you, O'Bannion. You're going to get to watch your slut perform first with me and then with Karl. And when we're through with her, she's going to watch you die."

As he grabbed for his weapon, Chantal lunged, plunging the sharp tip of the foil into the back of his hand. At the unexpected pain, Stephan screamed, distracting Karl just long enough for Caine to kick the gun out of his hand.

Then Caine fell on the blond man and began using his hands with startling efficiency. This was the man who'd tried to kill Chantal. The man who'd left her in that smoked-filled house to die. Blind with rage, he drove his fists into the man's face again and again until he lay unconscious.

"Caine! Caine! Please stop. You're going to kill him!"

Through the roaring in his ears, he heard Chantal's frantic voice. Shaking his head as if to clear it, he turned around. She was standing there, her foil pressed against Stephan's chest, her eyes wide with fright.

"You want to be next?" he asked Stephan, picking up both guns from the floor as he walked over to where the man lay.

"You may think you've won, O'Bannion, but you haven't. Fate has decreed that I kill the bastard princess, and I will not fail."

"Don't look now, pal, but your plan's gone down the drain," Caine said, uncurling Chantal's rigid fingers from the foil.

"Destiny will not be denied!" Stephan shouted. "The princess must die in retaliation for Princess Clea's death."

"He really is insane," she said faintly as Stephan let loose with a long, incoherent tirade against her family.

"Mad as a hatter."

"Drew was right." Her smile, as she looked up at him, only wobbled slightly. "You are a hero. You saved my life."

He brushed his fingertips down her cheek. "Then we're even. Because you saved mine."

The reluctant love he felt for her was so apparent in his eyes that Chantal had to bite her lip to keep from crying out his name. "Caine," she uttered simply.

It was only his name, but her tone spoke volumes. Before he could respond, Drew walked in the door, two FBI men right behind him.

"Nice of you to drop by," Caine said.

"Hey, you said you wanted first dibs on the guy," Drew said with a broad grin. "I figured you'd have everything under control by now." He put away his gun. "So your hunch about the cousin proved right, after all."

Chantal stared at him. "You knew about Stephan? How?"

Caine shrugged. "All this seemed so personal, I started wondering if your would-be assassin's grudge might be against your father rather than you. Remembering what you said about his first wife's insanity, I called the institution where she'd been hospitalized and discovered that she had committed suicide shortly before the first attempt on your life."

"Since that pointed toward a motive for revenge, we ran a check on all the family members and discovered that not only had Clea's nephew, one Stephan Devouassoux, recently visited Montacroix, but his credit card revealed that he was also in Washington, New York and Philadelphia on the same days as your exhibit," Drew tacked on.

"Figuring he'd try again, we asked Burke to tell him where you were, if he happened to ask," Caine continued, "which he did. But since we didn't have any hard proof that he was behind your rash of accidents, and simply wanting to know your whereabouts wasn't any crime, we've had the guy under surveillance ever since his call to you in Milwaukee."

"But you didn't say a word," Chantal said.

"I was going to, as soon as we got to L.A. But the way things were going between us, I didn't think you'd believe me."

Chantal looked down at the two men on the floor, one rubbing his battered face as he groggily regained consciousness, the other glaring up at her with an icy malevolence that chilled her blood. "I probably wouldn't have. It's so unbelievable. Stephan and I were always so close." She shook her head.

Displaying the tenderness that had been missing from their relationship during the past two days, Caine put his arm around Chantal's waist. "Ready to go back to the hotel?"

She was in no mood to argue. "Ready." Leaning against him, she allowed him to shepherd her to the car.

THE FOLLOWING DAY, Chantal was alone in her hotel suite, packing to return to Montacroix, when there was a knock on her door. Opening it, her heart soared when she viewed Caine standing there. She hadn't seen him since the FBI and the Los Angeles police had questioned her last night.

"Hi," she said, feeling unreasonably shy.

Caine looked no more comfortable. "Hi. I came to see if you're ready for your bags to be taken downstairs."

"The bellman could have done that."

"As you so succinctly pointed out three weeks ago, it's my job to carry all those bags. I like to see a job through to the end."

She forced a smile. "I'm almost finished. Would you like to come in and wait?"

"Sure." Clothes were piled high on the bed, colorful, expensive silks and satins, most of which he recognized. "I got a call from Montacroix this morning."

Chantal looked up from her renewed packing. He was standing in the bedroom doorway, military straight as always, his expression unreadable. "Oh?"

"Clea's father has been arrested for plotting your murder. Since there's no sign of mental instability, it doesn't look as if he's going to be able to use Stephan's insanity defense, so I suspect he'll probably be put away for a very long time."

She shook her head as she picked up a peach colored satin teddy that unstopped a flood of memories Caine had been struggling to forget. "Poor man."

Caine fought the urge to go to her. "That poor man tried to kill you, Chantal."

"I know." Tucking the teddy into a corner of the suitcase, she began folding the ivory nightgown she'd been wearing the first time he'd made love to her.

Desire slammed into Caine. He unrelentingly forced it down.

"But it's such a tragedy, Caine. So many years. So many lives."

"I talked with your father. He's relieved. But I think he's feeling a bit guilty about everything, too."

"Papa has this unfortunate tendency to believe that he can control the entire world around him," Chantal observed. *Like someone else I know,* she could have tacked on. "Whenever things go awry in his carefully constructed utopia, he believes it to be his fault."

When Caine didn't answer, Chantal fell silent, as well. "Well," she said at length, "I guess that's everything."

He'd never wanted a woman more than he wanted Chantal. Never needed a woman more than he needed her. "So, looks as if you're all set."

"I suppose so."

As Caine struggled to keep his expression from revealing his inner turmoil, he marveled at Chantal's ability to conceal her own thoughts so well. Her too-pale face was disconcertingly void of expression.

"I'm supposed to be downtown at police headquarters for a debriefing in thirty minutes, so Drew was scheduled to drive you to the airport," he said. "But I don't think Lieutenant Martin would mind if I changed our appointment to later this afternoon."

Chantal stared up at him, wondering if this was Caine's way of telling her that he'd changed his mind. But then she read the terrible finality in his eyes and realized that all he was offering was companionship to the airport.

"Drew's been doing all the driving up until now," she said. "He may as well continue."

Caine shrugged. "Whatever you want."

It was a statement Chantal didn't dare answer. She refused to give the man the satisfaction of knowing that her heart was breaking. Instead, she walked from the room, leaving Caine to follow with the bags.

They stood close together on the sidewalk in front of the hotel. "Chantal—"

"Yes?" Hope leaped into her eyes, only to fade away as she took in Caine's shuttered gaze.

"Take care."

"You, too," she managed through lips that had turned to stone. "And thank you. For everything." She turned away, then, unable to leave without one last bittersweet memory, she lifted her hand to his cheek. "You know, Caine," she said softly, "no one expects you to be bulletproof." Going up on her toes, she pressed her lips against his, igniting a quick flare of heat that was too soon gone.

Climbing into the front seat of the limousine, she quickly closed the door, continuing to stare straight ahead out the windshield until Drew had driven the car around the corner. Then she buried her face in her hands and wept.

After a time her sobs diminished, and Chantal drew in a deep, painful breath as she accepted the clean white handkerchief Drew extended across the center console.

"Thought you might need this," he said simply.

As she wiped her eyes, Chantal couldn't help wondering why she hadn't been smart enough to fall in love with a simple, uncomplicated man. A man like Drew Tremayne, for instance.

"You're going to make some woman a wonderful husband."

He grinned. "That's what my mama always says, right after she asks me how come I'm still not married."

"And what do you tell her?"

"That if I ever find the right woman, I'll move heaven and earth to get her."

And he would, too, Chantal knew. Drew was the kind of man who'd put his head down and forge full steam ahead. Depending on the woman he chose, such a damn-the-torpedoes, single-minded pursuit could either prove exhilarating or frightening.

"I love him, Drew."

"I know, honey. And I think you're a smart enough cookie to realize that he loves you, too."

"So where does that leave us?"

He reached over and took her hand in his. "Give him some time, Chantal. Caine's not as dumb as he looks. He's bound to realize that he can't live without a certain princess in his life." He shot her an encouraging grin. "In the meantime, there's a little going away present for you in the glove compartment."

Leaning forward, Chantal investigated, laughing in spite of her pain when she discovered the cache of chocolate-covered peanuts.

TWO NIGHTS LATER, Caine and Drew sat in a dimly lit neighborhood bar where the jazz was cool and the drinks weren't watered. "I always knew you were an idiot," Drew said, popping a handful of beer nuts into his mouth. "But I never realized you were certifiably crazy."

Caine lifted the bottle of dark beer to his mouth and took a long pull. "Now you're talking about Chantal."

"Who else? Do you have any idea how many men would commit murder to be in your shoes? She loves you, Caine."

"And I love her. But it's not enough."

"So you keep saying." Drew leaned back in his chair and took another handful of nuts. "You know, women have an unfortunate tendency not to wait around forever. Even for a man they love." Calm brown eyes observed Caine soberly. "Go to her, Caine. Before you spend the rest of your life wishing you had."

Drew wasn't saying anything that Caine hadn't been telling himself over and over again since he'd watched Chantal drive out of his life. "I'll think about it," he muttered, ignoring his friend's triumphant expression.

IT WAS A WARM spring evening, that special time between afternoon and night when the world seems to stop and catch its breath. The sun was a brilliant orange ball dipping into Lake Losange, turning the cloudless sky to jeweled tones of ruby, amethyst and gold. A light breeze rippled the sun-gilded water.

She was sitting on a rock, looking out over the lake, clad in a snug tank top and white shorts that displayed her long legs to advantage. It had been two weeks. Fourteen long and incredibly lonely days and even lonelier nights.

"Looks like good sailing weather."

At the sound of Caine's voice, Chantal closed her eyes briefly, then turned around. Noel's dream, predicting it would happen exactly this way, had been the only thing that kept her from going to Caine in Washington. She'd wanted to believe her sister; she'd clung to the happy premonition the way a seven-year-old clings to thoughts of Saint Nicholas. But deep in her heart she'd been afraid that it was only wishful thinking.

"Hello, Caine," she said with studied calm, wondering if he could see the galloping beat of her heart. "Whatever are you doing here?"

Her haughty tone was pure princess, but in her eyes he caught a glimpse of the Chantal he'd come to love. "I don't suppose you'd believe I came to bring you these." Reaching into his suit-jacket pocket, he pulled out a handful of silver-wrapped chocolate kisses.

She longed to go to him, but pride kept her where she was. "Since Switzerland is just across the border and world famous for its chocolate, I feel obliged to point out that it's a bit like carrying coals to Newcastle."

She wasn't going to make it easy on him. Caine wondered why he'd thought she might.

"I lied." He dropped the candies back into his pocket.

"Oh?"

"I didn't come all this way to bring you any damned candy."

"I didn't think you had." Something else occurred to her. "How did you find me out here?"

"Burke gave me a ride from the airport. Noel said you liked to walk along the lake this time of day."

"It sounds as if my family's orchestrating my life again."

"They love you.... I love you." He was amazed at how good those three simple words made him feel. Why had it taken him so damn long to say them?

"I know."

She was too calm. Too remote. He walked over to her, his stomach twisting into knots as he took both her hands in his and drew her to her feet. "And you love me," he insisted.

"I did." She took a deep breath, trying to turn away, but Caine wouldn't let her. "I don't any longer."

"And I thought *I* was a rotten liar."

"Even if I did love you," she said reluctantly, "and I'm not saying I do, what difference would it make? Someone once told me that love wasn't always enough." The hardness in her eyes was softening slowly, hesitantly. But it was a beginning.

"I've always thought you were an intelligent woman."

"I thought I was, too." *Until I let my heart run away with my head,* she could have added, but didn't.

"So why would such an intelligent woman pay any attention to an idiot jerk who didn't know what he was talking about?" The evening breeze ruffled her hair; Caine brushed it away from her face with hands so remarkably gentle that Chantal's breath caught in her throat.

"If I remember correctly, you were against marriage because of your career. It was too dangerous, you said. Have you changed your mind in a mere two weeks?"

"I may have been wrong about that," he admitted. "But it's a moot point. I've resigned from Presidential Security."

"But why?"

Caine shrugged. "Several reasons. One of them being all the guns I've had pointed at me in the past three months. I'm getting too old for that cops and robbers stuff."

"What will you do?"

"Drew and I are setting up a private security firm. Nothing dangerous, just surveillance—sweeping offices for electronic eavesdropping devices, that sort of thing." As nervous as he was, Caine managed a smile. "Fortunately, everyone in Washington is so paranoid about bugs, we've already got more jobs than we can handle."

"I'm pleased for you."

"Thanks."

Silence settled over them. "Why did you come here, Caine?" she asked finally, looking up at him, her eyes wide and vulnerable.

She'd already been hurt more than any one person deserved. Caine vowed that he'd never allow anything, or anyone—himself included—to hurt Chantal ever again.

"To ask you to marry me." He took a deep breath. "I love you, Chantal. And I want to have a family with you. Kids, dogs, a station wagon, the whole works."

"The big, sprawling house in the country," she said softly, remembering their conversation.

"With the wide front porch for watching our neighbors. Rose bushes in the front yard and a big tree in the back for a swing. And something I forgot to mention—a studio, with lots of high, wide windows and skylights for the family's resident artist." He framed her uplifted face in his palms. "No one has ever made me want those things. No woman until you."

A shimmering golden joy coursed through her. "There's something you need to know, Caine, before I give you my answer."

"What's that?"

"We are a little old-fashioned here in Montacroix. Although I realize that the rest of the world might consider it an anachronism, it is traditional to ask the father for his daughter's hand."

It was going to be all right. They were going to be all right. "I know. Burke warned me before I arrived."

"And?"

"And your father insists on the wedding being held in the palace chapel before I take you home with me to Washington. Your mother, as we speak, is planning the reception menu with the kitchen staff, Noel has been put in charge of floral arrangements and musicians, and Burke is on his way into town to bribe the parish priest into forgoing the usual four-week posting of the banns."

"My brother would never bribe anyone, let alone a priest."

"Correction, my mistake. It's not a bribe. It's a donation to the church building fund."

"My, my," she murmured. "Everyone certainly sounds in a hurry to get me married off."

Caine grinned, that rare, wonderful smile that Chantal knew would still have the power to thrill her when she was ninety.

"I think they're all anxious for me to make an honest woman of you," he said, lowering his lips to hers. Cupping the back of her neck, he lingered over the kiss. "So what's your answer, Princess? Are you going to make your family—and the man who loves you—very, very happy, or not?"

"I'll marry you, Caine, on one condition."

Caine didn't hesitate. "Name it."

As she twined her arms around his neck, the brightness of Chantal's smile rivaled the dazzling Montacroix sunset. "I won't darn your socks."

Bodyguards sometimes
came in small packages.

CHARADE

Evelyn A. Crowe

CHAPTER ONE

A LUMINOUS, engorged moon hung heavily in the stormy sky, its brilliance occasionally obscured by dark clouds streaking across its surface, dappling the ground below in eerie shadows. Clouds chased one another in a frenzied rush to gain force and forge into the darkness, wreaking their vengeance across the innocent Texas landscape. As if in answer to the whispered call for destruction, the leaf-rustling breeze picked up momentum until it sounded like the gasping breath of an unknown demon.

The wind huffed stronger, and the lone female figure moved with a surefooted stride across the rooftop of the Stone estate. Dressed to blend with the night, she was a dark phantom, and only her shadow was reflected on the ground below as the clouds deigned to part, allowing the moon's brightness to peek through.

A raised arm silhouetted against the sky lifted higher, and a nylon rope snaked out, encircling the brick chimney. The figure pulled on the rope, tightened it around the chimney securely and wrapped one end around her waist. Suddenly a strong gust of wind pushed at her back, and she came dangerously close to losing her balance and plunging three stories to the ground below.

Angrily she tugged on the lines, then took a deep breath and began to back down the slanted slate roof. Her bare toes gripped the sharp edges as she continued her descent into total darkness, cursing the menacing clouds for blocking out the much-needed light. She moved by feel and touch, and when she finally reached her goal she immediately planted her heels in the wide copper gutters. As she leaned precariously backward into the night, she knew the heady feeling of a bird ready to take flight.

Another gust of wind set the taut lines vibrating. The dark figure clutched her safety line and stabilized her slipping hold, grumbling through lips turned blue from the sudden drop in temperature.

With the agility of an eel she wiggled around for a better position in front of a small, round attic window. The diamond-tipped cutter scratched the outline of the pane, and the sound it made caused her ears to ache. She returned the cutter to its case, then pulled on the rubber suction cup adhered to the center of the glass. The stubborn window wouldn't budge, and she quickly gave it a series of strong taps before the pane came free.

One jean-clad leg worked its way through the opening, and a foot came to rest on a hard surface. A leather-encased shoulder went through next, followed by a dark cap. Perched on one leg, the woman suddenly lost her balance and in a hopping, jumping movement fell through the window and landed sprawled on the dusty attic floor.

She was in! An impish grin lit her face. No one expected a *cat burglar* to strike during one of Houston's legendary gulf storms. That was the very reason she had picked this night. Who would ever guess?

Stop playing games, my girl, and get to work, she reminded herself. *You have gold to collect.* Heaving herself up and dusting off her legs, she retrieved her penlight and made for the stairs, and the master bedroom.

Once there she found her way to the bathroom and pulled open the linen closet. Leather-covered fingers felt for the hidden latch and flicked it upward, causing the shelves to swing outward. Her light shone on the complicated panel of the electronic alarm system and she hissed in surprise. The system was already turned *off*.

She stood perfectly still and counted the seconds, trying to figure out the cause of this sudden feeling of unease. Then she shrugged. So the Stones had forgotten to turn on the alarm before they left for Europe. But that wasn't likely with the new system, or was it? Had they thought they'd switched it on and actually turned it off? She shrugged again. The system wasn't her problem now. What she wanted was to get her itchy fingers on the newly installed safe downstairs and the contents inside.

Like a homing pigeon, her inner radar guided her down the wide curving stairs to the double doors of the library. The pinpoint of light that she shone before her showed her the way around the furniture to the far wall. There was just enough moonlight coming through the floral-patterned drapes to allow her to see the large oil painting that covered the safe.

Quickly she reached up and ran her fingers along the edge of the ornate gold-leaf frame, hunting for the release catch. There was a click as the painting slowly swung aside.

Shasta Masterson lovingly caressed the shiny surface of the safe, her eyes glistening with devilment and the sheer ecstasy of having reached her goal. Giving one of the big dials a spin, she began to laugh softly, only to have her merriment choked off in midchuckle as she felt cold steel pressing painfully into the back of her neck. She listened to the deep, slightly accented male voice and stiffened.

"Make one move and you're a dead man!"

KANE STONE WAS JOLTED out of his nightmare. Though the intruding noise brought his conscious mind to an alert state, his subconscious was still reliving the loss and death of a man more like his father than his own flesh and blood one.

Sighing wearily, he lay motionless, afraid if he so much as closed his eyes again he'd see the horror of the hit-and-run accident and feel the sense of helplessness that had swept over him as he'd held the frail old body. But he did close his eyes again in exhaustion.

Before sleep could claim him, he wondered for the hundredth time what he was doing in his father's house. Memories had crowded in on one another the moment he'd stepped over the threshold. He'd looked up the darkened curved well of the staircase and the past had flashed so vividly around him that he'd cowardly turned his back. Refusing to face his demons, he'd made his bed for the night on the living-room couch. But even there the past wouldn't leave him in peace. How he'd hated this house and its owner—first with a young boy's passion and later with a grown man's strength. This hate had festered and exploded twenty-five years ago. He'd sworn then, at the tender age of twelve, never to return, and he had kept that vow—till now.

The noise came again, this time closer, and Kane pulled himself quickly up on one elbow, too quickly for his bruised ribs. He bit back a moan and eased his battered body into a more comfortable position to relieve the pressure and afford him a better view over the back of the couch.

A pinpoint of light weaved in and out of the darkness, passing so close behind the couch he could have reached out and grabbed the intruder. His fist was already on the move before he caught himself. *Not this time, you bastard,* he thought grimly. *You're not going to catch me unprepared.* He let the light continue on its way to the far wall, then, reaching for his weapon, he followed.

"MAKE ONE MOVE and you're a dead man!"

The words tingled along Shasta's spine. Once before she had looked down the barrel of a gun, and she didn't wish to repeat the experience. She winced as the gun ground harder into her neck, then inhaled deeply to calm the pounding of her heart.

"I said, not a move. Now spread-eagle."

Time seemed to stand still as she slid her hands out and up the paneled wall. In the distance thunder rolled across the land. The wind moaned, and fat drops of rain splattered against the windows in minuscule explosions.

Using his foot as a hook, her assailant forced her feet apart and back so that the only balance she had was her forehead resting against the cold wood paneling. It was a position used by law-enforcement agencies. She made a mental note of his expertise, reminding herself to stay quiet and try to glean as much information about this burglar as possible.

Judging from the distance and sound of his voice above her, she guessed him to be somewhere between six-foot and six-foot-two. And damn him, his after-shave was driving her crazy, reminding her of summer afternoons and warm sunshine—earthy and sensual. Thieves weren't supposed to smell good, were they?

"I thought I made myself clear in Paris. Didn't your friends relay the message to your boss? I warned him not to send his goons after me again. Maybe it's time to show him I mean what I say and teach him a little lesson in counterattack."

The husky voice stirred her hair, and a shiver seemed to slide down each vertebra, stiffening her whole body. It wasn't the soft accented voice causing the effect, but the menacing tone to his words.

"Keep still," he commanded as she twitched her shoulders, trying to relieve some of the strain.

Keeping the weapon pressed into the back of her neck, he ran his free hand around her ankles, then moved upward. Each calf was lightly touched, the outside of each thigh briefly frisked. When his fingers reached around to the inside of her thighs, she tensed and held her breath.

He stopped his search for a second, as if puzzled by something. "Scrawny thing, aren't you?" His hand wandered onward to her waist. "When did the company start hiring kids to do their dirty work? Or are you with the other group?"

Shasta knew he didn't expect an answer, and she wasn't about to open her mouth and give herself away—that would come soon enough. She grimaced as he clasped the zipper of her leather bomber jacket and yanked it down. His hand slipped inside the warm confines and quickly ran from ribs to armpit.

She heard his deep intake of breath and squeezed her eyes shut. Every muscle was tense as his fingers grazed the side of her breast then froze there.

"What the hell?" As if to confirm what he now suspected, Kane's hand cupped one nicely rounded, female breast.

"Son of a bitch." The shock didn't last long, and he leaned over and switched on a desk lamp. "Okay, baby. Let's have a good look at you."

His words weren't an endearment. He gripped the back of her jacket in a tight fist and hauled her upright. Without allowing her time to catch her balance, he spun her around and yanked off the knit cap. Brown shoulder-length curls tumbled out, bouncing in total disarray around her face. When she reached out to push the unruly mass from her eyes, her hand was slapped away none too gently. She yelped in pain as strong fingers gathered a handful of hair and pulled her sideways, twisting her face to the light.

Shasta inwardly flinched at the thought of having to face a gun again. Resignedly she opened her eyes, only to find them level with a bare male chest. Something was terribly wrong! A tall, half-naked thief who smelled good and talked with a French accent just couldn't be true. Lowering her eyes farther, she found herself gazing down the cold, menacing barrel of the weapon he held—an empty long-necked beer bottle, imported of course.

The heat of anger flushed her cheeks a bright red. She felt like a fool. Despite the pain she jerked her head back and frowned into her captor's face, ready to burst forth with a lengthy set of questions. Instead she simply gulped and stared, absolutely stunned.

"Well, pixie, you're a surprise."

Eyes as silver as newly minted coins flashed, and Shasta wondered dazedly whether she'd see her own reflection if she gazed long enough into their depths. She gulped again for air, lost in the masculine beauty before her. And he definitely was gorgeous—and very much a male.

A loud drumming filled her ears, and she felt a shortness of breath. She wondered how many other women experienced the same effects while gazing at him. He was the most beautiful, most decadent-looking man she'd ever seen.

It seemed a conspiracy against the female species that any man could possess those perfectly arched eyebrows and the double row of long, thick black lashes. Suddenly the hand in her hair tightened painfully and brought her sharply back to reality. Here she was, faced with possible death, and she'd been daydreaming and lusting after a thief.

"Welcome back." He smiled and Shasta watched, trance-like, as the chiseled lips mouthed the words, "No you don't." He shook her head roughly. "You're not going to fade out to never-never land on me again. Lady, I want some answers."

Shasta wasn't dreaming any longer. She'd seen that smile, and its resemblance to a tiger contemplating his next meal was unnerving. She knew instinctively that whatever she'd faced in the past was child's play compared to what this man could and would do to her. Beautiful he might be, but he exuded an air of cruelty, and she knew that nothing would stop him from doing exactly what he wanted. Keeping him distracted and off balance was her only hope to get away. Her free hand inched, unobserved, over the surface of the desk beside her, and she asked her own questions.

"What are you doing in *my* house? Who are you?"

"Your *house?*" He snorted, then smiled again, truly evil this time. "Do you usually sneak around your own house dressed like a Hollywood cat burglar?"

"I'm an actress," she lied, her fingers continuing their search. "I was getting into character."

He shook his head slowly and Shasta was momentarily distracted by the play of lights on his blue-black hair. She was about to give up hope of finding a weapon of any sort when the tips of her fingers nudged a round object, and her hand closed over a heavy, crystal paperweight. Bracing herself, she looked directly into his steady gaze, then her eyes traveled toward the open doorway. She made her body stiffen under his hands, her eyes widened and she smiled. "Come in, Julius. As you can see we have company."

"No, lady—" his voice rumbled with laughter "—that old trick won't wash."

Shasta made a lunge, then yelled out in pain as her head was snapped back and his other hand wrapped around her throat.

"I don't like games." His eyes narrowed to silver slits. "Talk." Fingers tightened around her throat, slowly cutting off her air supply.

How was she supposed to talk when he was choking her? She struggled for one deep breath of air, certain she was going to die, when suddenly a sharp blinding flash of light filled the room, followed instantly by window-rattling thunder. That brief second, when her assailant froze, gave her the chance she needed. She swung the heavy paperweight upward with all her strength. There was a satisfying thud, then the pressure around her neck eased.

Leaning against the desk for support, she rubbed at her bruised throat, inhaling deeply, trying to calm her shattered nerves. When she regained her composure, she looked down at the supine figure at her feet and nudged his side experimentally with a bare toe. Out like a light. She grinned.

A few seconds later she had his hands and feet secured with both their belts. Only then did she sit back on her heels and relax long enough to lay her fingers to the side of his neck, checking that the pulse still beat steadily. "While you're taking a nap, friend, I'll just make a few phone calls. Maybe when you wake you'll answer some of my questions. Don't go away now," she said, chuckling, as she pushed herself up and reached for the telephone.

With the receiver in one hand, she began to punch out the numbers while her other hand idly played with a small folder. "Damn it, answer, Jeff," she growled softly, her eyes wandering back and forth between her captive and the now-open folder. As the typewritten words came into focus, she slowly dropped the instrument back into its cradle and leaned across the desk toward the lamplight. She prayed she'd been dreaming. But, no, there it was, typed neatly on the official United States passport, and if that wasn't bad enough, his signature and photograph confirmed his identification.

Shasta looked up toward heaven. "Please," she begged in a pitiful voice. "Don't do this to me. You don't realize what I've been through this week, then to be so cruel as to throw this at me now." She let her eyes drop to the open passport, and this time she read the name out loud. "Kane Maximilian du Monde Stone." Her client's son.

The passport slipped through her fingers to the carpeted floor. What now, she wondered, her glazed eyes resting on the unconscious man.

Unconscious. The word rattled her out of her stupor and sent her vaulting over the inert form and out the door. Once in the big, modern kitchen, she yanked and pulled frantically at drawers, mumbling under her breath as she searched for a dish towel and filled it with ice. She raced back to her trussed-up captive, knowing he was going to be madder than a wet hen when he woke—to say nothing of the headache he'd have.

She threw herself down on the floor, slipped a needlepoint pillow from the couch under Kane's head and positioned the ice pack behind his left ear and the large lump she'd given him. Her fingers automatically went to the belt securing his hands before reason struck and she jerked back in horror. He'd never listen to what she had to say first. Shasta shook her head, recognizing Kane as the type who always came out of a corner fighting. She patted his hands gently. She wasn't going to give him any swinging room till she had thoroughly explored every possible explanation. Crossing her legs, elbows resting on her knees and hands cupping her chin, she settled down to wait for him to come to.

Kane groaned and Shasta adjusted the ice pack, her hands lingering a second longer than necessary on the springy black hair. She leaned back, intently studying the strong face, and whispered, "Well, Mr. Kane Maximilian du Monde Stone, welcome home." She reached out and lightly touched each arched eyebrow, then ran the tip of her finger back and forth over the fan of long lashes.

Lightning began to spark wildly outside, and everything faded around her as she sat on the floor, concentrating with an unnatural intensity on the man before her.

Thunder boomed overhead, but Shasta didn't feel the hammering vibrations. Rain drummed furiously against the house, bringing with it a coldness that penetrated every corner of the room, but she could only feel the heat of Kane's body.

"Do you know that you take my breath away?" Her eyes followed the path of her fingers trailing down the aquiline nose, outlining the flared nostrils. "I wonder if I'd ever have the nerve to say what I'm about to say if you were conscious?" she whispered. "From the moment you turned me around and I gazed into those soulless eyes, I knew you were mine." She caressed his square jaw with the back of her hand, smiling dreamily when the rough stubble of his cheeks tickled her sensitive skin. The clefted chin and deep lines bracketing his mouth seemed to beckon her light caress, and the tip of one finger moved to circle the sculpted lips. "You'll think I'm crazy, I know." She wondered if his lips would remain so impersonal pressed to her own. Moistening her parched lips, she said softly, "You're mine, Kane Stone," and leaned down to place her mouth on his.

Every breath he took seemed to be a sigh just for her. She allowed the tip of her tongue to trace the sharp lines of his lips before pulling back, reluctantly. For all she knew he might be married with a dozen children, but somehow she didn't think so. This man was hers, she knew it. To dispel any nagging fears, she picked up his passport from where it had fallen and flipped it open. Under "wife" there were three tiny, beautiful *X*'s.

"So, no wife—yet." Shasta grinned wickedly. She dropped her hand to his and let her fingers travel along the map of warm veins patterning one bronzed arm. He was tall, broad shouldered, slim hipped and lean. No surplus flesh there. He had the physique of an athlete, but shadows of exhaustion belied that exterior, faint half circles of fatigue under his eyes, lines of strain that deepened the furrows between his eyebrows.

Shasta jerked her hand back from Kane's ribs as he moaned in pain. She leaned down for a better view and sucked in a hard breath. His whole side was a mass of bruises. "What happened to you, Kane?" She picked up his tied hands and inspected the scraped and swollen knuckles. "I wonder who won? Looks like you gave as good as you got though." She brought his injured hands to her lips and kissed them lightly, noticing their long, slim fingered elegance. "But, my love," she began, only to be interrupted as Kane snorted in his unconscious state. She smiled. "You don't like the endearment? No, your footloose, fancy-free spirit wouldn't, but in time you'll get used to it."

Kane twisted his head back and forth, and Shasta stroked his brow to calm his movements, then replaced the dislocated ice pack. Her eyes caressed the broad chest, lingering on the mat of black hair that tapered off to a fine line down the center of his stomach and beneath the waistband of his jeans.

The temptation was too great, the pull too strong, and gently she laid her hand on his chest, barely touching the silken hair. She followed the path of darkness to the denim barrier, and though her fingers stopped, her eyes continued a very slow, very thorough journey to his bare feet. "Yes indeed, you're mine, and you can count on that!"

Maybe she *was* crazy. She'd spent the last ten of her twenty-seven years searching for this feeling, and she wasn't about to let it slip away. She was an incurable romantic. But what did the world expect when she was surrounded by a family of happily-ever-after marriages. She always felt odd man out, because up until now she'd never experienced that special something, that instant recognition her family talked about. Her brother teased her unmercifully, saying that her unnatural nerves of steel made a shield so that no romantic feeling could penetrate.

She wanted to touch Kane again and reassure herself he was real. She reached out, then stopped, laughing as she noticed her trembling hand. Amazed, she shoved the other one out and watched in fascination as it shook, also. Now! Now she'd proved Jeff wrong. She was just as normal as the rest of her family. She laughed aloud again. Her nerves of iron had melted away to flesh and blood.

KANE MANAGED to lie perfectly still, though his head ached abominably and the pain around his ribs made him want to double over. His jaw clenched as pieces of what had happened began to form a clear picture. To be bested physically by a woman was bad enough, but to be outmaneuvered and manipulated by a mouse—that's what really smarted, he conceded. And his big bad burglar was exactly that—a mouse with a tangle of brown hair, big brown eyes and a small pert nose that actually twitched enchantingly.

He was jolted out of his musing by her jubilant laughter, and the muscles along his jaw knotted at the sound. There was a long pause and then she laughed again, and this time he was forced to bite the inside of his cheek because he found the delightful noise contagious. The happy sound, half laugh, half giggle, came from deep down, a gut laugh. He wondered how long it had been since he'd heard the pure joy of uninhibited laughter. Certainly not from his so-called set, who usually gave a stiff, sophisticated whinny that grated on his nerves after too long an exposure.

Opening his eyes a crack, Kane assessed the situation correctly. He was expertly tied hand and foot with no hope of slipping free till his captor deemed it so or until help arrived. His gaze shifted to the woman sitting cross-legged beside him, her chin in hand. She was staring intently at him, and the sparkle in her eyes made him extremely uncomfortable.

"You can open them the rest of the way." Shasta grinned at the frown gathering across the wide brow. "I hope your head isn't hurting you too badly to listen to an explanation?"

Kane's gaze met hers and the frown deepened—partly in self-disgust, partly in anger. He watched warily as her full, lovely mouth stretched into a heart-stopping smile. He had to concentrate hard on staying angry in order to hide his inclination to respond to her smile. "Don't tell me there's actually an explanation? I guess now you're going to hand me the old line that this is not what it appears to be?"

"Well..." she drawled the word out.

"Baby, if you can come up with an explanation to convince me you're not a cat burglar, you're a better liar than I'd have suspected."

Shasta straightened, highly affronted at being referred to as a liar and being called baby. "First of all let's get a few things perfectly clear between us. You don't call me baby and I won't call you Maxie." He winced and she knew she'd hit the raw spot she'd aimed for. "Deal?"

"Deal." He couldn't help but smile this time. "If we're to have a lengthy conversation, do you think you could untie me?" He altered his expression to one of great pain. "These belts are cutting off the circulation in my hands and feet." She shook her head. "No! Come on now, what could I possibly do with my feet?" He gave her a smile that always worked on other women, but this one only laughed and shook her head.

"You can probably do more with your feet than most men can with an active pair of hands. Sorry, Kane."

Kane looked up at her, lingering over her wide brown eyes. He forced himself to concentrate once again on the situation and his anger. "You seem to know who I am. Am I entitled to a name along with this explanation of yours?"

"Shasta Masterson." She was thinking hard and fast, trying to find the quickest and most precise way to express herself.

He waited for her to go on, and when she didn't his lip curled and his next words came out in a cutting tone. "Ahh... that explains everything. Tell me something, Shasta Masterson, how much is this going to cost my father?" He ignored her start of surprise and narrowing eyes. "I mean, doesn't a burglar turn to kidnapping and ransom when his robbery plans are thwarted and he's caught? Let me give you some advice. Neither my father nor our company will pay. That, my girl, is Texas-American Oil's policy." He paused long enough to let his words sink in. "Now, be a good girl and *untie me!*" he exploded. He calmed down, but his next words were spoken through clenched teeth. "I promise you, you'll walk out of here and we'll forget we ever met."

Shasta's eyes widened as she listened to each word, then she stopped his angry struggle to get loose by throwing her head back and laughing. When she realized he had ceased moving and was glaring at her murderously, she reached for the leather knot binding his hands. She took a deep breath. "I know you're going to find this hard to believe." She stopped what she was doing, feeling he deserved her full attention.

"Untie me!" he demanded coldly. "Now!"

"Yes, yes. But you've wiggled around so this knot is hard to work loose." She continued to talk as she struggled with the stubborn strap. Her voice, usually sweet and slow with its soft Texas drawl, began to speed up. Words tumbled from her lips in a great rush. Syllables tripped and stumbled over one another in her haste to explain. While she wrestled with the belt, Kane punctuated her efforts at regular intervals with the command "Untie me." She looked up after her speedy speech and noticed the blank look on Kane's face.

"What it all boils down to is I work for Masters Security. We...I mean my brother, Jeff, designed and installed the alarm security system for your father. It's my job to find the flaws, and I did. The problem was, no one was supposed to be here." He still looked unconvinced and only held up his hands when she stopped working. She sighed and returned to her task.

"Honestly, Kane, I'm telling the truth."

"How did you get through the front gates? They were locked and are ten feet of wrought iron."

"I didn't go through them." She switched her gaze from his hands to his face and wished she hadn't. The wind-driven rain outside settled down to a steady humming noise in her ears. She felt herself wanting to drown in his silver eyes. Like calm water they seemed to promise everything and reveal nothing of the danger lurking within their depths. "I...I went over the gate." She tore her eyes away from his, her heart pounding like a big brass drum. She wanted to say something, anything, to break the silent hold he had on her. "Kane."

"Woman," he roared. "Would you finish untying me before my fingers and toes fall off?" The belt finally fell away and Kane sat up, pushed Shasta aside and began rubbing his hands together briskly before he reached down and expertly released his bound feet.

He turned the blaze of silver on her. "If what you say is true and you were running a test on the alarm system—" his mouth tightened "—what were you doing at the wall safe?"

Shasta smiled confidently. "We installed that, too."

Silence hung between them with only the flicker of lightning and the ominous rolling of thunder breaking the quiet. "I don't know whether to believe you or not? But I'll hand you this, lady, you're a cool one." Lightning split the sky again, lighting the room in an eye-blinking brilliance. Kane moved before Shasta knew what was happening. "Let's just see how calm and cool you really are?"

Before the thunder had time to follow the streaking light, Shasta found herself stretched out on the carpeted floor beneath Kane's full weight. Their eyes clashed and held for a moment, then his head came to rest in the curve of her neck and a low moan escaped his lips. Catching his breath, he raised his head. His eyes had turned the color of pewter and held a residue of pain. "What in the name of hell did you hit me with?"

She opened her lips to answer but was cut off by the pressure of his mouth on hers. Her first instinct was to fight, give him a good whack in his already sore ribs. She couldn't hurt him again, though, so she lay there unresponding. But, oh God, how she wanted to open her lips for him.

When Kane raised his head and looked down, the shutter of cruelty had left his face and been replaced with a hint of humor. "Well, I see you really are a cool lady. A shame I'd have—"

Shasta reached up, gathered a handful of his hair and pulled his mouth down to hers. This time her warm pliant lips met his, and as quick as a butterfly her tongue slipped between his parted lips. She felt him stiffen. Then, not to be mastered by a woman again, he took command and threaded his fingers through the shoulder-length curls, adding his own expertise to her kiss.

Shasta had thought to teach him a quick lesson in fair play between the sexes, but she realized this was no game, and though she wanted him and intended to have him, now was not the time to expose all her cards.

She opened her eyes and moved her head back, breaking contact. Thunder crashed overhead and the electricity blinked out, but the lightning highlighted Kane's features, casting his eyes into shadows. She gazed into them and felt herself succumb to their power. They pulled her like a leaf into a whirlpool of swirling silver water. Hypnotically she closed her eyes and gave herself up once again to the beauty of his mouth, savoring the firmness of his lips, the hardness of his teeth, the feeling of his warm breath blending with hers. They broke apart as the lightning struck once more, this time with all its fury, then it seemed to give up the fight and slip away into the night, the thunder reverberating in its wake, leaving them in total darkness.

"Hell..." Kane swallowed the rest of his comment, not sure if the heart-stopping sensation was from the kiss or this latest display from mother nature. He smoothed the springy curls back from her fevered brow and smiled into the darkness. She might be small, but she packed a most desirable punch.

"I don't think the lights are going to come on again," she breathed against his lips, allowing herself the luxury of teasing the corners of his mouth with the tip of her tongue.

"No," he whispered, his hand playing in the silken curls. "I guess there's nothing left to do but go to bed." He felt her stiffen. "Be reasonable. You wouldn't get one block on this street before your car was door deep in water. Besides—" his voice hardened "—I'm not one hundred percent sure I believe your story. I'd rather have you close by till I've checked you out. Okay?"

"I guess," she sighed. She knew only too well what happened to Houston's streets in a flash flood. Kane moved away and she followed him, her hand in his. She trailed behind him as he gave instructions where to turn, when to lift her feet to climb stairs, when to walk straight. Finally she felt the firm, high bed.

Kane turned back the covers, then touched her arm to signal her to climb in. Snuggling down, she pulled the blanket to her chin. "Good night, Kane." She heard his movements and assumed he was making his way to the door, but when the other side of the bed sank with his weight, she demanded, "What do you think you're doing?"

She felt a hand run the length of her leg and sat up. "Listen, Kane Stone—" She stopped, stunned speechless as something soft was tied firmly around her ankle. "What the hell...?" She tried to yank her foot away, but he held it firm as he tied the sash of joined neckties to the bedpost.

"Be still, damn it." His voice floated out of the darkness. "I'm making sure I get to check out your story. Cats have a way of sneaking off in the middle of the night. Just be thankful your tethers are silk and not leather."

The bed gave a few bounces before she settled down. "Well I'll be damned."

"We are both more than likely damned already." Why did he have an uneasy feeling in the pit of his stomach? He was attracted to her, though he hadn't figured out why. She certainly wasn't his type. Maybe that was the answer. He was tired of experienced, sophisticated women. Maybe for the next few weeks, while he searched for the information he'd come back for, he'd entertain himself and play with a mouse who went disguised as a cat burglar. He smiled. Things might not be as boring as he had anticipated. He was aware of her wiggling around, trying to find a comfortable position, and it irritated him to feel the tightening in his loins. "Keep still or you'll cut off the circulation in your foot," he said gruffly. "Go to sleep. I promise I won't take advantage of you during the night."

Shasta knew he was leaving. "Where are you going?" She hissed into the darkness, tugging frantically at her securely tied ankle. "Don't leave me alone like this."

"Afraid! You?" The sound of his laughter lingered long after he'd left the room.

Shasta wondered at the rusty rasp she'd heard—as if he'd forgotten how to really laugh. She certainly had her work cut out for her. Lying back, her arms folded behind her head, she decided she'd rest her eyes awhile and throw him off guard. Then she'd work herself free and follow him downstairs. Her eyes became heavier and a dreamy smile touched her lips as she thought of all the fun she could have teaching Kane how to enjoy life.

CHAPTER TWO

SHASTA OPENED HER EYES to an unfamiliar peach-colored ceiling. She wondered briefly why she was torturing her body by sleeping on her back, then tried to flip over onto her side. One leg seemed to be twisted at an odd angle, refusing to budge. She yanked it sharply toward her, then sat bolt upright with a yelp as pain shot through her ankle.

Once her befuddled brain was elevated she realized she was in a strange room, in a strange bed, and fully clothed. Gradually the previous night came back into focus, which wasn't easy at such an ungodly hour of the morning. Giving her foot an experimental tug, she leaned forward and in a few seconds was struggling grimly with a series of intricate knots. Reluctantly she grinned at Kane's sense of humor.

She persisted working at the taut silk, but with each pull the line of knots seemed to shrink. Frustrated, her fingers sore, she bellowed, "Kane!" and waited.

When he didn't answer, she propped her chin in her hand and contemplated the situation. She studied the length of silk, judging the amount of give at both looped ends—one around her ankle, the other around the bedpost—and the row of knots in between. As the seconds ticked by, she began to smile. Though short in stature, she was blessed with long legs and, as her grandfather put it, was "as limber as a double-jointed snake."

Shasta loosened the loop secured around the wood post so it could slide. Then, standing on her untethered leg, she did a slow split, working her foot up inch by inch until at last she slid the loop over the top of the tall post.

She collapsed amid a tangle of covers, then leaped off the bed. In a whirlwind of sheets, bedspread and trailing blankets, she bounded out of the room and down the stairs. Catching the scent of freshly brewed coffee, she marched into the kitchen, stopped in the doorway and yelled at the man calmly ensconced behind the morning paper. "That was a damn dirty trick, Kane Stone." Her nose crinkled in disgust when her words brought no response. She tried again. "You're a mean, vindictive man. You heard me calling you. What if I had needed to go to the bathroom?"

The paper vibrated a second, then lowered only as far as the bridge of Kane's nose. "Did you?"

"No," she snapped, sliding into the nearest chair and reaching for the coffeepot. She was more frustrated than she'd like to admit. His roving eyes had taken in everything from her bare feet, wrinkled and twisted clothes to her unruly hair before he slowly raised his paper shield.

"I'd like two eggs, scrambled. Bacon, crisp and blotted. Four slices of toast, crust trimmed and lightly buttered."

"So would I," she grumbled under her breath, her stomach jumping at each item he called off. Then she realized he was speaking to *her.* But just to be quite sure a cook wasn't lurking about, she searched out every corner of the kitchen before her vivid eyes flashed him a scorching look that should have melted him on the spot. Of all the nerve! She gently set the coffeepot down and leaned across the thick glass table. With both hands at the top of his morning paper, she pleated the sheets down to his lap. Their eyes met levelly. "I, Mr. Stone, can't cook."

"Figures." He shook both ends of the paper and folded it neatly.

She looked up into shimmering silver eyes, a deceptively sweet smile on her lips, and watched him struggle to keep his expression stern.

"You know, Kane, God won't strike you dead if you laugh out loud," she whispered, then pushed back from the table and left the room. She wondered what had happened to make him afraid to feel or show any emotion. Even his anger the night before, though loudly vocal at one point, had still been under rigid control. She was going to have her work cut out for her, and she still hadn't figured out a way to see him again after today.

Moving quickly across the hall to the living room, she winced at the sound of chair legs scraping on Spanish tile and ignored the heavy fall of footsteps behind her. She picked up her leather jacket from the floor, pulled a stethoscope out of an inside zippered pocket and inserted the rubber ends into her ears.

Kane leaned against the doorframe, watching as she walked to the huge painting on the wall. He smiled as she went up on tiptoe, her fingers searching for the hidden latch. Releasing the catch, she swung the ornate frame out, placed metal to metal and began to work the round cylinder dials slowly. His smile widened at her serious expression. Did she really think she was good enough to break the combination? He'd seen the trademark on that safe and knew the company's reputation. Besides, only two people in the world knew the magic numbers—his father and the German manufacturer.

The smooth tumbling clicks soothed her raw nerves. A smile twitched her lips as she recalled her brother's taunting words. "This time we gotcha, my girl. No one, but no one, can open the Stones' new safe."

Jeff and their cousin Daniel had spent weeks in conference calls between the German company and their New York representative to obtain this special locking system. They were so pompously sure of themselves they had laid a hefty bet that Shasta couldn't break the combination. They had even talked J. T. Masterson, her grandfather, into entering their so-called fun. Shasta knew heads were likely to roll in all directions tomorrow. If there was one thing J.T. hated worse than losing an argument, it was losing a sure-thing bet.

She couldn't restrain a soft chuckle. What none of her family of supersnoops had yet to discover was that she had designed the new lock system and sold her plans to the German company. It was the only way she could afford to indulge in her passion for fast, deadly, little sports cars.

Shasta purred with pleasure as she heard the last tumble of oiled metal. She reached up and pulled the handle, but before she could swing the round steel door open, Kane's hand clamped down on hers. In her total absorption she'd completely forgotten about him. She looked over her shoulder, meeting the renewed suspicion in his eyes.

"Kane, the only things in this safe are three Krugerrands and they're mine." She tugged on the handle, but he applied pressure to still her efforts.

He studied her expressive face. The big brown eyes were honest, yet there was a hard intelligence and perceptiveness in their depths that surprised him. For some unknown reason he wanted desperately to trust her, but he hesitated. The ease with which she'd opened the safe bothered him; she'd handled the whole operation so professionally. He knew it took a lifetime of experience to attain that self-assurance, and she didn't have the years, unless she'd started learning her trade from the cradle.

"Before you open the door why don't you tell me why three of your Krugerrands would be in this safe?"

A frown marred Shasta's brow. She had wanted him to believe her without proof, to take her word as the truth. Now she could see that it wasn't going to be that easy. She sensed his lack of trust for anything female and wondered what kind of woman had inflicted such deep scars.

She tilted her head and glared up at him, angry with herself for expecting so much so soon. Quickly she related the terms of the bet without adding any of the funnier sides of the story. She fell silent and waited for his reaction. The mask shuttering his face remained stonily fixed, his eyes mirror hard. Then, making up his mind about her, he smiled and dropped his hand.

Shasta didn't move—couldn't move if she'd wanted to. Her eyes were glued to his face, mesmerized by the power of his smile. Then, in response to the dazzling effect he was having on her, she slowly answered his smile with one of her own. She couldn't recall how long she stood there grinning like an idiot before she came to life at the touch of his finger caressing her cheek.

"Come back to me, Shasta."

"Yes," she breathed, and mentally gave herself a hard kick in the rear end. This just had to stop, she admonished herself. She was a woman of twenty-seven, not a love-struck kid. Spinning around, she pulled the safe door open and reached in for her winnings.

Her thoughts weren't on her victory but on the desire she'd seen in Kane's eyes and her own body's response. Her blood had warmed to that spark of life, and there was no doubt he knew exactly the effect he was having on her. She hoped she'd never have to drive him anywhere, because if she wandered off to dreamland she'd end up killing them both.

Shasta turned around reluctantly, keeping her eyes on the three big coins she juggled in the palm of her hand. "What time is it?" When no answer came she was forced to look up and meet his steady gaze.

"You really are quite lovely," he mused out loud, as if the realization was something of a shock.

"What time is it?" She tried again, her voice a hoarse whisper.

"About nine o'clock. Did you know your nose crinkles enchantingly when you smile?" His fingers traced her pert nose from the bridge to the tip, where he paused to tap the end tenderly.

"I have to go." Shasta fought for breath wanting to pull away from his touch, knowing he was deliberately baiting her, playing with her like a big cat teasing a tiny mouse before he pounces. She spun around, and marched away, picking up her jacket on her way to the front door. Kane Stone didn't play the game fairly. And that's just what this was to him at the moment—a game. He made his own rules as he went; and she'd have to stay one step ahead of him if she planned to accomplish her goal and stay alive.

She pulled open the door and stopped, staring blindly out over the wreckage of the front lawn. How was she going to stay one step ahead of him if she never saw him again?

She turned quickly and was jolted backward as she bumped into the solid wall of Kane's chest. "Well, I guess this is goodbye?" she said awkwardly, and held out her hand. Immediately she wished she hadn't as he took her fingers, lifted them to his mouth and lightly kissed them, his eyes twinkling knowingly down at her. Damn, she wished he'd say something. "Kane?"

"Yes." His smile widened.

"I'll have one of our men come out and replace the attic window." And she'd come along to supervise the job.

"Don't worry about it."

"No, no. We can't leave it like that." She turned away, her cheeks stained red. She felt like a fool standing there waiting for him to ask her out. Giving up, she spun around and stomped down the wide stone steps to the graveled drive.

Kane followed slowly, laughter twitching at the tight corners of his mouth. She was so damn adorable he wanted to grab her and give her a big hug. He watched the angry switch of her hips, the determined bounce in her walk, then hurried his own steps. When the object of his intense gaze came to an abrupt halt, he suddenly became aware of his surroundings. The storm with its high winds and torrents of rain had made a quagmire of the perfectly manicured lawns. He may never have liked his home when he was young, but he did appreciate its beauty. Now, all was in ruins.

As if on the same mental wavelength, Shasta looked back at the house and grounds and shook her head. The Stone estate sprawled over more than an acre of thickly wooded land in the older, wealthier section of Houston's Memorial area. The large brick Tudor house had sat like a jeweled crown amid the emerald-green vegetation and brilliantly colored flowers. Now several big trees and a multitude of shrubs had been uprooted and strewed across the grounds. The once-green lawn was covered with broken branches and a blanket of leaves and crushed flower petals.

Shasta was shocked. She hadn't realized the storm had wreaked such destruction. Remembering the rain and knowing Houston's streets were prone to flooding in record time, she set off at a run to the front gates, praying that the company van parked on the side street hadn't floated away. She was halfway up the wrought-iron gates when she was unceremoniously hauled down by strong hands gripping the waistband of her jeans.

"Are you trying to kill yourself, woman?" Kane yelled, settling her in his arms before he allowed her to slide down the length of his body to the ground. She'd been up that high gate before he knew what was happening, and when he saw her he felt as if someone had punched him in the gut. Why the hell should he care anyway? None too gently he set her aside, pulled out a key and unlocked the gate. "There, now you can walk out of here like a civilized human being." The thought of relieving his boredom with her company died a fast death. He'd be damned if he'd ask her out. She was nothing but a five-foot-four-inch, one-hundred-five-pound bundle of trouble. He'd had enough problems lately to last a lifetime. This was one temptation he could live without.

SHASTA COULDN'T SAY later what had happened. One minute she was on her way over the gate, the next she was hustled into the van and driving down the street, viewing Kane through the side mirrors and trying to figure out what had angered him so. Guiltily she realized she hadn't given a thought to her family and their concern about what had happened to her. She picked up the van's mobile phone and punched out the office number. When she received a busy signal on all the rotating lines, she tried her brother's house and then, out of desperation, her own home. All lines gave the same irritating signal. She sighed with relief, knowing that the phone lines were downed.

Two hours later Shasta parked the van in the parking lot adjacent to the tall office building that housed Masters Security. She stepped out, relieved to be on solid ground. The drive from the Stone estate to the Galleria area would normally have taken about fifteen minutes, thirty in rush-hour traffic, but this morning had been sheer chaos. She'd dodged downed power lines, driven around fallen trees, avoided flooded streets when she could and forged on.

She gazed up at the twelve-story glass-and-steel structure with pleasure. DeSalva's was as neat and sleek as its owners, who occupied ten of the twelve top floors and dealt with electronics in the oil industry, a highly competitive and secretive field. They felt fortunate that Masters Security was the tenant of the remaining two floors and an underground suite, and had put the company in charge of DeSalva's security.

Shasta grinned as she entered the building, showed her pass to the elderly guard and waited for him to sign her in.

"Everyone's about to pull their hair out trying to find you, Miss Masterson. You better hurry up."

"Thanks, Frank," Shasta said over her shoulder as she made for the row of elevators.

"You'll have to take the stairs," Frank called out. "Electricity's back on, but it keeps playing funny flickering games, so Mr. Brandon closed down the elevators."

Shasta waved and headed for the stairway, smiling. She could just imagine Brandon DeSalva trying to take over. He was the company's corporate attorney and a dream to look at, but he didn't take anything seriously in life except law and his older brother, Lucas. At times she wondered if law and Lucas were one and the same, the way everybody bowed at Lucas's feet. Though their many dealings had been all business, she had not missed the interest in his eyes. Lucas DeSalva with his rugged good looks was not her type. He seemed to have come to the same conclusion, because his interest had never developed further than that gleam in his eyes.

Shasta pushed open the big double glass doors to Masters and stepped into a madhouse. She paused a moment, listening to the three people arguing vociferously about the next step they would take to locate her.

"You can stop worrying. I'm here safe and sound, if a little wet." She grinned apologetically to the three angry faces now turned in her direction.

"Just where the hell have you been?" Jeff demanded. "Rena and I have been up all night trying to find you." He draped a long protective arm around his wife and glared at his sister for once again disrupting his well-ordered life.

"Sorry, but I couldn't call from where I was. You see—"

"And where was that?" Rena interrupted, a smile hovering around the corners of her mouth.

Shasta saw the twinkle in Rena's blue eyes. Her sister-in-law's looks were deceptive. She resembled the classic cold blond goddess, but in fact she was one of the warmest and most tenderhearted people Shasta had ever met. And Rena further endeared herself by keeping the family off Shasta's back when one of her harebrained ideas backfired.

Shasta couldn't hold back her smile, and as her lips turned up and her dark-brown eyes began to sparkle, she pulled her hand from her jacket pocket and held her palm open toward her brother.

Jeff gazed at the gold coins in disbelief and then groaned in defeat. "I should have guessed," he said tiredly, rubbing his hand wearily across his red-rimmed eyes.

Shasta wasn't fooled by his easy capitulation; she knew her brother too well. Every member of the Masterson clan carried one strong trait, they hated to admit defeat or give up. Jeff accepted the fact that he'd lost the bet, but he wasn't going to allow her to get off scot-free. She could see it coming—he was about to spring a guilt trip on her that would have her groveling for at least three or four days.

A mug of hot fragrant coffee was shoved into her free hand. She turned and nodded to Masters's top sergeant and peacemaker—Margret Sellers, their stylish, sixty-five-year-old executive secretary. "Thanks, Margret." She caught the woman's knowing look and went on meaningfully, "You're a lifesaver."

"Yes." Margret's lips barely moved as she lowered her voice. "You're more trouble than you're worth, young lady. When J.T. hears about this he'll have your hide."

"Now, Meg," Shasta wheedled softly. "What pappy doesn't know won't hurt him." She smiled brightly, knowing her grandfather's watchdog wouldn't tell on her.

Shasta also knew Jeff would never say anything no matter how mad he got. The Houston office of Masters, though two years in operation, was still on J. T. Masterson's "not sure" list. Shasta, Jeff and Rena had wanted to branch out on their own—Jeff and Rena because of Rena's parents' constant interference in their marriage, and Shasta because she figured it was time for a change. She'd been stuck at the head office in Dallas long enough, and the time was right to move on. It had taken the three of them months of long business discussions and involved meetings with J.T., and still they'd been forced to resort to pleadings and dire threats till their dear old tyrant agreed.

"Shasta," Jeff roared, making her spill her coffee. "I want to talk to you." He seized her arm and marched her into her office. When she smoothly slipped away, slid behind her desk and sat down, taking command, he realized his mistake. Frowning, he tried to shift the authority back to himself. "Shasta, you've pulled some stupid stunts before, but this takes the cake. Of all the—"

"Shut up, Jeff dear." She looked toward the open doorway and the two grinning women. "You two might as well come in. I have work for you."

"Work!" Jeff exploded. "You leave yesterday afternoon to check the security on the Stone estate, then waltz in here eighteen hours later..." He took a deep breath. "And—and you have the nerve to start throwing around orders without the least explanation as to where you've been all this time?"

"Hush, Jeff," Rena cautioned her husband as she perched on the arm of his chair, her fingers automatically going to the blond curls at the nape of his neck and stroking them soothingly. "Let your sister talk."

Shasta looked at the two of them and sighed enviously. They both had inherited their families' Nordic good looks, and she felt like the ugly duckling in a flock of swans. The entire Masterson family, from her seventy-two-year-old grandfather, who looked like an aging Cary Grant, to her mother, father, two older brothers and sisters, were all tall, beautiful and very fair. She couldn't figure it out. She'd come into this world short, with a curly tangle of brown hair and equally dark eyes, and had never attained the color and grace characteristic of the rest of the family.

"Jeff." Shasta picked up a pencil and twirled it between her fingers as she began relating all that had happened last night. From beginning to end she told her story, leaving out only her newfound feelings for Kane. She tried to be detached and impersonal, but an image of silver eyes and a smile that could melt the devil's own heart kept intruding and she would lapse into silence until Rena gently prompted her.

"Jeff, dear," said Rena, "when was the last time you saw that dreamy expression on your sister's face?" Three pairs of eyes studied Shasta.

Jeff was quiet for a moment, then smiled. "When I took her to the Black's Kennels to pick out a nice *little* dog for companionship and she fell absolutely head over heels in love with a mammoth puppy that grew into a full grown monster. Why?"

"Ahh, yes. Head over heels, did you say?" Jeff nodded and Rena reached across the desk, snatched up the pad Shasta had been writing on and shoved it under her husband's nose.

Jeff craned his neck backward to read the squiggling lines, which turned out to be Kane's name written repeatedly. "Don't tell me she's in love?"

Shasta lunged and grabbed the paper back. "Wait till you see him."

"Sexy?" Margret asked, her eyes twinkling.

Shasta leaned back and gazed up at the ceiling. "Sexy is entirely too tame a word for Kane." She mentally shook herself and glared at her grinning sister-in-law. Their interest made her nervous, and she squirmed uncomfortably in her chair. She wasn't ready to discuss her feelings just yet. "Listen, you three. Stay out of my personal life. I mean it!" Their smiles grew, and she tried to ignore them by going on with her tale.

"What I've told you sounds all very logical, right?" They agreed. "But something's wrong. One—Mr. Stone knew we were going to run a test on the alarm system while he was in Europe. So why didn't the old man tell us of his son's arrival? Two—somewhere along the way someone tried to beat the hell out of Kane." She stopped talking and let her eyes follow the tip of her pencil across the fresh sheet of paper, but she wasn't seeing what she was writing. She was seeing instead the long, ugly dark bruises on Kane's side and his grazed knuckles.

"Did you question him about his condition?" Margret asked softly.

"No, I was in a rather precarious position to be interrogating *him*. Besides, I don't think Kane's the type to reveal anything till he's ready. Damn!" She threw down the pencil. "Something's not right. Jeff, why would a man, a seemingly ordinary man, know how to do a professional body search? Believe me, he didn't miss a thing." Her cheeks turned pink, but her audience didn't interrupt. Jeff knew Shasta and her steel-trap mind, knew she was capable of sensing things the average person wouldn't detect, so he kept his questions to himself.

Shasta glanced unseeingly at her brother. "Why would this man use words like agency, boss, goons, fieldwork and counterattack?" Again she picked up her pencil and began to doodle. "Those aren't everyday words he was throwing around."

There were other things that bothered her, but she wasn't ready to reveal them. Kane seemed to be expecting another attack. Why? From his conversation while he searched her, it appeared he believed there could be more than one group after him. Why? And how could a man in perfect physical condition maintain such a jaded demeanor? It almost seemed to be an act. Why?

The pencil snapped between her fingers. She tossed the two halves down and looked at her brother. "I want you to put that whiz of a computer and your brain to work and find out everything you can about one Kane Maximilian du Monde Stone. Go through any agency you have to. If you run into trouble use our clearance codes, and if for some reason you're blocked there, call pappy." She and Jeff stared at each other in complete understanding. They were on to something big, and they could feel it in their bones. "I want to know everything there is to know about Kane."

"From birth?" Jeff's voice was tinged with excitement. His first love was his beloved computers; even Rena knew this and accepted it in good grace.

"From the womb, brother mine. Kane's in some sort of trouble, and I want to know what. After all," she said logically, "we are employed by his father and must look after *his* interest. Now get out of my office, all of you. I have a report to write up for pappy."

Jeff groaned and stood up. "By the way, sis, you neglected to tell me how you managed to breach my system."

Shasta grinned wickedly, her chin resting on her folded hands and her brown eyes dancing, enjoying his discomfort. "Through the attic window."

"That's not fair, you're so damnably small," he protested.

"Jeff, Jeff." She tried to interrupt his curses, then laughed. "Jeff," she shouted. "I hate to tell you this, but professional burglars don't come in stock sizes. Now, don't you think it's time you called pappy to tell him he lost his sure-thing bet, and your new system has some bugs to work out?"

Rena led a shaken Jeff to the door. "Darling, how does she get away with calling your grandfather pappy when everyone else in the family has to call him J.T.?"

"Damned if I know, Rena. You've been in this family for three years. Why the hell are you asking me this now?"

Shasta listened to them arguing all the way out of her office and smiled. Rena had a way of taking Jeff's mind off his troubles. She was of the old school, believing you could lead a man around by his zipper, and if by some small chance that didn't keep his attention, you totally confused him with meaningless chatter. It usually worked on Jeff, one way or the other. She tried to visualize the same tactics working on Kane and chuckled out loud. Kane was not the type to be led anywhere, and she pitied anyone who had the gall to try.

"Kane must be some man from that dreamy expression you're wearing. What are your chances?"

The question made Shasta jump, as if she'd been shot. She hadn't realized Margret was still in the room. "Not good, Meg. I think Kane has a connoisseur's taste. He's had everything that's beautiful, the crème de la crème. What would he want with me—yesterday's leftovers?" She dropped her chin into her small cupped hands and frowned.

"Shasta Masterson!" Margret yelled scornfully. "I can't believe you said that." She walked around the desk and pulled a surprised Shasta out of her chair, marched her through a side door and into a small washroom, where she positioned her before the mirror over the lavatory. "That, my dear, is an enchanting face."

"You're just prejudiced, Meg," Shasta shot back, but there was a hopeful note in the belligerent comeback.

"Listen to me, Shasta, you're no stunning picture-perfect beauty like the rest of your family, but you are pretty, and that loveliness also glows from the inside. You're small, yes, and you'd better quit moaning because there's not a darn thing you can do about it. And don't ever let anyone tell you men aren't attracted to small women because they are. It brings out their protective instincts."

Shasta opened her mouth and quickly snapped it shut as Margret went on. "Your hair is a shiny mass of curls, your eyes are big and round, and you've been blessed with thick lashes. Your skin's clear and healthy and you have a knockout figure for your size. And when you take the time with your makeup you're a head turner. So stop this self-pity. There's not a man alive who could resist you if you set your mind to it. My heavens, girl! Look how you twist J.T. and your father around your finger. That's no mean feat, even if they are family." Margret stopped her tirade and cocked her neat gray head in the direction of the ringing phones. "You think about what I've said," she ordered, and left the washroom.

Margret was right. She wasn't plain. But Margret's view was a woman's view, and she wondered what men really saw when they looked at her. Impatiently she combed her hair with stiff fingers. She was a mess and needed a bath and a change of clothes. From now on, she vowed, she'd take the time to give mother nature some help.

She grinned impishly into the mirror, showing all her small pearly teeth. Maybe, just maybe she had a better chance than she thought. After all, she'd caught the look of desire in Kane's eyes and that was a good starting place. She just had to figure out how she was going to see him again.

"The telephones are back to working and you have a call."

Jolted out of her musing, Shasta refocused her eyes on the older woman's reflection. "What did you say?"

Margret chuckled and snapped her fingers in front of Shasta's eyes. "A phone call." She stepped aside to allow Shasta by, then followed her out. "From Maximilian Stone in London."

AN HOUR LATER, Shasta emerged from her office to face the waiting threesome.

"Well?" They chorused in unison.

She struggled hard not to dance a little jig, as she'd done before she'd opened her door. She didn't want them to see just how ecstatic she was. "Mr. Stone has hired us for another job. It seems he's just been informed by the French Sûreté that his son was beaten up before he left Paris. He wants us to supply Kane with around-the-clock bodyguards till his business is complete in the States."

Jeff frowned, but it was Rena who asked the next question. "Did he know why Kane was attacked?"

Shasta sat on the edge of Margret's desk. "He said he didn't, but I don't believe him. I gave him an edited account of how I met Kane and touched on a few of my suspicions. He didn't sound shocked or surprised, nor did he offer any suggestions. For a man who's worried about his son's safety, he's shown a shocking lack of knowledge of Kane's troubles. He wasn't forthcoming with any answers to my direct questions, said I'd have to ask Kane." She jumped off the desk and began to pace the length of the reception area. "Jeff, is dad's old friend still with the French police?" She didn't wait for an answer and continued to pace.

"Who are you going to assign as Kane's bodyguard?" Rena opened a desk drawer and pulled out a manila folder. "Harry's free."

"No, Mr. Stone asked that I take care of this one personally," she lied. Shasta stopped her pacing, letting their vocal disapproval wash over her as she studied the Samantha Grey painting hanging in its solitary splendor on the Chinese-red wall. A small hunting party of Indian braves were mounted on their painted horses, but instead of the proud posture usually associated with them, their expressions reflected desolation, a pain that caught the onlooker's eye and held it for a long moment, till the gaze shifted and followed the Indians' line of vision. It took only a second to realize that the wide expanse of open plains was covered in the bleached bones of a great herd of dead buffalo and not melting patches of snow. The painting was appropriately titled *The Beginning of the End.*

Shasta shook her head in amazement. Who would have thought to have such a painting in an office decorated solely in an ultramodern decor. But Rena, who had done the decorating, had a flare for the unusual.

"Shasta. Shasta!"

She jumped, startled out of her thoughts, and answered, "There's no use arguing, Jeff. Mr. Stone was determined that I handle this." She didn't meet her brother and Rena's probing looks. Instead she caught Margret's narrowed glance and winked.

Margret smiled. "How do you think Kane's going to take your interference?"

Shasta's eyes danced with suppressed laughter. "Like a tomcat to water."

CHAPTER THREE

SHASTA SAT QUIETLY in the small confines of her recently acquired Porsche, oblivious to the purr of the engine and the sounds of the overworked air conditioner as it struggled gallantly to offset the rising temperature outside.

Houston weather never ceased to amaze her. One moment it could storm, threatening to wash the entire metropolis into the Gulf of Mexico and leave you praying for an ark. Then the sun, hot and bright, would pop out from behind angry clouds. The humidity would then rise far above its usual steaminess to a tropical swelter.

Shasta rested her chin on the top of the steering wheel, her attention on the open gate across the street. For the past hour, as she waited for the glazier's truck to leave the estate, she'd curiously examined the best way to break the news to Kane that he'd acquired a bodyguard. She'd let her imagination run free with possibilities and had come up with stories even she had to laugh at. But this seemed to be one time that a tall tale wouldn't suit. Only the truth would suffice, and she had a feeling that Kane wasn't going to take kindly to being watched and told what to do, especially by a woman.

She was roused from her thoughts by the sound of the old repair truck backfiring as it rumbled down the graveled drive and out onto the street. Shasta shifted gears and with a flick of the wheel sent the gleaming little black car across the street and up the drive, pulling to a stop before the front steps. Without hesitation she jumped out, dragging the suitcase with her. She bounded up the steps and punched the bell confidently. When nothing happened, she pushed briskly again, then nodded as she heard the chimes from within and the distant sound of footsteps on hardwood floors.

The heavy door swung sluggishly inward, and like a magnet automatically pointing north, her eyes were drawn slowly up the tall body.

"Did you forget something?" Kane drawled.

His tone set Shasta's teeth on edge, and as inconspicuously as possible she placed the toe of her shoe on the edge of the suitcase and nudged it an inch or two through the doorway. "No, actually I'm here because of my job." She smiled, the corners of her wide mouth turning up and freezing in place as her eyes roamed over him. He looked even better in the light of day, and the fact that he was fully dressed didn't hurt the dream. The casual elegance of dark-gray slacks with pleated front, immaculate white shirt opened at the collar and with sleeves rolled up only added to his male beauty. Kane wore his clothes with an easy nonchalance, and even dressed in rags he would have looked just as magnificent.

Shasta was keenly aware of her own neat appearance as she watched Kane's eyes run appreciatively over the length of her severely tailored suit, contradicting the softness beneath. She'd taken special care with her makeup, adding to the roundness of her velvet brown eyes and touching her lips and cheeks with color. She was glad she'd taken heed to Julie's teachings as she saw the renewed desire in Kane's steady gaze. Her foot pushed at the suitcase, moving it an inch farther.

"I know this is going to be a shock to you, Kane." She paused and extended her foot, shoving the case once more till it met an obstacle—Kane's outstretched shoe. They both looked down at the intruder crossing the threshold, then their gazes lifted and locked. Shasta tugged at the lapels of her jacket and straightened the pale-yellow silk tie at her throat. "May I come in and explain?"

"It rather looks as if you've come to stay." He raised an inquisitive eyebrow at the case on the floor, and when he received only a strained smile in reply, he stood back and waved her in. She was entirely too professional and sure of herself.

Before Shasta could get past Kane, he reached out and caught her shoulders, turning her to face him. Ready with a quick answer to any questions he might fire at her, she was startled to feel his fingers work at the waistband on her skirt and shift it slightly.

"Your seams were twisted. Lady cat burglars should always be neat," he said gently, his deep voice rumbling with suppressed laughter.

With that one deliberate act he had totally blown her cool composure and efficiency. Shasta slapped at his still-helpful hands, her cheeks flushed bright red, and she stepped back, picked up her suitcase and marched into the living room.

Devious, mocking devil. She dropped her case with a thud and whirled around. "Your father has hired me as your bodyguard. He seems to think you're in some sort of trouble. Are you?"

She waited in the suspended silence for the explosion, and when the long string of expletives eventually ran down to dire mutterings, she smiled in satisfaction.

"You can wipe that cat-and-cream grin off your face." His frown deepened. "I neither need nor want a bodyguard. You're fired."

"Can't!" She shot back, the bewitching grin spreading over her entire face, enhancing the mischievous sparkle in her dark eyes.

"What do you mean, can't. I can do anything I damn well please." He wished her nose wouldn't crinkle up like that when she smiled; it distracted his train of thought.

"Your father employed me. He's the only one who can fire me."

"Listen to me carefully, Miss Masterson. My father does not run my life."

Kane's eyes narrowed dangerously and his voice had sounded contemptuous, making Shasta wonder at the relationship between father and son.

"Now, I would suggest you pick up your case and go home."

Shasta shrugged helplessly. "I can't do that, Kane. Your father is one of our best clients. The security system for this house—" she waved an impatient hand around the luxurious room "—is just a small part of what Masters handles for your father."

"I don't give a damn—"

"But I do," she interrupted, her voice as hard as his had been. They fell silent, each assessing the situation.

"If it's money," Kane offered, "I'll double what he's paying you."

She shook her head vigorously, loosening the combs that anchored her hair away from her face. Her task was going to be harder than she had imagined.

"You can't get rid of me, because all I'll do is change tactics, and instead of acting as a bodyguard I'll set up a round-the-clock, close surveillance. I'm afraid you're stuck with me till you leave the country."

"The hell you say," Kane muttered under his breath, deciding to take a new tact. "Tell me something, Shasta, has my father ever seen you?"

She was idly roaming the room, striving to appear as self-possessed as possible, but his question caught her off guard. She spun around, nearly dropping the Lalique seagull she was examining. "I don't think so, why?" Her heart did a series of crazy beats as she gazed at him standing across the room. With his head thrown back and his silver eyes gleaming wickedly, he reminded her of an eighteenth-century pirate. All he needed to complete the illusion were the clothes and a flashing rapier. She could almost hear his *en garde* challenge. Shasta pushed aside her fanciful thoughts and carefully returned the fragile work of art to its resting place. Looking up, she asked, "Does it make a difference that your father and I have never met face to face?"

"My dear girl, if he'd ever seen you as you are now, he would have had a spasm at the thought of you passing yourself off as anyone's bodyguard." His eyes roamed disdainfully over her diminutive figure, taking in the wide eyes, the soft full mouth and the stubborn chin, now thrust out a little farther than before. "You're about as menacing and threatening as a dormouse."

Kane clenched his teeth hard. His long-buried conscience suddenly emerged, and he hadn't the heart to continue lashing out at her. She need never say a word to chastise him; all she had to do was cast those big eyes his way and he was lost. He turned his back on her, his mind rapidly going over other ways to rid himself of this watchdog when he felt the clamp of surprisingly strong fingers on his arm.

"You listen to me, you arrogant bastard. I might be small, but I'm as competent as any trained bodyguard in this country." She swung him around with little effort. "Would you like some references?" Her usually gentle temper rose with each word. Placing her hands on her hips, she inadvertently pushed her jacket open, revealing a dainty shoulder holster and the deadly compact twenty-caliber Beretta that snuggled securely under her left arm.

Kane spotted the weapon, his eyes widening in astonishment. "My God, an armed mouse," he choked out, then seeing the humor of the situation threw back his head and laughed uproariously.

Shasta's stillness should have warned him, but he was so caught up in the picture of an armed mouse with big expressive eyes that when he suddenly found himself lying stretched out full-length on the carpeted floor with Shasta sitting sideways on his chest, he could only continue to chuckle while gasping for breath. "Sor... sorry," he managed as a spasm of pain twisted his laughter to a moan.

Remembering his bruised and battered ribs, Shasta slid onto the floor beside him, but kept a firm hold on his arm. "Company policy, Mr. Stone. Bodyguards are armed at all times." When his lips moved to speak, she applied pressure, watching with a ruthless detachment as he flinched and snapped his mouth shut. She saw understanding dawn in the darkened eyes at her application of the art of pressure points. She smiled. "Yes, we *mice* must learn to fight dirty. Now, as for references..." She pressed her fingers a little to make sure she had his full attention. "Are you with me, Mr. Stone?"

"Oh, yes, madam," Kane growled, the muscles along his jaw knotting in anger. "Please, do go on. Believe me, you have my undivided attention." He noticed the fleeting softening in her glaring stare and relaxed.

"I hold a master's degree in criminology and am a licensed private detective, as is everyone with Masters."

"You mean you're not just another pretty face?" he drawled.

She pressed again, harder this time, and was momentarily pacified to hear the hiss of his indrawn breath. "Masters is not a second-rate security agency, Kane. We specialize in corporate and executive protection. We do security analysis and sensitive investigations and develop countermeasures to deter criminals. The security alarm system in this house is a minute part of our work. I don't spend my days just breaking into private homes."

"What do you do?" He moved his arm from beneath her slack fingers and placed both hands behind his head.

"I've delivered documents and merchandise around the world, trained executives who might be targets for terrorists or kidnappers, acted as bodyguards to a few rock stars, politicians, industrialists and the occasional high-ranking military bigwig."

Kane listened in astonishment as Shasta quickly listed her credits. He knew that she was downplaying some of her responsibilities and wondered at the chances she took. But the fact was, this pixie did a job that many men dreamed of but could never handle. For some inexplicable reason he wanted details of her work. He felt compelled to know what kind of chances she took, what kind of jeopardy she put herself in, and most of all he needed to figure out why a woman would want to involve herself in the hazards and dangers of the job. He'd never met anyone quite like her, and the change from dewy-eyed seductress to hard-eyed career woman intrigued him. What was really amazing, he realized, was the fact that in the last eight hours or so he'd laughed more than he had in months. And oh, what a delight she was. His mouse had a temper.

Kane reached out and fondled a silk curl that had slipped the confines of the tortoiseshell comb and now lay enticingly at her temple. He twisted the end around his finger and tugged lightly. When he met no resistance he continued to guide her head down till their breaths mingled and their lips barely grazed one another. "Who was the military man you acted as bodyguard for?" he whispered against her mouth.

What had happened to all her anger? Shasta felt the tip of his tongue slide across her lower lip and fought to think clearly. "General Howiser," she answered dreamily, "when he was stationed in Italy." She tasted and nibbled at his mouth, and finding the flavor of warm moist skin to her liking, she parted her lips invitingly for the kiss that never came.

"General George P. Howiser? My dear mouse! General Howiser was kidnapped over ten months ago, and the United

States is still negotiating with the Italian terrorist for his release."

Shasta gazed down into his silver eyes and said innocently, "Ah, but Kane, I wasn't the general's bodyguard ten months ago. I was fired!" Stretched out beside him, her arms crossed over his chest, she settled her chin on her folded hands and waited for Kane to gain control over his laughter.

"Fired!" he choked out. "Dare I ask why?"

"For some reason the general got it into his head that I was supposed to do more to his body than guard it. We had a mild disagreement, and the general didn't care for my manner of refusal, so he fired me. One week later the terrorist grabbed him."

Mindful of his injured side, Kane cautiously tumbled Shasta onto her back. With an impatient flick, he removed the combs from her hair and tangled his fingers in the thick waves. "You certainly pack a powerful punch for such a..." He stopped, knowing any adjective he used to describe her stature would be taken as a jest and only serve to inflame her temper once again.

Lulled in quiescence by the fathomless depths of his voice, Shasta grinned like a half-wit and nodded, heedless of the warning bells ringing in her head. Fascinated by the movement of his lips, she couldn't seem to drag her eyes from them. She almost sighed out loud with bliss as he lowered his mouth to hers. But instead of his earlier teasing kisses, this one was deep and long, edged with passion and feeding a newborn hunger in both of them. Kane was the first to break away, and Shasta wanted to cry at the loss.

"You know, Shasta," Kane breathed into her ear, sending a bone-jarring shiver through her body, "if you want to stay with me a couple of nights while I'm here, that's fine with me. But, sweetheart, I really don't need a bodyguard." Before Shasta could collect her thoughts he went on. "You have a sexy little body." One confident hand left her hair and moved slowly to her rounded breasts.

Kane's voice dropped to a smooth hypnotic timbre, and Shasta squeezed her eyes shut, frantically trying to think of her job. But her mind seemed to go blank as his fingers loosened the silk tie and the buttons of her shirt magically fell open with a mere touch.

"Your skin is like satin." Warm lips slid leisurely down the column of her neck to her collarbone, and he nipped along the ridge lightly, sending a hard jolt of desire through her. "Think of all the fun we can have. You can forget about your job and just enjoy yourself."

"Job? Job...job!" She kept repeating the word, whispering it till it finally sank in. Shasta's eyes popped open and she glared at her seducer. "Very clever," she grated, and rolled out of his reach. Coming to her knees, she quickly straightened her clothes, buttoned her blouse, and hopped to her feet. Where were her shoes? She didn't even remember kicking them off, but there were a lot of things that had eluded her in the past half hour. She looked up into Kane's mocking gaze and frowned. "You don't play fair."

"I wasn't aware this was a game," he warned ominously. "Shasta, I don't want a bodyguard, and I especially don't want a female hanging around my neck all day." Kane watched her closely as she searched for her shoes. "Come here," he ordered, and was surprised to see her grinning. She was up to something. He could tell by the odd sparkle in her eyes.

Shasta stood before him. "Would you be more at ease if we had a chaperon?"

As he studied her smug expression, he wondered what trap he was falling into, but it really didn't matter. All his determination to fight seemed to have dissolved. He unbuttoned and rebuttoned her blouse correctly while she stood docilely waiting for him to finish. Then he leaned down, pulled the absurdly high, high heels from under the couch, and one by one fitted them on her dainty feet.

"Okay, mouse." He tapped her nose lightly. "We'll try it your way for a while. I just hope this chaperon gets here soon and she brings food—I'm starving."

Shasta smiled agreeably. "Oh, Julie always comes prepared. But why don't we go out to eat now? I'm hungry myself." She turned to pick up her purse, then stopped. "What did you call me?" she demanded indignantly.

"What?"

"Just a second ago." She glared at his amused expression. "It sounded suspiciously like mouse—again."

"It did? I don't remember. Maybe you're hearing things." He began to move purposely toward her with a hungry look she immediately recognized, one that had nothing whatever to do with food.

She backed away, then spun around. "Come on, I'll treat you to a real Southern meal that will have your epicurean taste buds crying for more." She threw the words over her shoulder and headed for the front door, one hand groping in the depths of her purse in search of her keys.

Kane followed, stopping only long enough to pick up his jacket from the back of a chair. They walked out into a hot, muggy night, though the sky was clear and the stars gleamed brightly around a fat luminous moon.

Shasta heard Kane's footsteps crunching behind her as she rounded the back of her car. Even though he appeared world-weary, he was still gentleman enough to open a lady's door. As the car door swung open, she stepped forward and collided with his broad shoulders. "Hey," she all but shouted. "What…?" Seeing what he was up to, she used her smaller size to advantage. She slipped under his arm and stood barring his entrance to her car.

"I'll drive." He held out his hand and snapped his fingers impatiently.

Shasta clutched her car keys to her heart. "Drive my car?" she squeaked. "No!"

"Come on, sweetheart, I don't like to be driven by anyone."

"Tough! And if you do that with your fingers one more time, I'll give you these keys where you least expect them." She slid into the seat and started the powerful engine with an angry roar. "If you're hungry I suggest you hop in or I'll leave you to fend for yourself." She stuck her head out, looked up and smiled impishly. "I promise you I'm an expert driver." With that she pulled the door shut with a force that squelched any thoughts he might have of bullying her into changing her mind.

She waited patiently as Kane buckled his safety belt before sending the car careering down the drive with a squeal of rubber. As she turned onto the street, she glanced down at Kane's white knuckles, which threatened to pop off his kneecaps, and bit back a laugh.

"How long did you say you've had your driver's licence?"

"I'll have you know I rated highest in evasive-driving techniques."

"Well for God's sake, slow down. We're not trying to lose anyone now. I'd appreciate it if me and my stomach arrived at the restaurant at the same time."

"Oh, but this car was made for speed."

"On speedways, not city streets."

As Kane grumbled on about drivers, Shasta quickly glanced in the rearview mirror. She had that peculiar tingling in the back of her neck, an instinctive warning she'd learned to pay close attention to. "Have you ever had chicken-fried steak?" Figuring Kane was more European than American and certainly not Texan, she didn't give him time to answer but went on to describe the state's culinary trademark. "They use a cut of beef called round steak and beat it till it's tender." The blue car behind them was slowing for the stop sign, carefully maintaining a safe distance.

Shasta pushed the indicator for a left turn, checked the oncoming traffic and turned right. The car behind them was now pulling up to the stop sign with its left-turn signal blinking, but it also turned right.

"Then you batter it like you would chicken and deep fry it till it's golden brown." Accelerating, she shifted and expertly negotiated a hairpin curve that led to a shadowy tree-lined street. The trailing car picked up speed in an effort to keep up. Not very professional, she thought, then returned to her description of their upcoming meal, hoping to keep Kane distracted so he wouldn't notice they were being followed.

"They absolutely drown the steak in thick gravy and it tastes like heaven." The blue car was now far enough back that she could carry out her next maneuver.

"The mashed potatoes are light and fluffy, and the fried okra are gilded nuggets of ambrosia." Speeding up, she hooked a sharp right turn and headed down a back street.

"But the pièce de résistance is the hot peach cobbler topped with a huge scoop of vanilla ice cream." She outmaneuvered her followers and pulled up behind them, tailing them till they realized they'd been set up and sped away—but not before she'd memorized the license number and made note of the two male occupants. There wasn't any doubt Kane was their target. But why was he under surveillance and by whom?

There was a rustle of movement beside her, and Shasta looked sideways, her forced smile dissolving slowly as she met Kane's remote gaze. Quickly she returned her attention to the road ahead, and they continued their drive to the restaurant in brooding silence. She wondered dismally if dinner was going to be as strained as the atmosphere in the car.

DINNER WASN'T AS BAD as she had anticipated. Apparently the food not only appeased Kane's appetite but helped change his mood. Shasta took the long way back to the Stone estate, and the companionable silence was broken only by Kane's questions about her career and the history of Masters Security.

Slouched down in his seat, Kane leaned his head back and closed his eyes. "Your grandfather must be quite a man to have started a business from a one-man detective agency and built it into the dynasty it is today." He rolled his head back and forth on the leather headrest, fighting to keep his eyes open.

"Oh, J.T.'s a very determined man." Shasta adjusted the temperature of the air conditioner and slowly eased to a stop. "My father wanted to go into the diplomatic service, but J.T. wouldn't hear of it. He decided the only way to hold dad was to get him a wife. He had the young woman all picked out—a Southern belle from Kentucky with a long pedigree and an influential U.S. senator for a father. It seems the senator was being blackmailed for something in his past and had privately hired Masters. So, instead of going himself, J.T. talked dad into taking the job. Well, you can guess what happened. Dad met mom and they did exactly what J.T. knew they would, fell in love on sight." She didn't want to tell Kane just yet that it was almost a tradition among her family to fall in love at first sight, usually in the most unconventional places and circumstances.

A snort of disbelief came from the passenger side and Shasta smiled. She put the car into gear and pulled away from the stop sign. "I take it by that disgusting sound that your opinion of love at first sight leaves a lot to be desired?"

"You could say that."

"Or is it love you distrust?" She waited for an answer, and when only silence greeted her question, her shoulders sagged in disappointment. She should have realized it was going to take more than the ability to make him laugh to capture this man. He didn't dislike women; on the contrary, he appeared to be a man who enjoyed women to the fullest but didn't respect or trust their motives.

They reached the open gates of the estate, and Shasta pulled to a respectable stop in front of the house without making Kane grab for the dashboard. As he moved to open the car door, Shasta's fingers pressed urgently into his arm.

"Kane, did you switch on the burglar alarm before you shut the front door?" She felt a familiar tingling at the nape of her neck.

Kane followed her gaze, his eyes mere slits as he took in the heavy carved door, flung wide open. "Looks as if I forgot, doesn't it? But I did close and lock the door. Stay put."

He was out of the car in a flash, but Shasta was faster and paced him as he vaulted up the stone steps. Silently she cursed her stupidity as she dug around in the depths of her purse for her gun. If she hadn't given in to his fierce refusal to sit down to dinner with a woman packing a gun, she wouldn't have been scrounging around for her weapon like a fool.

They reached the open door at the same time and both stopped, alertly surveying the situation. "You stupid woman," muttered Kane. "Get back in the car."

Shasta took immediate exception to his remark. "I'm your bodyguard," she replied sharply. "I go in first." She stepped in front of him, but a hand of steel clamped down on her shoulder.

"Have you totally lost what few brains you have? Someone could still be in there," he whispered angrily, trying to pull her back. He was rewarded for his efforts by his arm going completely numb.

Shasta lost all her composure and yelled at him at the top of her voice. "I have the gun, you fool." Never in all her years had she met a more pigheaded man who seemed bent on having his way no matter what the cost. Couldn't he see that she knew what she was doing and wasn't some helpless female?

"Then give it to me and stay out," Kane barked. "And if you ever disable me like that again I'll strangle you. Now," he bellowed, "give me that damn gun!"

Shasta snarled at his outstretched hand and slipped through the yawning doorway and into the dark hole of the living room. Her back to the wall, she moved, inch by inch, her hand out in front of her feeling for the light switch. With a quick flick of the switch, the overhead chandelier bloomed into a soft glow. Down on one knee, her arms extended, Shasta swept the gun from side to side, ready for the intruder to pop up. She felt Kane's presence behind her and whirled around, her back to the shambles of the room. "Don't you *ever* interfere with my job again." She glared at him, her eyes as cold as winter leaves. "I'm a trained professional and know how to handle situations like this. I don't need some fool playing macho man. You're a civilian and don't know how to handle yourself."

Kane growled something under his breath and stomped out, heading for the stairs, hiding the smile that would have caused her temper to explode like a bomb had she seen it. Oh, but his mouse had a fine roar.

"Where do you think you're going?" she demanded, following him up the stairs at a run.

"To see what damage they've made of my things."

The entire house was a wreck. Every drawer from the bathroom to kitchen had been emptied onto the floor. Furniture had been toppled and slashed, and stuffing was scattered everywhere. But the Renoirs and Degas were still hanging in place, and the statues and other pieces of art had been left untouched. Shasta checked the rooms carefully, remembering the insurance list that Masters had inventoried. Whoever had ransacked this house, she mused, was a professional looking for something special and definitely in a hurry.

Shasta found Kane sitting at the kitchen table calmly drinking a cup of coffee. She poured a cup for herself and sat down across from him. "I've called the police." He nodded, his face contorting before he lowered his head into his hands and began to laugh.

She glared at him, sipping her coffee till he had stopped. "You find the sight of your father's house turned into a garbage pile funny?"

"No, but I find the sight of us arguing and yelling at the front door while the burglars were sneaking out the back rather amusing. It reminded me of one of those old B-movies."

A tiny smile struggled to turn up the edges of her mouth, but the seriousness of the situation won out. "Do you want to tell me anything before the police arrive?"

Kane's eyes glimmered like the surface of a newly polished mirror. "What's to tell?"

"I thought you might like to explain a few things."

He picked up his cup and studied the contents before looking directly at her. "I have nothing to say."

Shasta was about to contradict him when the doorbell chimed. Angrily shoving her chair back, she left the kitchen, mentally cursing Kane's stubbornness. She suspected he knew exactly what the intruders were looking for and it all tied in with Paris, his beating and the blue car following them. Stepping over strewed papers in the entrance, she yanked open the door and faced three uniformed policemen and a detective. "Hello, Bill, I thought you'd quit smoking?"

Bill Davidson removed the half-smoked cigarette from the corner of his mouth and flipped the glowing ember into the night. "I thought so, too, till we got your call." His smile belied his gruff tone. "Why is it, Shasta, that every time I hear from you there's always trouble?"

She returned his smile and stepped aside to let the others enter. "Could be the line of business you're in, Bill." Tall and lanky, Bill was a former basketball player who'd been on the force too long and seen too much. She was pleased to notice that his recent transfer from homicide to burglary had taken some of the tension and strain from his face.

Shasta spotted Kane leaning nonchalantly against the living-room doorway. She introduced the two men, then disappeared into the room, shadowing the three policemen as they checked the doors and windows for signs of forced entry.

As they searched, Shasta hurriedly gave Bill a rundown on all that had happened earlier, including their uninvited escort.

Bill made copious notes in a small spiral book while Shasta talked. When she finished he pulled out a cigarette from his shirt pocket and stuck it in the corner of his mouth. "Don't frown, it'll make ugly lines." He tapped the end of the unlit cigarette. "I've had my quota for the day. This is just a pacifier." His eyes bore into hers. "Is there anything else you've neglected to tell me?"

Shasta hesitated, then gave him the blue car's license number.

"Withholding, Shasta?"

"No, just a feeling that the number isn't going to do you any good. Besides, Jeff will have a rundown on the car before you can get back to the station and put it through your computers."

"True." Bill shrugged helplessly. "Are you trying to tell me that the men dogging you and Mr. Stone weren't the same who broke in here?"

"Oh, I'm ninety-nine percent sure they're one and the same. It's just too pat for them not to be."

An hour later they found the burglars' means of entry—the housekeeper's rooms off the kitchen. A windowpane had been cut and removed to allow access to the lock. As the police questioned Kane, Shasta listened grudgingly, admiring his ability to talk about everything, answer all their questions and still tell them absolutely nothing. She was so deeply absorbed in his mastery of evasion and prevarication that she nearly jumped out of her skin when the telephone blared beside her. Yanking the receiver up, she shouted, "Hello!"

"Shasta!" Jeff Masterson sighed with relief. "Where the hell have you been? Rena and I have been trying to reach you for hours."

Shasta matched her brother's sigh. Sometimes family could be the worst possible pain in the backside. "Kane and I went to dinner, Jeff. Now what's wrong?"

"Shasta, I know sometimes you think I'm a worrywart, but please listen to me very carefully." Shasta leaned against the wall and waited for the long harangue she knew was coming.

"Do I have your full attention?"

"Yes, Jeff."

"Okay. I want you to get out of that house—now." He waited for his words to sink in before continuing. "We'll send Julie over till we can assign someone else. But not you, sis. This one's rotten to the core, and I'd rather not have you exposed to the stench."

"Jeff, what are you rattling on about?" She straightened up and gripped the phone hard in anticipation.

"Don't go thickheaded on me now, sis. I've just scratched the surface on Kane's background. He's a..." Jeff searched for adequate words to describe Kane, and finding none, he tried again. "He has a reputation that would curl the devil's toes."

"Ahh, come on, Jeff," Shasta said scornfully, and relaxed. "What wealthy, single man doesn't have a reputation? Even you had one, and that was laughable." Her eyes followed Kane around the room: the ease with which he moved; the haughty way his head would tilt; the insolence in the curve of his lip; the intelligence in his unusual eyes.

"Damn it, sis. I checked some old articles about him, then called that society barracuda, Hanna McCoy. Shasta, the man's rolling in money, his friends are the European jet-set crowd. You know the kind. The ones that have no aim in life but to abuse and destroy everything they touch. She told me of Kane's parties and women, of gambling in Monte Carlo for sums of money that would even raise J.T.'s eyebrows." Jeff stopped long enough to catch his breath but not long enough for Shasta to interrupt. "There were skiing jaunts to St. Moritz and that Chilean resort in the high Andes. Hanna told me outrageous stories of barbarian acts in every sun spot in Europe. And women, Shasta, always women—world beauties who run as wild as he does. He's—"

"Jeff, what Kane appears to be and what he is are two different things." She turned her back on the room and spoke quietly into the receiver. "You've always trusted my instincts before, why not now?" She explained about the car following them and repeated the license number to be traced. Then she told him of the break-in at the Stone house. "Collate the new developments with what we already know, and I think we'll find another piece to the puzzle and maybe what kind of trouble Kane's in." As for his past escapades, she dismissed them flippantly and chuckled when she heard her brother's teeth grind together in frustration. His interest was piqued, though, and he was fighting an internal tug of war. "Call Julie—explain that I'm taking Kane to my house."

She turned and found Kane standing behind her. Startled, she jumped back, bumping her head against the wall in the process. "How long have you been there?" she demanded, ignoring Jeff's confused mumbles as the receiver slipped from her hand.

"Not long." Kane reached out to rub the back of his knuckles against her cheek, and his eyes locked with hers. "The police are through and want to know where they can reach me. I told them that was up to my bodyguard." He'd expected an outbreak of laughter at his words and was surprised that the men had taken them seriously.

"My home. Bill knows the address." She smiled, wanting to drown in the invitation in his eyes. Her smile widened as he tapped the tip of her nose.

"I believe someone's trying to get your attention." Kane pointed to the telephone resting on her shoulder and walked toward the waiting men.

"Sorry, Jeff." She was still in a daze from the passion she'd seen in Kane's eyes. Maybe her chances were better than she'd thought.

"Shasta! I don't like this setup," Jeff grumbled over the phone. "Just remember one thing. Kane Stone is not one of those injured animals you're always dragging home…sis, he's already rabid."

CHAPTER FOUR

THE DRIVE ACROSS TOWN to Shasta's home was accomplished in record time, even with the detours caused by the storm's havoc. Shasta kept quiet, realizing the man slouched comfortably beside her was deep in thought. She hoped his self-absorption would eventually lead to him answering some of her questions.

Periodically, she checked her rearview mirror to verify they were still being followed. This time she didn't even attempt to lose their escort. Jeff would trace the licence number, and she'd soon find out who was so interested in Kane's movements.

The street signs changed colors, announcing that she was now out of Houston's city limits and in her own neighborhood of West University, a small well-established community completely independent from the big city that surrounded its perimeters. Enormous trees formed a green leafy canopy over narrow streets, casting bypassers in a shower of shadows and bespeckled sunlight. Old homes, which until a few years earlier had begun to deteriorate, had been restored and now showed off their graceful lines in proud homage to past architectural fancies.

J. T. Masterson insisted that all his grandchildren invest in real estate, and Shasta had begrudgingly followed his orders. It wasn't the investment she minded, but the fact that owning a home had a stigma of permanence, another step in keeping her tied down to family and job. And even though each year she planned her escape from the restraint on her life the noose seemed to tighten.

She wheeled the car up the driveway of her home and wondered if she'd ever be able to break away and live the life she had envisioned years ago. Was it all just a dream? Sighing, she flipped off the ignition and returned her attention to the man climbing out of the car. What were his thoughts about the night's events? She slammed her door and turned, meeting that shuttered look once again.

"You're sure this Julie won't mind picking up my luggage on her way here?"

"Julie's used to running errands." She worked the key into the lock, and because the door was old and tended to stick in wet weather, she went through her usual ritual to open it. She kicked the bottom left corner three times, pounded above the lock twice then applied her shoulder with a good push. The stubborn door swung open amid Kane's chuckles and he followed her in, his eyes everywhere. In a brief flash Shasta wondered what he thought of her home. There was no opulence here, only warm colors and a homey comfort.

While Shasta quickly began to pick up scattered magazines, Kane inspected the living room with interest, pleased to see that the room reflected her personality. A woman with a softness and sweetness, yet strong and capable. All the furniture from the couch to the chairs seemed to invite his tired body to collapse; the pale-coral and green prints were a soothing balm, and the overstuffed couch a beacon to his sore muscles. Healthy greenery sprouted from gleaming copper pots, and fine pieces of glass sculpture—Steuben and Lalique—picked up the light and reflected a multitude of bright colors over the surface of the hardwood tables.

He studied one corner of the room a long time before he realized what was hiding among the profusion of a leafy schefflera and lacy ferns. Two antique wooden carousel horses were cleverly placed among the small forest. Their once colorful bodies were now pale and blotched, enhancing their camouflage. He smiled at the whimsical setting, and his smile grew as he realized one of the animals was a unicorn.

Kane's abused body and tense muscles began to relax. He was feeling a certain serenity when a low growl from the open doorway caught his attention and he went perfectly still. A huge black-and-brown Rottweiler lumbered toward him slowly, its head down, teeth bared and a low menacing rumble coming from its throat. Kane felt the hairs stand up on the back of his neck as he gazed into bottomless black eyes that were glued to his, their intent clear. He was about to become dinner for this one-hundred-eighty-pound monster.

"Baskerville, behave," Shasta called out quietly, and Kane watched the pony-size dog turn immediately into a cavorting puppy, jumping and hopping around Shasta in ecstasy at having his master home. Shasta introduced man and beast, and Kane couldn't decide who was more leery. He held out his hand for Baskerville to sniff and prayed that those jaws would never decide to clamp down on him.

Still watching Baskerville take his measure, Kane asked, "Why is it that little women always have huge dogs?"

Baskerville, having judged Kane safe, trotted over to Shasta, wagged his docked tail and whined pitifully.

Looking down irritably, she scolded, "No, Baskerville, you know you can't. You go lie down and behave yourself." Another whine followed this order, but Baskerville picked himself up and padded to his favorite place before the fireplace, a place that allowed him full view of his master. Shasta was watching the dog's play for attention with amusement when she remembered Kane's question. "Maybe the reason small women have big dogs is to keep men with free hands at bay."

Kane still eyed Baskerville apprehensively. The dog was still making faint growling noises deep within his throat. "Is that why you got him? Men trouble? And where did you come up with the name Baskerville?"

Shasta finished straightening the room, then went behind the bar. She rested her elbows on the hardwood surface, chin in hands, and smiled. "I picked him out because he was the runt of the litter and I felt sorry for him. I named him after an old novel that I must have read a thousand times, *The Hound of the Baskervilles* by Doyle." She began to pull out liquor bottles from behind the bar. "What would you like to drink?" When he hesitated she tried a little cajoling. "I'm going to have one, please join me." Ever since they had left the Stone estate, Shasta had been toying with an idea. Maybe she could get him drunk, she mused, and get some answers to her questions.

"Scotch, if you have it." He settled down on the feather-soft couch, and it felt so good that he kicked off his shoes and stretched out, something he would never have done anywhere but here. With that thought he frowned. Now why, he wondered, did he feel at home here? But he didn't get a chance to think of an answer, because at that moment a cold glass was pushed into his hand. He took a hefty swallow and nearly choked. The drink was practically three-fourths liquor. His eyes narrowed as he watched Shasta sit down across from him, her drink suspiciously light in color. He had a sudden feeling it was going to be a long night.

"How did you get those bruises, Kane?" She didn't look at him as she sipped her diluted drink.

"I fell down a flight of stairs?" He closed his eyes wearily, the alcohol warming his insides.

"I'll believe that only if you can convince me that those skinned knuckles happened when you grabbed on to a ninety-year-old woman who was tumbling head over heels beside you."

"What woman?"

"Exactly!"

Kane opened one eye and stared at her smug expression. He sighed, drained his glass and leaned his head back. "Listen, Shasta. How I got my bruises has nothing to do with you."

"Don't they, Kane? I'm your bodyguard now." She saw his lips tighten and frowned. "I think for both our safety I have a right to know what kind of trouble you're in."

"I'm *not* in trouble!"

Exasperated, Shasta took a sip of her drink, eased her shoes off and propped her feet up on the coffee table, her toes wiggling in agitation. "Let me put this another way. If you're in danger, then as your bodyguard, you've put me in the same danger."

He didn't seem to have heard a word she'd said. "Are you awake, Kane?" When she only received a grunt for an answer, she jumped up. She was supposed to get him drunk, not put him to sleep. Music! That was the thing—loud music.

Hurriedly she flipped through her record collection in growing desperation. She didn't have any fast music; all her albums were romantic mood music. Then she came across an old Pointer Sisters album and found the ideal song. In a few seconds a trumpet blared out the beginning notes to "Boogie Woogie Bugle Boy," and she watched in wicked delight as Kane's body bounced about three inches off the couch.

"Bitch," he grumbled grumpily, but he couldn't hide his smile as she danced over to him, picked up his glass and headed for the bar. He tried to keep a stern expression as she mixed their drinks, all the while dramatically lip-syncing the words to the earsplitting music, and she looked even more comical when the music abruptly ended and her mouth was left hanging wide open.

Kane whirled around, every muscle tense, as he spotted the man standing by the stereo, his body in half shadows. As the man stepped out into the full light, Kane leaped over the back of the couch, only stopping himself from making the final lunge when he heard Shasta call out.

"Julie!"

"Julie?" Kane grabbed his injured side, his breath coming hard and fast.

Neither Shasta nor Julie had moved during Kane's aborted attack, each stunned at the speed and precision of his maneuver.

"I ain't never seen a man move that fast," Julius Bridger said admiringly, his bushy gray eyebrows working like woolly worms.

Shasta introduced the two men, and Kane shot her a look that could have melted steel. He quickly sized the old man up, but changed his mind after their handshake. Julius Bridger was not much taller than Shasta but was in amazing condition for a man his age, an age Kane determined must be somewhere between sixty and sixty-five years old. His face showed his misspent youth as clearly as if someone had written it for all to see. Deep lines were etched across a wide forehead and pleated between his eyes. His nose looked as if it had been broken at least four times, judging by the number of lumps on the crooked bridge. But it was Julius's smile that robbed his round face of total ugliness, a smile so sweet that the sheer impact was enough to throw any opponent off guard.

Shasta watched in amusement as the two men eyed each other in the same manner as Baskerville and Kane had taken each other's measure. She was curious to see if Julie would take to Kane, and was rewarded by a nod as Julie left the room.

"I'll put Mr. Stone's luggage in the guest room. Then I'll make you something to nibble on."

Shasta's grin widened. Cooking was Julius's star of approval.

Julius was no sooner out the door than Kane's hands clamped around her shoulders. "You little devil. All the time you knew I thought Julie was a woman."

"Yes, but..."

"I ought to turn you over my knee, but I have a feeling I'm not the only one you've pulled that particular trick on." His hands glided to the sides of her face as if they had a mind of their own. Before he realized what he was doing, Kane leaned down and kissed her, a hard quick kiss that left her wanting more. He stepped back, away from temptation. "I take it Julie is spending the night in this house?" As an afterthought he added, "Who is he, or better still, what is he to you?"

Disappointed at the termination of his kiss, Shasta searched his face, trying to glean some reason for his harried retreat. But the only answer was a sparkle in the depths of his eyes before he turned away from her. "Julie has the room over the garage and lives there most of the time, though sometimes he stays at Jeff and Rena's, and then there are times when he gets so fed up with us he hotfoots it back to Dallas and J.T.'s quiet household."

"He's a servant then?"

"Julie!" She laughed. "Not Julie." As she mixed their drinks, Shasta tried to explain. But how did you describe thirty years of love and devotion to one family? How did you tell of a man who would give his life for yours, and almost had on one occasion? "First of all you'd better know that years ago Julie was an ex-convict fresh out of prison."

Kane accepted his drink, followed her to the couch and sat down, grimacing as the strong liquor stung his throat.

"He'd been in and out of juvenile detention halls and prisons all his life, and when he got out the last time he was determined never to return. But life outside was hard and lonely." Shasta stirred her drink absently. "Julie was a first-class safecracker and cat burglar in his youth, and I guess loneliness and itchy fingers got the best of him. The only problem was, this time he picked the wrong man to rob."

Shasta glanced over the rim of her drink and watched Kane's eyes as they roamed freely and hungrily. He looked up and their glances met.

"Go on," he said, feeling a fool at being caught.

"He tried to rob my grandfather's home and was caught," Shasta plunged on. "J.T. was so impressed with Julie's expertise he made him an offer he couldn't refuse, and hired him that very night. I don't know all the details, but Julie has never left us. He helped raise Jeff and me, but he answers to no one but grandfather."

There was more. Kane could hear the love in her voice when she spoke of Julie. He had a feeling that Julie was a father figure and probably the only person who truly understood the workings of her mind. He made a mental note to become friends with one Julius Bridger. "Did Julius teach you his trade?" There was a note of disapproval in his voice.

Shasta frowned at his tone. She had become immune to the criticism of her job by others, but she had somehow thought that Kane would appreciate her work. "Yes, he's quite famous in his field, or he was, and—" she glared belligerently at him "—he taught me everything he knows."

The man in question blocked an argument by entering with a steaming tray of hors d'oeuvres. "Your favorite, Shasta—crab-stuffed fried wonton and rumaki." He grinned at her and, setting the silver tray down, left the room.

Shasta pushed the food toward Kane and jumped to her feet. Excusing herself, she rushed after Julie into the kitchen. "Okay, what was that look all about?"

The little man shrugged and began cleaning up his mess. "I saw the way you were drooling over him."

"I was not."

Julius turned around and stared at her, one fuzzy eyebrow climbing slowly to his hairline. When she had the grace to blush, he nodded and continued to wipe off the stove.

"Okay, okay, so I like him." Julius snorted and moved his cloth over the refrigerator door with Shasta at his heels. Changing the subject before it became too personal, she asked, "Did you search his things before you brought them in?"

"Yep."

"Well!" she demanded in exasperation.

"Nothing that wasn't supposed to be there."

"Damn."

Julius sniffed and continued his clean up with Shasta right behind him. She had a feeling of déjà vu and realized that all her life her arguments with Julie had taken place in the kitchen while she followed him around like a puppy, pleading her cause.

"Your brother's not a happy man tonight, Shasta. Not happy at all about this here setup. And I ain't too sure myself."

"Oh, Julie, honestly. It's the only way." She walked up beside him and yanked the dish towel out of his hands. "Listen to me and quit worrying. I need your help for a week, maybe a little longer." Her voice became wheedling. "I have to finish up on the Thomas case and won't be able to accompany Kane during the day, so would you be a sweetheart and stick with him?"

"Follow Kane? You gotta be kidding!" He jammed his fists on his hips and glared at her. "Have you taken a good measure of that man? He's used to doing things his way, and if he catches me he'll kill me, or worse." Whenever he was excited, Julie's sharp black eyes glittered with a diamond brightness. "Did you see the way he moves?" He shook his gray head. "You know how I hate violence."

"Please, Julie," Shasta said, pouting. "This is very important to me."

Julie was weakening. He knew he couldn't refuse her anything, but he had to have the last word. "Shasta Masterson, I've done a heap of things for you I wouldn't have done for no one. I've bathed you when you was a baby. I've cleaned up after you when you was sick. I've even chased some of those loose-handed men away. But now you're asking me to follow the devil."

Shasta gave him another pleading smile aimed straight for his heart.

"Okay, Miss Priss, but there's a limit to what I'll do. I'm telling you right now, that limit has just reached its peak."

Shasta planted a big wet kiss on his scratchy cheek and hurried back into the living room. "I'm sorry, Kane, but Julie needed to know what we wanted for dinner tomorrow night." She picked up his empty glass, fixed him a fresh drink and resumed her seat.

"Julie cooks?"

"Yes, a gourmet cook. Cordon bleu, as a matter of fact." She reached for an appetizer and stopped. The small tray was empty. "You ate all the hors d'oeuvres?"

"Some, but not all."

Shasta followed Kane's gaze to where Baskerville lay, his docked tail thumping the hardwood floor louder and louder. "You let my dog eat crab-stuffed wonton and rumaki?"

Kane chuckled. "He didn't say please, just kept growling at me, Shasta. Then he walked over and helped himself. I didn't think it prudent to argue." Kane's shoulders began to shake as he watched the nefarious hound cover his head with his paws at his beloved's disapproving looks.

"Bad dog," Shasta scolded. "I'm surprised. It's usually not food I have to watch for, but—" She broke off, calling herself all kinds of a fool. Here she was trying to pry information from a man who should be roaring drunk by now, and all she could talk about was Baskerville's problem. She leaned back, prepared to start over, only to be interrupted once more by Julie.

"I'm heading for some shut-eye, Shasta." He handed her a folded piece of paper and mumbled, "Telephone message," then left the room.

Shasta sighed. Quiet at last, she thought, and rested her head against the back of the wing chair. She unfolded Julie's note and read the spidery handwriting. "Car parked across street, two men watching house." She crumpled the paper and stuck it in her pocket. So, whoever was following Kane intended to stay on the job around the clock. It was only ten, and she wondered worriedly why Kane's tongue wasn't loosening up. But they had plenty of time—all night if that's what it took. Reaching across the table, she snatched up his drink and hurried to the bar. This time she increased the alcohol content, hoping for quicker results.

"Did you know you were being followed, Kane?" She decided to try a direct approach and see if he would be equally honest.

"Yes."

"How long have they been with you?"

Kane's eyes turned a deep pewter with anger, but he calmly picked up his drink, evading her question. "By the way, congratulations are in order. You're an expert evasive driver. Those were classic maneuvers you executed on the way to the restaurant." He took a sip of his drink, then gasped. "Are you trying to permanently damage my insides, Shasta?"

Before she could come up with an appropriate answer the telephone rang, and she cursed vigorously under her breath as she walked toward the squat instrument. Heaven was conspiring against her again. She just knew there was trouble on the other end of the line. "Hello, Jeff."

"Is he still there?"

Shasta sighed, leaned her hip against the edge of the bar for support and smiled apologetically across the room at Kane. "Yes, Jeff."

"Don't let him out of your sight." There was a long pause, then Jeff asked, "Did you hear me?"

Shasta was momentarily taken aback by his change of tune. "Ah, yes, of course." She watched in dismay as Kane pulled himself up off the couch, picked up his shoes and moved toward her. His eyes gleamed, as if laughter lurked in their depths. "Hold on, Jeff." She dropped the receiver onto her shoulder as Kane spoke.

"You're busy and I'm tired. If you'll tell me which room is mine, I'll say good-night."

"The first on the right at the top of the stairs. But it's early, Kane!" she wailed, dropping the phone and following him out the door. At the bottom of the stairs he turned and placed his hands on her shoulders.

"I know it's early." His lips twitched at her disappointed expression. "But I really am tired, Shasta. Besides, I've had too much to drink." Kane touched his lips to her forehead and quickly slipped up the stairs.

Shasta stomped back to the living room and snatched up the telephone. "I hope you're satisfied, Jeffrey Bernard James Masterson! You just ruined my plans for the evening."

"Me? But, sis, what kind of plans?" He quickly recovered and demanded, "Is this all the thanks I get for staying at the office till midnight, hunched over this computer, neglecting my wife and child so you can yell at me?"

"It's not midnight and stop whining." Shasta picked up the phone, walked over to her chair and settled down for a lengthy conversation. "What did you find out, Jeff?"

"You know, Shasta, Rena's not very happy with me tonight. She had plans for us to go out to dinner."

Shasta apologized profusely to soothe his injured feelings. Geniuses were the pits. She cajoled him out of his bad mood and calmly demanded again what he'd found out about Kane.

"You were right about there being more to the man than there first appeared to be," he admitted grudgingly. "After I recovered from the shock of his decadent life-style, I decided just for the hell of it to search for a military record. Shasta, Kane was in the Vietnam War as a Green Beret attached to an S&D unit."

The awe and respect in her brother's voice puzzled her. "What is an S&D, Jeff?"

Jeff's tone was filled with male scorn. "S&D, sister dear, is a Search and Destroy unit that usually worked directly under the Central Intelligence Agency. Do you know what that signifies? Kane was a CIA agent and more than likely still is."

"But, Jeff, that was during the war, and the war was over years ago."

"Come on, Shasta. You know better than that. Once an agent, always an agent. They don't like to let go of their trained men. But listen to this. When I tried to check further, I was blocked by a high-priority code. We have the clearance, but I didn't want to use it till I discussed it with you." Jeff was quiet for a while as he let this information sink in. "Oh, and sis, that license number you gave me, it was a rental car, issued to a Jess K. Raco, an employee of High Tech Offshore Exploration."

Shasta could hear a shuffling of papers and smiled at her brother's disorder. She picked up a pencil and pad and wrote down the names he'd just given her. At her brother's next words she sat upright.

"There's something funny here, though. High Tech Offshore is only a small subsidiary of another company." Jeff groaned into the receiver. "Do you know how long it took to run down the parent company? I'll tell you—two hours. But listen to this. High Tech is just one in a long list belonging to one man—" He paused, deliberately dragging out the suspense.

"Jeff!"

"Tramble Carter Baldwin, Jr., 'Old Tram' to his friends. The president and chairman of the board of U.S.A. Oil. And, Shasta, our Mr. Raco's name also appears on their payroll. Quite a coincidence, wouldn't you say?"

"Yes." Shasta felt a growing dread. If Kane was mixed up with U.S.A. Oil, then the trouble was about as serious and dangerous as you could get. Oil companies didn't fool around being nice guys. Damn, Kane. He should have known that since his father owned Tex-Am Oil. Another thought struck her. "Jeff, does Kane have any stock in his father's business, and if so, how much?" She waited while Jeff noisily shuffled papers again.

"Yeah, sis. He inherited twenty-five percent of Tex-Am stock from his grandfather. I know what you're thinking. Baldwin's trying to force Kane into selling him his shares and then he'll initiate a takeover. But you're wrong. There was a clause in the old man's will stipulating that Kane can't sell his shares to anyone but his father. From past gossip, that's been a bone of contention between father and son over the years."

"Kane wanted to sell?" Shasta asked.

"No! That's just it. Max has harassed his son for years to sell out to him, but Kane wouldn't. It's not a money issue, either. Kane's grandfather left him his entire fortune, and that must stick in Max's craw. That same gossip has it that Kane wasn't Max's son but the old man's. Now don't get all upset, it's just hearsay and you know how that goes."

"None of this makes sense, Jeff. I think we're starting at the wrong point. Kane was assaulted in Paris. Wrap up your search here and begin at that end." She absently said good-night and hung up. What had Kane done to make oil-company goons trail after him? No answers came as she sat there gazing off into the darkness. Baskerville, sensing her agitation, laid his big head on her knee and whined sympathetically. Shasta automatically scratched behind his ears as she tried to fit together the pieces of the puzzle. But she didn't have all the parts and was left frustrated. Kane was not what he appeared to be, and she wondered how many layers she'd have to peel away before she reached the real man. Then she realized it didn't make any difference who or what he was, she wanted him just the same.

Shasta shooed Baskerville away, turned off the lights and climbed upstairs. Outside her bedroom she stopped and stared longingly at the closed door across the hall. Were his thoughts of her this night? She'd seen the masked desire in his eyes throughout the evening and wondered if, alone and warm in his bed, he was dreaming of her.

KANE LAY IN THE DARKNESS, his hands behind his head, listening to Shasta's light footsteps on the stairs and down the hall. When they stopped momentarily, his pulse increased its tempo and his breath was caught in the back of his throat. He didn't need that kind of involvement, but, damn, she was hard to resist.

The fact was, he'd thought over her earlier words about his danger becoming hers and realized she was right. By allowing Shasta to continue her job he was placing her right in the middle of his problems. When he'd given in to her bullying about his father's orders, he'd thought it would be a way to pass a few boring nights. The problem was, he hadn't expected her to be so professional and thorough in her work. His boredom wasn't worth her life—or his piece of mind.

Kane closed his eyes, straining to hear any movements from the other room. He could barely make out the sounds of running water and took a deep breath as erotic pictures ran rampant through his mind. He'd have to get rid of her. But how? And there in the night an idea formed and took root. The only way to keep her out of danger was to force her to quit. A smile, sharp and conniving, curved his mouth. After he got through with her she'd be so exhausted she'd beg to quit.

CHAPTER FIVE

IN THE EARLY HOURS of the morning, before the sun harnessed the night and rode the moon down, a strange wailing pierced the dark. Shasta shot bolt upright and cocked her head, listening again to the unearthly howling. As a child the sound had driven Shasta under her covers for safety, but now it sent her leaping from bed and flying down the stairs.

Panting for breath, she arrived at the kitchen door, shoved it open and skidded to a stop as a giggle escaped her lips. Kane stood in the center of the room, frozen in motion, a sandwich in one hand and an open bottle of beer in the other. Baskerville was planted directly in front of him, his massive head thrown back, jaws wide open and long white teeth gleaming in the light from the open refrigerator door. The ungodly sound he was producing was guaranteed to give anyone who heard it nightmares for days.

Shasta erupted with giggles as she watched. Kane, still shocked, moved only his eyes and Shasta marveled at how menacing he looked in his thigh-length robe, which revealed a tantalizing amount of chest and muscular, well-shaped legs. His steady stare threatened her early demise if she didn't call off her dog.

"Do something before he decides it's me he's going to eat instead of this sandwich."

Galvanized into action by the desperation in Kane's voice, she swallowed her laughter. "It's not food he's after." Snatching the bottle of beer from his hand, she walked over and filled Baskerville's bowl. The happy dog lapped loudly, his tail wagging so fast it defied detection. "You were drinking Baskerville's beer and he takes exception to thieves." She turned around in time to see Kane reach for a chair and sit. He threw back his head and laughed uproariously.

Shasta joined him at the table. "It's true. Baskerville's drinking problem is the deep, dark family secret around here." She pulled out a chair and sat down, fascinated by the sight of Kane's shattered composure. "If you had opened two beers, that would have been a different matter. Baskerville would have been delighted to share with you." She clucked her tongue at his ignorance. "But to insult him by just opening one was unforgivable. You could have saved us all that infernal racket he made."

Her words broke the last thread that held Kane together, and he groaned loudly. "Please, no more. My ribs can't take it."

Baskerville joined them, heading directly for his newfound buddy. He licked a bare knee in heartfelt thanks, then padded off to bed, a loud belch sounding over his shoulder.

Shasta's eyes followed the retreating dog with amusement. "When I first brought Baskerville home he was a skinny runt. Unfortunately my father was here on a visit and told me to give my poor pup a bottle of beer to improve his appetite." She sighed. "That was my first mistake. I believed him. My second was in doing it! So now I have a dog who loves beer and has to be watched carefully."

She stood up and flipped on the overhead light. Picking up the mangled sandwich from the floor, she asked, "Would you like me to make you another one?" Kane shook his head and continued to watch her as she cleaned up.

When she began to wipe off the table, Kane reached out and ran one finger around the short hem of her nightshirt. Shasta looked down in surprise, realizing by his touch that she'd forgotten a robe. The only thing that saved the cotton nightshirt from being completely transparent was its peacock-blue color.

"That's an intriguing little number." Kane would have continued his finger's exploration, but Shasta stepped back and out of his reach.

"What are you doing awake in the middle of the night?" Self-consciously she crossed her arms under her breasts, which only added to Kane's pleasure as the material pulled tight across her chest, unveiling a fascinating shadow of dark nipples. Shasta followed the path of his eyes and dropped her arms.

Kane's gaze lifted slowly to her face, his eyes heavy with desire, his mouth pulled taut at the corners as thoughts spun around in his head. "To tell the truth, I'm not used to going to bed quite so early." His gaze returned to roam her body freely. "Besides, all that alcohol you tried to force down my throat only succeeded in keeping me awake."

Shasta's cheeks flushed a bright red. "Well..." she hedged, then grinned. "I tried. You must have a great capacity for alcohol?"

"I do."

"You're good at keeping your mouth shut, too, aren't you?"

"I am."

"I'll bet you'll even deny that the men who are following us and those who ransacked your father's house are one and the same?"

"Right."

"And you're not going to tell me why those two men would want to put an around-the-clock tail on you, are you?"

"No, love."

She sighed, her shoulders slumping dejectedly. "I didn't think so." She slipped into the chair across from him. "You know of course that we'll find out *everything,* Kane? It would make things much easier if you'd just tell me."

Kane shook his head. "I can't do that, Shasta."

"Why?" she demanded. "Is someone threatening you? Who are you trying to protect, Kane? Your father?" Her voice trailed off as she looked at him closely. Kane was trying to smile, but Shasta could see additional lines of strain bracketing his mouth. Her gaze dropped to his side, and she saw how firmly he was holding his ribs. "You've hurt yourself again." She moved to his chair, her hand on his arm to aid him in getting up. "Come on, I've got something that will help."

Kane, in pain, didn't argue but allowed her to assist him out of the kitchen. They were passing the entrance to the living room when she stopped, her arms easing their hold on his waist. The snoring from within caused Kane's lips to twitch and Shasta frowned at both man and beast. "Bad dog!" she yelled, and Baskerville whined but didn't come fully awake. "Some fine watchdog," she grumbled as she guided Kane up the stairs.

"Shasta, stop!" Kane's shoulders shook as he slowly mounted the steps, his hand clamped on the banister. The woman was going to be the death of him if he stayed around here for long.

A few moments later, seated on a dainty, spindly legged vanity stool in Shasta's bedroom, Kane looked around in puzzlement. The room, for some reason, was a shock. He'd expected the same homey comfort as the rest of the house, but here in her domain were ruffles and lace, colors of old ivory and the palest yellow. The room was romantic and feminine, and it made him uneasy.

Kane tried to relax and take some of the pressure off his side. Despite his pain he was thoroughly enjoying watching Shasta. The show she was unconsciously putting on was better than any strip show he'd ever seen, and he followed her with his eyes as she bent, stooped and reached, searching through a linen closet that had been turned into a medical supply cabinet. "Are you a hypochondriac?" he asked, eyeing the impressive array of articles.

Her answer came muffled from the depths of the closet. "Of course not. It's just my line of work tends to attract injuries."

Kane wasn't listening. His eyes were glued to the flash of smooth white flesh that beckoned and titillated his senses till he questioned his sanity in wanting to rid himself of this tasty morsel. She had captivated and aroused his interest more than any woman he'd ever met, but there was a gleam in her eyes that threatened his freedom. He knew he should leave with the next strong wind, and yet she held him with her sparkling smile.

Kane raked his fingers through his hair, forcing himself from the outrageous path his thoughts had taken. He had no intention of staying around long enough to get involved, he told himself scornfully. He'd come to get information—to find a murderer—then return to Europe and his old way of life. He wasn't about to let an enchanting pixie sway him from his goal, and he certainly wasn't going to permit her to become so involved in his troubles that she could get hurt.

"Here it is!" Shasta spun around, a wide, thick roll of elastic bandage in her hand. "Take off your robe and stand up," she ordered. When he remained seated, staring at her, she demanded impatiently, "Did you hear me?"

Kane stood slowly. "I heard, but think you're—"

"Now don't be childish, Kane," she broke in. "I'm not going to hurt you. I'm just going to wrap your ribs to relieve the pressure. Now drop the robe."

Without further comment Kane did as she ordered. Untying the looped belt, he shrugged the robe off his shoulders, his eyes sparkling.

Shasta blinked rapidly at the sight of Kane's naked body in all its beauty.

"Someday maybe you'll let me finish what I started to say." Kane's teeth flashed brighter than a beacon at the color staining Shasta's cheeks.

Spinning around, Shasta yanked a large warm towel from the heating rack. "The sight of a nude man does not shock me, Kane." But her hands shook as she held the towel out to him. Forcing her eyes to remain on his face, she silently cursed his slowness, wondering if it was deliberate or from pain. When he at last secured the towel with a final tuck, she allowed her eyes to meet his and frowned. He was having entirely too much fun at her expense. "Hold up your arms." She placed the end of the wrap in the center of his chest. "Now hold these ends in place."

Kane mutely did as he was told, and the next few minutes stretched into eternity. His fists clenched, and a fine sheen of perspiration broke out on his forehead as she bandaged him, but it wasn't the viselike wrapping that was causing him such discomfort. It was the touch of her hands on his body; the brush of a breast against his arm; the feel of her arms reaching around his back and bringing her body within a fraction of an inch from his that was driving him mad. "Are you through?" he growled, exhaling slowly, his breath stirring her fragrant hair.

"I'm just about finished." Shasta lowered her head and coughed. She had always been taught to fight fire with fire, but now she began to doubt the soundness of that advice. The firm bulge beneath the towel was evidence of her revenge. The only problem was, her game had backfired. In the process she'd managed to become equally excited from touching Kane, and now she tried hard to mask her own heavy breathing by humming softly to herself. Hurriedly she fastened the metal clamps and spun away, only to have her shoulders caught in a firm grip and whirled around.

"Oh, no, mouse. You'll damn well finish what you started."

She gazed up at him, her velvet brown eyes wide and round and full of innocence. "I don't know what you're talking about." Her chin quivered slightly as the tips of his thumbs traced the bones along her shoulders to the base of her neck.

"You love to tease and play games, don't you?" He pulled her close. "But this time it got out of hand." Her body was touching his. "I saw the look in your eyes." His breath fanned her cheek as he leaned down to whisper in her ear, and a shiver raced across her skin like a gentle breeze. "I can read your body's message to me. No, don't say a word." He placed a finger firmly against her lips to stop the flow of denials he saw in her darkened eyes. But she couldn't hide the pounding of her heart as he touched the pulsing artery in her neck.

Shasta swallowed painfully. His deep rumbling voice with its pronounced French accent and his mirror-bright gaze were as hypnotic as a pendulum. Kane's charm was dangerous. He was a man accustomed to getting what he wanted with a minimum of effort. He'd been waited on hand and foot since a baby and denied nothing. Shasta sensed all these things about him and grimly realized that she wasn't capable of resisting or breaking his record of conquests. She could no more turn him away than any other woman. Knowing this, she snuggled into his embrace, as trusting as a newborn lamb.

Kane's mouth claimed hers. He pulled her against his waiting body, the hunger of her response answering his desire. With an expert movement he shifted her body sideways and his nimble fingers deftly released the buttons of her nightshirt.

Shasta stood naked before him as his eyes savored her softly rounded body. Without a word she turned and walked to the edge of the bed, grasped a handful of bedcovers and yanked them to the footboard. She felt the heat of Kane's body close behind her and relaxed, knowing instinctively that his hands were already reaching for her. Like a young willow bending in an untamed wind, she leaned into his warm flesh and snuggled back into arms that cradled her small frame in strength and security. If there was love only in *her* mind, that was all right, too. This was her man, and she was about to receive him into her body and be as close to him as any human could.

Both hands covered her rounded breasts, his palms rubbing the pert nipples to flowering peaks. "You're so damn tiny. I'm not going to hurt you, am I?"

Shasta's mind, heavy with desire, took a long second to register his question. "No, Kane. You could never hurt me." A husky chuckle sounded above her head and she looked up, only to be locked against his chest.

"I don't know whether to take that as an insult or a compliment." His hands pressed her hips to his own hardness, and her sleepy brown eyes widened.

"Oh, I . . ." Her words were lost in the dark cavern of his mouth as he eased her onto the bed. She rolled onto her side, facing him and tried again. "You know—" But his mouth claimed hers in a deep kiss that touched off a singing in her ears. She savored his warm velvet tongue with her own, and her hands kneaded the flesh of his shoulders. Lost in the feel and touch of him, she fought to regroup her thoughts and pulled away from his kiss. The mischievous lights in her eyes should have warned him. "I promise to respect you in the morning."

"What?" She'd completely disoriented him again.

"Well, we've only known each other a short while, but I can keep my mouth shut. I mean, I don't kiss and tell."

"Oh, God, no Shasta. Not in bed—not now! Please, don't make me laugh."

"But, Kane—" she pouted as her fingers traveled down his spine, over the bandage that strapped his abused ribs, to the firm muscles of his buttocks "—making love should be spiced with laughter." Before she could slip her searching fingers around his hips to his stomach, he captured her hand in a steel grip.

The pressure was released as he pulled her hand to his lips and smiled into her eyes. He inserted her fingers, one by one, deeply into his mouth, where he gently sucked on each, then pulled it out slowly. While he played his erotic game he watched her changing expression. "Is that something to laugh at?" She shook her head, and he listened carefully to the sharp intake of breath as his other hand worked its own special brand of magic between her thighs. His touch was gentle, yet there was a firmness in each caress, each stroke; a sureness and expertise.

Shasta planted tiny kisses along his jaw to the strong brown column of his neck, then to his chest, where her tongue played temptingly around a hardened nipple. Kane's chest ceased to move, and the rhythm of his breathing was suspended. Quickly capturing her face, he guided her mouth up to his.

Concerned about his ribs, Shasta rolled Kane to his side, but he edged back. She gave up agonizing over his injuries and lost herself in the soundless world of their lovemaking.

Kane gathered Shasta's hands in his and held them above her head. He lowered his mouth, taking hers in a quick kiss before his lips began a journey designed to drive her to a world of exploding light.

"No, Kane." Her voice came out a breathless plea, and she wondered if he heard her halfhearted denial.

"Oh, yes, mouse." His teeth nipped lightly along the sensitive skin on the inside of her thigh. "Did you think I wouldn't want *all* of you?" The trail of his words left a brand on her flesh that she knew she would never be able to erase or forget.

Kane raised his head, and Shasta looked into eyes that promised heaven. She shivered in anticipation as his head dipped again and his lips teased and tantalized, driving her crazy. He took the breath from her lungs and the beat from her heart, and she called his name in a hoarse voice that sounded as though it belonged to another human being.

Later, as she lay in his arms, Kane smiled, then slipped between her legs, filling her, burying himself in her body. Her eyes opened lethargically and her mouth curved sweetly. "You're going to hurt yourself. Why don't we change places?" she murmured softly.

Kane lowered himself fully onto her, his thrusts slow and deep. "Not necessary, love." His own breath came fast as he maintained the pace till Shasta groaned and wrapped her legs around his hips, increasing their rhythm. Kane followed her movements, matching the tempo till both froze in time and space, then collapsed in a tangle of arms and legs.

Shasta lay deathly still, a forearm thrown across her eyes, as dawn's light slipped between the slightly parted curtains and spilled across their naked forms like an eager voyeur. Her breathing was placid and unbroken, as if her body slept but her mind refused to surrender. *Why,* an inner voice screamed over and over again. *What had gone wrong?* The feel of cool air drifting across their damp skin brought Shasta back to reality. Without thinking she reached down, caught the edge of the sheet and pulled it over them. Kane shifted his weight and she began to move away. He cuddled her close, his lips grazing her ear with light kisses.

"Please, Kane. Not again." She ground her teeth together at the sound of his muffled chuckle.

"Did my lovemaking wear you out, baby?"

She'd always despised being called baby, she'd even made an issue of it on their first meeting. But she couldn't bring herself to call him Maxie in retaliation. The name just didn't fit. Besides, Kane was too sexy to insult with that wimpy nickname, and somehow his French accent took away the sting of insult.

"Don't call me baby," she muttered weakly. "And no, Kane, you didn't, as you so crudely put it, wear me out." The bite in her voice brought his head up off her neck with a jerk. "I wouldn't call what you did making love. Sex, yes, but there were no finer feelings there. I sincerely doubt that you're capable of anything so deep."

His silver eyes darkened ominously and he leaned across her, his body holding her immobile.

"You're playing a dangerous game, lady. Don't lie there and taunt me." He brought his face a breath away from hers. "I satisfied you, love, and if you try to deny it, I'll do it again and again. Only this time you'll wish I hadn't."

"I would never try to repute your prowess, Kane. You're a considerate lover. An expert in the arts of making a woman feel alive in every nerve of her body. You know all the right buttons to push. There probably isn't a man alive who could surpass your expertise." Shasta watched his brows come together with each compliment, and after a brief pause she went on. "It's just a crying shame that you feel nothing in return. You watched, gauged and analyzed my every response, each move choreographed and staged as if you were programmed like some robot."

Kane rolled onto his back and laughed at the lace canopy above him. "I've never heard such rot in all my life. What the hell do you want from me?" Raising himself up on his elbow, he reached out and grabbed her chin. "You got exactly what you've been asking for from the moment we met."

"Did I?" Shasta flinched inwardly at his tone but refused to back down. She had to make him understand. "I expected to have a warm giving man, not a stranger who dictated each move. Where was the spontaneity, the adventure and the fun? You're inhuman."

"And you're crazy." Kane shoved the covers back and lunged out of the bed. As he straightened, he grabbed his side and inhaled deeply.

"Am I crazy, Kane?" Quickly she moved in front of him and blocked his retreat. She reached out to place her hand on his chest but was stopped as Kane's fingers curled around her wrist. "Why don't you want to be touched?" His grasp tightened, and Shasta stood her ground, lowering her voice to a pain-laced whisper. "Every time I wanted to stroke or caress you, you intercepted me. Why? Why did your eyes never change color with your desire or the intensity of the moment?" Her heart ached for him. "Because you had to be in total control—master of your emotions."

Kane released her wrist as if he'd been holding a red-hot iron. "Stop it, Shasta! You don't know what you're talking about."

"Oh, I think I do. What happened to you, Kane? Where did your passion and capacity for love go?"

"Love!" he snarled, and caught her by the shoulders. "For years I watched that overrated word tear my mother apart. You see, she loves *all* men. And passion, Shasta—what does passion get you but obsession. My father's ruling passion is Texas-American Oil. Passion and love tore them apart. It destroyed my mother and will more than likely be the final weapon to kill my father." He pulled her close and stared down into her eyes. "Don't confuse love with lust or sex. I've been around a lot longer than you have. I'm older and have seen and experienced what people do in the name of love. They lie, cheat, steal, do unspeakable things to each other and, yes, even kill—all for love!"

Kane let go of her shoulders, but instead of stepping away, he rubbed her arms briskly to return the circulation. "Hell, I didn't mean to blow up like that. But, mouse, you could drive a man to murder with your pushing. Fair warning, don't do it again."

The golden sparkle returned to Shasta's eyes. "Kane Stone, I don't know what sort of people you've been around, but it's obvious that they, and you, know nothing about life." She laughed. "Strange how, with all your sophistication and intelligence, you could be so ignorant. And since you're going to be in town for a while and we'll be *so* close, I just might take you in hand and teach you how to be a human being—human enough to want to feel again and enjoy life."

"If I had about a hundred years you might have some luck." His fingers trailed lightly across the collarbone to the base of her neck, then dropped to brush the tops of her breasts and slowly circle her nipples. "I think I'll let you start right now."

"No!"

"Hmm."

"The next time you and I end up in bed I intend to have Kane the man, not a mechanical clone."

"You're joking?" Kane's hands moved over her stomach in an erotic pattern and Shasta stepped out of his reach.

"You needn't give me that look, either. I won't change my mind." She whirled around, picked up his robe, handed it to him and guided him to the door.

A second later Kane stood in the cold hallway wearing only gooseflesh and carrying his robe. The loud click of the lock on Shasta's door brought him out of his stupor and sent him hurrying to his bed. He lay there on his back, his head cradled in his hands and a frown etched across his forehead. It seemed to him that for every step he took forward in his plan to rid himself of Shasta, he was forced three steps backward.

Shasta was also wide awake. She glanced at the bedside clock and groaned. In two hours she'd have to get up and go to work. She reached over and snatched up Kane's pillow, hugging it to her breast. She sighed. There would be no self-recrimination for this night, she decided. What did disturb her, though, was knowing what she had to do. Changing Kane's perception of life wasn't going to be a piece of cake. She snuggled down farther into the warm covers. But, by heaven, she vowed, she was going to change his outlook on love—she had to for both their sakes. Whether she would win in the end remained to be seen, but Kane had a right to walk in light and love; he'd lived in darkness long enough.

Her eyelids began to droop in exhaustion and a tiny smile turned one corner of her mouth upward as a thought slipped across her mind. Despite his many faults, Kane *was* a wonderful lover, and she'd listened to the unspoken desires of his heart and body and willingly succumbed to them. There was a lot to be said for his methods.

CHAPTER SIX

"MIRROR, MIRROR on the bathroom wall, who's going to tell the devil he's in for a fall?"

Shasta grinned at her reflection and dabbed on additional makeup to cover the faint shadows under her eyes. Squaring her shoulders, she straightened her poppy-red silk blouse and checked to make sure she'd completed tucking the shirttail inside her white linen pants. She readjusted the white lizard-skin Judith Leiber belt, centering the large gold buckle, then picked up the matching handbag and marched out of her room.

She paused outside Kane's closed door, her hand raised hesitantly as she listened for any signs of awakening life. Hearing only the quiet of the house and the familiar sounds of Julius cooking breakfast, she dropped her fist and hurried on, the smell of freshly ground coffee drawing her like a parched person to water.

Shasta stopped in the open doorway of the kitchen and leaned against the frame, smiling. The air was filled with the delicious fragrance of hot croissants, thick sliced ham frying in butter and a spicy omelet guaranteed to open sleepy eyes. Julie was in his element in the kitchen and worked efficiently, his hands quick and sure as he and Kane discussed the merits of cooking with truffles.

Still unnoticed, she shifted her attention to Kane, who was propped nonchalantly against the center cooking island, sipping his coffee. Dressed in a multistriped polo shirt, snug-fitting white shorts and clean tennis shoes, he made a devastating sight for any woman. She hadn't had time to appraise his body last night, but as she eyed his beautifully shaped legs and enticing derriere, she remembered that his stomach muscles had been hard as a washboard. His wasn't the body of a decadent playboy. Kane was a man who, for whatever reason, kept himself in top physical condition at all times.

Baskerville barked, announcing her arrival and bringing her lustful thoughts to an end. She looked down at her faithful dog planted firmly at Kane's feet. "Traitor," she scolded, and received another playful bark as if to confirm her accusation. "That's fine, Baskerville, but who are you going to butter up to when Kane leaves?"

Baskerville's clipped ears perked up, and he cocked his head thoughtfully, then lumbered over to give her hand a wet apologetic kiss. She patted his head. "That's it, monster, keep all your options open." Accepting a cup of coffee from Julie, she nodded at Kane.

"Good morning." He eyed her over the rim of his mug, eyes alight with devilment.

"Morning," she mumbled in return. "I hope you slept well?"

"I did, and you?"

"Like a log."

They were both lying. Neither had had any peace of mind during the remainder of the early-morning hours.

"Shasta," Julie interrupted their silent clash, "wash your hands, breakfast is ready." He shoved his fists on his hips as he demanded, "And tell this overgrown drunkard to get out of my kitchen. Every time I open the refrigerator he's got his head inside breathing on my food and hunting for his bottle before I can stop him."

Baskerville knew he was being talked about and sat quietly, his massive head swinging from Julie to Shasta. Realizing he was in for another scolding from his master, he curled his lips in a mock snarl, growled at everyone in the room, then padded out, his head high and his docked tail pointed toward heaven.

Shasta sighed. "Another normal morning," she said to Kane, and smiled. "They love each other, really they do." Setting down her cup, she stepped to the sink to wash her hands. "Did Julie tell you that I have to go to the office this morning, so he'll stay with you till I can wrap up the case I'm on?" She reached for the tap, but Kane stopped her by taking her hands in his.

"He told me, and I informed him it wasn't necessary for him to hang around here all day." Kane quickly buttoned her cuffs, which she'd left undone, turned on the water and handed her a towel to dry her hands with. "I'm just going to laze around and give my ribs a chance to heal."

Shasta eyed his casual attire suspiciously.

"Believe me, Shasta, I'm quite capable of keeping myself entertained. Besides, I noticed you have the new Robert Ludlum novel, and I'd like to read it."

WHY DIDN'T SHE trust him? Later, at the office, she asked herself that question again, remembering his bland, innocent expression as they'd parted. Kane Stone hadn't seen innocence since he'd passed his first birthday. She picked up the telephone and quickly dialed her number. When the ringing went unanswered, she slammed down the instrument. She'd been duped. Her only consolation was in knowing Julie was trailing Kane. Julie on a job was like a bulldog with a bone.

"Well, well. What's put the bloom in your cheeks, or should I say whom?"

Shasta glared at her sister-in-law lounging gracefully against the doorframe. "I thought you were going to take Lizzie to the zoo? By the way, how is my angel of a niece?"

Rena straightened slowly and glided across the room to perch on the corner of Shasta's desk. "You won't distract me from my purpose, you know. But since my husband's so engrossed in this Kane project, I'll indulge you. Lizzie's fine, if you consider going through the terrible two's with a vengeance fine. And the reason we're not at the zoo is because last night the poor angel got bored and decided to change the color of her hair like mommy does. Do you remember when I wanted Jeff to take me to the Virgin Islands two months ago and he wouldn't?" Shasta nodded. "Do you also remember I threatened to dye my hair bright red if he didn't?" Shasta nodded again. "Well, your little angel found the red coloring and dipped her pigtails. She's now the youngest punk-rock kid in Houston."

"You could have it cut, Rena," Shasta suggested, laughing.

Rena picked up a pencil from Shasta's desk and expertly wove it between each finger with amazing dexterity. "Ah...now that's where you're wrong. You see, the reason for the aborted zoo excursion is that Lizzie likes her new hair color. She keeps dragging me to the television and pointing out those groups on the rock videos. Tell me something. How can you argue with a two-year-old who's been raised watching and believing what she sees on television? I mean, really, Shasta, 'Sesame Street' and Big Bird would never steer her wrong. I told the little monster no haircut, no zoo."

Shasta cleared her throat. "Has Jeff seen her yet?"

Rena eyed her sister-in-law, displeasure stamped on her beautiful features. "My dear Shasta, your brother—you notice I stressed *your*—spent the night here waiting for J.T.'s friend, Monsieur Duval of the French Sûreté, to return his call." Rena slipped off the edge of the desk and pulled the nearest chair closer for an intimate chat. "Now that we're off my problems—" she leaned forward eagerly "—what's he like?"

At that moment Jeff stormed into the office, saving Shasta from Rena's probing questions. Clothes crumpled and wrinkled, his blond hair standing out in all directions, Jeff looked every inch the absentminded professor. He waved the wad of papers in his hand and tripped over a loose shoelace. Rena jumped up and grabbed his arm, rescuing her husband from total destruction.

"Sis, you're not going to believe this!" He flopped his long body down in the chair Rena had just vacated. There was excitement in his voice, the eagerness of a hunter who, after days of tracking, has finally caught a glimpse of his prey. "While I waited for Duval's call last night, I decided to go ahead and use some of our government access codes."

Jeff tried unsuccessfully to press out the creases and frayed edges of the roll of papers on his lap. "Do you recall me telling you I hit a dead end searching Kane's military background? He wasn't discharged, and payroll still shows his salary being deposited in a Paris account, yet his service record doesn't show any order assignment."

"Jeff, that was years ago. What does all this have to do with now?"

Jeff frowned and said absently, "There's still those three blank years." He scratched his head thoughtfully as Shasta's question finally penetrated. "Oh, it's important. Are you ready for this? After busting my buns trying to trace Kane for that missing three-year span, I'll be damned if I didn't just happen to fall onto his name on another government list. Would you believe Kane Stone is registered as a diplomatic envoy attached to the United States government?" Jeff's blue eyes, though red rimmed and shadowed, sparkled with triumph.

Distraught, Shasta raked her fingers through her hair, destroying what little order she had achieved that morning, and yelled in total confusion and frustration, "None of this makes sense. If Kane's a diplomat, why are oil-company goons making a shambles of his father's home and following his every move?" She stared at her brother and braced herself for more. Jeff had that smug expression she recognized only too well. He was about to drop another bomb, and he wanted to make sure everyone felt the fallout.

Rena studied her husband and snuggled beside him, her arm thrown around his shoulders and her hand patting his arm encouragingly.

Shasta exhaled loudly, resigned to wait out the suspense in a calm ladylike manner. She folded her hands on the desk top, gritted her teeth and smiled sweetly at her brother. "What else?"

Jeff made a show of shuffling his papers, and she realized he would have continued getting his own back for the trouble she'd caused him, but his excitement over the new find was too great.

"Mr. Duval with the French Sûreté returned my call about an hour ago. We had a delightful chat. By the way, he said to be sure and remind grandfather that he still owes him two hundred francs."

"Jeff, so help me!" she said threateningly.

"Duval was familiar with Kane's name. As a matter of fact, the French police would like another interview with him concerning the murder of an American professor named Melvin Kimble."

"Murder!" Shasta breathed. "Kane! They want to talk to Kane about murder?"

Jeff's voice grew serious. "Yeah, seems this professor was killed in a hit and run, and Kane was in someway connected with the old man."

"They don't think Kane was the driver, do they?"

"No! Kane was with this Kimble fellow when he was hit." Jeff scratched his head again thoughtfully. "Or at least he was near him. I didn't get all that down."

Shasta's heart resumed its normal beat, and she exhaled the breath she'd been unconsciously holding. "It seems the deeper we dig into Kane's past the more confusing and involved it gets."

"I hate to burst your bubble of excitement, but has anyone thought of just *asking* the man himself what's going on?" Rena's lips tightened as two pairs of eyes damned her as an ogre determined to ruin their fun. She jumped up and glared at them. "Okay, so I don't understand the thrill you two get out of mysteries and puzzles." She looked down her perfectly sculptured nose at them. "I keep forgetting I'm the normal one around here." Throwing up her hands in defeat, she gave her grinning husband one more scorching look, laced with a sensuous invitation, and stomped out. "I'll just go home and see if Lizzie's changed her mind."

Shasta hid her smile as Jeff hastily gathered up his papers from his lap and the floor and followed Rena out the door, a bright gleam in his tired eyes. She picked up the telephone and dialed her number, slamming the instrument down after the tenth ring. It would have been to her advantage, she realized, if she had taught Baskerville to answer the telephone. Rena's words came back suddenly about enjoying the thrill of excitement, and she realized her sister-in-law was right. She tried her number again, and as the ringing continued, she prayed that no matter where Kane was, Julie was not far behind.

KANE STROLLED the sidewalks of downtown Houston with familiarity, though it seemed to him that the skyline had changed. New towers of glass and steel in unique shapes and sizes sprouted out of the concrete like tenderly nurtured plants. The sun's rays bounced and flashed off miles of tinted glass and polished steel, washing the milling lunch-hour crowd in a shower of brilliance.

Kane glanced over his shoulder and searched a knot of people for anyone showing an unusual interest in his movements. He'd been walking the streets for an hour, getting his bearings before making his move. Now he picked up speed, his long-legged stride eating up the distance between him and his followers. Crossing the street with the crowd, he entered the mammoth bronze portals of The Park, a new covered shopping mall in the heart of the city. The mall was the hub of a series of above-street walkways connecting numerous office towers and creating a shopper's delight. Kane passed specialty shops and restaurants without slowing his pace and exited at a side entrance, crossed the street and calmly stepped into the lobby of the Four Seasons Hotel. Again, without slowing down, he left the hotel through another door. On the street once more, he began another series of twists and turns through department stores and restaurants. Checking over his shoulder, he smiled. He'd lost the two men who had been tailing him, but there was still one more. With a wicked gleam in his eyes he speeded up his steps and entered a crowd of pedestrians waiting for a light to change. When the surge of people stepped off the curb, Kane quickly moved to one side, then headed down another street, where he turned the corner and stopped, waiting.

Julius Bridger, his breath coming fast, trotted around the same corner after Kane and ran straight into a solid chest.

"You following me, Julie?"

"That's right." Julius dusted off his vest and pulled at his jacket fastidiously, checking to make sure his pocket watch hadn't been lifted—a habit left over from his youth and one he had never been able to break.

Kane pushed up the sleeves of his navy linen sports jacket to his elbows, slipped his hands into his pants pockets and leaned against a granite wall, regarding the dapper little man insolently. "Want to tell me why?"

"Shasta's orders."

"I see."

"I don't think so."

"How's that, Julie?" Kane stared coldly at him, demanding the truth.

Julius studied the toe of one shoe distastefully, then rubbed it behind the opposite pant leg to remove the spot marring his spit shine. "She's got a bee in her bonnet that you're in danger and being followed."

Kane smiled wryly. "Just between you and me, Julie, she's right."

"I seen them." Julius smiled, his bushy gray eyebrows wiggling. "You done a real fine job of losing them. I doubled back to see what they was up to and seen them heading for their car. Do you know who they are?"

"I think so." Kane pushed away from the wall and started down the street, his pace slower so the little man beside him could keep up. "How about a drink? I'm sure you're thirsty after that long morning stroll."

"You said it." Julius rubbed his hands together. "I could do with a cold beer. There's no peace at Shasta's to enjoy one with that hound of hers kicking up a fuss and drooling all over you."

Kane paused under a cool, green canopy that covered an unusual set of double doors. A sculptured picture in hammered brass, copper and silver depicting a long line of charging bull elephants spread from the door down one entire outside wall. The magnificent work of art brought a wry twist to Kane's lips as he reached for the thick brass elephant tusks that served as door pulls.

"You ever been in Harry's Kenya, Julie? No? Then you're in for a treat." He held the heavy door open and waved the other man into the world of African safaris. The wall around the bar area was lined with stuffed animal heads that made the patrons feel as if they were sitting in a restaurant deep in the heart of Africa. Kane ordered a martini for himself and a beer for Julie, then settled back in his chair. "Tell me about Shasta and her family."

Julius took a hefty swallow of cold beer and studied Kane for a long second. Then, as if deciding to trust him, he said, "Got to you has she?"

"You could say that," Kane ruefully replied.

Julius sipped his beer, his expression thoughtful. "First of all, you have to know that Shasta is the baby of the family and was a big surprise." He lifted his gaze to Kane's. "There's only ten months between Shasta and Jeff, and there are the two older children. John's thirty-nine and Virginia's thirty-seven. See, Jeff was planned and Shasta was a slip up." Julius crossed his arms on the table and leaned forward. "Jeff was real sick as a baby and Shasta's parents had their hands full, so Shasta was left to her grandfather, a nanny and me. We raised that kid till she got old enough to take care of herself."

Kane snorted disbelievingly.

"You listen here, mister," admonished Julius, "if you think she can't take care of herself, you're a big fool and in for a shock. I ain't seen nothing she can't do." He was quiet for a second then chuckled, "'Cept those woman things." Julius caught a glimpse of Kane's interest and leaned forward conspiratorially. "She never learned to cook, doesn't like to clean house and has no taste in clothes or style. Why, hell, half the time either me or Rena does her shopping. She don't even carry her own charge cards, I do." Suddenly Julius clamped his lips together. "I'd be in your debt if you'd forget what I just told you," he said stiffly. "Shasta'll kill me if she knew."

Kane laughed and agreed, but continued to probe. "Do all the Mastersons work in the company?"

"Everyone down to second cousins."

"No black sheep?"

Julius threw back his head and laughed. "Black sheep. I guess that's as good a description as any." He saw Kane's puzzled expression and explained. "Shasta's the family black sheep, troublemaker or whatever you want to hang on her. She's the only one in the entire family with the dark coloring. All Mastersons are tall, blue-eyed blondes, and it's been the bane of her life. She's also the only one who wanted to work outside the company. That caused a row, I can tell you. But she's the apple of her grandfather's eye, and if she was to be hurt..." Julius's forehead pleated and his eyebrows dived inward. "Well, I wouldn't give the man any odds on staying alive long."

The two men stared at each other in perfect understanding—one giving warning, the other accepting.

Kane sighed in defeat. He'd been trying to find an avenue of escape. Now he realized he'd have to handle this affair carefully, or he'd end up with the entire Masterson family on his back. "Julie, I need your help. What I've come to Houston to do could get dangerous. I don't want anyone to get hurt, so how do I persuade Shasta to give up this bodyguard business, or better yet, make her quit?"

Julius smiled. "Can't! She senses danger and that's all it takes. You ain't very smart, are you? You haven't figured her out yet. She thrives on adventure and excitement and, mister, you reek of danger and mystery. She's on to you till she's tired of the game, or she's done what she has to do. Either way, you ain't going to shake her till she's good and ready to be shook."

Kane cursed long and low, shoved his chair back and stood up. "Let's get out of here." He threw down a twenty-dollar bill, and they walked out of the cool dimly lit room into a searing, humid afternoon. Julie was about to flag down a taxi when Kane stopped him, informing him he needed to pick up some dress shirts.

The two men returned to Shasta's house hours later laden with boxes and bags. Julius, finding himself amid the elegance of Sakowitz, talked a reluctant Kane into helping him choose a dress for Shasta. After the first show of distaste, Kane plunged into the world of silks, chiffons and sequins. Julius, pushed aside in favor of Kane's European taste, could only stand back and think of the hell this little shopping expedition was going to cause. If Shasta ever found out—he gulped—the fur was going to fly.

AS THE SKY GLOWED with a scarlet sunset, Shasta pulled up to a red light and stopped. Picking up the mobile phone mounted on the dashboard, she punched out her home number. Busy! For the past two hours she'd received the same signal and wondered who Kane was talking to. The light changed, and she shifted gears with a grinding noise that expressed her mood. At least, she thought, she now knew that Kane and Julie were home. Turning down her street, she gunned the deadly little car into her driveway and squealed to a stop. Flinging the door open, she was out of the car and through the back door in a shot. "Where the hell was everybody today?"

Standing at the kitchen sink peeling shrimp and arranging them artfully around an iced bowl, Julius waved her to silence. He pointed to the living room, explaining that Kane was on the phone, then proceeded to tell her about their day—omitting the shopping spree and the fact that three new day dresses and four evening dresses now hung half hidden in her closet, not to mention the shoes and accessories he'd tucked away.

"Who's he been on the telephone with for so long?"

"I ain't got the foggiest idea, but it's not just one person. He has his little black book open."

"Black book indeed!" She snorted in disgust. "Julie, where's that satin thing Rena gave me last Christmas?" She stormed out of the kitchen and headed for the stairs, Julie right behind her.

He grabbed her arm to stop her. "Shasta Masterson, never tell me you're going to wear that to dinner?"

Her eyes were filled with determination as she met Julie's scandalized gaze. "Fight fire with fire," she quoted one of his famous sayings. "Julie, I'll be damned if he's going to make dates and have me follow them along as his bodyguard. If Kane Stone goes anywhere, it's me he'll take."

Julius studied her for a long second. "If you're serious about this, then for heaven's sake wear the robe that goes with it." He frowned furiously, showing his disapproval in every stiff line of his body as he turned and walked away. But as the kitchen door closed behind him, he cackled out in gleeful joy and rubbed his hands together. Baskerville trotted in from outside, his nose busy following his mistress's trail. Julius smiled and patted the dog's head. "You best stay out of the living room tonight, beast, cause Shasta Masterson is about to meet her match."

Upstairs, water splashed onto a tiled floor as Shasta angrily finished her bath. She quickly dried off, dabbed Joy everywhere a pulse beat and some places it didn't. There would be no repeat of last night, but she would keep his interest high just in case he had other ideas. She held out a delicate porcelain-pink floor-length slip before her. Without further thought she slipped it over her head and stood before the full-length mirror. Her fingers touched the pale gray lace that barely veiled the tops of her nipples then dived to a plunging vee. She picked up the matching wrap robe, trying to arrange its folds to cover her slinky outline. But the clinging material only seemed to add emphasis to her slim, shapely body. A woman could get herself into real trouble in an item like this, she conceded warily, then wondered at her sanity in wearing it for Kane. Swallowing her nervousness, she quickly ran a brush through her tangle of soft loose curls, slid her feet into pink high-heeled slippers, hiked up her gown to her knees and marched out the door and down the stairs.

Shasta stood in the living room, her heart skipping a beat as she watched Kane's eyes lift at her entrance. With pure pleasure she observed the heavy droop of his eyelids as his conversation broke off in midsentence. She had definitely made an impression.

"I'll call you back, Boston." He hung up, then stood, his gaze glued to the petite vision gliding across the room toward him.

Shasta lowered her voice to a husky whisper. "Would you fix me one of those?" She tapped the rim of his crystal glass, which was still suspended halfway to his mouth.

With a jolt, Kane came to full attention. His mouth tightened. "What game are you playing now? After last night I'd have thought you would—"

"No game, Kane," she interrupted. "I just wanted to get into something more comfortable before dinner." Her cheeks flushed at the lie and the look in his eyes, and she hoped the dim lighting covered her uneasiness. She followed him slowly to the bar and leaned her elbows on the hard counter, affording Kane a tempting view.

"You know, Shasta, you can't ignore talking about last night or pretend it never happened just because it didn't go the way you wanted. And, goddamn it, if you don't straighten up I'll take you here and now on the floor."

Shasta jerked upright, then stepped back as Kane reached across the counter, a paring knife in his hand. She watched as fascinated as a bird before a cobra as he snipped off something from her sleeve then handed it to her. Shasta looked down to find a price tag lying across her palm and her eyebrows rose at the figures stamped on it. "Rena's totally out of her mind paying this for a few pieces of fabric stitched together," she mumbled, turning to Kane, her eyes glistening with laughter. "Should I leave and come in again?"

"No, mouse," Kane said with a chuckle. "You've done enough damage to my libido for one night." He guided her to a chair, handed her a martini, then plopped a boiled shrimp in her mouth before she could think of a comeback.

"I wish you wouldn't call me mouse." She scowled at him. "I've had to deal with nicknames all my life. I hate them, really I do, Kane."

"Sorry, but this one you'll have to get used to."

"It's not very complimentary."

"To me it is."

She leaned back in her chair and sipped her drink. "Did you have a nice restful day? How are your ribs, by the way?"

Kane grinned. "My ribs are fine, thank you, and you know I went downtown today."

"Why?"

Still standing beside her chair, Kane leaned down and gave her lips a hard kiss. "What an inquisitive little hardhead you are," he murmured, and was saved from further questions by Julie's timely arrival announcing dinner.

Through mushroom bisque to lobster thermidor, Shasta kept him totally fascinated with her chatter, regaling him with stories of Jeff's computer genius and Rena's new troubles with Lizzie. He was completely captivated and genuinely surprised when Julie placed a large wedge of chocolate-chip cheesecake and a cup of coffee before him. And he, who didn't care for lobster, now ruefully remembered he'd cleaned his plate, never realizing what he'd eaten.

"Who were you talking to on the telephone for so long?" Shasta watched the curtain fall across his features. Why, she wondered, did she have the feeling that those phone calls had something to do with her, and she didn't think they were full of goodwill.

Kane took a bite of cheesecake, his hard gaze fixed on her puzzled expression. "The calls were to some old friends letting them know I was in town. By the way, bodyguard, I hope you're free all night because I'm going to be renewing some friendships."

"What about the men following you?"

"What about them? I guess they'll have some long hours, now won't they?"

SHASTA WOKE in the middle of the night to the feel of a cold wet nose nudging her bare arm. A soft persistent whine penetrated her sleep-fogged mind. She opened one eye and stared at Baskerville. He whined again, then bumped her arm, his toenails clicking urgently on the hardwood floor.

"What's the matter, boy?"

Baskerville growled this time, his feet working like pistons even though he remained in the same position. Shasta threw back the covers, yanked open the bedside drawer and pulled out her gun. She flipped off the safety and checked the clip to make sure the gun was sufficiently loaded. Baskerville might be a clown with a drinking problem, but he was also a trained guard dog and every inch of him was screaming trouble. This was no stray cat or dog intruding into his territory, but a human he didn't know.

Her adrenaline pumping, Shasta ran down the stairs and was at the back door in a flash. She slid the lock aside, eased the door partway open and motioned the now-bristling dog to be quiet as she listened. When no unfamiliar sounds were forthcoming, she studied Baskerville's aggressive stance. "You're sure, boy?"

A low angry growl answered her whispered question. Then she heard the noise and froze, her body still as the night as the first faint sounds of someone tampering with her locked back gate reached her. Baskerville tried to push her away from the door, but Shasta again waved him away. "Let's wait till they're all the way in so..." She trailed off, her heart pounding with excitement as she heard the squeak of a rusty hinge.

Counting slowly to ten, she opened the door wide and gave Baskerville the silent hand order to attack. One hundred eighty pounds of killer bounded soundlessly out the door. Unlike some guard dogs, Baskerville was more menacing because he was trained never to let his victim hear him. An intruder would turn on stealthy feet and find himself staring into a snarling face that nightmares were born of.

Shasta brought her gun up to the ready position in both hands, ready to step outside and follow Baskerville before he tore his captive apart. Suddenly her perfect night vision was blinded by the brilliant blooming of the overhead light. She blinked and spun around, her temper rising as she spotted Kane standing in the kitchen doorway, his hand suspended on the light switch. Confusion reigned as a scream, growls and loud cursing flooded the backyard. Kane sprinted across the room, making a grab for the gun.

In a quick reflex motion, Shasta chopped his hand down and out of the way. "What do you think you're doing?" she yelled as they collided into each other. She didn't wait for an answer as Baskerville, caught off guard by the commotion in the house and his master's angry voice, gave a loud yelp.

Tangled in Kane's arms, Shasta squirmed to be free, and without thinking she elbowed him in the side, delighting at his grunt of pain. But he held her struggling body till Baskerville came charging up the steps, eyeing Kane and growling deep in his throat, his jaws still clamped around a strip of a man's pant leg.

"You damn fool woman!" Kane let her go and stepped back, shaking his numbed hand up and down. "I wonder why I'm forever leaving myself unprepared for your tricks? You'd think I'd have learned by now, wouldn't you?"

Shasta glared up at him as she knelt to check Baskerville. "I don't have anything to say to you right now," she ground out between clenched teeth. Baskerville yelped as Shasta found and touched a large lump on the top of his head. She wrapped her arms around his thick neck and talked baby talk to him while he whined even more pitifully for sympathy. "See what you and your Machiavellian secrets have done. Baskerville has a knot on his head the size of a baseball, and our burglar got away." She pushed Kane out of the way and yanked open the refrigerator door as Baskerville whined even louder.

"Damn it, Shasta—"

"Don't talk to me. Not yet—not till I've calmed down. Of all the macho, stupid, asinine . . . the nerve of rushing me when I have a loaded gun in my hand. I would have thought with your training you'd have known better."

She didn't notice Kane's steely expression or the shutter that seemed to fall in place over his eyes. Retrieving a bottle of beer, she tucked the cold container under her arm and pulled out a handful of ice cubes. Baskerville, spying the beloved brown bottle, moaned and limped slowly after her. "You faker, it's your head that's hurt, not your leg." She yanked out a dish towel from a drawer, dumped the ice in the center and rolled it up. Opening the beer, she knelt down in front of her dog and tied the towel around his massive head, positioning the ice on the swelling knot. Baskerville sat patiently as she completed her task, his tongue hanging out in greedy anticipation.

Shasta poured his beer, gave him another hug and picked up the strip of torn pants, inspecting it closely before she pitched it into the trash. She faced Kane and frowned, furious all over again at this interference. "Why can't you let me handle things my way?"

"God only knows!" Kane declared coldly. "You've proved you don't need my help."

Shasta pulled out a chair and sat down. "Kane, this has gone on long enough. You're going to have to tell me who's after you and why."

"No, and after tonight I think I'd better go to a hotel." He joined her at the table.

Shasta's stomach twisted at the thought of his leaving, and her gaze traveled over the broad shoulders under the smooth material of his robe. She wished she had handled last night's fiasco better, realizing now that she had cut off her nose to spite her own face. She was the one missing his touch. Cold and unemotional as she had accused him of being, she could still enjoy being held in the warmth of his arms. He was looking at her with amusement, and she tried to bring her thoughts back to the present.

"Will leaving here stop whoever is after you?" She scowled at him fiercely, and his lips twitched involuntarily. "I'm your bodyguard whether you like it or not. You can leave my house right now, but it won't change things or solve the problem. If I have to, Kane, I'll just set up a twenty-four-hour surveillance. Besides," she said, grinning, "you seem to be so protective of me now, just think what you'll feel knowing that I'm sitting on some dark street—alone—watching you."

Kane sighed in defeat. "You are without a doubt the most hardheaded woman I've ever had the misfortune to meet."

"Yes, I know." She folded her hands over one of his. "Kane, it's time you told me what's happening and how dangerous it's going to be."

Kane pulled his hand free and brought her palm to his lips. "This is not a case of the more you know the safer you'll be, mouse. Those men out there want something they think I have.

But more important, I want something I know they have, and I intend to get it. So, if your mind is made up and you insist on following me around—okay. Just don't interfere in what I'm doing." He kissed the other palm, but his features had taken on that inscrutable, passive look again. He laid her hands down gently on the table, shoved his chair back and stood. "You'd better get all the sleep you can, because if you plan to keep up with me, you'll only have a speaking acquaintance with your bedroom."

Shasta bit her lip as the sardonic glint in his eyes returned. After all, she reassured herself, what harm could a few nights out on the town do? At least she'd be with him.

CHAPTER SEVEN

WHAT HARM could a few nights out on the town do? Shasta wondered tiredly how long ago she had asked herself that question. Weeks, months ago? She felt as if she'd passed a year of sleepless nights, endless traveling and parties; a never-ending stream of smiling faces. And always they would return to Houston so she could be at work bright and early.

She pulled up the low-cut bodice of her strapless, black taffeta gown and frowned. Her closet seemed to have sprouted evening dresses lately, a development she'd have to check into when she had the time. She sighed and slumped in her chair, then straightened abruptly as she caught Kane's mocking gaze across the table. It had taken her a couple of days to finally figure out what he was up to, and when she did, her determination to keep up the pace he had set increased. She gave him a challenging smile. If he thought by dragging her all over the country he could tire her into quitting....

Shooting Kane another enigmatic look, she pointed her nose in the air and gazed around the smoky room filled with people in Valentino gowns flashing twelve-carat diamonds. They all looked blissfully ignorant of life and eternally young.

Where was she? Shasta's eyes glazed over as she tried to remember. There had been so many clubs, restaurants and private parties over the past two weeks that she'd lost all track of time and place. "Dallas," she mumbled out loud, and a self-satisfied smile lifted one corner of her mouth. The Rio Room—a chic, *very* private club. She wasn't as confused as she'd imagined.

Leaning back, Shasta eyed the voluptuous redhead hanging on Kane's every word. She'd been pushed aside more times than she'd like to count. Women seemed to take root on Kane's arm. After days of trying to deal with her jealousy, a jealousy Kane spotted and played on, she soon realized that he was only paying lip service to their attentions. Kane was too busy watching *her* and sending out scowling looks to warn any interested males that she was private property and to keep their hands off.

Shasta shifted position, eased her sore feet from her shoes and picked up a glass of champagne, pretending to take a sip. Her gaze roamed the room, picking out familiar faces. Wealthy leeches, her grandfather called them, people he had little patience or time for, though he and the Masterson family could match most of them monetarily. But J.T. separated the two classes, the working rich and the parasites with eight-figure quarterly incomes from inheritances or oil royalties. Shasta shivered to think what he was going to say when he learned of her activities these past two weeks. She closed her eyes wearily and pressed her hands over her aching stomach.

Each night was a marathon in travel and food as Kane dragged her on his jaunts. Was it yesterday or last week, she wondered, that she had flown to New York in Texas-American's company jet? There Kane had hired a caravan of limousines outfitted with bars stocked with iced champagne. Their party had arrived at a white Georgian house with a black lacquer door. A private restaurant, Le Club had a regular clientele that included politicians, socialites, Wall Street turks and Hollywood sheiks.

When was it she had walked New Orleans French Quarter in the early-morning mist, breakfasted at Brennan's, lunched standing up at the long white marble bar of Acme Oyster Bar and dined that evening at the most romantic place in town, the Court of Two Sisters? *Sunday,* Shasta recalled. She had been in New Orleans on Sunday, and after a day spent in revelry she had managed to talk Kane and his friends into sitting still long enough for her to savor café au lait and hot beignets, those puffy squares of fried pastry covered with powdered sugar that New Orleans was famous for.

Shasta's stomach rebelled at the thought of food, and she dug around in her purse for another antacid tablet. She'd dined like a queen on lobster from Maine, fresh salmon from Alaska, raw oysters from the Texas Gulf, stone crabs from Florida and caviar from Russia. Her palate was well traveled; she only wished her insides would settle on firm ground.

"Are you ready to leave?"

Kane's whispered question jolted her out of her thoughts and she looked up, her eyelids heavy with fatigue. He molded her evening wrap to her shoulders and, with his arm around her waist, guided her out into the night.

Shasta inhaled deeply of the bracing air, but instead of reviving, she slumped tiredly against Kane as he led her to the waiting limousine. Before she realized it, she was comfortably secured in Kane's arms and snuggling her head against his chest. When they switched to the small jet, she nestled into his warm body and began to play lazily with the pearl studs of his ruffled tuxedo shirt. "I'm so tired I could sleep for a year."

"I know. We'll be home in about forty-five minutes."

Shasta opened her sleepy lids and looked out the round window to see the sun's brilliant colors streak the horizon in a burnt-orange glow. "I'll have about two hours before I have to dress again and go to work," she murmured. "Thank heaven I'll be through with the Thomas case today." She closed her eyes and thought about the job. Thomas Jewelers were being systematically robbed of their precious diamonds. The thefts were so cleverly committed that it had taken them four months to realize what was happening before they had called in Masters. Shasta almost chuckled out loud as she recalled the ingeniousness of the eighteen-year-old runner, a close friend of the owners, who hand delivered loose diamonds from one branch store to the other. Somewhere along the way he would stop, heat the wax seal and open the package, help himself to two or three stones and replace them with high-quality fakes. He'd then reseal the package and reharden the wax with ice.

It had taken Shasta and two of her co-workers weeks to figure out his scheme and then confront him before calling the police. Between tying up the case and Kane's marathon partying, she was exhausted.

Shasta cuddled closer to Kane and tilted her head back into the crook of his arm. "Now that I'm free, I'll be able to catch up on my sleep during the day like you've been doing." Her fingers picked a stud loose and dropped it into his breast pocket before going on to the next one. "You know, of course, that your plan is not working? I'm not giving up."

Kane's answering grin sent her blood pumping through her veins. With deft hands he quickly worked out the pins holding her hair in place. After a few seconds the floor lay strewed with the tiny pieces of metal as his hands began massaging her scalp. "I think I'll have to concede this round to you, my mouse."

"Good! Then you're not going to try to turn me into one of those women who cling to you with adoring eyes?"

Kane snorted at the thought.

"Do you truly call those people your friends, Kane? They live such a useless existence."

"So do I, Shasta."

She dropped another stud into his pocket, letting her fingers play for a brief second on the soft hair on his chest. "Do you?" Suddenly fed up with the game they were playing with each other, she began to tell him what Jeff had found out, and as she talked she felt his body go taut at each new piece of information. The more she talked, the angrier she became with his continued silence, and she began telling him things she'd never planned to, though she did have enough wits to refrain from mentioning the murder of Melvin Kimble.

Kane cursed long and vigorously. "Your brother doesn't fool around. How in the hell did he get this information?"

Shasta dropped another stud into his pocket, then slipped both hands into the opening of his shirt, loving the feel of his warm flesh beneath her hands.

Kane clasped her wrist hard and pulled her resisting hands from his body. "Back off, Shasta."

His command came out slow and precise, his accent more pronounced than she'd ever heard it. Shasta straightened slightly in his lap, realizing for the first time that Kane was magnificently drunk, that the sensuous indolence and dissipation she'd witnessed over the past two weeks was controlled drunkenness, as if that was the only way he could endure the mindless chatter and boredom of his so-called friends. As she moved away, Kane grabbed her hips and pulled her back down, making her conscious of the growing hardness beneath her thigh.

"I asked how Jeff obtained all this material about me?"

"Computers and codes. I told you Masters had access to files very few are privy to." Kane's hand glided to her shoulders, and the tips of his fingers played like a soft breath along the tops of her breasts. She stared into his heavy lidded eyes and shook her head. "No. You're not human enough yet."

Kane threw his head back and laughed disbelievingly. "Mouse, you must be numb from the waist down."

Shasta knew with the wrong word or action he would lose control, and she'd be on the receiving end of his temper. She snuggled against his chest. "Tell me about your childhood—your mother and father."

Kane laughed again, but this time the sound under her ear was harsh and grating. "I never had a childhood, ma chérie. From the cradle I was being groomed to take over Tex-Am Oil. I grew up watching mother and Max yelling and fighting. Max wanted me in the business, and because he did, mother didn't. So they each, in their own way, used me as a pawn in their power plays. The funny thing is, I think I would have liked to have learned the family business and even taken it over someday. But I saw very early Max's obsession and knew he would only let go when he was in his grave. As for mother, she's just another vain woman afraid of growing old and losing her looks." Kane was quiet for a long minute.

"Who's Melvin Kimble?" She slipped the question in softly and waited. Only his even breathing met her ears, and she realized he'd fallen sound asleep.

AT FIVE TO EIGHT the next morning, Shasta straightened the pile of papers on her desk, rubbed her gritty eyes, then closed the folder of the finished Thomas report. Unable to sleep once she and Kane arrived home, she had jumped into a cold shower and headed for the quiet of the office to complete her work. Now she'd be able to give her full attention to Kane's troubles, whether he wanted her to or not.

"Hello there. You're here bright and early." Rena grinned at her from the doorway. "Want another cup of coffee?"

"Sure, and come join me, Rena, I want to ask you a question."

Shasta waited until her sister-in-law was seated, then asked, "Rena, have you ever regretted throwing over your English duke and running off with Jeff? I mean, did you truly know Jeff was the love of your life? Could you feel it in your bones?"

Rena started to make one of her witty remarks, then stopped as she saw the pain in Shasta's eyes. "Oh, dear. You've got it bad, haven't you?" Shasta nodded. "What about Kane?"

"I don't know." She looked down at her hands. How could she explain the feeling she had? Maybe she was more like her family than she'd thought. "You're going to think this is nuts, but I feel it here." She tapped her heart. "Kane *has* to love me. He just refuses to admit it." She propped her elbows on the desk top. "I'm in limbo. I don't know if I should wait or force the issue. Even though he doesn't think so, he *is* capable of love and tenderness." She shook her head and closed her eyes. "He's a stubborn man, and it's probably going to take a lifetime to bring him around. Any ideas?"

"Not offhand, but give me some time and I'll come up with something." They both fell into a thoughtful silence shattered by Jeff's entrance.

"Ah, ladies, gossiping on office time again, for shame." His neat appearance after weeks of disorder was in its own way a warning. He had exhausted every avenue in his part of the investigation and would now wait for new instructions. In the meantime he'd spend every spare second with Rena and Lizzie. He folded his long frame down beside his wife and pitched a thick folder on Shasta's desk.

"That's the rest of Kane Stone's report." He peered closer at his sister and remarked cheerfully, "You look like death warmed over. Why don't you take the rest of the day off and get some rest?"

Shasta fingered the fat file. "Summarize what's new here, *please,* Jeff."

Jeff was momentarily diverted by his wife's smile. "Oh, yeah... There's nothing more on Kane, though I sure would like to find out about those blank three years. I checked to see if anything earthshaking was going on in our government during that time and could come up with one item—a CIA operation involving a defected Russian laser scientist. There was a big stink over it, though. It seems our man lost him somewhere in Europe and they sent in a special agent to find him and bring him home." Jeff shrugged. "You know me!" He grinned sheepishly. "I got interested and started to check the file for more information when I was cut off, and not more than five minutes later, J.T. called raising hell. I stepped on someone's toes and they immediately informed J.T." Jeff shuddered. "I then had to explain the entire Stone case."

Shasta groaned in sympathy, knowing how thorough her grandfather could be. "Did you find out anything on this Kimble character?"

"Funny you should ask." Jeff wiggled his eyebrows in a poor imitation of Julie. "You know how strange we thought it was when Julie told us that Kane kept going downtown? Though he always ended up at Tex-Am Oil's office building, he usually made several trips by U.S.A. Oil. Well, sister dear, Professor Melvin Kimble was once employed by U.S.A. Oil in their research department. He'd been with them ten years, then suddenly one day just up and quit. And, get this, the next day he went to work for Max Stone at Tex-Am Oil." Jeff held up his hand to stop the spate of words he saw forming on Shasta's lips. "Wait. You have to hear the rest. Max Stone hustled Kimble to France and there, sister dear, we come to a dead end. It seems the professor dropped out of sight, and nothing's turned up about him until his murder in Barbizon, France, some weeks ago."

Shasta stared at her brother, her mouth hanging open. "Oil, Jeff! This is all about oil!" Her excitement dissipated, and she pressed her fingertips to her temples. "Oh, hell and damnation! I can't think straight I'm so tired. But somewhere I know there's a clue that ties all this information together." She dropped her hands and opened her eyes. "I'm going home to take a long nap, then, maybe, I can figure this out."

"Not yet, you won't," Margret said from her position by the door.

Shasta grinned. J.T.'s watchdog had slipped in unnoticed and overheard every detail.

"There's a Mr. Harold Winsome here to see you." Shasta flipped the pages of her appointment book frantically.

"No, you won't find his name there, but he says it's urgent." Margret stood aside as Jeff and Rena left the office, then closed the door. "He's vice-president of security at U.S.A. Oil!"

Shasta swallowed hard. Things were moving too fast, and her mind wasn't clear enough to handle it all.

"Coincidence, do you think?"

"I doubt it. Meg, have you talked to pappy?"

"This morning, and he has a message for you—'tread lightly.'" She smiled at Shasta's grimace. "Do you want me to send in Mr. Winsome?"

"Yes." Shasta closed her eyes again and sighed. "I don't know much else that could happen to surprise me in this case."

SHASTA GRIPPED the steering wheel of her car so hard her knuckles whitened. Her words to Margret had been the understatement of the year! Of all the nerve! No, it was bald-faced gall, that's what it was. That slick Mr. Winsome in his three-piece pin-striped suit, that smooth-talking snake who had just slithered into her office and... and... Shasta gritted her teeth together. This was all Kane's fault, she thought grimly.

She wheeled the Porsche into the driveway, slammed the door and marched in the back door. She passed Julie without a word and stomped into the living room. There she stopped, hands on hips, surveying the scene before her with angry eyes. Kane lay stretched out on her couch, a magazine covering his face as he caught up on his sleep and recovered from his hangover. And to make bad matters worse, her faithful dog lay curled up on the end of the couch, a place he knew meant severe punishment—no beer!

"I hope you're satisfied," she yelled, and both man and dog jumped as if they'd been shot. "I have just been propositioned, offered a bribe, had my professional integrity smeared, called a liar, threatened, been accused of harboring a murderer, referred to as 'toots' by the lowest form of life, and it's all your fault."

Kane blinked and Baskerville eased off the couch and half crawled, half ran from the room. "But, mouse..."

"Don't you dare 'mouse' me," she yelled again. "This mess you're in is over some stupid synthetic-fuel formula."

Kane was off the couch and gripping her shoulders almost before the last words left her mouth. "What do you know about the formula?" he demanded.

"I know you have it, and U.S.A. Oil is willing to pay any price or do anything to gain possession. Kane, you're hurting me." She'd finally cracked the feelings he'd kept so well hidden. His usually reckless expression had been replaced by one that was cunning and dangerous. She rubbed her arms and sat down.

"I had a visit from a Harry Winsome a while ago. He offered Masters a contract to handle their worldwide security. I politely refused his offer, explaining that there would be a conflict of interest as we already represented one oil company. He then proceeded to drop not so subtle hints and insinuations of bribery. When I continued to say no, he began to get a little testy. The snake in the grass then offered me a personal bribe of an amount that took my breath away." Shasta glared at Kane. "All that was required of me was to obtain a synthetic-fuel formula now in your possession. I hadn't the faintest idea what he was talking about and told him so. That's when he got nasty, and Jeff escorted him from my office—"

Shasta paused to let the impact of her next words carry their full weight. "He said that Masters could be charged as an accessory in harboring the murderer of Melvin Kimble." She jumped up and shouted, "You, Kane," then began to pace the floor, her temper rising rapidly as she watched his smile turn into laughter.

"So, the weasels are getting nervous, are they?"

Shasta stopped, his question hitting her like a blow. "You bastard. You've been using all of us as pawns." She thumped her head with the heel of her hand. "The trips downtown, the lack of concern at being followed, the visits to Tex-Am Oil. You deliberately led them in circles while you concocted your devious plans. Damn you."

"Now, Shasta, calm down."

"Calm down? I'll calm down when you tell me what's going on and what you're up to? Well?" she demanded.

Kane was at her side in two strides, his hands caressing her arms, his voice husky with sincerity. "Will you trust me, Shasta?"

"No! Are you out of your mind? Why should I?" She tried to shrug off his hands.

"I can't tell you...."

"Hah."

"Everything right now." His eyes captured hers and she quickly glanced away. "I didn't kill the professor, Shasta. You know that, don't you?" She nodded, still not looking at him. "Trust me?"

"No. Not without a good reason. Besides, Kane," she wailed, "why won't you let me help you?"

Kane sighed. "Because these men play for keeps. Masters is top in its field, I'll grant you that, Shasta. But in all this time have you realized that we're not only being followed by people for U.S.A. Oil but by the government, as well. No, you didn't know because they're the best. And while the oil people were willing to let us fly all over and simply wait for us to return, the government men were with us every second. They never missed a city or a restaurant or a party."

Stunned, Shasta sat down and stared at Kane. "Are they after the synthetic-fuel formula, too?"

"Yes."

"Are you going to give it to them?"

"No."

"Why? They are our government men, aren't they?"

"Yes, and you needn't get that excited look. They won't make a move—not yet. Not till they see what U.S.A. Oil and I are up to. If we try to make a deal they may step in. Right now they're merely our watchdogs." He reached out, captured Shasta's stubborn chin and forced her face to his. "Shasta, the less you know about the formula, the better off you'll be."

"You do have it, don't you?" She sat back, her mind working furiously over the advantages of such a discovery. "Does it work, Kane? There've been so many different attempts."

Kane sat down across from her and picked up her hands. "It works. Better than anyone could ever imagine. But it's dangerous, Shasta." He studied her puzzled expression, then went on. "The Saudis are violently against our research. Our government would like nothing better than to have a blade to hold over the necks of the oil-producing nations. The oil companies here would like to see it destroyed. Remember that the Saudis stopped us from stockpiling oil with a firm warning. Our coal-conversation program is wildly optimistic and so is the shale extraction. The idea of synthetic fuel is more than a savings for the consumers, it has worldwide implications. But all this is not the issue here. There's already been one murder over the formula, there could be others."

"That's what I don't understand, Kane. Why kill the goose that laid the golden egg?"

"Shasta," he said scornfully. "No oil company in their right mind wants a cheap alternative to oil. That would cause a catastrophic financial disaster that would only end in bankruptcy for them. What would you do if you were wealthy beyond imagination, greedy, ruthless, and someone you couldn't buy came along and threatened your very existence?" Kane shook his head at Shasta's blank expression. "No, you couldn't contemplate murder, but there are men—and governments—who could and do."

"If what you say about the big oil companies not wanting a synthetic fuel on the market is true, then why would your father invest so much time and money in the formula's development?"

"Because what few people know is that Tex-Am Oil is in bad shape, the result of poor investments, the lowering of oil prices, cutbacks and, of course, the economic decline. Also, remember that Tex-Am is primarily a family-owned corporation without the heavy cash flow of U.S.A. Oil. Max is becoming a desperate man and will grab at any chance of recouping his losses. So he jumped at the idea of newfound wealth and power. He set up the research lab with his own money, thinking he'd discovered a way out of his problems. Now, one person is dead, and I intend to find the man responsible!"

Shasta's breath hissed through her compressed lips in horror. "You've set yourself up as bait, haven't you? Whatever it is you want, you're going to trade the formula." She jumped up and began to pace back and forth. "You can't do it."

"Shasta. Shasta!" He matched her steps for a few seconds, then laughed. "Will you stop that? It's not as bad as it sounds." She opened her mouth to contradict him, but he placed his fingers across her lips. "You're tired. Why don't you go up and rest before we go out tonight."

"And that's another thing, Kane Stone. I'm tired of being dragged all over the country and sick to death of your worthless, boring, corrupt, malicious friends."

"We're not going out of town."

"They drink too much—"

"We're going to a gallery showing."

"They're shallow and vain and sick."

"Samantha Grey."

Kane smiled as she stopped her tirade and gazed up at him, delight shining in her big eyes. He should never have come here. Every second he spent in her company he was courting danger. She'd become his Lorelei and the warmth and comfort of her home his island. She was luring him to disaster, he knew, but her small, funny face had become so dear he couldn't bear to leave just yet. Kane tossed aside his wayward thoughts. "Boston called the other day to let me know about the show."

"Boston?"

"Really, Shasta, for someone who says that Samantha is her favorite artist, you show a shocking lack of knowledge about her. Boston Grey—Samantha's husband."

"The singer Boston Grey?"

Kane grinned at the typical female reaction to Boston's name. "One and the same." He took her elbow and firmly walked her out of the living room.

They both stopped as Julie and Baskerville scrambled up from their listening positions on the bottom step. Kane frowned. Shasta sighed and said dismissingly, "You can't have any secrets around here. I don't know why I even try."

She disengaged her arm from Kane's and turned to him. "I'm not through with this formula business yet, you know. It's just that I'm too tired to argue with you and need some time to think of a plan." She poked the center of his chest with a finger. "I don't want you to think you're going to run this scam on your own." She tried valiantly to look severe, but her sparkling eyes gave away her excitement. "Besides, I don't think it's fair that you have all the fun."

SHASTA STARED into the mirror of her vanity, batted her eyelashes and grinned. Turning her head sideways, she critically studied her makeup job and nodded, pleased with what a little sleep and a persistent hand could achieve. She checked the temperature of the heat rollers adorning her head and wondered what other women did to pass the time while their curlers cooled down. "Becoming gorgeous is such a boring job," she said to her reflection, and waited as if she expected an answer.

When a deep masculine voice said, "Yes, but it's worth every second," Shasta screamed and spun around on the stool.

Kane, as elegant as ever, sauntered over and set a frosted glass of white wine before her. "You'd better hurry, Shasta. Boston wanted us to be there early." One finger hooked itself under the fallen strap of her cream satin teddy and slowly pulled it back on her shoulder. Kane leaned down to give her a quick kiss.

But Shasta had other ideas, and her arms slipped around his neck, her tongue invading his mouth. Then, pulling away, she turned back to the mirror and lifted her eyes to his. "I do believe you're beginning to become human. Mind you, my job is not nearly completed, but we're making headway." She began to absently undo the spiky rollers, her attention still on Kane.

"Here, let me help or we'll be all night." He contemplated the job at hand for a second, then started where Shasta should have, at the neckline working upward.

Enjoying the novelty of having the man she loved working on her hair, Shasta sat calmly, eyes closed. "You're very good at this. Have you done it before? Ouch! I take that back, you're terrible. Ouch!"

Kane chuckled, playfully slapping her hands away, and continued pulling on her hair till all the rollers had spilled onto the vanity table or rolled across the floor. "This is a first." He toyed with the soft fat curls, loving the feel of the silken strands slipping through his fingers. "Hand me your brush."

Shasta frowned at his reflection. "I put those jumbo rollers in for a reason. If you go and brush my hair to death it'll only spring back into curls. Go away. You're making me nervous."

He leaned forward, his breath tickling the back of her neck. "How nervous?" His warm lips moved behind her ear, and his hands slid from her arms to gently cover her breasts. "This nervous?" He placed tiny kisses in the curve of her shoulder. "Or this nervous?"

"Kane, I thought you said we were in a hurry?"

He threw up his hands in surrender and stepped back as she meticulously ran the brush through her hair, pushing it this way and that before she gave up.

She realized that Kane was beginning to change, whether he ever admitted it or not. There was a peacefulness about him that hadn't been there a week ago. "Are you going to just stand there and watch me dress?" she asked.

"I thought you might need some help." His eyes twinkled teasingly, and Shasta caught her breath. "You know, things like a stubborn zipper, a snap you can't reach, or assistance with your gun and shoulder holster, which I'm sure you're determined to wear."

Shasta giggled as she walked over to her bed and picked up the apple-red chiffon dress lying there. Kane's smile widened as she wiggled into it. "No, I intended carrying my weapon in my evening bag. It would ruin the line of the outfit." She picked up the sequined bolero jacket, slipped it on, then stepped into her shoes. "I don't know what possessed Julie to buy red. He knows I've never cared for this shade." She studied her reflection a long moment, still unsure. "What do you think?" She spun around, the wisp of fabric clinging to her body like a caress. "Do I look like a flashing traffic light?"

Kane's lips twitched. "No, the color looks great on you. And by the way, Julie didn't pick out this little number. I did." Shasta's mouth fell open. "You might be shocked, but not as much as I was to find myself in the woman's clothing department, thoroughly enjoying myself."

"You picked this out?"

"That, and a couple of others." He thought it prudent to say nothing about the other items he'd selected for her. She'd find out about them soon enough. "Julie said you didn't have any taste." He watched the bright color flush her cheeks and rephrased his statement. "I mean, he explained that you didn't have the time to shop."

"I'll kill him. I swear I'll wring his scrawny neck."

Kane laughed and grabbed her by the shoulders, hugging her close. "Don't be angry, Shasta. I did have a good time, and besides, it's not criminal to be lacking in fashion knowledge." Her body stiffened in his arms. Still smiling, he let her go, picked up her evening bag and took her arm. "Come on, if you arrive at the art gallery with that fierce frown on your face,

Samantha will think you don't like her paintings, and we don't want to upset Samantha—at least not right now."

"Why?"

"You'll see," he replied enigmatically, and marched her out the door.

CHAPTER EIGHT

THE HUNTER ART GALLERY, perched on the edge of the wealthy side of River Oaks, was teeming with art patrons and people with fat wallets. Shasta had expected a lavish elegance to the gallery and was surprised at the starkness of the decor. Then she realized that the white walls and subdued lights were designed to show off the art to advantage, enhancing the mood of each painting and high-lighting every detail. Someone jostled her shoulder, and Kane wrapped a protective arm around her waist, steering her through the swarm of people.

As soon as she saw Samantha, Shasta immediately knew what Kane had meant about not unsettling her. Samantha Grey was a tall, beautiful woman with a shocking shade of poppy-red hair and freckles, who appeared to be about ten months pregnant.

Kane guided Shasta through the crowd, smiling and nodding to acquaintances, but never slowing until they reached their goal. "Samantha, you look wonderful, but what's happened to Boston? He looks about two steps from the grave!" Kane held the pregnant woman at arm's length and studied her mischievous smile and twinkling aquamarine eyes. "Ah, I see, you're driving the poor man crazy."

"Of course."

Kane gently relaxed his hold on Samantha, shook hands with Boston, then introduced Shasta, who felt like a butterfly pinned to a board for inspection. Then everyone spoke at once, stopped and laughed.

"Boston," said Samantha, "why don't you take Kane and show him the painting I did for him?" As she watched the two men walk away, she commented to Shasta, "They're a devastating sight together, aren't they? I bet the blood pressure in this room has risen considerably and hearts are pumping overtime."

They were indeed a sight for any woman to behold. Walking dreams, Shasta thought. Both men were of equal height and had that incredible blue-black hair. But Kane's shoulders were broad, whereas Boston's possessed a more wiry physique, a whipcord leanness. There was also the difference in their eyes, one pair as dark as midnight and the other as light as the silvery moon. As the men strolled casually among the throngs of people, Shasta saw the stares that followed them and sighed. "Even my heart is pounding ninety to nothing."

"Kane always takes me by surprise every time I see him," said Samantha. "He's the most beautiful man I've ever seen, yet he's remained so totally masculine."

Shasta's grin widened. "I know, but it's extremely hard on my ego. Do you have any idea what it's like to walk into a restaurant and have him get all the admiring looks and gasps—from *both* sexes?"

Samantha laughed hard, her hands holding the huge mound in front of her. At Shasta's concerned look she smiled and took hold of her arm. "Let's go find a place to sit so I can rest my back, and you can tell me everything about you and Kane."

If any other woman, with the exception of Rena, had commandeered her in such a way, Shasta would have bristled with resentment, but from the second she met Samantha she felt an instant rapport, an awareness of comradeship. And most of all there was that lovely twinkle in her aquamarine eyes that tickled Shasta's fancy. Here was another woman who saw the funnier side of life and men. They were no sooner seated than Boston and Kane were beside them. Kane passed Shasta a glass of champagne and rested his hands lightly on her shoulders as he watched Boston fuss around his wife.

Exasperated, Samantha drew Boston's attention to Shasta. "Did Kane tell you that Shasta is his bodyguard?"

Boston grinned. "Honey, I'm told that all you need is red hair and you'd be Samantha's counterpart. Heaven knows that another like her would be more than the male population could stand."

Shasta wondered if Boston's words were an insult or a compliment.

"Go away, both of you," Samantha ordered. "Surely you can put yourselves to better use than standing here. Go sweet-talk some of those gawking women into decreasing the balance of their checkbooks."

Kane kissed Shasta on the forehead, flipped down her skirt, which had twisted over one knee, and grabbed a reluctant Boston, leading him away.

"We'll never get to talk with all these people around, so I asked Kane earlier if the two of you would come over for coffee afterward." Samantha frowned up at Boston. "What are you doing back?" She tried to sound fierce, but Shasta could see that she was thrilled at the attention Boston showered on her.

"I just wanted to tell Shasta that if you needed anything to signal one of your brothers to fetch it." He looked at Shasta. "I don't want her getting up and down or walking all over the place."

Shasta nodded, and Boston gave Samantha a look that only husbands and wives understand before she, too, nodded in agreement.

"Who are your brothers?" Shasta's question was met first with blank surprise, then the two people staring at her broke into broad grins.

"Take a good look around," Boston told her, "and every time you spot an outlandish color of red hair you'll know. Samantha has six brothers and they're all here." He lovingly patted his wife on the back and left.

Shasta watched him go. She remembered all the times she'd seen him on television or lay listening to his records, fantasizing about her own dream man. She shook away her wishful thoughts. "He's very worried about you, Samantha. Is this your first?"

Samantha patted her stomach. "No. We have a two-year-old daughter named Rebecca, who looks just like her father. The reason Boston's so protective is that he's scared to death this time. But I'll tell you all that later. What I want to know is, did you really knock Kane out and tie him up at your first meeting?"

Shasta sipped her wine, refusing to meet Samantha's probing look, but when she finally raised her head, her eyes were filled with laughter. "He told you that?"

"He's told us everything about you, Shasta. Which is surprising in itself for a man as closemouthed as Kane. Though—" Samantha's searching gaze found Kane in the crowd "—I must admit I've never seen him quite so relaxed and animated before...even when he comes to the ranch." She stopped, realizing Shasta wasn't familiar with her and Boston's home. "We have a ranch out from Santa Fe, New Mexico," she explained, "and when we're in Houston we always stay at Kane's house." She saw Shasta's puzzled expression. "You did know Kane inherited his grandfather's house in River Oaks?"

"No, that's another little secret he's managed to keep from me."

"Oh, Kane's full of secrets, Shasta. Boston's known him for years. They've played around the world together, fought together, and still Boston says there's a part of Kane that remains private. I think it has a lot to do with his childhood and the fighting that went on between his mother and father. But Boston says no, that it's more to do with whatever it is Kane does." Samantha chuckled. "Heaven knows I've tried to find out, but it's useless."

They were interrupted by a steady stream of people congratulating Samantha, and by the time the well-wishers had left, Shasta spotted Kane and Boston making their way toward them.

"Now I wonder what they've been up to?" Samantha mused out loud.

"What do you mean?"

"Shasta, I know my husband like an open book, and his expression is entirely too innocent and angelic *not* to set off warning bells. If you know Kane at all, just take a look at his face and you'll know they've been up to no-good."

Indeed, Kane's expression was suspect. His smile was, too, and his eyes were darker than usual. Shasta searched his face more closely as he walked toward her, then dropped her gaze, frisking him with her eyes. Nothing!

"Don't ask questions," Kane whispered in her ear, his fingers biting into her arm as he hauled her up. "Sammy, I'm going to steal Shasta away for a minute and show her *my* painting." He gave a stubborn Shasta a nudge. "Walk."

Out of hearing distance Shasta asked, "Where have you been and what have you done?" She ground the question out between unmoving lips.

"Boston and I cornered one of the government agents following us and invited him outside to join us in a cigarette."

"You don't smoke." She glanced up and fought back laughter at his guileless expression. "And just how did you convince him to join you two? I'll bet he didn't come willingly."

"Well, no, not at first, but Boston and I convinced him it would be to his benefit to do so. Here's the painting Sammy did for me. What do you think?"

It took Shasta a minute to focus her thoughts on the painting, and when she finally did, she nearly choked on her champagne. The large oil painting depicted an Indian brave astride his horse, a blanket draped around him to protect him from the driving fury of a snowstorm, while his squaw held onto the tail of the horse and waded through deep drifts. "It's a beautiful painting, but sadly typical of man's behavior toward women. I suppose you told her exactly what you wanted?"

Kane chuckled as he guided her on to the next painting. "No, as a matter of fact, Samantha did it for me as a constant reminder that we're in the twentieth century."

"Quit changing the subject, Kane Stone. I want to know what the agent said." She tried to pull free of his hold, but Kane only tightened his grip.

"Now here's an interesting painting."

They circled the gallery, studying each work of art. Samantha's portrayal of the plight of the American Indian was beautiful but heartbreaking. Shasta wondered if the people who bought her paintings truly appreciated the passion behind each brush stroke. She sensed the rage and sorrow Samantha felt for the Indians and instinctively knew that it wasn't only Boston's Indian heritage that made her paintings so vivid but a real interest in the future of the first Americans.

Someone bumped her shoulder hard from behind, and Shasta took a quick step forward to regain her balance. As she turned to confront her clumsy assailant, she found an older woman gushing over Kane, asking about mutual friends and the painting he'd been studying. But the woman's interest wasn't in art. Her eyes devoured Kane with a greediness that both amused and revolted Shasta. She had to give him credit, though; when he wanted to snub someone he did it with finesse, and she smiled at the woman's stunned expression as he guided her away.

"One of your old loves, Kane?" she needled when he returned. Her question caught him as he took a sip of champagne, and he almost choked.

Kane took a firm grip on her elbow, but Shasta dug in her heels and forced him to look at her. Her small face was set in the stubborn expression he was becoming well acquainted with. He sighed theatrically and waited.

"Well! What did you ask the agent and what did he have to say? Come on, Kane, give."

"Not now, mouse, he's following us." She swore under her breath, and Kane shook her arm at the words he was hearing. He hugged her stiff body close to his side and bent down to whisper, "I wanted to find out which branch of the government we're dealing with. He's with the FBI. Now, does that appease your curiosity for a while? I'll tell you more later."

Shasta grudgingly nodded, her interest in his words reduced as his breath continued to tickle her ear. Teasing devil! He knew exactly what he was doing. "If you'll excuse me," she said, "I think I'll go talk to Samantha." With that she twirled away, leaving Kane to stare after her, his lips twitching and his silver eyes sparkling as he followed the swish of her hips.

Boston offered Shasta his chair beside Samantha, and as soon as he left, Samantha asked, "Are you going to tell me what's going on, or are you going to try and protect my delicate condition with lies?"

Shasta leaned her head back against the chair and began to giggle. She looked at Samantha and replied, "I'm sorry, Sammy, but I really can't tell you." Samantha's eyes sparked, and Shasta saw the anger building. "Client confidentiality, professional ethics! Honestly, Sammy." She held up her hands defensively. "I'm on a job. If Kane wants to tell you, that's all right, then we could talk about it, but otherwise I can't."

The disbelief and anger slipped away, and Samantha's smile returned. "I guess I'll take your word. It's just going to take me longer to get the story out of Kane and Boston than I'd like. But, make no mistake, I'll find out."

They were interrupted as Samantha accepted more congratulations from well-wishers, and Shasta searched the diminishing crowd for Kane. When she found him, she wished she hadn't. Two vibrant brunettes were hanging on either arm, raptly listening to his every word. She wondered how she would ever be able to deal with the beauties he seemed to attract.

"Shasta, Shasta!"

The repetition of her name and the jab of Samantha's elbow jarred her from her jealous thoughts.

"I want you to meet some friends of mine." She began to introduce them. "JoBeth Huntley, Lucas DeSalva and. . . ."

"Brandon DeSalva," the handsome blue-eyed man finished. "We're well acquainted with Shasta, Sammy." Both brothers turned to the women with all their Texan and Spanish charm.

"Hello, pixie, how's the security business?" Lucas asked, his rugged features lighting with pleasure.

Samantha's head swiveled from the grinning men to Shasta and back again before demanding, "Explain, please."

Shasta turned to Samantha but was interrupted by the arrival of Kane and Boston. Over the commotion of renewed friendships and introductions, Shasta whispered to Samantha, "Masters handles the security for DeSalva's, and we also lease two floors of the DeSalva building."

After the arrival of the DeSalva brothers, the gallery began to clear out more swiftly. The two men bought one painting after another, leaving only those previously sold or on loan for exhibition from their owners.

Any interest Kane might have had in his adoring brunettes dwindled when he overheard Brandon invite Shasta for a drink.

"Sorry, but we have other plans." He guided her swiftly away, explaining as they left the gallery, "Boston and Samantha have already gone, and I told them we would be right behind them."

Shasta inhaled deeply of the cool night air. Then she groaned, remembering the long two blocks they had to walk to the car.

"I told you to wear lower heels." Kane helped her over the high curb. In the area where the gallery was located, the streets were narrow and without sidewalks.

Shasta intertwined her fingers with Kane's as they set off down the street. "Want to tell me what else the agent had to say?" She tried to make out his expression, but the dimly lit street afforded little help. Shaking her hand free of his, she stepped in front of him and, walking backward, asked, "Does the darkness make you deaf, or are you trying to think up a good lie?" Kane gave a bark of laughter as she retired, panting, to his other side and valiantly tried to keep up with his long stride.

"Get out of the street." Kane tried to catch her arm, but she danced away, taunting him with a shapely thigh as the breeze lifted her skirt. "He said they were only ordered to observe and not interfere. They're playing their own game of wait and see, Shasta. Now get back here before someone runs over you."

As if Kane's words had conjured up a phantom, a car came careering out of the darkness like a locomotive. The headlights caught Shasta in a blinding glare, and for a moment she froze, like a startled deer before the fatal shot is fired. She didn't have time to scream a warning. As her mind cleared she dived for Kane, frantically thinking that the car would swerve toward him. And Kane, in the space of a heartbeat, extended his arms and grabbed Shasta. They collided, each trying to save the other. One of Shasta's high heels snapped and she fell to her knee, tearing the flesh on the pavement, and still the headlights bore down on them. Frantically Kane swung Shasta up against him and lunged over the high curb as the car roared by.

Tires squealed around a corner in the now-quiet night. Kane held Shasta to his chest, his heart hammering painfully against his ribs. "Bastards." He repeated the word several times as his eyes, dark and full of menace, followed the car's retreat. "Are you all right?"

Shasta mumbled against his shirtfront, shook her head free of his smothering hold and laughed. "Looks to me like you pushed too far and they shoved back."

Kane stared speechless into her dark-brown eyes. They flashed with excitement and an invitation he refused to pass up. "You're crazy, mouse. But, then, so am I." His cold lips touched hers, lightly at first, then he gathered her closer into the warmth of his arms, his mouth taking and giving, adding to the thrill of the night. Lowering her to the ground, he felt her flinch in pain. "What's the matter?"

"I scraped my knee when I fell."

Kane grabbed the torn shreds of her skirt and inspected her leg. He swallowed hard, scooped her up into his arms and took off toward the car.

"Kane, put me down. It's just a skinned knee."

"For once, Shasta, shut up and let me handle this."

She judged his temper and decided it prudent to let him have his way—this time. Before she realized how fast he could take control of a situation she was in the car and they were pulling up at a sprawling two-story, rose-brick colonial house in the center of River Oaks. Once again she was picked up, and Kane sprinted to the door.

"Ring the bell, mouse."

"Mr. Kane!" The butler's narrow face blanched with shock.

"Jones, where are Boston and Samantha?" He didn't wait for an answer but strode toward the living room with the almost soundless footsteps of the butler right behind them.

"Mr. Kane, they've brought that woman with them again. I told you the last time—"

"Not now, Jones. Please, just get me some hot water."

Shasta peered over Kane's shoulder as the ancient butler gave them a murderous glance. "Who's 'that woman?'" she inquired.

"What? Oh, Pearl is Boston's housekeeper, cook—I don't know what you'd call her. For heaven's sake, Shasta, quit asking me questions."

"Yes, dear." She received her second killing glance of the night.

Shasta was dumped on the couch, and amid concerned questions from Boston and Samantha, she leaned back and enjoyed the attention for a change.

Samantha dismissed Kane's orders and pulled up Shasta's torn skirt.

"I keep trying to tell him it's just a scrape, but he won't listen."

"It's a little worse than a scrape, Shasta. Boston, would you fix this up. I don't think Kane's capable right now."

Three pairs of eyes studied Kane's whitening features as he stared at Shasta's knee. Samantha took his arm, turned him around and led him quietly from the room.

"Well, there goes my hero!" Shasta laughed, her eyes twinkling as Boston accepted the first-aid kit and a bowl of steaming water from the haughty Jones. "Who would have thought the sight of a little blood would turn his stomach?"

Boston snipped away the leg of her panty hose below her thigh. "He's seen far worse than this, honey. I guess it's like what happened to me." He began to clean the area and Shasta hissed at the sting. "There are a lot of accidents on a ranch, and Kane and I've set our share of broken bones and doctored some nasty cuts. But not so long ago Samantha dropped a knife and sliced open the top of her foot." Boston sprayed on antiseptic, and Shasta clenched the arms of the chair. He looked up from his task, his jet-black eyes flashing with humor. "When I saw what she'd done and all that blood, I fainted—flat out on the floor. Here, hold this." He placed a large gauze pad over the wounded area and cut strips of tape. His next question took Shasta by surprise. "You know Kane's in love with you?"

Her face lit up with a bright smile. "I hope so. He's...."

Boston held up his hand, interrupting her. "He hasn't realized it yet, and when he does I think you're going to have a real fight on your hands. There." Boston positioned her foot on the low coffee table and began picking up the bits and pieces of paper he'd dropped. "I don't know how you two are going to work out your lives." He shook his head. "Believe me there are going to be difficulties. Kane's not used to answering to anyone. He's had only himself to think of, and now you've come along and complicated everything." Rocking back on his heels, he smiled at her. "He won't thank you, and don't ever say I didn't try and warn you." Boston gave her a brotherly pat on her thigh. "Now, rest that leg awhile."

"Did you really pass out?" she asked skeptically.

"Like a light."

Shasta looked at the famous singer and thought of the millions of women who would feel faint at the sight of him or the sound of his deep velvet voice, and she began to laugh.

"What's the joke?" Samantha stood aside as Boston tried to pass through the doorway.

"No joke. I was telling Shasta about the time I fainted when you cut your foot." He patted her large stomach. "Sit down, honey, you've been on your feet too long today. I'll be back in a minute. I want to have a talk with Kane."

Samantha kissed her husband, then eased her weight down on the couch beside Shasta with a weary sigh.

"Are you okay?"

"Now don't you start." Samantha rubbed her stomach. "They're just overactive tonight."

"They!" Shasta stared at Samantha's cat-and-cream smile.

"Kane didn't tell you? I'm surprised. He's done nothing but tease us since we found out. You're sure he didn't tell you?" Shasta shook her head. "There are two babies here, maybe more." Samantha laughed. "You can close your mouth. It's true."

"More than two?"

"Maybe."

Shasta spotted a bottle of Grand Marnier on the bar and hopped over, helping herself to a generous amount. "Maybe more?" she asked in awe as she sat back down.

Samantha's smile sparkled with anticipation. "That's the reason Boston's jittery and acting strange. Half the time he's so excited he can't sit still, and the other half he's so scared he can barely breathe." She settled back, folding her hands over her swollen abdomen. "Did you know Boston was an orphan? No? Well, he's always wanted a large family. Sometimes I think the only reason he married me was to be one of our clan." She was quiet for a long moment, her expression peaceful. "We planned the birth of Rebecca carefully, right down to the last second. Boston was there in the delivery room all ready to see his first child born." Samantha's face softened, then she chuckled. "I guess it got a little gruesome, because all I remember is that suddenly he was lying passed out on the floor. Now that I think of it, he got more attention from the nurses than I did. Anyway, this time he swore he'd be okay. Of course that was before we found out this was going to be more than one baby. Now he's about to jump out of his skin."

"Is it dangerous—multiple births, I mean?" Shasta asked, feeling a fool at her ignorance.

"I try not to think of the problems," Samantha said stoutly, but there was concern in the depths of her eyes. "How maudlin we're getting. What I wanted to ask you was if you'd go shopping with me tomorrow?"

"Should you?"

Samantha gave Shasta an exasperated look. "I'm not a total fool—though everyone seems to think just because I'm pregnant I've lost my senses. I'm well aware of my limitations. Besides, I'm dying to buy some new clothes for afterward, when I'm slim and trim again."

Shasta was torn between her loathing for shopping and her desire to help Samantha. Samantha won out. "I'd love to go."

"Liar!" Kane contradicted from the doorway. "You hate shopping with a passion. Hell, Sammy, she has a man named Julie buy all her clothes."

"Kane—"

"I even got hooked into one of his buying sprees and was hauled all over Sakowitz's."

"Kane—"

"She has without a doubt the worst taste in fashions I've ever seen."

"Kane Stone, you shut your mouth."

Boston and Samantha were laughing. Then Boston's expression changed and he frowned at his wife. "Sparky, I'm sorry, but I don't want you being seen with Shasta right now."

There was a gasp, and the room fell into an uneasy silence before Samantha spoke out. "What a terrible thing to say! You apologize to Shasta this minute, Boston." She struggled to get up, but gravity, weight and volume combined to make her efforts comical. "Well, don't just stand there laughing like a couple of idiots. Help me up, gentlemen—and I use the word loosely."

"Samantha. . . ." Shasta bit her lip to keep her voice steady. "Sammy, Boston's right. Kane's troubles have flowed over to me now." She gave Kane a speaking glance. "If I'm right, the men following Kane believe I'm important enough to be used against him. I've yet to get him to tell me everything, though that's going to change as of tonight. But from what happened this evening I'd say they've decided to escalate their plans and will use any lever they can." Samantha's unladylike snort brought a twitch to the corner of Shasta's mouth. "A pregnant woman would be an ideal target for use as a weapon against Kane."

"Well...." Samantha's lower lip protruded farther than usual as she stared pleadingly at her husband. "You'll tell me what's going on, won't you? You know how mysteries upset me." She turned her gaze back to Shasta and Kane. "Have you called the police yet?"

"No!" Both Kane and Shasta spoke in unison, but it was Kane who explained. "Samantha, there are too many people involved in this already. If the local police are called, there's a chance some nosy reporter will pick up on it and we'll really be in a hell of a mess. Besides, we've already had to call in the police about the break-in at my father's house."

Samantha was about to argue, but Kane held up his hand to stop her. "What could we tell them? We're sure it was the same blue car that's been following us, but we couldn't swear to it—everything happened so damn fast. We were too busy trying to get out of their path to take note of the license number. As for them parking outside Shasta's house and trailing us everywhere..." Kane shook his head. "There's no law against parking on the street or following someone as long as personal contact is not made and no verbal insult is given."

Samantha frowned. "Just what sort of trouble are you in, and what do you mean there are too many people involved already?" Kane's mouth tightened stubbornly. "Damn, can't you tell me something—anything? This whole business is unsettling me, and you know I'm not supposed to be upset in my condition." She realized her ploy hadn't worked as she glanced at the closed faces around the room. Samantha's bottom lip trembled a little.

Boston looked helplessly at Kane, who only shrugged. "She's your wife. You're on your own." Quickly scooping Shasta up into his arms before she could protest, he headed toward the door. "I'll call you tomorrow, Boston."

Boston opened the front door, and both men carefully eyed the empty street. "Yeah, do that, then I'll know nothing happened to the two of you on the way home." Shasta and Kane were halfway down the steps when he called out, "Take care of him, Shasta."

Shasta snuggled her head into Kane's shoulder and smiled. Oh, she intended to take very good care of him.

CHAPTER NINE

THE DRIVE TO Shasta's house was accomplished in a companionable silence, though Kane thought he could feel the sharp edge of censure in the air. "I think you should start wearing your gun from now on."

"Yes," she agreed, and the word hung heavily in the cool confines of the car.

Kane gazed at the woman beside him. She might be small, but she had the heart of a lion. "We need to discuss a plan of action."

Shasta halted her wandering thoughts and shifted her position in the seat so she could watch Kane. "I hope you're not going to try and persuade me to quit this time?"

"No, that would be pointless, wouldn't it? You're in this as deep as I am." Kane stopped at the red light, his mind's eye seeing again the headlights of the car rushing toward Shasta. He saw her startled expression, then her leap as she dived for him in an effort to push him out of danger. He swallowed hard. If he hadn't been alert, and if Shasta had been a larger woman, she would have accomplished her task and more than likely been killed in the process.

Kane felt the tightness in his chest increase to a steady ache. He'd been deluding himself all the while. He realized now that he'd never had any intentions of getting rid of her, and his two weeks of partying had been a challenge to see if she could keep up with the fast pace of his life-style. The light changed, and he drove on, his thoughts a turmoil. What had happened to him? Was he going through some stage? Surely thirty-seven was too young for a midlife crisis. But no matter where his thoughts led, they kept returning to a picture of Shasta as she leaped to save his life. The tight hand in his chest squeezed harder, and Kane sucked in a sharp breath as another thought rushed at him. He needed her! But he was damned if he understood why. For one thing, she was playing games with him, and he'd never allowed a woman to get the upper hand.

Kane shifted his weight and nervously drummed his fingers against the steering wheel as he tried to figure it all out. Hell, he'd enjoyed watching her try her tricks on him. He reveled in her sparkling smile and her big brown eyes so deceptively innocent. He found himself waiting for her tinkling laugh and a glimpse of her nose as it crinkled impishly. The feel of her skin, as soft as velvet; her small breasts round and firm; her hips so sweetly curved. Kane tried to apply the brakes to his thoughts, but they kept pounding at him for an answer. He wanted her now more than he'd ever wanted any woman, yet he was loathe to make the move. Afraid to...afraid! Why had that word popped out? He'd never been afraid of anything in his life. Certainly not a woman.

"Kane, you just passed my street!"

Cursing, Kane spun the wheel and made a U-turn. The car squealed around the corner and pulled into Shasta's driveway.

She watched him carefully as he got out and slammed the door. He was in a strange mood, and as yet she hadn't figured it out. He helped her out of the car, swung her body up into his arms and paused, as if waiting for her to make some remark. She smiled instead, gazing into the reflective mirror of his eyes, and was surprised to see confusion lurking in their depths. Tightening her grip around his neck, she kissed him long and lovingly.

"What was that for?" Kane whispered against her lips, his breath mingling with hers in a warm rush.

"For saving my life tonight." She kissed away the vehement denial she saw forming on his lips. "Yes, you did."

He carried her into the house, his thoughts a conflicting whirl. Baskerville met them at the back door and stretched his thick neck up. He sniffed Shasta's wounded knee and began a combination of whimpers and growls that set Kane's already ragged nerves crawling. He frowned down at the huge animal, who was glued close to his side, hampering his every step as he navigated with Shasta up the stairs. "What's wrong with him?"

Shasta buried her head in the curve of Kane's neck, her shoulders shaking.

"Shasta, make him stop!" Kane stood in the center of her bedroom trying to decide where to deposit his armful of giggling woman, while Baskerville continued to circle them, his strange cries getting louder.

"Baskerville, hush, I'm okay," she told him, but the big dog only sat in front of them, threw his massive head back and began to howl. "Put me down, Kane, or he'll never stop."

"What's wrong with him?" He refused to lower her till she reassured him that Baskerville wasn't going to go berserk and attack them both.

"He can't make up his mind whether to sympathize with me or give in to his jealousy and take a bite out of you."

"Me!" Kane gave her a look that spoke volumes regarding her pet's sanity.

"You're carrying me, and Baskerville doesn't approve."

"That's just too bad." Kane tightened his hold on Shasta and frowned fiercely down at her pet. "Traitor. Who's been slipping you food and beer? No more, Baskerville." Kane's voice was firm, and Baskerville, as though he fully understood, stopped midhowl. Kane lowered Shasta to the side of the bed, straightened up and rubbed the back of his neck. "You know, I think I'm going crazy. I find myself talking to that dog, and what scares me is I think he understands." Shasta flopped back across her bed and began to laugh again. "Good night, Shasta."

The door wasn't exactly slammed shut, but Shasta grinned at the solid bang it made. Kane was beginning to lose his cool exterior—chip by frozen chip. She eased off the bed and patted Baskerville, reassuring him she was going to live. "What do you think, old boy, are we ready to put plan number two into operation?" Baskerville showed his teeth in a sneer and stretched out on the rug beside her bed. "Don't be a spoil sport." She hobbled to the bathroom. "I intend keeping Kane around, so you'd better make up to him." She shut the door on another show of sharp, white teeth and curled lips.

An hour later Shasta lay between cool sheets, her hands behind her head as she planned her next maneuver. It was time Kane learned to relax and have some honest fun. Time, also, for him to face the fact that there was more to a relationship than sex, time to admit the truth of his emotions. There was a knock at the door and she called out, "Come in."

"I thought some warm brandy might relax you and ease the aches and pains away." He felt his stomach tighten at the inviting sight of her freshly scrubbed face and immediately regretted his good intentions. She seemed to have an invisible rope tied to him, and when she jerked, he jumped.

Shasta sat up and reached for the warm balloon glass filled with the fragrant liquor. "That was thoughtful. Thank you, Kane." She smiled, and his agitation slipped away.

"We need to talk." His voice sounded husky even to his own ears.

"Yes, we do." She patted the side of the bed and moved over.

"That's a dangerous position, Shasta. Can I trust you to behave?" He eyed her peach satin-and-lace nightgown hungrily.

Shasta returned his look in exactly the same way. Her eyes followed his bare legs up to the edge of his thigh-length robe, then slowly upward till she met his steady gaze. "I think I can control myself." She waited till he was propped comfortably against the pillows, then said, "I take it back, I can't control myself." She leaned over and whispered what she'd like to do, then watched, fascinated by the red that stained his cheeks.

When he could speak, Kane demanded, "Where did you hear such things—a nice Southern lady like you?" He was totally captivated by the combination of her fairy-tale innocence and wanton sensuality. Taking a hefty gulp of brandy, he let the liquor burn a path down his throat.

Shasta fluffed up her pillow and lay back, thrilled by her progress. She wondered how long it had been since he'd blushed at a naughty suggestion. "Have you decided what you're going to do? This standoff is beginning to be a bore."

There was a long thoughtful silence before Kane spoke. "U.S.A. Oil wants the fuel formula, and I want the murderer of Professor Kimble."

Shasta bolted upright from her lounging position. "You don't seriously think that if someone in U.S.A. Oil is responsible for Kimble's death they're going to come forward of their own free will, do you?"

"No. But I have a gut feeling. You see, *chérie,* I don't believe the murder was committed without the knowledge or orders of the owner of U.S.A. Oil." Kane's voice grew gruff. "I not only want the man driving the car, I want the man who ordered the murder."

"So?" she asked, still a little puzzled by his reasoning.

"If U.S.A. Oil turns over the killer in exchange for the formula, I'll know the upper echelon of the company was ignorant of the professor's death and that some ruthless vice-president went beyond his authority. But if there's no trade, then we'll know the orders came directly from the top—from Tramble Carter Baldwin, Jr., himself. And I want his skin."

The soft menace in his words sent a chill over Shasta's flesh. "If what you feel is true and there was an order to kill the professor, then there will be no trade and they will try to take the formula from you any way they can, right?"

"Right."

"They'll come after us then." Her eyes began to glow with excitement. "By the way, where is the formula, and why did the professor give it to you?" She met his stony stare and tried another approach. "The professor was more than just a friend, wasn't he?" Kane nodded, and she waited for him to go on, but he remained silent. She knew he hadn't truly faced his emotional attachment to the older man he'd spent so much time with. A great wave of pity for his inability to admit he was as human as the next person washed over her. She rolled over, positioned herself across his chest and gazed into his eyes. Reaching out a hand, she let her fingers lightly play up and down his cheek. "What happens now?" she whispered.

"We wait for them to make the next move."

"I wasn't referring to the goons."

"I gathered that. Shasta, don't." He captured her hand. "Stop these games before you get hurt. I want you, and if you keep this up I'll take you." The flesh tightened across his high cheekbones, and his mouth curved mockingly. "You needn't smile like that, either." He gathered her face in his hands and brought it close to his. "I've let you play because it amused me." One hand held her head secure while the other grasped her wrist and guided her hand downward to the hardness beneath his robe. "Tonight has been filled with tension and danger, and the edge is still there. Keep on and I'll take you whether you want me to or not."

Shasta knew he was telling the truth. She wasn't offended, knowing that in his own way Kane was being more honest about his emotions than he'd ever been. She realized that with another woman and under similar circumstances he would have done exactly as he said. But he cared enough for her to warn her. She touched his face with gentle fingers. "I love you, Kane."

She waited, her ears aching from the roar within. Then came the hiss of Kane's breath.

"Oh, no, mouse, don't," he whispered hoarsely. "Don't say that." He rested his forehead against hers for a brief second before he began to untangle himself from her hold. The covers became ropes binding him down. He kicked free and surged to his feet.

"Kane, loving someone is not a death sentence."

"You don't understand. I have to be free." He cleared his throat. "Besides, I'm too old for you."

Shasta stared up at him and began to laugh at his flimsy excuse.

"Ten years doesn't seem like much," he said, "and normally it's not." He retied his robe, straightened the lapels and looked directly into her eyes. "Shasta, I have a hell of a lot more miles on me than you could ever imagine, and they're miles you don't want to know about."

"I know more than you think, Kane. I—"

"No." He stopped her next words. "You know general facts about my life and a few supposed secrets, but you don't know some of the things I've done." Suddenly Kane couldn't breathe, and he turned to leave those sad brown eyes behind. He expected tears and recriminations, but only the sound of Baskerville's heavy breathing followed him to the door.

"You can't run forever from your feelings, Kane."

He stopped his hurried exit and looked back over his shoulder. "That's where you're wrong, Shasta. Unlike most people, I don't conform to rules or convention. I can run as far and as long as I please."

THE NIGHT SEEMED ENDLESS. Shasta twisted and turned till she finally gave in and swung her feet to the cold hardwood floor. Baskerville's head jerked up and he whimpered. "Go back to sleep, boy. I just need to think things out." She pulled the curtain back from the window, wrapped her arms around her body and sighed dejectedly at the sickle moon. Shadows moved back and forth on the street below as a gentle gulf breeze teased the tree limbs into a slow swaying motion.

Shasta rubbed her forehead, trying to find the relationship between her dreams and something Kane had said earlier. But each time she thought she had an answer, it would slip away, as elusive as her dreams. Mentally she reviewed their conversation, and still nothing came. She wished she could be free of this haunting...that was it! She grabbed the windowsill and squeezed hard to keep from yelling. Kane had said he needed to be *free,* and that was the problem. He thought that loving someone meant giving up his independence. Shasta smiled. If only she could make him see that she cherished her freedom, too, but that didn't keep her from loving him. Her eyes focused on the street below, and an impish grin began to grow. With a quick turn she was rummaging through her closet for a suitable outfit.

Ten minutes later, dressed in black shirt and jeans, Shasta slipped into Kane's room across the hall. She'd no sooner eased the door shut to keep Baskerville out when a hand clamped down on her shoulder. She jumped as if she'd been hit by lightning.

"What the hell are you doing sneaking in here in the middle of the night?"

Shasta shrugged off his hand and aimed the penlight into his face. "You're fast." She smiled up at him, watching the thunderclouds ride across his forehead. "How would you like me to show you a good time?" She wiggled her eyebrows suggestively.

Kane couldn't help grinning as he gazed into her flashing brown eyes. "Since you're dressed, I take it this adventure is to take place outside?"

"Right. Come here." She led him to the window, then paused before she pulled back the curtain. "If I let you in on *my* adventure, do you promise to follow my orders?" As her eyes adjusted to the darkness, she became aware of Kane's nudity, and her hand itched to reach out and touch his warm flesh. "What did you say?"

Kane snapped his fingers in front of her face. "Are you awake or sleepwalking?"

"Sorry, but I was distracted. Do you promise?"

"Yes."

"You'll do everything I say and not interfere?"

"I said yes, dammit."

"Good!" Kane's hand covered hers on the curtain. "Now. Get dressed in some dark clothes." She watched him like a voyeur in the dark, straining to see his every move and loving each shadowed hollow she could discern.

By the time she could put a leash on her thoughts, Kane was at her side. She pulled a small gun from the waistband of her jeans and handed it to him. "Tuck that away. I didn't have another shoulder holster." Without a word he did as he was ordered. "Ready?"

Kane grasped her arm before she could take another step. "Would you mind telling me the plan?"

"Our friends are back, but this time they're driving a gray car instead of the blue. I thought it might escalate things if we repaid their greetings earlier this evening."

"How?"

"Just follow my lead and back me up."

Kane held her at his side for a long moment, feeling the trembling tension in her muscles. She was like a thoroughbred before a race. Then he nodded his head and followed her, surprised to sense the same response in himself.

They slipped down the stairs, stopping only long enough in the kitchen for Shasta to call Julie, give him some orders, then convince Baskerville that his help wasn't needed. Once out of the house and in the darkness Kane was astounded at Shasta's catlike movements. She became a creature of the night as they eased from a crouching run to stand, breathing soundlessly, behind an old oak tree. She was one and the same with the darkness. As he followed in her wake, he realized for the first time that she was truly a professional. Till now he had tried to convince himself that she was only playing at work. But watching her move with all the professionalism of a trained warrior, he felt a sudden surge of fire running like molten quicksilver through his blood. Could he have met the female counterpart of himself? Or had he simply met his match? He brushed the thought away as absurd.

They squatted behind the bumper of the gray car and Shasta touched Kane's shoulder, motioning him to take the passenger side. She leaned sideways and whispered in his ear, "When you hear my voice, show yourself." He tapped her shoulder, signaling that he agreed, and they parted, crawling beneath the opened windows on either side of the car.

"Good evening, gentlemen," Shasta said conversationally. "Nice evening, isn't it?" The burly man in the driver's seat grunted in surprise, his hand sliding to his armpit as he turned his head and looked down the short but deadly barrel of Shasta's gun. "If I were you I'd place both hands on the steering wheel." The cold steel in her voice overrode any comments the man might have made. Kane ordered the other man to grab the dashboard. Guns were removed from their shoulder holsters, and Shasta clucked her tongue in mock disappointment. "Such fine weapons, a shame you've lost them." She stuffed the heavy gun into the waistband of her jeans. "When you explain how you were disarmed by a woman, you might tell your boss that he's made three mistakes so far. One in sending novices to do his dirty work, two in playing games with Mr. Stone here, and three—trying to run me down. Now, gentlemen, please strip!"

Kane chuckled from his side of the car as the two men blustered, then tried to reason, then began to beg. When Shasta didn't budge, but continued to glare at them menacingly, both men began rapidly shedding their clothing.

"Pitch everything in the back seat," Shasta ordered as she opened the car door. "Hand me the keys, please." The interior light flicked on, illuminating white pasty skin of the two men, but Shasta's eyes were trained on the clenched fist of the driver. "Don't even think it.... Now out!" She stepped back, affording the husky man plenty of room. When the two of them stood gleaming naked under the streetlamp, she pointed down the road. "Now, take a walk." She had to bite hard on her lip to keep from laughing at their appalled expressions. "Go on, get!"

They took off in a barefoot run down the center of the street, and Shasta sat down hard on the curb and began to giggle. She was soon joined by Kane, and they sat there following the men's retreat around a corner and out of sight.

"You little devil. I don't know when I've enjoyed myself more." Kane lay back on the damp grass and chuckled at the slender thread of a moon. Their laughter stopped at the sound of a siren in the distance. The high shrill came closer and Kane sat up. "You didn't."

"No, Julie did. I'll bet they have one hell of a time explaining to Tramble Baldwin this night's escapade, and how they were jailed for indecent exposure."

Kane wrapped an arm around Shasta's shoulder and pulled her close against his side. "You're one talented lady. But tell me something, Shasta. Why didn't you go into some form of law enforcement instead of working for Masters?"

"Originally that was my plan, but I was too small to meet the requirements of the police department, and when I talked to J.T. about the FBI or CIA, he marched me in front of a mirror and asked me if anyone would take this face seriously."

As he studied her disgusted expression, Kane had to agree with her grandfather. She was entirely too cute to look menacing, but the fact remained that she was an expert at what she did. Shasta was a confusing mixture of toughness, intelligence and femininity. Tonight she had showed him she was capable of entering his league. She had neatly turned the tables on him and proved she was more than just a pretty face. She was a woman who would be a buddy, friend and partner in adventure, as well as a lover. She'd played the game his way and on equal terms.

Shasta laid her head on his shoulder and looked up at him. "The night's still young. Why don't we make a surprise visit on these government men you say are lurking around every corner. Do you know where they are?"

Kane shook his head at her gutsy tenacity. "No, we will not interfere with their plans, and yes, I know where they are." He pointed down the street to a luxury recreation vehicle parked at the curb. "They're in there, and the week before they were in the telephone-repair truck at the other end of the street. The week before that they were in a city maintenance truck."

"But, Kane, that RV belongs to our neighbors the Parkers."

"Not now it doesn't." He stood, extended a hand and helped her up. "Our government borrowed it for the duration. We'd best get out of here before a police patrol car comes by. You might have pull at the department, but I bet we'd have some fast explaining to do as to why we're dressed like burglars and carrying an arsenal of weapons tucked in our jeans." He clamped her arm tightly as she stumbled along. "How's that knee?"

Limping beside him, she answered absently, "I'm fine, just a little stiff legged." Silently they moved down the sidewalk, their shadows cast before them from the streetlamp. Every step they took, their silhouetted images would lengthen and weave together on the cracked pavement. In an automatic reflex from her childhood, Shasta found herself avoiding the worn grooves in the cement. "Kane, are you still with the CIA?"

Unconsciously Kane fell into step with her, alternating the length of his stride to avoid the cracks. "Shasta, I haven't been connected with them since Vietnam."

"But, Jeff—"

"What your brother keeps digging up is something entirely different, and I'd advise him to stop playing gopher if I were you. He's liable to get caught in a cave-in."

"Then you do still work for some branch of the government?"

"You never give up do you? Yes! I sort of work for my country."

"How can you 'sort of work'?"

"Shasta...." He was out of breath, and the cracks in the pavement stretched farther and farther apart. He found himself helping Shasta over the distances too long for her shorter legs to cover. Stopping abruptly, he gazed up at what little moon there was and called out into the night, "I must be going insane! A thirty-seven-year-old man hopping along the sidewalk at two o'clock in the morning."

Shasta coughed back a giggle at his outraged expression. "Come on, Kane!" She grabbed his arm. "It's not as if I'm a total stranger. I do have government clearance. Who do you work for?"

Kane propped his shoulder against the rough trunk of an old pecan tree and sighed. "Okay, Shasta, you win. I do some work now and then for the WSA."

The light from the streetlamp shining through the thick foliage dappled his features in sinister-looking shadows. Something warned Shasta she was pushing too fast and hard, but the waiting she had endured over the past weeks had taken its toll. "What's the WSA and what do you do?"

Kane let the cool night air clear his head, pausing so long in the process that Shasta had to touch his arm to bring him back to the present. "The WSA is the World Security Agency—and the reason you've never heard of it is that that's the way the organizers prefer it. The WSA is international and works something like a combination of Interpol, the CIA and FBI. Except their investigations are more extensive and their restrictions aren't limited."

Shasta relaxed and joined him against the tree.

"I don't know if you realize it or not, Shasta, but wealthy, bored people can be the most corrupt in the world. Always greedy for new adventures, experiences and more money, they willingly become involved in many illegal activities. Because of my background and connections, the WSA approached me after Vietnam and asked me to help them."

He turned to face her in the darkness, his silver eyes shining eerily as a beam of light reflected off them. "You'd be surprised how foolish people can be. Because they're on some practically deserted balcony at St. Moritz or at a Chilean resort they feel free to conduct their business openly, foolishly discounting the fact that the man at the next table could be a threat, because he's one of their set." Kane jammed his hands into the pockets of his jeans and hunched his shoulders. "I resent those people making more money and getting cheap thrills off the weakness and misery of others. So I listen and report what I've heard and seen."

"Kane, wouldn't WSA help you or ask the FBI to step in and investigate what's going on here?"

Kane's mouth curved into a sour smile. "You're being naive. Besides, I tried that route and was told this is not a WSA concern. As for the WSA asking the FBI for help—" Kane chuckled humorlessly "—that would expose me as an agent of the WSA." He saw her question coming and headed it off. "Yes, they know who I am and who I work for, but an open admission is not done except in high-priority cases. And you know very well that our government agencies do not necessarily share information. Trades are made, favors are granted, but when they both happen to be working on the same case they can be amazingly closemouthed. Stupid, I know, but there is a professional jealousy and fear of exposing too much and endangering their sources or having leaks to the press." He closed his eyes and inhaled deeply of the moist night air. "The WSA suits my purpose. The way they operate they don't have all that government red tape and bureaucracy to wade through." He opened his eyes and smiled down at Shasta. "As I said, I just have to keep my eyes open and stay alert."

"But you do more than just listen and report, don't you?" Shasta asked softly, hoping her question wouldn't distract him and bring a halt to his openness.

"Sometimes," he said absently, then gave a harsh bark of laughter. "Would you believe that I've heard people openly discussing drug drops—times and places, Shasta? They sit there as bold as brass and talk about how their yacht will meet a certain ship and pick up their merchandise. They work out the details of rendezvous to retrieve works of art they've purchased illegally. And sometimes, just sometimes, you come across a few diplomats who are stupid enough to get caught in blackmail traps and are set up to leak vital information. Those civil servants are not all from the United States, either. There's a whole network out there that passes along secrets about military installations, government satellite movements, defection attempts and a multitude of other top-secret information. It's incredible!" He felt Shasta shiver beside him and pushed away from the tree. "Let's go in, it's getting chilly." He wrapped his arm around her shoulders and guided her across the lawn, so lost in his own thoughts that he didn't notice Shasta's silence.

Shasta was quiet, her mind furiously going over everything he'd told her. When she stumbled and he pulled her tighter to his side, she still made no comment. There was something in what he'd told her, or maybe his tone of voice, that set off bells of caution in her head. The old tingle in her spine was back, warning her that she'd stumbled onto a piece of a puzzle, but she couldn't totally connect it with what she knew. Whatever it was, she felt it was important and knew sooner or later it would come to her.

A haughty, rejected Baskerville met them at the door and lumbered at a reserved distance behind them as they climbed the stairs. "About earlier, Shasta." Kane stopped before her bedroom and clasped her shoulders lightly. "If I hurt you I'm sorry, but I think in the long run you'll see that falling in love with me would be complete folly on your part."

"Would it, Kane? I don't think so. Besides, there's not a whole lot you can do but accept it, because I'm already in love." Reaching up on tiptoe, she kissed his cheek, then slipped into her room, closing the door on his worried expression. She leaned back and sighed. It was a shame that he could see only decadence in himself. He had suppressed his compassionate side for so long he almost believed in his own image. Tomorrow, she thought, she would begin her lessons and make him admit he was worth salvaging and that he could love. Her plan, she realized, was underhanded, but she intended using his own weapons against him.

CHAPTER TEN

AT NINE O'CLOCK the next morning Shasta hung up the phone for the third time. She felt as if she'd had her ear plastered to the instrument for an eternity, talking and making plans as if her life depended on it. She refilled her coffee cup and took a hardy gulp of the hot brew, closing her eyes as the heat soothed her hoarse throat. Never in her entire life had she spent so much energy in talking, placating and downright begging. Looking across the kitchen, she checked the clock nervously, wondering what was keeping Kane, Julie and Baskerville. They'd set out more than two hours ago for their morning jog and should have been back by now.

The sound of distant, distinctive barking sent Shasta into immediate action. She pulled her chair around parallel to the table, thumped her elbow down on the writing pad, leaned back in a relaxed pose, crossed one leg over the other and began to swing a once-white tennis shoe back and forth. When the kitchen door flew open to admit three sweating, puffing males, she quickly took a generous bite of Julie's prize sweet rolls, waving her welcome as she slowly chewed.

"I thought I hid those," Julius wheezed, grabbing for the coveted rolls. But he wasn't fast enough, and Shasta encircled the plate with her arms. He flopped down in the nearest chair, Baskerville dropped with an exhausted grunt to the cool kitchen floor, and Kane casually poured himself a cup of coffee. Julius snatched up Shasta's half-empty glass of orange juice and gulped it down. "I'm too old to try and keep up with them two." He banged the glass down and glared at Shasta. "You sure J.T. ain't called and ordered me to get my tired bones back to Dallas?"

Shasta swallowed and shook her head, keeping her eyes glued to Julie's face. It wasn't concern for the older man that made her watch him so closely. She normally ran three miles a day, and he always paced her step for step. The fact was, she had had only a glimpse of Kane but figured that was enough for any red-blooded American woman to have at nine in the morning. She prided herself on her iron control. She wasn't going to gawk at him as if she'd never seen a male in jogging shorts. But her eyes slid toward the tall man against her will, drinking in the long, bare sweat-slick limbs. Her dark pupils dilated as she took in the brief shorts and wide expanse of naked chest. All the while the little voice in her head laughingly mocked her sound reasoning of the previous night. Hadn't she promised herself that she would handle her plans in a dignified manner and not fall apart like a drooling teenager at the sight of him? Shasta stuffed another big bite of sweet roll in her mouth and dragged her eyes from Kane's too-knowing gaze.

"I think I'll go shower." Kane set his cup down, but instead of leaving immediately, he squatted before Shasta and pulled her swinging foot to a stop. He tied the hanging shoelaces, checked the other shoe and retied its laces. "You're going to kill yourself one of these days." Without further comment he straightened and quietly left the room.

"You keep looking at him like you want to take a bite. Pretty soon he's going to start feeling for the missing pieces," Julius said, waving his hand before her eyes when she didn't respond. "Come on, kid. I ain't got all day. What have you been up to this morning? And you needn't turn them big browns on me. It ain't gonna work."

Shasta sighed as she shook the lingering vision of a firm male derriere from her thoughts. "I talked to Jeff." She reached for another roll and got her hand slapped for her efforts.

"You've had enough. Save some for Kane." Julius flipped off the towel from around his neck and buried his face in it, wiping away the last beads of moisture rolling down his cheeks. Shasta snatched a roll from the plate and took a bite, smiling at his reproving frown as he emerged from the towel.

"Don't come crying to me when you add three pounds to your backside."

"Julie." Shasta's expression turned serious. "Jeff's been driving me crazy about those three blank years in Kane's past. He's got this absurd notion that Kane's some superspy and has linked together a wild story about a Russian defector." Once again she felt a tingling along her spine as she related Jeff's questions to Julie. "He said you and J.T. could tell us more."

Julius rubbed the towel through his damp gray hair. "Damned if I know what Jeff's spouting off about, but then he ain't all there, either. Russian defector?" He shook his head again, his brow furrowed in concentration. "Wait a sec—" He tapped his temple repeatedly as if the gesture would hammer out the information. "A couple of years back, J.T. and I met one of his army cronies. Seems this here general was in intelligence after the war, and as the evening lengthened and the drinks came faster and stronger the general developed loose lips." Julie grinned and scratched his ear. "There wasn't any love lost between the CIA and Army Intelligence, and the general found it real funny to tell tales on his old adversary."

"The story, Julie," Shasta reminded him impatiently.

"Yeah, yeah. Hold your horse, miss. This old brain ain't what it used to be, and I got to think it out clear like." He was quiet for so long that Shasta wondered if he'd gone to sleep with his eyes open. Then he snapped his fingers with a loud crack that brought a growling Baskerville to all fours. "Stupid mutt. I remember now. All the kick up was about a Russian defector, some highfalutin scientist—did something with light."

"Lasers?" Shasta asked excitedly.

"Yeah. The CIA got him out of his country and as far as Lucerne with them commies hot on their tails. They wanted their boy back real bad. Well . . . now." Julius chuckled and leaned back in his chair while Shasta waited impatiently.

"Our gents lost their dove," he went on at last, shaking his head disapprovingly. "The general said every intelligence network throughout Europe was going crazy trying to find him. Anyway, Army Intelligence said they was sending in a special agent with the silliest code name I've ever heard of—Excalibur.

"Shasta, you should have seen the pure joy shining on that old man's face. He told us when the word went out of a new man in town everybody backed off but the Russians—they tripled their efforts. Seems this Excalibur was a feared troubleshooter of our government. And would you believe, in about six hours, news of spotting the defector started popping up all over Switzerland." Julie began to laugh softly.

"There were tales, Shasta, of drunken brawls and rumors of the Russian attending parties, hobnobbin' with the rich and famous. Sometimes there were stories of him being in two places at once—course it ain't possible, but the old general said that was this special agent's style, real classy. He loved to confuse and torment his enemy, and by setting the defector among well-known celebrities and wealthy people, no one could get close enough to nab him." By slow, stiff degrees Julius stood and began to walk toward the back door, heading toward his apartment over the garage.

Lightning skimmed up Shasta's spine. When Kane had talked about diplomats and defectors the tone in his voice had changed. Could he be? No! But why not? It all fit. "Hey!" Shasta yelled. "What happened?"

His hand on the knob, Julius stopped and looked back over his shoulder, his bushy eyebrows a straight line across his brow. "Why, three days later the American embassy in France had a drunken Russian singing a bawdy song on their doorstep."

"Whose doorstep?"

Shasta whirled around and almost sent her cup flying across the table at Kane's question. "Nothing . . . no one. Would you like some coffee?" She jumped up and began to pour. Her back to him, she inhaled deeply and scolded herself. Damn, she was a bundle of nerves. "I called Samantha while you were out running." She set the cup before him, pushed the plate of sweet rolls within his reach and handed him a napkin. Only after she sat did she allow her eyes to meet his, then wished she hadn't. Open suspicion was lurking in his face and she squirmed in her chair, praying she wouldn't be forced into giving up her secrets and plans just yet.

Kane raised his cup to his lips but stopped before taking a sip. He studied Shasta's bland expression and knew there was trouble brewing in that charming little head. She was up to something, and it was going to put him right in the middle of the fire. "How's Samantha this morning?"

"Oh, fine—fine," she answered, relieved that he had shifted those piercing eyes elsewhere. "Last night when Boston told her we couldn't go shopping, I knew she was disappointed and probably lonely for some female companionship. So this morning I fixed it so she and Rena could meet and go shopping together." Shasta watched the frown gathering across Kane's brow and knew he was worried. "I explained to Rena about Samantha, and she promised to take care of her. She will, Kane, honestly." The words kept tumbling out of her mouth in rapid succession no matter how she tried to slow down. She ran nervous fingers through her hair and once again tried to relax, but her head was so full of plans and schemes that she couldn't remain still.

She was saved any further attempts to cover her agitated state when Julie returned and the two men began their usual bantering while Julie cooked breakfast.

It wasn't till she had spoken that she realized she'd rudely interrupted their conversation.

"What did you say?" asked Kane.

"We're going out to dinner tonight. I've already made the reservations." She clamped her mouth shut on a tight smile.

"Oh, I thought you said you never wanted to see the inside of a restaurant again, not after the past two weeks?"

"Did I say that?"

"You did."

"Funny, I don't remember. Anyway—" she waved an airy hand "—you'll enjoy this one." She could feel the heat rise in her cheeks and turned her face away from Kane's penetrating gaze. Instead she met Julie's curious look and shot him a fierce, don't-give-the-game-away frown.

"What restaurant?"

"A Deux Inn." The name came out defiantly, and there was a jarring crash as the platter Julie was holding slipped from his hands and splintered on the floor. Baskerville yelped, jumped to his feet and staggered against the refrigerator in fright.

Kane followed the tense visual exchange between Julie and Shasta with restrained laughter, and before he gave Shasta's game away completely, he excused himself to make some forgotten telephone calls. Once in the living room he sat down in the nearest chair, trying to decide whether to laugh or cry. He'd heard of A Deux Inn, and though he'd never been there, he knew he was in for one hell of a night if he had correctly interpreted the bright gleam of determination in those big brown eyes. The pixie was out for blood—his. She had seduction on her mind, and he wondered if this time he could convince her he wasn't the right man for her? Kane rested his head in his hands and began to laugh.

Back in the kitchen Julius bent down and began to angrily throw broken pieces of china into a wastebasket. "You ain't taking Kane to *that* place. It ain't fair."

"Yes, it is—and yes I am." Shasta squatted to help, but Julie shooed her away.

"The man won't have a snowball's chance in hell of surviving. Besides, it ain't a proper place for you, either. What would your poor grandfather think if he found out?"

Shasta chuckled. "Why, you old hypocrite. J.T. would crow with glee and you know it."

"Maybe so," he grumbled reluctantly under his breath. "But I think it's a dirty trick to pull on an unsuspecting male." He retrieved the broom from the pantry. "I wish to heaven we never did the security setup on that place—it's downright disgusting."

"Then why did you walk around with your mouth hanging open? And I saw those sly looks you kept casting toward Pandora Smith."

"Her—the owner?" Julius ducked his head and sighed. "She's a fine-looking woman, though, ain't she? All bright and buxom." He cleared his throat. "But Pan's got nothing to do with you wanting to entertain Kane at her place."

Shasta grabbed the furiously moving broom and stilled it, making Julius lift his head. "I need to put some pressure on him, Julie."

"Dammit, kid, that kind of pressure could backfire on you."

"I know, but that's a chance I'll have to take."

Julius studied her sad eyes and patted her shoulder. "I ain't never going to figure out you young people—rush, rush, rush. Everything has to be *now*. What happened to courting? You know he cares for you—give it time."

"I can't," she whispered fiercely. "I'm losing control."

"Okay, okay. Don't start the waterworks," he said gruffly, pulling a handkerchief from his back pocket and pressing it to her nose. "Blow." Shasta batted the square of white cloth away with an impatient hand. "You be careful, mind you. That place will turn a mild-mannered man into a tiger—with fangs, and you better believe it." Julie avoided her searching gaze by pushing the broom in a vigorous motion. "Don't ask! It ain't none of your business."

THE SOFT TWILIGHT sheared the edge off the day and draped the approaching night with silken colors. Kane expertly drove the Porsche south with only Shasta's directions every now and then to break the quiet of the evening. She shifted in the leather seat beside him, straightening the skirt of her white linen sundress. Kane pushed the car harder, sending it flying down the road. At the increase in speed, Shasta turned around, scanning the spare traffic behind them.

"There's no one there," Kane told her. "I just wanted to feel some speed under me."

Shasta turned around again. "Oh, we have our escort all right. They're just keeping a safe distance behind. Julie found these." She opened her purse and brought out two tiny metal objects, one round like a button and the other a small square with a tiny wire antenna sticking out. Holding them in her palm, she showed them to Kane. "They were under the front and rear bumper."

"Are they still active?"

"Yes, indeed. I thought the goons and government men needed a nice evening drive." She rolled down the window. "Now, if you'll just pull up as close as possible to that produce truck we'll let them continue their journey in ignorance."

Kane maneuvered Shasta's car close to the ancient farm truck full of crates of peaches and tomatoes, and Shasta pitched the tiny transmitters over the side. Chuckling, Kane pushed his foot on the accelerator and the car shot forward like a bullet. They both waved to the bewildered farmer as they flew past.

Rolling up the window, Shasta began to fuss with her windblown curls, trying in vain to bring the soft strands back to order. She glanced sideways at Kane and thought how handsome he looked, casually elegant in white slacks and open-neck shirt, with a charcoal-gray sports coat. Reluctantly she focused her attention back to the road ahead, and spotting the discreet little sign announcing their destination at the next turn, she began to give directions once more.

The conditions of the dirt road forced Kane to slow down, and suddenly out of patience he demanded, "How much farther is this place? We've been driving for an hour and a half."

Shasta ignored his question. Leaning forward in her seat, she watched for the entrance. "Slower, slower," she ordered. "It's not far." Then she yelled, "Stop! Turn!"

Kane followed her directions, cursing under his breath and telling her what he thought of her navigating. He slammed on the brakes before a high steel gate surrounded by an equally high stone fence. The car's headlights illuminated the sign on the gate: A Deux Inn—An Inn For Two. A tapping sounded on the window beside him, and he turned to the guard there.

Shasta's name was checked off a list, then the guard pressed a button and waved them through the opening gates. "Have a nice evening."

Kane drove slowly, watching the gates roll smoothly shut in the rearview mirror. The sound in his head as they came together was like the clash of cymbals.

"Shasta."

"Why are we stopping?" she asked, afraid that any minute he would turn the car around and drive out—out of her plans, schemes and dreams. Out of her life. "Kane." She placed her hand lightly on his thigh, and her touch seemed to bring him out of his frozen state.

They drove down a long gravel road beneath a canopy of spreading trees that cut off the starlight. Finally they emerged before a huge old plantation house, softly glowing with amber lights that spilled out of the windows and open doorway. Two young men dressed in English footmen's clothing assisted them out of the car. They wished Shasta and Kane good-evening, then escorted them up a multitude of wide curving steps to the entrance. There they were met by a stately butler and behind him the tiny, gray-haired, voluptuous owner—Pandora Smith.

"Shasta, my dear. How wonderful to see you again." Kane stiffened at her words, then relaxed as she added, "I haven't seen you since you and your brother set up our security system. And might I say again, it works absolutely beautifully." Twinkling green eyes, heavy with mascara and fanned by laughter lines at the corners, turned to inspect Kane from head to toe. Then Pandora offered him her hand. "Mr. Stone, a pleasure."

Shasta watched, fascinated as Kane bowed over the older woman's hand and saluted her with a kiss on her fingers. They were both acting and thoroughly enjoying themselves.

"Shasta." Pandora touched her arm. "If you'll follow me, I'd like to take you to your table now. Everything is as you requested."

They followed their hostess through a set of double doors and down a candlelit hall with four closed doors on either side. Stopping before one of the ornately carved doors, Pandora inserted a card with Shasta's last name neatly printed on it into a slot and waved them inside. "You know the procedure," she said, and quietly shut them in.

Kane started at the hollow sound of wood meeting wood. The brief picture of a coffin lid being fitted into place flashed through his mind. His eyes were everywhere, taking in the red velvet hangings and overstuffed chaise longue. Tucked away in a corner was a small round table, beautifully set and surrounded by a padded high-back couch. Crystal and fine bone china winked mockingly in the candlelight. And when his ears picked up the barely audible sounds of music, one corner of his mouth lifted slightly. "It's a bordello," he whispered, loud enough for Shasta to hear.

"No, it's an inn. There's a main dining room on the other side of the house, bedrooms upstairs and cottages out back for people who wish to stay longer than one night. It's a special place for lovers."

"Lovers?" he repeated contemptuously. "When did we fall into the category of lovers? I wouldn't say one roll in the sack would qualify." Somewhere in the back of his mind he began to fully realize what Shasta had planned for him, and though the fantasy was exciting, he knew the outcome would be disastrous. He had to leave, and if insulting her wouldn't work... He reached behind him for the doorknob and gave it a firm twist. Nothing happened.

"It's locked." Shasta smiled and took hold of his arm, leading him to the comfortable couch. She moved the table out and guided his unresisting body around. When he was seated she replaced the table, imprisoning him.

"This is crazy, Shasta. You're wasting your time and money." He laughed, and though he tried to inject the proper note of humor, the sound was strained. "You didn't have to go to all this trouble just to get me in bed. Good God, woman! I've been trying to get back there since the first time. Why this elaborate show?" He leaned back and stared at Shasta, a muscle ticking wildly along his jaw.

Shasta widened her eyes in all innocence and looked at him with a wistful, almost injured air. "Why? I told you. You need to learn how to slow down and enjoy life." She slid in beside him and placed her hand on his thigh. "This is just one of the many lessons I have planned."

Kane studied her pose and relaxed. "I don't need to be taught how to enjoy life. I've been living it to the fullest for thirty-seven years. There's not a damn thing you can teach me that I don't know or haven't tried."

"Oh?" Shasta turned and pulled a three-tiered serving cart stacked with a variety of covered dishes to her side. She lifted one silver lid to reveal black caviar and transferred the iced bowl to her plate. "I wouldn't call what you've been doing living—existing, maybe, but not truly enjoying life. Don't forget, for two weeks I saw how you lived." She retrieved the plate of crisp, brown toast points and carefully scooped a generous amount of caviar onto a wooden spoon then let it drop onto the toast. "Why, just look at the changes already?"

"What changes—" He stopped, thoughtfully inspecting the table setting, then demanded, "Where in the hell is my silverware?"

"You don't get any. I'm going to feed you."

Kane shot her a strained smile. "I'm a big boy, Shasta."

She winked. "I know."

"And I can damn well feed myself."

Shasta ignored his outburst and picked up two liqueur glasses from the cart and a small carafe of chilled vodka. She set his glass before him. "Don't pout," she said, waving the delicious caviar under his nose. "It doesn't become a man of your great age and experience."

Kane snapped his teeth down on the caviar-laden toast and chewed, his silver eyes glittering dangerously in the candlelight. Then the humor of the situation struck him, and he began to chuckle. "You win, mouse. I'll do this your way—this once."

"Good. Now do as you're told and drink your vodka before it gets warm. I'm told this is the finest Pandora could find on such short notice. Do you approve?" She waited till he threw it back and nodded. She did the same with hers, finishing it in one gulp. Her voice was husky and tears filled her eyes as she gasped, "Wonderful." Picking up the wooden spoon, she fixed another piece of caviar on toast and popped it into her mouth. "You speak Russian, don't you?" Her heart began to beat erratically, and she wondered if it was the vodka warming her blood or the wary look on Kane's face. She quickly refilled their glasses.

"A little—enough to get by."

Shasta reached around and adjusted the volume of the music. She listened for a second to Boston Grey's deep voice crooning a love song, then lowered the volume to a mere whisper. She'd told Pandora she didn't want any instrumentals, but songs of passion and love. She wanted a soft background of words and phrases to entice Kane into a more eloquent state. "Does the name Excalibur mean anything to you?" Her eyes met his across the tiny expanse of the table.

Kane paled, and his face became a stark mask. "Where did you hear that name?" he asked softly, his fist clenched on the table. He forced his hand to relax and picked up the napkin from his lap and touched it to his mouth. "I asked where you heard that name?"

"Jeff was the first to put me onto it, then he told me to talk to Julie." She repeated what Julie had told her, all the while watching his carefully schooled features for any change. But he was an expert at hiding his feelings and revealed nothing. "Are you familiar with the code name?"

"Yes."

She waited, and when he was silent she started to ask the one question she'd been withholding since she'd heard the story.

But Kane stopped her, and the deadly calmness of his voice put her senses on alert. "If you want me to stay, you won't ask. On the other hand, if you want me to bust that door down and leave, then ask away."

Shasta smiled. He'd answered her question. "No more interrogations, I promise."

He returned her smile, reaching out to touch the satin curve of her cheek. "Wise woman." The tip of his finger caressed her jaw, then feathered a path to the base of her throat, where he pressed, feeling the pounding pulse under the skin. "Have I told you how lovely you look this evening?" His hand encircled her neck, his thumb tipped her head back and his lips whispered across hers, "All you need to set off that glowing face is a necklace of diamonds."

Shasta breathed in the fresh scent of his after-shave and pulled back. Whose seduction was this anyway? She clamped her teeth together and scolded herself for being easy prey where Kane was concerned. Reaching up, she removed his hand from her neck and brought it to her mouth, her tongue teasing his palm. His sharp intake of breath stirred her hair. "The only adornment a woman needs is a handsome man on her arm."

In a salute to her victory, Kane drained the small glass of fiery liquid. "Touché, mouse."

As far as Kane was concerned, the night fell apart after that one small concession. Shasta's triumph went to her head, and she laid siege to his scarred life with her love. She made him feel again, and newfound emotions surfaced, opening old hurts and wounds. He talked for what seemed like hours of his childhood and his family. He agonized over the war and the bitterness it had caused. He told her of his grandfather's love and his father's indifference. She plied him with food and alcohol in small but consistent quantities, enough to keep him talking. She whispered in his ear words that soothed the pain of remembrance, and her hands touched his body and aroused a deep passion, one he thought had been buried long ago.

"You're driving me crazy, Shasta—stop." Surprisingly she leaned back and reached for the serving cart once more. Kane winced, then shrugged. That cart was his nemesis, and like a witch she concocted a brew to keep him on the fine edge of frustration.

Shasta struck a match and brought it to the wick of a small oil lamp, then took two balloon glasses and warmed them over the flame, her fingers moving with practical grace. "My grandfather taught me this." Looking at him from under her lashes, she wondered at his thoughts and grinned. She almost had him where she wanted, just a little longer. She picked up an old bottle and poured a dark-amber measure into both glasses, setting one in front of Kane and keeping the other for herself. "Do you remember me telling you I loved you?"

Kane nodded, as fascinated by her movements as a cobra by a charmer. She opened a mahogany box, extracted a long, slim cigar and, holding it to her ear, rolled it between her palms.

"You told me not to love you. Why?" Satisfied by the freshness and age of the cigar, she took a pair of small silver pincers and snipped off the end, then held the cigar over the flame, turning it rhythmically between her fingers to warm it.

Kane raised his eyes to her face and found her watching him. Suddenly her actions were becoming deeply erotic. "I don't want you hurt, Shasta," he answered her hoarsely, then was forced to clear his throat like a callow boy before he could go on. "And I will hurt you. Maybe not now, but sometime it will happen. I'd rather die first."

She lowered her head to the cigar and gently closed her lips over one end, rotating the other end in the flames. "You love me?"

The aroma of fine, rich tobacco drifted across the table. Her hair, alight with a life all its own, swung down and framed her face. Kane drew in a shuddering breath. Shasta picked up her glass, dipped the end of the cigar into the cognac and held it out to him. Her question burned through him, and he opened his mouth in denial, but no sound came. She smiled.

"Yes." The word came out a growl, and Shasta's smile deepened as she raised her arm, brought the cigar to his lips and gently brushed her fingertips down his cheek. His teeth clamped down on the cigar as his eyes met hers. "It won't work."

"Shh, love." She leaned forward and struck a match, bringing the hot flame to the tip of his cigar. "Puff." Shasta moved back to rest against the padded couch. His answer was all she'd hoped for, an admission of love, yet she knew this was just the beginning, her job wasn't over yet. Kicking off her shoes, she stroked his ankle caressingly, then she moved her toes slowly upward till they touched a warm hardness; there they lingered, lightly kneading.

Kane felt perspiration pop out on his forehead and fought to get himself under control, but his admission of love had cost him dearly. Now his thoughts were centered on only one thing—Shasta, and the remembered feel of her under him as he buried himself in her loving warmth. Dear God, he thought, just once didn't he deserve to let go? His hand found her foot and fondled the smooth flesh. With a gleam in his eyes, he quickly ran his fingers up her calf to her knee, then to her thigh and farther still, encountering only bare flesh. "You're buck naked under that dress!" It wasn't a question but a statement, and her mischievous smile took what little control he had left. With a groan he shoved the table out of the way, pulled her onto his lap and brought his mouth to hers.

Shasta returned the ravenous kiss and felt the strength of his embrace and the seeking hand between her thighs. "Kane, Kane." She pulled back. "Not here. I have a place."

Loath to let her go, Kane stood with her in his arms. "More of your plans, Shasta?"

"Yes, love." She felt dizzy at her triumph yet fought to keep a rein on her happiness. There were so many questions to be asked, and she knew if Kane was pushed too hard her whole evening could blow up in her face. She warned herself to go slowly, to see if Kane, now that he'd begun to realize his life was changing, would open up on his own accord. Would he trust her enough to reveal the real man she knew was lurking within that worldly facade?

CHAPTER ELEVEN

SHASTA DIRECTED KANE to a concealed door at the back of the room, and with curses and giggles he maneuvered her up a narrow staircase to the landing above.

"Where to now?" He stopped, feigning exhaustion at the load in his arms, shifted her weight and fell against the nearest wall. He laughed as her seeking lips nibbled his earlobe. "I swear if you don't stop I'm going to throw you down on the floor and make love to you, Shasta!"

She raised her head from the curve of his shoulder. Loosening one arm from around his neck, she searched the pocket of her dress and triumphantly dangled an old-fashioned brass key before him. She squinted in the dimly lit hallway, trying to make out the number. "Room four."

Kane's long stride carried them down the hall to their room. He kicked the door shut behind them and with two steps pitched her squealing on the bed.

Shasta rolled over, came to her knees and quickly scanned the room, relieved that the heavy decor of their dining room did not prevail there. The bedroom was small, dominated by an oversize bed, and decorated in soft ivory lace, which lent a romantic air.

"I think you're more trouble than you're worth, Shasta Masterson."

A rosy hue colored Shasta's cheeks and her eyes brimmed with laughter. Jamming her hands on her hips, she demanded, "If I'm not worth the effort, then why, may I ask, are you stripping so fast?"

"Old habits die hard?"

Bounding off the bed, she slapped his hands away from his shirtfront. "I wanted to undress you." Kane dropped his arms to his side. She wanted him so badly, but she forced herself to move slowly, drawing out every second. Her eyes on Kane's face, she stepped back, reached behind and leisurely unzipped her dress, letting it fall in a white cloud at her feet.

Kane's breath caught painfully in his chest at the lovely, inviting body. He held out his arms and without hesitation she walked into his embrace. Smiling down at the curly brown head, he stopped her busy fingers on the buttons of his shirt. "I can do that a lot faster than you."

She retreated a step, watching as he disrobed, thankful that his eagerness was as obvious as hers. One by one each article of clothing was thrown aside, and when he stood before her naked, she could only stare for a second at his male beauty, the symmetry of hard muscles that defined his shape. She reached out with sensitive fingers to touch the smooth warm skin and mat of dark hair across his chest. Like a sleepwalker she moved, wanting only to wrap her arms around him, flesh against flesh, but to her dismay, Kane's hand gripped her wrist, halting her progression. Hurt shining in her eyes, she tilted her head back and met his troubled gaze.

"If I let you touch me now, mouse..."

"I love you, Kane. Don't hold back, don't think about yesterday or tomorrow—nothing matters." He slackened his iron hold and she moved quickly, wrapping her arms around his waist, her lips showering light butterfly kisses across his chest. "There's no other existence outside this room, just the two of us here and now. We have no past, no future, and the world may end at dawn. Don't throw away these precious moments." She waited for a sign from him and silently sighed as his hands slid down over her rounded buttocks, pulling her close to meet his desire.

Shasta loosened herself from his hold and began a slow silken path of kisses down his chest and across the hard muscles of his abdomen. Her knees touched the floor and Kane grabbed the bedpost as her hand gently stroked him. She touched and kissed, her lips warm and wet, till the groan rumbling in his chest erupted with a low moan of pure pleasure.

His fragile control snapped at the touch of her knowing mouth, and a feeling of release bloomed in him like a rose. He'd held back for too long. With her name on his lips he shuddered, and reaching down, he grasped Shasta by the arms and lifted her. Burying his hands in her delicate curls, he tilted her face and pulled her mouth to his for a slow and loving kiss. His tongue searched the moist sweet cavern, leisurely drinking the offered nectar.

Shasta took his hand and guided him to the bed. Playfully she pushed him backward, then followed him down, collapsing across his chest. Suddenly hesitant of her role as the aggressor, she wriggled in indecision, the mat of soft hair tickling her breasts and sending a rush of hot sensations through her. Her gaze met his, and she noted the sparks of light playing in his half-closed eyes, sparks that flared even brighter with her movements.

"It's your show, *chérie.*" His voice was ragged with hunger as he lifted her to straddle his slim hips. She touched him, and he caught his breath. "Now, Shasta," he whispered, his muscles taut with urgency as she brought him into the warmth of her body.

Shasta looked down into his gray eyes, her heart pounding heavily. She watched his gaze follow his hands as he caressed her thighs and stroked her hips. Fingertips moved as lingering as a kiss along her ribs to play and teasingly encircle each swollen breast. She arched her neck as he lightly strummed the dusky-rose nipples, making them harden to aching points. Shasta sighed and lowered her head, her eyes half-lidded slits of velvet brown as Kane massaged the tense muscles in her neck, then pulled her down to rest on his chest. His mouth touched hers, and his tongue traced the outline of her lips, sending a lick of fire across her skin.

Kane rolled her over and settled between her legs, his hands holding her head, his mouth clinging to hers as he set a pace designed to take her over the edge. "*Oui, mon amour.* Look at me. Look up and see what you've done."

Shasta opened her heavy lids in a haze of desire. Through the mist she saw him, and tears filled her eyes. His beautiful face was alive with expression and love. But it was his eyes that sent fat tears rolling unchecked down her cheeks. His eyes were no longer a soulless silver mirror; they shone with longing and tenderness, and a certain vulnerability.

He was free at last. Her heart sang as she held her arms open and he accepted the comfort of her embrace. Her legs wrapped around his hips, and he reveled in this prison.

"*Mon ange de feu.* My angel of fire," he crooned softly, then began to whisper endearments to her in his native tongue.

Though she was unable to understand all he said, the resonant sound of his deep voice talking to her of love was almost more than she could bear. She moved in unison with him and he loved her more. The culmination of their joining was so intense they were staggered by its depths. Too spent to move they lay cradled lovingly in each other's arms.

Finally their breathing quieted, and Kane levered himself on his elbows and stared down into Shasta's smiling face. "*Je t'aime toujours,* mouse."

Shasta touched the perfect arch of his eyebrow with the tip of her finger, then traced the bridge of his nose to his lips. "Ah, I know what that means. When will you teach me the rest?"

"Anytime or place you say." He grinned, then frowned. "Am I crushing you? You're turning the most peculiar shade of blue." Shasta laughed. "I forget how small you are, but that's understandable, you're such a fierce little thing." He attacked her neck with his lips, and as she struggled to avoid his tickling kisses, he eased his weight off her. Lying side by side, he covered his eyes with a forearm and let the silence of the room seep into his bones, bringing a peace he'd never known existed.

All his life he'd searched for this inner serenity. He thought of the years he'd spent running away from love, believing as his parents had that love was a burden. He'd vowed never to expose himself to such agony as theirs. At the back of his mind there had always been a nagging voice telling him he'd inherited the worst qualities of both his parents. Seeing the outcome of their union, he'd feared emotional involvement, despising it as a weakness. But now he knew that his father and mother had never loved each other. Max had married a young, flighty French heiress to gain entry into the European social set. And his mother, Jacqueline, had been fascinated by the older, rough-edged Texan.

Kane now recognized the bitterness and loneliness that must have slowly destroyed his parents' relationship. It was inevitable that their marriage would end, but they refused to give up gracefully. Instead they used Kane as a tool to vent their anger and frustrations, and in the process they had turned him into a cynical young man.

He wanted to believe he'd been wrong all those years and that Shasta's love for him was enough to erase the past. But was it? For a brief second he turned his head and studied her serene expression. She was so unlike any woman he'd ever met, so quiet and sure after their lovemaking. She needed no reassurance as to her abilities, no words of comfort. But his feelings were so new to him and he was still unsure. *Where do we go from here,* he asked himself. The question began gnawing at him. What did she expect of him now that he'd admitted his love? What did he expect of himself? He voiced his question and waited. "Where do we go from here, Shasta?"

Intuitively she knew the direction his mind was taking, but she refused to lay all her dreams and hopes on the table at one time. Her grandfather had taught her better than that. "Why, we find out who killed the professor and decide what to do with the synthetic-fuel formula."

The tranquility of the room shattered with her statement. She felt Kane stiffen beside her and she frowned at the ceiling, refusing to turn her head and look at him. She had a feeling the truth was about to come crashing down around her. Her breath hung suspended painfully in her chest, and then he spoke.

"There is no formula."

It was a long time before she could take sufficient air into her lungs to yell, and when she did Kane winced. "What did you say!"

"There's no...."

"I heard you the first time." She sat upright. The sheet fell to her waist but she ignored it, glaring at Kane. "Are we all to play your fool, Mr. Stone? Me, Jeff, Julie, the government and U.S.A. Oil." She rubbed her forehead. "I don't understand you. I try to figure you out, and every time I think I have, you turn around and pull something like this."

"I know the feeling, believe me, mouse."

She scowled. "Why? Why would you put everyone through this elaborate charade if you have nothing to bargain with?" Before he could open his mouth the answer hit her. "Of course, how stupid of me. It's the only way to force the issue. But have you thought about what they'll do to you—hell, us—if they find out there's no formula. What if they're willing to trade and you have nothing to give them? As smart as you've been, you can't manufacture a formula out of thin air."

Kane leaned back, his mouth a tight line. "You think I can't pull it off? Remember, they don't know, Shasta, and I have enough leverage to keep them running around in circles. Besides, if push comes to shove, I have enough of the formula to make them salivate."

"Wait a minute. Just wait." She snatched the sheet to cover herself and scooted back against the headboard. "Tell me everything from the beginning—from the first meeting with the professor till his death." She glowered at him, anger in every line of her body. "And don't give me that evasive look, either. This time I want it *all,* the whole story."

"It's long and complicated."

"We have all night."

Kane swung his bare legs over the side of the high bed and pulled the silver champagne stand closer. He popped the cork and poured the bubbly wine into two fluted glasses, handed one to Shasta before slipping back into bed.

"Why are you so reluctant to talk about the professor?" With a sinking heart she watched his expression become distant and withdrawn. Then he began to speak, and she sat very still so she wouldn't distract him in any way.

"I guess because the funny little man came closest to my expectations of what a father should be." Kane closed his eyes. "In the year I knew him he pried more out of me than I realized. We examined life together, and he had the strangest habit of calling me son. He would even introduce me to the locals as his son."

Shasta touched his arm, her fingers lightly stroking the tense muscles. "Start from the beginning. How did you meet the professor?"

"Have you ever been in Barbizon, France?"

"No."

"I have an estate there, one I use infrequently—only when I need to get away from everything and everybody and rest. About a year ago I broke my leg skiing at St. Moritz and went home to recuperate. You can imagine my surprise and anger to find that my father, in his typical high-handed manner, had commandeered the carriage house and turned it into a laboratory for a scientist to work on his synthetic-fuel formula. Hell, Max didn't even have the guts to hang around and explain. He left it up to Melvin. Then, Max had the nerve to call and tell me that since I was going to be staying for a while he would call off his guards and let me keep an eye on his new acquisition—acquisition!" Kane snorted. "That's my old dad for you, everything is a possession."

He picked up the champagne bottle and refilled their empty glasses. "I was furious and hadn't decided whether to kick Melvin out or just throw in the towel and leave, but the professor convinced me he really did need a guard and friend. It seems he'd been working for U.S.A. Oil for the past ten years, trying to come up with an alternate solution to the oil problems, when he realized he could possibly have the beginnings of a synthetic fuel. He took his discoveries to the executives of the company, who were encouraging but not overly enthusiastic. So he quit in disgust and took his proposition to Max—U.S.A.'s biggest competitor."

Kane sat up and stared fixedly into space. "When Melvin described his experiments I began to get as excited as he was." He turned to Shasta, reached out and pulled her to his side, absently stroking the skin along her hip. "Can you imagine a cheap fuel to run this country? Better still, a means of breaking the stranglehold the Middle East has on the world? It was a heady prospect that could tip the scales of power back in our favor, preventing more wars and destruction. Hell," he said, laughing, "I got so caught up I started hanging over his shoulder like some eager college student."

Shasta grinned at the image of a wild-eyed scientist in his laboratory with Kane at his heels. He caught her smile, kissed her cheek resoundingly and laughed, as if reading her mind.

"Barbizon's a quaint town with one main street and the feel of an old-fashioned village. I guess it hasn't changed much since 1830. There was a bistro the professor particularly liked, and every evening we'd walk there, sip calvados, and discuss the world and its problems. It wasn't till he got closer and closer to finishing the formula that I noticed the change. He began to drink more and argue harder and louder. His hope for world peace with the new fuel had diminished and he'd become cynical. I was on the verge of calling a doctor when he stopped drinking and going to the bar altogether. He spent twenty-four hours a day in that damned laboratory."

Kane stopped talking, the memories painful as he recalled his helplessness at watching his friend waste away with work and worry. "I tried—God, how I tried—to get him to open up. Then one evening I went to the laboratory, found it locked and realized Melvin was gone." Kane swallowed hard and Shasta hugged him close, her hands riding the rise and fall of his chest in a slow rhythmic caress. "I was scared. There'd been men snooping around and inquiries made in town. But I finally found him in the bistro with bag and baggage, and he was the drunkest I'd ever seen him. He said he'd finished the formula and was celebrating."

Shasta squeezed her eyes shut at the clipped emotionless tone of Kane's voice.

"We argued because he hadn't let me in on its completion. He was furious, but not with me. I could tell that. He seemed weighed down by some problem and it kept preying on his mind." Kane lay back, dragging her down beside him, and covered his eyes with his arm. "Melvin walked out on our fight. Right in the middle, up he gets, grabs his bag and staggers out. I was so mad I just sat there for a few minutes like a hurt child and let him go. When I finally did follow, I remember how surprised I was to see how far down the street he had gone." He paused, his lips a grim line in his pale face. "Shasta, the Rue de Fleury is a long main street and you can see down both ends for quite a distance. But the car came roaring out of the darkness—out of nowhere—with its headlights a bright beam heading directly for Melvin."

Shasta felt a chill creep over her skin as she remembered another evening and another car racing out of the darkness. She now understood Kane's desperation that night.

"I called out to warn him, but I don't know if he was too drunk to hear or if he was too ridden with his own demons to care anymore. The next thing I recalled was holding his broken, bleeding body all the way to the hospital, and later after they'd done what they could, I held his hand."

Kane cleared his throat and dropped his arm from across his eyes. He hugged Shasta closer to him in an effort to ward off the sudden chill seeping across his flesh. "Melvin regained consciousness once during the night. He talked to me as coherently as I'm talking to you now. But he was possessed with the formula and kept repeating over and over that he didn't want Max or anyone else to have it. He said he'd done what he had to do and explained that the formula would only corrupt whoever had it, that it could be turned into the ultimate weapon of power and no one could resist the allure. I remember his last words as they were burned into my brain—'Money can turn men into whores, but great power corrodes the soul, and even you, Kane, with all your wealth, can be corrupted by power.'"

Kane shivered and pulled the covers over them. He rolled onto his side and faced Shasta for the first time since he'd begun his story. "And he was right, Shasta! He knew—he knew the oil companies would destroy the formula to save their profits, the government would use it as a weapon against other countries, and he knew I could be seduced with the knowledge of what kind of power that formula could bring."

"Kane—"

"No, listen and let me finish, because I never intend to repeat all this again as long as I live. After Melvin died, I drove home thinking of what I could do with the formula—the good I might try to accomplish. But good has its evil side, and as Melvin said, power, not money, is the root of evil. He was right. When I got back to the estate I went immediately to the laboratory and forced open the lock, thinking I'd simply retrieve the ledger and lock it up for safekeeping." Kane chuckled. "You should have seen the place. Old Melvin destroyed every scrap of paper dealing with the formula. There wasn't anything left of his notes and books but a pile of ashes. That's when it hit me that he was right, and no one should be able to wield that much power."

Shasta touched his brow, wanting to smooth away the deep lines and erase the pain from his eyes. "What about the men who ran the professor down? How did you trace them to U.S.A. Oil, or are you only making a wild assumption?"

"Part fact, part guesswork. But they do seem to be extremely nervous, don't they?"

She had only one or two more questions to clear everything up. "What about the government men, Kane? Why are they holding back?"

"That I don't know, Shasta. It's definitely not like them to be so coy when they want something. I think, like Tramble, the government doesn't know if I have the formula—they're only assuming I do. But once they're convinced they'll step in and make an offer I won't dare refuse."

"But, Kane, there's no formula."

"That's the sticky part." He smiled recklessly. "All this maneuvering with Tramble to make him believe I have the formula will convince the government, also. Of course, their presence has helped to step up Tramble's efforts, you can be sure of that. We might be in for some fast talking to the government later but it will be worth the trouble."

Shasta snuggled closer. She'd had enough of formulas and agents. Her fingers played in the soft hair on his chest. "You sleepy?" she questioned, looking at him through her lashes, a recognizable spark in her dark eyes.

Kane removed her champagne glass, which she'd left balancing on his stomach, and set it aside. Her hand moved lower. "If I was, I'd be wide awake now, wouldn't I?" His lips took away her answer.

"I'm sorry about Melvin, Kane," she whispered against his mouth.

"I know you are. Now hush." And he kept her awake till the sun began to creep between the lace curtains to announce a new day.

JULIUS MET THEM at the back door, his bushy eyebrows a straight line of disapproval. He held out scraps of paper for both of them and slapped them into their outstretched hands. "I ain't your personal answering service. I got better things to do with my time." Wheeling around, he stomped over to the stove, checking the progress of his quiche. "Breakfast's about ready—sit."

Shasta grinned at the gruff old man, mischief dancing in her eyes. "Pandora sends her love and told me to be sure and tell you that she misses you. I didn't know you were seeing her." The back of Julie's neck turned beet red, and Shasta tried to hide her grin. "By the way, how did you know when we would get here?"

"Pandora called." Julius thumped a plate of homemade blueberry muffins and buttermilk biscuits on the table. "I was getting worried."

Baskerville butted Shasta's knee for attention, and she absently began to scratch behind his ear. "Why would you worry about me?"

"Wasn't you I was thinking of."

Kane ducked his head to hide his grin at Shasta's outraged expression. He quickly scanned the telephone messages, discarding ones from friends who had managed to trace him to Shasta's house. "I could have used a warning, Julie. A Deux Inn isn't for the fainthearted." He looked up when he heard Shasta's muffled laughter. She pointed to Baskerville and his eyes widened. The huge animal was stretched out full-length on the kitchen floor, making low whimpers as his oversized paws, one by one, pulled him across the cold surface. With a loud sigh and a last pitiful groan, he rested his massive head on the rim of his empty bowl and closed his eyes.

Shasta wiped the tears from her cheeks, looked at Kane's bewildered expression and broke up all over again. "Julie," she choked. "Have you been starving my dog?"

"Damn ham," Julius grumbled good-naturedly. "Always putting on a show." He grabbed a couple of blueberry muffins, cut a large wedge of quiche and dumped them into Baskerville's bowl.

Still laughing, Kane reared back in his chair as he glanced down at the last two messages in his hand. The amusement in his eyes hardened and the smile froze, leaving his skin pale and taut across his high cheekbones. Abruptly he excused himself and left the room.

"Kane!" Shasta was out of her chair immediately, but Julius grasped her arm firmly and held her back. "What's wrong?" she demanded, pulling free and glaring at Julie.

"Don't give me that look, kid. You still ain't too old for me to turn over my knee. Now sit down and let the man take care of his business."

"You seem to forget, Julie," Shasta's voice turned cold, "that Kane's business is our business. I have to know what's happening."

"Don't you use that tone on me, either, miss."

Shasta grinned sheepishly and slumped down in the nearest chair. "I'm overprotective, aren't I?" She gnawed at her bottom lip.

"It's okay." He patted her shoulder. "This love business is all new to you, takes a while to get the hang." He pulled up another chair and sat down. "But we got troubles, kid. Old Max Stone was beaten up in England last night. That was one of Kane's messages. The other was a call this morning from Tramble Baldwin, the president and chairman of the board of U.S.A. Oil."

Shasta whistled loud and long, and Julius nodded his head in full agreement.

"That ain't all. *We* got problems—big ones. There's G-men crawling all over Masters. Your brother's being held and interrogated there. J.T.'s fit to be tied. He says if you two brats don't clear this mess up real quick like, he's going to come down here and see for himself what's going on." He propped his elbows on his knees. "J.T. ain't a happy man. Seems he's been getting telephone calls all night about the Houston branch of Masters."

Shasta shivered at the thought of her grandfather's intervention. She'd witnessed too many situations in which he had to take over, and there wasn't anyone around who escaped the stiletto edge of his tongue. "But what are government men doing at Masters? What has Jeff done?"

"Well, now...." Julius sat up and smiled. "The boy got carried away searching codes and information on Kane. You know how he is with that damn computer. Once he gets going he forgets everything—he just went too far. But that ain't what worries me, he'll fast-talk his way out. What does concern me is the government's insistence to see the Stone file."

Shasta's face lost some of its color, then her cheeks flared an angry red. "They can't do that."

"They can do anything they damn well please and you know it. But don't fret. Margret has the file in a safe place, and she and Jeff are denying its existence."

"And Rena?" she questioned.

Julius chuckled. "She's playing the dumb blonde to the hilt."

Shasta sighed with relief. "I think it would be a wise move if Kane and I spent some time together alone."

She grinned conspiratorially at Julie. "Away from the city—say at the family lake house?"

Julius winked. "Yeah, Kane looked a little peaked. A couple of days' rest and fishing will do him a world of good. Want me to set it up?"

She nodded, then looked up as Kane walked in and sat down. "How's Max?"

"Bruised, but nothing broken. He doesn't have any idea who did it, and they never asked any questions. But it was a very professional job."

"A warning, Kane?"

He raised his head, his eyes blazing with anger. "I'd say so, especially when Tramble follows it up with a personal phone call." He cut himself a generous slice of quiche, poured some coffee and picked up his fork.

"How can you eat at a time like this?"

His silver eyes darkened momentarily and a suggestive smile touched his lips. "I have to keep up my strength. After all, I didn't get much sustenance last night. By the way, Tramble offered me two million for the formula."

She rested her chin in her hands and smiled. "And what did you tell him?"

"I wouldn't want to sully your delicate ears by repeating it, but I did tell him we might have a deal if he could locate the man who killed Melvin." Kane paused, broke open a hot, fluffy muffin and spread it with butter. "Of course he blustered about how sorry he was to hear of Melvin's death and that he'd do all he could to help. Lying old bastard." Kane's teeth snapped together around half of the muffin and his eyes glinted. "I'd like... never mind." He poured himself more coffee and cut another wedge of quiche.

"Do you always eat this way when you're upset?" she asked, awed by the amount of food he was consuming.

"Sometimes."

"What else did you tell Tramble?"

"I told him to think my proposal over for a couple of days and I'd do the same."

Shasta shivered at the wolfish grin on Kane's lips. "So we're back to the war of nerves again?"

Kane wiped his mouth, refolded the napkin, set his fork on his plate, then gazed up. She didn't like the look in his eyes. They were completely expressionless.

"Whatever you're thinking you're not going to do it without me."

"Now listen, Shasta!"

"No, you listen. You said I was in this as deep as you, so don't start trying to cut me out to protect me."

"They think I have the formula with me and know the government has more than a passing interest in us. They're getting desperate, and desperate men are unpredictable."

"Ah, now they're going to start playing rough." Excitement shone in her eyes. "Why don't we throw them all off balance by disappearing for a few days and give them time to think?"

Kane tried to frown at her suggestion but couldn't manage with her eager gaze on him. Hell, he thought, not only was she a mind reader, taking the very words out of his mouth, but she could just smile and twist him around her finger. He felt the first twinge of unease at her power over him, but a few days alone together were too tempting to pass up.

Shasta held her breath, and when he answered her with a smile she exhaled slowly. "We can escape to our family vacation home on Lake Livingston. Julie said he would help us, and no one will find us until we want to be found."

"Seems you've already planned this—" The explosive slamming of the front door froze every muscle in Kane's body. He didn't relax until he heard a female voice call for Shasta.

"Rena!" Shasta was halfway out of her seat when her sister-in-law bolted through the door, quickly grabbed the nearest chair and sat down. She was laughing so hard it took Shasta a few minutes to calm her down.

"Here." Rena yanked a thick manila file from the folds of Lizzie's worn and ragged blanket. "I've turned your niece into a criminal. There are government men all over the office hunting for this." She tapped the file. "Jeff is absolutely wild. I've never seen him so animated, not even on our honeymoon. You should hear the silver-tongued lies tripping out of his mouth to save his ass." Rena shifted her bright gaze to the other occupant of the table, and her next words choked in the back of her throat.

Shasta bit back a smile. She knew only too well the effect Kane had on women, but this morning he seemed bent on causing complete havoc and smiled his most beguiling smile at Rena. Shasta leaned across the table and gently tapped her sister-in-law's mouth shut. "You have yours, Rena. This one's mine."

"What?"

"Kane, if you haven't figured it out yet, this is my sister-in-law. Rena, meet Kane." Shasta shook her head. Never had she seen Rena's composure slip like this. She snapped her fingers before Rena's glazed eyes, and while her sister-in-law composed herself, Shasta quickly told Kane of the government men visiting Masters. "Rena, Kane and I are going to the lake for a couple of days. Julie will fill you in, but no one's to know."

"What?"

"Rena! Look at my lips when I talk." Exasperated, she started to repeat what she'd said when she caught the gleam of devilment in Rena's eyes. "You've had your fun. You've gawked at Kane, you've delivered the file—now go home."

Rena obediently stood up. She held out her hand to Kane, then yanked it back and tapped her fingers to her forehead. "How stupid! I almost forgot. Boston called me about thirty minutes ago. Samantha went into labor, and he rushed her to the hospital."

"She's not due for another month," Kane said, glancing from one woman to the other. "I don't know much about these things, but I do know Boston said the doctor wanted her to go the full nine months to ensure a healthy delivery for all the babies. What happened?" he demanded fiercely of Rena.

Rena retreated a step at the accusing look he turned on her. "I promise you, when we went shopping yesterday she was fine. I didn't let her overdo it, either. Boston gave me a long lecture on her condition." Rena picked up her purse to leave. "When Boston called he was so distraught. I told him I'd call you two, then meet him at the hospital." She was gone in a flash, Kane's hard gaze following her.

"Kane." Shasta laid her small hand on his arm. "Don't blame Rena."

"I don't, Shasta. I was just thinking how fragile life is. Besides, I know Samantha and how bullheaded she can be, but she'd never do anything to endanger her babies." He was quiet for a moment. "If anything happens to her, Boston will never recover. He worships her. We'd better clean up and get over there. He might need me." It scared him to think that Shasta's thoughts might be on babies—theirs. He hugged her briefly, wondering if she'd try to tie him down with a home and children.

He might be ready to admit he loved her, but anything else sent a chill of dread down his spine. Surely he'd suffocate and die in the daily routine of domestic life. A deep feeling of dread crept into his heart. He felt the weight of responsibility of Shasta's love and at the same time wondered if he was worthy of the gift. Could he change at this late date and accept the inevitable? What he needed was a stiff drink and a long overdue talk with Shasta.

CHAPTER TWELVE

WHO WOULD HAVE thought the birth of quadruplets would totally disrupt an efficiently run hospital? Shasta chuckled to herself, shifted the Porsche into low gear and switched lanes. Kane's fingers gripped his knee, and the smile she'd been holding back blossomed as he turned his tousled head toward her. Briefly she glanced at her own reflection in his sunglasses. She knew the darkened lenses hid red-rimmed eyes and the pained expression of a hangover. "Does your head still hurt?"

"Hmm."

"You're sure you don't want to drive?" He'd meekly slipped into the passenger side that morning without a single complaint.

"No."

"Are you able to talk intelligently yet?"

"Barely, and only if it's important."

Shasta ignored the slightly pleading note in his voice and plunged on. "Samantha looks wonderful considering what she's gone through. I was surprised they allowed her to have visitors this morning." Out of the corner of her eye she saw Kane sag a little lower in the seat. Poor man, he really had a bad headache. But his condition was understandable. Yesterday had been a day filled with tension.

They had arrived at the hospital forty-five minutes after Rena's departure. The entire time Shasta was trying to dress, Kane had followed her around, complaining about her slowness, arguing that Boston was alone, and would she please put her behind into fast gear. When they finally arrived they found the maternity waiting room filled with people—all men except for Rena, and the awestruck nurses who had used every excuse they could to stroll by. Shasta sighed. She would have done the same thing if she'd seen all those good-looking men in one small area. Samantha's brothers had turned out en masse—all six, plus her father and Uncle George. The eight men, all with bright-red hair identical to Samantha's, alternated between pacing the floor and arguing among themselves.

Boston sat calmly, his hands welded together, totally oblivious to the commotion around him. Hours later the head nurse smiled her way through a sea of bodies and told Boston he was the father of quadruplets—all fine, healthy boys. Boston stood slowly, shakily, then fainted into Kane's waiting arms.

"What was Lucas DeSalva doing there? I didn't know he was close friends with Boston," Shasta asked.

Kane ripped his sunglasses down and eyed her glassily over the rim. "He's not. Samantha's family breeds and raises quarter horses, so does Lucas. They've all been friends for years." He pushed the dark glasses back to shield his sensitive eyes from the early-morning sunlight bouncing off the hood of the car. "You seem to be in tight with him."

Shasta disregarded the question, remembering Lucas's concern at her association with Kane the previous day, and then the laughter in his face at her panic when she realized the men were going to take Boston out to celebrate the birth of his sons. She'd been forced to tell Lucas of her job as Kane's bodyguard, omitting the particulars of the case, and discreetly asked him not to let Kane out of his sight. Before she'd let Kane walk out of the hospital, she wrung a sworn promise from him that he wouldn't do anything more foolish than drink too much. Shasta weaved the little car in and out of traffic, changing lanes with a motion that brought a groan from her passenger.

"Must you, Shasta?"

"Yes, our followers are getting too close and it's important to keep them at the right distance."

"Could we stop this mad dash long enough to get a hot cup of coffee? I know I'd feel better." Shasta shook her head. "Ruthless damn female," he muttered, and closed his eyes.

"I'm truly sorry, Kane, but Julie's meeting us and I have to keep to the time we agreed on. If you hadn't—"

"Don't say it!" he groaned again, and slumped down.

Later, as the car began to slow down, Kane opened one eye to check his surroundings. "Shasta, why are we turning into the Sam Houston National Forest?" His head might feel the size of a basketball, but he still had enough sense to know that a person couldn't build a vacation home on federal land.

"I told you, Kane! We're meeting Julie and switching cars."

"Just when did you tell me all this?"

She laughed and slowed the low-slung car to a crawl as she drove over the deeply rutted road. "While I was putting you to bed this morning."

"Ah, I see. Would you please repeat the reason now that I'm in a more receptive frame of mind?"

"We're meeting Julie and changing cars in hopes that our friends behind us will continue to tail my car and get lost, then we'll be on our way to the lake house."

They passed picnic and camping areas in shaded groves. Cars and campers lined one side of the road as Shasta drove on, leaving the civilized world behind. Giant pines so fragrant their scent penetrated the closed confines of the car towered over them, and thick vegetation and vines scraped the doors as she maneuvered the narrow lane, jarring Kane's aching body. He was about to comment when they rounded a bend in the road and he spotted Julie standing beside a dilapidated army jeep. He groaned loudly this time, fighting the urge to demand if Shasta had deliberately picked this mode of transportation to aggravate his hangover. He'd been in too many similar vehicles and well remembered the rough treatment they inflicted on the human body. And this old relic with its worn camouflaged paint and rust spots looked as if it had refined the arts of torture. He opened his mouth to protest, but his words were cut off as Julie swung the passenger door wide and the aroma of hot coffee filled the car.

"Drink it fast, man. She's not about to stop the fun now."

Kane gulped down the scalding brew and followed Julie to the jeep. He leaned against a tall pine, silently blessing the shade it afforded, and ignored the conversation going on around him. But his serenity was shattered by the ear-splitting blare of the horn and Baskerville's urgent barking.

Julius eased the empty mug from Kane's tight grip and led him to his side of the jeep. "Cheer up. You're only about thirty minutes from the house and a nice comfortable bed."

Shasta took off at a gear-grinding, bone-jarring pace that snapped Kane's head back with a jerk. The rusty springs of the bucket seats squeaked till he thought his head would burst with the sound. "Stop!" he yelled.

The jeep bounced to a halt. Kane yanked off his sunglasses and glared at Shasta. They stared at each other for such a long moment that Baskerville, sitting on the floor between them, began to swing his head from one side to the other in puzzlement.

"Enough," Kane growled. "You want to tell me what's eating you? You seem bent on taking out your foul mood on me in the cruelest way possible. Now spit it out and let's be done with it."

Shasta frowned, her nose crinkling, but her eyes wide and blank. "Nothing's bothering me," she hedged as she ground the gears into low and eased the jeep around another mammoth hole in the dirt road.

"Don't go all female on me, mouse. I don't have the patience this morning to cope." Women, he thought irritably, could pick the most inopportune time to play coy. "Now what's the matter?"

She steered the jeep off the road and into a stand of thick trees. "We need to wait here until our followers pass." Pointing through the trees to the paved road beyond, she settled back comfortably, while Kane waited. "I received a call from Tramble Baldwin last night. He made me an excessively generous offer if I would turn over the formula. Of course your name wasn't mentioned in sharing the deal. This, he said, was just a little on the side."

Kane snorted and Baskerville growled in agreement. "What did you tell him?"

Shasta grinned, mischief dancing in her eyes. "That I'd think it over and get back to him. He dwelled on the importance of the discovery to America and reminded me that though you are a citizen you're more French than American."

Forgetting his throbbing temples, Kane laughed long and hard. "The bastard's slick, I'll have to hand him that. He covers all the bases." Kane relaxed against the worn, squeaking cushion and rested his hand on a brown paper bag propped between the two seats. A huge paw slapped down on his hand, holding him immobile, and he stared directly into Baskerville's snarling face. "Shasta," he whispered, "Shasta, what have I done now?"

"You have your hand on his beer," Shasta laughed, as she watched man and beast glare at each other.

Kane jerked his hand free and frowned at Baskerville. "I wasn't trying to steal it, boy... ah, hell," he said disgustedly. "Why am I explaining myself to a damn dog?"

"There they go." Shasta watched the second car drive slowly by and started the engine.

A few minutes later they were once again speeding down the highway, but this time the wind was whipping around them and tearing at their clothes. Talk was impossible. The air sucked the words away as fast as they were spoken. Kane shouted, then shook his head and gave up. He realized his head had ceased to pound, and he almost laughed out loud. His body must have figured it didn't need to add to his troubles; he had plenty dealing with the Mastersons.

Kane turned to look at Shasta and couldn't help but smile as he noticed that her head barely cleared the steering wheel of the old jeep. His amusement increased when he saw that she was pressing the gas pedal with the tip of her toe.

Shasta caught Kane's smile and relaxed her shoulders a fraction. They hadn't gotten off to a very good start, and she prayed it wasn't an omen of a disastrous vacation. Her plans required an atmosphere devoid of worry and tension for her to convince Kane she'd make an ideal life-time partner.

Her hands grasped the steering wheel, the skin pulling taut across her knuckles as she realized the enormity of her task. Kane still wasn't ready to totally accept his new-found emotions, and he'd made it only too clear that he didn't even consider a permanent commitment to be a part of his future. She could understand his distaste for the institution of marriage, though she didn't agree. But he'd never been in love before, and a change was definitely in order. He had so much love and tenderness bottled up inside that it would be a shock even to him when he discovered how deeply he could care for another person.

She'd studied every angle of their situation and decided against offering to live with him. Such an arrangement would have been too easy to walk away from if things got rough. She wasn't fool enough to think they would or could live in happy harmony forever; they both enjoyed a good fight too much.

Marriage was the only answer. But how did you propose to a man and make him think it was his idea? Shasta groaned to herself. She should have had a long talk with Rena or Samantha before she left town. If there were two women who knew how to get what they wanted from a man, it was those two.

Shasta pulled up to the four-way-stop sign at the main intersection in Coldspring, checked the traffic both ways and turned to the right. The quaint town was a step back in time, a place where people waved to strangers and stopped to chat in the town square on a busy Saturday morning. It was a place where a smile was sincere and a handshake was your word of honor.

An old brick courthouse and gazebo stood proudly among huge shade trees in the center of town, luring passersby to rest a spell and remember the past. The shops and stores surrounding the square had been remodeled with high, false clapboard fronts that teased the imagination with visions of a more leisurely yesteryear.

Shasta drove slowly around the town as she saw Kane's interest peak. People waved and nodded in friendly hellos and Kane waved back. She turned into a parking lot and cut the engine. "How do you like it so far?"

"What a lovely place. It reminds me of the small villages in Europe where people still take pride in their homes and town. But why are we stopping here?"

Shasta grinned. "Did you think the lake house stocked itself with food?"

"I see." He read the distaste in her expression correctly. "Your aversion to shopping extends to supermarkets, am I right?"

"Right."

"You want me to do it?"

"No, no." She kept a straight face. "Julie called ahead and ordered our supplies. I just wanted to get several things out in the open before we continue on our way. This is as good a place as any." She cleared her throat. "Julie meant it when he told you I can't cook, so it's up to you whether we eat or starve. Of course, we can come into town for every meal, but that's so inconvenient."

Shaking his head, Kane crawled out of the jeep. He'd never understand this woman. Turning to Shasta, he was pleased to see the blush creep into her cheeks. "We won't starve. I'm an excellent cook."

By the time they reached the turnoff to the lake house the sun had risen to its zenith and was beating down unrelentingly. Shasta carefully maneuvered through a narrow gate, then around a curved bend that brought them out onto a sloping lawn thick with blooming shrubs and manicured flower beds. The Mastersons' vacation home was not the small weekend cottage he'd envisioned, and he smiled in appreciation of the beauty before him.

Amid towering pines and live oaks sprawled a large split-level cedar house built on high stilts. Kane could make out a sluggishly moving creek running in front of the house and the bright blue of Lake Livingston beyond. Shasta seemed to read his mind and answered his question before he asked it.

"We're not actually on the lake but the creek. There's a boathouse built on the lakeside that houses a boat for skiing and one for bass fishing." She pulled to a stop and jumped out, heading for the flight of stairs and the back door. Baskerville bounded out, barking and running around with his nose to the ground.

Kane followed more slowly, his body suffering the combined effects of his hangover and the bumpy ride. By the time he climbed the stairs, which seemed to go on forever, he heard Shasta mumbling and cursing softly to herself.

"Shasta, don't tell me you don't have the keys?"

"Just a minute." She sat on the cedar step and emptied out the contents of her purse, rummaging through the items frantically. Looking up, she smiled wryly. "I forgot them, but—"

"Wonderful. We have six bags of groceries, a cooler full of Julie's goodies...." He sat down beside her and began to laugh. "What the hell? I couldn't care less about food. We'll just kill ourselves making love." He hauled her onto his lap and kissed her long and deep.

Her arms creeped around his neck, and she returned the slow movement of his tongue with her own. Pulling back, her breath coming fast, she grinned and held a small black leather case before his eyes. "There's one advantage in having a lover who's an expert with locks."

"Shasta, those are burglar tools and illegal to carry." He studied the stainless-steel instruments, which resembled a dainty manicure set. His frown deepened.

She flashed him an impish smile. "Don't preach! J.T. searches my purse every time we're together. I can't tell you how many sets I go through." Her nose crinkled enchantingly. "My contact is threatening to go up on his price. He's accusing me of reselling them for a higher profit."

Kane watched in fascination as she worked, and in a matter of seconds the lock clicked and the door swung open.

"I'm impressed—I shouldn't be, but I am." His eyes began to dance with laughter. "How long would it take to teach someone the art?"

"Oh, years and years of intense study to be as good as me." She leaned over and kissed him lingeringly on the lips. "And we can start anytime you say."

SHASTA STRETCHED LAZILY on the dock, lulled by its swaying motion. Between half-closed eyelids she studied Kane, who was lying beside her. His broad chest, slick with sweat, rose and fell in shallow even breaths that told her he was sound asleep. For the past four days theirs had been an idyllic existence, and as if by an unspoken mutual agreement, they refused to discuss U.S.A. Oil, the professor, the formula or anything remotely related to it. Instead they made love, sunbathed in the nude, and when they felt the necessity to talk, they told stories about their past, funny tales that kept them laughing for hours later. Kane told her of all the places he'd seen, and Shasta talked about her job and some of the crazy stunts she'd pulled during her career. She also told him of her sideline designing locks, explaining that the sale of the designs enabled her to indulge her passion for fast foreign cars.

But even in the tender moments they shared, Shasta sensed a tension in Kane. There was an uneasiness that lurked behind his darkened eyes and a wariness that warred with the gentleness of his voice. For the past few hours the warning tingling at the base of her neck had made her more alert to his moods.

Though he was trying his best to hide it, she sensed that something was terribly wrong.

The dock dipped precariously as Kane rolled over and sat up. He rubbed his face in his hands briskly, then stared off into space before he asked, "Why did you put your top back on?" Reaching out, he ran the tip of his finger down the wet valley between her breasts.

"I was beginning to get burned in the wrong place. I didn't want to deprive you of any of your pleasures."

"Me? You're the one who enjoys it so."

Shasta tugged at her brief yellow bikini top and sent him a scowl belied by her sparkling eyes. "I might ask you the same question." She slipped her fingers into the waistband of the scrap of fabric that covered him. "Why are you wearing these?"

"I wanted to get some sun on my front but didn't want to incapacitate myself and spoil your fun!"

"Touché." She grinned and lay back down. Kane did the same, bringing the palm of her hand to his lips and kissing her lingeringly. "What's wrong, Kane?" The question had been haunting her for hours.

Kane was silent for a long time, going over and over in his mind what he must say. The fickle sun dipped behind another dense white cloud, and he shivered as the air cooled his wet skin. He'd been dreading this moment for days, and he felt like a coward. He'd become so caught up in the wonder of loving that he'd blocked out the consequences. But last night as they'd cuddled together on the deck, gazing at the stars, he'd realized they'd come too far. He shivered again, remembering.

Dusk was slow in coming in the country—or so it seemed to Kane. They had spent the day out on the lake, fishing, enjoying the sun and just being lazy. As the afternoon lengthened, they went back to the lake house and cleaned up, and Kane cooked a simple meal of steaks and baked potatoes. Then they retired to the cedar deck with a bottle of wine to watch the darkness overtake the day. Stargazing had became a nightly ritual, one he had come to look forward to. The soporific drone of cicadas, the erratic flight of fireflies and the sound of the wind rustling through the tall trees brought a timeless peace that soothed away all the intruding yesterdays. They had been sitting quietly, listening to the approaching night, when the breeze brought the baying of dogs from across the creek.

Kane had felt Shasta tense as the barking animals began an earnest pursuit of their prey. Then suddenly there came a high-pitched scream, and the night grew still with death. Shasta hadn't spoken of the incident, but he knew she hurt and wept inside for the helpless animal. He could read her body and mind now, just as she could read his. They were one, and he felt the burden of that special gift. He would share her pain, and it scared him. She was too softhearted, too sensitive, and so very vulnerable now. It was then that he had faced the reality of what he'd allowed to happen and what he must do.

He wasn't good enough for her—she deserved better. He'd never measure up to her dreams and expectations, and the thought of the hurt and disappointment in those big dark eyes was more than he could handle. He knew if she ever found out of his past activities she would reject him. Better to put an end to their love now than let it be battered to death when the truth came out.

He turned to look over at Shasta now. "I asked you once before, where do we go from here, and you neatly evaded my question. I think you'd better answer it."

"Where would you like to go?" Shasta's heart pounded in her ears, and her palms began to sweat. She had sensed a feeling of doom all day, and now she knew it was upon her.

"To be honest, right now I'd like to be anywhere but here, having to go through this."

"I'll go where you go." She tried to interject a teasing note to her voice, but her throat ached and the words came out a hoarse whisper.

"You'd lead my life?" He snorted. "Come on, Shasta. You despise the way I live. But I do it for a reason—not very noble, but it does have its compensations. If you went with me, what would you do?"

"The same as you. Don't you think the World Security Agency would take me on if you tell them we're a team?"

Kane shrugged noncommittally. He knew for a fact that the WSA would be ecstatic to have her talents. "I don't know, but that's not the issue here, or an answer."

Shasta closed her eyes tightly and asked softly, "Is marriage out of the question?"

"Yes," he said harshly, and immediately regretted the curt tone. He tried to soften his reply with an explanation. "I told you once I was too old for you—that I had too many miles on me. I've done things that would sicken you." His face hardened. "I'm not good enough for you, Shasta. I'd corrupt your life and hurt you, then I could never live with myself."

Shasta's eyes shot open. "That's crazy!" She twisted sideways, rocking the dock and sending waves of water over the sides. "I know what and who you are...."

Kane laughed, and the savage sound made Shasta wince. "Don't be naive." He began to tell her the things the frivolous, vain and bored rich did for excitement, and he tried to convince her that he was exactly like the people she'd met. "Shasta, there's *nothing* I haven't done or tried."

"But—"

"No, really think about what I just said. Remember all the things you were taught were wrong, and then picture me doing them. I'm just like those friends of mine you despise so."

"Stop! We've gone through this before, and I didn't believe you then and won't believe you now. I've done a few reprehensible things myself." She began to gather her towel and get up, but Kane grabbed her arm and held her down.

"What you've done is child's play."

"I don't want to hear anymore."

"But you will, Shasta. You'll listen to every dirty little detail till I'm through."

She sat powerless in his verbal grip, torn between her love to shut his words out and a kind of fascination to know every facet of his life. Her face a stoic mask, she listened as he poured out his past. Her complexion alternated between a bloodless white and bright red, and every now and then she would flinch. The back of her eyes stung with unshed tears. She wanted to cry for him, for the devastating loneliness he must have endured.

When he had finished, Kane stared at her, his eyes depthless mirrors once again, his beautiful features expressionless except for the pale circle around his tightly held mouth. Shasta met his look squarely with an understanding smile that promised the world.

"Are you through trying to shock me? I don't give a damn about your past. It's the future I'm concerned about. I love you, Kane. You can't take that away or change my feelings."

"And your love washes the slate clean?" he yelled, exasperated at her stubbornness, yet deep down the tight knot relaxed its hold on his heart. She hadn't turned away from him in revulsion.... But it still wouldn't work. "I'm not the man for you. Even my work for the government is a sham—a way to assuage the boredom."

"Liar!" She came to her knees and faced him, rocking the dock so violently that water curled halfway across the wide platform. "Liar. You believe in good and right and your country."

Kane brought his furious face close to hers and bellowed, "You need a husband with a nine-to-five job who'll come home every evening to you and your children. I can't fill that dream."

Shasta flinched with each of his statements as if he had slapped her. She doubled her small fist and drew back without giving a second thought to what she was doing as she clipped him soundly on the chin. His head snapped backward a fraction, and he stared at her. His shocked expression would have been comical at any other time, but Shasta was so indignantly angry she could barely speak.

"You fool," she snarled. "Blind, self-centered...."

"Damn it, Shasta," he interrupted her tirade, rubbing his stinging chin. "That hurt."

Her eyes filled with tears, which she rapidly blinked away. "What would I do with a nine-to-five husband. I don't even work regular hours! After all I've tried to do and show you, you've never really seen me at all. You didn't listen to me. You—" she poked at his naked chest with a sharp fingernail "—don't know me at all. Damn you! I don't want a home. I can't take care of the one I bought. I never wanted—" Her words trailed off and she cocked her head, listening to the tone of Baskerville's vicious growls in the distance.

Shasta leaped to her feet and sprinted up the wooden steps, running with an urgency that set Kane in motion. He yelled a warning and followed, but she'd been too quick, and her head start had given her the advantage. As he cleared the top of the slope his heart stopped, and for a split second he froze at the scene before him. Baskerville had a man by the leg, his massive head shaking his prize back and forth.

The stranger yelled and cursed as he tried to aim his gun at the huge animal's head. But Baskerville kept jerking him around in circles, his razor-sharp teeth biting deeper as he pulled and tugged.

Kane felt as if he was moving in slow motion; his feet seemed to weigh a hundred pounds. Each step made him gasp for breath, and he thought his pounding heart would burst from his chest. In his mind he saw what was coming, and a scream ripped from his throat. The stranger had spotted Shasta flying up the grassy slope and raised his arm to fire.

Kane's line of vision narrowed into a long tunnel and all he could see at the same instant the gun fired was Shasta's graceful leap into the air. Her body arched high then tucked together in a ball as she flipped and landed on the ground in a rolling motion that brought her body against Baskerville's prisoner and brought them tumbling to the ground.

The invisible hold on Kane was released and he charged the remaining distance, kicked the fallen gun out of reach and set his bare foot across the struggling man's neck.

"Shasta, are you all right?"

"I'm fine." She glanced at him, her eyes sparkling with excitement and anticipation.

Kane shook his head and smiled, but the smile disappeared as he looked down. "Hello, Willie. What dark hole did you crawl out of?" The little man, no taller than Shasta, twisted his ferret face in a grimace. He opened his long thin mouth to speak, but Kane applied more pressure against his throat, choking off his words.

Shasta sat back on her heels stroking Baskerville, trying to persuade him to let go of the man's leg. Her head jerked up when she realized Kane knew the fellow, but she didn't have time to ask any questions. She caught sight of a moving figure over his shoulder and screamed, "Kane, behind you!"

Everything happened at once, but Shasta only had time to marvel at Kane and his expertise in an art she'd never mastered. He pivoted on one leg, as supple and fluid as a ballet dancer, while the other leg swung out and to the side like a sledgehammer as it connected with his assailant's middle, dropping him to his knees. Kane delivered a hand-chop to the back of the man's head that knocked him out cold. Shasta could watch no longer; her captive was attempting to grab her and his fallen gun at the same time.

Shasta dived across the little man, her fingers busily touching nerve points on his body. The man grunted and spewed out foul names as his arm lost its feeling. Frantically she grabbed Willie's hand and drew his arm forcefully between his legs. As she eased the pressure, she warned him, "You make one more move like the last and I'll ruin you for life. Baskerville, back off," she ordered sternly.

"My bloodthirsty mouse, that hurts me just to watch. Please let him go." Kane dropped the ropes he'd retrieved from the garage and quickly tied up the two assailants. "Go call the local law and ask them to come pick these men up. Then pack—we're getting out of here."

He stomped off, leaving the two men trussed up on the lawn with Baskerville standing guard. Shasta chased after him, grabbed his arm and swung him around. "We're not leaving here till we settle a few things, Kane. I won't let you end—"

"Listen to me, Shasta." His hands clamped down on her shoulders, and he gave her a tiny shake. "Willie over there is an ex-agent, a renegade for hire to anyone willing to pay his price. His fee is high, Shasta, because he's an expert at his job—extracting information." Kane crushed her to his bare chest. "Willie tortures people. I told you it was going to get dirty and dangerous, but I never envisioned a man of Tramble's stature hiring scum like Willie." He held her at arm's length, then let go and walked away. "The one drawback to employing a man of Willie's talents is that his victims never seem to live through his questioning. They meant to get the formula then kill us, Shasta. Now get moving. I want to have a talk with our two *friends* here before they're carted off."

Shasta did as she was told, her hands trembling as she dialed the number of the sheriff's office. She would follow his orders this time because she knew he was right to want to get back to the city. But if he thought he was going to get rid of her so easily, he was in for a big surprise.

CHAPTER THIRTEEN

THE RETURN TO HOUSTON was considerably rougher and faster than the original trip. The wind beat at them from all directions, making conversation impossible. Shasta had long since stopped asking Kane to slow down; her requests only met with grim silence as he pushed the jeep harder. Even Baskerville was out of sorts. He usually loved to ride in an open car with the breeze in his face, but he couldn't stand the stinging air whipping at his ears. He grumbled and growled at Kane's back, then finally gave up and stretched out on the floor in the rear of the jeep.

Shasta sighed with relief as Houston's city limits came into sight, and Kane was forced by law and traffic to decrease his speed. She shook her head a few times to clear away the lingering roar of the highway. Her appearance, she thought grimly, didn't bear thinking about. She knew her hair was in a wild tangle, and as she touched her hot, windburned cheeks she winced. She felt angered at the unjust turn of events. How could everything fall apart so quickly, she wondered. She wanted nothing more right now than a cool shower, a cold drink, and a quiet place to think. Kane pulled into the driveway, and Shasta climbed out and stomped up the back steps. Baskerville and Kane followed at a safer distance.

Julius's laughter greeted her as she marched in the kitchen.

"Who pulled you through the bushes feetfirst?" At her murderous glare he tried to adopt a somber expression, but he couldn't restrain his chuckles.

Kane tried to ease past Shasta in a manner that set Julius off again. "Oh, you're both hopeless," she muttered. "Kane! Stop right there, we need to talk."

"Later. Shasta, I want to get to the hospital and see Samantha." Kane turned away and she grabbed his arm. He gave her a piercing look filled with determination. "I won't change my mind."

"You at least owe me a few minutes of your time."

"I don't know what's wrong between the two of you," Julius interrupted, "but before you square off for battle you best let me pass on these here messages. Kane, you're to call Boston, the decorators finished with your dad's house and Tramble Baldwin called." Julius checked his list, then glanced up. "Shasta, Jeff's gone to Dallas to meet J.T. He left at your grandfather's request of course."

"Oh, dear." Shasta backed out of the kitchen, leading Kane with her.

"You're also to call J.T., Samantha Grey and Rena." Julius looked up, his expression full of curiosity and surprise when he saw that Shasta was taking Kane to her private room. His woolly eyebrows rose in shock as she opened the door, pulled Kane inside and quickly shut them in. "Well! Don't that beat all? You see that, you dumb mutt?"

Baskerville collapsed on the cool kitchen floor and closed his eyes.

Shasta leaned against the door. "How's your chin?"

"Fine. A little touchy."

"I won't apologize for hitting you."

"Hmm." Kane studied the room with genuine surprise. Julie had warned him earlier that this was Shasta's haven and no one was allowed. For some reason he'd pictured overstuffed furniture and walls lined with books, but what he saw came as a shock. There were bookshelves all right, but instead of the bound leather editions he'd expected, there were hundreds of locks in all sizes, colors and fashion filling every spare inch of space. A drafting table and tall stool were the only other furnishings.

"I can see I've caught you off guard again. This is where I design the locks that help support my foreign-car addiction. Damn it, Kane! Did you even try to see the real me?" She yanked a large ring of keys from his hand and put it back on the shelf with a bang.

"This isn't going to do us any good. I've made up my mind." He began to roam the small room.

Her heart sank like a stone in her breast. She blinked rapidly, telling herself she wasn't going to lose her temper, she was going to deal with this like an intelligent, sophisticated woman. "I'd like to sock you again," she yelled. "Put that down." She snatched a brass double-bolt lock from his hands and dropped it on the floor with a crash. "How can you possibly think I want roots and children? I want to be free—can't you see that?" She spread her arms wide. "Take a good look around you, Kane. I didn't want this house, I didn't decorate it, I don't cook, shop or clean. Nor do I want to—that should be obvious to anyone. And when did I ever say anything about babies? This might come as a shock to your male-chauvinist brain, but I don't want children, not for a long time, maybe never." She inhaled deeply and rocked back on her heels, glaring up at his beautiful, insolent face. "Can't you see *me?* I'm you, Kane."

He grimaced and his skin lost some of its color.

"It's true. I'm a female version of you. I thrive on excitement and danger. I want my freedom just as you do, but that doesn't mean I can't love and have a husband." Gazing into his cool eyes, she wanted to scream. He was the most stubborn man she'd ever met. "I love you, Kane. No—don't go."

"Shasta, I wouldn't be good for you. Hush." He laid his fingers across her lips. "You're upset—"

"Of course I'm upset," she mumbled around his fingers.

"We'll talk about it later when things have settled down some."

"You bet we will," she muttered. "You just bet we will." She followed him to the door and up the stairs. "What about the professor, Kane? You haven't said a word about what Willie and his partner had to say. And don't give me that look. You were alone with them for twenty minutes while I called the sheriff and threw our clothes together."

Kane turned and faced her, his expression taut. "It's useless, Shasta, I can see that now. My whole plan was a pipe dream from the start. I thought if Tramble wanted the formula bad enough, he'd make arrangements to turn over the killer. He's the type to bribe the man into giving himself up—with monetary compensations, of course. Remember, the tragic *accident*—and that's what Tramble's lawyer will call it—took place in France, not America. I doubt, with Tramble's money, the man would even have been extradited. So you see, it's over." He cupped her curved cheek, tenderly stroking its softness with his fingers. Then, suddenly aware of his actions, he jerked his hand away as if her flesh burned. "I don't want anyone else hurt or another death on my conscience so I've had to face the reality that in this case there will be no justice—though heaven knows it makes me sick to my stomach. Now I really have to clean up and get to the hospital." He walked into his room and shut the door.

Shasta stood staring at the closed door, her eyes narrowing with suspicion. His downtrodden act was not at all characteristic, and giving up wasn't his way. There was a sly glint in his eyes. It was all a bald-faced lie. Kane Stone would never retreat so meekly, no matter the danger to him or anyone else. But why did he find it necessary to make up such a story?

"Going to the hospital, like hell," she grumbled, and sprinted down the stairs. "Julie." She bounded into the kitchen, startling both man and dog. "Kane's up to something and I need you to follow him." She stopped to catch her breath. "And this time don't let him see you." Looking down at herself, she frowned. "I wish I could go, but it's going to take me hours to be presentable again. Will you do it? Please."

Julius wiped his hands on a dish towel and tugged off his apron. "Sure, kid. I could use some excitement and exercise myself. Want to tell me what's wrong?"

She kissed his lined cheek, and as quickly as possible told him of their two assailants and Kane's decision that he wasn't good enough for her.

"Well, he ain't."

"Julie!"

"No man's going to be good enough for you, kid. Not where me and your grandpappy's concerned. But Kane's as good as you're going to catch, so you better think of something to change his mind." He patted her shoulder awkwardly. "I better get moving."

A COOL SHOWER and a good long cry helped soothe Shasta's jangled nerves. She fluffed her hair one last time, then leaned closer to her reflection, inspecting her still-red nose. Why couldn't she cry prettily instead of looking like Bozo the clown? Even a generous application of makeup hadn't hidden the bright tip of her nose or the apple redness of her windburned cheeks. Her eyes filled with tears of self-pity, and she fought to hold them back. She should have remembered her grandfather's advice. He'd told her repeatedly that a person could map out his work, his life and a vacation, but never try to plan the course of love. And if you did, don't be surprised when it backfired in your scheming face. She was all out of ideas, strategies and maneuvers. Now she'd have to ride out the storm on intuition alone.

Shasta sniffed and surged to her feet. Action was what she needed to pull her out of the doldrums. Squaring her shoulders, she straightened the bodice of her pink-and-gray striped sundress and slipped her feet into a pair of wheat-colored sling-back pumps. As soon as Kane returned, they'd sit down and work out *his* problem. All they needed, she told herself fiercely, was to talk. And what if that didn't work and Kane was still determined to abide by his decision? Shasta dismissed the question, unwilling to face the heartache of the answer.

She wandered downstairs and into the kitchen, where Baskerville lay sleeping and unresponsive to her chatter. She even tried the magic word "beer," but still he slept on. "You're a wonderful watchdog, Baskerville," she said loudly, and only received a twitch of one ear in reply.

The house had an emptiness about it that she'd never noticed before when she was alone. Roaming from room to room, she touched familiar objects that now seemed strange to her. Even her workroom didn't calm her tension. All she could see was her life coming apart at the seams. She had to find a way to make Kane understand that he was wrong and his crazy idea that he wasn't good enough for her was ridiculous.

When the doorbell rang, Shasta almost fell over herself in her rush to have someone to talk to, even a salesman. She swung open the door with a bright smile of welcome that slowly died on her lips as she inspected the government badges held out to her.

"Miss Masterson, I'm Gill Ham and these two men are Richard Brown and Sam Willis. We're with the FBI and would like to speak with Kane Stone."

"He's not here." She was about to close the door, but one of the agents already had his body halfway inside. Shasta opened the door wider. "Do come in," she said sarcastically.

"We really do need to talk with Mr. Stone and would like to wait." All three were inside and edging their way toward the living room. "May we?" Before she could reply they made themselves comfortable around her coffee table.

Shasta had to bite back a grin at their audacity. She'd often used the same ploy. "I've no idea when Kane will be returning."

"We'll wait."

She smiled, not at their determination but the fact that she could have spotted them as agents on any crowded street. The government, she thought disgustedly, didn't have any imagination. In an attempt to be nondescript, the agents reeked of their profession. Her smile widened dangerously, and she decided to have some fun. Maybe a good laugh would help.

"Baskerville!" she yelled, injecting just enough anxiety in her voice to bring the huge dog at a run. She ordered him to sit, and he planted himself in the center of the doorway, his fathomless eyes alert to every move and gesture the men made.

"Now, Miss Masterson, there's no need for him."

"Well, Mr. Ham, a girl just can't be too careful these days, can she?" Besides, she didn't want to give the agents free access to her house. There was going to be trouble enough as it was without one of them talking to Kane before she had time to warn him.

"You're right," the agent agreed, and tried to ignore the fixed stare from the animal across the room. "Would it be too much to ask for a cup of coffee?"

"Yes, it would. I'm afraid I don't know how to make it."

The agent sighed. "Miss Masterson, let's stop dancing around the issue, shall we? You could be a great help to us and your country."

Shasta's big eyes opened wide. "Oh. How?"

"You know, of course, that Kane has a synthetic-fuel formula?" Shasta nodded eagerly. "We don't know if he's trying to sell the formula on the open market or to an individual."

"The formula's not for sale to anyone, Mr. Ham."

"Fine, fine. By that I take it he hasn't made any decision?"

She shrugged, her eyes beginning to flash with anger.

"You're a loyal American, Miss Masterson. You and your family have an impeccable reputation, and a scandal could seriously damage your good name."

"What scandal?" she asked softly. Baskerville recognized the danger signal in her low voice, and his lips curled over his teeth in a soundless snarl.

"Why, the one Kane's liable to bring down on your head if he decided to sell." He held up his hand. "I know you said the formula wasn't being marketed, but look at it logically. If the formula works, it could cause untold damage in the world economy. Even a rumor of such an alternative in oil resources could cause an all-out war. The Middle East would lose its revenue and set off a disastrous chain reaction if they began to pull their investments out of banks and call in loans. Miss Masterson, they wouldn't begin with us—America. They would start with our allies. Do you have any idea how much the Middle East has invested in the British pound sterling? The chaos it would cause if they dumped their investments would put the pressure on our government and make us answerable to the world. You do see that to let such a potential weapon be controlled by one individual is unthinkable? The discovery could be as explosive an issue as the bomb."

"I still don't see what this has to do with Masters."

"Why, Miss Masterson." He looked shocked at her ignorance. "If Kane decides to keep the formula for private enterprise, then Washington would have to step in, not only for the safety of the formula but Kane's personal protection. You know the leaks and false stories the papers are always printing. Your name would be linked with Kane's, your private investigator's licence revoked and suspicion thrown on Masters' ethics." His big white teeth flashed in a grin that reminded her of Baskerville's.

"With your help we could avoid any possible misunderstandings. If you would talk to Kane, I'm sure he would listen to *you.*"

The innuendo in his voice wasn't lost on Shasta, and her hand balled into a tight fist. "I see."

"We knew you would. You're an intelligent young woman. Brains and beauty, a resourceful combination."

"Yes." Shasta returned his smile. "If you'll excuse me, please." She didn't wait a second longer but marched out of the room, pausing only long enough to give Baskerville a hand order to stay.

A few seconds later she was standing in the middle of the kitchen, spinning around slowly, hunting for something to throw. She snatched up an oval platter from the counter and with a satisfied smirk on her lips held it firmly in both hands, raised it aloft, then froze. A picture snapped in her head, a scene of another throwing spree, after which Julie had made her pick up every sliver of glass then scrub the kitchen floor on hands and knees. She shivered with revulsion and gently returned the platter safely to the counter. But the inactivity didn't help her steaming temper, so she opened the pantry door, stepped inside and yelled, "Of all the unmitigated gall! Blackmail, coercion, threats. Wait till J.T. hears about this!"

She opened the door and stepped out, feeling a little better as she picked up the telephone and began to punch J.T.'s telephone number. It was time the game ended. Nothing could be done to catch the killer of the professor. She'd agreed with Kane on that. But she was sick of the three-way tug-of-war going on between Kane, U.S.A. Oil and the government. Besides, the turmoil was complicating her love life. She cleared the line and pushed a different set of numbers.

"U.S.A. Oil, Mr. Baldwin's office," the disembodied voice said.

"Tramble Baldwin, please."

"I'm sorry, but Mr. Baldwin is in a board meeting. May I take a message?"

"No, lady, you go get him. Tell him Shasta Masterson's on the line, he'll come." She waited, tapping her foot impatiently.

"Shasta, honey. Good to hear your lovely voice. What may I do for you today, sweetheart?"

Tramble's whisky-and-tobacco voice, laced with endearments, made her stomach lurch. She thought of Willie and his methods of extracting information.

"Nothing," she replied. "It's what I can do for you. If you want to know about the formula, be at my house in one hour." She hung up before he could ask any questions. Now all she had to do was wait and pray that Kane would be back soon. She sat down in the nearest chair and stared as if mesmerized by the wallpaper across the room. What had she done? Kane was going to kill her with his bare hands for interfering.

But the lies and evasion had to stop, now, before they went so far that no one would believe there wasn't a formula after all. If a false story concerning the formula were to leak to other interested parties they'd never be free; there would always be the threat of some foreign government believing the falsehood and coming after Kane. The agent was right; Kane would truly need someone's protection then. But all her rational thoughts didn't make facing Kane any easier. He'd warned her repeatedly to stop meddling. Maybe she was wrong. The problem was, she just couldn't keep an interest in a nonexistent fuel formula when her personal life was falling apart. She'd worried and fretted all day, fearing Kane wouldn't come back, then dreading having to face him again. She'd never felt as far away from Kane as she did now, all the while one thought kept running through her head—what if she couldn't convince him they belonged together?

Shasta didn't know how long she sat there, her mind grappling with her growing mountain of problems. The insistent ringing of the telephone finally jolted her out of her stupor. "Yes?"

"Shasta, Kane's just now pulling into the hospital parking lot."

"Julie, where have you been?" She mentally thanked her grandfather for his insistence that every family member have a mobile phone in their car. "Where are you?"

"In the car behind Kane. Don't ask questions, kid. It ain't easy keeping up with this slippery eel. Listen—when Kane left the house he stopped at a pay phone and made a call. Then, twenty minutes later I was following him across town. Shasta, he met Jason Leroy at the zoo, and they talked for a good hour." He paused to let his information sink in before continuing. "I think after the hospital he'll be heading home. If not, I'll call you."

Julius hung up before Shasta could say anything, and in any case her voice seemed to have deserted her completely. Jason Leroy, she mouthed silently. The name clanged in her head like a giant bell. Jason Leroy was a well-known electronics expert with a questionable past. He'd been accused many times of using illegal wiretaps and planting listening devices, but charges against him never seemed to stick, since the victims, usually large corporations, were unwilling to bring him to justice and expose themselves and their secrets. Shasta frowned fiercely in growing fear. What was Kane up to? But she knew. He was going to try one more time to trap Tramble Baldwin and to hell with the legalities.

SHASTA SIGHED, rested her elbows on the table and propped her chin on her folded hands—waiting was unbearable. She checked her watch and sighed again, deeper this time. It had been an hour and twenty minutes since Julie's call.

"Shasta. Honey! Could you call your dog off, sweetheart? I'd like to come out and talk to you."

A sly grin curved her lips as she listened to Tramble's pleas. " 'Fraid not, Tramble. But I'm sure that Misters Ham, Brown and Willis would be willing to listen to anything you have to say. The four of you have so much in common." She chuckled as she heard the grumble of curses and Baskerville's sharp bark.

Tramble had arrived blustering and oozing cordiality. From the minute he contaminated her threshold she'd been offended by his "good ole boy" act and his self-assurance that she was willing to hand over the formula. But she'd had her own small revenge in the look on his face when he realized his meeting included three government agents and a dog determined to hold him prisoner till Kane showed up.

The distinctive purr of an engine pulling into the driveway and the sound of a car door slamming sent Shasta flying to meet Kane. As he stepped into the kitchen she wrapped her arms around his neck and tugged his mouth down to hers. "Thank heaven you're home."

Kane could no more resist the full lips than he could stop breathing, so he closed his eyes and savored her warmth. Just one more time, he told himself, and gathered her into his arms, feeling her pliant body melt into his as he deepened the kiss. She was so small and soft he wanted to go on holding her forever. His hands slid down her back to her hips and settled her against him. "Hey." He broke away, his breath coming a little faster. "That's some welcome."

The back door opened and Kane glanced up in time to catch the look that passed between Shasta and Julie. "Ahh." He released Shasta and retreated a few steps so he could watch them both. "You're a better tracker than I gave you credit for, Julie. I never knew you were there today."

Julius frowned, his brow pleating into deep grooves. "I can be darn near invisible if I ain't watching my back as well as the front." Then he did something that shocked Shasta—he apologized. "I was under orders, you understand?"

Kane nodded, his gaze shifting back and forth between the two people. "Did you follow me to the zoo?" Julius smiled. "And you knew the man I met?"

"Yep."

"From Shasta's expression, I guess you called her?" Julius nodded and Kane shrugged.

"I want to talk to you, Kane." Shasta looked around, trying to figure out where she could achieve total privacy and still keep her four visitors from interfering. She reached around behind Kane, opened the pantry door, and gently pushed Kane backward.

Kane found a hanging cord and pulled it. A harsh light illuminated shelves of cans, bottles and jars. "I'll have to hand it to you, mouse. This is a strange place to hold a conversation." He began to laugh, then sobered when she refused to see the humor. "You're upset?"

"You can't do it, Kane! Jason Leroy is a criminal."

"Not true." He inspected the labels at eye level, feigning a disinterest that didn't fool Shasta. "Leroy's never been behind bars."

"A mere technicality. He's an industrial Peeping Tom."

"Shasta, stay out of this." He stopped his detailed inventory of the shelves and turned his blazing eyes on her. "I'm no longer your concern." She snorted. "Where's your other earring?"

"Wha . . . what?"

"You're only wearing one earring. Where's the other?"

Shasta frowned, her hands automatically searching the copious pockets of her sundress. "Here." She held up a small gold loop and he took it from her, turning her sideways to the light. "I won't let you hire Leroy, Kane."

"Be still." He inserted the minute piece of metal into her pierced ear and fastened it. "Now, turn all the way around."

She did as she was told, and he fastened the two center buttons at the back of her dress, which she'd been unable to reach.

"I wasn't hiring Jason, Shasta. I was buying merchandise." With his hands on her shoulders he spun her around.

"You were going to plant bugs in Tramble's office yourself?"

"And his home," he added. Leaning down, he whispered, "Now that you know, wouldn't you like to come along? Think of it, Shasta. You'd be pulling a job for real. No more playacting or pretending you're a cat burglar."

She stared up at him, a silly smile of longing on her lips and her eyes wide with excitement at the thought of the thrill and danger. But her good judgment intervened and her eyes hardened.

"No, Kane, and I'll stop you if you try."

Kane sighed. He knew his plan was doomed the moment Shasta was on to him. He had only wanted to see that look of pure joy light her face one more time. "Okay, no Leroy."

Her gaze narrowed on his face. "The truth?"

"Yes."

Shasta grinned. Then her lips twisted as she remembered the four waiting men. "Ah, Kane. . . ." She stopped and swallowed. "I've done something I know you won't be pleased about."

"What?"

"Actually, pleased is the wrong word. I guess you'll be quite angry, really."

He grinned. "You're hedging, Shasta."

"Yes, I know." She looked up and smiled her most brilliant smile. "We have company—four men."

"Mouse. . . ."

"Three government agents."

"You've left one out."

"And Tramble Baldwin."

Kane cursed long and low in several languages, and Shasta was thankful she couldn't understand what he was saying. "I know you're mad that I've interfered, but—"

"That's an understatement." He leaned against a shelf and crossed his arms over his chest to keep from reaching out and strangling her. "How did this menagerie of misfits come to be in your living room?"

Shasta told him as quickly as possible, then asked, "Why are the agents making their move now, Kane, after all these weeks of watching our every move?" His face, set in hard lines, wrenched at her heart. She wanted to caress away the deeply etched lines on his forehead and kiss his taut lips.

Kane shrugged. "Who knows, Shasta. But you can bet their following us was not the only ongoing investigation in this case. They could probably tell us a few things." He sighed. "For whatever reason, I'm suddenly glad they've finally showed their hand. I was beginning to get nervous with them always at our backs."

Shasta remembered something one of the agents had said concerning personal safety. "Kane, do you think they could have been protecting us all this time?"

"I wouldn't discount that theory altogether." He was thoughtful for a moment. "I think they're somehow wise to Tramble and felt his escalating efforts to obtain the formula for himself weren't healthy for anyone concerned. More than likely they've stepped in at this point to make sure I hadn't been coerced into making a deal." He scowled down at her. "Now I'm forced to face them and Tramble and explain that there's no deal in the making."

"All you have to do, Kane, is go in there and tell them you don't have the formula."

"You think it will be that easy, and they'll believe me?" he sneered.

"Yes, I do. After all, it's only Tramble you've been leading down the garden path."

"And what about Melvin, Shasta?" he asked softly.

Shasta shivered at the sudden drop of temperature in the pantry. His words were so frigid she could have hung icicles from them. For the first time she truly realized how angry and disappointed Kane was at having his plans altered. Though he had faced the fact that Tramble would get off free, he'd still hoped for justice. The sadness in his eyes made her want to cry at his loss and her interference. She took a deep breath, swallowing her misgivings for what she'd done, and forged ahead.

"I think I've figured out a way to get Tramble, Kane." She placed her hands on his crossed arms, but he stood stone still. "Kane, there's nothing we can do for Melvin. You've admitted and accepted that fact. But Tramble's a different story. We can make him pay if you'll just give it time."

"That's something I have plenty of. Go on."

"Tramble and your father are just alike. What's the most important thing in their life?"

"Their business—oil."

"Right. So, if U.S.A. Oil is Tramble's life, you take it away from him in slow torturous degrees. You do it in such a way that he's helpless to fight back." Shasta tightened her hold on his arms as she felt him stiffen. "You have the money to do it, Kane," she said excitedly as she saw her words begin to take hold and his features relax.

"Go on," he urged with genuine interest in his voice.

"A stock takeover. You buy up all U.S.A. Oil's stock and take the company."

"There's not enough stock on the open market to get controlling interest. Tramble made sure of that a long time ago."

"No, not on the open market. I know something that isn't public information. JoBeth Huntley is Tramble's niece. You remember JoBeth, don't you? She's good friends with the DeSalvas and is always hanging around them."

Kane nodded, picturing the tall, pretty blonde, who made the society pages with her fabulous parties.

"JoBeth's mother and Tramble were brother and sister. When JoBeth's mother got married, Tramble refused to acknowledge or accept the man. He wouldn't have anything to do with his sister again, but when she died he could do nothing about her will leaving the stock to JoBeth. Kane, JoBeth Huntley holds forty percent of voting stock, and she despises her uncle." She smiled into his animated face, marveling at the change. "With a little help from Brandon DeSalva we could discuss a deal with her."

"Why you Machiavellian-minded, crafty little witch." He cupped her glowing face in his hands and kissed her lingeringly. "Shall we go face our adversaries and put our dragon to rest?"

For the next hour Shasta was amazed by Kane's firm but eloquent denial of a synthetic-fuel formula. Cold, precise, his eyes never leaving Tramble's disbelieving face, he told them of the burned ashes of the professor's papers.

Though Tramble couldn't openly dispute Kane's statement with the agents present, he did manage to inject a skepticism as to Kane's honesty.

"You doubt me, Tramble? Why would I lie?" Kane leaned his shoulders against the fireplace mantel, enjoying the choked sounds coming from the older man's throat.

"To make a fortune for yourself, that's why, and you damn well know it."

Kane smiled. "I already have a fortune. What would I do with two?"

Shasta's attention swung back and forth between the two combatants. The agents, she realized, seemed content to allow Kane and Tramble to fight it out, while she held her breath waiting for Kane's cool facade to explode. But he kept calm and politely turned Tramble's every insult aside. She listened, stunned and unbelieving, as Kane apologized to both Tramble and the agents for leading them astray.

"You understand I was directing my own investigation, don't you?" He glanced over at Tramble, his message clear as to whom he held responsible for the professor's death.

When at last everyone seemed to be satisfied that there was no synthetic-fuel formula, the meeting began to break up. The agents left with a promise from Kane that he'd travel to Washington for a special meeting with some concerned parties.

Tramble hung back as the agents said their goodbyes, and as the front door closed he turned to Kane. "You better be telling the truth, Kane—" he looked pointedly at Shasta, "—because Willie didn't spend very long in that hick-town jail." He leaned closer, his florid face as close to Kane's as his short height would allow, and his gravelly voice held anger and suspicion. "If that formula's not ashes as you say, and it turns up...." He paused dramatically, and Shasta held her breath, her hand squeezing Kane's arm hard.

Tramble's cold blue eyes stared at Kane. "Accidents can happen and you could end up like old Melvin." He ignored Shasta's gasp and, shoving his Stetson on his head, sauntered out of the house.

"My God! Kane, he did it, he had Melvin killed."

Kane turned around, his face a stone mask. "I never doubted it for a second." Then he smiled, a smile that sent a shiver up and down Shasta's spine. "There *will* be a reckoning and retribution, though. I promise you that with your plan I'll make Tramble Baldwin pay—slowly, painfully. We'll have our justice, and he'll account for his sins here on earth."

Shasta collapsed into her chair. Closing her eyes, she again saw the look of menace and hate on Tramble's face. Yes, she thought, Kane would eventually have his justice. Men like Tramble didn't deserve anything less.

"All things considered, that went well, don't you think?" Kane poured himself a small amount of whisky and tossed it back in one swallow.

"You were wonderful—and surprising!"

"How so?" he added another splash of liquor into his glass and sat on the arm of her chair.

Shasta grinned. "You missed your calling. You should have been a snake-oil salesman." She began to chuckle. "The way you handled Tramble was brilliant. Did you see the joy on his face when he really began to believe that the formula had been destroyed? And his anger when you reminded him that if one old man could discover and develop a new fuel alternative, then someone else would eventually follow in Melvin's footsteps."

Kane smiled, but the humor didn't reach his eyes. He picked up her small hand and studied it for a long moment before turning it over and kissing the palm. "Shasta, I'm leaving—moving back to Max's house today. No, don't look like that. I told you this couldn't go on, that I wouldn't let it continue this way."

"Damn. I don't understand you." She snatched her hand from his and jumped up. "You're so hung up on your past. Haven't I made it plain enough that I don't care! It's done with—over—exactly where it belongs, in the past."

Kane rose slowly to his feet as if the weight of the world hovered around his shoulders. "And you don't see what I'm saying at all. The past has a way of resurfacing, and I don't know if I can change, Shasta."

She took a step toward him, then stopped. "I never wanted to change you," she whispered. "I love you just as you are—past and all."

Kane shook his head and walked out of the room, leaving his heart behind as he climbed the stairs to retrieve his packed suitcases. He had pulled Julie aside earlier and out of Shasta's hearing had asked the tight-lipped old man to drive him to his father's house. Now that he was at the back door, luggage in hand and Shasta following him down the steps, he wondered for the hundredth time if he was wrong. He stiffened his spine and kept moving, determined not to look back. But as he opened the car door to get in, his gaze swung automatically to the steps, where Shasta and Baskerville stood silently watching him leave. He hardened what was left of his heart to the tears on her cheeks, stumbled into the seat and slammed the door, keeping his eyes straight ahead.

As they drove off, Shasta's legs gave way and she sat down, her arm slung around Baskerville's neck. She couldn't believe he was really gone, that she hadn't been able to make him stay. "Stop it." She moved her head away as a wet tongue tried to wipe away her tears. "I'm all right. We'll just give him a couple of days alone, revise our plans and show up on his doorstep." She tried to force a note of optimism into her voice, but the enthusiasm was gone from her, and only a dull, hollow ache remained. "I can't have lost him, Baskerville. Mastersons are notorious for always getting their men—or women." But, she thought grimly, she was different from the rest of her family, the black sheep so to speak, and maybe their luck hadn't rubbed off on her. "Don't worry," she reassured the whining dog. "Somehow, someway, we'll get him back."

CHAPTER FOURTEEN

"SHASTA, YOU HAVE TO pull yourself together." Rena draped her body across Shasta's desk and snapped her fingers before her sister-in-law's fixed stare. "Margret's worried about you, and frankly so am I."

"I'm fine."

"No, you're not, and you're breaking my heart. I wish Jeff was here, he'd think of something. Oh," she growled, "I'd like to ring Kane Stone's neck."

"So would I." Shasta's lips twisted in a mockery of a smile. "So would I," she whispered. The past three days without him had been hell, and to make it worse she was alone. Her grandfather had finally ordered Julie to return to Dallas so they could accompany Jeff to Washington. It seemed that Jeff's fast talking hadn't soothed all the feathers he'd ruffled. Now J.T., both angry and amused at his grandson's plight, had had to step in and help him out of a sticky situation.

"Why don't you just go see him?"

Shasta slammed her fist on the desk and leaped to her feet. "Because, damn it, I haven't thought out a plan of action yet." Her once fruitful mind had dried up like a parched desert.

"Stop being so calculating, Shasta—just go over there."

Shasta dropped down in her chair, her body limp with indecision and lack of sleep. "I don't know if he's still there."

"Oh, he's there all right." Rena spun away quickly to keep Shasta's alert gaze from seeing the sudden uncertainly in her own eyes.

"Did you know that I had to dress *twice* this morning before I got my clothes right?" She turned worried brown eyes on Rena. "I know I'm forgetful and lax, but I've never done that before. Do you think I'm losing my mind? I mean, does love make you crazy?"

Rena almost choked with laughter. After all this time Shasta was finally beginning to show some interest in her appearance. Maybe there was hope for her after all. "No, Shasta, as usual you have a lot on your mind. I'm just a little surprised you noticed it at all."

Shasta grinned. "I think I'll go to the hospital and see Samantha and the boys. Maybe she's heard from Kane."

She had indeed. Samantha's accusing words hit Shasta like a blast the minute she stepped into the hospital room.

"What have you done to Kane?"

The two new friends glared at each other. Samantha was the first to break the tension as she took in the fatigue and hurt in Shasta's face. "Let me rephrase that question. What are you and Kane doing to each other? He looks terrible but you look even worse."

"You've seen him then? When?"

"He came by this morning," she said, and pointed to the nearest chair, motioning for Shasta to sit down. "You're ready to fall. What's happened between you two? I tried to pry some answers out of Kane, but he was as reticent as ever. Infuriating man! And Boston's no different. He knows but refuses to talk. Just looked at me with that smug smile of his. Here I am stuck in this hospital while my friends need me to help straighten out their problems, and he just laughs and gloats like some damn sultan." Her blue eyes flashed in anger. "Sorry," she said sheepishly, "but I'm going stir crazy."

Shasta smiled. Samantha's temper had become legend, but it was balanced by intelligence, beauty and a good sense of humor. She was the perfect match for Boston. Thinking of the two of them, Shasta felt her insecurities resurface, hammering away at her dreams of her and Kane together. After all, Boston and Sammy complemented each other, and she certainly couldn't say that of Kane and herself. They were too much alike.

"Kane's miserable, Shasta." Samantha tried again to prod some free information.

"So am I, and it's all his fault." Hesitant at first, she began to tell Samantha of Kane's conviction that he wasn't good enough for her, that he was using his past as a barrier.

"Do you know anything of his past, Shasta?"

The deep male voice made Shasta jump. Boston leaned against the door, his long body relaxed, but his black eyes were smoky with hidden secrets.

"Kane told me."

Boston pushed away from his lounging position. "I doubt he's told you all." He leaned down and kissed Samantha, then settled on the edge of her bed. "Kane's led a rather... adventurous life."

"Adventurous!" she sneered, and gave an unladylike snort. "He told me everything he possibly could to shock me."

Boston studied her for a long moment, and something he saw in her face must have convinced him that Kane had indeed spilled out his notorious past in detail and that Shasta didn't hold it against him. She watched as husband and wife exchanged meaningful glances, as if giving their final stamp of approval on her relationship with Kane.

"Did you know he's been partying nonstop since he left your home?" She shook her head, and Boston went on. "It's been in the society papers all week."

Shasta scowled. She hadn't seen a newspaper in three days. As a matter of fact, she thought grimly, the papers at home and at the office had mysteriously disappeared lately. Then it hit her. Rena, the early riser, had been coming by her house and stealing the newspaper off her front steps, and she had conspired with Margret to hide the office copy. Her plans for retaliation were interrupted by Boston's next statement.

"Kane leaves for Washington tomorrow morning, and after his meeting he's going to New York, then back to Europe." He watched dismay settle over Shasta's features. "He's also throwing a farewell party tonight."

Shasta's breath hung painfully in the back of her throat. Europe. She knew that if he left the country she'd never see him again, never be able to convince him that he was wrong to leave her behind. She gathered up her purse and stood.

"I have to go. Million things to do. Thank you, Boston," she babbled, then took a deep gulp of air. "I know by telling me he's leaving you've broken a confidence, and I appreciate it. Samantha, I'll call you later." She was at the door when she realized how rude she'd been. "I'm sorry. How are the babies and when do you get to take them home?"

Samantha laughed, a sound destined to lighten anyone's spirits. "They're wonderful, and I'd be even more ecstatic if Boston and I could agree on names." She reached out and pinched her husband's side. "As for taking them home..." She shrugged. "They need to gain at least a pound each before that happy event." Her expression brightened. "But I get to go home tomorrow, so call me there. Now go before I really start to bore you with parental pride."

Shasta waved, stepped out into the hospital hallway and squeezed her eyes shut. Kane leaving. Did he plan to go and never contact her again? A slow burning anger began to build at the injustice of it all. She was helpless, but she'd be damned if she would make it easy for him. What was the old saying about "Hell hath no fury like a woman scorned"? Well, he'd burned her, and she was determined that if he left he would carry a few more scars then he'd started out with. Her shoulders slumped, and she punched the elevator button. Who was she fooling? The torment would be all hers. She didn't want to inflict any more pain on Kane. But, heaven help her, she was going to see him one more time. Just once more she was going to try to make him see he was wrong. She glanced at her watch—three-thirty. She had at least four hours till she could crash his party.

ONCE HOME, Shasta paced the floor. What was she going to do with herself between now and the party? She wasn't used to waiting or sitting at home with idle time on her hands. She wondered what other women did all day. The answer came as she looked in the mirror. Her hair needed shampooing, her eyes were puffy from crying and circled in shadows from sleepless nights. Time to take herself in hand. A nap would help if she could stop the memories of Kane flashing through her head in a never-ending reel. It hurt to think those memories might be all she would have left.

When the doorbell woke her three hours later, Shasta groggily groped for her robe and struggled to get it on as she staggered down the stairs.

"Miss Shasta Masterson?"

"Yes," she said, her voice husky with sleep.

"Would you sign here please?"

She accepted the small package, tucked it under her arm and scrawled her signature across the receipt. "Thank you." The door closed with a snap, and belatedly she realized she'd forgotten to tip the young man. Who, she wondered, could be sending her something from Cartier's? She unwrapped the package and stared with dread at the embossed box. The tip of her finger outlined the monogrammed name tentatively, then with a sick feeling she flipped the hinged top open and gasped. On a bed of white satin lay a diamond-and-black-onyx panther-headed bracelet. The two meeting heads winked wickedly at her with emerald eyes when she touched the bauble. They seemed to be daring her to pick up the formal, cream-colored card and read it.

Shasta didn't know how long she stood there looking at the bracelet, but she quickly realized that she hated it on sight, and she snatched the card up to confirm what she already suspected. It was from Kane, and as she read, a red mist seemed to drop like a veil over her eyes. Closing them tightly, she wished she were back in bed and this was all a horrible nightmare. She couldn't believe this was happening to her as she reread the note.

> This gift is only a small insignificant object, but the only way I know to say "thank you." Also, I believe that if a woman doesn't have a handsome man on her arm, she should adorn herself with precious jewels.
>
> I shall never forget,
> Kane

Bastard! If she didn't have a handsome man! "I'll kill him," she yelled, then stopped, her breathing hard and fast. "No. I'll make him beg. I'll bring him to his knees." Fantasies were wonderful, but reality struck with the force of a sledgehammer. As far as Kane was concerned their affair was over. Was it worth the chance of more hurt and pain to confront him one last time? Her answer was yes. No matter what, she had to be the one to swallow her pride and give it another try.

An hour later she checked her appearance in the full-length mirror and smiled in satisfaction. For a brief second her gaze wandered from her reflection to the room behind her and she flinched. A rainbow of colors had spilled across the floor and her bed as she tried on outfit after outfit, discarding each in her frantic search to find the right dress. She'd finally settled on a two-piece Valentino silk. The dress was deceptively sexy with its strapless chemise of red dots on black and fingertip-length silk jacket in a reverse design of black dots on red. It was slinky yet innocent, sophisticated but naughty as it clung to her body, revealing only enough to tantalize. The barely black stockings added chic and mystery to her long legs. She was a little awed that she'd managed hair, makeup and clothes by herself. There was hope for her after all. Without another thought of the consequences she fled the house.

The night was clear and warm, the stars shining bright in the sky and the scent of the sea in the air. Shasta maneuvered her car down the street and turned into Max Stone's long graveled driveway. Bentleys, Cadillacs, Mercedes, Jaguars, several Porsches and a Rolls-Royce or two were lined respectfully together, bumper to bumper. Kane was indeed throwing a party. Judging by the glaring light streaming from every window and the blare of music, it was a farewell party to be long remembered. He was back among his so-called set and flying high.

She parked her car in the center of the driveway, slipped out and slammed the door. She took a deep breath as her steps faltered and her courage failed. All the way there she'd kept preparing herself for Kane's reaction to what she was going to do. Though he'd never been cruel to her, she knew he was capable of it. Rude, abrasive, sharp, he could be a cold-blooded savage with his words, and she knew he could devastate her in a second. Bracing herself, she ran up the steps and walked through the open door.

Tina Turner's soulful voice was pleading for everyone to stay together while people danced, milled around, laughing and talking, and Shasta was able to enter the room unnoticed. Her eyes scanned the crowd, then she turned abruptly to check out the other rooms when she didn't spot Kane among the guests.

"Shasta, Shasta Masterson."

The masculine voice was welcomingly familiar and she swung around in a quick circle to find its owner. "Lucas. Brandon." She waved, and they weaved their way toward one another.

"What are you doing here?" they all demanded in unison, then laughed.

"JoBeth dragged us. Said we were turning into a bunch of workaholics." Lucas grinned, his usually stern features lightening as Brandon groaned behind him. "The reason my gallant brother is sulking and dodging around is that there's a society columnist here trying to get his picture. Go away, Brandon."

"Maybe Shasta will allow me to hide behind her skirt?" Bright-blue eyes full of laughter and a spark of sensuality roamed over Shasta slowly. "Such a dainty little thing, isn't she, brother?"

Shasta was used to Brandon's teasing, but tonight was the first time she'd noticed the male interest in his eyes. "I'm looking for Kane. Have you seen him?"

Lucas scowled and shook his head. Brandon answered before his brother could stop him. "Last time I saw him he was upstairs in Max's private library."

She thanked them, excused herself and hurried up the long curved stairway. As she rounded the bend out of sight of Lucas and Brandon, her dread slowed her steps to a snail's pace. The husky tones of a woman's voice reached her as she neared the doorway. She stood there, feeling like an intruder and eavesdropper, though she didn't hear a word they said as her eyes devoured Kane. Dressed with his usual casual elegance in gray pleated slacks and a matching linen shirt tucked neatly in at his narrow waist, he was male personified. Shasta swallowed hard. Even with the world-weary lines etched deeper in his face and the cynical curve of his mouth twisted a little higher, he was still beautiful.

"Hello, Kane," she said softly. Shasta's gaze never wavered to the blonde draped across one corner of the big desk. She could only stare at Kane as he lounged gracefully near the woman.

Kane straightened, his surprise genuine, and for a brief second his expression lightened before the mask fell into place. "How are you?"

"I'd like to talk to you... alone, please." For the first time since she'd entered she looked pointedly at the other woman.

"I'll check with you later, Kane." The blond woman made to slip off the edge of the desk, but Kane stopped her with a motion of his hand.

"Stay, Karen, she won't be here long."

Karen settled back with a smug smile, and her hand moved intimately up and down Kane's arm.

"You want a stranger to hear what I have to say?"

"If it's going to be a personal conversation, maybe you'd better wait till tomorrow." He waved his hand around the array of scattered glasses, overflowing ashtrays and half-empty whisky bottles. "As you can see, I'm having a party."

Shasta leaned back against the doorframe as casually as possible, while inside she shook with weakness and dread. "But then you won't be here tomorrow, will you, Kane? You'll be in Washington." She reached in the pocket of the silk jacket and pulled out the unmistakable box. "I didn't want to believe this when I received it." How could he be so cool, standing before her with that damn woman touching him? She wanted to scream at her to go away and leave them alone. Instead she stared into bright-silver eyes that broke her heart with their icy depths. "I don't think I deserve to be treated this way."

"You didn't like my gift?"

"No, Kane." She took a step forward then stopped. "Kane, are you sure you want to do this? You know I don't care about your past."

"I think I made my position very clear," he said.

"You want to end our affair?"

"Hey," Karen interrupted. "I'd better leave."

"No," Kane ordered again, his voice harsh.

Shasta swallowed all her pride. "You don't want me anymore, Kane?"

He shook his head slowly. "No."

"What about love? I still love you." She persisted, determined, even if it killed her, that she would make him tell her exactly how he felt. If this was truly the end, then he was going to have to destroy the love she had for him.

"Love's overrated. You were different, you amused me."

She closed her eyes, wanting only to die. "Don't do this to us, Kane."

"There's no us, there never will be."

His words hurt beyond belief, but it was the tone that devastated her. She'd come prepared for his cruelty, and though his eyes were as cold as a winter moon, his words were spoken softly, full of understanding. How she wished to hear him call her Shasta, mouse; even baby, would be preferable to no name at all. The very omission was more insulting than if he'd slapped her face. Her fingers tightened around the forgotten jeweler's box in her hand till she threatened to crush it. There was an ache in her throat, and it hurt to breathe too deeply. He meant it when he said it was over, and no amount of talking was going to change his mind. She released her grip on her lifeline. "You'd better take this back. It offends me and would only remind me of what a fool I've been."

She pitched the box directly to him, but Kane didn't even make a move to catch it. Instead, he brought his glass to his lips and took a long drink of whisky. The box fell to the floor, and as it hit the clasp gave way and the bracelet spun on the floor, showering sparkles as the light caught and flashed the richness of the panther heads. The blond woman sucked in a ragged breath at its beauty.

"I guess this is goodbye then." She blinked rapidly, wanting only to get out of this room, but her feet seemed to have taken up a permanent relationship with the wood flooring.

"Goodbye, Shasta."

It was the use of her name that released her; the gentleness of each drawn out syllable was nearly her undoing. She whirled around and walked out, only to stop outside the door as she heard Karen gushing over *her* bracelet.

"Kane, honey, it's absolutely gorgeous. May I wear it?"

The gall, Shasta thought, and cocked her head to hear Kane's reply.

"Sure, baby. Keep it. I've no use for it anymore."

She hadn't realized she'd been holding her breath, waiting for his answer, hoping deep down that he would snatch the bracelet from the woman's hands and come after her, begging her forgiveness. But wishes don't always come true in the real world, she'd just found that out the hard way, and love was a fantasy she hoped she'd never experience again. The hurt was too damn painful. Straightening her shoulders, she continued on her way, seeing only what was before her; everything else was a haze of color, sounds and smells. She even missed the man lounging against the door, another eavesdropper whose rugged face was a study in puzzlement and anger.

KANE IGNORED the chattering woman beside him and walked over to the window, looking out on the driveway below. He deliberately blanked out his thoughts and tilted the glass up to drain the contents, trying to numb his body as well as his mind. His fixed stare caught movement below, and he edged closer to the window. There she was, walking slowly, carefully down the front steps. *It's best this way, mouse. You'll see and someday forgive me.* She reached her car and was opening the door. His knuckles whitened around the heavy crystal glass as he watched her make her way down the long drive. Standing there with bleak eyes, he followed her till the taillights disappeared out of the gates and turned onto the street. "Goodbye love," he whispered.

"Come on, Kane, let's party!"

He was startled from his stupor by a woman's shrill voice, and he turned savagely on her. "Get out of here, you stupid, greedy bitch."

"But, honey?"

"Out!" he yelled, and left the window to pour himself another drink. He'd done the right thing; he knew he had. So why did the feeling persist that he'd just ruined his life and nothing would ever be good again? Returning to the window, he gazed out, seeing only the bleakness of what was to come.

"You're a fool and an ass."

Kane turned his head, his eyes following Lucas DeSalva as he moved across the room in that peculiar soundless way of his. He frowned, irritation stamped clearly across his brow at the intrusion. "Back off, Lucas. This isn't your concern."

"Maybe, maybe not. But it looks as if I'm going to interfere all the same, doesn't it? I'll repeat, you're a fool to let her go."

Kane's gaze returned to the window and the dark night beyond.

"She's worth fighting for." Lucas sat on the corner of the desk, his foot swinging back and forth.

"You don't know what you're talking about—it's over."

"Is it?" Lucas pushed off the desk and walked slowly to the door. He stopped and turned. "Is it over when you'll see her everywhere you go? She loves you desperately, Kane, but she's a strong woman. She'll eventually get over you. Can you say the same? And late at night when you're unable to sleep, will you picture Shasta in bed with another man?" The color drained from Kane's face. "Can you accept the reality of another man making love to her? Shasta's a hell of a woman and not so easily dismissed."

"But not your type, Lucas?"

Lucas paused thoughtfully for a long moment. "No, not my style." He saw Kane's tense shoulders sag a fraction in relief. "She's too untamed for my taste, too much like you Kane. But she's Brandon's type." He let his words soak in, then went on. "He'd been sniffing around before you showed up." Lucas shrugged and lit a cigarette, watching Kane over the flame, grinning to himself at the other man's clenched jaw and the flash of anger in his unusual eyes. "I imagine after a little time passes she'll be receptive to his offer to help her forget. After all, Brandon can be damn amusing, and I'm also told from numerous sources that he's a strong, imaginative lover." He wheeled around, letting his last words float over his shoulder as he left the room.

Kane's brooding gaze followed Lucas's departure, the threat still hanging heavily in the air long after he'd gone. Hell, why shouldn't she have lovers? He didn't plan to remain celibate. But the thought of her with another man sent a chill through him, and he knew he'd never be warm again. Laughing brown eyes full of mischief haunted him. He picked up the nearest bottle of liquor, wrenched off the cap, put it to his lips and took several long swallows. The burning liquid didn't set the fire in his gut he'd hoped for; instead it seemed to freeze there like a lump of ice. Why couldn't he take what was offered? She didn't care about his past or what he was; she loved him just the same. He set the bottle to his lips and turned it up. Why?

The voice in his head that had told him repeatedly he wasn't good enough was strangely quiet. Kane upended the bottle once more and asked himself the question again. Why? Only silence and a kind of peace came in reply, and he suddenly realized that he'd forgiven himself for his unspeakable behavior in the past. He'd accepted responsibility for what he'd done to his life and others and was granted freedom from his own imprisonment.

The bottle dropped to the floor, its contents spilling in a great pool as Kane sat down in the nearest chair and buried his face in his hands. He'd do it right this time—step by step. Washington was tomorrow, then he'd return and take what was his—and she was his; right or wrong he'd never let her go again. Lucas was right. He'd been the biggest kind of fool and ass, and he'd spend the rest of his life making up for the pain he'd caused.

SHASTA PULLED INTO her driveway, totally oblivious to the fact that she was home. She didn't even remember the drive, and it was only Baskerville's frantic barking from the house that roused her out of her dazed state. Like a robot, she entered her house and went through her nightly routine. She knew this evening would hold no rest for her, and she'd never be able to close her eyes. As if she was numb to all that had happened to her, she calmly fixed herself a Scotch and water and curled up at the end of the couch. All the way home she had tried to put the rest of her life into perspective, but her mind refused to think about her future. Instead her thoughts wanted to relive the events of the last hour, and that she absolutely refused to permit. Kane was out of her life forever. It was over.

She relaxed her tightly clenched fist, rubbing her palms together to return the circulation and smooth away the nail marks on her skin. She had her life to lead, and there were going to be some drastic changes. The hard lump in her throat threatened to choke her and she sipped her drink, grimacing at the medicinal taste. She felt hot and cold at the same time and her eyes ached with unshed tears. She'd shed bucketsful for the past three days, and now was the time to plan, not wallow in self-pity.

Her chest throbbed painfully and she placed her hand over her heart, then almost laughed hysterically. What heart? Kane had torn it out that evening, and she'd left it lying on the hardwood floor of Max's library. She cleared her throat and shook her head to dispel the maudlin thoughts. That part of her life was over. Her hand trembled as she brought the glass to her lips.

Oh God, Kane. Why? The words screamed in her mind and she almost choked on the swallow she'd taken. No! He was no longer a part of her life, her future, and she must forget his very existence. But she'd made so many plans for them together. Again she put mental brakes to her thoughts.

The idea of returning to her daily routine was disheartening. Her eyes narrowed. Maybe Kane's desertion was the catalyst she needed to spur her on to other things. Maybe it was time she broke the ties with her family and sought the life she'd always wanted. There was a whole world out there, and she was ready for some danger and excitement. And there would be men in abundance willing to help heal the wounds.

Shasta squeezed her eyes tightly together. Who was she trying to fool? What man could even compare with Kane? For the little time they had shared he'd shown her what it was to be loved. Deep down she knew she'd never find that love again. There would be no fairy-tale, happily-ever-after ending now. Almost angrily she thought that her grandfather had lied to her—she wasn't like the rest of her family after all. She buried her face in her hands and for one last time wondered what she was going to do without Kane.

CHAPTER FIFTEEN

"SO IT'S TRUE, the formula's gone?"

Shasta absently took a sip of tea, her eyes studying Max Stone intently over the rim of the delicate china cup. She silently questioned her sanity for coming here. It hadn't been necessary for her to hand deliver the final report and file to Max, but even after a month's absence she wasn't ready to return home and face her family. She took another sip of tea and grimaced, thinking of the phone call that had awakened her early that morning. J.T. had tracked her down and ordered her return to the States—preferably Dallas—so he could personally give her a piece of his mind. And because she'd been sleepy and disoriented, and dreadfully homesick just hearing his voice, she'd agreed.

Kane's father thumped his cup down with a clatter, rose to his impressive height and stomped across the suite's sitting room to the well-stocked bar. After a few seconds he regained his dignity and faced Shasta. "After a year of hard work and an enormous outlay of money, it all went up in ashes. What a stupid, senseless waste! You're sure the formula was destroyed?"

Shasta nodded, refusing to give voice to his question—one he had asked repeatedly since she arrived at his hotel. Instead she eyed the silver tray crowded with sandwiches and cakes. The Dorchester was famous for their high teas and her stomach growled in protest of weeks of neglect. The soft muted sounds of pacing caught her attention, and she gritted her teeth. Max's muttering stretched her already frayed nerves to the snapping point. Not once since she had brought the twenty-page report to London had he inquired about Kane's health or whereabouts. His only concern was to establish the facts of the formula and to make absolutely certain that it might not one day surface and someone lay claim to what should have been his victory.

Max tipped the glass, draining the contents, and Shasta's throat tightened. Older and thinner than Kane, and with a thick head of salt-and-pepper hair, Max Stone fascinated and repulsed her.

"I appreciate you bringing the completed report to me in person." He smiled, but the calculating hardness in his eyes didn't soften. "The preliminary report you sent a month ago would have sufficed if Kane had bothered to tell his story."

"Kane's had other things on his mind lately. I'm sure he'll contact you soon." Why was she defending Kane, Shasta wondered.

"He's damn fool to think he could force Tramble to do anything. Besides, dead is dead. There's nothing to gain from digging further into Kimble's death. Let the French police handle the mess."

"Mr. Stone, Kane cared deeply for the professor...."

"Bull! My son cares for nothing in this world but his own hide and his pleasures." He eyed Shasta coldly, taking in her shapely, petite form and revealing face. His gaze honed in on her changing expression, and a sly smile slid across his mouth. "Well, well. Maybe I should reread that report and pay closer attention to what's between the lines." He returned to the chair across from Shasta and continued. "You know, Shasta—" he made a steeple with his fingers and rested his chin on it thoughtfully "—with your grandfather's reputation and your family's wealth, I wouldn't be adverse to a merger between the Stones and the Mastersons."

"What...what?"

"Come now, you're not going to try and tell me that you and Kane weren't—lovers? If you're as smart as I think you are, you're already carrying my grandson."

Shasta sat horrified by what he was saying, but his next words brought her up and out of her chair.

"With your family's power and prestige, and by my pressuring Kane, we could persuade him to accept his responsibilities. At some time his mother must have taught him about chivalry. He could be swayed into doing the correct thing and marry you. Maybe that would give him some purpose in life."

"Mr. Stone! I'm not pregnant, nor do I wish to marry your son." She hurriedly gathered up her belongings and stood. He was everything Kane said he was and more.

Max's defeat was as visible as a deflated balloon, and he sagged in his chair.

Shasta felt a pang of sympathy as age seemed to suddenly catch up with the old devil, but before she could voice any trite, consoling words, she hardened her soft heart. Blood ran true to form between father and son, she reminded herself. She felt awkward standing there with her purse in hand and her briefcase clutched to her breast while he stared at her. "If I don't leave now Mr. Stone, I'll miss my flight out of Heathrow."

Her voice snapped him out of his stupor and he apologized. "I'll call my chauffeur and have him drive you."

"That's not necessary."

"I insist." He rode with her in the elevator and together they walked out to the waiting limousine. "I'll be returning to Houston just as soon as my business is completed here, probably in a week, so if you have anything further to add to the report, give me a call at the office."

Stiff and correct, Shasta politely said the right things and crawled into the limousine, allowing herself to relax only when the car pulled away from the curb. For a few seconds she stared at the soothing calm of Hyde Park and the orderly greenery of trees and manicured shrubs. She leaned back against the rich leather and closed her weary eyes as the long car glided through London traffic.

She was going home. After almost a month of risk-taking and danger, she hoped she'd faced all her demons and conquered the ache in her heart. There were a few loose ends to tie up, then she would be off again. How she loved the freedom. The only thing she had to make sure of was that her work schedule would keep her out of France and Switzerland. Those two countries seemed to be Kane's favorites, and she knew that though she'd come to terms with her loss, she didn't have the strength to come face to face with him. She tightened her hold on her briefcase as memory upon memory stacked on top of one another. Dear God! Would she ever be free of his haunting image?

SHASTA'S SLOW STEPS carried her down the long corridor of the Dallas airport. Groups of people milled around the terminal juggling hand luggage and all-weather coats. Darkness had long since made its claim on the sky, bringing an unexpected nip in the air. As Shasta walked toward customs, fragments of conversations penetrated her jet-lagged state, and she smiled. The topic, of course, was the crazy Texas weather.

"Shasta, Shasta!"

She recognized Julie's husky voice before she spotted him and gave a little wave. She presented her passport to the overworked customs official and answered the necessary questions, but when he asked her to open the brown alligator briefcase she'd hand carried from London, she presented him with a small sheaf of permits and official documents.

The agent's face brightened with excitement, his black skin taking on a shine of anticipation after hours of boredom. "Mr. Lawerence is waiting for you in room two." He pointed over his shoulder with his thumb, his eyes eagerly searching for one of his co-workers to take over his position. Spotting a willing nod, he signaled and escorted Shasta to the room set aside for questioning and private business.

Shasta shot a speaking glance to a now-worried Julie, averting his uneasiness with a cock of her head and a bright smile. Ten minutes later she emerged, exhausted but relieved to be rid of her dangerous burden. A suave, fashionably dressed man now carried the brown alligator briefcase, tailed by two overdeveloped bodyguards.

"Damn, kid, you look beat," grumbled Julius. "Ain't no one told you you're supposed to sleep now and then? Was that Benoit Lawerence of Lawerence Jewelers?"

"Yes."

"And you were carrying diamonds for them from London?"

"Diamonds and other stones."

Julius's bushy eyebrows drew together. He clasped her elbow firmly and led her out to the waiting Silver Cloud Rolls-Royce. Shasta's eyes didn't even widen as Julius helped her in, then slipped into the driver's seat. She rested her head back and closed her eyes for a few seconds before she turned around. "Hello, pappy."

J. T. Masterson's heavy lids drooped farther over his eyes, concealing his concern, as he studied his granddaughter's strained face. "Burning the candle at both ends, Peewee?"

The childish nickname brought a lump to her throat and she swallowed hard before she could answer. "Looks that way, doesn't it? But I'm okay now." She forced a smile and tried to change the subject. "How's everyone?"

J.T. shook his silvery head and clucked his tongue, bringing another soft smile to Shasta's lips. She knew she was about to be reprimanded. "I taught you that maneuver, don't pull it on me."

"Yes, sir."

"And don't get sassy, either."

They were killing time and each of them knew it. They fell silent. Shasta sighed, dreading the inevitable, knowing that she was going to have to hurt her grandfather in order to have a life of her own. She let her gaze drift to the moving lights outside the car windows. The route home was one she could drive in her sleep, and when they reached the tree-lined streets of Highland Park she wondered if she would have the strength to fight her family. She was tired, emotionally and physically, and incapable of her usual logical judgment, a weakness J.T. would use to his advantage if necessary.

Julie stopped the car at the crest of the driveway and Shasta climbed out without looking at the Regency-style brick house she had called home for so many years. Dead on her feet, she dragged her lagging steps through the open door, mumbled a greeting to their butler, Sampson, and continued on her way to the living room.

She inhaled deeply, straightening her shoulders and turned to face her adversaries. Suddenly she was eager for this confrontation, wanting only to have it over and done with. But as she whirled around, she caught the concern and love on the faces of her beloved men and gulped down the harsh words she'd been about to pour out. "Oh, pappy." She walked into his arms and reached out for Julie's hand. "It's just a broken heart not a fatal disease. I'll get over it." She squeezed Julie's hand and leaned back in her grandfather's embrace.

"I best make us some hot chocolate," Julius said gruffly and left them alone.

"There's no use beating around the bush, Shasta. Kane has made a pest of himself trying to locate you. Something has to be done."

Shasta stiffened and turned away. "I don't want to see him, pappy. Not now when the hurt is still fresh."

"I think you should. No, I think you must," he said cryptically, struggling hard to hide the warring emotions churning with each heartbeat. Should he tell her that Kane was flying to Dallas tomorrow to meet with him? A crafty smile touched the corners of his mouth, then immediately disappeared as he caught her staring at him.

"No, pappy. In this case I know what's best for me. Kane will eventually get bored with his new game and give up."

"Don't you even want to know why he's raising so much hell looking for you?"

"Not particularly, no." But her heart contradicted her words with a pounding roar in her ears.

Her expressionless voice sent a chill through J.T. and he deemed it prudent to change the subject. He scowled at Shasta and motioned for her to be seated. "You have totally disrupted this family for a month." She opened her mouth and he held up his hand. "No, young lady. You're going to hear me out, then we'll see if we can't come up with some solution to your problems."

Shasta sagged back in her chair and angrily crossed her arms like a petulant child. She shifted her gaze from J.T. to Julie and sighed. It was a wasted effort to try to outmaneuver these two. She eagerly accepted the steaming mug of hot chocolate, liberally laced with cherry liqueur and topped with whipped cream. "I'm sorry if I've caused you to worry."

"Not me necessarily," J.T. lied. "But your activities and the overseas jobs you took had your mother and father up in arms against Julie and me. They called at least five times a day from Washington to see if I'd heard from you. By the time I answered the other daily inquiries..." His voice trailed off as he glared fiercely at her from under his heavy eyelids.

"Pappy, I can't go back to the Houston office—I'll suffocate and die there. This isn't something that's just happened recently, and it's not all Kane's fault, either, though our situation cleared the air." She jumped up and began to pace, totally exhausting her grandfather.

"Sit down," he ordered. "Now," he said, fighting to keep his expression stern. "Julie and I have had a long discussion about this, and he's in full agreement with you."

Shasta's mouth fell open and she shot a surprised glance at Julie.

"You ain't gone and forgot that I was in prison once? I know what it's like to be caged." He glared at J.T., then hastily amended his words. "It ain't fair to keep you penned in."

"As usual, Julie's gotten right to the point, though somewhat indelicately. What we've agreed to—"

"Now wait just one minute, you two. You're doing it again, trying to run my life."

"Well, hell, kid!" Julie burst out. "Someone has to. You've made a mess of things lately what with all your running around carrying jewels and such. I ain't never heard of some of the dim-witted stunts you've pulled this past month."

Shasta scowled at Julie, knowing he was right. At times she'd even scared herself with her recklessness. Shasta was a little ashamed now, facing the two men who had taught her above all else to be careful. Her gaze dropped to the Persian rug. "Sorry. I guess I did take some rather foolish risks."

J.T. snorted in disgust. "Now are you willing to hear us out quietly before you jump to any further arguments?" Shasta nodded. "Good. First of all I never, *never* want to hear of you carrying jewels again. You and I both know those are suicide runs."

"Yes, pappy." She sipped her hot chocolate then, concentrated hard on the floating glob of melting whipped cream.

J.T. allowed himself a tiny smile, knowing the meekness she portrayed for the act it was. "Second—you may leave the Houston office. But your investment in the company must stay to keep it solvent for Jeff and Rena's sake till I can think of something. They have their dreams too, Shasta, and it's only right you do this, since you're pulling out with no forewarning."

Shasta's head shot up, her attention riveted on her grandfather as his words sent a jolt of adrenaline through her tired nervous system. Was he going to let her go without a fight?

Like a mind reader J.T. answered her unasked question. "Yes, you're free. I'm just sorry I didn't realize I was doing wrong a long time ago. This old fool—" he pointed to Julie "—tried to warn me, but I was too bullheaded to listen. Now I figure any upheaval is on my shoulders." He smiled but shook his finger at her. "However, there are some rules."

Shasta's grin grew, happiness removing the tension lines in her face. "What rules?"

"As much as I'd like to think that Julie is loyal to me, I know I'd only be lying to myself. I'd never be able to keep him here if he thought you needed him. So it's up to you two to decide what you want to do. But I would like to make one suggestion." J.T. leaned forward and became serious. "No matter how smart, experienced and tough you think you are, there are always men just one step ahead of you. It's always better to have a friend at your back, and I'd sleep a hell of a lot better if I knew that whenever you plan taking a job in Europe you'd take Julie with you. He's moped around with his feelings hurt this past month till I thought I was going to have to send him after you."

The full force of her irresponsible actions hit her, and she jumped out of her chair and wrapped her arms around Julie's shoulders. She'd forgotten for a while that he'd practically raised her. He'd given her his greatest gifts, teaching her his trade and loving her unquestionably all her life.

"Forgive me, Julie, but this past month I just needed...." She trailed off, unsure of how to put her feelings into words.

"To put your head on straight after that man turned it around backward?" He ducked his head, blinking away the excess moisture that stung his eyes.

"Something like that," she said softly.

"If you would quit crying all over each other I'd like some thanks and appreciation, too." J.T.'s gruff voice made them laugh.

"Sure, pappy. Even an interfering old busybody needs a hug."

"Now don't get mushy, Shasta." He returned her embrace with a force that took her breath away. "You know how I loathe water spots on my suits." He held her at arm's length.

"Will you take some jobs from Masters now and then? Do you need any money?"

"Yes and no." She laughed at his disgusted expression. "It will be strange to be free-lancing on my own." Looking her grandfather straight in the eye, she went on. "But exciting. And I think you of all people can understand that feeling."

"Don't let all this go to your head just yet. You have to face Jeff and Rena and make your peace with them."

"Tomorrow, if you'll lend me the jet and pilot so I can get to Houston early. Then I think I'll go on to Aspen to ski awhile. Julie can meet me there later."

J.T. shook his head and got up. "Not even working a job yet and she's off on vacation." He turned at the door. "Don't forget the keys to the ski lodge." Then he mumbled, "I must be getting old. She's never needed a key in her life."

"WELL, IF IT ISN'T the family renegade sneaking back in town to clear out her office before anyone can catch her stealing away into the night." Rena's voice was as cold as her blue eyes.

Shasta knew there'd be a confrontation with her brother and sister-in-law, and somewhere in the back of her mind she had thought it would be Jeff who would give her the most trouble. "Listen, Rena...." She set the half-full box aside and walked toward her glaring sister-in-law.

"No, you listen, Shasta Masterson. You're making a fool of yourself. The way you're acting anyone would think you'd just lost your husband of twenty years to another woman."

"Rena!"

"Jeff's been almost out of his mind with worry." The crystalline-blue eyes turned even icier. "He blames himself for not stepping in and stopping the affair before it began. Damn you, Shasta, Kane Stone is not a god. He's only one man, and there are plenty of others in this world. Stop being a martyr and acting like you're the only one to suffer from a broken heart. Inflicting your tantrums on others is beginning to become boring!"

"Rena, please. Shut up! None of this—" she waved her hand around the office, indicating the piles of personal belongings "—none of this has anything to do with Kane."

"No?" Rena questioned, and a frown began to mar her smooth, pale forehead.

"No." Shasta smiled at her confusion. "Sit down. There are a few things you should know that even Jeff, bless his heart, doesn't know about me." She told Rena of all her destroyed dreams and the restraints that had held her back. "So you see, now's my chance."

"I didn't know you felt this way, Shasta." She was genuinely shocked, and her wide eyes and open mouth expressed her surprise more than words. "We've been friends—close friends for four years, and I never understood why you were so unhappy at times." Her eyes narrowed. "But Kane's part of this, isn't he?"

Shasta couldn't help but chuckle. Rena was as much a romantic as her brother.

"Shasta, you can't give up everything and everyone you love because of a disastrous affair."

"Rena, you're not listening to what I'm saying. Stop thinking love and romance. Think freedom. Did you know that years ago J.T. talked me out of joining the FBI and the CIA? That was one of many shattered dreams. Now I'm going to do exactly what I want for a change."

"But Kane..."

The continued reference to Kane was getting on her nerves. With a great deal of willpower she'd deliberately forced him from her thoughts, refusing to think of what had been between them. She'd made her mind numb to any intruding memories, and Rena's constant reminders were upsetting the fragile hold she had on her overtaxed emotions.

"You say you want to be free. Free to do what?" Rena began slowly and nonchalantly unpacking the box sitting on top of Shasta's desk. "Oh, I know financially you're fixed for life whether you ever work another day or not. You're too old and set in your ways to be of any use to those government agencies." She smiled at Shasta's grimace. "Well, really, don't they like to get their recruits young and brainwash them or something? And please don't tell me you're going to continue this mad, dangerous dash you've been on lately? You'll give the entire family heart attacks."

Shasta gently removed the box from Rena's clutches and began to throw her personal belongings back in it. "I won't be so reckless anymore."

Totally exasperated, Rena pulled the box out of Shasta's hands and automatically rearranged the mess in an orderly fashion. "Are you going to continue working as an international courier?"

Shasta nodded. "I promise I'll be very careful."

"What about Julie and Baskerville?" Her voice cracked a little as she went on. "What about Lizzie, Jeff and *me,*" she wailed softly. "Will we ever see you again?"

The box was torn from Rena's hands and sent flying across the room, the contents spilling in a rolling heap on the floor. "Damn you, Rena Masterson, don't you cry." Shasta grabbed her arms and shook her hard. "I'm not going to change my name and move to another country, for heaven's sake. The way you talk you'd think I was dying or something." Rena's limp body collapsed without further assistance into a nearby chair. "Now, this time you listen to me. Julie and I have worked out a happy arrangement to our problems. As for Baskerville, he goes with me unless I'm in Europe."

She moved back to the side of the desk and with a slight hop sat on the edge. The bright smile she gave Rena should have set off warning bells in the woman's head. "You know how Lizzie loves Baskerville, and I thought that since you're the official dog sitter I'd leave him at your house in between jobs." Her smile slipped a little at Rena's blank look. "He's on the wagon now and hasn't been any trouble, has he? Rena, say something."

"Baskerville's fine—so is Lizzie, and you're right, she worships him to the point that she only rides on his back three or four times a day, now that we've explained he's not her personal pony." Her expression was still a little vague as she said absently, "That's not what's bothering me." She sighed. "I was just thinking how little I really know about you. Unfortunately, like the rest of your family, I've only seen what was on the surface or what was convenient for me to see." She slipped out of her chair and hugged Shasta. "I hope you'll be happy at whatever you decide to do, and don't worry about Jeff. I'll take care of him."

"And what, dear wife, are you planning to do to me?" Jeff asked from the open doorway. His tall good looks were marred by a distinct untidiness that was evident only when he was tied to his computer. He ran his fingers through his thick blond hair, and his eyes slid away from Shasta's steady stare. "Hi, sis."

"Jeff, Shasta was explaining—is something the matter? Are you sick?" Rena was all concern, and Jeff quickly gave her a kiss on the cheek to ward off any further questions.

"Nothing's the matter," he said, his voice a little too hardy to convince Shasta that he wasn't up to something.

"Okay, out with it," she demanded, and Jeff jumped. "What have you done?"

"Me? Listen, sis. I talked to J.T., and he's explained everything. I hate to see you leave, but if it's truly what you want then I'm all for it."

"Jeff, you're trying to evade my question. What are you up to?"

Jeff fidgeted around the office, ignoring his sister's sharp gaze and his wife's thoughtful one as he absently picked up and replaced objects off the desk and shelves. "Well, actually, there is a problem." He pulled out Shasta's chair and sat down, folding his hands together to still their nervous twitch. "The McKinneys' security system was completed yesterday, and I need you to check it out."

"But, Jeff—"

"No," he said sternly and frowned, shocking both women. "This is still part your company, and you made the McKinney commitment in good faith, so you'll stick by your word. *I* insist." He seemed proud of his firm stand, and his square chin stuck out farther.

Shasta eyed Jeff suspiciously, then leaned over the desk and kissed him on the cheek. "If I have to work tonight, I'd better go get my equipment organized." She picked up her box of personal belongings and headed for the door.

"Oh, Shasta." Rena stopped her. "You'd better call Samantha and Boston. They left for Santa Fe last week, but she's called nearly every other day wanting to know if we'd heard from you." Rena chuckled. "You know Sammy, at first she tried to hide the fact that she was also trying to find out your whereabouts for Kane. Then out of guilt, I guess, she confessed her duplicity. She's afraid that when you find out you'll think she was only calling to help Kane and not truly concerned about you. So please call her if only to ease her conscience."

Shasta agreed. She gave one last glance around her office and prepared to leave, but she still couldn't take her gaze from Jeff's guilty expression. Why, she asked herself, did she have a funny feeling in the pit of her stomach and that familiar tingling at the back of her neck? The warning signs were all there, and why did Jeff's nervousness bring with it the strange sensation that her grandfather had something to do with his discomfort? She shrugged. After all, there was nothing her grandfather could do to interfere with her life now!

CHAPTER SIXTEEN

KANE STOOD at the long line of windows in the lobby of the Adolphus hotel, heedless of the opulent grandeur around him. Limousines, taxis and expensive cars loaded and unloaded their elegant passengers as he watched, searching each elderly man for something familiar in a face, a hint of Shasta in the coloring or the flash of a smile.

He rubbed his damp palms along his pant leg and gave a bark of laughter. Anyone who saw him and noticed the perspiration that gathered periodically across his forehead would think it was a blistering day and that the hotel's air conditioning wasn't working. Actually a blue norther had hit Dallas and the temperature was dropping steadily. What Kane was feeling was raw fear.

It had been a month since the night of his party. A month of trying to track Shasta down, but to no avail. He scowled, the signs of fatigue and worry biting deeper into the hollow caverns of his face. In his own conceit and arrogance it had never once crossed his mind that when he returned to Houston she wouldn't be waiting for him. All his life women had fallen at his feet, but he should have remembered that Shasta was an original. With his usual insolence he hadn't even considered her disappearing and leaving him flat. Why hadn't he gone straight to her that night? Because, he derided himself, he was a pompous boor whose easy conquests had gone to his head and impaired his judgment. He'd made mistakes in his life, but underrating Shasta was the worst of them all.

Now he'd come begging to her grandfather, J. T. Masterson. He, who had never felt it necessary to explain his actions, was in for a rough time. Shasta's entire family was aware of his search. He'd seen to that with all the hell he'd raised, but his demands had only met with stony expressions, vicious tongue lashings and threats that if he didn't stay out of her life, his own wouldn't be worth living.

How could he have been so stupid as to leave Houston without going to Shasta's? He berated himself over and over with the same question. The only answer he could think of shamed him deeper than any event in his past. If he'd gone to Shasta that night she would have won, and he couldn't accept losing control of his situation. To hell with male pride! When he'd realized his own motives he was even more outraged. He thought he'd learned to behave like a modern, intelligent man, and it rankled to know that he was a throwback to the primitive Neanderthal, dragging his woman around by her hair. Shasta certainly had her work cut out to straighten him up—if he ever found her.

He was sweating again. The thought of dealing with Shasta's grandfather sent a shudder through his body. Over the past month he'd heard enough about J.T., the shark, to last a lifetime and then some. Kane quickly unbuttoned his vest, shifted his shoulders beneath the confines of his coat and grimaced. The conservative gray pin-striped suit ill suited his finicky taste. His tailor at London's Turnbull & Asser would have hysterics if he knew he'd bought off the rack. He rebuttoned the vest and shoved his hands in his slacks pocket, then pulled them out again to check the time. The old devil had kept him cooling his heels for twenty-six and a half minutes.

Kane began scanning the traffic outside again when he froze, a feeling of hope and dread coursing through him as a vintage Silver Cloud Rolls-Royce glided to the entrance of the hotel. Porters and doormen snapped to attention as the luxurious car pulled to a stop. As he watched, the back door swung open and Julie stepped out. He turned, his hand extended to assist the passenger, and Kane grinned as the helpful offer was declined with a whack across Julie's palm by a thin gold-tipped cane. Then his attention focused on the silver-haired old man who descended from the car and straightened to his full height; he cut an impressive figure, and there was enough hauteur in his expression to shrivel the strongest of men.

Kane's head began to ache, his lips were dry and his eyes felt like a pound of sand had been poured into them. His palms were as sweaty as a teenager's on his first date. With a flash of wry humor he thought he might faint, his heart was pounding so hard in his chest. But he pulled himself together as he watched the two men entering the hotel's glass portals, and he moved to meet them.

"Mr. Masterson." He stuck out his hand to receive the older man's firm shake and a once-over, lightning glance from those disconcerting cobalt-blue eyes. "Julie, it's good to see you again." He looked back at J.T. "Thank you for seeing me."

The old man shrugged and pointed with his cane to a nearby table. "Shall we sit over there out of the way of prying eyes and big ears?" At Kane's raised eyebrow, J.T. laughed. "Shasta's cousins have been checking you out, seems they're better at the game than I thought." He turned to Julie. "Remind me to give the boys a bonus."

Kane should have known he was being watched, but his mind was distracted by more important things, and he plunged into his prepared speech. "Mr. Masterson. . . ."

"Might as well call me J.T." He lowered himself slowly into an antique French chair, placed his cane between his legs and folded his hands over the crooked handle.

"J.T., I have to know where Shasta is. I've exhausted all means of finding her, and everywhere I turn I meet stone walls. Even her father doesn't know, or else he's not telling."

"My son is going to run for Congress and can't be bothered with his daughter's problems at the moment. And you needn't clench your jaw at that, young man. I'm the one who can control Shasta and my son's wise enough to be aware of that fact, so he's left it to me to settle this mess." He leaned forward, studying Kane. "We're a close family, and what hurts one hurts us all. You've managed to cause us a great deal of pain lately."

Kane wondered if he would get a chance to explain or if every time he tried he was going to be interrupted. He looked at Julie, caught the laughter in his eyes and frowned. He could find no humor in the situation. "Believe me, J.T., from the very beginning I've been aware of the problems I've caused. I tried to explain this to Shasta, but she wouldn't listen. Now I want to make up for all the hurt, but how can I do that if I can't find Shasta. Where is she?" He was fast losing patience. A month of worry and wanting had taken its toll. He refused to play a cat-and-mouse game with this old man any longer. "Where is she?" he demanded once again, his eyes flashing with determination.

"I'd like to establish a few facts before I tell you—if I tell," he corrected himself and smiled.

"No, sir," Kane shot back. "I'll tell you nothing. What's between Shasta and me is private, and until we settle our problems it's our affair."

J. T. Masterson had never been talked back to like this and it didn't sit well. He sent a grinning Julie a murderous look. "You find this amusing. You set me up, didn't you? Told me Kane would come crawling on his hands and knees and I could have some fun." Julius threw back his head and laughed. "You keep it up, you old goat, my day will come." He returned his attention to Kane and quickly stuck out his cane as he saw the young man rising to leave. "No, stay. I apologize, but I'm an old man with little to entertain myself with these days, and Julie and I are always pulling tricks on each other. I'm sorry you're the brunt of one of his jokes."

"If you won't tell me where Shasta is, then tell me where she's been and I'll pick up the trail from there." He couldn't believe what was happening to him. Here he was fighting for his life, and two overgrown jokers were having fun at his expense.

"For the past month she's been working on her own." Shasta's grandfather frowned fiercely at Kane. "She was moving from place to place like a person possessed."

"Where is she?" Kane demanded.

J.T. studied Kane more carefully this time and saw the haggardness in his face. "She was working as a special courier carrying merchandise from Antwerp to Tel Aviv and Lisbon for a while."

Kane's face lost all color, leaving his skin a pasty white. The Antwerp route could only mean the diamond market and the most dangerous run any courier could make. He bolted out of his chair, but Julie's next words stopped him.

"She ain't working over there no more, Kane. She's going free-lance and will be hopping around all over the place soon."

Kane's heart resumed its normal beat and he sat down. "Where," he said hoarsely, "is she now?" The he did something he'd never done in his life, he begged. "Please!"

J.T. pulled out a business card, turned it over and wrote something on the back. He held it between two fingers, as if to tear it up if he didn't receive the answer he wanted. "I can only assume by this urgency to see me and your reaction to what she's been up to that you care a great deal for my granddaughter. But I want to hear it from your lips before I hand her over to you."

Kane swallowed his pride and his anger. "I love Shasta, Mr. Masterson, and I'll do anything I can to get her back." J.T. handed him the card and Kane memorized the address before he looked up. "I've hurt Shasta deeply and for that I'm truly sorry, but at the time I thought I was doing the best thing for her."

The older men shook Kane's hand, and as he turned to leave, Julius stopped him. "There's something you better know that J.T. ain't told you." He shot an irksome glance at his friend and employer, his bushy eyebrows a straight line over his eyes. "Early tomorrow morning Shasta leaves for Colorado, so don't put off talking to her. Good luck." He clasped Kane on the shoulder and smiled tightly. "You're going to need it."

A BLUE NORTHER swept over Houston as the sun was sinking deeper into the sky. The crisp air could set teeth to chattering in the unprepared, those doubters who didn't believe that in a matter of minutes Houston's balmy temperatures could drop to near freezing.

Shasta was a believer. Bundled in light down-padded clothes and leather jacket, she sat on the edge of a red tiled roof, cursing the tangle of ropes in her hands. Her salty vocabulary grew even spicier as the chill wind bit at her nose and exposed cheeks.

"If it isn't just like Jeff to insist on a systems check on a night like this!" she grumbled out loud, her words forming a puffy white cloud before her. But then, she conceded, it wasn't Jeff's fault at all. Who could predict Texas weather? "I should have listened to the forecast. At least the local weatherman came close to the facts."

She shook her head and pulled the knit cap farther down on her head. In the past month she'd begun talking to herself. Kane's fault. She could lay a number of other strange changes at his feet. His desertion had almost been her undoing, but she'd managed to pull herself together. To learn that he was trying to find her infuriated her beyond belief. To face him again, then have him walk away a second time would have been too much to bear.

Shasta snapped the stiff rope in her hands in a quick movement that dislodged Kane's image from her mind. There was work to be done, and if she didn't want to become a frozen fixture on the rooftop, she'd best get busy. Jumping to her feet, she caught her balance on the chimney and gazed upward. The change in weather had cleared the sky and left the stars glittering like diamonds and the full moon glowing like translucent pearl. She shivered with a sudden feeling of déjà vu. There'd been another night when she'd been on a rooftop beneath a bright full moon. A tormented laugh filled the air and echoed off in the darkness. It was ironic, but from where she stood she could just make out Kane's father's house. Her eyes stung sharply behind the lids, and she stomped her cold foot in anger and frustration, then had to grab the edge of the chimney to keep from sliding forward.

Carefully, methodically, she buckled the harness around her waist, attached the iron hook into the loop on the belt and adjusted the ropes on the small block pulley secured around the chimney. Backing away from the stationary anchor, she slowly let the rope play out between her fingers. When her heels touched the edge of the big glass skylight, she squatted and pulled out her burglar tools, rapidly working the lock open and propping the glass panel securely back. She fished out a tiny flashlight with a high-intensity beam, flashed it around the darkened bedroom below and chuckled.

Jeff truly thought he had her this time. Besides the usual security system he'd installed hidden sensors that reacted to weight and vibrations. Her cunning brother had secured the little devices under the carpet, so that if anything over the weight of two pounds touched them they would send off a whole orchestra of alarms that would blast the peaceful night apart. She had to admit he was a genius, except for one thing. He'd designed his system from the original blueprints of the house, and studying them with him later, she'd seen what he hadn't. While making a tour of the house several months earlier she'd realized that Jeff's blueprints were not complete. The lady of the house had changed her mind at a later date and a skylight had been added to the master bedroom.

Shasta lowered herself down into the yawning hole, stopping midway to allow her vision to become accustomed to the darkness. The first thing her eyes discerned was the shape of the massive king-size bed below. She fished out her tiny flashlight from its special case clipped to her jacket pocket, and a thin stream of light sliced through the blackness. Mentally measuring the space she had to traverse, she returned the flashlight to its holder. Pulling on the ropes, she lowered herself down farther and aligned her body over the middle of the bed—directly across from the huge oil painting hanging above the headboard.

With one powerful move she tipped her body down so that she hung suspended horizontally over the silk covers. Now all she had to do was swing like a pendulum till the momentum carried her to the painting, where she could anchor herself to the frame and open the safe on the other side. She began to wave her arms back and forth, the motion widening the swing of her body.

"Come on," she huffed, the leather harness digging deeper into her stomach and ribs. This was harder than she'd envisioned, and she should have practiced it a few more times before venturing out. "Come on, come on," she muttered again as her fingers barely missed the edge of the ornate frame and she was carried backward. She took one more lunge, her body curved into a half circle, and with all the momentum she could muster she arched outward. But this time she didn't budge an inch. Instead, the snap of the ropes made her lose the rigid control she had on her muscles and she sagged like a rag doll.

"What the hell!" she exclaimed, hanging doubled over at the waist. She took a strangled breath of air and swung herself back into a vertical position, her hands grabbing the ropes in front of her.

"Hello, mouse."

Shasta threw back her head, her eyes riveted to the shadowed outline of the man above her. The numbness she'd tried so hard to hold on to had begun to fail her, and in the past few hours more and more memories of Kane kept creeping into her thoughts. She'd argued and scolded and fought a mental battle with herself, but still the heartache kept rushing back at her like a gushing river overflowing its banks. Now to look up and see him, to hear his voice—she squeezed her eyes tightly shut for a second in pain.

Kane shook the ropes playfully, shaking Shasta back and forth. She mumbled a few choice words under her breath.

"What did you say? Come up here."

"I said go away, Kane. I'm not moving from here till you leave. We have nothing to say to each other, so go away."

"It's cold up here, Shasta, and I have to talk to you." Without another word he stood, and with the aid of the pulley began to haul her now limp body upward. He groaned at her dead weight. "You could help some."

"I'm going to kill you, Kane," she yelled. "How dare you show up here after running out on me. You're a coward, Kane Stone, and I don't want anything to do with you."

"Oh, I dare, mouse. I dare a damn lot lately." He remembered the month he'd spent worrying about her, trying to find her, as he grimly pulled on the ropes. With one last gut-straining tug, he pulled her out of the black hole she'd been dangling in. His breath came in great foggy puffs as he slid down the side of the chimney to sit on the cold tiles. "I think I just gave myself a hernia," he moaned.

Shasta hooked a leg on the sill and crawled over the edge of the skylight, her eyes never leaving Kane's face. She sat down cross-legged just out of his reach, yanked off her knit cap and glared at him, her eyes snapping with temper and a hidden excitement she wasn't prepared to admit. "How did you get past Baskerville?"

Kane caught sight of Shasta's feet and smiled tenderly—she was wearing one black sock and one white one. He sobered his expression immediately as he met her angry glare. She was out for her pound of flesh. "I could have gotten past Baskerville without the beer bribe I brought. He was very happy to see me."

"Of course," said Shasta sarcastically. "You were always sneaking him food and giving him extra bowls of beer. He got fat so I put him on a diet and what happens? He sees his easy touch return and forgets he's supposed to be guarding my back.

Traitor!" she yelled into the night, and received an answering whine.

"He's right, Shasta. I am easy." Kane took several deep breaths. "I love you and want you back."

"Don't you dare say that to me! Never again, do you hear me?" She glared at him, her soft full mouth a tight line. "You love only one person—yourself."

"That's not true." He leaned forward in an eager attempt to convince her, but Shasta scooted back, keeping herself out of his reach. Sighing, Kane leaned back as casually as possible. "Didn't they tell you I came back for you?"

She laughed, a hurt sound that wrenched at his heart.

"Oh yes, they told me. And you had your nerve after what you said to me."

"Damn it, Shasta. I made a mistake. Believe me, I realized it almost the instant I sent you away."

"You definitely made a mistake," she agreed. "And coming here is just another to add to your list. I don't want you." She stuck out her chin, her eyes mere slits. "You were different, you amused me, but not anymore. And don't think for one minute that you're the only man in the world for me. There are plenty out there willing to help a girl forget." Her poison arrow hit its mark, and she watched Kane flinch. Why then didn't she feel elated that she'd managed to penetrate his thick hide and return a little of the pain she'd suffered?

"No, mouse," he said softly, "your love couldn't have been so shallow that you're over me this quickly. I know you."

"Know *me?*" she whispered back. "When did you ever try? Every time I showed you who I was, you turned a blind eye. You kept comparing me to other women and your standards for them. You never saw me."

"I did, Shasta. But it's hard to admit that a woman can be so much like a man and still remain loving and feminine." He sent up silent thanks that she was willing to talk and not just throw him off the roof. Shifting his weight, he edged a fraction of an inch closer. If he could only get her into his arms. "Someone told me recently that I was a fool and an ass. He...."

"Was right."

"Yes, he was." Kane moved another inch. "Believe me, I've suffered this last month never knowing where you were or who you might be with." He didn't mention his wild jealousy at the thought of her making love to another man. "Come on, Shasta, forgive me," he wheedled, and smiled a smile destined to bring women to their knees.

"No," she pouted. "Why should I?" She was no different than the rest of the women falling victim to his charms, she realized. Faced with the power of his sensual magnetism, she felt her anger begin to drain away. She rubbed her hand across her eyes. He'd become so much a part of her life—of herself—that at first she hadn't been able to believe it was truly over. There were times when the very air would stand still and she would hear a French accent or see a man who resembled Kane. She would smell his after-shave in the middle of the night and reach for him, only to realize that the fragrance was coming through an open window. He had haunted her like a shadow, never leaving her but only disappearing with the light of day. But she knew she was strong, and as long as she didn't come face to face with him she could make it. She rubbed her hand across her eyes once more as if the action would make him vanish.

Kane had caught the change in her voice and moved a little closer. "Forgive me because I love you."

"No. When you hurt, Kane, you go for the throat. I don't ever want to go through that again."

Kane realized in that instant that Shasta thought he was only coming back for a short while, then would leave her again. He lunged toward her, caught her arms in an unbreakable grip and pulled her, fighting and struggling, across his body, forcing her to straddle his lap and tuck her legs on either side of his hips. He wrapped his arms around her, crushing her small frame to him to stop her escape.

"No, no, no," she wailed. His warmth and strength were her undoing, and a month of holding back broke free as her shoulders began to shake with deep sobs.

"Don't, Shasta. Please, mouse." Awkwardly he patted her back as she cried into the curve of his neck. "Please. Your waterworks are going to freeze my ear off." He received a watery chuckle and squeezed harder.

Shasta drew back and wiped her eyes with the sleeve of her jacket, then turned her liquid brown eyes on Kane. "Why did you do that?"

"What?" Kane smiled as her nose crinkled in distaste when she realized her leather jacket wasn't absorbent. He pushed up his own jacket sleeve and offered her his flannel shirt cuff.

"Why did you touch me? I could have made it if you hadn't." She clasped his hand and rubbed her freezing wet cheeks across the warm material of his shirt. "I can't go through this business of breaking up again, Kane."

He chuckled and dropped his hands to her hips. "Neither can I."

Suddenly aware of how intimately they were touching, Shasta wiggled.

Kane grinned. "Feel how much I've missed you. No, don't say anything, just listen and stop moving around." He closed his eyes for a second, savoring the warmth of her next to him, and when his lids opened, the moonlight showed how dark with desire his silver eyes had become. "I can't believe I'm in this condition sitting on a rooftop in the middle of a norther." Shasta tried again to shift her weight off his lap, but he stopped her. "Don't. No matter how much I complain it feels good just to have you so close."

"Kane, please let me go." His condition was beginning to affect her.

"Not till I'm through talking. Maybe having to contend with two things at once will dull that sharp brain of yours. Be still."

"I'm cold."

"Tough. This is the only way I could be sure we'd be alone." Looking at her, he couldn't help the smile that touched his lips.

"You're laughing at my red nose." She sensed that he was about to launch into a serious conversation, and she wanted to put it off as long as possible. What was he going to offer her this time? First a diamond bracelet to say goodbye... Now was he going to suggest she become his mistress for as long as he wanted?

"Shasta, you're not listening to me." He shook her shoulders gently. "I said that we'd better get married as soon as possible. I have this feeling that if we wait much longer, J.T. will come after us with a shotgun."

"Married! J.T.!"

"Besides, how would it look for an up-and-coming congressman to have a daughter flaunting her freedom."

"Congressman."

"Who's been feeding you birdseed? You sound like a parrot repeating everything I say."

"Daddy?"

"You didn't know?"

She shook her head, then for the first time truly realized what he was saying. "Marriage. You want to marry me?" She flung herself against his chest and lay there, laughing and crying as she tried to soak it all in. He told her of his meeting with her grandfather and Julie. "Marriage? You're sure?" Snuggling further into his embrace, she began to nibble the warm skin above his collar, her lips edging slowly to his ear. She took his cold lobe in her mouth and warmed it with her tongue.

"You didn't—" he sucked in a breath "—give me an answer."

"To what?" she asked, planting tiny kisses along his jaw.

"Shasta, it's too cold out here for these games." He jumped as her hand slipped between their bodies.

"My fingers are cold." Her innocent gaze met his.

"I want you to say—yes."

"Yes," she repeated, and slid her other hand down farther to the warm haven where their bodies touched.

"Stop that." His long, planned speech melted away at her touch. He pulled her hands out. "You'll marry me?" he persisted, wanting a clear answer to the first proposal of marriage he'd ever made.

"Hmm." Shasta licked her cold lips and his eyes followed the movement hungrily. "What happened in Washington?"

It took Kane a long confused moment to realize that she'd changed the subject. "Devil. The meeting went fine. I had to convince certain interested parties that I didn't have a formula for synthetic fuel."

Slanting a look at him from under long lashes, she asked, "Do you think that WSA will allow me to work with you?"

"That's taken care of."

She immediately bristled. "Oh, is it? Just when did you fix things up? And I'd like to know another thing, why the sudden change of heart? When you left for Washington, marriage was the furthest thing from your mind." She was angry all over again and tried to move, but Kane held her securely in place.

"I realized that nothing I've done in the past could compare to the stupidity of giving you up." He wasn't ready to tell her of the hell he'd gone through. This love business was still too new for him to completely reveal his vulnerability to her. It would take time for him to learn to share every part of his life with another person. Openness was not his strong suit, and he'd have to start taking her into his confidence. But he loved her, and love was something he'd never envisioned for himself. Everything else would fall into place with time. He grabbed a handful of delicate curls and pulled her mouth to his. "I'll answer anything you want, but first answer me this." He studied her lovely face and swallowed. "Tell me there were no men in your life this past month."

He was jealous. She could see it in his darkened eyes. "No one, Kane. I just said that to hurt you."

Kane closed his eyes for a brief second in relief. "Now what questions must I answer before we can get off this damn rooftop and into a warm bed?"

Shasta smiled then threw her head back and laughed, a tinkling sound that went straight through him. "Just a few more." She struggled with her expression, then finally gave in and continued smiling at him. "Are you going to buy my clothes?"

He frowned. "You know I don't have any taste or knowledge of fashion."

"Okay, agreed."

She snuggled against him, crinkled her nose and touched the cold tip to his. While he was being so magnanimous, she went on, "I've always wanted a Lamborghini."

"Absolutely not. No! Don't do that." He squirmed away from her hands. "No, Shasta. I will not buy you a car for you to kill yourself in. I have you now, and I'm not going to lose you."

Shasta jumped up, held out her hand to him. "Come on, Kane. We have a job to finish."

"That's not funny, Shasta. We're going to your house, crawl between warm covers and make love till dawn." He looked at his watch. "Well, maybe midnight—I've had a rough time this past month."

Shasta ignored him and, whistling began to refasten the leather belt around her waist. "Straighten out those ropes, will you?"

"Now you listen here Shasta Masterson...." But she was already over the edge of the skylight, and he felt the jerk of the rope in his hands. He held it firmly and yanked backward bringing Shasta's head up. Brown eyes aglow with excitement peered at him over the windowsill and he was lost. Like a thief in the night she had stolen his heart with that look. He sighed, if nothing else, life was going to be fun—and, by the looks of it, busy. Bracing himself, he began to play out the rope.

Shasta disappeared into the darkness, then her head popped back up again, a smile flashing bright and loving. "I love you."

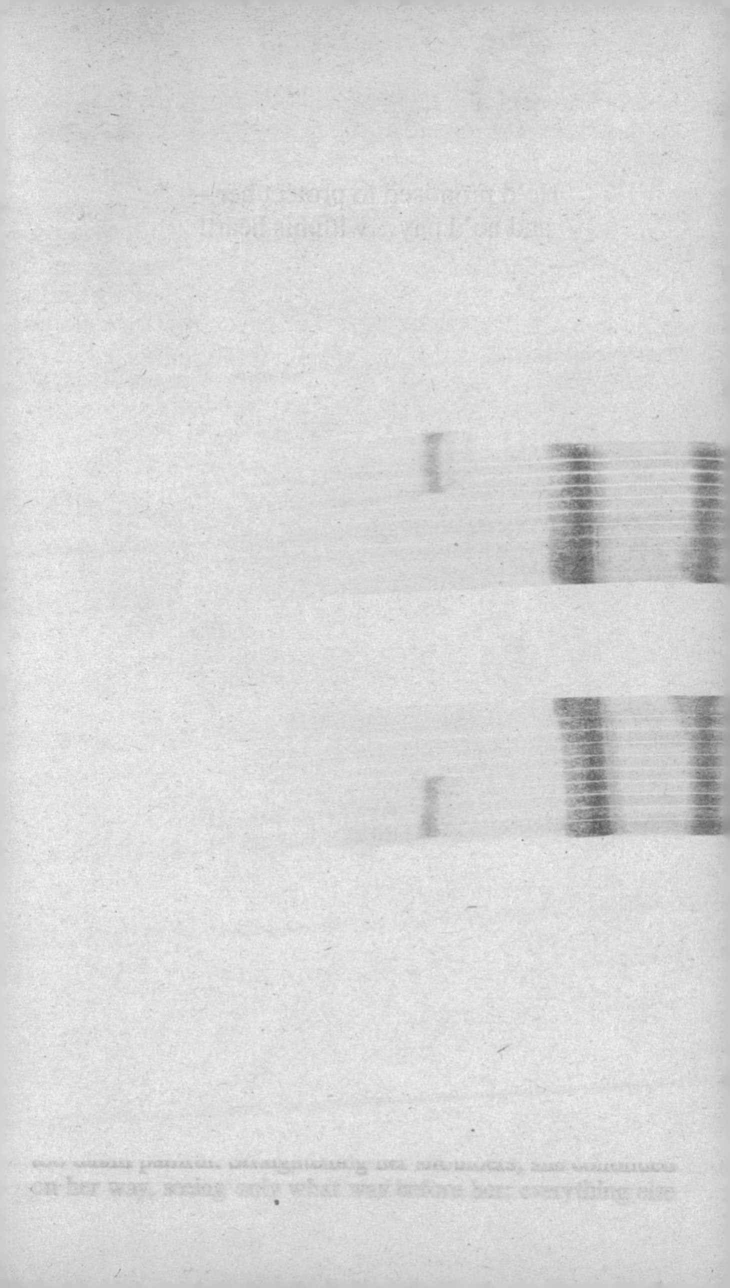

He'd promised to protect her—
and he'd pay…with his heart!

THE HONEY TRAP

Pamela Bauer

PROLOGUE

Vienna, Austria

"IT WOULD SEEM your wife did not board the plane in New York."

To the untrained ear, the man's English was flawless. But American Peter Lang, a linguist whose area of concentration was the Slavic languages, detected the slightest trace of a Russian accent in the softly spoken words.

"Not on the plane . . . no messages. . . ." The lifting of broad shoulders was accompanied by a dubious shake of his head.

"I know she's coming," Peter insisted, trying to keep the anxiety from his voice. "Her connecting flight to New York was probably delayed. Airplanes in the United States are seldom on schedule." At this point he didn't dare think that his wife had chosen not to join him in Vienna.

"Wouldn't she have left a message for you had that been the case?" The man frowned as if puzzled, then began edging away from the waiting area.

"We aren't going to leave without her, are we?" Peter didn't want to beg, but he knew he would if it was necessary.

"We have no choice. We cannot delay your departure without putting the entire operation at risk. By this time tomorrow, the whole world, including your wife, will know where you have gone."

"But I was assured she could go with me," Peter protested.

"Had your wife cooperated, yes. But I don't think I need to tell you the danger you will place yourself in if you remain here. Even in a country like the United States, where convicted murderers are allowed back on the streets after a short incarceration, espionage is still a crime punishable by life imprisonment. No woman is worth that."

"It isn't my wife I want with me. It's my daughter. I'm afraid that if I leave now I may never see her again."

"If you end up in prison, you will be no good to your daughter...or your son. Or have you forgotten about your son?" The man gave a twisted smile.

"It's because of my son that I'm here, as you well know," Peter reminded him. "I've waited a long time to see him again."

"First we must get you safely out of Vienna and to your destination. There you will be reunited with your son and our agents will do all they can to see that your daughter joins you, as well. In the Soviet Union you will be a hero, receiving great respect from those who will be your pupils. You will have a position of great honor. Your son will have a father, and who knows..." He paused, giving Peter another twisted smile. "Maybe Svetlana will be assigned to Little America, too."

"Just let me check to see if my wife is on the next flight." Peter started toward the reservation counter, but an arm of steel stopped him.

"*If* she is still coming," the man began in a tone that matched the hardness of his grip, "someone will be here to escort her and your daughter to the Ukraine."

"I prefer to wait for them myself," Peter said, squaring his shoulders defensively.

"That would be foolish," the other man warned. "It would be to your advantage to continue to cooperate until our mission is complete. You have been successful in securing all the necessary information, and now it is imperative that we return with that information as quickly as possible." Subtly he turned and nudged Peter toward the exit.

"What possible harm could a couple of hours make?" Peter backed away from the subtle pressure and laughed nervously as panic began to swell inside him.

This time there was no twisted smile, only an icy glare. "We have our orders."

Peter wanted to tell him he could shove his orders. The mission wasn't complete and wouldn't be until he had his daughter. Before he could utter another word, however, he felt a piercing sting in his left arm. Within seconds he was surrounded by several men, all dressed in identical dark suits.

With incredible difficulty, he tried to resist sinking into arms ready to support him as his legs buckled and a great cloud of haziness descended upon him. He could feel himself slipping from the haziness into the darkness, yet he was powerless to stop the slide. Before the world was gone entirely, he heard his own voice, as though it were coming from a great distance.

"I need Steffie," he mumbled, then fell unconscious.

CHAPTER ONE

Melbourne, Florida

"IS STEFFIE ALL RIGHT?" Clara Summers hesitated in the doorway of the hospital room, her face as pale as the stark white sheet draped over the small child asleep in the crib.

"She's fine, Mom." Ronni Lang rose from the vinyl-covered sofa to greet her mother with a reassuring hug, then gently led her over to the crib. She understood her mother's anxiety; just the sight of her daughter lying perfectly still in the hospital bed was enough to send a chill down her own spine. "Really, Mom... she's fine. She's just sleeping."

"You don't sound so sure of that," Clara whispered, her eyes taking in every inch of her granddaughter. She lifted the sheet and with loving fingers caressed the little arms poking out of the hospital gown. "When I heard your voice on my answering machine, telling me Steffie had taken an overdose of cough syrup, I had these horrible visions of—" She broke off with a shudder.

"I know, Mom." Ronni placed her hand on her mother's shoulder. "I'm sorry you had to hear about it that way. But honestly, she's going to be fine."

"Are you sure? Her cheeks look flushed." With tender fingers, Clara smoothed the delicate curls that hung like tiny red corkscrews on Steffie's forehead, then pressed her fingertips against the rosy cheeks.

"Her cheeks are always flushed when she sleeps. And you don't need to whisper. The doctor said she probably won't wake up until morning... the cough syrup made her more than a little drowsy."

Clara murmured a few words of endearment over the sleeping child, then kissed Steffie's fingers before tucking them back under the sheet. With a sigh, she stepped back from the crib and faced Ronni, her hands on her hips. "I don't understand how this could have happened. How did Steffie manage to get into cough syrup? I thought you kept all your medicines in a locked cabinet."

Ronni, too, had moved away from the crib and was standing next to the window, where the lingering rays of the setting sun cast striped shadows across her face.

"It didn't happen at my house," she explained with a gentle toss of her head. "I wasn't even with Steffie when it happened. Lisa was watching her so I could finish packing."

"Oh, Veronica, you didn't leave her in Lisa Bergstrom's care," her mother admonished. Ronni recognized the tone as the same one Clara used whenever she felt her daughter wasn't giving her granddaughter the attention she deserved. "Didn't I tell you that sooner or later something like this would happen?"

Normally Ronni would have defended her next-door neighbor, as she had often done in the past whenever her mother had questioned her friendship with the artist. But guilt was already fluttering inside her like a trapped butterfly. Her mother wasn't saying anything Ronni hadn't already said to herself. Right now, however, what she didn't need was to be defending herself to her own mother.

"Mom, you always do this to me. If Steffie gets an upset stomach, it's something I've fed her. If she's got a cold, I didn't dress her properly." She turned to stare out at the city she had lived in nearly all of her life, both arms wrapped tightly across her chest. "That's my daughter lying in that crib. Don't you think I know that Steffie wouldn't be here if I hadn't left her at Lisa's?"

After a few moments of uncomfortable silence, Ronni felt her mother's hand on her elbow. "I wasn't blaming you, Veronica."

The words sounded stiff to Ronni, but considering how difficult it was for her mother to express her feelings, they were enough to cause Ronni to give her mother's hand an understanding squeeze. "I know you weren't, Mom. You're just worried about Steffie . . . the same as I am."

"You seem to forget, Veronica, that she's not like other children," Clara reminded her, glancing back at the sleeping child. "She's so delicate."

"Mom, she's a typical fifteen-month-old baby," Ronni insisted. It never ceased to amaze her how one small child could turn her normally reserved mother into such a softie. Even thirty years after her discharge from the army, Clara still looked a bit like a drill sergeant, with her gray hair pulled back into a French roll. Ever since Ronni could remember, her mother had never been demonstrative. Gestures of affection were usually initiated by Ronni, who often attributed her mother's cool reserve to her military background. Yet with Steffie she was a doting grandmother.

"You still haven't told me what happened," Clara said, lowering her slightly overweight frame onto the vinyl sofa.

Ronni leaned back against the window ledge and began to explain. "Remember how I told you Lisa's little girl, Angela, had that same flu virus Steffie had last week?" Seeing her mother's nod, she continued. "Well, it was Angela who gave Steffie the cough syrup. Lisa's always commenting on how Angela likes to play mommy to Steffie. Apparently Steffie was coughing so Angela decided to be a good mommy and give her some cough medicine."

"And where was Lisa when all this was happening?"

"She'd gotten a long distance phone call and took it in her studio. She said she was only out of the room a few minutes."

"But long enough for a five-year-old to feed cough syrup to a toddler." Clara shook her head disapprovingly. "Any mother can tell you it takes only a few minutes for something to happen with children. That medicine shouldn't have been anywhere near Angela's reach."

Ronni exhaled a long sigh. "No, it shouldn't have, and I'm sure Lisa's learned a lesson from this. I know she feels terrible about what happened."

"I suppose we should be thankful it wasn't anything worse than cough syrup that Steffie swallowed. When will you be able to take her home?" Clara asked, glancing once more at the crib.

"The doctor wants to keep her overnight as a precaution. I'm going to sleep here just in case she should wake up."

"Would you like me to keep you company?"

"Thanks, Mom, but if you're going to leave for your cruise tomorrow morning, you need to get a good night's sleep."

"Oh, I'm not going to go... not until I make sure Steffie's recovered completely." Clara waved her hand in a dismissive manner.

"Mom, she's fine," Ronni insisted. "In fact, the doctor told me there's no reason Steffie and I can't leave for Vienna tomorrow."

"You're not still going to see Peter, are you?" Her face had a look of near horror.

Ronni ignored her mother's shocked expression and reached for her purse. "That reminds me. This all happened so fast I haven't been able to call Peter." She rummaged through the leather shoulder bag until she found a small business card, which she passed to Clara. "Would you see if you can reach him? He's probably worried sick about us."

"If he is, it'll be the first time," Clara muttered.

No one knew better than Ronni just how true her mother's words were, yet she couldn't help but say, "Mom, even though Peter will soon be my ex-husband, he's always going to be Steffie's father."

"She doesn't need a father like that," Clara stated brusquely.

"I think we'd better end this discussion right now. It's obvious you and I have different opinions about the importance of a father in a girl's life." This time it was Ronni's tone that was stiff.

"Obviously we do. I happen to believe a father should love his daughter and take care of her. So far, Peter Lang hasn't shown me he's capable of doing either one."

"That may be true, but I think Steffie should have the opportunity to know her father if she chooses." She paused before adding quietly, "I never had that choice."

"You sound as though you blame me for that," Clara retorted, the stiffening of her back revealing even more than the tone of her voice.

"Blame you? Mom, I never expected you to get married again just so I'd have a father." Ronni studied her mother. "Why do you always get so defensive when I bring up the subject of fathers?"

"I'm not defensive," Clara said huffily. "It's just that I did my best to bring you up properly after your father died, and now, ever since you've been separated from Peter, you seem to want to blame everything that goes wrong on the fact that you don't have a father."

Ronni could see she had upset her mother, and immediately felt contrite. "Mom, as a single parent you were the best, and I'll always be grateful. But that doesn't mean I don't often wonder what it would have been like if Dad hadn't died." Her voice softened. "All I have is a couple of photographs. I never had the chance to get to know him. It would help if you would just talk to me about him."

But as usual, Clara had no inclination to talk about William Summers. "He's been gone twenty-five years, Veronica."

"But you must have memories."

"I've already told you about him—dozens of times. I don't really know what else there is to say." There was an edge to her voice, and her white-knuckled grip on her purse echoed her agitation.

Ronni could see from the set of her mother's jaw that even if there had been anything else, she wasn't going to say it. She had her drill-sergeant look firmly in place, and after twenty-eight years, Ronni knew better than to ask any more questions.

She wasn't surprised by her mother's unwillingness to talk about William Summers. As a child, Ronni had always been afraid to mention her father's name, for it would invariably put her mother in a sullen mood. Initially Ronni had believed it was because Clara had loved him so deeply and couldn't bear the pain she felt at the memories. As time went by, however, Ronni began to wonder if her mother's reticence was truly due to grief. The older Ronni became, the more she began to suspect that her mother and father's marriage had been a troubled one, despite her mother's contention that William Summers would always be her one and only true love. Of course, Clara would never discuss such personal feelings with her daughter, and dispiritedly Ronni gave up trying to find the answers.

"I guess you really can't compare the two situations. My father's dead. Steffie's is alive. The courts will determine whether she'll have a father," Ronni finally said. "At least this will be the last time we'll have to visit Peter. To be honest with you, Mom, I feel much better about us visiting him rather than him visiting us. I don't want him here in Florida," she stated firmly.

"Well, I for one will be happy when you're both back home safe and sound." There was a hint of relief in Clara's response.

"Does that mean you'll call him for me?"

"I guess I can tolerate speaking to the man for five minutes," she reluctantly agreed as she stood up.

"Thanks." Ronni reached for her mother's hand and squeezed it gratefully. "Tell him I'll phone as soon as I've arranged another flight."

Clara nodded and stepped back over to the crib. "I don't care what you say, she looks delicate to me." She lifted Steffie's hand and surveyed the little wrist. "Is that a rash on her arm?"

"Mmm-hmm. She must be allergic to the metal in her Medic-Alert bracelet. She probably inherited the allergy from me. You know I can't wear anything but sterling silver."

"Can't you get this one in sterling?"

Ronni nodded. "I've ordered one for her. I had hoped it would come before we left for Vienna."

"The poor little dear," Clara crooned affectionately, then brushed a butterfly kiss across Steffie's forehead. "She's had her share of problems. First she was born premature. Then there was that bout with pneumonia. Now this." She shook her head regretfully. "Is it any wonder I worry?"

Absently Ronni ran a hand across the crib railing. "No, I guess not. Mom, you will call Peter as soon as you get home, won't you?"

"Yes, although I'm sure that by now he's checked with the airlines and learned you never boarded the plane. Don't you think it would be a good idea to wait a day or two before you reschedule your flight?"

"I'll think about it, all right?" She steered her mother toward the door. "Now I want you to go home, finish your packing and think about all the fun you'll have on your vacation. By the time you return from your cruise, Steffie and I will be back from Vienna, and we'll have dozens of stories to share."

When Clara would have left with only a wave of her hand, Ronni reached for her mother and gave her a hug. "Thanks for coming."

Clara mumbled a good-night and made Ronni promise to call her first thing in the morning.

After she'd gone, Ronni considered her mother's suggestion carefully. Maybe she shouldn't be in such a hurry to leave for Vienna. The thought of calling Peter and telling him Steffie was too sick to travel danced tantalizingly before her. Each time she'd seen her husband in the past two years it had taken her weeks to get over the emotional upheaval their meetings always created. Yet the sooner she confronted him about the divorce, the sooner she would be able to get on with her life.

She studied her daughter as she slept so peacefully. Steffie was such a beautiful child; it hardly seemed fair that she should have two parents who could barely utter a civil word to each other. Or that she hadn't been conceived out of love, but a futile attempt to salvage a hopeless marriage. It was because of Steffie that Ronni would go face Peter. She only hoped that his feelings for his daughter weren't as fleeting as the light summer rain that evaporated before it ever reached the ground.

THE HEAT WAS RELENTLESS. Scorching. Suffocating. It sucked every inch of air out of Logan McNeil's body until his lungs felt like two raisins. His clothes clung to him, damp from the moisture that seemed to pour from his skin, while the heat robbed him of his strength, his determination, his sanity. Yet he knew he had no choice but to sit in the car and wait for the signal. Just when he thought he could no longer bear another minute of waiting, he saw the woman in the black-and-white polka dot dress getting a drink at the water fountain.

Logan climbed out of the car and headed for the opposite end of the park where several wooden barricades surrounded a newly erected bronze sculpture. Ignoring the sign that warned the area was closed to the public, he climbed over the wooden barrier and headed to the right of the massive sculpture. As soon as he spotted the wooden bench, he saw the drop—a package wrapped in what looked like old newspapers. But before he could reach the bench, a shiny red ball went rolling past him, followed by a little girl with long blond curls and the most angelic face Logan had ever seen.

"What are you doing?" he asked when she fell to her knees beside the bench.

"I have to get my ball," she answered breathlessly, smiling up at him.

"Wait," Logan called out. "I'll get it for you. My package is under there, too."

"It's all right. I can reach it," she said, and crawled under the bench.

Before Logan could say another word, an explosion sent a rocket of fire mushrooming around him. Pain engulfed him, blinding him to everything but the furnace of heat threatening to drag him into its abyss. He reached for the screaming child, but she eluded his grasp, and he cried out in frustration. With a feeling of desperation he frantically grasped at thin air, until the pounding in his head reached such a tempo he thought he'd die. In a natural reflex he closed his eyes, only to discover when he opened them again that the world around him was in total darkness.

"I can't see! I can't see!" he repeated, panic-stricken.

Logan awoke from his nightmare with a start. He heaved a long shuddering sigh of relief at the sight that greeted him. The old iron bed with the faded pink chenille bedspread, the aging chest of drawers with its brass knobs, the still life on the wall of a bowl of fruit. He wasn't in southern France, but southern Florida. Automatically he reached for the dark patch that covered his right eye. His peripheral vision was gone, but he wasn't blind. He knew, however, that the tormenting nightmare would continue to haunt him, because even though he wasn't blind, the little blond girl had been killed in the explosion.

The room was stifling and close, and Logan could only guess that his air conditioner had gone on the blink again, as it had a habit of doing with greater frequency now that it was July and the humidity rose higher than the temperature. Logan wondered if there wasn't a fault in the electrical circuit, as the large ceiling fan had ceased to whirl, as well. Suddenly he realized that the pounding he had heard in his head was actually someone knocking on his front door.

With only a pair of khaki shorts covering his lean frame, he rolled off the bed and stumbled out to the kitchen, where he splashed cold water in his face and swiped at the slick sheen of perspiration glistening his torso. Grabbing a bottle of imported beer from the refrigerator, he opened it on the side of the counter, then took a long swallow, welcoming the cool relief with a satisfied sigh. When the knocking persisted, he reluctantly started toward the sound, but changed his mind in midstride. There was only one person who knew his whereabouts.... The thought brought a frown to his face.

Slipping out the back door, he crept around the side of the house until he was close enough to the porch to snatch a glimpse of his visitor. To his surprise, a feeling of homesickness washed over him at the sight of the heavyset man banging impatiently on the front door. Quietly Logan stepped up onto the wooden veranda, then drawled softly, "You look like a man who could use a cold beer."

Startled, the gray-haired man turned around. "It's good to see you again, Logan," he said sincerely. He thrust his hands into the pockets of his pants, as though unsure whether he should embrace the younger man.

Logan had no such qualms. He set the bottle of beer down on the porch railing and wrapped his arms around the slightly rounded shoulders. Watching the other man's eyes dart nervously about their surroundings, he said, "It's true what Hemingway said, Doc." Logan looked off in the near distance, where sun lovers littered a beach strewn with seaweed. "People don't stare in Key West. I doubt if anyone down here would even care that a United States senator was talking to a beach bum."

Doc glanced around self-consciously. "Maybe we ought to get a megaphone so you can announce it to the world," he said dryly, propping one leg up against the porch railing.

"You're looking well, Doc," Logan remarked, taking in the older man's familiar face, a face he remembered better than his own father's. But, then, Doc was more like a father to him than his own dad had been. As a youth he'd spent most of his free time in the campaign office of Senator Potter rather than on the farmstead of Lawrence McNeil.

"I'm still thirty pounds overweight and I smoke too much." As if to confirm his statement, Doc unbuttoned his light blue suit jacket and extracted a cigarette from his shirt pocket. "How do you stand this heat?" he asked, wiping his brow with the palm of his hand.

"This is nothing compared to what I've been in over in the Middle East. You want a beer? It's about the only thing that's going to cool you down here. My air-conditioning's on the blink."

"Is that all you've got?" He gestured with his cigarette toward Logan's bottle of imported brown beer.

Logan nodded. "At least I drink it cold." He smiled, remembering how Doc used to chastise him for not drinking the beverage warm. "Wait here and I'll get you one."

When Logan returned, Doc had removed his suit jacket and was fanning himself with an old newspaper Logan had left lying on the porch. "How did you find me?" Logan wanted to know, handing his friend the bottle dripping with moisture, then added, "or shouldn't I ask?"

"You certainly didn't make it very easy for me." He expelled a steady stream of smoke as he talked. "You don't need to worry. No one knows I'm here—not even Smithson."

"You actually came without the Senate's number one congressional aide?" Logan arched one eyebrow and raised his bottle in a mock salute.

"Smithson's loyal and discreet, but that doesn't mean he needs to know my every move. Besides, he's visiting his mother in Cocoa Beach." Doc raised his beer bottle in acknowledgment, then after taking a swallow said, "You're looking much better than the last time I saw you."

"Yeah...well, hospital patients seldom look good, do they?" Logan's lip curled cynically at the memory.

"I thought maybe the bandage would be off by now."

Doc had a habit of looking him squarely in the face, which annoyed Logan now that he was forced to wear the black eye patch. The loss of sight in his right eye had been an emotional as well as physical adjustment, leaving him reluctant to be around people. He wasn't sure which bothered him more—the way people would stare at him curiously or the way they would deliberately look away at the sight of the patch. When he responded now, his voice carried his annoyance. "It doesn't matter much. I can't see with or without the patch."

"Wounds take time to heal, Logan," Doc reminded him.

"Well, that's one thing I've got plenty of, isn't it?" He was peeling the silver label off the bottle with his fingernail.

"You're still seeing a specialist, aren't you?"

"There's one in Miami I see."

"And?" Doc prodded.

"He says exactly what all the others have said. It's a fifty-fifty shot. The eye might work again, and again it might not."

"What about the rest of you?"

"Fit as a fiddle." Logan avoided looking at Doc as he spoke, but stared out at the Gulf of Mexico, where the sun, in its daily descent, was bathing the shrimp fleet in a golden serenity. Even though Doc was like a father to him, Logan felt uncomfortable with his concern. "Doc, you didn't come all the way down here to inquire about my health."

The senator smiled without revealing any teeth. "Logan, I need to ask a personal favor of you. I need your help with something."

Logan's immediate response was a humorless laugh. "A man in your position doesn't need an old broken-down case officer."

Doc chose to ignore the sarcasm. "Oh, yes, I do. I need you to help me find someone."

"In case you hadn't noticed, Doc, I don't see so well anymore." Defiantly he snapped the elastic band holding the black patch in place, then took another long swallow of beer. "Have you forgotten that the Company retired me? I don't look for people anymore . . . only fish."

"Fish?" Doc made a disgruntled sound. "Then it's true? You really are spending your time taking tourists out to look at a bunch of fish swimming around in the ocean?"

"The coral reef is more than 'a bunch of fish swimming around in the ocean,'" Logan gently chided. "There's another whole fascinating world out there in the reef. You know, I think if I had to do it all over again, I would have studied marine biology in college," he said thoughtfully.

"And the United States would have missed out on one heck of an agent. You're the best I've ever seen in intelligence work."

Seeing the intensity in the older man's face, Logan said, "I *was* the best. I think you're forgetting about what happened in France. I lost the big one, and I'm not just talking about the sight in my right eye, Doc. I don't have what it takes anymore."

"That's rubbish, and you know it," Doc exclaimed. "What happened wasn't your fault. You were betrayed."

"I was careless." With the admission came a sigh of remorse. "Look, if you're trying to recruit me back into service, you're wasting your time. I like being a conch here in Key West."

"You don't look very happy to me," Doc remarked, grinding his heel on the remainder of his cigarette.

"I'm as happy as I deserve to be." Bitterness laced his words.

"I've never known self-pity to be one of your faults, Logan." The older man shook his graying head. "What happened to that patriotic kid from Kansas and his strong sense of justice?"

"He finally admitted to himself that he couldn't right every wrong in the world."

Doc gave him a shrewd look. "Are you sure you don't mean it's easier not to try?"

Logan could see the disappointment in his mentor's eyes, and it still had the power to disturb him. Why was pleasing the senator so important to him? "Doc, I wouldn't be any good to you. I've lost it—that ruthless, cunning drive that makes the ends always justify the means."

"Aren't you even a little bit curious about why I've come?" Doc tempted him.

Logan could feel his interest growing, but he didn't want to let the senator know that. Instead he chose sarcasm. "You've got more children I can lead to the slaughter?"

Doc tightened his fists and shook his head disapprovingly. "I've got a child you can save from the slaughter," he told him with more than a hint of reproach in his tone. He pulled a snapshot from inside his shirt pocket and handed it to Logan, who gave it a cursory glance.

Clutching a striped beach ball was a wide-eyed baby with a toothless grin and a dusting of red fuzz on its head. But it was the woman kneeling on the patterned blanket beside the baby who drew Logan's attention. She was wearing a one-piece swimsuit of jade green that left little to the imagination, although it generated quite a bit of activity in Logan's imagination. Her features weren't as stunning as her figure, but there was something rather appealing about the almost gamine face framed by blond curls. It was a happy face, as though its owner possessed a zest for life.

"I didn't realize the Senate Intelligence Committee was involved in child protection services." Logan's attempt at irony couldn't disguise his curiosity.

"It isn't, and you know that."

"Then why show me the picture of the baby? Just who is it you want me to find? The baby or the woman?" As much as he hated to admit it, Logan was intrigued.

"Both. They're mother and daughter. Veronica and Stefanie Lang." Doc extracted another cigarette from his shirt pocket. "Actually, I know where they are. What I need is information."

As Doc lit the cigarette, Logan noticed his hand was shaking. It was so out of character for the senator to be nervous about anything, Logan found himself asking, "What kind of information?"

When the senator hesitated before answering, Logan prodded, "Are you in some kind of trouble because of this woman?"

Doc shook his head. "Not in the way you're thinking." He took another swig of beer. "Andrew left a few things at the house the last time he visited. That picture was one of them."

Suddenly Logan understood the reason for the senator's concern. "If this is Andrew's girlfriend and you want her investigated, I'll give you the name of a private investigator in the Melbourne area."

"It's not as simple as that," Doc cut in impatiently, pulling a second photo from his pocket and handing it to Logan.

It was a wedding photo, and Logan quickly recognized the bride as a younger version of the woman in the picture with the baby. "Andrew's girlfriend is married to someone else?"

"That's not the worst of it." He exhaled a narrow stream of smoke. "I think the child may be Andrew's. There's a very good possibility that Stefanie Lang could be my granddaughter."

Logan could see how disturbing the whole idea was to the senator. "I know it's probably not easy for you to accept that your son is involved with a married woman, Doc, especially if there's an illegitimate child involved. But if you're worried about your political career, I don't think the public would hold you accountable for your son's personal relationships. I mean nowadays, the idea of a senator's son having an affair with a married lady is probably not even newsworthy."

"It would be if that lady's husband was under investigation by the Senate Intelligence Committee. Smithson found that photo in one of the case files that came through the office last week—the one concerning certain defense secrets that have been ending up in enemy agents' hands."

Logan whistled through his teeth. "Andrew's lady is married to a spy?"

"An alleged spy. His name's Peter Lang. That's why I need to know what her relationship to Andrew is, and whether Stefanie could be my granddaughter."

Logan was silent for a few moments, as though deliberating whether he should say what was on his mind. When he did speak, all traces of sarcasm were gone. "Do you have any reason to suspect that Andrew has any connection whatsoever to this Peter Lang?"

"That's what I need to find out. I need you to prove he doesn't." The words were almost a whisper, a plea filled with pain. "You know as well as I do that when it comes to electronic technology, Bartron has had a distinctive edge in the marketplace, which is why they've been awarded some of the largest government contracts for the space program. Peter Lang was working for Bartron when Andrew was hired. Although they weren't in the same department, they did work together in the same plant." His voice faltered. "I can't believe my only son could be a traitor to his country, Logan."

Logan's immediate reaction was the same as Doc's. He felt stunned by the implication. Although he and Andrew had been at odds throughout most of their lives, he knew him well enough to feel relatively certain that he wouldn't betray his country.

Logan glanced at Doc, hardly believing they could be having this conversation. Then his espionage mentality asserted itself, and he knew it was possible that Andrew could be a spy. He had seen firsthand what money, desire for revenge and thirst for intrigue could make people do. Andrew had always lived in the shadow of the senator, never quite measuring up to his father's expectations. But was that shadow dark enough to turn him into a traitor?

"I need you to find out what you can before the authorities get dragged into this. Because sooner or later they'll make the connection between Andrew and the Langs," Doc explained anxiously.

Logan looked again at the picture of Veronica and Stefanie Lang. "What do you know about this woman?"

"Smithson's done a little investigating for me and uncovered a few things. She's a schoolteacher, been married to Peter Lang for eight years, which means she married him when she was only twenty. The only reason she was mentioned in the Agency's report was that she's still legally married to her husband, although they've lived apart for several years. Actually, Smithson had trouble finding any information on her at all."

"Can I have this?" Logan flicked the photo in his hand.

"Does that mean you'll help me?" Doc asked carefully.

For the first time, Logan noticed the shadows beneath the senator's eyes. "This is really troubling you, isn't it?"

The wooden railing creaked as Doc rested the bulk of his weight against it. "I knew Andrew was seriously involved with someone a couple of years ago. He became very secretive about his private life, and I guessed that it was because the woman was married. He knows I'm old-fashioned when it comes to that sort of thing. Smithson checked it out and discovered it was her—Veronica Lang."

"So you think the baby is Andy's?" Logan was studying the picture again, trying to pinpoint any similarities between the baby and Andrew.

"Yes. Just look at her hair—it's the same shade of red as Andrew's. And he's crazy about her. He says it's because she's his godchild, but I'm convinced she's his daughter. Veronica lived with him for a while around the time Stefanie would have been conceived. The thought that I might have a granddaughter innocently caught in such a mess..." Doc's voice trailed off. "Logan, you're the only one I can trust with this. I'm not asking for myself but for the child."

Cautiously Logan said, "If I agree to help you, I'm going to have to talk to Andy."

"Do you think that's wise? I mean, knowing the way he feels about you?" Andrew Potter had made no secret of his feelings for Logan. In his eyes, Logan had usurped his role as son and was everything his father had hoped he would be. Their friendship had been a stormy one, and in recent years, the few occasions they'd been together there had always been friction between them.

"You want the truth, don't you, Doc?" When the older man agreed, Logan added, "No one will have any reason to suspect me. As far as the rest of the world is concerned, I'm out of intelligence work. You said no one knows you're here, right?"

"Smithson thinks I'm in Washington." Doc reached over and withdrew a legal-size envelope from inside his suit jacket pocket and handed it to Logan. "All the information I have on Veronica Lang is in here."

"What about the baby's birth certificate?"

"It's in there, too. It shows Peter Lang as the father."

"Where's this Lang now?"

"Employed as a linguist for an American firm in Vienna. During his tenure at Bartron, he never worked in any of the departments requiring security clearance. He translated technical manuals into foreign languages, but of course it's probable that he had contacts in all the right places. You can read about it in there." He pointed to the envelope fat with papers, which Logan was absently tapping against his palm.

"Are you going back to Washington tonight?"

Doc nodded. "I've got a cab waiting around the corner to take me to the airport."

"Does that mean you won't join me for some supper at Bubbles?" Logan knew of the senator's weakness for pasta.

"It wouldn't be wise, Logan." Doc's smile was filled with regret. "When will you leave for Melbourne?"

"As soon as I've cleaned up, although if I went looking like this, Andrew would simply believe the rumors floating around that I've lost my mind." He rubbed his fingers along his unshaven jaw.

"You do look a bit like a drunken pirate. By the way, I have a new secure telephone . . . courtesy of the government." Doc rattled off a string of digits. "Got it?"

Logan nodded. "I'll contact you as soon as I've talked with Andrew."

"I appreciate this more than I can tell you, Logan." This time he didn't hesitate to embrace his friend. "It's not hard to see why Andy fell for someone like her. She's easy on the eyes," he said, indicating the photo.

Logan gave a sardonic chuckle. "She looks like she should be singing in the church choir, not married to a spy."

"I figured if she could charm Andrew, she could charm anyone. Maybe I should tell you to be careful. We don't have much information on her, which is rather odd."

"You don't need to worry about me, Doc. I can take care of myself—even when it comes to pretty little blondes." He poured the last few drops of beer onto the parched lawn.

But long after Doc had disappeared out of sight, Logan found himself staring at Veronica Lang's picture and wondering how a guy like Andy could have attracted such a beautiful woman.

CHAPTER TWO

"VERONICA, I can't find Peter."

"What do you mean, you can't find him?" Ronni asked her mother, propping the telephone receiver between her ear and her shoulder so she could fold the hospital blanket she had used during the night. "Did you try his office?"

"I have been calling all over Vienna looking for that man," Clara declared a bit indignantly. "His home phone has been disconnected and his secretary at his office told me she hasn't seen him in two days."

Ronni would have sworn she could feel the hairs rise on the back of her neck. "Something's not right, Mom. Why would his phone be disconnected? That's the number he gave me to call in case of an emergency."

Clara made a derisive sound. "As if you could ever turn to him in an emergency."

Ronni let her mother's comment pass. "There must be some logical explanation. Are you sure his secretary understood what you were asking her?"

"Yes. I'm telling you, she didn't know where he was. She seemed a little perturbed with me—as though I were responsible for his failure to show up for work."

"I wonder where he could be? It's not like him to miss work. Despite all his faults, he's always been very conscientious when it comes to his job." She gnawed unconsciously on her lower lip. "Now what am I supposed to do?" she pondered aloud.

"You'll have to wait for him to contact you. I left a message for him at his office, as well as at the airport in Vienna. He should be calling you sometime today... if he's going to call you." It was obvious from Clara's tone that she didn't think he would.

"I guess that means we won't be leaving for Vienna today," Ronni concluded.

"I really think it's better if you don't," Clara agreed. "Listen, Veronica, I'm just getting ready to call the taxi to take me to the airport, but I'm still not comfortable about leaving you like this. Has the doctor been in to see Steffie yet?"

"Yes, and he's given her a clean bill of health. She's sitting up in the crib, stacking plastic rings on a peg."

"Oooh... let me say goodbye to her," Clara pleaded.

Ronni held the receiver next to Steffie's little ear and watched her daughter reach for the spiral cord. While she fought the battle to keep Steffie from pulling the cord from the phone, Ronni could hear her mother cooing endearments. Finally Steffie gurgled a garbled sound and Ronni snatched the receiver away.

"There, Mom. She says she loves you, too." Ronni looked at the cherubic face, which was starting to wrinkle in displeasure at having the telephone yanked out of her grasp. "We'd better say goodbye. I think I hear the breakfast cart out in the hall."

As soon as she had hung up, Ronni dressed Steffie in a one-piece terry-cloth romper, then set her in the high chair the nurse's aide had wheeled into her room as soon as dawn had broken. Whereas Steffie was bright eyed and full of energy, Ronni felt stiff and headachey. Unlike her daughter, she hadn't slept well, having tossed and turned on the lumpy couch, waking each time the nurse entered the room to check Steffie's vital signs.

Now, without a shower and change of clothes, Ronni was feeling distinctly out of sorts. Actually she was feeling downright irritable. She longed for the comfort of her small, but homey two-bedroom rambler with its peeling paint and missing roof tiles. If she didn't go to Vienna she could cash in her ticket and hire someone to paint the house and repair the roof. In her present frame of mind, she could have easily made the decision without a second thought.

"I must really be tired," she told her daughter, who was trying to force the plastic rings onto the peg in the wrong order. "Your mama always gets silly when she's tired." Ronni gently eased the red plastic ring from Steffie's hand and gave her the yellow one, instead. Steffie immediately shoved the yellow ring into her mouth, as though she could tell by its taste whether it was supposed to be the next one on the peg. After a couple of chomps on the plastic, she managed to slip it onto the stack of colored rings with a squeal of delight.

"Way to go, Steffie!" Ronni clapped her hands, then, seeing Steffie's breakfast being carried into the room, slipped the final red ring in place before whisking it off her tray. "Time for breakfast," she announced, tying a large plastic bib around her neck.

While Ronni spooned creamed cereal into Steffie's mouth, her thoughts drifted to Peter. Deciding to visit him in Vienna had been a difficult decision, one she didn't want to have to reconsider. Now faced with the opportunity to change her mind, she felt unsettled, and just as nervous as when she had originally made the decision to go. The fact that her mother hadn't been able to reach him only added to her uneasiness. Why had his phone been disconnected? Now she would have to go home and wait for him to call her. Once again, Peter had her waiting for him, as so often had been the pattern in their relationship.

Steffie's little fingers had discovered the oatmeal and, as usual, were tracing patterns across the high chair with it. By the time she had finished her breakfast, oatmeal graced her red curls, her ears and Ronni's elbow.

"Steffie, my darling, I do believe we're making progress," Ronni proclaimed as she wiped away the cereal with a wet cloth. "None on your nose!" She accentuated each word with a tap of her forefinger on the tip of Steffie's tiny nose.

Her daughter's response was to grab the washcloth and suck on it.

"Here. Chew on this for a few minutes while I get our stuff ready, and then we'll go home." Ronni gently eased the washcloth from Steffie's mouth and handed her a teething biscuit, which she proceeded to gnaw on, humming contentedly to herself.

As she did every day, Ronni turned on the local morning program on TV to catch the latest news and weather updates. Dividing her attention between Steffie and the movie review being given, she gathered up the few toys Steffie had been playing with in her crib and began stuffing them back in the diaper bag. One of the plastic rings had rolled under the crib, and Ronni had to scoot down on her hands and knees to retrieve it. It was only as she stood back up that she happened to glance once more at the overhead television.

Expecting to see the face of the movie critic, Ronni gasped at the image staring back at her from the television. For an instant she couldn't talk or even breathe, for the photo on the screen was of Peter.

"Oh, my God!" she exclaimed, her hand flying to her gaping mouth. Why was Peter on the national news? Her immediate thought was that he must have been killed in an accident, but then she saw the filmed footage that followed, and she quickly reached for the TV's remote control to turn up the volume.

"U.S. officials caution that it is too soon to speculate on the impact the thirty-nine-year-old linguist's defection will have on U.S. intelligence. Lang was employed by Bartron for seven years, but it is not known whether he had access to top secret defense information or was merely the liaison in a network of spies. Unofficially we've received word that Lang will be holding a press conference later this morning concerning his defection to the Soviet Union."

"Defection to the Soviet Union!" Ronni repeated, sinking down onto the couch. Peter a *spy*? No, it couldn't be. She shook her head in disbelief. There had to be some mistake. He was proud to be an American. Hanging on the wall in his parents' home was a picture of him with the president of the United States, taken the day he was one of fifty high school students honored for writing essays on the topic "What it means to me to be a citizen of the United States."

Peter would never give up that citizenship! When Ronni had suggested they get rid of his old navy uniform, he had protested indignantly, telling her it represented not only his time spent in the service, but freedom itself. He would never willingly leave it all behind. How could he? She jabbed at the button on the remote control to switch channels, hoping to catch another news report that would repudiate what she had just heard. But after a rapid succession of images on the screen, she knew there would be no such report.

Suddenly the disconnected phone number made sense. As did the Swiss bank account she had stumbled across when she had cleaned out an old chest he had hidden in the attic. And the many business trips he had always been so secretive about. At the time she had thought he was seeing another woman, that he was betraying her. But he wasn't just betraying *her*, he was betraying his country, and the thought filled her with revulsion.

She was married to a stranger. A dangerous stranger. A spy. The notion was both revolting and alarming. But it was only as she looked at Steffie, happily munching on her teething biscuit, that she realized how angry she was with that stranger. What would the consequences of Peter's actions be for her and Steffie? A chill ran down her spine.

She reached for the phone and immediately dialed her mother's number, letting it ring at least a dozen times before accepting that her mother had already left for her vacation. Who could she turn to? Certainly not Lisa—not after yesterday. She started to dial her mother-in-law's phone number, but stopped after the third digit. Evelyn and Marshall Lang hadn't spoken to her since her separation from Peter, and by now they were probably in their own state of shock.

Names of several of her friends flashed through her mind, but there really was only one person she knew she could count on to help her through this mess. She quickly dialed his number, silently praying he'd be home. When she heard his voice, she practically cried in relief.

"Andrew, it's Ronni."

"Ronni! Oh, thank God you didn't go with him! Where are you? I've been trying to reach you since yesterday morning."

"Andrew, is it true about Peter? I just saw the news and I—" She broke off, choked with emotion.

"Ronni, listen to me. It's important that I talk to you before..." He changed thoughts in midstream. "Where are you?"

"I'm at the hospital. Steffie accidentally swallowed some cough syrup and she had to stay overnight. That's why we missed the plane."

"You missed the plane," he repeated.

There was a queer emotion in his voice that Ronni was unable to identify.

"How's Steffie?" he went on. "She's all right, isn't she?"

"She's fine, Andrew, but I don't understand why Peter did this—"

"Listen to me," he cut in. "I want you to bring Steffie over here as soon as she's released from the hospital. Will you do that? Will you come directly to my house?"

Ronni had never heard Andrew sound so distraught.

"Of course I will, but you have to tell me what you know about all this. Did you have any idea that Peter was—"

Again he interrupted her. "I really don't think we should be talking about this on the phone. For all we know, they could already have a bug on my line."

Ronni automatically pulled the receiver away from her ear and gave it a cursory glance. "They? Who's 'they'?" A frown wrinkled her brow.

"The government's going to be questioning anyone who's had any connection whatsoever with Peter. I did work at Bartron when Peter was there," he reminded her. "What time do you expect Steffie to be released?"

"The doctor's already been in. I'm just waiting for the nurse to bring me the forms."

"Have you talked to anyone else about this?"

"No. I just saw it on the television. I tried calling my mother but she'd already left for her vacation." Ronni massaged her temple where a dull ache was rapidly becoming a throbbing pain. "My God, Andrew! This is all so horrible. I don't know what I'm going to do!"

"Ronni, you're going to have to trust me on this. It's important that you come directly to my house and not talk to anyone, all right? At this point we don't know who we can trust. Do you understand what I'm saying?"

"No, I don't understand any of this!" she exclaimed, raising her hand in a helpless gesture of frustration. "Yesterday I was supposed to meet my husband in Vienna. Today I learn he's a Soviet spy and you tell me I shouldn't trust anyone. Next I suppose you're going to tell me I'm in danger."

There was a prolonged silence and Ronni gasped. "Oh, my God—we're not in danger, are we?" She glanced anxiously at Steffie.

"No, of course not," he denied. "I'll just feel a lot better when you and Steffie are here with me and I know you're safe. Peter was hanging around people with few scruples . . . people who'd stop at nothing to get what they want."

"But Steffie and I don't have anything they want!" she protested.

"I know, I know," he said soothingly.

But she was not calmed. When a nurse slipped quietly into the room, Ronni lowered her voice. "Look, Andrew, I've got to go. Steffie's nurse is here."

"All right. Remember what I said . . . and please, be careful."

"We'll be there soon." As she hung up the phone and turned her attention to the nurse, Ronni tried to shake off the sense of foreboding that had descended upon her. Like a thick fog, it pervaded her emotions as well as her logic, and she couldn't help but worry that Peter's actions had jeopardized their safety. By the time she was ready to leave the hospital, the apprehension was close to becoming panic, and she was surprised that her wobbly legs were able to carry her and Steffie out to her car in the parking lot.

All the way to Andrew's, she tried to make sense out of what she had heard on the television, but there seemed to be no explanation for Peter's behavior. If he had been planning his defection all along, why had he arranged for her to come to Vienna? Unless— She nearly ran a stoplight at the realization. *He thought that she would consider going with him!* It was almost too bizarre to consider, yet what other explanation could there possibly be?

More than anything, what she needed right now was a friend. Thank goodness Andrew was there for her, just as he had been more times than she could remember. He had helped her through the most painful period of her life. She knew she could trust Andrew. With her mother away, he was the only person she could really turn to.

She only hoped Andrew would have some answers to her questions. It wasn't like him to sound so worried. Images of James Bond spy scenes came to mind, and automatically her eyes moved to the rearview mirror, as though expecting to find someone tailing her. But none of the drivers behind her looked like anything except impatient motorists disgusted with traffic. She heaved a sigh of relief, but still found herself glancing into the rearview mirror from time to time.

Not a single car followed her off the freeway exit to Andrew's, which led her to believe she was letting her imagination run wild. She was glad Steffie had fallen asleep in her car seat, for she didn't need her daughter to witness her paranoia. If Steffie sensed her mother's tension, she'd be fussing, and whining, as well.

Ronni smiled at the sight of the little head that dipped to one side of the car seat. Steffie looked so peaceful, so totally unaware of all the craziness going on around her. If only she would never have to know the horrible truth about her father.

Ronni made the final turn onto Andrew's street and her smile vanished. In front of his home were a police car and an ambulance, both with their red emergency lights flashing. She pulled into the driveway and parked next to the house. Without waking Steffie, she slipped out of the car, leaving the door wide open as she rushed toward the house.

"What's happened?" Ronni asked a police officer who was filling out a form on a clipboard.

"Are you a relative of Mr. Potter's?"

She shook her head. "No, but I spoke to Andrew not more than an hour ago and he asked me to come right over...he's expecting me."

"From what I can see, your friend has had a heart attack. The paramedics are with him right now," the officer told her, his face grim.

"A heart attack? But he's only thirty-three," Ronni squeaked.

The policeman could only lift his shoulders regretfully.

She hurried toward the front door, but was met by two uniformed men carrying a stretcher bearing Andrew. His face was ashen white, his eyes closed, and an oxygen mask rested over his mouth. Ronni was shocked by his appearance. Only two days ago they had had dinner together and he'd been the picture of health. Now he looked like the shadow of death.

"Andrew, are you all right?" she asked. "It's me...Ronni."

Andrew's eyes fluttered open, then widened in recognition, and Ronni took his hand in hers. "He's trying to tell me something," she said to the paramedics as she trailed alongside the stretcher with Andrew's hand clinging to hers. She bent closer to him.

"Steffie?" he mumbled through the oxygen mask, his eyes searching about frantically.

"Steffie's fine," she assured him. "She's in the car. Don't try to talk now. Save your strength."

The hand that wasn't clutching Ronni's reached up and pulled the oxygen mask away from his face. "You've got to be careful. Don't trust—" Suddenly his face took on a deathly green pallor, and his eyes bulged. He was no longer looking at Ronni, but at the man who had just stepped into view.

"What are you doing here?" Andrew managed to croak, just seconds before the paramedics forced the oxygen mask back into place despite his reluctance to have it hampering his ability to speak.

Ronni's eyes flew to the man who had caused her friend such distress and she nearly gasped. Standing across from her was a suspicious looking dark-haired stranger. At first she thought it was the eye patch that gave him a menacing appearance, but his jaw was hard, and there was something somber about the planes of his face. He was either hiding secrets or sorrow. In any case, Ronni didn't want to know which.

"I'm a family friend. What's happened?" He was speaking to the paramedics, but staring at Ronni.

"Coronary. We've got to get him to the hospital right away," one of the attendants stated.

Andrew continued to mumble inaudible words, waving his hands wildly in Logan's direction. Maybe the paramedics didn't notice his obvious distress at seeing this so-called family friend, but Ronni knew that Andrew was definitely upset at the man's presence. And with good reason, she thought. The stranger was watching her with an intensity that was at odds with the concern he'd voiced for Andrew. He had a height advantage of at least six inches over her, and next to Andrew's pale figure he looked rugged and strong.

"Is he going to be all right?" she asked the paramedic as Andrew was lifted into the ambulance.

The man shrugged. "We're going to do everything we can to assure he is. Are you a relative?"

Again Ronni shook her head. "Only a close friend."

"Then I'd call before you make the trip to the hospital. Only immediate family members are permitted in the coronary care unit."

Ronni nodded, a bit dazed by the speed at which everything was happening. Within seconds the ambulance doors were being shut and the vehicle was moving away from her, taking out of sight the one person she could trust. If it wasn't for Steffie asleep in the car, she would have climbed inside along Andrew and gone to the hospital with him. Now all she could do was watch the flashing lights disappear around the corner until she was left standing alone with a man dressed in a Hawaiian print shirt, navy blue shorts and wearing an eye patch.

Ronni cast a suspicious look in his direction. Who was he and where had he come from? Andrew's reaction was enough to convince her he wasn't a friend. She wanted nothing to do with the man and would have walked away without another word to him, but he was determined to speak to her.

"You must be Veronica Lang."

The fact that he knew her name rooted her to the spot. Seeing her surprise, he added, "Andy told me about you... and your daughter, Stefanie. I'm Logan McNeil, an old friend of the family's."

Ronni detected a hint of a challenge in the way he stared at her, and she realized he was deliberately trying to intimidate her into looking away from him.

Logan McNeil. The name didn't sound familiar to Ronni. She thought about offering her hand—in fact, wiggled it nervously at her side—but settled on nodding in acknowledgment. One dark eye scrutinized her and she was the first one to break eye contact, looking in the direction of her car. "I think I'm going to go to the hospital... just in case."

"You won't be able to see him. You heard what that guy said—immediate family only." This time the tone was more icy than polite.

"That may be the case, but I'd still like to be there." Her ash-blond hair was tied back with a green ribbon, but the wind had loosened several strands and they were skipping across her face. She brushed them away with shaky fingers.

"I'm going to have to call his father," Logan stated soberly.

"You know Senator Potter?" The tilt of her head challenged him.

"Yes. I said I was an old friend of the family's," he returned, meeting her challenge with a chilling glare.

Her answer was a look that said she was skeptical of everything he said.

"I grew up on the farm that bordered the senator's back in Kansas. Andy and I used to play tag in the cornfields," he explained evenly.

Ronni regarded him carefully. The few times Andrew had confided in her about his family, there had always been a bitterness in his tone. He hadn't wanted to talk about his childhood, except he'd told her that his best friend had grown up to be Mr. Perfect—the kind of man his father had expected him to be. Somehow she couldn't see Andrew aspiring to be like this man, who looked as if he should be playing guitar with the Beach Boys.

"Were you here when it happened?" he asked her when she remained silent.

"No, I only arrived a few minutes before you did." She tried not to stare at him, but there was something compelling about the expression in his eye. She thought she detected a flicker of admiration, and for just an instant, she experienced a feeling of déjà vu, as though they had stood staring at each other some other time, some other place. It was an odd sensation, one that sent goose bumps along her flesh and at the same time brought a flush to her cheeks. Suddenly a child's cry carried on the summer air, breaking the silence.

"That's Steffie." Ronni turned and walked toward her car, followed by Logan. When she saw him appraising Steffie through the window, her initial apprehension returned and Andrew's warning echoed in her mind. *Don't trust anyone.*

"You'll have to excuse me." Ronni climbed in the car and started up the engine, her thoughts on getting away as fast as she could. As she backed out of the driveway, she saw Logan walk over to the policeman, say a few words, then proceed to enter Andrew's house.

Ronni wondered what he had said to the cop. That he wanted to use the phone? Who was he really, and what was he doing at Andrew's? And why had Andrew reacted so strongly to his presence? Maybe it was better if she didn't know. Right now she was so confused that all she wanted was to take Steffie and run far, far away from all this madness.

All the way home, her mind held vivid images of Logan McNeil digging through Andrew's desk drawers, searching through his personal belongings with that one, dark brown eye that had seemed able to gaze right into her soul. She could still hear the rich deep timbre of his voice, and the way her name had rolled off his lips in an almost familiar manner. The memory was enough to cause her to shiver, and then to wonder. If he knew her name, did he also know her address?

CHAPTER THREE

WHEN RONNI ARRIVED HOME, she found a white van with the blue-and-red call letters of a local television station painted on its side parked out front. Standing on her doorstep was a reporter with microphone in hand and a cameraman at his side. It was obvious that they were filming, and Ronni wondered of what possible interest her modest home could be to anyone.

As soon as she drove her Honda Civic into the driveway, the reporter came rushing across the yard with the cameraman in tow. Ronni was undoing the strap on Steffie's car seat when her door was flung open and a microphone thrust under her nose.

"Mrs. Lang. What can you tell us about your husband's defection? Isn't it true you had arranged to go with him, but your daughter's illness prevented you from joining him?"

Ronni shrank from the microphone and shook her head distastefully at the appearance of the television camera over her shoulder.

"I don't know anything!" she insisted, trying to shield Steffie from the camera's probing eye. "Please, leave us alone." She clutched Steffie against her chest and with head down got out of the car and made her way over to the front door, ignoring the camera and the questions that were being fired at her in an almost hostile fashion.

She fumbled with the lock as Steffie wiggled impatiently in her arms, eager to be set down. Through the metal door she could hear the telephone ringing. With her purse and the diaper bag slung over one arm, and the baby close to her hip, squirming like a worm, Ronni had to lean against the door and give it a shove with her shoulder to get it open. As a cool blast of air greeted her, she quickly slipped inside, then shoved the door shut with her rear end. Before she answered the telephone, she deposited Steffie on the living room floor, dropping her purse and the diaper bag beside her.

"Hello." She was slightly out of breath by the time she reached for the phone.

"Mrs. Lang, this is Bill Mason from the *Times*. I want to ask you—"

"I'm sorry, I can't talk right now," Ronni interrupted, in no mood to face another reporter. She replaced the receiver with more force than was necessary, only to have the phone ring again. She took several calls in succession, each of them from reporters wanting to ask her about Peter. And she told every one of them the same thing—that she had no comment. Only, with each successive call she became more annoyed by the questions, until finally she left the receiver off the hook.

Steffie had found Ronni's yellow plastic laundry basket that doubled as a home for her stuffed animals and was happily tossing the furry creatures around the living room. When the doorbell rang, Ronni was tempted to ignore it, thinking that it was probably the television reporter persistently pursuing a story. Reluctantly she went to see who it was, and was relieved to find Lisa and Angela Bergstrom on her doorstep, looking concerned.

"Hi. We wanted to see how Steffie was doing," Lisa greeted her. "I tried calling, but your line's been busy."

"I know. Come on in," she answered, stepping aside for the two of them.

"Here." Lisa handed Ronni a small stack of envelopes and a tiny package as she walked past. "I grabbed your mail. I wasn't sure if you still wanted me to take it in for you."

"Thanks." Ronni casually glanced at the return address on the slim package and said, "This must be Steffie's new Medic-Alert bracelet."

"How is she?" Lisa asked nervously.

As if she knew she was being talked about, Steffie came toddling out into the hallway, a big smile erupting at the sight of Angela.

"As you can see, she's fine." Ronni scooped her into her arms and smoothed the red curls back from her face. "Why don't we go into the kitchen, and I'll get us some iced tea and the girls can play?" She set Steffie back down and watched the two little girls make a beeline for the toys in the living room.

"Ronni, I think you ought to know that a television reporter was at my house, asking all sorts of questions about you and Peter," Lisa told her as she followed her into the kitchen. "Of course I didn't tell him anything," she quickly added.

Ronni paused with her hand on the refrigerator door. "A reporter was at your house?"

"Yes, and I know he's been here, too, because I saw him in the yard. Ronni, what's going on?"

"You haven't heard?"

Lisa shook her head.

"Peter's done something horrible. It was on the news this morning. I thought the whole world would know by now." Ronni filled two glasses with cold water, then briskly stirred in the instant tea.

"How horrible is horrible?"

"It's worse than anything I could ever have guessed."

"Does this mean you're not going to Vienna and getting the divorce?"

"Peter's not in Vienna, Lisa." She handed her one of the glasses.

"Did he come back here?"

"No. According to the news, he's not coming back—ever."

"And that's bad news for you?" Lisa questioned, lifting one eyebrow.

Ronni considered not telling her friend the whole story, but she knew it would only be a matter of time before she learned what had happened. She didn't realize, however, how difficult it would be to admit what Peter had done. She took a deep breath to steady herself, then said, "Lisa, the reason he's not coming back is that he's decided he wants to live in the Soviet Union. Peter has defected."

"Defected? Why would he defect unless he's a..." Her voice trailed off in disbelief. "Ronni, you don't mean he's a...a..." She couldn't seem to speak the word aloud.

"Spy," Ronni completed soberly.

"A spy!" Lisa finally said, a distasteful fascination in her tone. "You're kidding, aren't you?"

Ronni took a sip of her tea. "I still can't believe it myself, but it's true."

"And all this time you never had any idea what he was doing?" There was a flicker of incredulity, then amazement on Lisa's face.

"Of course not!" Ronni denied emphatically.

"No wonder the television cameras have been prowling the neighborhood," Lisa said, slowly shaking her head. "This is incredible!"

"I've had to take the phone off the hook. Reporters keep calling, asking all sorts of awful questions. Then there was that guy waiting for me when I got here." She raised her arms in helpless supplication. "Look at me. I've slept in my clothes, my hair's all greasy and I don't have a stitch of makeup on. This is how I looked while they were filming me."

"You don't look that bad," Lisa sympathized, setting her glass on the counter. "You probably feel worse than you look." She moved over to the window, where she lifted the lace edge of the curtain.

"What are you doing?" Ronni asked.

"I wonder if they've got the house under surveillance."

"Surveillance? Who would have us under surveillance?"

"The government, Ronni." Her neighbor was looking at her rather oddly, almost suspiciously. "The FBI's probably going to be involved. Spying is pretty serious stuff. I mean, it's not like committing a misdemeanor."

"Peter hasn't lived with me in almost three years," Ronni shot back defensively.

"That doesn't matter. You are still legally married to the guy."

Lisa was moving from window to window, lifting curtains and shades carefully, as though she expected someone to be watching her. Ronni followed her from room to room until they came to her bedroom.

"I don't see anything that seems out of the ordinary, but there is a guy out there in a pickup who looks a little odd, although he doesn't exactly look like an FBI agent." Lisa's voice was barely a whisper.

Ronni pushed her aside and stole a peek out the window. "Where? I don't see anything."

"Look around the corner—behind that overgrown bougainvillea Mr. Klemmons refuses to trim."

"Oh, no!" Ronni moaned as her eyes spotted the orange pickup with Logan McNeil sitting inside. "What's he doing out there?"

"You know him?" Lisa narrowed her eyes again suspiciously.

"Not really." Ronni let the curtain slip back into place, then went back into the living room, where Steffie and Angela were playing.

"Well, who is he?" Lisa asked, trailing after her.

"He says he's a friend of Andrew's." Ronni chewed on her lower lip.

"You mean Andrew's in on this whole mess?" This time Lisa's eyes widened.

"No! Of course not," Ronni vehemently denied. "Andrew's had a heart attack. He's in the hospital."

"A heart attack? When did that happen?"

"Just this morning." Suddenly Ronni was feeling distinctly uncomfortable with the way Lisa seemed to be absorbing every bit of information. It was as though she had a morbid curiosity about her friend's predicament, and Ronni was beginning to regret telling the woman anything at all. "Look, Lisa, if you don't mind, I'm really tired and I'd like to take a shower and get cleaned up. I also want to call the hospital and check on Andrew's condition."

"Oh, sure, I understand," Lisa replied, although Ronni detected a coolness in her tone. "Steffie can stay with me if you want to go visit Andrew," she offered.

Ronni knew she couldn't accept, not after what had happened. Diplomatically she said, "I don't think it would do me any good to go. If he's in the coronary care unit, they won't let anyone but family in."

Lisa moved toward the door, pausing on her way out to say, "I'm really sorry about Peter. If I can help in any way, let me know." She looked anxiously at Ronni, who assured her she would, then thanked her for the offer.

Unlike Ronni, who was relieved to see Lisa and Angela leave, Steffie was unhappy with the loss of her playmate. Still suffering from the effects of the cough syrup, she was rubbing tightly balled fists across her eyes and fussing. Usually Ronni read her a story and rocked her in the big wooden rocking chair before putting her down for her nap, but in her present state of mind, she found Steffie's whining to be just another source of irritation. With a brisk movement she swept the little girl up into her arms and carried her into the nursery.

"Steffie, you need a nap."

But Steffie didn't appreciate her mother dumping her in the crib. While Ronni pulled the shades and wound up the clown music box, she stood against the side rails, screaming in protest.

"Steffie, go to sleep," Ronni ordered before closing the door on the red-faced child. As she moved around the living room picking up Steffie's scattered toys, the muffled sounds of her daughter's crying penetrated the hard barrier her frazzled nerves had built around her heart. She reached for the book of Mother Goose nursery rhymes and returned to the bedroom.

"Come on, pumpkin," she said, giving Steffie a kiss as she lifted her from the crib. "Just because the rest of the world has gone crazy doesn't mean we have to join them, does it?" she said softly, settling into the wooden rocker. With Steffie sagging against her bosom, Ronni read several rhymes, gently rocking the chair, until after only a few minutes, the tiny red lashes were fanned out across plump cheeks and Steffie was asleep.

Ronni had just deposited her back in the crib, when the doorbell rang. A quick look out the living room window told her it was two men dressed in dark blue suits and stark white shirts. Leaving the chain lock in place, she slipped the door open just far enough to speak to them.

"Mrs. Veronica Lang?" one of the men asked as the door partially opened. Before Ronni could either confirm or deny his assumption, a badge was shoved into the crack in the door. "I'm Doug Mahoney and this is Stan Wicklund. We're from the Federal Bureau of Investigation and we'd like to ask you a few questions."

Ronni released the safety chain and stepped aside, allowing the two men to enter. She led them into the living room, where they chose to sit side by side on the peach-and-blue camelback sofa. Ronni took the wing chair across from them.

"Mrs. Lang," the man who had identified himself as Doug Mahoney began, "I'm sure you must know why we're here."

"I'm assuming it's about Peter," she returned steadily, clasping her hands in her lap.

"When was the last time you saw your husband?"

"I'd appreciate it if you'd refer to Peter as my ex-husband," Ronni insisted. "We're in the process of getting divorced. We haven't lived together in over two years."

"Are you saying you haven't seen him in two years?"

"No, I saw him at Christmastime. We have a daughter and he came to visit her."

"And you haven't spoken to him since then?" While Doug Mahoney asked the questions, Stan Wicklund wrote furiously in a small notebook.

"Not in person. He's called on the telephone, but I haven't seen him. He travels a lot and recently he's been living in Vienna," she explained.

"Weren't you yourself planning on joining him in Vienna yesterday?"

"Yes, I had planned a trip to Vienna," Ronni answered candidly. "I was supposed to take our daughter over for a visit and our divorce was going to be finalized."

"So why didn't you go?"

"My daughter, Steffie, had an accident and we had to spend the night in the hospital. As a result, we missed our flight."

"Then had your daughter not been taken ill, would you have met him in Vienna and gone with him to the Soviet Union?"

"No! Of course not!" she protested, straightening in her chair.

"You just told me the only reason you didn't join him was that your daughter was ill," Doug Mahoney reminded her.

"That was because I didn't know what he was planning!" she exclaimed. "There's no way I would have gone to Vienna if I'd had even the slightest hint he was a spy."

"Then he is a spy?"

"He must be if he's defected, mustn't he?" She was getting flustered by the way he wanted to put words in her mouth. "Why are you asking me? You're the ones who are supposed to know about this kind of stuff." Ronni realized he wasn't simply asking questions but interrogating her, and it was obvious from his tone of voice that he was suspicious of her.

"So you're saying that until today you had no knowledge he had any connections to the Soviet Union?"

"No," she replied firmly. "I told you. We've lived apart for nearly three years."

"I thought you told me it was two years?"

"It's been two years since we tried a reconciliation, but we've been legally separated for three years."

"Yet you were married and living together when he worked as a translator for Bartron?"

"Yes."

Mahoney withdrew several black-and-white photos from his coat pocket and set them out on the coffee table in front of her. "Do you recognize any of these people?"

Ronni thought the pictures looked like mug shots. She studied them carefully, but didn't recognize any of the faces. When she looked up at the agents, she noticed that while she had been studying the photos, they had been studying her reaction. "Why are you looking at me like that? Should I recognize these people?"

"You're the one to be answering that question, Mrs. Lang."

His suspicious attitude angered her, and it was increasingly difficult to keep that anger in check. "Look, I don't know what you came here hoping to hear, but I can assure you it was probably a greater shock for me to learn about my husband's activities than it was for you."

"If that's the case, Mrs. Lang, you won't mind if we ask your cooperation in not leaving town until we've concluded our investigation."

"Leave town? I've got no reason to leave town." She saw both men glance toward the suitcases that still sat packed and ready to go in the hallway, then exchange guarded looks, which had Ronni wondering if anything she said would make them think any differently. Apparently she was guilty by association.

"Good." Both men stood at the same time. "Then you won't mind if we put a tap on your phone. It's for your own protection, Mrs. Lang."

"Protection?" Ronni rose from her chair. "Why would I need protection?" she asked, her voice rising slightly.

This time it was Stan Wicklund who spoke. "Your husband was only a small part of a spy ring—a ring that's still operating here in Florida. Until we identify who your husband's contacts are, it's in your best interest to have our protection." He snapped the cap of his pen in place and tucked his notepad into his breast pocket. "Keep in mind one thing, Mrs. Lang. There are two sides to this game. We're the side you can trust."

Ronni looked at his beady little eyes and never felt more dubious in her entire life. The one person she would have given her trust to implicitly was lying in a hospital bed, fighting for his life. These men were strangers—as Peter was to her right now. The thought brought a chill to her skin.

Doug Mahoney reached inside his pocket and produced a business card. "Here's the number I want you to call should you receive any information that might help us, or—" he paused dramatically "—if you need our help."

Ronni accepted the card. "I don't see how I could possibly help you. I've already told you everything I know."

"For your sake, I hope that's true."

Again she resented the implication that she wasn't being honest with them. "What possible reason could you have to think otherwise?" she asked.

Doug Mahoney's answer was another warning. "Your husband was trading secrets with devious people, Mrs. Lang. People who would stop at nothing to get what they want."

"And I told you I don't know what my husband was doing," she said adamantly. "I do know that I don't have anything that could be of interest to anyone."

"I hope you're right." He glanced around until he spotted the telephone on the desk, then walked over and turned it upside down.

"What are you doing?" Ronni asked.

He paused to look at her. "You said you didn't mind if we monitored your calls."

"I don't, but are you sure it's necessary? The only people who have been calling are pesky reporters."

"Oh, it's necessary, Mrs. Lang," Doug Mahoney assured her as he fished a small round disk from his pocket and placed it on the underside of the telephone. Signaling Wicklund, he moved toward the door. "We'll be in touch." Again he paused. "A word of advice. I'd be careful who you trust. As I already said, your best bet is to call us."

FROM HIS SPOT behind the overgrown bougainvillea, Logan watched the feds leave Veronica Lang's house. Judging by the expression on her face as she showed them out, she hadn't found their visit reassuring. Wicklund and Mahoney were not the smoothest when it came to interrogation, and he was a bit surprised the Bureau had assigned them to this particular case. Judging by the expressions on their faces, they weren't overjoyed with their assignment, either. But, then, he couldn't really blame them. It simply wasn't a case for the likes of Wicklund and Mahoney.

But, then, it wasn't a case for him, either. He was no longer with the Agency, and even if he was, this case would be under the jurisdiction of the FBI, not the CIA. Even Doc had suggested they let the feds handle it from now on, since Peter Lang had gone and put all of his cards on the table.

Logan knew he should start up his engine and drive away. There were other ways of learning about the paternity of that baby without getting involved with this case. All he had to do was drive away and forget he had ever met Veronica Lang.

But that's where he was having a problem. He *had* met her. And during that brief meeting, something had happened that wouldn't let him forget. There was something about her and that baby that was calling him to take an interest—besides the fact that she had a beautiful face with perfect white skin and gentle blue-gray eyes. The photo Doc had given him hadn't nearly done her justice. The kinky blond curls were now smooth, chic tresses, and although her shapely legs were hidden by the long skirt of her sundress, she had a graceful way of moving no photograph could capture. After the murky world of espionage, she was like a breath of fresh air and sunshine.

From the information Doc had given him, things weren't adding up. He couldn't figure out why she would have married a slimeball like Lang in the first place, let alone be a partner to what he had done. Nor could he believe she had been Andy's mistress. Both ideas were equally repulsive, and it was because he wanted to prove Doc wrong that he decided he wouldn't drive away.

He would pay her a short visit. Just long enough to find out the answers to a couple of questions that were bothering him. Unofficially he wanted to learn the truth about Andy before the feds did—for Doc's sake. At least, that's what he told himself was the reason for walking up to Veronica's house and ringing the doorbell.

Just as she had with the feds, she kept the chain lock in place, only opening the door a crack.

He could see the fear in her face and wondered if it was him or the feds who had done a pretty good job of scaring her.

"How did you know my address?" she asked through the narrow opening in the door.

Logan was beginning to suspect it was him and he didn't like the feeling one bit. "I found it in Andy's desk," he lied.

She gave him a look that left little doubt about what she thought of his riffling through Andrew's desk.

"Why have you been watching my house?"

She caught him off guard with that one. "What makes you think I have?"

For an answer she slammed the door shut on his face. Logan rapped on the door with his knuckles. "I'm sorry, Veronica. Please open the door. I need to talk to you about Andy and I have something to show you." He knocked again, a knock accompanied by another plea, and was just about to leave, when the door opened once more.

"What is it you need to tell me about Andrew?" she asked.

He could tell by her tone of voice that he had found a vulnerable spot. "Do you think maybe you could let me in? I'm not crazy about carrying on a conversation through a crack in the door, and it is rather hot out here."

"I'm not in the habit of letting strangers in, Mr. McNeil."

"What did you call those two suits who just left?"

"They at least had identification." She flung the words back at him. "I don't even know who you are."

"I told you. I'm a friend of Andy's."

"He's never mentioned your name to me," she said skeptically.

"Andy doesn't call me 'Logan.' Ever since we were kids I've been called 'Mick.' It's short for McNeil," he explained.

The door closed again, but this time he heard the chain slide open and the next thing he knew she was gesturing for him to step inside. As he walked past her, he said, "Then you do know who I am? Andy has spoken of me?"

"Yes, but I'm not sure he'd approve of your being here," she told him, indicating he should follow her into the living room.

"Aha." He bobbed his head knowingly. "I guess you know that we're not exactly best friends anymore."

"I guess I do," she returned dryly. "You've got five minutes to convince me differently."

CHAPTER FOUR

"I DON'T SUPPOSE I could get a nice cold glass of water," Logan said, giving the suitcases in the hallway an interested glance as he followed her into the living room. He moved casually, looking very relaxed as he gazed around.

"Wait here and I'll be right back," she told him, noticing how he was taking in the contents of the room with a sweeping glance. When she returned with a bottle of spring water, he was nosing around her desk, but didn't look the least bit guilty at having been caught doing so.

"Make yourself at home," Ronni said wryly, handing him the bottle of water.

He transferred the newspaper he had been holding in his hands to under his arm. "Thanks, but tap water would have been fine." He held the bottle up in a gesture of gratitude, then twisted off the cap and took a long swallow before setting the bottle down on her desk.

Ronni quickly slipped a coaster under it.

"Oh, sorry." Logan shrugged, then turned his attention to the telephone.

"What are you doing?" she asked when he found the small metal disk Doug Mahoney had attached to her phone.

"The suits left a calling card."

"I know. It's a phone tap."

He gave her a look that said, "Are you for real?" then shook his head. "It's a bug. As in microphone." He held the disk up between his fingers. "This little thing will pick up whispers from a distance of twenty-five feet."

"You mean they can hear everything we're saying?"

A hint of a smile creased his cheeks. "Not anymore." He toyed with the device briefly before slipping it into his pocket. Then he picked up the bottle of water and the coaster and moved to the sofa, where he sank down, setting the water on the coffee table—this time with the coaster beneath it. Unlike the FBI men, who had looked very uncomfortable sitting on her sofa, Logan appeared completely at ease.

She tried not to let his presence affect her, but her eyes were drawn to his strong, tanned legs, so she lowered her gaze to his feet, bare except for a pair of worn huaraches. "Maybe you ought to tell me why you're here, Mr. McNeil." Instead of sitting, as she had done with the FBI men, she remained standing with both hands on the back of the chair.

"The name's Logan." He lifted the bottle to his lips and took another long drink. "And as I told you, I came because of Andy. I was hoping you could answer a few questions for me. It was quite a shock to arrive at his house and find him being taken away in an ambulance."

"I think the shock effect was mutual. It was also rather obvious that your being there was upsetting Andrew. Why is that, Logan?" She said his name for the first time, and found that she liked the way it sounded.

"You have to understand that Andy and I didn't exactly part on friendly terms the last time we saw each other. Have you ever met Andy's father?"

Ronni shook her head. "Andrew's not very close to him."

"No, he's not, and unfortunately I may be partly to blame for the distance between them. You see, the senator's been like a father to me, which hasn't always made it easy for Andy and me to be friends."

Ronni suspected that what he said was probably true. She knew that Andrew's estrangement from his father was due in part to his own feelings of inadequacy as a son. He had often told her that he hadn't been able to measure up to the standards of his father. If Logan McNeil was the man he had to compete with for his father's affection, it wasn't so hard to understand why. Despite the fact that he was dressed more for the beach than a boardroom, there was something commanding about him, an inner strength that would refuse to be subdued by anyone. Ronni's eyes roved over muscular legs dusted with wispy dark hairs and her heartbeat quickened. Yes, next to Logan, Andrew would definitely look wimpy.

"The reason I went to see Andy this morning was to try to patch things up between him and the senator." Logan sighed. "I only hope it's not too late."

"Too late?" Her eyebrows drew together. "Are you telling me that Andrew might not make it?"

"When I spoke to the senator, he told me the hospital had informed him that Andy had slipped into a coma. He's flying down to see him later today."

Logan saw her grab the back of the chair for support, and her face paled. She looked as though a feather could knock her down. There was a lost little girl quality about her, which elicited an enormous rush of sympathy from him. But just when he thought she was about to burst into tears, she surprised him with her composure.

"Isn't there some way I can see him? I know they said only family, but..." She shrugged helplessly.

"It's probably not a good idea. The press is bound to be sniffing around once the word gets out that it's the senator's son who's hospitalized. If you do go, you run the risk of creating a headline."

"Me?" She gave him a look of surprise.

He pulled out the newspaper that had been tucked under his arm and spread it open for her inspection. Timidly she closed the short distance between them until she stood directly in front of him. As he held the paper up for her perusal, he saw her eyes light on the picture of Peter. She took the newspaper from his hands and began to read the front page story. It only took a minute before she was rustling the pages to find the continuation of the article. Then came a gasp, and Logan knew she had spotted her own picture on page eight. He watched her read on, her face coloring with emotion at the press's interpretation of her relationship with her husband.

"Who told them all this stuff?" she asked, her blue-gray eyes flashing. "They've twisted practically everything they've written about me. They made it sound as though *I'm* a spy!" she told him with a look he could only describe as one of total bewilderment. As though she suddenly realized that perhaps Logan shared the newspaper's sentiments, she declared emotionally, "I'm *not* a spy!"

At that moment, Logan thought she could have been holding government secrets in her hands for all the world to see and he would have believed her. She made such a lovely picture standing before him, her cheeks flushed, her eyes sparkling, as she protested her innocence. He held up his hands defensively.

"I didn't say you were." He realized as he spoke the words that he really didn't believe she was.

"When people read this, they're going to think I am." She waved the newspaper in disgust. "How can I expect strangers to understand any of this when I can hardly believe this is happening?"

Just then the phone rang. When Ronni hesitated before answering it, Logan said, "Aren't you going to get that?"

"It's probably another reporter," she replied, still not making any attempt to move.

"Do you want me to take it for you?" he offered.

Ronni sighed. "No, I'll get it."

Logan followed her across the room and stood beside her while she answered the phone. He was fast coming to know that Veronica Lang had a face he could read like an open book and this phone call was upsetting her. He was about to pull the receiver from her hands, when she slammed it down onto the cradle and thrust her fist close to her mouth. Logan put both hands on her shoulders to still her trembling.

"Who was it? What's happened?" he demanded, but she didn't say anything. "Veronica, tell me what's wrong."

When she looked up at him, it was with eyes that silently begged for comfort and understanding. "It was a woman. She said I have something she wants, something that doesn't belong to me, and that as long as I give it back to her, nothing will happen to me or Steffie." Her lip quivered and she immediately pulled it in beneath her teeth.

"Did she say what it is that you're supposed to have?"

"No. I was so frightened I hung up on her. Logan, what could I possibly have that she'd want?" Her fingers were clinging to his shirt sleeves. "Whoever it was had my phone number. That means they'll probably have my address, too."

This time her voice did break and Logan found himself wanting to choke Peter Lang for putting such a lovely lady into such a predicament. It was obvious she was caught up in a web he had spun.

"It could have been a prank phone call," he told her, knowing his explanation was feeble. "Now that your name has been in the paper, you're probably going to be the target of all sorts of kooky phone calls."

"Oh, that's just terrific," she moaned, letting go of his shirt and slipping out of his grasp. "It's bad enough that the public thinks I'm some kind of spy. Now I'm going to be the target of lunatics, as well."

"Maybe you should take your daughter and get away for a few days. Go somewhere the press can't find you," he suggested.

"I've never been one to run away," she told him, stiffening.

"It's not running away," he insisted, as the phone rang again. This time when he offered to answer it, she didn't protest. He smoothly got rid of the reporter, then turned to Ronni.

"Don't you have some friends or relatives you can go stay with for a while?"

Ronni shook her head. "My mother left this morning on a cruise. There really isn't anyone else I can turn to, now that Andrew's in the hospital." She tried to appear composed, but she felt so weary, so confused and so frightened. And worst of all, she felt alone. Dejectedly she dropped down onto the chair beside her desk. "Since all of this has happened, I don't even know who I can trust."

Logan hunkered down beside her and gave her an intense look. "You can trust me."

She responded with a nervous little laugh.

"I'm serious." His gaze moved slowly over her face.

"Are you inviting Steffie and me to stay with you?"

She gave him an incredibly beautiful look of disbelief that had Logan's insides doing gymnastic maneuvers.

"It's quiet and you'd be away from the nosy reporters and crank phone calls." His offer took him by as much surprise as it did her, and he immediately regretted his impulse. What in the world had possessed him to utter such an invitation? The last thing he needed at this point in his life was to be responsible for a woman and her child.

She gave him a look that was narrowly suspicious, before relaxing and smiling weakly at him. "It's very kind of you to offer, but I don't know you and you don't know me," she said.

"I feel as though I know you. Andy's spoken about you often enough." The second statement was a lie; the first wasn't. He did feel as though he knew her, and it wasn't because Doc had handed him a dossier on her. Her blue-gray eyes were softly disarming him, and he searched them for some clue as to why they should hold such an appeal for him. There was really nothing extraordinary about her eyes, yet they seemed to captivate him.

"I'm surprised Andrew talked about me to you." She seemed to be wondering what he could possibly know about her.

"Do you mean you're surprised he talked about you, or just surprised that he talked to me at all?" There was a hint of challenge in his voice.

"Both, I guess," she replied candidly, a bit uneasy he was able to read her mind. "It seems odd that he would discuss me with you, yet he seldom mentioned your name to me."

"Well, Andy can be rather odd at times." His mouth twisted wryly.

"That's not a very nice thing to say about a friend," she chided.

"You're not going to try to tell me that Andy's always spoken fondly of me, are you?" he asked with a lift of one eyebrow.

Her reply was a gentle toss of her blond head.

Looking at Logan, Ronni could understand why two men who had been best friends as children could be adversaries as adults. If they had been alike at all as children—which she seriously doubted—they were now as different as night and day. Quiet, timid Andrew would be no match for such an aggressive, virile man as Logan.

"Andrew seldom spoke about his family or his background," she told him, and was about to explain further, when the telephone rang again.

Once more Logan took the call. When he had gotten rid of yet another reporter, he said, "You really should try to get away for a few days. They're going to continue to call until all this business with your husband is settled."

"But those men from the FBI told me I wasn't supposed to leave."

"You have a right to your privacy." He could see that she was carefully weighing her alternatives. "Look, I'm not sure whether the FBI can do anything to stop the harassing phone calls, but if you'd feel safer contacting them, I understand."

For Ronni, it was strange that she should be more inclined to trust this man than the FBI agents, but she did. Despite the eye patch that gave him a sinister look, there was integrity in his face, and intuitively she knew that she could trust him. "Are you sure we wouldn't be imposing on you? I do have a toddler."

He shrugged. "It's not a problem. I live alone." He glanced down at his watch. "How soon could you be ready to leave?"

Ronni hesitated before answering. Despite his invitation, she wasn't convinced he really believed it was a good idea. She had the strange feeling he would have been pleased with either a yes or a no. Or was she simply projecting her own feelings on him? She wanted to say yes and she wanted to say no. She decided to go with her instincts.

"I guess I could leave as soon as Steffie wakes up from her nap and she's had her lunch." She looked down at her wrinkled sundress. "I'd also like to shower and change my clothes."

"I've got a couple of things to take care of, and I want to call the hospital and check on Andy. What if I come back in say, an hour and a half?"

"That should be fine." As she walked him to the door she said, "Thank you, Logan. I'm not sure what I would have done if you hadn't come by today. It's as though I went to sleep last night and woke up this morning in somebody else's life."

One look into her delicate face convinced Logan that he had done the right thing by inviting her to his place. "It'll all work out," he promised.

There were two things on Logan's mind as he drove the short distance to the public phone in a nearby shopping mall. The first was the threatening phone call that Veronica had received. His gut reaction had been that it wasn't a prank. If he was right, she needed someone to watch over her—which accounted for his second thought.

She was a woman he *wanted* to watch over. Through the years he had met many women, but never one who aroused his interest the way Veronica did. There was something about her wide, sensual mouth that made him want to forget the reason he was with her. Whenever he was in the same room with her, he found himself wanting to believe every word she said. He knew now that his first instincts concerning her were right. She was no spy, but an innocent victim. Unfortunately she had hit the nail right on the head. She did wake up in someone else's life—Peter's life of espionage.

Doc had instructed him to find out about the baby and her involvement with Lang. He had found the answer to the latter question. Now all he needed to learn was the baby's paternity. Personally he hoped Doc was wrong. The thought that Veronica had had a child with Andy was not a possibility he wanted to consider, let alone accept. Just the notion that she could have slept with him was disturbing enough. It was only because he was certain that her relationship with Andy had been platonic that he would be able to find the answer for the senator.

Logan expected Doc to agree with his conclusion. Little did he know he would end up wishing he hadn't called the senator once more.

"I think you'd better leave the Lang woman alone," Doc advised him as soon as Logan told him what he had discovered.

"Leave her alone? I thought you wanted me to find out about the baby?"

"I do, but now that the feds are involved, it's probably better to leave it in their hands."

"I'm not so sure you're right. They've got Mahoney and Wicklund on the case, and they're more concerned about proving she's a spy than they are about protecting her and the baby."

"And you think she needs protecting?" Doc clicked his tongue disapprovingly. "Logan, you aren't telling me that you're going to be the one protecting her?"

"As a matter of fact, I am." Unbidden came the image of blue eyes appealing to him for help. "I'm going to take her down to my place for a few days."

"Logan, your job is over. Finished. You've told me you don't think she's involved in Lang's activities. That's all I expected of you after everything that's happened. If you want to find out about the baby, do so in Melbourne. I'm telling you, it's not a good idea to take her out of there—not with the feds involved."

"Doc, I know what I'm doing." He ignored the little voice in his head that wanted to argue that point.

"Ha!" The senator laughed sarcastically. "You're the last man I'd expect to be swayed by a pretty face."

"It's got nothing to do with her looks," Logan lied, as her face swam before him. "I've talked to the woman and I'm telling you she's not involved in this spy ring. She's an innocent bystander, only I have a feeling that she'll get dragged into it in a very unpleasant way if I don't help her."

"I can't believe you're talking this way. A couple of hours with the woman and you're ready to absolve her of any guilt," Doc said impatiently.

"As far as I can see, her only crime was marrying a heel like Lang."

"I wouldn't be so sure of that. Smithson's uncovered some rather interesting information concerning your *innocent* Mrs. Lang."

Logan didn't like the feeling he had in the pit of his stomach. "What information?"

"Clara Summers and her daughter, Veronica, were killed in an automobile accident twenty-five years ago. It seems that your Mrs. Lang and her mother are using dead people's identities." There was a heavy silence until Doc finally said, "Logan, are you still there?"

"I'm here," Logan said wearily. "Doc, there's got to be an explanation."

"Yeah, I'm sure there is," the senator returned dryly. "I didn't think a smart boy like you needed an old codger like me to explain it to you, however."

"I'm telling you, you're wrong about her," Logan persisted.

Doc groaned. "From that tone of voice I know there's nothing I can say that will change your mind, is there?"

"You won't tell anyone where we are, will you?"

"Of course not." The words had the intensity of a promise.

"Thanks. I'll keep in touch—I'm going to probably need your help. There's some strange stuff going on."

"I'll say," Doc said under his breath.

"How's Andy? Has there been any change?"

"None. He's still comatose. I'm catching a plane down there in a couple of hours." There was a weariness in the senator's voice. "I feel as though I've already lost him, Logan. Even if he pulls through, I'm afraid of what the feds are going to uncover."

"Don't give up hope, Doc."

"You be careful, Logan. I may have already lost Andrew to a honey trap. I don't want to lose you, too."

Logan didn't want to think about Doc's warning, but the knowledge that Veronica and her mother had assumed identities was a fact he couldn't ignore. Long after he had hung up, he couldn't help but echo Doc's sentiments. Could he be wrong about Veronica? The fear, the concern for her daughter, the pleading of her innocence—were they all orchestrated for his benefit? He didn't think so. There had to be some explanation about her identity. But no matter who she was, he knew he couldn't just walk away from her.

She was like the apple Eve handed Adam. Only now there were two worms wriggling their way into his apple—the fact that she might have had Andy's child and the knowledge that she wasn't who she pretended to be. He knew that if the apple was going to be sweet and juicy, he needed to get rid of the worms.

Instead of returning to her house feeling protective of her, he felt annoyed. Doc had planted a tiny seed of doubt. Not even the beautiful smile of relief she greeted him with would ease his mind. He forced a smile to his lips, then quickly glanced away, not wanting to notice how appealing she looked.

She had changed into another sundress, but this one was a bright pink and had part of its back missing, exposing a lovely expanse of flesh. On her feet were a pair of thongs with a large daisy in the center of each, and her hair fell softly around her face.

"How's Andrew?" she asked, genuine concern in her voice.

The mention of Andrew's name in such an endearing tone reminded him that she might have been the man's lover, and that thought annoyed him more than the idea that she could be a spy. "There's no change. He still hasn't regained consciousness," he said curtly. "Are you ready to go?"

She was about to answer, when the sound of tiny bare feet thumping on the floor announced Steffie's arrival. Logan looked down and couldn't help but smile at the wobbly toddler. Steffie gazed up at Logan and burst into tears.

Ronni lifted her up into her arms, kissing her cheek soothingly, repeating softly, "It's okay, Steffie. This is Logan. He's a nice man."

But Steffie wanted nothing to do with him. She turned her face away from his inquisitive gaze and buried it in her mother's shoulder. When Logan attempted to take her hand in his, saying, "Hi, Steffie," she pulled her hand away and cried all the louder.

"She's recently become frightened of unfamiliar faces," Ronni said in an apologetic tone.

Logan simply shrugged. "Where are your things?" he asked brusquely.

"Everything's right there," she replied, nodding toward the hallway.

Logan took one look at the pile of things and rolled his eyes. "You're not bringing all that!" Besides the two suitcases, there was a playpen, a jumbo box of disposable diapers, the diaper bag, the car seat and a large catchall that was filled with toys.

"I do have a fifteen-month-old child," she reminded him with a thrust of her chin, wondering what had happened to the friendly man who had issued the invitation to his home.

"I'll have to make several trips," Logan said, picking up the suitcases.

Ronni went to check that the back door was locked. Passing through the kitchen, she noticed that the package containing Steffie's sterling silver medic alert bracelet still sat on the table. "We'd better take this along," she told her daughter, then slipped the package into the diaper bag.

"I'm not sure this is going to fit," Logan said a moment later, hoisting the folded-up playpen under his arm. "Does this have to go?"

"Unless you have a crib at your place. That's where Steffie sleeps."

"And that?" He pointed to the car seat.

"That's her safety seat. You'll need to attach it to the seat belts in your car."

"Pickup," he corrected her. "Let me get this monstrosity out first." He staggered through the doorway with the playpen under his arm and Steffie eyeing him suspiciously.

Ronni slung the diaper bag and her catchall over her free shoulder, so that when Logan returned for the final load, all that was left was the jumbo box of diapers. Scooping the box under his arm, he motioned for her to precede him out the door.

"Is that it?" he asked, as she managed to get the door closed behind them.

"That's it." When Logan relieved her of the diaper bag and carryall, she shifted Steffie to her other arm and inserted the key into the dead bolt.

"How far is it to your place?" she asked, walking toward the pickup.

"We should be there by dark."

"Dark?" She stopped beside the pickup and looked at him with questioning eyes. "Just how far is it?"

Logan had opened the door and was fiddling with the buckles on the car seat. "You can put her in. I think I've got all the straps in the right places." He gestured for her to place Steffie inside.

"Where *do* you live, Logan?" she asked, settling Steffie in her seat.

"Didn't I tell you?" He waited until she had climbed in beside Steffie, then he slammed her door shut and walked around the front of the truck to the driver's side. As soon as he was seated behind the wheel, he put the key in the ignition and said, "Key West."

CHAPTER FIVE

"KEY WEST? That's over three hundred miles from here," Ronni exclaimed.

"Yeah—Florida's a big state, isn't it?"

"You're taking us all the way down to Key West?" she asked.

"You said you wanted to go where you wouldn't be disturbed. I can guarantee you won't be disturbed in Key West." Noticing that her hand had moved to the door handle, Logan started the truck and pulled away from the curb before she could have any second thoughts about going with him. "Don't you like the Keys?"

"It's not that. It's just that I had assumed you lived in the Melbourne area."

"I'm only here because of Andy." He took the corner a bit faster than he should have, but only because he had spotted a suspicious-looking gray sedan in his rearview mirror. They were being followed.

Steffie had been fussing ever since he had climbed in beside her, and if it wasn't for the fact that his eyes were darting back and forth between the rearview mirror and the road, he would have made an attempt to pacify the child. Right now, however, he needed to concentrate on losing the tail.

"You missed the entrance to the freeway," Ronni commented when he cut in front of a bus in order to make it through a yellow light at the intersection.

"I'm not going to get us lost," he snapped, taking a quick left that had the tires squealing and Ronni complaining.

"Do you think you could slow down? Please keep in mind that you have a child riding with you."

"It's kind of hard to forget," he returned dryly. "She's been crying ever since I got into the truck."

"I think it must be a stage she's going through." Ronni had to raise her voice to be heard over Steffie's whining. "Normally she loves riding in the car. It usually puts her to sleep."

Logan shot a dubious look in her direction. By the time they finally reached the interstate, he had lost the gray sedan, but Steffie's whimpering had become a wail. When Logan reached up to adjust the rearview mirror, Ronni turned around to peer out the back window.

"Is there someone following us?" she asked. "Is that why you've been driving like a road warrior?"

"I think 'road warrior' is a little extreme," he said. "And no, there isn't anyone following us—at least not anymore."

"You mean there was?" She waited for him to elaborate, but he didn't. "Was it the FBI?"

"Probably." By now Steffie's crying was no longer easy to ignore. "Do you think she'd quit that bawling if I were to turn the radio on?"

"I doubt it," Ronni replied, bending over to dig into the diaper bag.

Logan looked at Steffie and wiggled his eyebrows. He gave her a smile, saying, "Coochie coochie coo," which only caused the little girl to cry harder. "My God, she's having a temper tantrum."

"Steffie doesn't have temper tantrums," Ronni insisted. She pulled a stuffed animal out of the diaper bag. "Here. Lookey, Steffie. Here's your favorite Pooh bear." She jiggled the mustard-colored stuffed animal in front of her daughter, who was twisting and stretching in an attempt to get closer to her mother and farther away from Logan.

"I don't think she's going to shut up as long as she's sitting next to me," Logan remarked. "Maybe you ought to take her on your lap."

"I can't. It's not safe."

"Well, maybe we ought to forgo safety for the sake of sanity," he retorted.

Again Ronni reached into the diaper bag, and this time withdrew a pacifier. "Lookey, Steffie—here's your plug," she said, trying to force the rubber nipple between screaming lips. Steffie grabbed the pacifier with her little fist and threw it up in the air. It ricocheted off the ceiling and landed with a thunk somewhere near the gas pedal.

"That's not a temper tantrum?" Logan asked sarcastically before reaching down to retrieve the pacifier. "What about giving her a piece of candy? I've got some Lifesavers in the glove compartment."

"Soothing a child with sugar is not healthy," Ronni returned primly.

"Having a child screaming for six hours in a car is not healthy, either," Logan countered, nearly out of patience.

"Maybe you should pull off the highway at the next exit and I'll take her out of her seat until she calms down," Ronni suggested.

Without another word, Logan shot off the next exit and brought the pickup to a screeching halt on the side of the road. He climbed out, slammed the door, then stomped around to Ronni's side and pulled her door open in a dramatic gesture of chivalry. Ronni unfastened Steffie's seat belt, then climbed out of the car, murmuring soothing words to Steffie, who was clinging to her neck for dear life.

"What are you doing?" Ronni asked when Logan started to unstrap the car seat.

"Moving this contraption next to the door. She's not going to ride peacefully as long as she's sitting beside me. You'll have to sit in the middle," he told her.

As much as Ronni hated to admit it, he was probably right. When Steffie was finally quiet and Logan had finished strapping the seat onto the passenger side, he looked at Ronni and said, "Got any ideas on how you're going to get her back in?"

"No problem," she replied with a look that bordered on hostility. "See, Steffie. You get to ride next to the window," she told the toddler as she attempted to slide her back into the car seat. Steffie's response was to tighten her arms around Ronni's neck and squawk.

"She's bucking again," Logan said smugly.

Sighing, Ronni backed away from the truck with Steffie in her arms.

Logan glanced around the area where they were parked. "You wait here," he said, then started off toward a roadside café about fifty yards away. With his departure came silence from Steffie, and Ronni wondered how on earth they were going to make it all the way to Key West when Steffie was so obviously frightened of Logan.

It wasn't long before he returned, carrying three large paper cups, three plastic spoons and a bundle of napkins.

"How about some ice cream, Steffie," he said softly, handing Ronni two of the paper cups, two long-handled plastic spoons and the pile of napkins. "A milk shake isn't unhealthy, is it?"

"No, she loves ice cream," Ronni replied graciously. "Thank you." As soon as Steffie realized she was going to get the milk shake if she was strapped in, she willingly went into the car seat.

When all three of them were back in the pickup, Logan started up the engine and drove back onto the highway. Ronni was grateful her daughter had stopped fussing, although she wasn't so sure she was going to be any more comfortable sitting next to Logan than Steffie had been.

The cumbersome car seat forced her to sit closer to him than she would have chosen. His shoulder was touching hers, his half-naked thigh pressed against her cotton-covered legs. She could smell his after-shave—at least, she figured it had to be after-shave, for he didn't look like a man who wore men's cologne. She tried to disregard the tiny dark hairs that covered his forearms and legs, the large fingers that were wrapped around the steering wheel, and especially the dark patch over his eye, a patch that gave him a mysterious look.

While Logan drank his milk shake through a straw, she fed Steffie with a red plastic spoon. Now the only sounds in the pickup were the air conditioner fan, Logan occasionally slurping through his straw and Steffie humming as she savored each spoonful of ice cream. Before the cup was even half-empty, Steffie's head began to droop to one side, and she soon fell asleep.

Before long the silence became uncomfortable, as Ronni sat with Steffie's half-consumed milk shake as well as her own full cup. Several times she glanced in Logan's direction, hoping he'd initiate some sort of small talk, but he didn't. It was only when she finally spoke that he turned his head to look at her.

"Would you like some more?" she asked, as he stuffed his empty cup in the litter bag hanging from the radio knob. "Steffie didn't finish hers and I haven't even touched mine."

"If I'd known ice cream would put her to sleep we could have stopped sooner," he commented, his voice low.

"As I said, she usually falls asleep in the car, but she was crying so hard she couldn't relax. It's been a stressful day for both of us," she explained.

"I think she's a little scared of me, Veronica."

"I wish you'd call me 'Ronni.' All my friends do. In fact, my mother's the only one who calls me 'Veronica.'"

He shrugged. "Then 'Ronni' it is."

"I really don't think Steffie's afraid of you because you're you." She chuckled nervously. "What I'm trying to say is she seems to have developed an aversion to men in general. Just last week when we were in the grocery store she burst into tears when this kindly old gentleman said hello to her."

Ever since they had been in the truck, Logan had been wondering if she was aware that in order for him to see her he needed to turn his head. He wanted to give her the opportunity to ask about his eye patch if she was curious about it. "Well, I can't really blame her for being scared. My patch does have a piratical touch."

"What happened to your eye, Logan?" she asked gently. "Was it an accident?"

As much as he hated talking about his injury, Logan felt a bit relieved that she had come right out and asked him about it. The injury was too recent for him not to feel self-conscious, yet he appreciated her directness. His response was just as straightforward.

"Yes, it was an accident," he said soberly. "There was an explosion. I could have been badly burned, but I was fortunate in that regard. Debris went flying in all directions and several small particles became embedded in my right eye. I didn't lose my eye, only my vision."

"Then you can't see out of it at all?" Again there was a gentleness in her voice, which made it easy for him to talk to her about a subject he usually avoided.

"Not at the moment, but the doctors tell me that could change. Only time will tell for sure."

"Does it bother you?"

"If you mean does it hurt, the answer is no. If you're asking if it bothers me to be without the sight in my eye, the answer is yes. I bump into things because I'm not used to being blind on my right side and I've had a hell of a time adjusting to having no depth perception. It's one of those things you take for granted until you try to catch a baseball or you go to park your car and discover you're three feet from the curb."

Ronni closed one eye and found herself surprised at how her vision became altered. For one thing, she was acutely aware of the outline of her nose.

"Is it a strain for you to be driving such a long distance?" she asked.

"Not as long as there isn't a child crying all the time," he said, the charm of his smile taking the sting out of his words. He wished it would have been possible for her to be sitting on his left side so he wouldn't have to turn to see her. He wanted to be able to look at her without it being so damn obvious.

"I'm sorry. I was simply going to offer to drive part of the way."

"It's not necessary," he told her smoothly, then adjusted the rearview mirror, positioning it so that he could glance into it and see her face, rather than the traffic behind him. That way he wouldn't have to keep turning his head to get a glimpse of her. He would also be able to read her expressive face when he questioned her about Andy, a subject he was eager to discuss.

"Have you known Andy long?" he asked casually.

"About five years. Why?"

He shrugged. "I was just curious about how the two of you became such good friends."

Ronni heard the emphasis on the word "friends" and felt a bit defensive. "Actually he was a friend of my husband's. Peter and Andrew worked together at Bartron. I only met him because I took a computer class."

When Logan didn't respond, Ronni felt the need to explain. "You see, Bartron offers an evening program of computer classes for employees and their spouses. When I took the introductory course, Andrew was my instructor. He's a whiz with computers."

"Yes, I know."

"When it came time to take the second course in the series, I had a scheduling conflict, so Andrew offered to teach me at home. Since he was living alone, I cooked him dinner in exchange for his helping me with my computer instruction."

"I see."

"And that's how we became good friends." This time it was she who emphasized the word "friends."

"And your husband didn't object?"

"There was nothing to object to," she lied, knowing full well that Peter had more than objected to her friendship with Andrew; he had accused her of having an affair with him. Yet she wasn't ready to reveal anything so personal to Logan.

Logan was watching her in the rearview mirror and knew by the expression on her face that she was lying. Either Peter Lang was as jealous as hell of her friendship with Andy, the computer whiz, or her relationship with Andy was more than a friendship. Logan preferred to believe it was the former. No man in his right mind would welcome a woman who looked like Ronni having a friendship with another man—even one as meek as Andy.

"Andy told me he's Steffie's godfather," he said, watching her closely in the mirror.

"Yes." She wanted to say that Andrew had been more of a father to Steffie than Peter had ever been, but there was something in Logan's tone that disturbed her. "He's very good with children. I often tell him he would have made a wonderful schoolteacher."

"Is that the voice of experience talking?"

"You do know I'm a teacher, don't you?"

"Yes. I saw that paperweight on your desk—the one that said 'A teacher's three favorite words are June, July and August.'"

"That was a gift from one of my students." She smiled in recollection. "Even though I love teaching, it's nice to have the summer off, especially now that I have Steffie."

"You don't teach summer school then?"

"No. I never have. Before Steffie was born, I always spent my summers as a volunteer at a summer camp for mentally handicapped children," she answered quietly.

That was something that hadn't been in the senator's file on her, and made him realize how little information the file had actually contained. "It sounds like an admirable way to spend a summer."

She appreciated his praise. "Unfortunately Peter didn't share your sentiment. He couldn't understand why I would volunteer to teach kids when I could get paid for it."

"That type of work probably has rewards greater than any of those with monetary value," Logan remarked.

"Oh, it did," she assured him, her eyes sparkling as she talked about a subject dear to her heart. "I can't tell you how exciting it is to see a child who has been struggling for weeks with something so simple as printing a letter of the alphabet finally succeed. It's true I gave a lot of time to those children, but what they gave me in return was something I wouldn't haven't given up for anyone—not even Peter."

He didn't miss the determined angle of her chin or the decisiveness flashing in her eyes. "Did you have to make sacrifices for him?" he asked.

Ronni nearly answered candidly, but she stopped herself, a bit embarrassed at how easy it would be to reveal her private life to a near stranger. "I'd really rather not talk about Peter, if you don't mind."

Logan shrugged. "It's all right with me. He's probably not worth talking about."

Again there was an uncomfortable silence, until Ronni finally said, "You're right. He's not worth talking about, and just the mention of his name makes me angry. I should have divorced him two years ago."

"Then what the paper said was true? You are still legally married?"

"I was a signature away from being free of him," she confirmed.

"It's too bad you weren't free of him before he defected. It might have saved you a lot of grief."

"You don't think the press would be hounding me if I were his ex-wife?"

"You probably wouldn't be under suspicion the way you are now."

"I'm not a spy, and I don't understand why you offered to help us if you think I am." She looked up and met his gaze in the mirror.

He was the first one to turn away. "I haven't said you are."

"Well, I'm not," she insisted, suddenly feeling too tired to be arguing with him. She'd had little sleep the night before and the motion of the vehicle was causing her eyelids to droop. Suppressing a yawn, she looked first right, then left, wishing for something soft to lean against. Sitting in the middle, she had either Steffie's car seat or Logan's shoulder to turn to. She placed her arm along the back of the car seat, turning her chin into her shoulder. Within a few minutes, she was asleep.

Logan wondered why she had stopped trying to convince him of her innocence. He glanced in the rearview mirror and once again saw traffic. When he turned his head and saw Ronni's neck bent awkwardly over the car seat, he wanted to reach out and pull her into his arms, cradling her so that her creamy smooth cheek would be cushioned against his shoulder rather than the plastic molding on the car seat. But the picture the two of them made was one he was loath to disturb.

Again he found himself questioning his judgment in offering to help her out. He could feel himself being drawn into their predicament, and if he wasn't careful, he could easily lose his objectivity. So far, he hadn't learned who she really was or whether Steffie was Andy's daughter. What he had discovered was that she was as genuine a woman as he had ever met. Despite what Doc had told him about her identity, he found himself attracted to her and wanting to know everything about her—and not for Doc's sake. From what he could see, she had become entangled in a web of intrigue and he was going to do everything in his power to get her untangled.

He thought about that web of intrigue as the truck ate up the miles and miles of coastal highway on the way to Key West. The beauty of the palm-lined beaches and the sparkling waters of the Atlantic Ocean were lost on him, for his mind was preoccupied with trying to connect the information Doc had given him with the woman sleeping beside him.

After several hours of silence, Logan began to wonder just how exhausted mother and daughter could be. Not even the noisy congestion of rush-hour traffic on the Miami interstate had aroused either one of them.

It was Steffie who woke first, uttering a few words of gibberish. Logan turned to look at her, giving her a quick grin. "Hi, Steffie." He waited for the tears, but there were none.

Craning her little neck in his direction, she simply said, "Ba."

Ronni shot upright, straightening the bodice of her sundress as she did. She greeted Steffie with a lip-smacking kiss that Logan could hear but didn't see. It had, however, the power to arouse all sorts of images in his mind.

"Where are we?" she asked, looking out and seeing water everywhere as the truck ventured across a long bridge toward a cluster of cottages and wharves reminding her of a New England fishing village.

"We're in the Middle Keys."

"Already?"

"It's after six," Logan told her.

Ronni checked her watch. "I can't believe we slept that long. Do you think we could find a rest stop? Steffie needs to have her diaper changed and she's probably hungry."

"I should stop for gas, anyway. We're not far from Grassy Key, which is where a friend of mine owns a small resort. Actually it's more of a fishing club, but I know the restaurant serves kids' portions."

Cooter's Fishing Club was located just off the main highway and was comprised of waterfront cottages, a saltwater lagoon and an informal restaurant that overlooked the marina. As it turned out, Cooter, Logan's friend, was out deep-sea fishing, but the restaurant staff treated Logan with an easy familiarity.

While Ronni took Steffie to the rest room to freshen up, Logan managed to get a table on the patio and arranged to have a high chair brought outdoors. He was sipping on a beer by the time she and Steffie had finished washing up and joined him.

"Care for anything to drink?" he asked, getting up to help her settle Steffie in the high chair.

"Iced tea, please," she told him, as he signaled for the waitress. "And milk for Steffie." She sat down across from Logan and opened the soda crackers that had been sealed in plastic wrap on the high chair tray.

"It's lovely here, Logan," she said, looking out across the lagoon to where a flock of egrets stood in stark white contrast to the blue-green water, patiently waiting for their prey.

"You should see it at sunset. The water changes colors so many times it's impossible to describe or even photograph. It has to be experienced." He handed her a menu. "The specialty is fresh shrimp steamed in beer. There should be a children's menu slipped inside there, too."

Ronni found the extra sheet of paper indicating what choices were available in children's portions and gave her order to the waitress as soon as she brought their beverages. "With Steffie one learns to be fast," she told Logan, with a faint smile.

Once their food arrived, it didn't take long for him to see what Ronni was referring to. She spent more time attending to the toddler's food than she did her own. Steffie smeared applesauce all over the high chair tray, as well as herself, tossed several mushy French fries in the direction of the diners across the aisle and splattered her milk on everything within a three-foot radius. When it was obvious that Steffie was no longer going to sit quietly in her chair, Ronni warned Logan that they should probably leave.

"But you haven't finished. Maybe you should get her some ice cream," Logan suggested, and before she could reply, he had signaled the waitress and was ordering a dish of vanilla ice cream.

Steffie's fidgeting ceased the minute the tulip-shaped dish of ice cream was set on the table. When Ronni reached for the spoon, Logan said, "Do you think she'd let me feed it to her? That way you could finish your meal."

Ronni hesitated, looking apprehensively from Logan to Steffie, whose little fingers were reaching impatiently for the glass serving dish.

"I think she's probably used to the patch by now," Logan told Ronni in an aside.

She's not the only one, Ronni thought, noticing for the first time how really handsome Logan was. With or without the patch he would be devilishly attractive. He didn't, however, look the type to be spooning ice cream into a toddler.

"If we weren't in a public place she could try to feed herself," Ronni said, then reluctantly passed him the spoon. She watched as he slid his chair closer to Steffie's, then thrust the spoon into the small mound of ice cream.

"I'm afraid I haven't had much experience with this kind of thing," he said, looking a bit uneasy as he gingerly held the spoonful of ice cream out in front of Steffie, who quickly opened her mouth and accepted it with an appreciative hum.

"You don't have any children of your own?" Ronni asked, surprised at how easily Steffie had become accustomed to Logan's presence.

"No. I've never been married," he replied.

"Why not?" The words seemed to pop out before she could think about them. "I'm sorry. That's a rather personal question."

He shrugged. "It's all right. I haven't married because I guess what they say about some careers and marriage not mixing is true."

"What do you do, Logan?" she asked, suddenly feeling as though she'd done all the talking during their ride in the car. "Andrew never mentioned what your career was, only that you were the best at everything you ever did."

He gave a sardonic chuckle. "Hardly the best. If I were, I wouldn't have this," he said, gesturing at the patch. "At the moment I don't have a career. I guess you might say I'm in one of those mid-life crises. Of course, I have an excuse, since I was injured on the job and I'm down here to recuperate." He was toying with the neck of the empty beer bottle. "Since I'm not very good at doing nothing, I've been dividing my time between helping a friend get his boat seaworthy and exploring the reef."

"Snorkeling or scuba diving?"

"A little of both, but I prefer snorkeling."

"Me, too, although I haven't been able to go very often since Steffie's birth."

As if Steffie could tell her mother was talking about her, she began to squirm and wiggle her way out of the high chair.

"I think it's time to leave," Ronni said, dropping her napkin on the table. "I'd better wash her up in the rest room."

"I'll take care of this," Logan said, picking up the check, "and meet you back at the truck."

In the ladies' room, Ronni set Steffie on the vanity top, then found the square piece of terry cloth she carried in a plastic bag for emergency cleanups. "Let's get all that sticky applesauce off that pretty little face," she said aloud, moistening the cloth and dragging it across Steffie's rosy cheeks. "Let me see those hands, too," she coaxed, swabbing in between each of the little fingers.

Lifting the Medic-Alert bracelet, she dabbed at the irritated skin underneath. "Mama's going to have to put some cream on that before you go to bed tonight," she told Steffie, them remembered she had stuck the sterling silver Medic-Alert bracelet in the diaper bag.

Ronni groped for the package. "Aha. Here it is," she said, quickly tearing open the brown wrapping paper. "Lookey, Steffie." She dangled the new bracelet in front of her daughter's wide-eyed face. "A new bracelet!"

Carefully she unclasped the old chain, then fastened the new one in place. "Now you won't get any more itchy rash." Steffie briefly fingered the silver links. "Isn't that pretty?" Ronni asked, holding the little wrist up in the mirror for inspection.

She almost tossed the old bracelet in the waste receptacle, but changed her mind and dropped it into the side pouch of the diaper bag. "We'd better not throw that one away, Stef. You never know when we might need it."

Steffie responded with her usual "Ba," then reached for her mother's outstretched arms, and together they went to find Logan.

CHAPTER SIX

THE EVENING AIR was balmy and Ronni could hear the faint sounds of calypso coming from somewhere farther down the beach as she stepped out of the pickup and onto the gravel drive beside Logan's house. Like many of the homes in Key West, it was painted white, with flamingo pink shutters. Although a bit awed by its location, she was disappointed by its size. The house had a veranda extending around three of its sides, but they were tiny sides. As Logan led her through the gate in the wrought iron fence and past a towering poinciana that appeared to be larger than the house itself, her first thought was that there wasn't going to be enough room for the three of them.

Once inside, her suspicions were confirmed. There were only four rooms—a kitchen, bathroom, living room and bedroom. Logan deposited her things in the latter.

"You don't have to give us your room," Ronni told him, eyeing the sparsely furnished bedroom. "I could sleep on the sofa and Steffie has her playpen."

"It might be easier for her to get to sleep if you can shut the door," he reasoned.

Ronni shrugged, then looked around the room, trying to visualize where she could put the playpen. "We'll probably have to push the bed up against the wall to fit the playpen in here."

Logan gave first one end of the bed a shove, then the other. "I'll get some clean sheets for you as soon as I've brought in the rest of the stuff."

"Let me help," she offered, but he dismissed her with a wave of his hand and disappeared out the door.

Ronni did a quick visual inventory of the room, which seemed to lack any personal touches that would identify it as Logan's habitat, and she wondered how long he had been living here. It could have been a hotel room; there were no traces of his occupancy other than the pair of running shoes next to the dresser.

Logan returned lugging the cumbersome playpen under one arm and the box of diapers in the other. "I think one more trip ought to do it," he told her, unfolding the mesh playpen, then wiping the dampness from his forehead with the back of his hand.

Ronni acknowledged his efforts with a nod. There was something about seeing Steffie's playpen in this hotellike room that brought the stark reality of her situation into focus. Despite the fact that Logan was practically a member of Andrew's family, he was virtually a stranger to her, yet here she was, sleeping in his bed, sharing his home. Unconsciously she tightened her arms around Steffie, who grunted in protest. Ronni kissed her cheek, then set her on the bed so that she could rummage through the suitcase for her nightgown. When Logan returned with the rest of their things, she was wrapping a sheet covered with rainbows around the playpen pad.

"If it feels a little warm in here it's only because the landlord didn't get the air-conditioning working until late this afternoon." He pulled the chain on the ceiling fan and the blades whirled faster. "It should gradually cool down."

"I think I'll let Steffie sleep in her diaper," Ronni said as she continued to make the playpen into a bed, tossing Steffie's Pooh bear and a lightweight blanket onto the pad.

Logan stood in the doorway watching her, admiring her gracefulness, her beauty. "Do you want to feed her anything before she goes to bed? I think there might be some ice cream in the freezer."

Straightening, Ronni smiled at him. "I think she's had enough ice cream for today. She usually has a bottle of milk before she goes to sleep."

"I'm afraid I don't have any milk, but it'll only take me a couple of minutes to run to the convenience store. There's one right around the corner. What about in the morning? What will you need?"

"Maybe some juice? I brought her cereal and fruit along." Steffie was clinging to her mother's leg in an appeal to be picked up. "I'll give her a bath while you're gone," Ronni said, scooping the child up into her arms.

"Make yourself at home, and I'll be right back."

Ronni waved a weak hand in his direction, then turned her attention back to Steffie, who had crawled across the bed to the nightstand and had discovered a paperback novel. Before she could mangle any of the pages, Ronni gently eased the book from her grasp, noting that the author was one of her favorites, too. When Steffie made a grab for the cord of the clock radio, Ronni scooped her into her arms and went to look around the rest of the house.

"Lookey, Steffie." She paused next to a life-size statue of an old sea captain that appeared to be standing guard at the entrance to the living room. "Now where do you suppose this came from?" she mused aloud, giving the wooden statue a thorough appraisal. "I guess it does sort of fit the decor," she added, noting the eclectic assortment of furniture in the room. One look at the rattan couch had her doubting that Logan would be able to use it for a bed.

Near-empty bookshelves lined the walls, and Ronni wondered if the house had been some writer's retreat. There was a calendar featuring the artwork of Georgia O'Keeffe, but it was last year's calendar. A cassette player sat on one of the shelves, and when Ronni pressed Play the sound of Al Jarreau filled the room. "He can't be all bad if he likes Al Jarreau," Ronni whispered to Steffie, punching the Stop button.

Although sparsely furnished, the house was neat and clean, with pine floors throughout except for a sea-green linoleum in the bathroom and the kitchen. Like the rest of the house, the bathroom was small, with enough room for a shower stall only—no tub. The compact vanity top was cluttered with shaving things, shampoo and a can of men's hair spray. There were no feminine traces anywhere, which made her suspect that what Logan had said was true. He did live alone. She opened a louvered closet door and found a stack of linens, all neatly pressed and folded. "He probably has a cleaning lady," she told Steffie, whose wide eyes looked around the place with the same curious gaze as Ronni's.

Stepping into the kitchen, Ronni saw a drop-leaf table and apartment-size appliances. She opened the refrigerator door and made a face. Two shelves of imported beer, a roll of salami and a partially disintegrated head of lettuce greeted her. The usual condiments lined the shelves of the door, but there was no butter in the butter keeper. "At least there aren't any creepy things growing inside,'' she said to Steffie, then closed the door.

A peek into the freezer compartment revealed one lonely frozen dinner entrée. Investigating the cupboards, she found sparse contents, as well, and Ronni knew she would have to go to the grocery store in the morning if they were going to stay for any length of time.

Since there was no tub, she was giving Steffie a bath in the kitchen sink when Logan reappeared with a bag of groceries. His first thought was that the two could have been a Norman Rockwell picture. Steffie's little feet and hands were busy splashing playfully while Ronni attempted to wash her slippery body. Logan reflected he had never seen a more heartwarming scene. ''Don't you ever take her bracelet off?'' he asked, noticing Steffie was still wearing the silver chain around her wrist.

''It's a Medic-Alert bracelet,'' Ronni explained, lifting Steffie out of the sink and onto the towel draped across the countertop. ''She needs to wear it at all times so that if she's ever in an accident the medical personnel will know that she's allergic to penicillin.''

''What would happen if she did accidentally receive penicillin?'' he asked.

''She'd probably only get a severe case of hives, which is what happened when we first discovered the allergy. When she was six months old she had an ear infection that the doctor treated with a form of penicillin. But there's always the possibility of more serious complications, which is why I have her wear the Medic-Alert bracelet.'' Ronni wrapped the towel around Steffie and lifted her into her arms. ''I'm going to get her ready for bed. Would you mind filling that bottle with milk?'' She nodded toward the table, where Logan saw a plastic bottle with a Minnie Mouse figure painted on its side.

''Skim? Whole? Two percent?'' He raised his eyebrows inquisitively.

''Whatever you bought is fine.''

''I got one of each,'' he said with a crooked grin, producing three cartons of milk from the brown sack and setting them on the table. ''I wasn't sure which one was best.''

Ronni couldn't hide her smile. ''Whole for tonight.''

Logan filled the bottle, screwed on the nipple, then handed it to Ronni, who bestowed the most beautiful smile of thanks he thought possible. While he put away the groceries, he could hear her reading Steffie a bedtime story, and at one point, he couldn't resist peeking around the corner to get a glimpse of the two of them. They were lying side by side on the bed, Steffie with the Minnie Mouse bottle clasped in her hands, Ronni holding the book of nursery rhymes. Listening to the gentleness in her voice, he knew it was impossible that she could be involved in Peter Lang's activities.

Ever since Doc had told him of her false identity, he had been reviewing everything that had happened in the past twenty-four hours, thinking he must have missed a clue somewhere. His intuition told him she was innocent, yet he'd been an agent for too many years to totally disregard the fact that two and two weren't adding up to four.

He didn't want to admit it, but the truth was he was letting his feelings cloud his judgment. He'd always prided himself on his ability not to get emotionally involved in any case. But, then, he'd never felt so overwhelmingly protective of anyone. Only it wasn't just protectiveness Ronni aroused, he was thinking when she returned to the kitchen, where he was sitting at the drop-leaf table, drinking a beer.

Seeing that Logan had opened a bottle for her, Ronni sat down across from him. "This tastes good," she told him, after taking a sip of the cold liquid. "Thanks." She trailed her fingers down the side of the moisture-laden bottle.

"You look tired." He didn't want to be concerned about her, but he couldn't help it. She did look tired.

"I didn't sleep very well last night."

"I don't suppose you did." He hadn't intended the words to sound quite so sarcastic, but from the slithering expression she gave him, he knew she thought he had.

"The reason I didn't sleep well last night was that Steffie was in the hospital," she stated quietly, her chin lifting just a fraction as she spoke.

"The hospital?" he repeated.

"Yes. She accidentally swallowed some cough syrup, so we both spent the night there. For your information, Logan, I didn't know about Peter's defection until this morning."

"The newspaper article implied—"

"The newspaper was wrong," she cut in. "I heard about Peter's defection the same way millions of other people did—on the morning news—only I was at the hospital waiting for

Steffie to be released. Now it seems her accident was a blessing in disguise."

"Why do you say that?"

"We were supposed to fly to Vienna yesterday and meet Peter. He agreed to the terms of the divorce, but he wanted to see Steffie one more time before it became final. Now I think he was planning to steal her from me and take her with him when he defected." When her bottom lip began to quiver, she stilled it with her teeth.

Logan studied her intently, wanting to believe her. The woman was gentle and compassionate. He could see it in her face; he could feel it in his bones. There was no way she could ever be cunning and ruthless.

After taking another swallow of beer, he asked, "Ronni, do you know what a honey trap is?"

She looked at him with eyes as innocent as Steffie's. "No. Should I?"

"Not unless you're pretending to be somebody you're not." He wanted her to be the one to tell him who she really was. But if he was expecting an admission of anything, he couldn't have been more wrong.

She was up and out of the room in a flash. Just as quickly she returned, clenching her shoulder bag. "This isn't the first time you've insinuated I'm not Ronni Lang!" She reached into her purse and pulled out her wallet, whipping out several credit cards before extracting her driver's license. "Look. That's me! Veronica Summers Lang." She slid her license across the table. "Five-foot-five, one hundred ten pounds, twenty-eight years old."

Logan stared at the photo and saw a beautiful, innocent face—as innocent as the eyes that were pleading with him across the table.

"I don't understand any of this." Her expression was troubled. "Why did you bring me here if you're suspicious of me?"

"Because I..." He nearly said *because I saw a woman I was attracted to*, but he stopped himself. "Because I knew you were a friend of Andy's and I didn't believe you could be involved in anything as nasty as the newspaper implied."

"I'm not!" she denied. "If I'm guilty of anything, it's marrying a man for all the wrong reasons."

"You weren't in love with Peter?" He knew he wasn't asking the question from a professional perspective.

"I thought I was at the time, but it didn't take long for me to see that the things I thought I loved in him were things I'd hoped to find in a father." She slowly put her credit cards and driver's license back in her wallet, then sat down again and faced him across the table.

"At nineteen I was looking for a man to tell me what to do, to take care of me," she reflected. "I guess as time went on, I realized I didn't need a father, I needed a husband. Peter wanted to be in complete control of my life. If he'd had his way, I would have been staying home with babies right from day one of our marriage. I wanted to finish my education and teach a few years before we started a family."

"He disapproved of you working?"

"'Disapproved' isn't a strong enough word." She frowned, then shook her head slightly at unwanted memories. "He always blamed our troubles on the fact that I wanted a career, when the truth was he's a very manipulative person. It's funny I didn't see that when we first started dating."

"Maybe because at nineteen you didn't want to see it," Logan suggested.

"I wouldn't be honest if I said I didn't enjoy having a man in my life who wanted to take care of me," she admitted. "Not having a father, I never had someone to do that for me."

"Is your father dead, Ronni?"

"Umm-hmm. He was killed in a car accident when I was a child. I don't even remember him." She sighed and lowered her eyes. "I know that doesn't excuse my marrying a man much older than me. I really tried to make the marriage work, Logan."

There was a weariness in her voice, Logan thought, as though the struggle hadn't been worth the effort.

"We were separated for more than two years before I finally contacted an attorney," she finished.

"It sounds as though you gave it a fair chance," he commented, not wanting to be drawn to her, but unable to stop himself.

"I didn't want to make any hasty decisions, especially not where Steffie was concerned. I grew up without a father and I know what that's like. I wanted her to at least have the opportunity to know hers, to choose to see him if she wanted." Her mouth curled cynically. "Now look what he's done to us. He's got kooks and weirdos calling our house... the government's questioning my integrity…" Her voice cracked until it was barely a whisper. "Our lives could even be in danger." Then she lost what little control she still possessed and began to cry.

Logan was normally not a man to succumb to a woman's tears. But when it came to Ronni, he found he wasn't behaving normally. He rose from his chair and pulled her into his arms, smoothing a hand over her blond head as he murmured, "It's all right. We've gotten rid of the kooks and the weirdos…and the government agents will soon get to the truth."

"If he's done anything to put my baby in danger…" she said, sobbing.

"I'm not going to let anything happen to you or Steffie. Look at me, Ronni." He held her at arm's length and raised her chin with his forefinger. "You're safe with me." He wiped away the tears under her eyes with his thumbs. Ronni's gaze held his, then much to his surprise, she kissed him.

It was a kiss salty with tears, a kiss Logan would have liked to last longer than the time it took to say thank you. But as her lips moved lightly over his, he realized that that was exactly what she was doing—expressing her gratitude. She ended the kiss just as his libido kicked in.

"You do believe me, don't you?" She gazed up at him with pleading eyes.

This time his answer was a kiss, not sweet and gentle as hers had been, but demanding and intimate, surprising both of them with its intensity. A powerful surge of desire spread through him as her lips softened and opened beneath his. While her hands found his nape, his were moving up her back, drawing her closer, until he could feel her body burning hot with a pleasure he wanted to share.

Somewhere in his brain a tiny warning sounded, but he couldn't bring himself to let her go, not when she was matching each rhythmic stroke of his tongue with an incredible caress of her own. When he felt her nipples tighten against his chest, every muscle in his body seemed to harden. But the tiny warning kept growing stronger, burrowing its way into the desire that was sending tremors through his body. Reluctantly he pulled his mouth from hers.

He tried not to notice that her lips were rosy from his kisses or that she was breathing just as raggedly as he was. From the way she was looking at him he knew she had been as hungry to taste him as he had been for her. Not trusting his self-control, he turned away from her. "You'd better get some sleep." Unlike his insides, his voice was surprisingly cool. "If you need anything, I'll be in the next room."

"Thank you—for everything."

Her voice was like soft velvet, threatening to unravel his resolve.

"Do you need to get anything from the bedroom before I..." Her voice trailed off.

"No, I'm fine." He avoided meeting her eyes. "Just try to relax and get a good night's sleep."

Later, it wasn't Ronni who was having trouble sleeping but Logan. The sounds coming from his bedroom provided his imagination with vivid images of the woman sleeping in his bed. Every time the old iron bed squeaked he had visions of her rolling over. Was she, too, like Steffie, sleeping without a nightgown? The problem was, he knew how appealing she looked asleep. Her full lips parted ever so slightly, her golden lashes created a thick fringe on creamy smooth skin. And her even breathing caused her chest to heave ever so slightly—just enough to remind him that it was indeed a most noticeable chest.

He grumbled, then shifted his cramped legs, trying to find a more comfortable position on the rattan couch. But each position felt more uncomfortable than the previous one. He knew it wasn't only because he was scrunched up like a pretzel that he was miserable. No matter how many explanations he arrived at regarding Ronni, there was still the unanswered question of who she really was and why she and her mother were using dead people's identities.

He didn't need for Doc to tell him it was common practice for a Russian female spy to assume the identity of a dead person as a cover for clandestine activity. Could Ronni be a Russian? He didn't want to even consider the possibility. She'd looked so innocent when he asked her if she knew what a honey trap was. And he certainly didn't want to think she might have responded to his kisses in an attempt to entrap him with her sexual wiles. If she was a honey trap, he was falling very neatly into it. Look at what a couple of kisses had done to him.

He punched his pillow. He wouldn't think about it. There had to be a logical explanation for her false identity. As for the tail he'd lost leaving her home—was there a logical explanation for that? He had an uneasy feeling that it wasn't the feds—

which left the KGB. If the Russians were interested in her, it could mean that the threatening phone call she'd received wasn't simply from some prankster. She and the baby could be in real danger... another reason for him to be worrying.

He'd put himself in a position to protect the two of them. Logan McNeil, one eyed and still a little weak in the knees, was now responsible for the safety of a mother and child. He'd already caused one child to be killed. What made him think he could protect this one? His reflexes were slow, he was blind in one eye and he was sorely lacking confidence in himself as a protector of anyone.

There was only one thing for him to do. He knew several people in the CIA with contacts in the Soviet Union—agents who owed him more than the time of day. It was time he called in his markers. While Ronni and Steffie slept, he made a few important phone calls. When he did finally manage to fall asleep, it was only after he'd decided that he wouldn't become emotionally involved with Ronni until he'd proven her innocence.

RONNI AWOKE the next morning to the smell of freshly brewed coffee. She glanced at the digital clock on the nightstand and was surprised to see it was after eight. Usually Steffie was her alarm clock—waking every morning at six-thirty on the dot. Ronni's eyes automatically moved to the playpen. It was empty.

She quickly threw back the sheet and scrambled out of bed, slipping into her cotton kimono as she crossed the room. Barefoot, she made her way to the kitchen—and breathed a sigh of relief. Logan was seated at the kitchen table, balancing Steffie on his knee and trying to feed her breakfast. Steffie, with a dish towel wrapped around her neck for a bib, had little clumps of scrambled eggs oozing through her fingers. There were blobs of grape jelly smeared all over the tabletop, as well as all over Logan's white slacks.

Ronni's first thought was that Peter would never have bothered to feed Steffie at all, especially if it meant holding her on his lap. Unless Ronni could assure him that Steffie wouldn't make a mess, Peter hadn't wanted to hold her period.

"Good morning." Logan was the first to break the silence.

"Hi." He was gazing at her rather curiously, and suddenly Ronni was conscious of the fact that she'd just climbed out of bed and her hair probably looked as though a bird had been nesting in it. Self-consciously she smoothed a hand over her head. "I'm sorry. I usually wake up when Steffie does."

"It's all right," he told her, still giving her a rather close scrutiny.

"From the look of things, it's hard to tell who's been feeding whom." An involuntary smile tugged at her lips. "I'm afraid she's made a mess of your clothes," she said apologetically, trying not to notice the firm muscles shaping the tank top he wore.

Logan glanced down briefly. "Yeah, well, other than a couple of days around the holidays when I usually go visit my brother and his wife, I haven't had much experience with kids. I made her scrambled eggs because that's what my nephews always seem to be eating whenever I'm there."

Ronni eyed the remains of the breakfast on the table. "That's fine."

"She didn't eat much," he said, then set the squirming toddler down so she could greet her mother.

Leaving a trail of scrambled eggs in her wake, Steffie wobbled toward Ronni with arms outstretched. In one hand she carried a soggy piece of toast, which she held up for her mother's inspection.

Ronni lifted her into her arms and kissed the only part of her that wasn't covered with food—the top of her head. "Good morning, Steffie. I bet you have more breakfast on you than in you," she said, walking her fingers playfully across chubby arms. She looked over at Logan. "I think I'd better take her in the shower with me."

"You go ahead and I'll clean up here." He stood and began clearing away the dishes, grateful for the diversion. When Ronni had lifted Steffie into her arms, Steffie's foot had caught the hem of the kimono, giving him an enticing view of bare thighs and weakening his resolve not to regard Ronni in anything but a platonic manner.

The memory of how she had felt in his arms last night and that image of bare flesh stuck with him as he heard the sound of the shower running. To take his mind off such thoughts, he decided to cook breakfast, so that by the time Ronni and Steffie were dressed, the aroma of green peppers and onions wafted tantalizingly through the house.

"You didn't have to go to any trouble for me," Ronni told him when she saw that two places were set at the table.

He shrugged away her comment. "It's no trouble. Aren't you hungry?" he asked, reaching over to turn down the volume on the portable television that sat on the countertop.

"It smells wonderful," she admitted. "Is there anything I can do to help?"

"There's fresh juice in the refrigerator and the coffee's over there." He waved toward the space-saver coffee maker suspended beneath the cupboard.

Ronni filled two mugs with coffee, then poured two glasses of orange juice, while Logan slid an omelet onto each of the plates, then gestured for her to be seated. As soon as she sat down, Steffie wanted to climb onto her lap. Knowing the child would be in her food unless she had toys to keep her occupied, Ronni went to find the large plastic carryall.

"That ought to keep her busy for a few minutes at least," she told Logan when she'd returned and dumped its contents in the middle of the floor.

"She's quite a bundle of energy for such a little thing," Logan commented, as an awkward silence seemed to crop up between them.

"Yes, she is," Ronni replied, wishing she could think of something more clever to say, but after last night, she was feeling self-conscious. Had she been so lonely that a simple kiss could ignite such a reaction? Actually she wasn't sure it had been simply a kiss, which was why she felt compelled to discuss it with him. "Logan, about last night."

When he looked up from his food, his face had a neutral expression. "You needed a little comfort and I provided it," he said with a slight lifting of his shoulders. "Maybe that's all we should say about it."

All morning she had fretted over what had happened, wondering if he, too, had experienced the powerful sexual attraction she'd felt for him. Now that he was telling her he'd kissed her to comfort her, she felt disappointed.

When she didn't speak, he added, "I'd be lying if I said I didn't find you attractive, Ronni. But right now there are two things preventing me from letting that attraction grow. At this particular time in your life you're very vulnerable. You're also still married—at least legally."

"And I've Peter to thank for both of those things, don't I?" she said with a brittle smile.

Logan reached across the table to cover her hand with his, but she slipped it out of his grasp.

They continued to eat in an uncomfortable silence for several minutes before he said, "I called the hospital earlier this morning."

Ronni held her fork poised in midair. "Is Andrew worse?"

"There's been no change in his condition. He's still comatose. Senator Potter wanted me to tell you he would call us if there was any news."

"I still can't believe Andrew had a heart attack. He's too young and he's also heart smart. He's the one who's always telling me I eat the wrong foods and that I should watch my cholesterol."

Logan didn't want her to know what he suspected—that Andrew's heart attack might have been induced as a means of silencing him permanently. At least the police had been able to confirm that Ronni had arrived after the paramedics. He didn't want to even consider that she might have tried to eliminate Andrew, although the possibility that someone else had loomed largely at this point. It was a disturbing thought—not only because it could mean Andrew was a traitor, but because it could mean that Ronni had been his honey trap.

"This is really very good," she said between mouthfuls of food. "It isn't exactly what I expected for breakfast—not after I saw the contents of your refrigerator last night."

"Breakfast is about all I can handle—farm-boy skills, I guess. Normally my idea of cooking is to pop frozen lasagna in the microwave." He pushed his half-empty plate aside and wrapped both hands around his coffee mug. "Actually I haven't had much of an appetite since my accident."

His mood had changed again—something Ronni was coming to expect. One minute he was friendly, the next he was aloof. There was another silence, with the only sounds in the room Steffie banging a squeaking rubber hammer on the floor, Ronni tapping her fork against her plate and the hum of a commercial jingle on the television.

Finally Logan got up and scraped the remainder of his food into the garbage disposal. When he dropped the plate and cup into the sink with force, Ronni knew she had to say something. She quietly got up from the table and approached him from his right side. Unable to see that she was coming up behind him, he unwittingly turned around and bumped into her.

"I told you I can't see on my right side," he snapped, angry with himself more than her for feeling like a clumsy clod. "Are you all right?"

"I'm okay," she assured him. "I'm sorry if I startled you."

He sighed. "No, I'm the one who's sorry." He wanted to tell her how frustrated he was feeling, but the picture on the television had captured his attention. Reaching across the counter, he turned up the volume.

Ronni followed his movement, then her eyes widened in horror as she recognized the man on the black-and-white screen. Seated at a table with two other men, an array of microphones in front of him, was Peter.

She moved closer to the television, her face paling at the sight of her husband. Blue eyes that had been sparkling just moments ago became cloudy, as her long, thin fingers grasped the edge of the counter for support.

As flashbulbs went off and television cameras rolled, Peter Lang held his press conference. So great was Ronni's anger, she found it difficult to breathe. Never in her life had she felt such a rage toward another human being. But, then, never before had anyone ever assaulted her character in such a despicable manner.

In a most convincing tone Peter told the world, "I want it made public that I chose to make my home in the Soviet Union. I was not forced to leave the United States. All I ask now is that my wife and daughter be allowed to join me as they had originally planned."

CHAPTER SEVEN

"HE'S LYING!" Ronni exclaimed, her fists in tight balls. "We weren't going *with* him. We were going over to visit him so that he could see Steffie and I could get the divorce papers signed. That's all!"

She stared at the television contemptuously while Peter continued with his statement.

"I want to send a message to my wife, and that is this—Ronni, you must know how much I love you, and how much I want both you and Steffie here with me. Please don't keep my daughter away from me."

Several reporters asked questions. Peter gave vague responses, but it wouldn't have mattered what he said, for all Ronni could think of was how he'd lied about her joining him. As soon as the news segment was over, she switched off the television angrily.

"How can he even think I'd let him have Steffie?" She shook her head in amazement. "He hasn't wanted to have anything to do with her in fifteen months. Now all of a sudden he's trying to make it sound as if he's a devoted father."

"Maybe since he's given up his freedom he's realized how important the two of you are to him," Logan suggested.

Ronni's response was a guttural sound of disbelief. "I don't understand why he's doing this to us. I never thought he would be vindictive, but what other reason would he have to lie like that? Everyone is going to think that I'm one of...of...*them*." She said the word as though it were bile in her mouth. Reaching for her purse, she dug through it until she found what she was looking for—the FBI agent's number.

"What are you doing?" Logan asked, as she picked up the telephone and started to dial.

"I'm calling the FBI."

Logan crossed the kitchen and took the phone from her hand. "If you think the FBI was hard on you yesterday, what do you suppose they're going to say after this?"

"But I'm innocent, Logan," she declared vehemently. "I don't have anything to hide. Oh!" she groaned in frustration, rubbing fingers across her temple. "I should have never left my home. Now I probably look guiltier than ever."

"But you're not guilty." He realized that as he said the words, he wasn't simply trying to console her, but that he truly believed them. "And if you had stayed in Melbourne, you would have had to worry about the press hounding you, crank phone calls and who knows what else."

"But what am I going to do? Hide out here?" She felt totally confused.

"I wouldn't exactly call it hiding, Ronni. You simply chose to get away for a few days rather than subject yourself to harassment," Logan reasoned.

"To me it feels like I'm hiding and I shouldn't be. I've done nothing wrong." Her eyes sought his, and found the trust she so desperately needed. "You really are a friend, Logan, and I'm sorry about sounding so ungrateful. I do appreciate you helping us. The next time I see Andrew, I'm going to tell him his suspicions about you are unfounded. I don't know what Steffie and I would have done if you hadn't chosen yesterday as the day you were going to make amends with him."

Logan felt more than a twinge of guilt. He debated whether he should tell her his real reason for going to see Andrew. What would she think if she knew that in addition to being a close friend of the Potters, he was also an ex-agent—an ex-agent whose initial interest in her was for the same reasons as the FBI. He knew that emotionally she was getting close to the breaking point. Revealing his identity now might only confuse her further. Besides, his interest in her went beyond Doc's inquiry. The memory of the taste of her lips made the decision for him.

He took her hands in his. "You've got my help if you want it, Ronni. You can stay here as long as you like."

She bit her lip indecisively. "You really don't think I should call the FBI?"

"Why don't you let me see what I can learn from Senator Potter? He's on the Senate Intelligence Committee, so he should be able to find out if the government is close to cracking the spy ring Peter was involved in."

"How long do you suppose that will take?"

"Hopefully not more than a couple of days. As soon as the government uncovers Peter's contact, your name will be cleared. It won't matter what Peter does or doesn't say."

She looked skeptical. "It's just not fair. I shouldn't need to have my name cleared."

"I know that, and it won't be long and the rest of the world will, too." He lifted her chin with his finger. "Trust me, Ronni. It'll all work out."

Ronni studied his face and wondered why just looking at him made her want to believe that everything would be all right. To her surprise, she did trust him. "Do you really think the senator will be able to tell you anything?"

"He's in a position that affords him information unavailable to the FBI."

She could only nod her agreement.

"Does that mean you want to stay?" he asked.

Again she nodded.

"Good." He took her hands in his. "The first thing I think we ought to do is clear your mind of any thoughts of Peter the Terrible. How would you and Steffie like to see where I've been spending most of my time lately?"

"You don't need to entertain us, Logan."

"I want to, Ronni," he said sincerely. "I'd like to take you out on the reef and show you some sea life."

"That sounds wonderful, but Steffie hasn't learned how to swim yet."

"I'm not talking about diving. When I said I was helping a friend of mine get his boat seaworthy, I didn't mention what kind of boat it was." He reached for the captain's hat that sat atop the refrigerator and slipped it onto his head. "Ever been on a glass-bottom boat?"

"No, I can't say that I have—despite having lived in Florida almost all my life."

"You've been to Key West before, haven't you?"

She shook her head. "I've been to Key Largo, but that's as far I've made it down the Keys."

"Then we should play tourist. I think it'll do you both good to get out on the Gulf, in the fresh air, and forget about everything that's been happening on the television and in the newspapers."

The thought was too appealing to even consider refusing. She simply agreed.

And she was glad she did. Logan took them past picturesque old buildings, fresh with paint and framed with hibiscus, to Mallory Square, where statues of bearded fishermen and sea captains much like the one in Logan's living room graced the sidewalks. There they boarded the Old Town Trolley for a sight-seeing tour of the city. For lunch, Logan chose an outdoor café with picnic tables overlooking the marina; the specialty of the house was conch chowder and key lime pie. He also managed to find a quaint ice cream parlor, much to Steffie's delight.

At the marina, Logan introduced her to Casey Stevens, a friend of his who not only operated the glass-bottom boat, *Rosemary's Baby*, but ran a charter seaplane service, as well. When Casey offered to take the three of them on an aerial tour of the Keys, Ronni took a rain check, uncertain whether Steffie would be a good flier.

Once they'd boarded the glass-bottom boat, Ronni was happy with her choice. The two-hour narrated cruise from the Gulf of Mexico to the Atlantic Ocean took them into a fascinating world of underwater beauty. It wasn't long before Ronni discovered that Logan had more than a passing interest in aquatic life.

Steffie, as it turned out, was a better sailor than her mother, giggling and cooing as the boat churned its way through the reef. Most of her attention was on the large group of children, who enthusiastically vocalized their excitement at seeing big basket sponges and schools of porkfish and grunts. Ronni's attention was on Logan, who enthusiastically pointed out the variety of corals on the reef, as they looked through the glass panels in the ship's hull. Throughout the trip, she couldn't help but be impressed by his knowledge of the reef.

Ronni learned a lot about Logan that afternoon. As patient as he was with Steffie, he could also be rather intimidating, especially in a crowd. Part of his uneasiness in public she knew was due to his lack of sight on his right side. He was careful to make sure she was always on his left, and although he didn't seem self-conscious about his eye patch, she could see that he was uncomfortable with the crowded sidewalks and streets, where getting bumped and jostled about was common even for those who had full vision. By the end of the day, she knew that had it not been for his wanting to show her and Steffie a good time, he wouldn't have mingled with the tourists.

She brought up the subject later that evening after Steffie had been bathed and put to bed. "Thanks for today, Logan," she said when they'd finished the chicken and barbecued ribs he'd ordered from a local carryout restaurant.

"It was my pleasure," he responded, lifting his wineglass in a salute.

He'd changed into a white knit shirt, and Ronni noticed how it made his tanned skin appear even darker.

"I know it's not always easy with a child Steffie's age in tow," she continued.

"Steffie was one of the bright spots," he told her with an indulgent smile.

"You don't like crowds, do you?"

He shrugged. "I can tolerate them."

"You should have said something. We could have just as easily gone to the beach, or even stayed here." She looked at the man seated across from her and wondered how she could know so little about him, yet at the same time feel as though she knew so much.

"There aren't many uncrowded beaches in Key West. And I wasn't lying when I said I enjoyed today. In fact, it's been a long time since I've laughed so much." He was looking at her as though she'd accomplished some miraculous task.

"Steffie does have a way of creating funny scenes," Ronni agreed lightly, not wanting to see in his face that same tenderness she'd seen the night before—just after he'd kissed her. "I've always said that to be a parent one must have a good sense of humor." She promptly rose and began clearing away their empty plates, for she'd caught a glimpse of that tenderness and it frightened her.

She was at the kitchen sink when she heard his chair scrape against the floor. Next he was at her side, only inches from her; yet Ronni could feel her skin tingle as though he were touching her.

"You're fun to be with, Ronni," he told her. "Your students are lucky."

Like the gentle ocean trade winds that carried the scent of frangipani and wild orchid, his compliment carried a sweet, heady fragrance that affected Ronni in a manner that was more intoxicating than any perfume. "Thank you," she said softly.

She stole a look at him, then wished she hadn't, for there was no levity in his face, but an intensity that left no doubt in her mind that he was very much attracted to her.

Unconsciously her lips parted, and had she known he could read every emotion on her face, she would have turned away from him. The way he was looking at her made her feel as though her stomach were smiling, and even if she'd wanted to look away, she wouldn't have, for his expression had her mesmerized.

When he caught her face between his hands, she felt sapped of any rational decision-making powers. He lowered his head to taste her mouth with his own, a feather-light kiss that began as gently as a whisper, caressing her lips with the promise of intimacy.

It was that promise that made Ronni forget she hadn't known Logan but a few days, made her forget she'd vowed not to let what had happened the night before repeat itself. With a shiver of pleasure, she instinctively opened her mouth to his, not wanting the kiss to end before she had felt the warmth of his tongue moving over hers.

When it did finally end, they were both trembling. Cheeks that were already flushed deepened to a rosy bloom as Ronni realized how her body had moved sinuously against his in a sensuous quest. She tried to pull free of him, but his arms firmly stopped her.

"Look at me, Ronni," he commanded, when her eyes focused on his feet. When she raised her eyes to his, he brushed his lips gently over hers. "There's no point in denying we're attracted to each other."

"You said this morning—"

He raked a hand through his hair. "I know what I said," he cut in impatiently, as though he wished he could forget the words he'd uttered. "Unusual circumstances have more or less thrown us together, but had I met you under ordinary circumstances, I'd still have the same feelings for you."

"Do you have feelings for me?"

For an answer, he caught her mouth with his, not gently tasting, but hungrily taking possession. Ronni responded with equal passion, shuddering at the intense need his touch created. He moved his hands over her, stroking, caressing, pulling her closer so that she could feel his need for her. His warmth seemed to seep into her bones, causing her to quiver with desire. She heard him groan, but it was only as he pushed her away that she realized it was a groan of displeasure. The phone was ringing.

Ronni watched him reluctantly inch his way backward to answer it, never taking his eyes off her. Upon hearing the voice on the other end of the line, however, he turned his face to the wall. When he glanced at her over his shoulder, she realized he was uncomfortable with her listening to his phone conversation. Awkwardly she motioned to him, indicating she would wait for him in the living room.

He didn't stop her, which made her wonder who it was on the telephone. If it had been the senator, wouldn't he have wanted her to stay and hear the report on Andrew? Although Logan deliberately kept his voice low, Ronni could make out bits of his conversation. Unconsciously she found herself straining to hear more, especially when she caught such phrases as "take her to Russia" and "disobey orders."

Ronni's pulse sped up. Who was Logan talking to? And why was he talking about going to Russia? She crossed the living room, then pressed herself to the wall, following its path until she was next to the open archway. Holding her breath, she leaned as close as she could to the entrance, and listened. Logan's voice was low, but there was a hint of impatience in it that caused it to carry.

"I'm here with the baby and her mother. You're going to get what you want."

Ronni bit down on her lower lip. Why was he talking about her and Steffie, going to Russia and disobeying orders all in the same conversation? Fear as she'd never experienced swelled inside her, making her legs tremble and her throat tighten. Suddenly Andrew's words echoed in her mind like a broken record: *"Don't trust anyone. Don't trust anyone."* She tried to push away the recollection of how distressed he'd been to see Logan, but the memory forced itself to the front of her thoughts, and she found herself questioning Logan's integrity as fear clouded her thinking.

By the time he joined her in the living room, she was seated on the sofa, trying to appear composed. She was hoping he would tell her about his conversation and erase all the doubts that had materialized from the bits and pieces she'd overheard. He didn't.

He took one look at her sitting like a frightened child on the sofa and his tone became distant. "That was the senator. He told me to tell you there's still no change in Andrew's condition." Unaware that she had overheard parts of his phone call, he could only draw one conclusion from her obvious discomfort: she was unhappy about what had happened before the phone rang, and was worrying that he would expect her to take up where they'd left off.

Ronni could see that Logan was avoiding her eyes and guessed it was because he was lying about the phone call. "Did you ask him about the investigation?"

"Yes. They still don't know who Peter's contact is." He had thrust both his hands in his pockets and was jiggling his loose change.

"Did he say how long he thought it would take for me to be cleared?"

He shook his head. "All he could tell me was there had been a couple of leads they were checking out."

"Does he think it's a good idea for me to be here with you?"

"He's not going to send the feds down here, if that's what you're worried about," he snapped.

If she was worried, it wasn't because she was troubled about the FBI finding her. She was confused over her feelings for Logan. Just minutes ago she'd been in his arms, trusting him completely. Now a single phone call was responsible for the doubts that filled her head, unsettling her so that she questioned whether her trust was misplaced. He was looking at her oddly, which only made her more apprehensive.

"It's getting late," she said, glancing nervously at her watch. "Well, actually, it's not late, but it's been a long day and..." Slowly she got to her feet.

Sensing her uneasiness, he said, "I think I'm going to go out for a walk."

"Then I guess I'll say good-night now," she said stiffly, avoiding his face.

His good-night was equally stiff. As soon as he'd gone, Ronni began searching the small living room. What she was looking for, she wasn't sure. Maybe something that would put to rest the doubts the phone conversation had created. Glancing through the few titles on the bookshelves, she found nothing out of the ordinary. She noticed, however, that there was something sandwiched between two of the hardcover novels.

When she pulled down one of the books, several pieces of paper fell to the ground. Bending to retrieve them, she discovered that they weren't simply pieces of paper, but envelopes containing letters.

There were three of them, each looking as though it could easily come apart at the seams. A glance at the addresses told her they were indeed Logan's letters, but they hadn't been sent to him here in Key West. One had an East German address, whereas the other two had been sent to him in Czechoslovakia. What on earth would Logan have been doing in Czechoslovakia?

With shaky fingers she removed one of the letters from its envelope, carefully unfolding the fragile paper, only to discover she couldn't read its contents. The letter was penned in a foreign language—one she didn't recognize. A quick glance at the other two letters revealed they'd been written by the same person—someone who identified himself simply by the letter A. Again she scrutinized the envelopes, but there were no return addresses. Who was this "A" and why was he writing to Logan in what looked to her like it could be Russian?

Once more she felt a growing wave of panic threaten to rob her of her breath. Logan couldn't have anything to do with the Russians . . . he was Andrew's friend—wasn't he? Of course he was. Andrew had mentioned him on several occasions, although he hadn't ever shown her a picture of Logan McNeil. Maybe this man was an impostor—a Soviet impostor. Could that have been why Andrew was so upset when Logan had appeared?

Now the panic wasn't just taking her breath away, but her composure, as well. She shoved the letters back in between the books and looked around in confusion. "We have to get out of here," she said aloud to the empty room.

No. She was overreacting. Rubbing her palms up and down her bare arms, she paced the room. Logan couldn't possibly be a spy. He was trying to help them. Then a frown wrinkled her forehead. Was he really helping them, or simply attempting to keep them away from the government agents?

She had to leave, but how? Steffie was asleep, and even if she were awake, Logan had the keys to his pickup in his pants pocket. She'd have to think of a plan—a safe escape for her and Steffie.

While she prepared for bed, she tried out and rejected dozens of ideas. She came to the conclusion there was only one way she would be able to leave Logan, and that was to take his pickup. But she needed to get hold of his keys.

Since she couldn't risk leaving in the middle of the night, she'd have to wait until morning. If she loaded everything—including Steffie—into the pickup while Logan showered, she could sneak into the bathroom and lift his keys from the pocket of his slacks. Because there was no lock on the bathroom door, all she had to do was slip in and slip out. He wouldn't even have to know she'd been there.

It seemed easy enough. But as she climbed into bed and thought about what lay ahead, she began to have doubts. *If* he was a spy, she and Steffie were in terrible danger. What if he caught her trying to leave? Would he have a gun? He didn't wear one, but that didn't mean there wasn't one in the house.

She reached for the flashlight on the nightstand, then crawled out of bed, stubbing her toe on the playpen as she groped around in the dark. She searched through each of the dresser drawers but found nothing except underwear and socks. Next she went through the narrow closet, where she uncovered a few shirts and some snorkeling gear, but no gun. That left only the front hall closet. Expecting Logan to return any minute, she hated having to look there, but fear gave her no choice.

It was in that closet that she found it—a small silver handgun, hidden behind a shoe box on the top shelf. The gun was no bigger than the palm of her hand, but to Ronni it looked too large even to grasp. She'd never handled a weapon before and she certainly didn't want to start now. Again fear made the decision for her.

Gingerly she picked the piece up, holding it away from her as though it were a stick of dynamite. She carried it into the bedroom and carefully stuck it in her purse, which she in turn placed atop the tall dresser. She wouldn't even pull the gun out of her purse unless it became necessary. Oh, God, how she hoped it wouldn't be necessary, for she wasn't sure if she would be able to point it at another human being. All she wanted was to take her daughter and leave.

WHEN RONNI WOKE the next morning after a restless sleep, the first thing she did was check to see if the gun was still in her purse. It was and she heaved a sigh of relief. She'd half expected Logan to come storming into the bedroom the night before, demanding to know what had happened to the gun. Since he hadn't, she could only hope he had no idea what she was planning.

She wished she didn't have to face him at all, but while she was quickly packing up her belongings, she could hear him moving around in the kitchen. Taking a deep breath, she opened the bedroom door and called out to him, "If you want to use the shower first, go ahead. I'm going to feed Steffie her breakfast before I have mine." She closed the door and leaned against it, then nearly jumped out of her skin when he rapped on the other side.

"I need to get some clean clothes," he told her as she slid the door open a fraction of the way.

"Oh! Sorry," she said with a weak grin, then reluctantly swung the door wide open. At first she was worried he would notice her suitcases standing beside the door, but he went straight to the dresser and pulled out a pair of briefs from the drawer, giving her an idea. When he had what he needed, he tossed her a faint smile and went straight to the bathroom.

As soon as she heard the shower running, Ronni flew into motion, pulling open the closet door and grabbing every pair of slacks inside. Then she rummaged through the drawers of the dresser until she'd pulled out every pair of briefs and shorts she could find and added them to the pile on the floor. She raced out to the kitchen to get a large green plastic garbage bag, then rushed back to the bedroom, where she frantically shoved the pile of clothes into the bag.

She didn't think her heart could beat any faster than it was when she dragged the suitcases, the big green bag and Steffie's carryall past the closed bathroom door. When everything was loaded into the back of the pickup, she grabbed Steffie and the diaper bag and installed them in the cab of the truck.

"You wait right here for Mama, pumpkin," she told Steffie as she strapped her into the car seat. "Let's hope this isn't one of those mornings when he takes a short shower," she said, then gave Steffie a bottle filled with juice and hurried back into the house. She went straight to the bedroom, where she pulled the gun from her purse before slinging the leather bag over her shoulder.

Taking a deep breath, she squared her shoulders and headed for the bathroom door. The sound of water running bolstered her confidence, and with gun in hand, she made her move. The minute she opened the door she saw that the keys weren't in Logan's pants pocket but on the narrow wooden shelf below the mirror. She didn't realize she'd been holding her breath until her lungs practically collapsed with relief. She wouldn't have to step into the bathroom at all. She could snake her hand in and snatch the keys. What she hadn't counted on was the shower curtain being zipped open and a drenched Logan catching her in the act.

He stood there stark naked, soapsuds cascading down his tanned body as the hot water continued to bounce off him in miniexplosions of moisture. Just who was more startled was a toss-up. Ronni let out a shriek; Logan appeared to be at a loss for words. The gun was in her left hand, while her right hand seemed frozen, inches from the wooden shelf and the keys. It was in that instant that Logan's eyes met hers, and before she could grab the keys, his voice was booming in her ears, stopping her hand's progress.

"Are you looking for something?" There was a seductive quality to his voice, and Ronni realized he thought she'd come to beguile him.

She tried to keep her eyes from running down the length of his body, but he was a fine specimen of a man and it wasn't every day she accosted a man in the shower. It was also the first time she'd seen him without the black eye patch, and except for a slight bruise under his eye, there was no evidence of a loss of sight. He had a hint of a smile on his face and Ronni noticed he made no effort to cover himself with either the washrag or the shower curtain. For a brief moment she found herself wanting to indulge in the pleasure of looking at his body, but she quickly brought herself back to her senses and nudged the door open, exposing the gun in her hand.

When Logan saw the weapon his provocative smile disappeared. "What are you doing with that thing?" he demanded.

Carefully she transferred the gun from her left hand to her right. "I don't want to have to do this, Logan, but I need the keys. I'm taking Steffie and leaving." She was surprised at how steady her voice sounded, considering how fast her heart was beating.

"Leaving?" He turned the water off. "And where do you plan on going?"

"Just away," she said shakily.

"Away from me, isn't that what you mean? Ronni, you must know I'd never hurt you or Steffie." He made a move as though to step out of the shower.

"Logan, please. Don't move." She raised the gun until her arm was nearly straight out in front of her. "Just let me take the keys and leave."

"I'm hardly in a position to stop you, am I?"

Again he smiled, and Ronni had to fight hard not to listen to the voice in her head that told her she was being ridiculous to think Logan could be one of the bad guys.

Slowly she reached for the keys, expecting that Logan would try to stop her. But he didn't. Nor did he move when she took his clothes and tucked them under her arm. "I'm sorry," she found herself mumbling, then immediately chastised herself for feeling guilty about leaving. She raced through the kitchen and out the back door.

Despite the fact that her hands were shaking so badly she could barely get the key in the ignition, she managed to start the engine and back out of the driveway. She half expected a naked Logan to come running out of the house after her, but he didn't. As she headed toward the highway, she kept seeing images of him naked, remembering the feral look on his face as she surprised him in the shower. It was difficult to believe that he was on the wrong side, that he could have been part of a scheme involving Peter. But because of Steffie, it was a chance she couldn't take.

By the time she reached the highway, Steffie had almost finished her bottle and was looking peacefully content, unlike her mother, who felt as though a war were going on in her head. There was only one road out of the Keys and she was on it, and so far, she'd seen nothing to indicate that Logan was following her. How could he? Even if he were to find a pair of pants and somehow manage to borrow a car, he would have a hard time catching up with her. Yet as she drove across the series of bridges connecting the Keys, she continually checked her rearview mirror, keeping her foot steady on the gas pedal.

More miles stretched between her and Key West, and she began to believe she was actually going to escape Logan. As she followed the road signs toward Miami, she relaxed a bit and thought about the next step in her plan. She would stop at Evelyn and Marshall Lang's home in Miami, and from there contact the FBI.

When Steffie began to fuss, Ronni reached into her purse and withdrew a small plastic bag filled with teething biscuits. "Here, sweetie. Munch on this until Mama finds us a nice place to eat," she said, handing one to Steffie.

Steffie eagerly grabbed the hard biscuit and immediately began gnawing on it, humming as she did so.

Ronni looked back over her shoulder one final time. "It won't be much longer and we'll be far away from Mr. Logan McNeil. Then we won't have to look back anymore," she said, wondering why the thought was not a comforting one.

CHAPTER EIGHT

LOGAN BANKED the seaplane slightly and squinted through his aviator sunglasses at the highway below. Despite his altitude and the fact that the automobiles looked like crawling bugs, he'd been able to spot the bright orange pickup easily and had been following it as it sped across the highway. Several times the truck had left the highway, cutting down side roads, then doubling back, as though its driver were trying to determine whether she was being followed.

Logan could imagine her looking everywhere. To her left. To her right. Behind her. Everywhere. Everywhere but up—which was why he'd been able to tail her without being noticed. It also helped that he was an experienced pilot who knew how to vector from time to time and stay in her blind spot.

He still couldn't believe she'd pulled a gun on him. It had been a humbling experience for an ex-agent, although he didn't know which was worse—her pulling the gun or leaving him without any pants. He wondered what she'd done with all of them. Were they in the pickup? They certainly weren't hidden in the house—he'd made a thorough search and hadn't found a single pair. Even his swim trunks were gone. He was a bit surprised that she'd left him his underwear.

If it hadn't been for Casey, he might still be sitting in his skivvies. Instead he was sitting in the cockpit of a seaplane in a pair of Casey's walking shorts. Glancing down at the baggy shorts, he wondered if it wouldn't have been smarter to wear his skivvies. Although Casey was the same height as Logan, he was probably a hundred pounds heavier. On Logan, Casey's baby blue walking shorts looked like oversize boxers and had probably produced just as many smirks as his underwear would have.

"Beggars can't be choosers." He could still hear Casey's mocking tone as he'd handed him the pants. Logan would have loved to wipe the grin off of his friend's face, but he really couldn't afford to be ungrateful when the man had offered him the use of his seaplane. Rather than try to catch her in Casey's Jeep—which Logan knew had a tendency to stall at the most inopportune times—he'd accepted the offer. With only one route out of the Keys, it hadn't taken long for him to spot the orange pickup.

He thought back to the day he'd leased the vehicle, remembering how he'd debated whether it might not be better to lease a car rather than drive around in what the salesman had called an "ultra orange machine." But he'd wanted a pickup, so despite its color, it had become his. Now it was because of that color that he was able to maintain his position tracking Ronni.

And track her he did until she reached the bridge at Plantation Key. At that point he flew on ahead and landed at a marina in Key Largo. There a friend of Casey's handed Logan a set of keys to a silver Mazda. The marina was situated right off the highway, so all Logan had to do was move the car to the edge of the parking lot and wait for the pickup to come by. He didn't have to wait long. As it went cruising by, Logan started up the Mazda and was soon driving behind it.

He stayed far enough back, so that even if Ronni saw the silver Mazda, she wouldn't be able to recognize him. Compared to some of the routes he'd traveled while tailing suspects, following Ronni was relatively easy. Except for a brief stop at a gas station, where she had the attendant fill the tank while she took Steffie into the rest room, she continued to follow U.S. 1. Instead of taking the exit going north, however, she surprised Logan by heading toward Miami.

At first he thought she must have missed the turnoff that would have led her to Melbourne. But when she left the highway and began traveling down a residential section of the city, he knew she hadn't planned on returning to Melbourne—at least not right away. So where was she going? More important, who was she going to see?

He still didn't understand what he'd done to frighten her into running away. Ever since the phone call from Doc she'd been uneasy in his presence. Even if she had overheard his end of the conversation, he didn't think he'd said anything that would have precipitated her leaving. Which left the other possibility—the one that gave credibility to Doc's assertion about Veronica Lang. Logan hated to think he could be wrong about her, but as he followed her into the city of Miami, he had to admit that the possibility that she'd left to meet a contact did exist.

He tailed her for several miles until she finally pulled the pickup into the cement driveway of a modest brick home across the street from a church. Logan drove into the church parking lot and watched Ronni get out of the car with Steffie in her arms. Up to the front door the two of them went, where Ronni rapped on the brass knocker. After several minutes she rapped again, but still no one came. Frowning, she hustled Steffie back to the truck. When she didn't start the engine, Logan wondered if she had decided to wait for the residents of the brick house to return.

He didn't have to wonder for long. Within minutes Ronni was out of the pickup and walking over to the mailbox at the foot of the driveway. Logan watched her slip a piece of paper inside, then get back in the truck and drive away. On his way after her, Logan passed in front of the mailbox. He debated whether he should intercept the message. But then he saw the name stenciled on the mailbox: Mr. and Mrs. Marshall Lang. Peter's parents. They were as straight as an arrow according to Doc's report.

He breathed a sigh of relief. Ronni *wasn't* a spy looking for her contact. She was simply searching for someone she could turn to. He didn't look at the message Ronni had left for her in-laws. Nor did he glance around to see if anyone else was interested in it. If he had, he would have seen the gray sedan that was parked around the corner.

But Logan was too worried about following Ronni to suspect that anyone would be following him. They were in the midst of rush-hour traffic and several times he nearly lost her. He was relieved when she finally pulled into a motel parking lot. Steffie appeared to be fussing as Ronni hauled her out of the car, and he could only surmise that the little girl was probably the reason she was looking for a place to sleep.

He watched her come back out with Steffie, who didn't seem any happier than when they'd gone in, then get in the truck and drive around to the side of the building, where she parked directly in front of room 112. As soon as she had unlocked the door and taken Steffie inside, Logan went to see the clerk at the registration desk.

Minutes later, he emerged with a hotel key and two cans of soda. He pulled the silver Mazda into the spot that was directly across the courtyard from the pickup, then unlocked the door to his room, which by no coincidence was directly across from Ronni's. Next he turned the knob on the air conditioner to high, then closed the red-and-blue plaid drapes on the large window.

As was typical of economy-motel drapes, when closed they left a gap of about half an inch either in the center or at the sides. He chose to have the gap in the center. Then he turned on the radio on the TV set, settled himself in a square chair and propped his feet up on the other square chair. Through the gap in the curtains he was able to observe Ronni's room without any problem.

Although there was little to observe. Logan watched her carry the two heavy suitcases into the room, one at a time. A member of the motel staff came by with a crib. Then there was no movement until around dinnertime, when room service brought her a tray. Logan, too, ordered room service, then groaned when the tray arrived and he got a look at the economy-motel cuisine. Hungry, he ate the food, anyway, still keeping an eye on Ronni's room through the gap in the curtain. He was washing the meal down with his third cup of coffee when Ronni and Steffie emerged.

For the first time since he'd known her, Ronni was wearing shorts. Other than the quick glimpse of thigh he'd caught yesterday morning, he hadn't seen much of her legs, for she usually kept them hidden beneath the long, flowing skirts of the sundresses she liked to wear. The sight of slender bare legs was enough to cause his pulse to dance. Ronni and Steffie headed for the children's playground connected to the swimming pool area. Again Logan was able to observe simply by sliding his chair to the end of the window and adjusting the gap in the curtain.

He watched Ronni place Steffie in the dolphin-shaped swing and push her back and forth until the child giggled merrily. Then they both climbed the elephant slide and slid down its metal trunk, shrieking with glee. When Steffie toddled toward the large sandbox, Ronni followed her. She plunked herself down to one side and began scooping sand into a plastic bucket nestled between Steffie's legs. Logan wished he could run outside and join them, but until he was certain she wasn't making contact with anyone, he couldn't risk it.

As the sun began to sink low in the sky, Ronni brushed the sand off Steffie, then carried her back to room 112. Again Logan found himself wishing he could join them. Images of Steffie's red head covered with suds and Ronni's wet shirt clinging to her breasts as she bathed her daughter in the kitchen sink filled his mind, only to be replaced by the memory of how her body had responded to his during their brief but passionate embrace.

He found himself glancing at his watch more frequently as every hour seemed to get longer and longer. After watching the room for nearly seven hours, Logan was tired and there was a dull throbbing in his right eye. He was tempted—even in an economy motel—to stretch out on the bed. It was obvious from the absence of light in Ronni's room that she had gone to sleep. She wasn't a spy. He'd bet his life on it. So what did he expect was going to happen in room 112 tonight? Of one thing he was certain. If anything was going to happen, he wasn't going to miss it. So he popped the top on his second can of soda, which was now warm, propped his feet up and watched some more.

By midnight the neon Full sign on the motel's carport was lit, and there was little activity anywhere. Logan decided to stretch his legs and go for a walk around the parking lot. He crossed the asphalt driveway, stopping to lean against the fence surrounding the kiddie playground, where just hours earlier Ronni and Steffie had frolicked. He regretted not confronting her when it was still daylight. If he were to go pounding on her door in the middle of the night, she would really be frightened. After much deliberation, he decided that first thing in the morning he was going to get things straightened out.

As he was about to step out of the shadows and into the light, he noticed the gray sedan parked across the street. A chill began at the base of his spine and his heart started to beat a little harder as he recognized the car that had been following him when they'd left Melbourne. When two men materialized—one big, one small—Logan's eyes darted to Ronni's darkened room before quickly returning to the two men. The prickly sensation along the back of his neck told him they weren't there by invitation.

They started across the motel parking lot, and Logan's heart began to pound even harder. He watched them slip into the shadow of the overhang and walk the entire length of the motel until they came to room 112. There they paused, as though searching for a key, and Logan felt his body go rigid before a shot of adrenaline electrified him into action.

Logan knew his catlike footsteps wouldn't betray his presence, but he wasn't so sure about his heart. It beat so hard in his chest he felt he could have aroused the sleepiest guest in the motel. As he hurried across the parking lot, he could see they were picking the lock, but before he could reach Ronni's room, the bigger man had slipped inside. Just as he lunged at the man standing guard outside Ronni's room, he saw the light go on and heard Ronni frantically cry out, "Get away from my baby!"

Logan easily took care of the smaller man with a blow to the stomach that caused him to double over in pain. Another quick left sent him to the ground, where he lay half in and half out of the open doorway. But the bigger man caught Logan by surprise, coming at him from his blind side and landing a fist to his jaw that sent him reeling backward.

Flat on his back and momentarily stunned, Logan struggled to clear his head. Slightly dizzy but aware that Ronni and Steffie were in danger, he willed his weak muscles to work together and staggered to his feet, only to see the big man's fist coming at him again. Only this time his fist never had the chance to connect with Logan's flesh, for brittle words split the air.

"Stop or I'll shoot!"

Logan looked past the man's shoulder and saw that Ronni had both her hands wrapped around his gun and was aiming it in their direction. The big man slowly backed away from Logan, who by now was steady on his feet. With deliberate steps, Logan moved closer to Ronni.

"Are you all right?" he asked, noticing the wild expression in her eyes.

She nodded, swallowed with difficulty, then said, "Steffie's crying."

Logan glanced over to where Steffie sat, looking lost and forlorn in the crib, then gave Ronni a reassuring nod. "She's okay and everything's going to be fine. Just keep the gun on these two." Then he turned his attention to the intruders and snapped, "You...up against the wall...both of you." He quickly patted each of them down in a thorough search that produced two weapons.

"Well, well, well," Logan slowly said as he carefully examined the guns. "What have we here? Looks to me like Russian-issue automatics."

"Did Peter send you to take my baby?" Ronni demanded, her cheeks flushed and her eyes flashing as the gun wavered unsteadily in their direction.

Neither man uttered a sound.

"I think you're wasting your breath, Ronni. They look like the silent types to me." Logan pulled out the bigger man's wallet and checked the identification inside. "It says here this is Fred G. Miller. He's even got a union card that says he's a member of the local carpenters' union. Pretty authentic-looking stuff, *Fred*," Logan remarked dryly. "These automatics must come in handy when you're building houses, eh?" He tucked one of the guns into the waistband of his shorts, then handed the other one to Ronni. "Either one of you got anything to say to the lady before she leaves?"

Again both men remained silent, until Logan finally said, "I didn't think so." He shoved Fred's wallet back into his pocket, then ordered, "On the floor, both of you, and put your hands behind your backs." As both men fell facedown on the floor, Logan turned to Ronni. "If either one so much as bats an eyelash, shoot him." Then he moved over to the bed and began ripping apart a sheet.

"What are you going to do?" Ronni asked nervously.

"I'm going to tie them up and then we're going to get the hell out of here," he said, as his fingers worked quickly tearing the sheet into long strips of cloth. In a matter of minutes he had bound and gagged each of the men until they reminded Ronni of mummies.

"There. That ought to hold them," Logan said soberly. "You can put those down now," he told her gesturing to the guns she still held tightly in her hands.

Ronni gave them a distasteful glance before handing them to Logan. Then she went over to the crib and lifted Steffie into her arms. With eyes closed, she rocked the whimpering child in her arms, whispering soft words of comfort as she clung desperately to her daughter.

Logan wished he could have wrapped both of them in his arms, but he knew that what was important right now was for the three of them to leave. "Come, we'd better go," he advised, placing a hand on her shoulder. "Where are your things?"

"In the closet . . . and some are in the bathroom," she replied anxiously.

"You've got five minutes to get everything together. I'm going to go settle our bills. When I get back, we'll leave." He started toward the door.

"You're not going to leave me alone with them, are you?" she called out in near panic, motioning to the two men on the floor.

"They are tied up," he reminded her. His words, however, were of little comfort to her, he saw, especially after the trauma she had just experienced. "All right," he conceded. "You take Steffie and go settle the bills and I'll pack your things. You'd better get dressed first."

Ronni glanced down at her cotton nightgown and blushed. "I'll only be a minute," she told him before disappearing into the bathroom. When she returned, she was wearing the same pair of shorts and top she'd had on earlier in the evening, which Logan found was an even greater distraction than the two intruders. "I'm ready," she said, carefully stepping around the two bodies on the floor, then shivering when one of the men groaned. "I've got to get out of here."

Logan opened the door and gestured her outside. After he had pulled the door shut behind them, he said, "I want you to wait for me in the lobby. As soon as I have everything loaded into the truck, I'll drive up to the front door, all right?"

"Logan, about those men . . . are they really Russians?"

There was a faint tremor in the fingers that reached for his arm.

"Ronni, I don't think this is the right time to be discussing this. Once we're out of here I'll answer all of your questions." He tried to steer her toward the reception area, but she hesitated, confusion clouding her eyes.

Suddenly she started to tremble, and Logan wondered if the shock of what had just happened was finally making itself felt. "They were going to kidnap Steffie. If you hadn't come along . . ." Her voice quivered with emotion.

"What's important is that I did come along and you and Steffie are safe. But, Ronni, that might not be the case if we don't leave," he snapped a bit impatiently.

For several moments Ronni just stared at him, then, as if she suddenly realized the gravity of their situation, she dug into her purse and pulled out the keys to the truck. "Please hurry" were her parting words.

CHAPTER NINE

"WHERE ARE WE GOING?" Ronni asked as the pickup pulled away from the motel, this time with Steffie sitting between Logan and her.

"Someplace you'll be safe," Logan replied.

"I'm beginning to wonder if there is such a place," she said wearily.

"You can quit looking over your shoulder," Logan told her as he headed north on the interstate. "No one's following us."

"How can you be sure?" Ronni asked, wishing she could be like Steffie, who was already drifting off to sleep.

"Those two thugs weren't in any condition to hop in their car and come after us," Logan said dryly. He winced as he rubbed his jaw.

Ronni caught the action and said, "You probably should have put some ice on your face. It looks like it might be a little swollen."

"It would have looked a lot worse than this if you hadn't pulled the gun out when you did," Logan told her, assessing the damage in the rearview mirror. "That big guy had an iron fist."

"If you hadn't come along I wouldn't have had time to get the gun out of my purse. They would have taken Steffie." Her voice was choked with emotion. "I don't know how to thank you."

"You could start by trusting me, Ronni," he said bluntly.

"That seems like a fair request," she agreed. "Logan, how did you manage to find us?"

"I borrowed Casey's seaplane. While you were driving the pickup on the highway, I was flying overhead." A smile played with the corners of his mouth. "I've been following you ever since you left the Keys."

"I thought it seemed too easy," she said, sighing.

"Ronni, why did you run away?" He shot her a puzzled glance.

For several seconds she stared at him, before finally saying, "Because I was frightened."

"Of me?" he asked in disbelief.

"I was so confused. And you weren't making it any easier," she replied, feeling rather foolish now.

"Confused about what?"

"About who the good guys and the bad guys are," she said impatiently, throwing her hands up in frustration. "The FBI said one thing, Andrew said something different, then you said something else. I didn't know who to believe."

"Why didn't you just tell me you were confused? Why did you have to run away?"

"I overheard your phone conversation last night. You were saying something about orders and having to go to Russia."

"I was talking to the senator about your predicament. Is that why you were so nervous when I came back into the living room?"

"You were acting so secretive, and then when you went for your walk, I found several letters on your bookshelves.... Letters that were addressed to you but sent to places in Czechoslovakia and East Germany. Unless I was mistaken, they were written in Russian."

"You thought *I* was a Russian spy?" He punctuated the question with a laugh.

"After everything that's happened in the past few days, can you really blame me?" she asked, her voice rising. "Why were you getting mail written in Russian at an East German address?"

Logan shook his head and exhaled a deep sigh. "Ronni, there is absolutely no reason for you not to trust me. East Germany and Czechoslovakia are only two of the many foreign countries I've lived in working for the government. That career I told you about—the one I left behind—was with the CIA. I'm an ex-agent. You don't need to fear me."

Instead of being reassured by his admission, she was dismayed. "You're a spy?"

"Not a spy in the sense that your husband is a spy," he said defensively, resenting the look of distaste that had spread across her face. "I spent most of my career as a counterintelligence officer, tracking down double agents or agents who defected."

There was a silence while she seemed to be digesting what he'd just told her. When she did finally speak again, her voice was small and distant. "Is that what you're doing now? Tracking down Peter?"

He shook his head. "Peter was never one of our agents. His isn't a case of a U.S. agent gone bad," he explained. "He was recruited as a civilian. And as I told you, I no longer work for the CIA."

"If you're not tracking down Peter and you're no longer with the agency, why did you come after me and Steffie?"

Logan had been asking himself that same question, and had only learned the answer when he'd seen those two thugs breaking into her hotel room. He wondered what she would say if he told her that he was falling in love with her and didn't want to lose her. He doubted she'd be very receptive to such a declaration at this time. There hadn't exactly been a flash of admiration in her eyes when he'd announced he was an ex-agent. So instead of telling her he was finding it difficult to stay away from her or that he wanted to be her hero, he decided simply to tell her the truth—at least, part of the truth.

But before he could say another word, she was angrily demanding, "Were you hired to spy on us?"

"No!" he denied vehemently.

He might as well not have said anything, for she continued on as though she hadn't heard him.

"That's why you were so suspicious of me, isn't it? You were supposed to be finding out if I was a spy. All this stuff about being a friend of Andrew's and wanting to help us out was just a way to find out if I was working with Peter."

"Initially, yes," he admitted, "but that was before Andy had his heart attack, before the feds became involved and before I met you." He wished she would at least look at him instead of staring out the window. "Senator Potter asked me as a personal favor if I would do a little investigating to find out if Andy was in any way connected to Peter. He wanted to know if there was any evidence that could possibly link his son to the spy ring."

"Are you saying that Senator Potter thinks Andrew is involved in this mess?" Her eyes widened as this time he did manage to get her attention.

"Before Peter's defection it was only speculation," he said solemnly. "Now it appears that it's probably true."

"True? How could it possibly be true? Andrew is a good, honest man. I've known him for five years. I even lived with him for a short period. I would have known if he was involved in anything clandestine."

Her defense of Andrew annoyed him. "You mean the way you knew about your husband's clandestine activities?" Immediately he regretted his words. "I'm sorry, Ronni. That wasn't fair. The truth is, one thing that all spies have in common is an ability to dissemble. They're capable of leading two separate lives at one time. I don't want to think that Andrew is involved in this mess, either, but until I hear officially, one way or the other, I have to tell you, it doesn't look good."

"Is that why you went to see him the day of his heart attack? To *accuse* him of being a spy?"

"I wanted to prove he wasn't," he insisted. "The senator has been like a father to me. If there's any way I can spare him pain, I will. I'm on your side, Ronni. I hope Andrew is innocent, too."

She studied his face, wanting to believe him. "But you don't think he is, do you?"

"It might be a case of Andrew having to clear himself. Until he's well enough to be questioned, he'll remain under suspicion. The FBI knows what I know—that he worked for Bartron the same time Peter did, that they were friends...." He paused, as though deliberating whether he should say more, then finally added, "that you two are quite close."

She gave a mirthless chuckle. "That explains the treatment I got from the FBI. I must be their number one suspect, although for the life of me I can't understand why."

"They're only doing their jobs," he rationalized.

"And you would know all about that, wouldn't you, Logan?" She laughed bitterly. "Oh, damn. Why did you have to be one of them?"

"One of them?" He thought it was a good thing he was driving, or else he would have been tempted to shake her. He tightened his grip on the steering wheel. "You make it sound as though I should apologize for wanting to protect our right to freedom. I'm an ex-one of them," he reminded her. "And because I am an ex-one of them I was able to prevent those two goons from kidnapping Steffie." This time he was the one who laughed sarcastically. "You're going to have to forgive me for not understanding this, Ronni, but for some reason I thought that if you knew I was an ex-agent you'd be able to trust me."

"I do trust you," she told him. "It's just that..." She wondered how she could explain her disappointment in learning his real identity. The truth was, she had wanted to believe he had helped her and Steffie because of a personal interest, not because of some favor he owed a senator. She had foolishly let her emotions sway her into believing he had risked his life because he cared about her, and now he was telling her his presence in their lives had nothing to do with his feelings for her.

"What do you want to do, Ronni? I can either take you to stay with me or I can take you back to Melbourne," he stated simply.

"We'll go with you, Logan." She surprised herself with her quick response.

Other than an indolent shrug accompanied by a muttered "Good," he made no effort to indicate he was pleased with her decision. "You'll be safe with me, Ronni."

"I know." She lowered her eyes, acutely aware of the change in his tone. She wished she knew what he was thinking, but unlike her, he was so good at masking his emotions. "Logan, what about those men we left back at the motel. Won't they try to find us?"

"They'll try all right. That's why I don't want to return to my place. Men like that seldom give up until they get what they want."

"They want Steffie," she said, her voice faltering. "I think Peter sent them to take her away from me."

"Ronni, it's not likely that KGB agents would attempt a kidnapping simply because an American defector wants his daughter with him," he reasoned. "There must be more to it than that. I'd have to say that phone call you received wasn't simply a prank. It's possible they hoped to use Steffie as a bargaining tool to get what they're really after."

"And what would that be?"

Logan shrugged. "If we knew, we wouldn't have to be driving around in the middle of the night, looking for a place to sleep."

"Just where are we going?" she asked.

"A friend of mine who is no way connected to the government has a place in Fort Lauderdale," he answered. "That's about an hour's drive. Maybe you should try to get some sleep."

She wanted nothing better than to take his suggestion, but every time she closed her eyes she saw the big, muscle-bound man standing over Steffie's crib. As exhausted as she was, what she needed more than sleep was the assurance that Steffie and Logan were right beside her. Rather than watch the Florida coastline speeding by, she fixed her eyes on Steffie's face, appreciating the serenity in the delicate features. Occasionally she'd glance at Logan's expressionless face and wonder what would have happened had he not followed her to Miami, and such thoughts would bring a shudder.

The remainder of the trip to Fort Lauderdale was accomplished in silence, but it wasn't an uncomfortable silence. When Logan pulled off the interstate and slowed for a blinking amber light in a deserted intersection, Ronni straightened in her seat and asked, "Where are we?"

"About five minutes from our destination," he told her, taking a road that led into a residential section.

Except for the streetlights, the neighborhood was dark until they came to a bungalow with a small illuminated yellow globe over its door. Logan parked the truck in the driveway, then offered to carry a sleeping Steffie inside. Ronni followed him up the narrow walk to the door, where she saw two doorbells, and she realized that the house was actually a double bungalow.

Expecting to see a man who had been a classmate of Logan's at the Naval Academy, Ronni was surprised when a woman answered the door and welcomed them inside. She reminded Ronni of a petite version of her mother, only she had a much warmer smile and a very soft, soothing voice. She didn't seem to be the least bit put out that she'd been awakened at three in the morning, and Ronni could only wonder if Logan had previously brought over other visitors under such strange circumstances.

"I'm sorry to get you out of bed, Mabel," Logan apologized, bending to press a kiss on her cheek as they stepped into the hallway separating the two apartments.

"You know I don't mind," she said, brushing aside his apology with the wave of a wrinkled hand. She unlocked the apartment door on the left. "I've put clean linens on the beds, but I'm afraid the refrigerator is empty. You didn't tell me you were bringing a baby,'' she admonished gently, looking lovingly at Steffie, who was still asleep on Logan's shoulder.

''Mabel, this is Ronni and her daughter, Steffie,'' he said casually.

''Such a beautiful baby,'' Mabel crooned affectionately.

''Thank you.'' Ronni felt an instant rapport with the older woman and began to relax just a bit. ''And thank you for fixing the beds.''

''If there's anything you need, I'm just across the hall.'' She pulled the key out of the lock and handed it to Logan, but addressed her words to Ronni. ''Would you like some milk? I'm sure Steffie'll want to eat as soon as she wakes up in the morning.'' She lowered her already soft voice to a near whisper.

''You're right, Mabel. I would like to borrow some milk if you don't mind,'' Ronni replied gratefully.

''Not at all. I'll get some for you right away.''

''While you do that, I should get the bags out of the truck,'' Logan said. ''Should we put her down on one of the beds?'' He was looking at Steffie as he spoke.

''I've got an old crib I keep in the garage, but I'm afraid it's all dusty and will need a cleaning before you can use it,'' Mabel offered.

''Maybe we can get it in the morning,'' Ronni suggested. ''She'll be all right with me for tonight.''

''We can move the bed up close to the wall in this room,'' Mabel told her, leading the three of them into one of the bedrooms. Instead of flicking the switch to the ceiling fixture, she turned on a small brass lamp sitting on the nightstand between the twin beds. In no time, both beds were rearranged so that together they formed one large one against the wall. While Ronni turned back the covers, Mabel fetched two more pillows from the closet.

''Maybe if you put these along the side, she won't roll off,'' she suggested, aligning the pillows lengthwise after Logan had gently deposited Steffie on the bed.

''I'm sure she'll be fine until I lie down with her,'' Ronni said softly.

''Which means I'd better get the suitcases so we can all get to bed,'' Logan stated in a low voice.

''You wait here with the baby and I'll go get that milk for you,'' Mabel insisted in a whisper.

During the few minutes they were gone, Ronni casually surveyed the apartment. Like Logan's house, it had only one bathroom, which meant they would be sharing, but at least now that Logan had his own bedroom she wouldn't have to worry about getting up in the night and running into him asleep on the couch. The apartment itself seemed less intimate than his house, a feeling that disappeared the minute he came back inside.

As he carried in her suitcases, she wondered how long she would be staying with him. Some of her uncertainty must have shown. After setting the luggage in the bedroom, he took her hands in his.

"I wish I could erase that frightened look from your face," he whispered.

It felt so good to have his concern, his gentleness. She wondered what he would say if he knew she wanted nothing better than to curl up in his arms and retreat from the world. She wished now she hadn't made such a fuss over his being an agent. But the truth was, she had hoped his interest in her had been responsible for his offer to help them.

She was attracted to Logan McNeil in a way she'd never thought it would be possible to be attracted to a man, and during their drive from Miami, she'd found herself tempted to tell him she wanted him to care about her, not simply feel responsible for her. If there was a frightened expression on her face, it was because being with him was a danger—a danger to her heart.

She was saved from having to say anything by the appearance of Mabel, who brought not only a carton of milk, but a plate of cinnamon rolls, as well. If the older woman hadn't looked so tired, Ronni would have invited her to stay awhile. The air between her and Logan had become charged with emotions she wasn't sure she was ready to face. But after slipping the milk in the refrigerator, Mabel said good-night and Ronni knew she was going to have to face being alone with him.

She told herself they really weren't alone. Steffie was in the other room. Then she looked at him and remembered what it felt like to be kissed by him and she shivered.

Logan mistook the shiver for fear. "I'm going to keep you safe, Ronni. Both of you."

"I know you will," she said softly.

He walked over to a wooden cabinet in the corner of the living room and slid open the door to reveal several glass decanters. "Why don't you let me pour you a brandy? It'll help you sleep."

Ronni didn't object, sinking down onto the leather sofa while Logan filled two glasses with the amber liquid. "This is a nice place," she said, glancing around the room.

"It belongs to Mabel's son, Josh, my old college roommate. He uses it as a winter retreat when he needs to get away from the snowy cold in Maine."

"How long do you think we'll be here?" she asked when he handed her a snifter of brandy.

"It should only be a matter of days before the government uncovers Peter's conspirators." He sat down beside her. "I've been in contact with a couple of our agents overseas and I'm expecting to hear something shortly."

"Does the FBI know we're here?"

Logan shook his head. "No one does, not even the senator. I think it's better that way—at least until we can figure out what it is those men wanted from you. What I'd like to do first thing tomorrow is go over all your recent conversations with Peter, and hopefully something you'll tell me will give us a clue to what it is they're after."

Ronni pushed the hair back off of her forehead with a tired hand. "We can do that, Logan, but I honestly don't think it'll help. Peter and I haven't exactly had lengthy telephone conversations recently. And when we did talk, it was usually to argue over our divorce agreement."

"Until either the feds or my contacts come up with something, it's the best we can do."

She sipped the brandy, letting it warm her insides. "Tell me something, Logan. What causes people to become traitors? As many faults as Peter had, I'm still having trouble understanding why he would do something like this."

Logan shrugged. "There could be any number of reasons, but I'd say the number one lure is money. Unfortunately trading secrets can be very profitable. Was Peter in debt?"

"Probably not more than any other person, although I do know that he had a Swiss bank account. I came across it one day when I was cleaning."

"That doesn't surprise me. As for the other reasons, often the people recruiting spies will look for someone with an alcohol or drug problem, or someone who's dissatisfied with a job."

"Peter had a lot of problems, but as far I know, he was never into drugs. And he seemed to get along all right with his employer, although he always seemed to resent authority." Ronni swirled the brandy in her glass pensively. "He often talked about getting even. I just never thought I'd be the one he wanted to get even with." She couldn't prevent the shudder that overtook her.

"You should get to bed," Logan said, taking the half-empty glass from her. "Listen to me, Ronni." He helped her to her feet so that she was facing him. "You're safe here. No one, and I repeat, no one, knows where you are. You can trust me."

"I do trust you, Logan. And I'm sorry about running away. It seems so foolish now...especially the way I did it." She could feel her skin warm at the recollection of catching him naked in the shower. He smiled, and she knew that he remembered those few minutes, too.

"By the way, where are all of my pants?"

She dropped her gaze to the baggy blue shorts, and felt a giddy sort of guilt that made her want to giggle. "They're in the back of the pickup in a large green trash bag."

"Great. That means I won't have to go out in public like this again." He managed a big foolish grin. "I have to confess, it was rather humbling for an ex-agent to be caught not only with his pants down but with his own gun."

"I can't believe I did it. I'd never even held a real gun in my hands, let alone point it at someone," she confessed.

Logan laughed.

"What's so funny?" she asked.

"That gun wasn't loaded. I haven't used it in years. Contrary to what the public believes, agents seldom carry guns."

"If you knew it wasn't loaded, why didn't you try to stop me?"

He shrugged. "I guess because at that point I still wasn't convinced you weren't working with Peter." He paused, then added with a half grin, "And there was the possibility that you had found the bullets."

"You mean we stopped those KGB agents with an empty gun?" Again she shuddered, and a wave of weariness washed over her. "I was fortunate you were there," she said softly, her eyes misting over with emotion. "And it doesn't matter why you were there. I'm just grateful you were. I don't know how I'll ever be able to thank you."

"I thought we'd already settled that."

He encircled her in his arms, and the space between them disappeared. "It's called trust."

Then he lowered his head until his lips were only inches from hers, and she could feel his breath caressing her cheek.

She wrapped her arms around his waist and in the seconds before his lips found hers, her eyes looked trustingly into his, telling him much more than words could ever say. Need, desire and promise were all there, and Logan could see that she wanted him the way he wanted her.

His lips moved slowly over hers, softly at first, as though he were reassuring her that he'd never hurt her. For Ronni, it was a kiss that seemed to warm every tiny hollow in her body, yet at the same time reminded her there were places that needed more than warmth; they needed his touch. She moved her arms upward and slid them around his neck, pulling him closer to her as those other places in her body began to ache with her longing for him.

Not quite sure whose body was trembling, Logan responded to the suggestive thrust of her body against his, tightening his hold on her with hands that pulled her intimately against him. Her mouth opened beneath his, and the kiss was no longer sweet but provocative, echoing the hunger they were both feeling for each other.

A groan came from deep in his throat as Ronni let her tongue find his, and instinctively she moved against him in an intimate invitation. Had he wanted to, Logan wouldn't have been able to resist. This time he heard no warning bells, only the wild beating of his heart. Her skin was warm and delectably sweet as he feverishly kissed her neck and her ear, inhaling the ambrosial scent that was hers alone.

Ronni whimpered as his hand inched its way downward and found a burgeoning breast. Through the thin cotton of her shirt, he caressed the beaded tip, while she exhaled a shuddering sigh. When he slipped his hand inside her blouse, her knees threatened to buckle.

"If you keep kissing me like this, I might just melt away," she said breathlessly, her eyes smoky with passion.

Logan eased himself down onto the sofa, deftly pulling Ronni on top of him so that she was cradled in his arms. Then his mouth was crushing hers, and soon they were no longer sitting but lying side by side, legs entwined on the sofa.

"I want you, Ronni," he said thickly.

"I want you, too."

Her voice was whisper soft, yet radiated sensuality. Her admission made him forget she was still legally Mrs. Peter Lang and that she was using a dead woman's identity. It made him forget that she could have been Andy's lover and that the FBI suspected her of being a spy. It made him forget that she could be a honey trap. Right now all she was was a woman he wanted to be a part of, a woman he needed to be a part of him.

While fingers frantically fumbled with buttons and zippers, Logan thought of nothing but what it was going to be like to love her. His breath nearly stopped when her fingers found the hardness of his desire. The last vestiges of self-control were slipping away and Logan's breathing became hoarse as his body moved in an involuntary response to her exploring hands. Sounds of love were all around them . . . the sound of clothes being removed . . . the sound of lips trailing kisses across warm flesh . . . the sound of sighs created by caresses . . . the sound of Steffie crying.

As if they both became aware of her whimpering at the same time, Logan and Ronni raised their heads. "Steffie's crying," he said aloud, as though he couldn't quite believe it himself.

"Yes."

Logan didn't think he'd ever heard the word uttered with such anguish. For a couple of seconds, they stared at each other, then both laughed. "I'll be right back," she whispered before getting up from the couch.

Logan slowly sat upright, taking a long, deep gulp of air as he watched Ronni walk out of the room. Although it was only a few minutes, it seemed like an eternity before she returned. Only she wasn't alone. Steffie was in her arms, her face red from crying, her eyes narrowed to tiny slits as she came from the dark into light. Logan silently groaned.

"I think she needs a drink of water," Ronni explained, her eyes telling him she was just as disappointed as he was that Steffie was awake.

Logan remained seated on the sofa, waiting while Ronni took the child into the kitchen. He heard the cupboard open, the faucet being turned on, the soothing words of comfort—and Steffie's stubborn whining. The two of them came back through the living room, Ronni looking frustrated, Steffie looking wide-awake.

"I'm going to put her back down," Ronni told him as they passed by.

Logan nodded. "I'll wait for you."

"Ba?" Steffie stretched an arm out toward Logan, who returned the gesture saying, "Bye-Bye."

The two of them disappeared into the bedroom, and almost immediately he heard Steffie begin to cry. It wasn't a sound one could easily ignore, and after a few minutes, he got up and walked into Ronni's room.

"Is she all right?" he asked from the doorway.

"I think it's the strange bed. I'm afraid she's not going to fall back to sleep unless I lie down with her," she said apologetically.

Logan didn't think he'd ever been more disappointed about anything in his lifetime. But Steffie was scrambling across the bed, gurgling and smiling at the sight of him, dissolving his frustration into an almost comic relief. He leaned over and planted kisses on both Steffie's and Ronni's cheeks, then tossed a "Sweet dreams," over his shoulder and sauntered out of the room.

CHAPTER TEN

"LOOK WHAT I FOUND. Not only did Mabel have an old crib in the garage, but this high chair, as well," Logan told Ronni when she waltzed into the kitchen the next morning with Steffie on her hip. He proudly displayed the worn but sturdy wooden high chair he'd just finished scrubbing, tossing his sponge into a bucket of soapy water. "It's missing the pad, but I stuck a towel in here so she won't slide out." He rapped on the wooden seat hidden beneath a blue terry-cloth hand towel, then slid the high chair up to the table.

He was dressed in khaki trousers and a salmon knit shirt that was unbuttoned at his throat, and to Ronni he'd never looked more attractive. "That'll be fine," she said, suddenly self-conscious about what had happened the night before.

Logan reached for Steffie, who willingly went into his arms and received a "Good morning" and a kiss smack-dab in the center of her nose, producing a gleeful sound from the toddler. Ronni looked on enviously.

As though he could read her mind, Logan asked, "Does Mom want a good morning kiss, too?"

She laughed softly. "Not on my nose."

"What about right here?" he asked, trailing his thumb across her lower lip.

No part of him touched her except for his thumb and his warm breath, yet she trembled. Before she could answer, his lips captured hers briefly—too briefly for Ronni, who after last night knew how long a kiss could be.

"Good morning, Ronni," he said with a lazy drawl.

"Good morning," she repeated, swaying slightly as she folded her hands behind her back.

"You smell good... like apples and sunshine," he told her, his breath just a bit more irregular than it had been. "Did you sleep well?" he asked, turning away from her to slip Steffie into the high chair.

"Did you?" she countered. The two words had the power of a magnet, drawing his attention away from Steffie to her.

"I had a little trouble falling asleep," he confessed with a wry smile. For several moments neither one of them spoke, as though silently commiserating about what hadn't happened the night before. Steffie's fussing brought them both back to the present. "Can she have some of this?" he asked, reaching for the box of cereal on the table.

"I'm going to give her some oatmeal, but she can munch on those until I get it ready," Ronni told him, moving over to the refrigerator.

Logan sprinkled a small mound of the toasted O's on the high chair tray. "It's probably a good thing Steffie awoke when she did last night," he said, pulling out a chair and sitting down at the table.

Of all the things he could have said, those were not the words Ronni expected or wanted to hear. She masked her disappointment, however, focusing her attention on the task before her. "You could be right," she said evenly, despite feeling very uneven at the moment.

"We shouldn't be rushing into anything we both might end up regretting."

There was silence except for Steffie's soft familiar hum—the one that accompanied her munching on the cereal. Ronni emptied the packet of instant oatmeal into the bowl, grateful now that she hadn't gone and told him she'd nearly knocked on his door last night after Steffie had fallen asleep.

"You're vulnerable right now, and I'm probably the last man on earth you should be getting involved with," he continued in a tone that sounded as though he were not only trying to convince her, but himself, too.

"It's all right, Logan," she managed to croak, furiously mixing the required amount of water into the cereal before sticking it in the microwave. "You don't need to let me down easy. I understand." Although she really didn't. For the first time in her life she felt as though she might have found a man who was right for her, only to have him tell her he was wrong. Her eyes filled with tears, and before she could stop them, they trickled down her cheeks. When she turned, he was standing next to her, having crept up behind her. She tried to move away from him, but he caught her by the shoulders.

"You don't understand," he said, brushing a silky strand of hair away from her face. With a sense of urgency, he pulled her into his arms. "I'm sorry, Ronni. I don't want to hurt you."

"You're not," she mumbled into his shirtfront, trying to push out of his arms, but he held her forcefully, possessively.

"Look at me," he ordered, and she lifted her tear-stained face to his. "All I'm saying is that maybe we should take it slower. We don't have to come to a complete stop." The tenderness in his expression held her more tightly than the brute strength of his arms. "You've been through so much these past few days, right now I think we should concentrate on getting things back to normal. Why don't we take things slow and easy?"

"Slow and easy," Ronni agreed, forcing herself to ignore the way her mouth ached for his.

As though he knew what she was thinking, he gave her a quick, hard kiss, then eased himself away from her, putting some distance between the two of them in the small kitchen. When the timer on the microwave chimed, he said, "Why don't you get Steffie fed and then after breakfast we'll work at normal, okay?"

During the next few days, Ronni was surprised at how normal everything did seem. It was almost as though she and Steffie had planned a vacation and met Logan and Mabel along the way. Together the four of them would walk to the ocean, which was only a few blocks away, with Logan carrying Steffie on his shoulders. At the beach he'd build castles in the sand that Steffie would mischievously demolish with her shovel and a gleeful shriek.

Other than an occasional phone call from a public telephone booth, Logan gave no indication that he was involved in solving a spy case. After the first morning, when he'd questioned her extensively about her relationship with Peter, he hadn't spoken of the defection or any of the possible consequences. He was acting as though they were on some sort of holiday. They spent days at the beach and evenings playing three-handed cribbage with Mabel.

Ronni was grateful for the older woman's presence, for she enjoyed the stories Mabel told about Logan and her son, Josh. Ronni could tell that Logan was uncomfortable being the subject of conversation, but short of taping Mabel's mouth shut, there wasn't much he could do. Despite Mabel's frail appearance, she was a lot like Ronni's mother—strong willed.

Mabel's presence also helped alleviate the tension between Ronni and Logan, a tension that seemed to be growing with each passing day as Ronni found herself becoming more anxious about her feelings for him. Living together provided an intimacy neither one could deny, yet he managed to keep his distance from her, while an inner battle constantly waged in her between wanting and not wanting him. The better she got to know him, the more she was attracted to him. She often found herself wondering if it was because he was someone she could lean on, which only complicated her feelings for him. If there was one thing she had learned from her marriage to Peter, it was not to be dependent on a man.

At first she'd found Logan's attentiveness reassuring, and she'd wanted him to be the rock she could cling to while she floundered in uncertainty. But as she became more dependent on him, she began to worry that she was enjoying having him take charge of her life. The thought was frightening, since it reminded her of her relationship with Peter and the control he'd exerted over her. She wanted to tell Logan how she felt, only the problem was, how could she explain it to him when she didn't understand it herself?

Her frustration finally surfaced one evening after she'd bathed Steffie and put her to bed. Instead of telling Logan her fears, she confronted him on a totally different issue.

As usual, Logan could tell by a glance at her face she was upset about something. He'd been sitting at the table, doing the *New York Times* crossword puzzle, when she'd swept through the kitchen, banging cupboard doors along the way.

"What's up?" he asked innocently.

She stopped banging long enough to prop her hip against the table and say, "You don't fold your towels correctly."

"I beg your pardon?" Logan looked up, pencil poised.

"In the bathroom." She cocked her head. "The towels . . . when they're wet. You fold them over at least four times before you hang them up and then they don't dry."

"At least I hang them up. Isn't that better than leaving them in a pile on the floor?" He grinned, then realized she was not amused.

Without another word, she spun around and vanished out of the kitchen. Logan followed her, easily overtaking her shorter stride. He grabbed her by the hand and pulled her into the bathroom.

Good-naturedly he said, "If you show me the *proper* way to fold a towel, I'll make sure it won't happen again." Once more he tried the grin. Again it failed.

"Just forget it," she retorted somewhat sullenly. "It's not important."

"If it wasn't important you wouldn't have brought it up." He still had a hold of her hand, and was gently massaging her palm with his thumb. He could feel the tension in her. "Go pour us a couple of brandies and I'll refold my towels."

She pulled her hand out of his. "Will you please stop telling me what to do? You're taking charge of my life as though you were my... my..." she stammered.

"Husband?" Logan supplied, arching one eyebrow.

There was a gleam in his eye that dared her to deny the sexual attraction between them. She did.

"No, my father," she shot back stubbornly, stalking out of the bathroom.

Logan followed her into the living room. "There's not a paternal bone in this body where you're concerned."

"Then quit hovering over me like I'm a child who needs to be told what to do."

"I'm not trying to tell you what to do," he denied calmly. "I'm trying to protect you."

"Protect?" she repeated. "Do you realize that when we're not in this apartment, you don't let us out of your sight for a single minute? If anyone even glances at Steffie, you look as though you're ready to sprout fangs. Sometimes I have to peek over my shoulder when I go use the ladies' room just to make sure you haven't followed me in there. Logan, I appreciate your trying to protect us, but you're suffocating me."

Unbidden came the memory of a little girl with blond curls being enveloped by the flames of the explosion. He winced, then turned away from Ronni, the color slowly draining from his face.

"Logan, what is it?" she asked, seeing him sink down onto the couch, his head in his hands. She dropped down on her knees beside him, propping herself at his feet. "I'm sorry. I didn't mean to sound ungrateful," she apologized, placing a hand on his thigh. "It's just that after being married to a very possessive man who tried to run my life for me, I'm not very good at dealing with someone wanting to protect me."

"If I seem overprotective, it's only because I'm trying not to make the same mistake twice." He raked a hand through his hair.

"What mistake, Logan?"

For several moments she thought he wasn't going to tell her, for that neutral expression of his was back in place. But then he said, "The explosion I told you about—the one where I injured my eye—also caused the death of a five-year-old child. A little girl named Michelle Donet."

"And you feel responsible for her death?"

He made a guttural sound. "I was responsible."

"But I thought you said it was an accident?"

He made another derisive sound. "'Carelessness' would have been a better word."

There was no mistaking the emotion in his voice. It was pain—the pain of a man who couldn't let go of guilt, and it brought an ache to Ronni's chest. "Tell me what happened, Logan," she gently urged.

"Ever hear of a dead drop?" he asked. When she shook her head, he continued. "That's when an agent will leave something in a prearranged spot to be recovered by another agent. It's a way of passing information, which is what I thought I was doing when I arranged to pick up a package in a park in the south of France. What I didn't know was that the agent who was passing the intelligence information wasn't only working for the U.S. The package I was supposed to retrieve carried explosives, courtesy of another foreign government." He shook his head at the painful memory.

"And the little girl?" she carefully prodded.

"I had arranged for the exchange to take place in a newly remodeled section of the park that wasn't yet open to the public. And it was deserted, except for one little girl who'd somehow managed to get into the closed area. Before I had a chance to recover the package, her ball rolled under the bench where my package sat. When she went to fetch her ball, she bumped the package, triggering an explosive that was meant for me."

"Oh, Logan, I'm sorry." The words felt so inadequate, but she didn't know what else to say.

"I tried to reach for her, but it was like grabbing thin air. I couldn't save her from the fingers of fire that seemed to swallow her up right before my eyes." He rubbed his hands across his face as though he were trying to erase the memories.

"Surely you can't blame yourself for her death, Logan?"

He shot her a look that told her he did. "I should have been more careful. As I look back now, I see so many things I could have done differently," he reflected, staring absently into space. "I should have figured it out that he was a double agent."

"You were betrayed, Logan. It's sad that an innocent child was killed, but you can't blame yourself." She wanted to ease his pain, but she felt as helpless as someone trying to put out a forest fire with a bucket of water. "You have to accept that it was an accident."

"I want to, but I keep seeing that angelic face." He shook his head in remorse.

"Is that why you quit the Agency?" she asked.

He sneered. "Quit? They retired me. Oh, I could have had some desk job at headquarters, but my fieldwork days were over. Now I'm not even sure if I'd go back if my eyesight were to return." He absently rubbed several fingers across his jaw. "Sometimes I wonder if subconsciously I didn't slip up because I was tired of living on the dark side of humanity."

"You didn't enjoy intelligence work?"

He considered her question seriously before he answered. "At one time I did." He shrugged. "Maybe one can only do that type of work for so long. It's a murky world, one of deception and betrayal."

"Whatever made you go into it?"

"That was the senator's doing. I guess I had always wanted a career in the government. Politics wasn't for me, so I chose a field where I thought I could make a difference. Save lives, protect our freedom."

He sounded like a disillusioned little boy, and Ronni couldn't help but respond. "You *were* protecting our freedom, and now, you're protecting me and Steffie," she told him, reaching for his hands.

He sighed heavily. "The problem isn't protecting you and Steffie."

He looked at her, and for once she didn't see the unfaltering assurance that was usually there. Gently she asked, "Then what is the problem?"

"I'm afraid I've developed an obsession."

"Are you obsessed with protecting us?" she asked in a husky voice.

Slowly he trailed the tip of his finger across her cheek until he found her mouth. It had been three days since he'd kissed her, yet her lips felt moist, as though his mouth had just brushed hers. He wanted to feel those lips again, and he knew that she wanted it, too.

He leaned forward until his face was only inches from her. "I'm obsessed with wanting you."

The words caressed her cheeks, like silken whispers of longing. "That doesn't sound like a bad obsession to me," she murmured. Her lips parted in anticipation of his kiss, but it didn't happen.

With a groan, he slumped back against the couch and dropped his arm across his eyes. "It's a fantastic obsession," he said in an almost agonized drawl. "Except we agreed to take things slow and easy."

She closed her eyes, wanting to scream in frustration. For days she'd been fighting her feelings for him, denying the longing that swept through her whenever he touched her or came near her. How could he even think slow and easy after so much had happened between them? Infuriated by his self-control, she wanted to yell at him, *I don't give a damn about what we agreed to do. I* need *to be loved by you.* However, she wouldn't have been able to bear the humiliation should he reject her a second time. Instead she swallowed her frustration and slowly got to her feet.

"It's late. I think I'll turn in."

She paused, giving him the opportunity to say something, but he remained silent, and her hopes that he would change his mind and ask her to stay with him were dashed when he finally uttered, "Good night."

She crept into the bedroom, where Steffie lay sleeping in the green glow of the numerals on the digital clock radio. Instead of undressing right away, Ronni sat down on the end of the bed, mulling over her conversation with Logan. She'd known that he was self-conscious about his eye, but he'd always seemed so sure of himself; she never expected that he would lack self-confidence. For the first time since they'd been together, she felt as if she were the stronger one, and it gave her hope that he might need her just as much as she needed him. She wished now that she hadn't been so quick to say good-night. Hoping that he would still be up, she tiptoed out of the bedroom, only to find the living room empty. It took her a couple of seconds before she realized that he was in the shower—his second shower of the day.

A smile inched over Ronni's face at the thought. She hurried toward the door and, before she could change her mind, turned the knob. This time when she entered the bathroom, there was no gun in her hand. Unlike the house in Key West, where there had been only a shower stall with a plastic curtain, this house had a tub with a glass enclosure. Billowing clouds of steam rose above the top of the panels, but she didn't notice, for her eyes were drawn to the male silhouette discernible through the tinted glass.

Softly she closed the door, then leaned back against it, mesmerized by the blurred naked image. Arms lifted, hands rubbed, and Ronni stood there staring, And absorbing. And appreciating. And anticipating. While she watched, she peeled off her clothes. Hers did not join his neatly folded ones on the vanity, but fell in a heap on the floor. She placed her watch beside his, then took a deep breath.

With a trembling excitement, she quickly closed the distance between her and the tub. Heart hammering, skin tingling, she slid the glass door open and was greeted by a rush of steam. At the movement of the glass panel Logan swung around, and Ronni's breath caught in her throat.

Soapsuds were coasting down the sleek sheen of tanned flesh like icing on a cake. Wet, his hair looked almost black, but it was his eyes that were responsible for the fluttering in her stomach. After their initial look of surprise, they had darkened with another emotion, and were making a thorough assessment of every inch of her naked body. Whether or not he saw out of his right eye didn't matter; she felt as though he did, for both eyes were blazing with desire.

A fine mist had begun to glisten on her skin, when she heard him say, "Aren't you going to come in?"

She turned away long enough to step in behind him. Logan slid the glass door shut, then pulled her under the pulsating stream of hot water, maneuvering her so that her backside was fitted close to his front side.

"Ah! It's hot!" she exclaimed, and she wasn't only talking about the water temperature. She was wrapped so tightly in his arms she could feel the evidence of his arousal burning against her flesh.

"Too hot?" he asked, as rivulets of water ran down her breasts and his hands molded her to him.

"Uh-uh" was the only reply she was capable of uttering, for in his hands was the bar of soap, and he was gliding his lathered fingers across her swollen breasts.

Ronni leaned back against him, and his hands slid lower until she felt their circling motion on the flat of her stomach. She closed her eyes at the exquisite sensations his large hands created as they worked a magic of their own on her skin. He pressed kisses into her neck, nipping at her earlobe before saying, "Does this mean you don't want to take it slow and easy?"

"Uh-uh," she moaned, shivering as his hands slid even lower. "Do you?" She heard the bar of soap drop, then he was turning her around to face him.

"I just want to take you," he said, before crushing her mouth with his. As they kissed, she pressed hard against him, wrapping her arms around his neck.

"Here?" She managed to pull her lips away from his long enough to ask the question.

Logan's answer was to place his hands around her trim waist, then with one swift movement lift her up. Her legs slid around his waist as he guided her down onto him. Holding tightly to him, she cried out his name in a moan of pleasant surprise at the ease at which their bodies were united.

In her mind she had already lived this moment, but never had she expected such exquisite joy as her body moved with his, establishing a private rhythm that only the two of them would ever share. Deliberately, intently, they moved together with a hunger they both understood, a hunger they couldn't have leashed had they wanted to.

It was dazzling, it was delightful, and it was all too soon done. Although they had tumbled over the edge of ecstasy, neither one wanted to still the shuddering, and it was with spent sighs that their heartbeats slowed.

He nuzzled his face in her wet breasts, savoring the sweetness that was threatening to fade. Ronni felt her feet touch the bottom of the tub, and she groaned.

"What's wrong? Did I hurt you?" Logan asked as his hand snaked around her to turn off the faucet.

She opened her eyes and touched his face with a kind of wonder. "Uh-uh. I just don't want it to be over."

He smiled, a devastating smile that held more than a hint of wickedness. "Did you forget? I'm the one who said we were going to take this slow and easy." He slid open the glass doors and reached for a large fluffy towel, then began to dry her skin, smoothing the towel over her shoulders and down her arms. When he reached her breasts, the tips hardened. "They don't think it's over yet, either," he said, pressing a kiss on each nipple.

He continued to towel her dry, arousing all sorts of feelings that never really had a chance to be put to rest. She gasped as the towel slid across her bare thigh, then journeyed up and down each leg. Weak and trembling, she watched him take several quick slashes at his own wet body before dropping the towel on the floor.

"Now it's time for *slow and easy*," he said huskily, then picked her up and carried her into his bedroom.

IT WASN'T STEFFIE who woke Ronni the next morning, but Logan, as he attempted to slip from under her without disturbing her sleep.

But after the night they'd shared, even asleep Ronni was in sync with him and she stirred the minute the warmth of his shoulder disappeared. "Where are you going?" she murmured, pressing her hand against his bare back as he sat up.

He leaned over on one elbow and smiled down at her. "Just thought I'd better test my legs. I'm not sure I can still walk."

A lazy, dreamy grin lit up her face. "It was wonderful, wasn't it?"

Logan kissed her twice, first on the lips, then on her breast, where he pillowed his head. "Unbelievably wonderful. I still can't believe you came into the shower."

"Actually I was going to show you how to fold your towels, but you insisted on showing me soap tricks," she teased, her fingers rumpling his dark hair.

He chuckled and positioned himself so that he had a hand on either side of her head and was looking into her eyes. "I have no scruples when it comes to finding naked women in my shower...." He lowered his face even closer and whispered, "Or in my bed."

"You're not sorry, are you?"

"Does this feel like a remorseful man?" he asked, shifting so that she could feel his arousal.

She laughed seductively as she felt desire flare—loving the power she had over him—loving the power he had over her.

"What about you? We didn't exactly act like two responsible adults," he said softly.

"If you're worried about any possible consequences, you don't need to be. I'm on the Pill," she told him with an understanding smile, while her hands, as if long familiar with his body, were finding his erogenous zones. "Now wouldn't it be wonderful if we didn't have to get out of this bed all day?"

"Ummm-hmmm. It would be," he agreed, his breath growing ragged. "I'm surprised your daughter isn't awake."

"Her biological clock is a little off schedule—probably because of all the moving around."

"Your biological clock sounds perfect," he said, pressing his ear to her breast.

"I've never felt this good—not in my entire life," she said when he looked up at her.

"Me, neither," he admitted, gazing into her eyes. "Who said obsessions can't be healthy?" He gave her one more long, satisfying kiss before hauling himself out of bed.

"Do we really have to get up?" she asked with a catlike stretch, admiring his naked form as he moved around the bedroom in search of some clothing.

"We promised Mabel we'd take her to the botanical gardens this morning," Logan reminded her, slipping into a pair of pants. "She wanted to be there when they opened."

"Then the botanical gardens it'll be," Ronni declared, wrapping the sheet around her body toga-style as she marched past him, a crooked grin on her face. "We'll be the first ones in line."

As soon as Ronni glanced outdoors she doubted there would even be a line. A heavy rain relentlessly pelted the streets, and after talking to Mabel, Logan decided they would save the gardens for another day. He did, however, suggest that he and Ronni take Steffie for a drive. When they stopped at a gas station, Ronni knew their outing was serving a dual purpose—Logan needed to use the pay phone. There was no telephone in the apartment they were occupying, and she could only guess that to protect Mabel, he never used hers. He still hadn't told

Ronni if he'd heard anything about Peter, and she realized that she could no longer pretend the entire problem would go away if she refused to think about it.

"Are you going to call the hospital?" she asked as he parked the truck.

He paused with his hand on the door handle. It was the first time in several days that she'd mentioned the hospital and it reminded him that she had feelings for the senator's son. "There hasn't been any change in Andrew's condition. I would have told you if there had been," he said, an edge to his voice.

"I know that." She saw the defensive look on his face and wondered why the subject of Andrew always created such tension between them. "Maybe I'm just feeling a little guilty. I mean, Andrew's lying in some hospital, fighting for his life, and I'm here with you in what seems to be almost paradise."

The fact that she'd alluded to the night before as "almost paradise" made Logan want to take her straight back home to bed. But her concern for Andrew raised the same old questions in his mind. Automatically his eyes flew to Steffie's red head. Had Ronni found "almost paradise" in Andrew's arms, too? After last night he could no longer ignore the questions he had concerning her relationship with Andy. He needed answers and he needed them now.

"If Andrew is fighting for his life, it's probably because of his own making. And before you waste any more energy feeling sorry for him, maybe you ought to consider that he could be one of the reasons Steffie was nearly kidnapped." The words came out more harshly than he'd intended.

"You have heard something, haven't you?" she accused.

"No, I haven't. And I don't have any concrete evidence, only my gut reaction. But if I'm right, I have to tell you, Ronni, it disturbs the hell out of me to think of your relationship with him."

"And what if you're wrong?" she countered, her voice rising.

Once again her defense of Andrew irritated him like salt on an open wound. "Well, I don't think I am, but even if Andy is innocent, that still doesn't make it easy for me to accept your relationship with him." At this point he didn't care if the whole world knew he was jealous.

"My relationship with him?" she repeated. "What could you possibly object to in my relationship with Andrew?"

"You need to ask me that after last night?"

She looked out the rain-splattered window and quietly said, "Logan, don't do this."

"Don't do what?"

"Don't try to control every aspect of my life for me. I've already been in a marriage where my husband tried to tell me who I could and could not have as friends. I won't let anyone control me that way ever again."

"Friends? Is that how you describe your relationship with Andrew?"

"What else could it possibly be?" She gazed at him, totally perplexed.

"What else, indeed!" he answered sarcastically.

"Logan, you know Andrew." She dismissed his statement with a laugh.

"And according to Senator Potter, you knew him quite well yourself," he retorted.

"I don't know what it is you're accusing me of, but I don't like the sound of your voice." The tilt of her head challenged him.

Logan drummed his fingertips on the steering wheel. When he finally spoke, he looked not at Ronni but Steffie. "One of the reasons Senator Potter asked me to investigate you was that he wanted to find out if Steffie was his grandchild."

Her blue eyes widened. "Steffie his granddaughter? Didn't you tell him that's highly unlikely."

"Highly unlikely? Andrew's got pictures of the two of you all over his house. You were living with him at the time of Steffie's conception. What's so unlikely about someone assuming the child is Andrew's?" he argued.

"You may be a friend of the senator's, but you don't know Andrew if you need to ask me that question." Seeing his puzzled frown, she said, "Logan, Andrew is gay. When I moved in with him, he was involved in a relationship with another man."

Logan was momentarily stunned by the information. After a lengthy silence, he finally said, "I didn't know."

"Neither does his father. Andrew has always been concerned that it might somehow affect the senator's political career," she said quietly. "I thought you would have known, since the two of you were once close."

"Not *that* close," he said under his breath. He sat staring out the front window. "I can't imagine how Doc is going to accept this."

"Does he have to find out?"

"Wicklund and Mahoney might not be the smoothest investigators, but they are thorough."

"Andrew's private life is his own business," Ronni declared in his defense. "He's never hurt anybody with his actions."

"Not that you know of," Logan added grimly.

"Why are you so critical of him?" she demanded.

"Why are you always defending him?" he countered.

"Because I happen to believe Andrew is a good person. When my reconciliation with Peter ended in an ugly scene, he was the one person who was there for me. He's been like a brother to me, and more of a father to Steffie than Peter ever wanted to be. And right now I'm having a very hard time accepting that he could be anything but a friend of ours." Her voice broke and a trembling hand covered eyes wet with unshed tears.

"Look—" he leaned over Steffie's car seat and pulled Ronni's hand from her eyes "—I don't want him to be guilty any more than you do. And if there's any way I can prove he's innocent, I will." He raised her fingers to his lips. "You wait here while I make a couple of phone calls, okay?"

Ronni nodded, holding back her tears as Logan climbed out of the truck and dashed into the public phone booth. He'd parked as close as possible so he could keep his eye on Ronni and Steffie. First he tried calling the senator. When there was no answer, Logan felt relieved. He knew it was going to be difficult to keep information from his mentor, and he wasn't ready to discuss the reason he was certain Steffie was not the senator's granddaughter.

He had better luck with his second phone call, which was to one of his agency contacts. "What do you have for me, Max?" Logan asked, keeping his eye on the pickup.

"Your suspicions about a honey trap were right, Logan." The voice came as sharp as a lightning bolt and Logan felt a prickly sensation along the back of his neck. He wouldn't have been able to keep from staring at Ronni's face had he wanted to.

"It seems our Peter Lang took himself a mistress—a Russian female agent who went by the American name Holly

Conrad." Logan closed his eyes and breathed a sigh of relief. "Whether or not he knew she was an enemy agent at the time he started fooling around with her is debatable. At any rate, she's one of the reasons for his defection. But I think the main reason was his son."

"His son?" Logan frowned.

"Yeah. It seems Holly—or I should say Svetlana—was pregnant when she was ordered back to her country. Lang was promised the three of them would be together in Little America. As a linguist, he'll be useful to them there, teaching all those Russkies how to speak like homegrown Americans."

"How old is the baby?" Logan asked.

"Less than a year. Pretty good leverage to use to get Lang to defect, wouldn't you say?"

"Yeah, if he needed to be coerced," he said sarcastically. "Do you know how long he's been working for them?"

"Intelligence estimates maybe as long as five years. At least, that's how long it's been since he was first seen with Svetlana."

Logan glanced over to where Ronni sat looking as though she couldn't hurt a single soul if she wanted to, and he felt an eruption of anger at Peter Lang. How could any man have cheated on someone like her? "What about the public plea for his wife and daughter?"

"Probably staged by the KGB. Word's out Lang left some valuable information behind. She must be in possession of it."

"She doesn't have the foggiest idea what it could be."

"It's got to be something big. They've got their top agents working on this one."

"I'll check with Doc and see if he's come up with anything. And Max, thanks." Logan replace the receiver with a grimace. In less than an hour he'd heard enough to make his stomach feel like the inside of a volcano. Andy was gay and Ronni's husband was an adulterer. How could he relay such information to two people he cared about? The senator was hundreds of miles away; Ronni was several feet from him. He was going to have to tell her something.

He ran the short distance back to the pickup and quickly climbed inside. He didn't start the engine, but turned to look at her.

His concern for her must have shown on his face, for she said solemnly, "You've heard something, haven't you?"

"There's no news from the hospital, but I did find out some information about Peter," he told her honestly. "Have you ever heard of Little America?"

Ronni shook her head.

"It's an intelligence training school in the Ukraine where Soviet spies are taught to think and behave like Americans. It's a model of a small American city, complete with department stores and fast-food restaurants. Newspapers are American, so is the currency, and English is the only language spoken, so that when the trainees are sent to the U.S., they'll know how to talk and act like Americans. Peter's going to be an instructor there."

"Peter a teacher?" She blinked at him, surprised. "That's rather ironic."

"Why do you say that?"

"He always scoffed at the teaching profession—at all levels. One of the reasons he went to work for Bartron was that he said there was no money in teaching."

"It could be that as an instructor in Little America he'll hold a position of honor. Although he's going to discover that honor has different meanings to different people."

"He's always been the kind of man who's done what he wants, when he wants. It's hard to imagine him in such a rigid environment," she said pensively. "What if he doesn't like it and wants to come back?"

"You mean redefect?" At her nod, he said, "There have been instances where we've traded jailed operatives for our own people. In Peter's case he would probably face criminal charges if he were to return to the U.S." She had a faraway expression in her eyes, and for just a brief moment he felt threatened by her feelings for another man. "Would you want him to return?"

"No."

The response came swiftly and firmly, pleasing Logan. "I don't think it's something you need to worry about. I doubt he'll be back," he told her confidently.

"I'm wondering what's going to happen with our divorce. He never signed the papers," she said unhappily.

Again Logan felt a surge of anger at Peter Lang. "It'll all work out," he said, then turned his attention to the key in the ignition.

"Is that it? Was that all you learned?"

"That's it," he lied, looking out the windshield rather than at Ronni. As they drove home, he debated whether he should have told her everything he'd found out about Peter. Even if she was through with the marriage, how would she react to learning that her husband's defection was the result of a honey trap—that it wasn't simply a case of greed driving him to become a traitor. Personally he didn't want Ronni to know that Peter had been having an affair with a Russian spy while he was married to her. Or that he'd had a son with that spy. Or that the son was the reason he'd chosen to give up his citizenship. Because if she did react strongly, he just might think she still harbored feelings for the man, and that thought was unbearable.

Parts of the puzzle were slowly falling into place, although one of the pieces he'd found today troubled him. If Peter Lang had such strong paternal feelings, why would he leave without his daughter?

CHAPTER ELEVEN

AFTER HIS CONVERSATION with Max, Logan knew that as much as he dreaded calling the senator, he had no choice. When he finally managed to reach him the following afternoon, Doc was able to confirm Max's information, and Logan learned the reason for the KGB's interest in Ronni. When Peter Lang had defected, he'd taken classified information on several strategic defense weapons. He had left behind, however, the code that would access electronic control of the weapons. According to Doc, that information was on a computer microchip stolen from Bartron. Despite Logan's assertions that Ronni knew nothing about any missing microchip, Doc wasn't convinced she wasn't somehow connected to its disappearance. Logan assured the senator that he would speak to her about it. Because of Mabel's presence, however, that wasn't possible until late that evening.

"We need to talk." He stilled Ronni's hands, which were busy clearing glasses off the kitchen table. Just minutes earlier he and Ronni had been playing cribbage there with Mabel.

"Something's bothering you, isn't it? I thought you seemed rather preoccupied during dinner." A frown transformed her serene expression into one of apprehension. "What's wrong?"

Logan wished he could tell her that everything was all right—even though he knew it wasn't. He nudged her toward the living-room sofa and pulled her down onto his lap.

"I was finally able to reach Doc this afternoon."

"And?" She looked at him expectantly.

"I know why the KGB are following you. Apparently when Peter defected, he made off with a pile of military secrets. For some reason, though, he left behind the one piece of information that would make those secrets worth anything."

"Why would he do that?" she asked, puzzled.

Logan sighed. "If only we knew the answer to that question. Right now all we do know is that the information everyone is looking for is on a programmable computer microchip that is so small it's not even easily seen with the naked eye. And from everything that's happened, you're the primary candidate for having it in your possession."

"That's ridiculous! I don't have any computer chip!" she protested. "I haven't even seen Peter since last Christmas." She dismissed the idea with a toss of her head.

"He's been back to the United States at least three or four times since Christmas, Ronni."

Surprised, she said, "I had no idea." Slowly she shook her head. "He must not have wanted us to know he was here. I can understand he didn't want to see me, but why wouldn't he want to see Steffie?"

He squeezed her hand in an effort to reassure her. "It doesn't make sense to me, either, unless he was so deep into espionage he couldn't risk it. There's a strong possibility Peter didn't obtain that information without inside help. Someone who was an expert in computer technology."

Ronni sighed. "You mean Andrew, don't you?"

"Whoever it was at Bartron, he was clever enough to prevent the theft from being discovered until after Peter defected."

She nibbled on her lower lip thoughtfully. "There's something I think you ought to know, Logan. Peter once questioned whether Steffie wasn't Andrew's child—just as the senator did."

"He didn't know Andy was gay?"

She shrugged. "Oh, he knew all right, but in his perverse mind he couldn't understand how any woman could live with a man and not sleep with him. Then, when Steffie was born with red hair, he drew his own conclusions."

"He doesn't deserve a beautiful child like Steffie," Logan told her quietly.

"No, he doesn't," she agreed, a lump starting to form in her throat. "And I can't tell you how many times I wished he wasn't her father. I still remember when the doctor told me I was pregnant. I burst into tears. Not because I didn't want to be a mother, but because I knew that my baby hadn't been conceived out of love."

Logan reached out to gently stroke her hair, then pressed his fingers across her cheek. "Did he force himself on you?"

"No, but it was an unpleasant, meaningless act that left little doubt in either of our minds that there was nothing to salvage from our marriage," she said, keeping her voice low. "I didn't see him again until he came to the hospital the day after Steffie was born. And I can count the number of times I've seen him since, which is why I don't understand how anyone could think I have knowledge of some missing microchip."

Right now her eyes were more gray than blue, Logan noted, as they became cloudy with alarm.

"What about by mail? Did he send you anything recently... any packages?"

"No. He didn't even send Steffie a present on her first birthday," she answered, unable to hide her disappointment at his thoughtlessness.

Logan absently rubbed his thumb over her hand while he stared into space. "I keep thinking that your not going to Vienna must somehow be the key to all this. At first I thought Peter deliberately left the microchip behind as a type of insurance for you and Steffie joining him in Little America. But he had no way of knowing you weren't going to be on that plane." He paused, then added, "Did he ask you to bring him anything in Vienna. A package of any sort?"

"There was only one thing I was supposed to bring him—the divorce papers," she said sharply. "I just don't see how I could possibly have any connection with this microchip."

"Unfortunately the KGB believes you do have some connection to it, which would account for the kidnapping attempt," he said soberly.

"And what about the U.S. government? Do they think I have it, too?"

He wished he could tell her the FBI believed her story, but he knew how important it was to be honest with her, so he answered truthfully. "I'm afraid they do."

"But do they think I have it because I'm working with Peter—or do they think I have it but don't know I have it?"

Logan couldn't help but smile at her innocence. "I don't think they're sure themselves. You *were* scheduled to meet Peter in Vienna, which by the way is a nest of KGB activity. I've done everything in my power to convince Senator Potter you're innocent."

Anxiously she asked, "And do you think he believes you?"

"He's not as convinced of your innocence as I am," he admitted. "But, then, he doesn't know you the way I do." He twirled a strand of her blond hair around his finger. "With everything that's happened to Andy, I think he's letting his emotions cloud his judgment. Of course, he thinks I'm letting my feelings for you cloud my spy common sense."

"And just what are those feelings, Logan?" she asked, her eyes searching his.

He brought the strand of hair to his lips. "Do I need to tell you after last night?"

His voice had become husky, reminding her of how it had sounded when he'd murmured words of endearment and passion.

"Some things can never be overstated," she said softly, her eyes on his mouth.

The vulnerability on her face tugged at his heart. He wrapped his arms around her, hugging her close as he burrowed his face in her hair. He wanted to tell her that he loved her, but he wasn't quite sure if he was ready to admit it to himself. It had all happened so fast. He hadn't expected their lovemaking to unleash such an overwhelming need for her, an all-consuming desire to be with her.

"Let's go to bed," he whispered into the perfumed hollow of her ear.

"Yes," she said simply, then giggled as he attempted to rise with her in his arms, but somehow in the process managed to send them both tumbling back against the cushions.

"Some kind of hero," he grumbled as Ronni playfully slid off his lap and got up.

"I don't need a hero. I need you," she told him with desire dancing in her eyes.

Logan stood, too, and this time easily lifted her into his arms, then carried her into the bedroom.

IT WAS HOURS LATER when Ronni awoke. Slivers of moonlight were tracing patterns on the wall and she wondered what it was that had caused her to wake from such a peaceful sleep. Warm and secure in Logan's arms, she could hear his even breathing. But it wasn't enough to feel the powerful muscles of his chest. She needed to see him, to look at his face, softened by repose.

As she gingerly attempted to reverse her position, she felt the hand on her hip caressingly move across her thigh and a pair of lips nuzzle her nape.

"Can't sleep?" he murmured, raising his head to examine her face.

"I'm sorry. I didn't mean to wake you." She traced the outline of his lips with her fingertip.

"I love waking up next to you," he whispered, pulling her closer, his hands gently stirring the embers of passion, barely extinguished from their earlier lovemaking.

Ronni sighed dreamily, shifting her hips to welcome his touch more easily. They'd only been together a little over a week, yet what she was feeling for him was so strong she couldn't bear to think of what would happen to them once she was no longer in any danger and she could return to her home in Melbourne. "What's going to become of us, Logan?"

"We're going to find the missing microchip and return it to the U.S. government. My contacts are working on this, Ronni, and it's only a matter of time until we learn who Peter's conspirator here in Florida is."

He sounded so confident, so optimistic, she couldn't do anything but nod in agreement. His words, however, did little to ease her concern. More important than unraveling the mystery she'd been caught up in was her worry over what would happen to their relationship after that mystery was solved. Right now, she didn't want to think that she might lose Logan, for that would be a greater danger than any other peril she'd encountered.

"I really don't think it'll be much longer," he told her, his hands traveling across her naked flesh.

"Do you still believe that Andrew's involved?"

The mention of Andrew's name stilled his roving hands and he shifted uncomfortably. "Ronni, I think you should know that Andy saw Peter when he was in the States in May."

"Yet he never told me." Sadness etched her words. "Why would he do something like that—especially when he knew that Peter was behind on his child support payments?"

He wished he could get her to accept that Andy wasn't the paragon of virtue she thought he was. "The obvious reason would be that he, too, was trying to keep Peter's visit secret."

She sighed. "Maybe. Have you told Doc about Andrew being gay?"

Logan exhaled a ragged breath. "I couldn't...not with everything else that's happened. He's worried enough over Andrew's physical condition." He propped himself up against the pillows, pulling her into the crook of his arm.

"But you did tell him Steffie wasn't his granddaughter, didn't you?" she asked, resting her cheek against his chest.

"Yes. I think I was able to convince him Andrew isn't Steffie's father, although it wasn't easy."

"If the senator believes that I'm a spy, I would think he'd be relieved to know that his son didn't father my child." Bitterness laced her tone.

"Don't be too hard on the man, Ronni. He's only seen pieces of the puzzle. If he knew you the way I do, he wouldn't have a doubt in his head." His hand was again tracing patterns on her skin, traveling to places warm and soft. "On second thought, I don't want him knowing you the way I do. I don't want any man knowing you the way I do."

"No man ever has, Logan." His hand had found the now familiar spot where he could reawaken desire with a tender caress. "You've touched me places I never even knew existed. You've created such a hunger in me I find myself lost in erotic daydreams, wishing for nighttime to come so that we can be together. We've only known each other a week, yet you know me more intimately than anyone ever has. I have no secrets from you," she whispered. "You seem to be able to see right through me. Only you know the real Ronni."

"The real Ronni," he repeated. He slid his hands to her breasts, where he gently circled her nipples with his thumbs. "You definitely are real." Then he looked deep into her eyes and said, "Even if you aren't really a Ronni."

Despite the fact that he was nearly driving her insane with his touch, she was lucid enough to hear him clearly. She stiffened, but he didn't seem to notice. "Umm, you taste good," he said, replacing his thumbs with his lips.

"Logan, what did you say," she asked, shifting beneath him.

"I said you taste good," he repeated.

"No, before that."

Puzzled, he looked up at her.

"You said something about even if I'm not Ronni." She was frowning. "What did you mean?"

He could see that she was more than curious, she was disturbed. "I just meant that it doesn't matter to me what your real name is. There are good reasons for people to change their names. I know you're not a spy," he continued. "That's all that matters."

Ronni sat up and reached for the lamp. "Change my name? Logan, what are you talking about?"

The sudden burst of light caused Logan to squint uncomfortably. Ronni had pulled the sheet up over her breasts and was looking at him inquisitively. As Logan gazed into her bewildered face, he realized that she had no idea what he was talking about. Could it be that her mother had never told her the truth? Twenty-five years of using an assumed identity meant that Ronni was only three when she became Veronica Summers.

"Logan, tell me what you meant!" she demanded, pulling her knees up to her chest and clutching the sheet.

There weren't enough derogatory adjectives to describe what he thought of himself at that moment. Reluctantly he said in a low voice, "You and your mother are using assumed identities."

She laughed nervously and brushed a strand of hair away from her face in an almost childlike gesture. "That's absurd! Where would you get such a crazy idea?"

"Because you've been under investigation by the government," he said in an even lower voice. "The day Andy suffered the heart attack, Senator Potter informed me you and your mother were using false identities. That's one of the reasons I was so suspicious of you when we were traveling to Key West."

"I don't understand. Are you trying to tell me that my mother and I aren't Clara and Veronica Summers?" Again there was disbelief in her face, and the color was slowly disappearing from her cheeks.

"Clara Summers and her daughter, Veronica, were killed in an automobile accident in Madison, Wisconsin, twenty-five years ago."

Her face grew even whiter. "No!" She shook her head defiantly. "I'm Veronica Summers," she insisted. "You're wrong! I've got a birth certificate and..." Her eyes met Logan's and tears slowly began to spill down the paper-white cheeks. "Tell me it isn't true," she pleaded.

"I'm sorry, sweetheart. I thought you knew." He tried to pull her into his arms, but she stiffened and pushed him away.

Impatiently she swiped at the tears with the palm of her hand, then said, "My mother's best friend lives in Madison. We're originally from Eau Claire, which is where my father died." Her brows drew together in a frown. "That is, if he was my father. If I'm not me, then maybe he's not him." The look she gave Logan was almost desperate. "Oh, my God, if I'm not Veronica Summers, who am I?"

He took both her hands in his. "You're still you, Ronni. A name doesn't change who you are. It's the person inside that counts. You're bright, compassionate, beautiful, and it doesn't matter what name your mother gave you."

"But everything she told me about my family must have been a lie!" she sobbed. "That must have been why she never wanted to talk about my father." She wrenched her hands free of Logan's, climbed out of bed and started to pull on her clothing. "This is horrible!"

"What are you doing?" he demanded.

"I'm getting dressed." Restlessly she prowled the room, searching for the garments that only hours earlier had been scattered about in passion. "I need to talk to my mother." She was trembling so badly she had to sit down on the bed to pull on the lacy underwear. "She'll be home the day after tomorrow and I intend to be in Melbourne when she arrives."

"Ronni, it's after midnight." Logan got up and donned his pants.

"I don't care what time it is," she said irrationally, then shrugged away from his second attempt to take her into his arms.

This time Logan was not about to be rebuffed. Lovingly but firmly, he gathered her trembling body close, cuddling her in the same way he'd learned to soothe Steffie when she was having one of her temper tantrums. "I know this has been a shock, and I'm sorry, Ronni." He kissed the top of her head. "I would never have mentioned it to you if I had thought you didn't know about it."

"Logan, please take me back to Melbourne," she cried, as the tension slowly eased out of her body.

"I wish I could." He continued to massage the back of her head, holding her tenderly, gently rocking her. "But until that missing microchip turns up or the feds crack the case, it's just not safe for us to leave here."

When the tears were spent and she appeared to be back in control, Logan loosened his hold on her.

Ronni eased herself from his grasp and put a little distance between them. "I've got to go back, Logan. Don't you see? I don't know who I am. All this time I've been thinking I'm somebody I'm not."

Calmly Logan asked, "So what are you going to do?"

"I'm going to go to my mother's apartment and search until I find something—I don't know what—but something that will tell me who I am."

He watched her flitter around in search of her shoes. "And are you going to wake up Steffie and drag her out of here in the middle of the night, putting her life in danger because you have to search your mother's apartment?" He raked a hand through his sleep-tousled hair. "Ronni, have you forgotten that the KGB caught up with you when you stopped at your mother-in-law's house? Don't you think they'll have someone watching your mother's house, as well?"

"You tell me. You're the spy," she said nastily, kicking his shoe out of her way with a vengeance.

He ignored her gibe. "What if you go there and you don't find what you're looking for? You'll be putting two lives at risk for nothing."

"Nothing? Finding out who I am is certainly not *nothing* to me, Logan."

"Of course it isn't," he said consolingly. "But you don't know if your mother has any documents that will tell you what you want to know. As far as you can tell, she's the only one who knows the truth, and she's not even there. All I'm asking is that you give me a couple of days. If I haven't heard something by then, I'll take you to see your mother in person . . . I promise."

He could see her prickly edges softening. He extended a hand to her and said, "Come on, Ronni. Trust me. I haven't let you down yet, have I?"

She placed her hand in his and let him pull her back down beside him on the bed. Her body slouched against his.

"First thing in the morning I'll call the senator and my other contacts, all right? Maybe there'll be some good news and we'll be able to leave tomorrow." Slowly he began to ease the cotton shirt from her shoulders. Ronni didn't protest, but allowed him to undress her as though she were a child.

When she was once again naked, he gently laid her back on the pillows.

"Don't leave me, Logan," she called out softly when he would have gotten up from the bed to fold her clothes.

He moved her skirt and blouse to the end of the bed, then climbed in beside her. "I'm right here, Ronni." He placed a butterfly kiss on her forehead. "Don't worry about a thing. I'm going to take care of everything. I promise."

She snuggled down close to his bare chest and murmured, "Right or wrong, I'm glad."

"Shhh. It's definitely not wrong." He kissed the top of her head.

But as right as it felt to be in his arms and let him take care of her, Ronni couldn't help but wonder why she seemed destined to have a man take charge of her life for her. At the moment, however, she was too emotionally drained to deal with those feelings. Right or wrong, she needed Logan, and clutching him to her, she fell asleep.

RONNI AWOKE to find herself alone in the bed and Steffie babbling from the other room. Logan was neither visible nor audible. She felt a moment of panic when she reached Steffie's room and there was still no sign of him in the apartment. Carrying Steffie into the kitchen, she found a note on the table saying he had gone to fetch a newspaper and some milk, which by now Ronni knew meant he had gone to make a few phone calls.

There was no indication he had eaten any breakfast, so after feeding Steffie her usual oatmeal and fruit, she whipped up some pancake batter and made a fresh pot of coffee—partly because she was hungry, but mostly because she needed to keep busy. Ever since she'd awoken, her thoughts had been consumed with questions about her identity, the biggest one being why. *Why* had her mother assumed a dead woman's identity?

Until last night, she had thought her worse nightmare was Peter's defection. Now she could only wonder if she would ever be able to make the nightmares end. She tried to remember what her life had been like back in Melbourne. Her students, the other teachers at the school, even the school building itself, were out of focus in her memory. All except Billy Johnson.

Billy had been one of her second-grade students, who had spent an inordinate amount of time asking her the same question—did hospitals ever get their babies mixed up? Because their family life unit dealt with babies being born in hospitals, Ronni hadn't paid much attention to what seemed to be normal curiosity. Billy was more inquisitive than the average child and asked more questions than the rest of the second grade combined, so Ronni didn't find anything unusual in the boy's query.

It soon became apparent that Billy wasn't simply preoccupied but troubled. It was only when she had her students bring in family pictures for the bulletin board that she learned the reason why. Everyone was eager to have his or her photograph tacked to the cork board—everyone except Billy.

"Billy, didn't you bring a picture of your family?" Ronni asked.

"Yes, Mrs. Lang," he dutifully replied, but she could see he was reluctant to hand her the snapshot of five people gathered around an elderly couple. "That's me and my brother, Aaron, and my sister, Heather," he told her, pointing to the three children in the photo.

"And your grandma and grandpa, and your mom and dad," Ronni finished for him. "Although you wouldn't have had to tell me that was your dad," she said, indicating the tall man behind Billy. "You look just like him."

Eyes that had been downcast gazed up at her in joyful disbelief. "I do?" he asked with a look similar to the one he'd given her when she'd told him he'd scored the highest in the class on his math test.

Ronni studied the picture carefully. "Yes, you do. Especially in the eyes. But I think you have your mother's nose."

"My mother's nose?" he repeated, unconsciously wrinkling his nose.

"Well, actually it's your nose, but you're very lucky to have one that looks just like your mother's," Ronni told him with a grin.

By now Billy was beaming. "Do you really think I look like them?"

"Yes, but I'm surprised you haven't heard that before."

"Uh-uh," he said solemnly.

"Never" would have been more accurate, for at parent conference time, Ronni had learned that the standard line around the Johnson household was "Where did Billy come from? He doesn't look like anyone in the family. Do you suppose they got him mixed up in the hospital?" What adults had viewed as playful teasing, Billy had taken to heart. At age seven, he was suffering from an identity crisis. He didn't know who he was, despite a birth certificate and two parents who assured him he was their son.

At the time Ronni had been compassionate and had done everything she could to reassure Billy that he really was Billy Johnson. Only now, however, did she really understand the traumatic feelings the small child had had to deal with.

Billy *was* his mother and father's son. She didn't even know if she was an adopted or a natural child. She'd always assumed her mother had given birth to her, but if her mother had changed her identity when Ronni was three, could it be possible that—

"We're going to have frothy orange juice if you stir any harder."

Logan's voice brought Ronni out of her daydream. She removed the wooden spoon from the pitcher and turned her attention to the pancake griddle.

"You were up early," she commented, hoping he'd say he had some news—any news—for her.

"I went for a walk." He had a carton of milk in his hand, which he placed in the refrigerator. "Are you all right?" he asked over his shoulder as he reached for a cup of coffee.

"I'm fine," she replied, knowing perfectly well that she wasn't, but she was determined to be strong for him. She poured two large round circles of batter on the griddle. "I still want to go back to Melbourne, though."

"Just one more day," he pleaded, holding up one finger.

Silently she wondered how she could take one more day. Aloud she said, "If you think it'll make a difference." She thought she heard a sigh of relief at her agreement.

"Why don't we take Steffie to the park? Or maybe we should go to Ocean World and see the porpoise show? Mabel told me they have dolphins and sea lions that you can feed. I think Steffie would like it. What do you say? It would do you good to take your mind off things," he coaxed.

Carefully she flipped the golden-brown pancakes, then looked at him. "All right, but I can't help but wish we were driving back to Melbourne."

Little did she know that her wish was about to come true.

CHAPTER TWELVE

RONNI HAD INVITED Mabel to accompany them to Ocean World, but she had politely declined as she had already made plans to spend the day with friends. It was a typical summer day—very hot and very humid. Ronni thought it was too hot to be strolling through a marine-life park with a fifteen-month-old child, but Logan was determined to take them. So she tied a bonnet under Steffie's chin, smeared her with suntan lotion and smiled when Logan opened the door for her.

They hadn't gone more than six blocks from the house when Ronni realized she'd left without Steffie's pacifier.

"Logan, we're going to have to go back," she said regretfully. "Steffie doesn't have her plug."

He shrugged, saying, "No problem."

They were near the entrance ramp to the highway, where cars sat bumper to bumper, barely moving in the heavy traffic. It took quite a bit of patience to turn the vehicle around under such conditions, but Logan managed to accomplish the task without losing his temper—which was what Peter would have done had he been behind the wheel. Something so trivial as forgetting Steffie's pacifier would have provoked an outburst of hollering and disparaging comments from Peter, but Logan didn't seem affected at all by the inconvenience.

"I'm really sorry, but I'm afraid if we don't go back she'll get cranky on us," Ronni apologized.

"We're in no hurry," he told her, giving her an understanding smile.

Again she found herself comparing the two men, and as usual, Logan appeared to have all the positive qualities Peter had lacked—patience, honesty, optimism and a sense of humor. It was no wonder she was attracted to him. He was everything she'd always hoped to find in a man, and just looking at him made her feel like smiling. What she had with Logan made her relationship with Peter seem empty and cold. She felt more intimate with Logan after knowing him only eight days than she had after eight years of marriage with Peter. And for the very first time in her life she wasn't lonely.

As the truck retraced its path down a street bordered by canals, Ronni could feel herself relaxing, despite the delay because of traffic and Steffie's absent pacifier. When Logan turned onto Mabel's block, she could see the palm trees lining the boulevard, their fronds gently swaying in the hot summer breeze, and she marveled at how comfortably familiar the neighborhood felt to her after such a short time. She was about to tell Logan she would run inside for the pacifier if he would wait in the car with Steffie, when he made an abrupt turn into a driveway several houses from Mabel's.

"What are you doing?" she asked as he brought the pickup to a halt beside a strange house.

"Mabel's got company," he said by way of an explanation, rolling down his window. "Two men with bodies by Schwarzenegger."

Ronni leaned forward to look around Steffie's car seat. "I can't see anything," she said, craning her neck to peer through a thick green hedge that separated two yards.

"They've slipped around to the back door. My guess is once they realize there's no one home they'll move inside." His voice was barely over a whisper.

"You think they're KGB?"

"I don't think they're selling vacuum cleaners," he returned dryly.

"But how did they find us? You said not a soul knew where we were?" There was a hint of panic in her voice.

The question was a sobering one for Logan—one he didn't want to answer right at the moment. Only one person knew of their whereabouts, and it cut like a knife to think that someone he trusted could have betrayed him. "Do you think anyone's home here?" He nodded toward the Spanish-style stucco house whose driveway they were occupying.

"There's a child's tricycle out back," she observed, "and laundry on the clothesline."

"Here's what I want you to do. Leave Steffie with me and go knock on the door. Tell whoever answers to call the police. Say you think someone is robbing your aunt's home," he instructed calmly.

"You want to call the police?" she asked, surprised.

"I don't want those two Tarzan types busting up Mabel's place." Seeing her apprehension, he added, "The local police aren't looking for you, Ronni."

"No, you're right." She unbuckled her seat belt.

"All you have to do is tell the person who answers the door to call the police, then come right back to the truck, okay?"

She nodded, exited the pickup and on wobbly legs went up to the house.

Logan watched as a young woman who looked to be about the same age as Ronni answered the knock. She appeared to be listening intently as Ronni made a sweeping gesture with her arm that had the woman looking first at Logan and Steffie, then in the direction of Mabel's place. The young woman nodded vigorously before closing the door, and Ronni came hustling back to the truck.

Logan leaned over to let her in.

"She's calling right now," Ronni said a bit breathlessly, quickly sliding back into the truck. "Now what?" she asked.

In answer, Logan shifted into reverse and backed out of the driveway. He drove to the end of the street, positioning the pickup so they could easily see Mabel's back door. "Now we wait for the police to get rid of them for us," he told her with a smug grin.

Within minutes the whine of a police siren could be heard and the two Schwarzenegger types came bounding out of the house. "Surprise, surprise," Logan mumbled as the two men were caught red-handed fleeing from the house. Logan and Ronni watched the pair get frisked and handcuffed before being escorted to a squad car. It was only after they'd been herded into the back of the police vehicle that Logan drove the truck around to the front of the house.

"Let me handle everything, all right?" he told Ronni as he parked behind a second police car, which had arrived ahead of them. She consented with a nod, too disconcerted to protest. "I want you and Steffie to wait here until I get everything straightened out. It shouldn't take long." He reached across to give her shoulder a reassuring squeeze before leaving.

Ronni watched him head straight for one of the policemen. Hands gesturing demonstratively, he spoke to the officer, occasionally glancing in her direction. At one point during the conversation, the officer took a couple of steps toward the truck, then stopped, obviously swayed by something Logan had said. But what? she wondered.

When Logan and the policeman disappeared into the house, she wanted to rush in after them, for the two Schwarzenegger types had spotted her sitting in the pickup and were staring at her with venomous expressions. She deliberately turned her back to the window, but they still managed to put an icy feeling in the pit of her stomach and it wasn't until Logan came back outside that she was able to relax.

He opened his door and with one hand on the roof of the truck leaned in to speak to her. "They didn't have time to do much damage inside, although there is a bit of a mess. Mabel's apartment wasn't touched—only ours."

"Do you think they were looking for the microchip?"

"Probably. As far as I could see, nothing's missing. According to the police, the men didn't have any stolen goods on them when they were apprehended."

"What are we going to do now?"

"We're going to pack our things and get out of here just as soon as we possibly can."

"Who were those men?" she asked, as the police car carrying the two intruders pulled away from the curb, its red lights flashing.

Logan looked up and waved a hand at the departing policemen before saying, "It doesn't matter. We'll be out of here just as soon as the police have finished and I've had a chance to talk to Mabel."

Ronni didn't ask any more questions. She simply followed Logan's instructions, waiting until the second police car had gone before she went inside. Except for the contents of several drawers being dumped on the floor, there was little damage to the apartment. An eerie feeling washed over her at the thought that some stranger had handled her things, and if she'd had a choice, she would have left her belongings behind. Instead she found herself packing for the fourth time in a week.

As she gathered up Steffie's toys, she couldn't help but wonder where they would go next. She was tired of running, tired of living in strange places and tired of being under suspicion. She longed for her little house back in Melbourne, leaky roof and all. She wondered how much longer it would be before the missing microchip turned up and she was cleared of any wrongdoing.

When Mabel returned, Ronni realized that as anxious as she was to return to Melbourne, she was sorry she wouldn't be seeing the woman who in a short time had become very dear to her. She felt her emotions rise in her throat as she tried to say goodbye to the older woman.

"Thank you, Mabel, for everything," Ronni managed to get out with only a slight break in her voice. "I'm sorry our visit had to end this way."

"It's not your fault those hoodlums broke in," she told her.

Ronni glanced at Logan, who indicated with facial expressions that Mabel had no idea of their true situation.

"I'm happy I was able to help out," Mabel finished.

"Oh, you did help us—more than I can tell you," Ronni assured her. "This past week has been wonderful because of your hospitality. And I know Steffie is going to miss you."

"Can I give her a hug?" Mabel asked, opening her arms wide.

Ronni released Steffie with a smile, touched by the woman's obvious affection for her daughter.

"I want you to promise me you'll come back for a visit," Mabel insisted, cuddling Steffie close to her bosom. "Do you hear that, Steffie?" She turned her attention to the little face gazing into hers. "You make sure your mama brings you back so I can see how big you've grown."

Steffie gurgled a sound that seemed to agree, and they all laughed.

"You have to promise you'll come visit us, too," Ronni said, tears springing to her eyes. "We're only a couple of hours up the coast. We can take you to the space center."

"Oh, I'd like that," Mabel replied with a warm smile. "I'll bring the cribbage board." When she handed Steffie back to Ronni, she said in a low voice, "You've got a good man this time, Ronni. And if there's one thing I've always said, it's this—a good man is a treasure. I know it's going to work out for the two of you." She winked conspiratorially and grinned.

"I hope you're right," Ronni said, returning the smile. She watched as Logan hugged Mabel, noticing that he had slipped something into her hand. As soon as they'd waved goodbye and were back on the road again, she asked him about it. "What did you give Mabel back there?"

"Money for new locks. I thought she'd feel better if she changed all of them."

Ronni exhaled a long sigh. "I hope our staying with her hasn't put her in any danger."

"With us gone, there'll be no reason for anyone to bother her," Logan assured her. "And if it's any comfort to you, the police told me they'd watch the house for the next few days."

"She didn't know why we were there, did she?"

"No. I told her you were having trouble with your ex. She didn't pry any further."

Ronni smiled to herself. "She's so sweet. I'd hate to think I was responsible for anything happening to her."

They were stopped at a red light and he said, "Ronni, look at me." When she did as he requested, he stated convincingly, "Nothing's going to happen to Mabel."

"I hope you're right," she said wearily. "Logan, where are we going?"

"Back to Melbourne. I've got to find some answers."

"Me, too, Logan," Ronni replied. "Me, too."

THE DRIVE from Fort Lauderdale to Melbourne was accomplished in near silence, except for Steffie's chortling. Both Ronni and Logan were lost in their own thoughts—she wondering about her identity, he feeling betrayed by someone he'd thought he could trust.

It was dark by the time they reached Melbourne. Logan found a motel and checked them into a two-bedroom suite with a crib for Steffie. Ronni was grateful he was taking charge of everything, for she was simply too weary to deal with any other problems just now.

After seeing that Steffie was fed and bathed, she put her to bed, then took a long hot bath herself, hoping to ease the tension in muscles cramped from riding in the pickup as well as from stress. As she soaked, her thoughts returned to her mother and to what possible reasons she could have had for changing their identities. Ronni found none of the explanations comforting, as repeatedly her mind imagined the worst possibilities. Could her mother be a criminal? It seemed preposterous even to contemplate such an idea.

But, then, it seemed preposterous that she had lived practically her entire life pretending to be someone else. Right now she was a twenty-eight-year-old woman without a name. She leaned back and closed her eyes, murmuring, "The spy's wife without a name," then groaned at the painful reminder.

Legally she was still married to a spy, but it wasn't true that she didn't have a name. She had a name all right; she just didn't know what it was. Only her mother had that information, and that thought brought a rush of fresh anger. At least tomorrow she would find out who she really was, for right now that was more important than anything else.

Suddenly the bathwater felt cold. Shivering, she reached for a towel just as she heard Logan knocking on the door.

"Ronni, are you all right?" he called out, concern in his voice.

She quickly climbed out of the tub and slipped on her cotton kimono before opening the door.

"I'm fine, Logan."

She stood before him, her skin devoid of any makeup, yet having a rosy hue. She looked so fragile, yet Logan knew there was a strength beneath that dainty exterior.

"You were in there so long, I was worried you might have fallen asleep in the tub," he said lightly, seeing the almost forlorn expression on her face.

"I was thinking," she told him as she walked past him and out into the small sitting area.

Once more he experienced a feeling of helplessness, for he knew that nothing he could say would chase away that lost little girl look. Worse yet was the knowledge that he was responsible for her troubled thoughts. All he had wanted to do was protect her, yet he'd ended up causing her pain.

"What smells so good?" she asked, wrinkling her nose.

He had shoved both his hands in his pockets. "I ordered a pizza. You didn't eat much at dinner and I thought you might be hungry."

His thoughtfulness brought a tiny rush of warmth to the coldness inside her, but her stomach rejected the idea. "It smells good, but I'm not sure I can eat anything."

Logan pulled out one of the bar stools for her, gesturing for her to be seated. "Just sit with me," he urged, easing himself onto the stool across from hers and opening the cardboard box. Again Ronni thought how nice it was to have him taking charge of everything. Even if it was wrong, it felt so good to have him look after her. It was a wonderful feeling—being cherished—which was exactly how he made her feei.

When he slid a napkin bearing a triangular piece of pepperoni pizza toward her, she smiled weakly. "You don't take no for an answer, do you?"

"Not where you're concerned." He licked a drop of tomato sauce from his finger. "Try it. It's not bad for motel pizza."

She picked off a slice of pepperoni and popped it in her mouth. "Do we have anything to drink?"

"Pick your poison. The room's equipped with a portable bar." He dug a key from his pocket and dangled it in front of her.

"What are you having?" she asked.

"A beer."

"That's fine with me, too."

"You sure?"

Seeing her nod, Logan took two beers from the portable bar and set them on the counter. After he had eaten three pieces of pizza and she was still staring at her first slice, he said, "I was hoping this would help you to relax." He covered her hand with his. "It'll be over soon, Ronni, and then you'll be able to go home."

She didn't say a word, but simply lifted her shoulders and nodded, her eyes still on the now-cold piece of pizza.

After several moments of silence, he finally said, "I'm sorry, Ronni."

She glanced at him in surprise. "Sorry? For what?"

"For telling you about Veronica and Clara Summers. I've hurt you, and it's the last thing I wanted to do."

"Oh, Logan, it's not your fault," she said on a weary sigh, taking his hand in both of hers, her fingers gently moving over his knuckles in a soothing manner. "It's my mother who's hurt me. I keep telling myself she must have had a good reason for doing what she did, but what I don't understand is why she kept it from me. Why couldn't she have told me the truth? It seems rather ironic that Andrew's father knew, yet I didn't."

Logan took a long sip of beer and rubbed a hand over the back of his neck before answering. "There's something I haven't told you," he said soberly.

Ronni could see that that something was deeply disturbing him. "What is it?" she asked, her concern mirrored in her eyes.

"You know that I was very careful not to make any calls from Mabel's." She nodded. "And I can assure you that none of the calls I made from the public phone booths could have been traced to the Fort Lauderdale area." He toyed with the flip top of the aluminum can. "I was determined that no one would know where we were staying."

"Then how did they find us at Mabel's?" she asked, a frown knitting her brow.

"There was one person who knew where we were. I thought I could trust him, that he would be the last person on earth who would betray me. He was a man I would have given my life for because I thought he was a man of honor, loyalty."

She could see the pain it was causing him to admit his mistake, and for just a moment, she forgot about her own unhappiness. "Who was it, Logan?" she asked gently.

It seemed to take him forever to finally tell her, and then the words were barely audible. "Senator Potter."

"Oh, no, Logan. You don't mean you think Senator Potter sent those men after us?" She shook her head in disbelief.

"The only way anyone could have found us was through Doc," he said grimly.

"But what about your contacts? All those people you've been getting information from?"

"None of them knew where we were, Ronni. Only Doc had that information."

"There could be another explanation," she said optimistically.

"No, there couldn't." The look he gave her was so intense she didn't rebuke his statement. He climbed down off the bar stool and ambled over to the sofa, where in the shadows of the dimly lit room he dropped down onto the soft cushions, propping his feet up on the coffee table. He leaned back and closed his eyes. "Somehow Doc is connected to Peter," he said in an agonized drawl.

"But why would he ask you to investigate me if that was true?" She had followed him over to the sofa, and sat down beside him, placing her arm along the back of the sofa. "It doesn't make any sense."

"I haven't quite figured that out," he admitted. "You could have been a smoke screen, or maybe something backfired in his plan. He tried to discourage me from getting involved with you, but now I have to wonder if that wasn't his way of keeping me interested. This way if the KGB agents weren't successful in finding the microchip, he had me ready and waiting to return it to him."

"Are you saying you think he's the ringleader of whatever Peter was doing?"

"I've been searching all day for answers that would tell me he isn't." He shook his head disconsolately. "I wish there were something—anything—that would convince me he isn't."

Ronni found the taut muscles in Logan's neck and began to knead them. "What are you going to do?" she asked softly.

"I'll have to go to the FBI with what I know. The man's head of the Senate Intelligence Committee. I just can't do nothing and hope that I'm wrong about him."

She could see that he needed to justify his actions to himself, more than to her. "Of course you can't. It's the only thing you can do," she agreed.

"But how can I turn him in? He's been like a father to me, Ronni," he said, dropping his head into his hands. "Ever since I was knee-high I took in every word he said as though it were the gospel truth. I campaigned for him and helped him get his position on the Senate Intelligence Committee. I would have died for him. I didn't think a finer man existed. How could I have been so wrong about him?"

Ronni continued to knead the tense muscles as he talked.

"The funny thing is, I used to envy Andy because Doc was his father. Ninety percent of our squabbles were because I'd get so damn jealous that Doc was his father and not mine. I couldn't understand how Andy could talk so disparagingly of him. When Andy would tell me I didn't know the real Senator Potter, I practically laughed in his face. Now I have to question whether Andy might not be a victim in this whole mess."

"Logan, what about your father?" she asked.

"What about him?" He lifted his head to look at her.

"You always talk about Doc as though he were a father to you, yet you never mention your own father. Is he alive?"

"Oh, yes, he's alive," he said, lifting one eyebrow. "He's still running the family farm in Kansas—with the help of my brother."

"You have a brother?"

"Two of them. Lawrence, Jr. and Allen. One's a farmer, the other's a farm machinery dealer, which is why they get along better with my father than I do," he told her dryly.

"Was your father expecting you to follow in his footsteps?"

"Probably, but not necessarily farming, just something related in agriculture. He loves the land and he has a hard time understanding why anyone would not want to live that kind of life. It's all he's ever known and all he's ever wanted for his family. So you can imagine how he felt about a career like mine."

"I bet he's proud of you, Logan."

He gave her a skeptical look. "He's got a funny way of showing it if he is."

"You speak to him regularly, don't you?"

He shrugged. "As regularly as any other adult child does, I suppose. We're not estranged, Ronni. We're just not that close. For some reason, I always found it easier to talk to Doc." He steepled his fingers beneath his chin. "My dad was always a patriotic man, but Doc was more than patriotic. He represented justice and equality and all the other values that were so important to me when I was a student. Public service was his life. He's my hero, Ronni. He can't be a spy." The last few words were a plea.

She looked at him and realized he was just as disappointed in Doc as she was in her mother. "I hope you're wrong about both Andrew and his father."

He sighed heavily. "We'll soon find out. Before I contact the FBI, I'm going to go visit Andy. I want to see for myself what condition he's in. I believe he's the key to this whole mess. I only wish I didn't have to leave you and Steffie alone here."

"That's something I wanted to talk to you about," she said, facing him squarely. "My mother's plane is coming in tomorrow morning at eight. Steffie and I are supposed to be picking her up at the airport."

"You'll have to call the airlines and leave a message for her to take a cab."

It sounded like an order to her and she immediately took offense. Annoyed, she asked, "Why can't we go get her?"

"Why?" He flashed her a look of disbelief. "Have you forgotten there are several men out there who would like nothing better than to find you? That your daughter was almost kidnapped?"

"Of course I haven't," she retorted, not wanting to admit that she had. All she seemed capable of thinking about was who she could be, and it made her feel guilty to realize that she could so easily forget what had happened to Steffie.

When she didn't say anything for several seconds, he stood up and walked over to the phone. "Tell me the name of the airlines and I'll call for you."

Reluctantly she gave him the information. As soon as he had completed the call she asked, "Will you at least drop me off at my mother's apartment on your way to see Andrew?"

Logan frowned. "I like that idea even less than you going to the airport."

"Why?" She stood up and confronted him.

"Why?" he repeated, practically glaring at her. "Because I've got no way of protecting you if you go to your mother's without me."

"But I need to see her," she pleaded.

"And you will. As soon as I've had a chance to talk to Andy and after I've contacted the FBI. I'll take you to see her myself."

"But I don't want to wait. If you think you're disillusioned with Doc, imagine how I feel about my mother. She's been lying to me for over twenty-five years."

"I know how important it is to you to learn your real name," he said, his voice softening, his hands covering her shoulders. "And believe me, I do understand how you're feeling, but it's not a good idea for you to go traipsing over to your mother's. We've been through all this before, Ronni."

"It's not just learning who I am, but learning who my father is. Right now I don't know if my father is dead or alive." She turned to him with pleading eyes. "Don't you see? I've spent a lifetime wishing I had a father. It's possible that I do."

"What makes you think your mother hasn't been telling you the truth about him?"

"That's just it. She hasn't told me anything about him. All I have are a couple of photos and precious few details."

He took both her hands in his. "All I'm asking is that you be patient. It won't be much longer before the spy ring is broken and the missing microchip is found. Once that happens, you and Steffie will be safe and you'll be able to return to a normal life."

"I doubt my life will ever be normal again," she said wearily.

"It'll all work out, Ronni. Trust me."

When he wrapped his strong arms around her and whispered those words in her ear, it was impossible not to. And when he made it clear that it was her decision whether they slept together that night, she chose to share his bed, needing the comfort of him. As they made love, the exquisite pleasure of their intimacy, the oneness of body and mind, made everything else seem unimportant. All that mattered was her need to be his always.

But long after their passion was spent, Ronni found herself worrying that she was giving this man too much control in her life. She couldn't deny her feelings for him even if she had wanted to. He was her treasure, just as Mabel had said. She knew, however, that come morning, nothing he was going to say or do would prevent her from contacting her mother.

CHAPTER THIRTEEN

RONNI KEPT ONE EYE on the bathroom door and the other on Steffie as she dialed her mother's phone number. She figured she had about fifteen minutes—which was how much time it usually took Logan to shower and shave each morning. When a busy signal sounded in her ear, she replaced the receiver with a frown. She immediately tried the number again, only to get the same annoying busy tone, a pattern that kept repeating until finally, after seven of the fifteen minutes had elapsed, her mother answered. Ronni hadn't been talking to her for more than three or four minutes, when she saw the bathroom door open and Logan come out.

"I need another razor blade," he announced, the lower half of his face smothered in shaving cream.

Startled, Ronni quickly averted her head, nearly pulling the phone off the desk in an effort to turn her face away from him. "I've got to go now. I'll call you later," she told her mother in a low voice before hanging up.

"Who were you talking to?" Logan asked as soon as she had replaced the receiver. He had a towel draped over his bare shoulders, a pair of white slacks covering his legs and he was looking at her as though he already knew the answer.

As usual, the sight of his bare chest did funny things to her stomach, but she forced her eyes back to his face. "I called my mother," she answered, standing with her arms crossed over her chest and seeming more defiant than she felt.

He appeared to be counting slowly to ten. "Why would you do that?" he inquired calmly but intensely.

"Because I knew she would be calling me as soon as she got home and I didn't want her to worry when there wasn't an answer at my place." The lie came easily to her lips. She knew it was a lie and so did he, but she wasn't about to explain again her almost desperate need to speak to her mother. "We were supposed to meet her at the airport," she reminded him. "Mothers have a tendency to worry when their daughters aren't where they're supposed to be. I wanted to make sure she knew that we were all right."

Logan didn't respond, but stood staring at her. His silence was worse than his censure, and she almost wished he'd shout at her rather than stand there coolly assessing her.

"I only talked for a couple of minutes—not long enough for a call to be traced," Ronni pointed out.

He narrowed his eyes suspiciously. "How much did you tell her?"

"Practically nothing. She asked about Vienna—I told her we didn't go. Mostly she talked about her vacation. Oh—and I also told her about Andrew's heart attack."

"Did she mention Peter?"

"Yes, but only in regard to us not going to Vienna. I'm sure she hasn't heard about his defection. She probably hasn't seen a newspaper since she's been away."

"I know you're anxious to see her, Ronni, but I want you to promise me you'll wait here until I get back from the hospital."

She moved closer to him. "I know you're only trying to protect us, Logan, but I wish you'd reconsider. I really don't want to stay here alone. If you don't want me going to see my mother, can't we at least go to the hospital with you?"

He shook his head. "It's better for you to stay put. No one knows you're here." When she would have protested, he added, "I'd never forgive myself if anything happened to either one of you." Steffie had crawled over to Logan and was pulling herself up by the leg of his slacks. He bent over and scooped her into his arms. "Will you and Steffie wait here for me?" he asked, looking at Ronni while Steffie's fingers gingerly poked at the shaving cream.

Ronni watched how tenderly he held her daughter, as he carefully wiped her soapy fingers with the towel. Seeing him with Steffie evoked such a warm feeling inside her chest it was hard not to do as he requested. "We'll wait," she finally told him.

Logan kissed both of them on the cheek, then grinned sheepishly as they each wrinkled their noses at the foamy shaving cream that accompanied his kisses. Then he set Steffie down and gave Ronni a long hard look before going back into the bathroom to finish shaving and getting dressed.

Despite Logan's optimistic frame of mind, Ronni couldn't help but feel a sense of foreboding. When he kissed her good-bye, she wanted to beg him not to go without her, but she knew her protest would be in vain.

Standing beside the plate glass window in their room, Ronni watched his lean figure cut across the motel's asphalt parking lot. With each step he moved further away from her, taking with him her sense of security. When she saw him climb into the pickup, a wave of panic swept over her. It was like an explosion of fear, and she had the horrible feeling it would be the last time she would ever see him.

Frightened by such a thought, she grabbed Steffie and went running after him. But by the time she was able to race through the lobby and out into the parking lot, the orange pickup was gone. For the first time since she and Logan had been together, she felt totally alone, and the feeling was overwhelming.

She went back to the room and waited, just as he had instructed her to do. But there was little comfort to be found in a strange motel room, and although she tried to give her undivided attention to Steffie and her toys, her eyes kept returning to the telephone. Anxiously she waited for it to ring, wanting so desperately for Logan to call and tell her the microchip had been found . . . that she could stop worrying about anyone trying to take Steffie from her. But it didn't ring, and the waiting became unbearable as her attention repeatedly strayed to the telephone and her wristwatch.

By midmorning, Ronni was jumping every time she heard a noise in the hallway. Convinced that something horrible had happened to Logan, she wrestled with several different plans of action until she finally came to the conclusion there was only one person who could give her any peace of mind—her mother. So, despite Logan's warning not to leave and knowing that her mother's apartment building might be under surveillance, Ronni scribbled a note for him telling him where she would be and set her plan in motion.

With her blond hair swept up beneath Logan's captain's hat and her slender curves hidden by his Hawaiian print shirt and a pair of his khakis, Ronni hoped that if she couldn't pass for a man she would at least look very different from the Veronica

Lang whose picture had been splattered across the newspapers. Before calling a taxi, she scrubbed her face clean of all makeup, emptied the contents of her purse into Steffie's diaper bag, then headed for the gift shop in the lobby, where she purchased a pair of men's sunglasses and promptly perched them on the bridge of her nose.

When she climbed into the taxi, she couldn't help but cast a suspicious eye around the motel parking lot; nor could she keep from looking over her shoulder as the taxi pulled out into traffic and headed across town. Without the confines of a car seat, Steffie scrambled and wriggled about in the back of the taxi, and it took all of Ronni's energy to try to hold her still.

When they reached her mother's apartment complex, she told the driver to circle the block before stopping. Acting as though it wasn't an unusual request, the driver followed her instructions, allowing Ronni the opportunity to scrutinize the neighborhood. By the time the taxi came to a halt in front of the apartment entrance, she had seen nothing untoward, but that didn't prevent her from running the short distance between the taxi and the building. Once inside the lobby, she jostled Steffie from one hip to the other as she waited impatiently for her mother to answer the intercom.

"Come on up. Grandma's waiting for you," Ronni heard her mother say before a buzzing sound signaled that the security door was unlocked. Instead of waiting for the elevator, Ronni took the stairs to the third-floor apartment, to find her mother waiting for the two of them with a big grin on her usually taciturn face.

"Come to Grandma, pumpkin," she cooed, taking Steffie from Ronni's arms and smothering her with kisses.

"Welcome home, Mother," Ronni said dryly as she closed her mother's door and leaned against it.

"Oh, it's good to be home," Clara declared, cuddling Steffie and making her giggle. "I missed you so much. Wait until you see what I brought back. You wouldn't believe all the bargains I found in the duty-free shops—it was like paradise." She finally turned her attention to Ronni and gasped. "Veronica! What on earth are you doing in those clothes?" she asked, her face wrinkling in surprise.

"It's a long story," Ronni said wearily, removing the captain's hat and running her fingers through her hair. "Maybe we ought to sit down," she suggested, despising the weakness that had invaded her body now that she was finally in a position to learn the truth about her identity.

"Just set those packages on the floor," Clara instructed, waving an arm in the direction of the sofa, where the bargains were spread out from end to end. "Look at these darling sunsuits I found for Steffie in Saint Croix," she exclaimed, producing several colorful cotton outfits and holding them up for Ronni's inspection. "There were so many things to choose from I could have spent all my time in the shops." She started rummaging through a large shopping bag. "I wonder what I did with the swimsuit I bought for her."

There was only one subject Ronni was interested in discussing and it wasn't Steffie's new clothes. She glanced impatiently at the sunsuits, then set them aside. "Mother, I need to talk to you."

"I'm listening," Clara told her, rattling two gaily painted maracas in front of Steffie while she hummed "La Cucaracha."

Ronni grabbed the gourds before Steffie's little fingers closed around them. "She'll end up putting those in her mouth, and you don't know what kind of paint is on them," she admonished, the sharpness of her tone causing her mother's eyebrows to draw together.

Ronni's actions brought a cry of protest from Steffie. Immediately Clara began to bounce her on her knee. "Maybe I should get her the doll I bought for her in San Juan."

"If you'd set her down on the floor, she'd find her box of toys and entertain herself," Ronni remarked testily. "Then we could talk. I have something important I need to discuss with you."

Clara set Steffie down on the plush blue carpet. "Very well, but why don't I get us something cool to drink? Then you can tell me what it is that's bothering you." She started walking toward the kitchen, but Ronni stopped her.

"Mother, I don't need something cool to drink," she snapped.

Clara gave her daughter an inquisitive glare, then slowly sat back down. Two eyebrows arched. "No, I guess you don't. I think you'd better start by telling me why you're dressed like a man," she said, asserting herself with a thrust of her chin. Before Ronni could reply she added, "And why couldn't you tell me where you were when you phoned this morning? Why weren't you at home?"

"Steffie and I haven't been home since the day you left," Ronni said on a weary note, rubbing her temples with her fingertips.

"Well, for goodness' sake, why not?" Clara asked, her features softening with concern. "I thought you said you didn't go to Vienna."

"We didn't." She laughed sarcastically. "We went to Key West and to Miami and Fort Lauderdale," she said, counting off the names on her fingers.

"Whatever for? Not to avoid Peter?" Clara made a fretful sound. "He's not here in Melbourne bothering you again, is he?"

"I doubt if Peter will ever come back here again, Mother," she said bitterly. "That ought to make you happy. It's what you've wanted all along—for Peter to be out of our lives."

"I've only wanted for you and Steffie to be happy," Clara answered stiffly. "I don't know what's going on here, dear, but ever since you walked through that door you've been looking at me with that wounded expression you always toss at me whenever you're angry with me."

Ronni looked at her mother and tried to control the rush of conflicting emotions that threatened to turn her into a raging interrogator. "I need some answers," she said as calmly as she could. "And you're the only one who has them."

"Answers to what?" Clara frowned.

"Answers to the questions such as, who I am. Or maybe we should start with who you are." She looked at her mother as though she were seeing her for the first time.

"What do you mean, who am I?" Clara attempted to dismiss her question with a chuckle.

But there was no answering humor in Ronni's voice. "You know what I mean, Mother," she said soberly. "Who are we?"

"Veronica, you're not making any sense." She gave her what Ronni called her military scare-'em look, but Ronni wasn't scared. Then she pursed her lips and said, "And I don't appreciate your tone of voice. You're angry with me. Why? What's happened?"

"What's happened is I want to know who I am. That's something you never thought you'd have to tell me, isn't it? How long were you planning on keeping it from me? Forever?'' Ronni tried to keep her anger under control, but her voice rose sharply, so sharply that it startled Steffie, who looked anxiously from her mother to her grandmother, then uttered an uncertain wail.

''Keep your voice down. You're frightening Steffie,'' Clara rebuked her. ''As well as me.''

Ronni took a deep breath, hoping to slow down her hammering heart. She sat clutching her hands so tightly her knuckles were white. ''I want to know who I am, Mother,'' she repeated, calmly yet firmly. ''Twenty-five years ago Veronica and Clara Summers were killed in an automobile accident.'' Her gaze didn't waver from her mother's. ''We're not dead, Mother.''

Clara's face paled and she grabbed the wooden arms of her chair to still her trembling. For the first time in twenty-eight years, Ronni saw fear in her mother's face. ''Who told you this?'' she asked in a raspy voice.

''It doesn't matter who told me. What matters is who I am, and at the moment, I don't have the slightest idea who that is.'' She had to use every ounce of self-control not to lose the little bit of composure she was so desperately clinging to.

''You're my daughter, that's who you are,'' Clara said unequivocally. ''We may have used someone else's names, but you are my flesh and blood, Veronica.''

''So it is true,'' Ronni said slowly, her shoulders slumping. Until she had heard her mother's admission, there had been that slender thread of hope that Logan was wrong. Now she knew he had spoken the truth. Denial was impossible. ''Why, Mother?'' she gasped. ''Why did you do it?''

Obviously upset by her daughter's discovery, Clara made a fretful sound, then said, ''I didn't have any choice. Twenty-five years ago it was the only alternative.''

''Alternative?'' Ronni looked bewildered. ''Alternative to what?''

''To living in continual fear.''

''Fear of what?''

''Not what, but whom.'' After what seemed like a long silence, Clara swallowed with great difficulty before quietly saying, ''Your father.''

''My father?'' Ronni thought the lump in her throat would constrict her breathing it was so large. ''You were afraid of my father?'' she whispered.

"Yes, and with good reason."

"But you said he was killed in a car crash when I was only three."

Clara looked down at her hands, which were now folded in her lap. "There was no car crash," she admitted in a low voice. "We divorced when you were two."

"Divorced? You mean, he's still alive?" The thought that her father could be alive sent a chill down her spine.

"I don't know whether he's alive or dead, nor do I want to know," Clara replied unevenly. "He made my life so miserable the short time we were married that I have no remorse about what I did."

"What did you do?" Ronni asked faintly.

"I did the only thing I could do to make sure he would never hurt either one of us again. I changed our names and moved far away from him."

"But how? Why did we end up with dead people's names?"

"I had a friend who worked in the Department of Vital Statistics. We'd been in the army together, and she was also my maid of honor at my wedding."

"You mean Marie Spenser?"

"Yes. Maybe you remember her. She visited us several times when you were just a little girl."

Vaguely Ronni recalled a matronly woman who had a tinkling laugh and smelled of lilacs.

"Well, she knew of the problems I was having with your father," Clara continued. "She had warned me against marrying him in the first place. You see, I met him while I was in the service, which was automatically one strike against him where Marie was concerned. She didn't trust soldiers."

"Then he was a military man?" Ronni asked, hungry for any information at all about her father.

"Not a career man. He had about six months of his tour of duty left when I first met him. We were both stationed in New Jersey."

"Did you get married while you were in the service?"

"Oh, no." She shook her head. "I only had four weeks left to serve when I first met him. After I was discharged, I went back to Eau Claire and got a job with the telephone company. During the next few months we corresponded by mail until he was discharged from the army. One day he turned up on my doorstep and a week later we were married."

"You must have loved him if you married him." It was more of a question than a statement.

"Oh, yes, I loved him very much in the beginning. I couldn't believe my luck when he asked me to marry him. He was so handsome, and women were after him like you wouldn't believe."

There was a dreamy look on her mother's face that Ronni had never seen before.

"He had what my mother would have called a silver tongue. He could charm the socks off a girl."

"But you had problems in your marriage?" Ronni prodded.

"He could be loving and tender, but he could also be violent. Little did I know that our life would be so troublesome—one minute tranquil, the next minute chaotic." She grimaced at the memory. "At first I excused his abusive behavior, blaming it on his upbringing. He told me that in his family a man would lose his honor if he didn't keep his woman in line. You know me, Ronni. I'm no shrinking violet. I can defend myself pretty well, but he had such a violent temper."

"You mean he struck you?" Ronni's mouth dropped open in horror and she clutched her stomach. All her life she had visualized her father as being a kind, gentle man. She didn't want to hear that he could be cruel.

"More than once. When I learned I was pregnant with you, I begged him to get some counseling with me, but he refused. Not even when I nearly had a miscarriage."

"He hit you when you were pregnant?" Ronni winced, feeling as though she were breaking out in a cold sweat as the picture became even uglier.

Clara nodded slowly. "He pushed me and I fell. When the doctor told him I could have easily lost you, it seemed to shake him up pretty badly. He didn't touch me again for the remainder of my pregnancy. I was so happy, because I thought we were finally going to be able to work things out and that he had changed."

"But he didn't change, did he?" Ronni said somberly, her eyes misting with unshed tears.

Clara shook her head sadly. "After you were born, it started all over again. The lies, the fighting, the accusations and the physical abuse. Finally I couldn't take it any longer. I was afraid that if I left him alone with you, he'd hurt you, too. So I moved out. He threatened to kill me if I left, but I took refuge at a women's shelter."

"Didn't the police do anything?"

"Oh, there were restraining orders and whatnot, but the authorities weren't overly anxious to get involved in domestic disputes—especially back then. Women didn't have the rights they have now. I wanted to run far, far away, somewhere that he'd never find us. But I had to wait for the divorce proceedings. Your father hired himself a hotshot lawyer who persuaded the judge that he should be allowed to have you every other weekend."

"Even though he was abusive?" Ronni shrieked in disbelief.

"I'm afraid so. In court, he appeared as the wronged party and had a whole parade of witnesses who testified that he was a devoted father and husband. And I had made the mistake of not reporting his abuse to the police."

Clara sighed. "I was determined not to let him take you away from me for even one hour, let alone a whole weekend. Marie offered to let me stay with her in Milwaukee, so we moved in with her. When he found out where we were, he caused trouble, and I was beginning to think we'd never be safe from him. It was then that Marie suggested I take you and move out of state. Knowing your father, I figured he'd find us no matter where we went. That's when Marie came up with the idea of assuming new identities."

"But wasn't it illegal? I mean, you just can't go take other people's names!"

"Veronica, I was desperate," her mother explained. "Because Marie worked in the Department of Public Records, she knew of a woman and her small daughter who had been killed in an automobile accident. She provided me with copies of their birth certificates and it was then that I decided to use their names so that no one would ever know where we were. Ironically the woman's name was Clara, which was similar to my given name—Clarissa."

"But what about the rest of your family? Didn't they care that you were going to disappear out of their lives?"

"I've always told you the truth about them. One of the reasons I went into the army was that I was alone. My father was killed in World War II and my mother died the summer after I graduated from high school. Except for a few cousins, I didn't have any other family, so it really wasn't hard for me to leave Wisconsin. When I moved to Florida, I closed the door on that life and began a new one."

"But using other people's names... it just doesn't seem right," Ronni protested. She could hardly believe that her rigid, rule-abiding mother had been able to take such measures.

"I only borrowed their names. I didn't pretend we actually were those people. All I wanted was a fresh start for the two of us. Is that so wrong? To want to give your child a new beginning?"

Ronni was too numb to make any judgments. She walked over to the bookshelf and picked up the photo of her father her mother kept in a silver frame. "That's why you never wanted to talk about him, isn't it—all those times I questioned you about him and you would always change the subject." She studied the photograph as she talked. "I always thought it was because after his death you found it too painful to talk about him." She traced the outline of his face, the strong jaw, the wide grin. It was a face she had memorized years ago—a happy face. "He was so handsome," she said wistfully. "It's hard to believe he could have been so cruel."

Clara had been watching her daughter's fingers caress the picture. "That man isn't your father, Veronica," she said quietly.

Ronni shot her mother a quizzical expression. "This isn't my father?"

Clara shook her head.

Ronni's eyes flew back to the picture, looking distastefully at the face she had loved all of her life. "If this isn't my father, who is it?"

Square shoulders lifted. "I have no idea," Clara admitted.

"Mother, you've been telling me for twenty-five years that this man is my father." She held the photograph out in front of her in an accusatory manner. "Now you're telling me that not only is he not my father, but you don't even know who the man is?" she asked incredulously.

"After your father and I were divorced, I went to work for a photographer. There was a box of unclaimed photos... that's where I found that picture and the ones you have." She watched Ronni return the silver frame to the shelf as though it burned her fingers. "You were too young to remember your father, so I took those pictures home with me to create a memory of a handsome, gentle father for you."

Ronni closed her eyes, feeling a sense of betrayal. "What about my real father? Do you have any pictures of him?"

"No. I destroyed all reminders of him. I wouldn't have been able to pretend he was a good and decent man if I had had to look at his picture every day."

Ronni glanced over at Steffie, who was chomping on a rubber toy. "Did he have red hair?"

"Oh, yes. It was like burnished copper. I used to think what a shame it was that such glorious red hair was wasted on a man."

"What about all those pictures in the photo album—the ones of our relatives—are they phonies, too?" she asked bitterly.

"No, they're not!" Clara denied vehemently. "Those are your family. Most of them still live in Wisconsin. If I have any regrets, it's that you didn't have the opportunity to know them—even if they were distant relatives."

"What about my father's family? I must have had grandparents and aunts and uncles on his side, as well." She held her breath, waiting for the answer, as the thought of discovering a whole new family threatened to overwhelm her.

"Yes, and I'm sorry you weren't able to know them. But that wasn't my fault, Veronica. Your father gave me no other choice."

"Are they still alive?"

Clara shrugged. "I don't know. It's been twenty-five years."

"Were they from the Wisconsin area?"

"Yes."

"And what about your friend Marie? Does she still work in the Office of Vital Statistics?"

"Yes, she does, but surely you're not thinking of trying to find them." A look of agitation flickered in her eyes.

"I can't even begin to look for them unless I know their names."

There was a silence while Ronni waited for her mother's answer. Clara sat licking her lips as though debating whether she should tell her.

"Don't you think I have a right to know, Mother?" Ronni demanded.

Clara's eyes met hers and she said, "It's Locken. You were christened Cynthia Louise, after my mother."

"And my father's name?"

Ronni saw her mother swallow with difficulty. Her lips trembled as she said, "His name was Ronald Locken, but everyone called him 'Ronnie.'"

CHAPTER FOURTEEN

"THAT'S WHY YOU REFUSED to call me 'Ronni'—because that was his name." She spoke the sudden realization aloud, a wistful expression lingering in her eyes.

"In twenty-five years, no one has ever suspected a thing. Why now? I don't understand how you could have found out," Clara mused. "What happened while I was gone?"

Ronni gazed out the window to the street below, wondering how everything could look so peaceful outside when her life was in such a turmoil. She moved away from the window and slumped down onto the sofa. "A whole lifetime seems to have happened," she muttered. "I keep thinking I'm going to wake up and discover it's all been a bad dream." She leaned her head back and closed her eyes. "I'm not who I thought I was . . . the man I thought was my father isn't really my father . . . my husband isn't who I thought he was." A tiny moan escaped her. "If only it were a nightmare."

"Do you hate me, Veronica?"

Ronni opened her eyes and saw uncertainty in a face that had always been so stoic. She wanted to reach out and put her arm around her mother's shoulders, but something stopped her—pride, anger, confusion—she didn't know which. She had always been the one to reach out and do the touching, but at this moment her feelings were too raw, too complicated for her to respond.

"Oh, Mom, of course I don't hate you," she answered honestly. "I wish I could tell you everything is all right, but it's so hard for me to absorb it all—especially after what Peter's done." Seeing her mother's puzzled expression, she added, "I forgot. You haven't heard about Peter, have you?"

"What's he done now?" Clara asked, the worry lines at the corners of her eyes deepening.

"It's such an awful story, Mom, I don't even know where to begin," she said on a weary sigh, rubbing her fingers across her forehead. "Remember how you couldn't locate Peter for me when Steffie was in the hospital?" She didn't wait for a response from her mother, but continued. "The reason you couldn't find him was that he wasn't in Vienna. He was in the Soviet Union."

"The Soviet Union?" Clara's brow wrinkled. "What was he doing there?"

"Working for the KGB." She waved a hand impatiently. "The day you left on your cruise, Peter defected to the Soviet Union."

Clara grimaced in horror. "Are you saying he's a spy?"

"I'm afraid he is, and that's only the beginning of it." She sighed heavily. "Not only was he betraying his country with his little spy games, but he made it appear as though I was involved in the whole sordid mess," she said bitterly. "My picture was in the paper and there was even a television reporter on my doorstep, looking for a story about me."

"But that's ridiculous!" Clara protested in outrage. "Anyone who knows you would know you couldn't possibly be involved in any such thing. Didn't you go to the authorities?"

"I didn't have to. They came to me with all sorts of questions—or I should say accusations, thanks to Peter. He set me up so that the FBI suspected I was his conspirator."

"I can't believe all this! How—how could he do such a thing?" Clara sputtered indignantly.

"Quite easily, believe me, Mom. He held a press conference, during which he announced to the world that the reason I had been planning my trip to Vienna was so that I could join him when he defected."

"But that's a lie!" Clara nearly choked in anger. "I knew he was a lowlife, but I never would have thought he could be so vindictive! And probably all because you wanted to divorce him."

"The story gets worse," Ronni warned her. "If it was simply a case of my having to prove I wasn't a spy, I would have been able to defend myself." She let her glance stray to her daughter, who was busy stacking blocks on the floor. "Putting Steffie's life in danger is something I'll never forgive him for. It was a mean, despicable thing to do. He's not worthy of having her call him 'Father.'" Her voice broke with emotion.

"What do you mean, Steffie's life is in danger?" Clara shot forward in alarm.

"Peter arranged for us to come to Vienna because he was planning to take Steffie with him when he defected. After we didn't show up, he tried to kidnap her."

"How could he kidnap her? I thought you said he was in Russia?"

"He is. He sent someone else to do it. Two creepy guys. It was awful." Ronni shuddered at the memory. "I don't know what I would have done if Logan hadn't been there."

"Logan?" Clara looked at her inquisitively.

"Logan McNeil. He's a friend of Andrew's," Ronni explained. "I met him the day Andrew had his heart attack."

Clara raised a finger in the air. "Now that you mention Andrew, that reminds me. He called earlier this morning and asked me if I knew where you were. I told him you'd be coming over later today and I would have you call him when you arrived."

"Andrew called here?" Ronni felt goose bumps travel the length of her body. Had Logan already been to see him? Was that why he'd phoned? "That must mean he's out of his coma."

"He didn't sound much like himself, but I suppose that's to be expected, considering he had a heart attack and was comatose," Clara remarked thoughtfully.

Ronni got up to use the telephone. "Do you have the number to the hospital? I think I'll try calling him."

Just as Clara reached for the phone book, the intercom buzzed. She handed the directory to Ronni before going to answer the door.

"Western Union. Telegram for a Clara Summers." The voice came smoothly over the intercom.

Clara pressed the button allowing the delivery man access to the secured apartments, then turned back to Ronni. "I hope it's not bad news. I always associate telegrams with bad news."

Ronni paused in her search for the telephone number as her mother's words registered in her consciousness. She looked across the room to where Clara stood with one hand on the doorknob, anticipating the messenger's arrival. Intuitively an alarm sounded in her brain.

"Mother, wait!" The words spilled out in a sudden panic, but her warning came too late. The door was swinging open and within seconds it had swung shut, only this time the two men who had been on the outside were now on the inside. Immediately Ronni recognized them as the men who had tried to kidnap Steffie in Miami.

"What are you doing?" Clara demanded as they muscled their way into her apartment.

With lightning swift reflexes, Ronni bolted into action, sweeping Steffie into her arms.

The smaller man pulled a gun from inside his suit jacket pocket and waved it in the air. "No one needs to get hurt if you just cooperate."

"You can't take my baby. I won't let you," Ronni cried out bravely.

Clara gasped as the armed man began to move slowly across the living room. When she would have rushed to Ronni's side, the second man stopped her, stepping in front of her with his arms folded across his chest, the sheer size and strength of him enough to intimidate any woman.

Ronni clung to Steffie, inching backward as the man advanced until she came up against the wall and could go no farther. He continued to stalk her, while she stared at him with beseeching eyes. When he was close enough that Ronni could see the pores on his face and smell the cigar smoke on his breath, he stopped.

For the first time in her life Ronni thought she knew the meaning of the expression "frightened to death." No matter how hard she tried, she couldn't seem to get any air into her lungs, so great was her fear.

"Give it to me," he demanded, looking her squarely in the eye, the gun close to his chest. He held out a hand.

Ronni squeezed Steffie so tightly the little girl squealed in protest. She tried to speak, but nothing would come out, and she was forced to answer with a toss of her blond head.

"I said give it to me," he bit out between clenched teeth, raising the gun until it was so close to her face she thought she could feel its cold metal despite the fact that it didn't touch her skin. "I want the bracelet." He enunciated each word carefully.

"Bracelet?" she finally managed to croak.

"The baby's bracelet." He waved the gun at Steffie's wrist.

Ronni's heart was pounding so hard she thought it would put a hole in her chest.

"Hand it over and no one has to get hurt."

She slowly nodded. Then, despite Steffie's wriggling and her own arms feeling like Jell-O, she managed to unclasp the Medic-Alert bracelet and drop it into the man's callused palm. He pocketed the silver chain, then motioned for the other fellow to leave. Both Ronni and Clara stood like mannequins, watching the two men swiftly cross the room and vanish out the door.

Clara was the first one to jolt into action, rushing over to bolt the chain lock in place. "Quick! Call the police!" she exclaimed. When Ronni made no move for the telephone, she repeated, "Ronni, call the police!"

"And do what? Report that someone came in here and stole my daughter's Medic-Alert bracelet?" Her voice quivered as she spoke.

There was a knock on the door and Clara jumped. "Don't answer it! Whoever it is shouldn't be here.... I didn't open the security door downstairs!"

Both women stood looking at each other like a couple of frightened rabbits, until Ronni finally said, "This is ridiculous," and walked over to peer out the peephole in the door.

As Ronni fumbled with the lock, Clara demanded in near hysteria, "What are you doing?"

"It's all right. It's Logan."

"How could he have gotten in the building?"

"I don't know, Mother," she replied a bit impatiently. "Maybe he picked the lock." Disregarding her mother's protests, Ronni opened the door, only to be lambasted by Logan.

"I should have known you wouldn't wait for me," he scolded, shaking his head in anger. "Why did you leave? Don't you realize how dangerous it is for you to be out on your own?" He looked her up and down. "And what are you doing in my clothes?"

Ronni held up her hands, trying to stop his outburst of anger. "Logan, listen to me. Those men were here—the ones who tried to kidnap Steffie. Only they didn't want her, just her bracelet."

Logan's eyes flew to Steffie's bare wrist. "And you gave it to them?"

"I didn't have any choice. They had guns." She shivered at the memory, holding Steffie close for comfort.

"How long ago did this happen?" he asked.

"Not more than a couple of minutes."

Logan rushed over to the window and looked down at the street below. "There they are." He raised his index finger to the glass. "They're getting into a blue Buick." Before Ronni could stop him, he was tearing out of the apartment, calling over his shoulder, "Lock the door, and for God's sake stay put this time."

"Logan, wait!" she shouted after him, but he paid no attention to her plea.

"Mom, take Steffie." Ronni shoved her daughter into her mother's arms. "I have to go after him."

"But you heard what he said," Clara protested. "'Lock the door and stay put.'" she mimicked sternly.

"I can't, Mom." She frantically reached for the diaper bag, dumping its contents onto the middle of the floor. "Oh, where is it?" she moaned, combing through the bibs, bottles and baby powder splattered across the carpet. Within seconds she was clutching Steffie's old Medic-Alert bracelet.

"I hope I can catch him," she yelled as she went running out of the apartment and down the corridor to the stairwell. She raced down the three flights of steps, her hair flopping against cheeks flushed with fear. Breathless, she came flying out of the entryway, only to discover that she was too late. There was no sign of Logan or the pickup.

"Damn!" she cried out in frustration, jiggling the Medic-Alert bracelet in her hand. She was tempted to run back upstairs and get the keys to her mother's car, but she knew her chances of finding Logan were next to none. She hadn't even seen in which direction he'd gone. There was nothing she could do but wait and pray that he wouldn't catch up to the other two men.

"I was too late. He was gone," she told her mother as she dragged her weary body into the apartment. She plopped down on the sofa and absently toyed with the bracelet.

"Why did you go after him?" Clara asked, setting Steffie back on the floor.

Ronni shifted her gaze from the bracelet to her mother's face. "You saw those men. They had guns—which means Logan is putting himself in danger, and all over a worthless bracelet. But he didn't give me a chance to explain."

"I'm beginning to think you've lost your senses, girl. What are you talking about and why did you go running after the man like that?" She clicked her tongue disapprovingly.

"I went after him because I'm in love with him and I didn't want to see him get hurt," Ronni declared emotionally.

"In love with him?" her mother parroted in disbelief. "How long have you known this man?"

"Ten days, but it seems like I've known him a lifetime," Ronni told her, a bit of wonder in her voice at the realization. "And I do love him," she added defiantly.

"Love?" Clara snorted. "I can't believe any of this." She threw her arms up in the air. "First you tell me Peter's a spy, then two men with guns force their way in here. They take Steffie's Medic-Alert bracelet, although for the life of me I can't figure out why, and now you go chasing after a guy with one eye because you tell me you're in love with him."

"He has two eyes, Mother," Ronni corrected. "He wears an eye patch because he was in an accident and he's still recovering from the injury."

"Maybe you'd better tell me who this man is and why you think you're in love with him," Clara ordered in her maternal voice as she sat down opposite her.

"I am in love with him," Ronni insisted. "And I already told you—he's a friend of Andrew's. They were childhood friends in Kansas. And if you're worried about his credentials, you don't need to be. He's very close to Senator Potter and he's also worked for the government."

"He's a politician?" She arched one eyebrow, and Ronni could see how her mother would find that rather difficult to believe. From the way he dressed, not many would believe he worked for the government in any capacity.

"No, not that kind of government work. Before he was injured, he worked for the CIA."

"You mean he's a spy?" Clara looked as though that was even more difficult to believe.

"Sort of," Ronni hedged. "It doesn't really matter. The point is he did intelligence work for the government. He's a good man. Instead of looking for things wrong with Logan, Mother, you should be feeling grateful to him. He saved Steffie from being kidnapped and helped me get through the most difficult time of my life."

Her mother gave her a disapproving look. "Are you telling me you've been living with that man?"

"I didn't have anyone else to turn to." Ronni stood and walked over to the window. "I told you—after what Peter did,

I didn't exactly receive an outpouring of sympathy from my friends."

"Why didn't you just go to the authorities for help?"

Ronni continued to stare out the window. "The authorities were one of the reasons I needed Logan's help. After Peter held that press conference and announced to the world that I was planning on defecting, too, the FBI treated me like I was a spy. And after everything that had happened, I wasn't sure whom I could trust."

"Are you sure you can trust this Logan?"

"Oh, yes, Mother. I'm sure." Her response had been automatic, and she knew that if there was one thing she was certain of, it was her wholehearted trust in Logan.

"Is he the one who found out we weren't the Summerses?"

Ronni turned back to her mother and nodded. "It puzzled him for a long time. You see, it's not uncommon for Russian spies to assume dead Americans' identities when they infiltrate the country. At first he thought I might be one of them—a Russian pretending to be an American."

"Then those men who took Steffie's bracelet were Russians?"

"All I know is that they're the same ones who tried to kidnap her. But I guess Logan was right all along. They really didn't want her, only the information she had."

Clara frowned. "What information could a child possibly have?"

Ronni held Steffie's Medic-Alert bracelet up to the sunshine streaming through the window. "Whatever it is, it must be in this." She examined it carefully, but could find no evidence that it opened. "Apparently Peter must have somehow attached the missing microchip to this bracelet, although I don't see how."

"What do mean, missing microchip?" Clara demanded, getting up and walking over to stand beside Ronni.

"According to Logan, Peter had been selling American defense technology secrets to the Russians for years. When he defected, he left behind a microchip that supposedly contained information necessary to break some sort of intelligence code. Until those men burst in here, I had no idea where he could have put that information. Now it's obvious he must have slipped it into Steffie's bracelet somehow."

Again she studied the bracelet, turning it over and over. "Logan told me a microchip is so small it would be difficult for the naked eye to discern. Maybe that's why I don't see it, although it does look as though there's a flaw on the underside. What do you think?'' She handed the bracelet to her mother.

Clara peered at the metal, scratching it with her fingernail. ''It's hard to tell. There are all sorts of marks on this, but they could be from Steffie banging it.'' She gave it back to Ronni and said, ''You think those men wanted her bracelet because it contained defense secrets?''

Ronni nodded. ''Peter must have somehow attached the microchip when he was home at Christmas, believing that when we traveled to Vienna to see him, we'd be bringing it with us.'' She dangled the silver chain from her fingers. ''What he didn't expect was that Steffie would get a rash from the bracelet, and I would replace it with a sterling silver one.''

''So those men took the sterling silver bracelet, when all along it was her old metal bracelet that had the information.'' Clara glanced nervously at her daughter. ''What's going to happen when those men discover they've got the wrong bracelet?''

Ronni pressed her hands to her temples and shook her head. ''I don't know.''

''I think you'd better call the authorities—now,'' Clara advised.

''I think we should wait until Logan gets back before we do anything.''

''Wait?'' Clara repeated in disbelief. ''You don't even know if he's coming back. Those men had guns, Veronica.''

The cold fingers of fate seemed to reach out and wrap themselves around Ronni. ''Mother, for Pete's sake. Of course he'll be back. He's an ex-CIA agent,'' she said with more conviction than she was feeling. It worried her that he had gone after them—especially when it hadn't been necessary. She felt a spurt of anger that he hadn't given her the opportunity to tell him she had the missing microchip.

''I still think you should call the FBI,'' Clara said, bending over to pick up Steffie, who was beginning to fuss. ''Steffie's probably hungry. Why don't I make her some lunch while you make that phone call?''

Ronni was not about to be railroaded by her mother. ''We'll all have lunch,'' she announced firmly. ''Then, if I haven't heard from Logan by the time we've finished, I'll call.''

Clara didn't look pleased, but she acquiesced. The three of them ate lunch, although Ronni spent more time pushing food around on her plate than putting it in her mouth. As soon as they'd finished, Clara offered to read Steffie a story, and got her ready for her nap while Ronni cleaned up the kitchen. Ronni was staring out the window, hoping for some sign of Logan when her mother reappeared.

"Well? Did you make that phone call?" Clara asked.

Ronni glanced at her watch. "No, I didn't. Can't we give him another half hour?"

"All right," Clara reluctantly conceded. "But come away from that window. You know what they say—a watched pot never boils." She pulled a deck of cards from the desk drawer. "Why don't we play some gin?"

Ronni wanted to decline, but her mother was already sitting down at the dining-room table, shuffling the cards. Reluctantly Ronni pulled out a chair and sat down across from her. "I tried calling the hospital, but they wouldn't let me speak to Andrew. They said he isn't able to use the phone," she commented, picking up the playing cards her mother was dealing her.

"That's odd...considering he called here this morning." Dark eyebrows peppered with gray drew together. "Do you suppose he's taken a turn for the worse?"

"I don't think so. When I spoke to his nurse I was told he probably would be moved out of the cardiac care unit today. What's strange, though, is that she was under the impression he hasn't been able to use the telephone since he was admitted."

"Of course he has," Clara said, rearranging her cards. "He called me."

Ronni chewed on her lower lip. "I was thinking about that. What if it wasn't Andrew who called this morning, but someone pretending to be him? Maybe it was someone connected with those men who took Steffie's bracelet." She drummed her fingers on the table. "I wonder if there's a tap on your phone."

"For heaven's sake, Veronica, this is worse than a James Bond film." Clara slapped her cards down and placed both palms on the table. "If you're not going to call someone, then I will." She started to stand, but Ronni put out her hand to stop her.

"Please wait just a little longer," she begged. "Logan is convinced that Peter's contact here in the States is working within the government. If he's right, it wouldn't be wise for us to call."

Clara eyed her skeptically, then sat back down. "Do you realize how long he's been gone?"

Again Ronni looked at her watch, and frowned. "Too long. If he would just call so I could tell him about the bracelet." Ronni tossed her cards into the center of the table and got to her feet.

"If you're going to go look out that window again, I'm going to go make us a fresh pot of coffee," Clara said.

Ronni did cross the room and peeked out the window at the street below. Then she began to pace, until finally Clara shoved a magazine in her hand and ordered her to sit down and read. Ronni had little interest in the weekly news magazine, but flipped through the pages to appease her mother.

As she was glancing at the magazine, however, one photo managed to catch her attention. It was of Senator Potter and several other congressmen. Upon closer inspection, Ronni noticed a familiar face in the background, although the caption beneath the photo didn't identify the man.

"What are you looking at?" Clara asked, when Ronni muttered an unintelligible comment under her breath.

"This picture of Andrew's father. It just made me realize something," she said thoughtfully. Suddenly the intercom buzzed, causing Ronni to practically leap off the sofa and rush for the door. Her heart turned over at the sound of Logan's voice.

She was waiting at the elevator when the doors slid open and he stepped out. She launched herself against his chest, wrapping her arms around him possessively. "You're all right," she cried, tears of joy streaming down her face as she looked up at him.

"I'm fine," he assured her, appreciating her exuberant welcome. "You weren't worried, were you?" he asked, covering her tears with his thumbs.

"Of course I was. Those men had guns," she told him wide-eyed. "Come inside," she urged, steering him toward her mother's apartment, where Clara stood guarding the door with a posture that made Ronni want to salute her as she ushered Logan past her.

With an arm wrapped around his waist, Ronni led Logan into the living room, where she pulled him down beside her on the sofa.

"Tell me what happened," she said.

"I lost them. I thought I had them and . . ." He snapped his fingers. "Like that they were gone." He raked a hand through his hair. "Some hero, eh?" He laughed sardonically.

"Thank God you didn't catch them," Ronni exclaimed.

He looked at her quizzically. "Ronni, this means they've got the microchip. It was in Steffie's bracelet."

"I know it was in Steffie's bracelet. I figured that out for myself," she gently chided him. "But, Logan, they don't have Steffie's bracelet."

Confused, he said, "You're not making any sense. You told me you gave them Steffie's bracelet."

"I did," she admitted. "But you came exploding in here, then went tearing out before I could explain to you that Steffie has *two* Medic-Alert bracelets." Her eyes lit up in excitement as she pulled Steffie's original bracelet from her pocket and held it out in front of Logan. "If Peter put the microchip on a bracelet, it's got to be on this one."

Logan took the bracelet and examined it carefully. "What makes you think it's on this one?"

"This is the bracelet Steffie's had ever since she was diagnosed as being allergic to penicillin. She's worn it for months, and I wouldn't have bought a different one except that she developed a rash on her wrist. Thinking it was the metal in the bracelet, I ordered her a sterling silver bracelet that was hypoallergenic."

"And Peter didn't know she had the extra bracelet?"

"No. It only arrived the day we left for Key West. I put it on Steffie's wrist when we stopped for dinner at Cooter's place. I almost threw the old bracelet away, but decided to stick it in the diaper bag in case something happened to the new one." She smiled in relief. "Little did I know how important it was."

Logan looked bewildered and Ronni playfully punched him on the shoulder. "Look happy. The microchip is in your hands. Trust me."

CHAPTER FIFTEEN

"IF ONLY WE'D KNOWN that this little thing was what they were looking for," Logan remarked, jiggling the bracelet in his cupped hand. His expression changed from one of relief to uncertainty. "The problem is, now that we've found it, what do we do with it?"

"Does that mean you still suspect Senator Potter?" Ronni asked.

Before he could reply, Clara stepped forward and said with a slight edge of annoyance in her tone, "Since Veronica's not going to introduce us...I'm Clara Summers." She offered Logan her hand. "Are those two men going to come back here when they realize they don't have the right bracelet?"

Logan stood up and acknowledged her introduction. "I'm Logan McNeil, and I'm afraid I don't have the answer to your question, Mrs. Summers."

Ronni could sense her mother's readiness to cross-examine Logan, for there was disapproval in her narrowed eyes and her pointed chin. Before Clara could pounce on his reply, Ronni gave her a warning glance and said, "Mother, why don't you get us some coffee?"

Ronni half expected her mother to tell her to go get the coffee, but Clara excused herself and disappeared into the kitchen. As soon as she was gone, Ronni slipped her arm through Logan's and asked, "Are those two men likely to come back?"

"If they think you still have the microchip, yes," he answered truthfully.

"Can't we give it back to the government? Surely you can trust the FBI."

"So far the FBI's been unable to find the key man behind the conspiracy. He's covered his tracks pretty well." Logan arched both his eyebrows. "The microchip might be the only way we can identify who was working with Peter."

"Have you told them you suspect the senator?"

Regretfully he said, "I can't—not until I'm certain he's the one."

"What did Andrew say when you talked to him?"

He shook his head. "Nothing that would incriminate his father."

"Mom said he called here earlier this morning asking for me."

"He did call...right after I spoke to you this morning," Clara confirmed, returning with a silver tray laden with cups and saucers, which she set down on the glass-topped coffee table.

"Are you sure it was him?" Logan asked, accepting a china cup from Clara. "He didn't look to me as though he'd be strong enough to use the phone. I was only allowed to talk to him for ten minutes."

"But why would somebody call and pretend to be Andrew?" Ronni asked suspiciously.

Logan took a sip of the coffee. "I don't know, unless it was simply a way of finding out if you and Steffie were here."

"Could it have been the senator?" Ronni asked over the rim of her cup.

Logan shrugged and looked as though he didn't want to even consider the possibility. "He was supposed to meet me at the hospital this morning, but he never showed up."

"Why would Senator Potter pretend to be his son?" Clara asked with a puzzled frown.

Ronni ignored her mother's question and said to her, "Logan uses sugar in his coffee." Clara, who had been hovering beside the two of them with her arms folded across her chest, reluctantly went back to the kitchen.

Ronni waited until her mother was out of sight before saying, "Logan, are you sure the senator doesn't know Andrew is gay?"

"Yes. Why do you ask?"

She reached for the newsmagazine on the coffee table and began flipping through the pages. "While you were gone I happened to be glancing through this and I noticed something." She found the page she was looking for, then held the magazine out in front of him. "See this picture?"

"What about it?" he asked, glancing at the photo of Doc and several congressmen on the Capitol steps.

"See that man in the background—the one with the mustache?" She cocked her head as she peered over his shoulder.

"Yeah, that's Smithson. He works for Senator Potter," he stated simply. "He's been his personal aide for at least five or six years." He held her gaze, waiting for her to continue.

"Then I don't see how the senator could not know that Andrew's gay. That man—" she tapped her fingernail on Smithson's face "—was Andrew's lover."

"Smithson?" Logan was obviously caught off guard by her announcement. She could see the disbelief in his face, and something else—maybe anger?

"Andrew never called him by that name, but I'm positive that's the man," Ronni said confidently. "I only saw him once or twice, and that was by accident. You see, Andrew got very upset that I'd seen him at all. Although he himself had told me about his homosexuality, he became rather embarrassed that I'd actually discovered who his lover was."

"Andrew's a homosexual?" Clara muttered under her breath, nearly dropping the sugar bowl in reaction to Ronni's statement. "How come you never told me?" she admonished her daughter as she slowly lowered her ample figure onto the chair.

"It's not something one broadcasts, Mother," Ronni replied. "Andrew's private life was none of my business. I knew he had men friends, but with the exception of this guy, I never saw any of them."

"Are you sure it was him?" Logan looked again at the man in the picture.

"Yes, that's him. Although I think their affair ended shortly after I found out about it." Ronni glanced at her mother, whose mouth was gaping. "Don't you have some cookies or brownies to go with the coffee?"

"In the freezer, but..." Clara's voice trailed off.

"Pop them in the microwave and they'll be fine," Ronni said pointedly, causing Clara to excuse herself and disappear once more into the kitchen.

"She doesn't look like a dragon to me," Logan commented softly after she'd retreated again, remembering how Ronni had told him her mother was so tough she could puff smoke without a cigarette.

"You haven't seen her in her command mode yet," Ronni said dryly. "And don't you dare say I look like her," she warned.

"You do look like her, especially when you point your chin at me," he teased. He brushed a quick kiss over her pursed lips, then quickly slipped back into a serious mood. "Tell me about Andy and Smithson."

"At first I thought I was responsible for breaking them up, especially because I had to move in with Andrew after Peter and I separated. But Andrew assured me that my staying with him wasn't a problem, since this guy lived out of town and theirs was a long distance affair."

"And he never mentioned that this guy worked for his father?" Logan asked.

"No. All I knew was that because of both of their reputations, secrecy was important. I promised Andrew I'd never mention it to anyone, and I never did. In fact, I had forgotten all about it until I saw that picture."

Logan regarded the photo pensively. "He could be the honey trap."

"What do you mean?" Ronni asked.

"Do you remember when I asked you if you knew what a honey trap was?"

"Yes, when we were in Key West," she replied. "Does it have something to do with spying?"

"A honey trap is a sexual seduction—a common recruitment device spies often use," Logan explained. "Usually it's a female who seduces a male, then threatens to reveal that she's been sleeping with him unless he gets the information she wants. It's a type of blackmail."

"And you think that's what might have happened to Andrew, only in his case the person doing the seducing wasn't a woman but a man?" Ronni suggested.

"It would explain a lot of things—including why those men were able to find us in Fort Lauderdale. Smithson knows every move the senator makes, and even though I asked Doc not to tell anyone where we were, it wouldn't surprise me if Smithson was able to get the information out of him. Doc trusts him implicitly."

"Does this mean that Senator Potter is innocent?" she asked encouragingly.

He exhaled a long sigh of relief. "This is the first time in the past two days that I thought there's a good possibility he is innocent," Logan replied, a look of hope on his face. "You know how difficult it was for me to believe he could be guilty. The problem is, how do I go about proving he's innocent?" He contemplated the question, staring absently into space.

"Can't you just contact the FBI and let them handle it?"

He let his face slip into a grin. "That would be Plan B."

Ronni could see that he was scheming, and a flutter of apprehension had her cautiously asking, "What's Plan A? You're not going to do anything dangerous, are you?"

"Plan A is a little meeting with Mr. Smithson and the senator," he said smugly.

"Did I hear someone say 'dangerous'?" Clara asked, returning this time with a plateful of cookies. "What are you two up to?"

"Logan has a plan that will trap the man responsible for all the horrible things that have been happening to me and Steffie," Ronni explained in a tone more befitting a mother speaking to a child than a child speaking to a mother.

"I hope his plan doesn't involve you," Clara said anxiously.

"You can relax, Mrs. Summers," Logan reassured her. "I wouldn't let Ronni anywhere near this guy."

"What do you mean you won't *let* me?" Ronni asked indignantly, hands on her hips. "I'm the one who recognized Smithson from the photo, and if I want to come with you, I'm going to come with you."

"You're not coming with me," Logan said firmly. "Catching spies is my business, Ronni, not yours."

"Veronica, listen to the man," Clara advised. "He knows what he's talking about. My goodness, we've just had two men with guns break in here and steal Steffie's bracelet!"

"There must be something I can do," Ronni lamented.

"You can give me the keys to your house," Logan said. "And Steffie's bracelet. And I'm going to need to use the telephone."

An hour later, Ronni accompanied Logan to the lobby of her mother's apartment building, where they waited for a man called Nat. Six-foot-tall and an ex-marine, Nat was the bodyguard Logan had arranged to stay with Ronni and her mother while he was gone. Although Logan felt comfortable with the arrangement, Ronni wasn't—not because she resented having a bodyguard, but because she didn't want Logan going alone to her house.

"You're worrying over nothing, Ronni," Logan told her when she expressed such sentiments. "I've been in intelligence work for over ten years. I'm not going to get hurt."

"You were the one who said desperate men are dangerous," Ronni reminded him, trying to control the shivers of apprehension that made her want to fling herself against the door and not let him leave.

"If our suspicions are correct and Doc is innocent, it'll be two against one." He laid his hand on her cheek. "Trust me."

Ronni reached up and covered his hand with hers. "I wish you'd let me come along. I promise I won't get in the way. I could hide in one of the bedrooms. You wouldn't even know I was there." She looked up at him beseechingly.

"I wish I could say I want you to come with me, Ronni, but the truth is it's better if you wait here."

"But I want to be there, Logan. Do you realize what this guy has done to me? He's blackmailed Andrew into committing treason, he's helped convince the FBI that I was involved with Peter, and worst of all, he's put Steffie's life in danger."

"He's one of their best," he acknowledged with a sigh. "For five years he's managed to fool one of the sharpest men I know."

"Logan, what are you going to do if Senator Potter was in on all of this?"

"He wasn't." The words were swift and positive. "I'd bet my life on it."

"You sound awfully confident."

"Didn't I tell you? I've got a sixth sense when it comes to detecting spies. When I see someone I know is legit, I get a flutter right here." He nudged his rib cage with his fist.

"Is that what happened when you met me? You got a flutter right there?" She touched the same spot.

"With you, the flutter was in an entirely different place," he said huskily. "Actually it was more of a throb."

"And when did you first notice this... ah... throb?" she asked, his nearness causing her body to respond in a natural way.

"When Doc showed me a picture of you. You were wearing the most delicious green swimsuit." He smiled dangerously. "I took one look at you and I told Doc you weren't a spy."

"Do I have this...ah...throb to thank for your helping me and Steffie?" She inched her fingers teasingly between the buttons on his shirt.

"I suppose it played a part in my decision to come after you," he confessed with a seductive grin.

"You did have a few doubts along the way," she reminded him.

"When you've been an agent as long as I have, it's hard not to be suspicious of your own mother." He reached out and caressed her cheeks with his fingertips. "I want you to know something, Ronni. When it comes to what's happened with us, there are no doubts."

"For me, neither," she told him, turning her head so that her lips met his palm.

He leaned over and kissed her long and hard. "I'm not going to let anything happen, I promise," he murmured.

"It'll all work out." They both knew she wasn't talking just about Smithson being apprehended. "If I'm frightened at all, it's only because I'm worried that when it's all over you're going to walk out of my life." She looked at him with pleading eyes.

Logan reluctantly released her. "This isn't the time or the place to be talking about that." He glanced over his shoulder and out the glass doors. "Nat's coming across the street."

Ronni reached up and wiped the smeared lipstick from his mouth. "I love you, Logan," she told him just seconds before the bodyguard entered the lobby. Logan looked as though he was going to say something to her, but Nat greeted him with a big grin and a raised hand.

"Hey, Mick!" He slapped Logan's hand in a high-five manner. "It's good to see you, buddy."

Logan slapped the outstretched hand back and smiled warmly. "Nat, this is Ronni. She and her mother are going to wait upstairs until I get back."

Ronni shook Nat's big burly hand and returned his grin. "Hi, Nat. It's nice to meet you. I'm going to walk Logan to his car, then I'll take you upstairs."

Nat looked to Logan for confirmation.

Logan nodded, then tapped Nat on the arm. "I appreciate your coming over," he said gratefully, then opened the door for Ronni.

As soon as they were outdoors, she said, "You weren't kidding when you said he was big." She glanced back over her shoulder and saw the blond giant standing in the doorway. "I think his arm is bigger than my leg."

"What frightens me more than confronting Smithson is the thought of leaving you alone," Logan said with more emotion than she was expecting to hear in his voice. "If I can't be there to protect you, I want to make certain the guy who is can handle the job."

"But if Smithson is Peter's contact and he knows you're bringing the microchip with you, there isn't much chance that he'd send anybody here, is there?"

"It's a chance I'm not going to take." They had arrived at the pickup, and the apprehension she was feeling about him leaving was written all over her face. Logan hooked a finger beneath her chin and said, "Hey, don't look at me as though I'm walking into a firing squad."

She lowered her eyes. "I'm sorry. I'm just a little nervous."

He quickly pressed one last kiss on her mouth, only it wasn't a quick kiss, but a slow, lingering caress that left both of them breathing a little harder. Logan leaned his forehead against hers and said, "Relax, it's a piece of cake."

She pressed her hands against his chest, unwittingly finding the shoulder holster, and she stiffened. "I thought you said agents seldom carried guns?"

"This is seldom," he said, looking away in the distance.

She bit on her lower lip. "Please don't go, Logan. Let the FBI handle this," she pleaded.

He returned his gaze to her, searching for understanding. "Ronni, I can't. If Doc is guilty, I have to be the first one to know."

Unsteadily she nodded.

"Look, I've got to go." He grabbed her one last time and planted one more long, hard kiss on her mouth. "I love you, too, Ronni," he murmured, then signaled to Nat that he was leaving.

"Be careful," she called out as he climbed into the orange pickup.

He rolled down the window. "It'll all work out. Trust me."

Ronni could only nod and wave goodbye. Long after his truck had disappeared out of sight, she stood staring at the street, until finally Nat called out to her to come inside. Slowly she walked back to the apartment building, her mind racing ahead to what would happen when Logan confronted Smithson and Doc in her home. She tried not to think about that meeting, forcing her thoughts to images of what it would be like when it was over. She would be cleared of any involvement with Peter, she could go home again and she and Steffie would be out of danger.

What would happen to Andrew she could only speculate on. Even if his involvement was the result of being blackmailed, she assumed he would be tried and sent to prison. Not only was Steffie going to lose her father, but her godfather, as well.

And she herself would still be married to Peter, but in love with another man. Logan had said he loved her. Those three words had unleashed a torrent of hopes and dreams, which she'd been secretly harboring ever since she'd discovered how much she loved him. She knew, however, that just because he'd said he loved her didn't mean he wanted to make a commitment.

It was a lot to ask of a man—accepting the responsibility of parenting a child. She wasn't just a married woman; she was a married woman with child. And they hadn't had time to talk about what the future held. They had been too busy discovering each other.

ALL THE WAY to Ronni's house, Logan's thoughts were filled with images of her tear-stained face, how appealing she had looked begging him not to go. He was just as apprehensive as she was—not about trapping Smithson, but about what was going to happen to the two of them. In a very short time Ronni and her daughter had managed to become a part of his life—a part he didn't want to lose. Yet when all this craziness was over and he was no longer needed to protect them, would she still want him in her life? As much as he wanted to believe that she loved him, he knew that circumstances had played a big part in their relationship. Maybe she was simply in love with the dangerous secret agent image he represented.

As he parked the pickup beside her house, memories of the last time he'd been there rushed to greet him. Automatically his gaze flickered to the large, overgrown bougainvillea on the corner, and as he expected, there sat a television repair van. So far so good.

He climbed out of the truck and followed the cement walk to the front door. As soon as he was inside, he found the telephone in the living room, pulled a small metal disk from his pocket and placed it on the underside of the cradle. Then he went to the refrigerator, extracted a bottle of spring water and looked curiously around Ronni's house while he waited for his visitors.

He didn't have to wait long. Smithson pulled into the narrow driveway, carefully maneuvering the large town car. Logan watched him open the door for the senator and help him out in his usual attentive manner. Doc looked even more haggard than the last time Logan had seen him. His suit was slightly wrinkled, his gray hair less than immaculately groomed. He appeared troubled and tired, and Logan's heart balked at what he knew he had to do to the old man. He wanted to console him, not interrogate him. But he couldn't—not until he was absolutely certain that Doc wasn't involved in the spy ring.

Smithson on the other hand looked impeccable. Despite the heat, he wore a three-piece pin-striped suit without a wrinkle in it—not even a crease in the pants. Logan had often wondered how anyone could sit down and not wrinkle his pants, but Smithson had always managed it. His hair was cut shorter now, and his mustache was gone. He looked as honest as a judge, and Logan had to remind himself that beneath that gentlemanly facade lurked a deceptive mind.

"You made good time," Logan said by way of a greeting, as he opened the door for them to enter.

"The hospital gave me your message as soon as I arrived," Doc explained, following Logan into the living room. He had withdrawn a handkerchief from his pocket and was blotting his forehead.

"Are you all right, Doc?" Logan asked, gesturing for the two men to be seated.

Doc dismissed Logan's concern with a wave of his hand. "I'm fine. I'm just a little warm." He accepted Logan's offer of a chair, but Smithson expressed a desire to remain standing.

Logan searched for some signs of anxiety in the younger man, but there was none. He figured it could mean one of two things: either Smithson didn't suspect that Logan knew he was Peter's conspirator, or else he was confident that no matter what happened, he would get the microchip. Logan hoped that it was the former. He also wished that he had Smithson's confidence, for right now his insides were churning. He wasn't sure he could play charades with Doc, yet he knew he had no choice but to give it his best shot.

"Warm, eh, Doc?" Logan shoved his hands in his pockets and stood looking down at the older man. "You wouldn't be nervous about seeing me, would you?"

Doc gave him a puzzled look. "This whole business of the microchip has me nervous. Do you realize how important that tiny piece of information is?"

"Maybe you ought to tell me why it's so important to you," Logan suggested, an edge to his voice. He raised a hand to his forehead and gently massaged his temple.

Doc caught the gesture and asked, "What's wrong with you? Is your eye bothering you?"

Logan gave a couple of quick shakes of his head. "It's nothing."

"Where's the microchip?" Doc asked.

"It's right here." Logan reached inside his pocket and withdrew the bracelet, dangling it in midair.

"A bracelet?" Doc looked quizzically at him.

"Surprised?" Logan asked.

"You mean to tell me the microchip is in that bracelet?" The senator appeared skeptical.

"Very good, Doc," Logan said sarcastically, and just as Doc was about to reach for the chain, Logan stepped back and snatched it out of his reach. "But you can cut the ignorant number. You know damn well the microchip is in the bracelet. That's why you sent those two goons to steal it off Steffie Lang's wrist." With the accusation came the appearance of the gun, as Logan smoothly pulled it from under his arm.

Doc gasped and fell back against the sofa cushions. "What the hell are you talking about?" he demanded.

"I'm talking about treason. You know, selling secrets to foreign governments," Logan said, pointing the gun at his mentor.

"Logan, you can't possibly think that *I'm* involved in the Lang affair," Doc challenged.

Coolly Smithson spoke up in defense of his boss. "Come on, Logan, you're out of line on this."

"I think not," Logan went on. "I knew there had to be someone on the inside—a top brass. You fooled the feds—you even fooled me—well, almost. Why did you do it, Doc? How could you have set me up like that?" he asked painfully.

"I didn't set you up!" Doc emphatically denied. "Logan, you've got to be sick if you think I'd do such a thing. Sit down and put that gun away."

The senator attempted to rise, but Logan pointed the gun directly at his face.

"You're right about one thing, Doc. I am sick," Logan rasped. "I'm sick at heart to think that someone I loved like a father could have done this to me."

"I can't believe you would think such a thing of me," Doc said, again protesting his innocence.

Smithson finally spoke up. "Logan, are you certain about this?"

"Of course he's not certain," Doc interjected. "He's confused. I don't know why or how he came to such a conclusion."

"It's over, Doc. You can save your defense." Logan turned to Smithson. "Take this and keep him covered while I call the FBI." He handed the gun to Smithson, then walked over to the desk and started to dial.

"Smithson, quit waving that gun around," Doc ordered. "Let him call the feds. They'll tell him how wrong he is." He made a move to get up again, but Smithson pushed him back with the point of his gun.

"Nobody's calling anybody," Smithson declared in a threatening tone of voice.

Logan glanced over his shoulder and saw that Smithson didn't just have the senator covered, but was aiming the gun at him, as well. "Hey, be careful where you're pointing that thing," he said uneasily.

Smithson chuckled nastily. "Sure, Logan. Just as soon as you've put down that telephone and given me that little silver chain. After all, we want to make sure it reaches the proper authorities, don't we?" he said with a smirk, his palm outstretched.

Logan stood staring at Smithson for several seconds before he finally uttered, "You?" He gave him a look of disbelief that could have won him an Academy Award.

"I'm waiting for it, Logan," Smithson reminded him.

Slowly Logan replaced the telephone on its cradle, then walked over to Smithson and dropped the bracelet in his hand. Smithson's fingers quickly snapped shut around it.

"Now move over there next to Doc and keep your hands up over your head where I can see them," Smithson directed, gesturing with the gun.

Logan did as he was told, eyeing Smithson suspiciously as he sat down beside the senator. "You're not going to get away with this," he warned.

"Who's going to stop me? You?" He chuckled sarcastically. "It's no wonder the Agency retired you. Admit it, Logan. You've lost it. Or maybe I should say you met someone smarter than you, Mr. Spy Catcher."

Doc was sputtering and shaking his head in disbelief. "You were the mastermind behind Peter Lang?"

"Have been for five years, Doc," Smithson confessed proudly. "Since the day you hired me." With one hand, he examined the bracelet, scratching a small metal piece on the underside. "Bingo! There it is. Right where it's supposed to be." An evil grin spread across his face. "Thanks, fellas." He slipped the bracelet into his pocket. "This little piece of jewelry is going to set me up for life. I'll finally be able to return home."

"Home?" Doc queried.

"Leningrad." Again Smithson smirked. "There's no place like home, is there?"

"You're a Russian? But what about your credentials? I had you thoroughly investigated before I ever hired you," Doc insisted.

"Kenneth Smithson was created to be the perfect congressional aide...and he was," he said smugly. "I don't think I've ever seen a more impressive résumé. Amazing what contacts in the right places can do, isn't it?" He gave a little laugh. "We worked well together, Senator, and I enjoyed our partnership...especially now that it's given me the opportunity to return home a hero."

"You disgust me!"

When the senator would have lunged at the man, Logan grabbed him.

"Stop it, Doc. He's not worth getting shot over."

"You really are washed up, aren't you?" Smithson directed his loathing at Logan. "First you hand me the gun, then you expect me to walk out of here with the two of you still breathing." He shook his head disbelievingly. "When I leave, I leave two dead fools behind."

"Tell me how Andrew is involved in this," Doc demanded.

"Ah, yes, Andrew."

Smithson appeared to be considering how much he should tell the older man, and Logan knew it was time he intervened with some questioning. "As long as we're dead meat, why don't you tell these two fools just how many people were involved in this Peter Lang affair?"

"Does it bother you that you weren't able to crack it?" Smithson chided.

"All right, so you fooled me," Logan admitted. "But how do I know it was you who masterminded this whole scheme? Maybe Andrew was the brains behind it."

Smithson laughed. "Andrew followed orders I issued." He looked at the senator. "Your son is bright, Doc, but he's spineless."

"How did you trap him? Was it the Lang woman?" Doc asked, and Logan held his breath waiting for the answer.

"What makes you think he had to be trapped? Andrew is just as greedy as any other man," Smithson replied.

"He did it for money?" Doc asked, and Logan could see the agony on the lined face.

"What's wrong, Senator? Does it bother you to think that your son could sell his idealism for material things? It shouldn't surprise you. You've known all along that Andy doesn't share your patriotic sentiment. He's not righteous and strong like Logan here. He's weak, Doc. But you've known that all along, too, haven't you?"

"Isn't that what attracted you to him in the first place?" Logan asked, hating to have to bring up the subject, but knowing he had no choice. "You got a thing about weak men, Smithson?" There was no way either man could have missed the double meaning.

"Logan, are you saying that Andrew and Smithson were..." Doc's voice trailed off, his face paling.

"Lovers," Logan finished for him, hating to have to be the one to say the word.

A small bead of perspiration lined Smithson's thin lips. "How did you find out?"

"I'm glad you're not going to deny it," Logan said soberly. "You know, you were good, Smithson. You fooled Doc. You fooled me. Luckily Mrs. Lang saw your picture in a magazine. Apparently Andy didn't keep your affair as secret as you had hoped. Tell me, did you blackmail him into spying for you, or was he already mixed up with Peter Lang?"

He pressed his lips together so tightly they almost disappeared. "Andy's more like his father than he wants him to believe he is. Fortunately his feelings for his father were strong enough to want to keep his sexual preferences private."

"So you threatened to expose him if he didn't cooperate," Logan inserted. "So what happened to this wonderful arrangement?"

"Andrew began having an attack of conscience, especially when Peter told him the microchip was going to be delivered on the wrist of his daughter. He did as he was told—saw to it that it was affixed to the baby's bracelet, but he threatened to expose all of us if anything happened to either the child or its mother," Smithson explained.

"So you countered his threat with one of your own. You made sure that Andrew had a change of heart—literally—injecting him with a drug that nearly stopped his heart permanently," Logan accused.

"I can't believe you'd do such a thing!" Doc exclaimed, gaping at the man who'd been his trusted aide for the past five years.

"Oh, it's true, Doc," Logan assured him. "That day you visited me, Smithson here flew to Melbourne."

"You told me you had to visit your mother," Doc said to Smithson.

"All those visits he supposedly made to his mother—convincing you he was a dutiful son—they were actually visits to Andy," Logan continued.

"Well, well, well," Smithson said. "The old one-eyed agent isn't as foolish as I thought." His eyes flew to the gun in his hand, and in an almost panicky move, he squeezed the trigger.

"Sorry, Smithson," Logan said when the only sound heard was the click of an empty barrel. "I don't like to carry a loaded gun." He shot him a wicked grin.

Immediately Smithson dropped the gun, but when he would have reached inside his coat pocket for his own weapon, a voice called over Smithson's shoulder, "Freeze!"

Smithson had no choice, for a heavy-duty Magnum was aimed directly at him.

Logan looked up to see Wicklund and Mahoney searching Smithson for any other weapons. "It's about time you two showed up," he said, a hint of relief in his voice. "I was beginning to worry."

"You're the one who said you wanted time to get the whole story," Stan Wicklund reminded him with a crooked grin.

CHAPTER SIXTEEN

LOGAN WANTED NOTHING more than to rush right over to Clara Summers's apartment to see Ronni, but the senator was slumped wearily on the sofa. Even though his face reflected no emotion, he looked like a broken man, and Logan wondered if there was anything he could say that would ease the heartache the man was suffering.

As soon as the others had gone, Logan sat down beside him and put a hand on his sagging shoulder. "I'm sorry, Doc. I didn't mean to be so hard on you, but it was the only way I knew how to get Smithson to confess."

Doc seemed to be lost in a world of his own and didn't respond.

Worried, Logan asked, "Are you okay, Doc?"

"How could I have been so blind?" he asked quietly, closing his eyes as he shook his head regretfully. "Smithson is right—I am an old fool."

"You've never been a fool in my eyes," Logan said sincerely.

Doc stared at his hands. "How long have you known about all this?"

"I only put the final pieces together this afternoon. I went to the hospital looking for you this morning, but you and Smithson hadn't arrived yet. You see, you were the only person who knew we were staying in Fort Lauderdale. When the KGB agents showed up there, I figured it had to be someone in your office."

"Or me?" Doc looked him in the eye. "You did think it was me, didn't you?"

Logan wanted to lie and tell him he'd never lost his faith in him, but he'd never pulled any punches with Doc, so he told him the truth. "I wouldn't be a good agent if I hadn't suspected you. But deep down in my heart I knew that you were innocent. Although I must confess it's not easy being objective when people you care about are involved."

Dejectedly Doc said, "I've lost everything, Logan. My son...my job—I'm going to have to resign from the Senate."

Logan didn't try to pretend otherwise. "You're the one who's been telling me for quite some time now that this was going to be your last term, that you wanted to go back to the farm."

"Yes, well, I didn't want to leave with my tail tucked between my legs." He smoothed a hand across the thin spot on the back of his head. "There'll be a formal investigation. I haven't anything to hide," he said proudly.

"I didn't think you did," Logan assured him. "Tell me, Doc, how much did you know about Andy's part in all this?"

"The first indication I had that he could be involved with Lang was when I came to you. Like you said, sometimes you lose your objectivity with people you care about. As I look back now, I can see the signs were all there, but I chose to ignore them." There was self-recrimination in his voice, then he chuckled and shook his head in amazement. "I thought that all those weekends Smithson spent in Cocoa Beach he was visiting his mother."

"He fooled me, too, Doc," Logan admitted. "You're the one who told me that a good agent isn't fooled but betrayed."

"I was betrayed by my right-hand man and my own son. That kind of betrayal makes a man feel foolish."

"Smithson was a pro—and a damn good one. He knew exactly what he was doing and for what reasons. Andy, on the other hand, was a victim—maybe not an innocent victim, but still a victim. Tell me something, Doc. If Veronica Lang had been the honey trap, would that have made it any easier for you to accept Andy's treason?"

Doc considered the question carefully. "No, I guess it wouldn't have," he finally said. "I only wish Andrew had come to me and told me what was happening. Did he think I wouldn't understand about his homosexuality?"

"Knowing Andy, he probably figured it would be one more reason for you to be disappointed in him. Or maybe he hasn't truly accepted his homosexuality himself. And you have to remember, he didn't want to blemish your reputation with ugly gossip. It was that vulnerability that allowed Smithson to use him. The threat of exposure was all he needed to keep Andy in line."

"Andrew is going to end up in prison," Doc said sadly.

"More than likely, although at this point we don't know to what extent he was involved. It's possible he could get a reduced sentence depending on his testimony. Andy must have been ready to go to the authorities, otherwise the Russians wouldn't have tried to kill him."

Doc sighed. "I hope you're right." He heaved his large frame up off the sofa. "I guess I'd better get over to the hospital. I told Wicklund and Mahoney I'd meet them there."

"Do you want me to come with you?" Logan offered.

"I guess I'll need a ride," the senator said, patting his pockets. "Smithson took the keys to the town car."

Logan threw his arm around the rounded shoulders and said, "Come on. I'll show you what it's like to ride in an ultra orange machine. I can drop you off on my way to get Ronni."

As it turned out, it was quite late by the time Logan got back to Clara Summers's apartment. The meeting with Wicklund and Mahoney had been a painful one for Doc, as Andrew, with the doctor's permission, had talked with the FBI and openly admitted his involvement with Smithson. Logan had hung around to the bitter end, hoping his presence could in some small way compensate for the misery he knew Doc was suffering. As eager as he was to get over to see Ronni, he couldn't leave the senator to face such adversity alone.

He had called Ronni from the hospital and learned that she had decided to spend the night with her mother, since Steffie had fallen asleep shortly after dinner. When Clara admitted him to the apartment, Logan saw Nat sitting in front of the television with a bowl of popcorn on his lap, while Ronni was curled up on the couch, asleep.

Logan wanted to run over and kiss her awake, but he forced himself to settle up with Nat, exchanging a few words and a handshake while Clara turned off the television, then gently nudged Ronni's shoulder. Startled, Ronni awoke, stretching like a cat before noticing that Logan was ushering Nat out the door. Clara discreetly announced that she was going to bed, and as the dead bolt clicked shut behind Nat, Ronni joyously rushed into Logan's arms.

"I'm so glad it's finally over," she said when he had finished telling her about Smithson's arrest. "It is over, isn't it, Logan?"

"I can't guarantee that the FBI won't want to speak with you again, but at least they know you were simply an innocent bystander caught up in circumstances beyond your control."

"Andrew wasn't innocent, though, was he?" she asked solemnly.

Logan shook his head. "It's true that Smithson was blackmailing him, but he was involved, more so than we first thought. Andy was the one who put the microchip on Steffie's wrist."

"It wasn't Peter?"

"No. Apparently Andy went out and bought a Medic-Alert bracelet identical to Steffie's, had the microchip affixed to the metal—sort of a false front so you couldn't tell it was there. Then, before you were supposed to leave for Vienna, he made the switch."

Ronni's brow wrinkled. "It must have been when he invited us over for dinner. He said it was a bon voyage supper."

"Peter was supposed to make another switch, substituting an identical bracelet for the one with the microchip once you got to Vienna."

"Only we never made it to Vienna," Ronni said solemnly. "That must be why Andrew told us to come directly to his house the morning of his heart attack. He wanted to get the microchip off of Steffie's wrist." She shook her head in disappointment. "When the paramedics were wheeling him out to the ambulance, he pulled off his oxygen mask and asked about Steffie. I thought he was worried about her health, when all along he was only worried about getting the microchip back."

"He does care about her," Logan said in Andrew's defense, which only drew a skeptical look from Ronni. "Apparently Smithson had promised Andy that the transfer of the microchip would be the last assignment he would have to complete. At first Andy refused to be a part of anything involving you and Steffie, but Smithson warned him that if someone else was assigned to the task, he couldn't promise you wouldn't get hurt. So Andy did the job, thinking he would at least be able to protect the two of you."

"Did he know that Peter was going to defect?"

"Not until it was too late to stop you from going to Vienna—or at least he thought it was too late. That's when he started making his own threats about exposing the spy ring if anything happened to either you or Steffie. When Smithson got word that you never made it to Vienna, he had two problems on his hands. One was to retrieve the microchip, the other was to silence Andy, who by now was close to telling his father everything."

"Are you saying that Smithson tried to kill Andrew?" Her eyes widened in disbelief.

"You were right about Andy being in good health. As it turned out, his heart attack was drug induced. Smithson paid him a visit shortly before you and I arrived at his house."

"I don't know whether to be angry with him or to pity him," she said sadly.

"I'd say you're entitled to do both." He studied the tumble of blond hair framing her face and tucked a strand behind her ear.

"I think I'm too numb to know what I'm feeling," Ronni said flatly as tears blurred her vision. "All I know is it hurts."

Logan pulled her into his arms and gently rocked her. "I did everything I could to protect you, Ronni, but there simply wasn't any way I could protect you from the emotional pain of all this," he said regretfully.

"I'm just happy you're here for me," she whispered, taking comfort in both his strength and his gentleness. "Steffie fell asleep before you called, otherwise we would have gone home."

"I think it's a good idea that you're staying the night here. You look tired."

"I am, but what about you? Where are you going to stay? You can use my place if you like," she offered, a smile creeping across her face.

Logan knew the inevitable moment had come. He had to tell her he was leaving. "I'm not staying in Melbourne tonight. I'm going back to Washington with the senator."

"Tonight?"

She looked at him in alarm, and his resolve nearly crumpled. "The sooner all this gets cleared up, the better. Unofficially I'm involved in the investigation. Plus there are a few matters I need to attend to in Virginia."

"Virginia?"

"That's where the pickle factory is." He grinned, then added, "CIA headquarters."

"How long will you be gone?"

He shrugged. "I'm hoping it won't take more than a few days…maybe a week. I figured you probably wanted to spend some time with your mother—after everything that's happened."

She wanted to say she needed to spend some time with him, but she didn't. Suddenly she felt unsure about his feelings. Had she read too much into his declaration of love?

"Did your mother have the answers you were looking for?" he asked, concern in his voice.

But Ronni didn't want his concern. She wanted him to stay with her—to tell her everything was going to be all right, that he still loved her. Nervously she answered, "She told me what happened and why we're using other people's names."

"Do you want to tell me about it?"

She shrugged. "There's not much to tell really. She's not a criminal," she was quick to point out.

"I didn't think she was."

No, he wouldn't have, Ronni thought. If Logan was anything, he was just. She'd turned away from him and was absently fingering a clay pot her mother kept on the bookshelf. It was an art project Ronni had made in the fourth grade, and despite its childlike design, it still held a treasured spot in her mother's home. "She did it to protect me."

"That sounds like a pretty normal reaction to me—wanting to protect the ones you love," Logan remarked.

Ronni rubbed her hands across the lumpy clay pot. "Yes, I guess it is." She gave him an abbreviated version of the story her mother had told her. By the time she'd finished her eyes reflected no emotion, yet Logan knew better.

"You still feel betrayed by her, don't you?"

His voice was gentle and understanding. But, then, she knew it would be. He understood her the way no one else ever had.

She nodded. "Maybe if Peter and Andrew hadn't done what they did, I'd be in a better frame of mind to try to understand my mother's behavior. What's funny is that in my head I do understand, but my heart still aches, Logan. Maybe my father was a real jerk—just like Steffie's—but I feel cheated out of the chance to find that out for myself." She pushed her hands into her pockets and shrugged. "I know this probably doesn't make sense to you... it doesn't make much sense to me."

"I think you're going to need to give it some time," Logan advised.

At the mention of the word "time," Ronni felt a flutter of panic. They needed time with each other, time that wasn't filled with fear and danger, time to talk about their future together. But he had just told her he was going to be spending time away from her. She wanted to scream at him, *Don't go to Washington, Logan, please.* She didn't need to shout it out aloud, for her expressive face said it all.

Logan felt torn. Here was a woman he loved, a woman who needed him, yet the senator needed him, too. There was also his professional obligation to complete the investigation. And in his heart he knew that he and Ronni needed the time apart to examine feelings, to make sure their romance wasn't simply a result of two people being thrown together in the excitement of intrigue and danger.

"I hate leaving. If I could stay with you, I would," he told her, moving closer to her. "But there's one thing I've learned about you. You're a strong woman, Ronni. You're going to get through all this."

"It's 'Cynthia,'" she corrected. "My real name is Cynthia Locken."

He hooked a finger under her chin and turned her face up to his. "You'll always be 'Ronni' to me."

"Is there an always for us, Logan?" she asked, raising her eyes to his.

He couldn't immediately assure her there was, for he wasn't sure himself, and if there was one thing he always wanted to be with her, it was honest.

When he didn't reply right away but stood studying her face, she said, "You don't think there is, do you?"

"It's been a wonderful ten days, Ronni...ten days I'll never forget..." he began, but she cut him off before he could tell her everything it had meant to him.

"But that's all it was, right? Ten days out of your life." She bit down on her lower lip—so hard she was surprised she didn't draw blood. At the same time the phone rang, and on wobbly legs she went to answer it. "It's for you," she said flatly, handing him the receiver.

Feeling awkward, she escaped into the kitchen, opening the refrigerator and appraising its contents, despite not being the least bit hungry. She pulled out a pitcher of orange juice and poured herself a glass, only to jump when she heard Logan's footsteps behind her.

"Do you want some juice?" she blurted out.

He simply shook his head. "That was Doc. He managed to get a private plane to take us to Washington. They're waiting for me at the airport."

She nodded in understanding, although she wasn't understanding anything. Why was Logan leaving her when they had so much unfinished business? She moved her gaze from his face back to the glass of orange juice. "You'd better get going, then." Her voice was stilted, her movements jerky. "I want to thank you, Logan, for everything. I'll always be grateful for what you did for me and Steffie."

"Look at me, Ronni," he commanded, turning her around to face him. "I'm not going to be gone forever," he told her, hoping his words would erase the worry on her face. "I wouldn't be honest with you if I said I knew what the future holds for us. But I want you to remember this while I'm gone. It's not over between us." Then he kissed her, a deep, possessive kiss that left her with no doubts that indeed it wasn't over between them. It couldn't be.

REPEATEDLY DURING the following weeks, Ronni relived that kiss, as well as all the other intimate moments they had shared during their brief interlude together. For that's what their experience seemed like with him gone—simply a brief interlude of fantasy in which she had met the man of her dreams, only to have reality intrude.

Logan's business took longer than he expected, and the longer he was gone, the less hope she had that their relationship would ever be anything other than a fantasy. He seemed to be in her thoughts day and night, and she was powerless to resist the images that haunted her.

In the morning, she'd imagine how wonderful it would be to have him wake her with a caress, his head beside hers on the pillow. While she made breakfast for Steffie, she'd remember how Logan had stood at the stove, taking great pride in what he called his "farmboy skills," cooking up breakfast for the three of them. As she cleaned house, she'd wonder if he would want to move into her little house or if they'd look for a bigger place. Would they even live in Melbourne, or would he want to go back to Key West? At the grocery store she'd pass the frozen food section and want to load several of the microwavable entrées into her cart, knowing he thought of them as staples.

And as she folded the freshly laundered linens, she'd think about the night they had argued over the wet towels, chiding herself for getting upset over something so trivial.

Several times he had phoned, but the phone calls were brief and never contained the news she wanted to hear—when he would be coming home. As insecure as she was feeling about their relationship, Ronni was beginning to believe Logan didn't want to return. She wondered if he was having second thoughts about severing all ties with the CIA, especially when she went to see Andrew and he implied that Logan would be encouraged to return to intelligence work. The longer he stayed away, the more she worried that she and Steffie weren't going to be included in his future.

Once the press broke the news of the congressional aide and the senator's son, Ronni's story appeared to be of little interest to the media. She was amazed at how easily her life did return to normal. So much had happened, so many things had changed, yet life seemed to go on as though nothing had happened, nothing had changed.

After several conversations with her mother, Ronni was able to piece together enough details about her father and his family that she felt she had sufficient information to search for them. Clara gave her the addresses she had, even though it was unlikely that after twenty-five years they were correct. Ronni wrote them all down and tucked them away in the top drawer of her jewelry chest, uncertain about what she was going to do with them. There were still five weeks left before school started again—plenty of time to journey to Wisconsin. She told herself she was waiting until emotionally she felt rested, when the truth was she was afraid to leave in case Logan returned and found her gone.

Little did she know that Logan was conducting an investigation of his own. Tracing the background of one Ronald Locken, he discovered that Ronni's father was indeed alive and well in Wisconsin, working as a plumber for Ronni's uncle, a general contractor. Although he had remarried since his divorce from Clara, he was single again, but the father of a second daughter, twenty-four-year-old Kelly Locken. From the pictures Logan had seen, Kelly resembled Ronni, but had red hair and lots of freckles. Besides several cousins and distant relatives, there were also paternal grandparents, who were retired and now living in Naples, Florida.

It was with this information that Logan packed his bags and prepared to leave for Melbourne. Between testifying before the Senate Intelligence Committee and following up on his medical treatment, he had been forced to stay away from Ronni far too long. He had thought that a little distance between them would enable him to better understand their relationship. But the only thing distance had done was frustrate him with longing for her.

It had also prevented him from being the one to tell her about Peter Lang's death. When word had arrived that the defector had been killed in an automobile crash in the Soviet Union, Logan had nearly told the Senate Intelligence Committee they could stick their investigation—he was leaving. However, as usual, his strong sense of duty had prevailed and he had stayed, and Ronni was notified of Peter's death by someone from the government. He doubted whether the official report included any details of the accident. Few people outside the Agency knew that unimportant defectors often succumbed to "accidental deaths" in the Soviet Union.

Now Logan no longer needed to worry about such matters. His work was completed and there was no reason for him not to return to Melbourne. The question that had his stomach tied up in knots as the big jet landed in Florida was, did Ronni want him to return?

It had been three weeks since he'd been gone. Except for brief telephone conversations sandwiched between important meetings, they'd hardly spoken to each other. And those conversations had done little to ease his anxiety about whether she still felt the same for him as he did for her. There was only one way to find out her true feelings, he told himself as he stood up to retrieve his carryon bag from the overhead compartment of the plane. Face-to-face. With a deep breath, he followed the rest of the passengers out the exit, a smile on his face at the thought that she was waiting for him.

A half hour later the smile was gone, as was a good share of his optimism. She hadn't been waiting for him at the terminal. There weren't any messages for him at the information desk, and there was no answer when he telephoned her house. He was on the verge of letting insecurity overrule his logic and doing something drastic—like taking the car he'd just rented and driving all the way back to Kansas. Then he berated himself for acting like some kind of fool in love. Ronni wasn't the kind of person to convey messages with her absence.

A quick phone call to Clara Summers revealed that Ronni had left Steffie with her grandmother so that she would be free to pick him up at the airport. However, Clara was under the impression that Logan's plane wasn't due in until later that evening, which would account for Ronni's absence. Clara also mentioned that Ronni had planned to spend the afternoon shopping, which would explain why there was no answer at her house. Clara suggested that he stop by and pick up a key to Ronni's house, then go wait for her there.

Logan took Clara's advice, and after stopping off for a brief visit with her and Steffie, he drove to Ronni's home. When he arrived, he could see that her car was parked under the carport, but she was nowhere in sight. After several minutes of knocking on the front door and ringing the doorbell, he inserted the key in the lock and stepped inside.

The first thing he noticed was a small mound of shopping bags dumped in the middle of the carpet. A pair of red espadrilles looked as though they'd been kicked off in a hurry, and as the air conditioner switched off, he realized there was another sound in the house—running water. She was in the shower.

Trying—unsuccessfully—to keep from smiling, he tiptoed across the carpet toward the bathroom. The door was wide open, and for a moment, he simply lingered in the doorway, listening to the sounds of her splashing in the shower. Then, almost without any conscious effort, he began prying loose the knot in his tie. He couldn't see her through the dark blue plastic curtain, but he could hear her moving around, and the thought of what she looked like nearly drove him wild. He'd taken off his trousers, but was wearing his shirt, his tie undone but still dangling around his neck, when she opened the shower curtain and let out a bloodcurdling scream.

Then she threw a wet washrag at him, cursing, "Damn you, Logan McNeil! You nearly scared me to death. What are you doing here?"

Her outburst startled him, stopping his hands in the middle of what they were doing—removing his underwear—so that now he stood before her with his briefs down around his knees.

"What does it look like I'm doing?" he retaliated dryly as he realized what a comic sight he must be. She slowly looked him over from head to foot, then met his gaze, noticing for the first time that he wasn't wearing the eye patch.

"Your eye... is it all right?" she asked hopefully.

"As right as rain," he replied with a grin. "Well, not exactly as right, but almost." He reached over into his suit jacket pocket and pulled out a pair of eyeglasses. "I'm supposed to wear these," he said, placing them on the bridge of his nose. "What do you think?"

"I think for a guy who has his underwear down around his knees they look pretty good."

They both laughed and he stepped out of his briefs.

Then the humor disappeared from his face, replaced by another emotion, one Ronni had longed to see for three weeks. "And I think you're even more beautiful than ever," he said as his eyes seemed to be savoring every inch of her.

"Oh, Logan, I've missed you so," she cried as she reached for him. Her fingers were trembling as she helped him undo the buttons on his shirt.

"I love you, Ronni, and I want to marry you," he whispered as he carelessly tossed aside the silk tie.

Ronni stopped and looked up at him. "What?"

He took both his hands in hers and kissed her fingertips. "I had planned on taking you out to dinner and proposing over champagne, but I have to know right now what your answer's going to be. Will you marry me, Ronni?" he asked again.

"Of course," she answered without hesitation, a grin lighting up her face.

"Of course," he repeated, lifting her off the floor. Then he carried her into her bedroom, where he deposited her in the middle of the bed. He sat down on the edge to remove the last of his clothing—his shoes and socks. Then he was lying beside her, holding her close as he said, "I need you... now and forever."

"And I need you," she returned softly, loving the feel of him as his weight pressed down on her. "I feel as though I always have and I always will."

He smiled at her, kissing her, caressing her, letting his hardness insinuate itself between them so that she could feel his desire for her. "I never thought I'd find what I've found in your arms," he murmured as his tongue tasted her hot flesh in its most sensitive places.

Then he was lying on top of her, covering her body with his strength, his warmth and his love. As exquisite pleasure drove all thought from her head, Ronni cried out, "Promise me this will never end."

"I'll love you forever, Ronni," he said on a ragged breath, his body emphasizing his words with its intimate rhythm.

Afterward they lay together, side by side, content with the silence, wanting to absorb being together after a long absence from each other, touching, comforting, appreciating.

"I've missed you, too," Logan said, pulling a sheet up around them when their bodies had finally cooled down. "I wanted to come when I heard about Peter, but it didn't work out."

"It's all right, Logan. I know how important your testimony was." She rested her head on his chest. "It's probably better that you didn't see me. I couldn't cry for him or feel any sort of loss. Somehow that doesn't seem right. Despite everything he did, he was still Steffie's father, yet I felt as though someone had told me a stranger had died."

"Did anyone ever tell you his story? I know you've heard how Andy and Smithson were involved, but what about Peter?" He gently played with her fingers. "I want you to know that I'll never lie to you, Ronni. If you ever want to know anything, all you have to do is ask."

"To be honest with you, Logan, I don't think I want to know. If he did it for money or for revenge—what does it matter now?"

"It doesn't. It's all over, and as I told you a long time ago, I never thought he was a subject worth talking about."

"Then let's not." She hugged him tightly. "I'm moving forward with my life. Steffie and I are making a new beginning."

"Does that new beginning include an overprotective, bossy beach bum?"

"Beach bum? Does this mean you're not going back to work for the CIA?" She looked up at him.

"What makes you think I'd want to?"

"Andrew hinted you might, and I talked to the senator."

"You called the senator?"

"No, he called me. He wanted to apologize for sicking you on me," she teased, planting a tiny kiss on his chin. "Actually he did apologize, He told me how he had suspected that I was Andrew's honey trap, and despite your protests in my defense, he continued to believe that right up until the time Smithson confessed."

"What he didn't expect was that we would get caught in a honey trap of our own." He cupped her face with his hands and kissed her.

"But this is more than a sexual seduction," she said throatily.

"Yes, it is," he agreed, nuzzling her neck. "Much, much more, which is why Doc called you. He knows how I feel about you."

"He also wanted to tell me a few things about you."

"Such as?"

She lay back against the pillow in an indolent pose. "Let's see," she drawled. "He said you have too keen of a sense of duty and responsibility and that you're a Soviet expert and that you help out with the Special Olympics every year."

"Sounds like you two had some conversation," Logan said dryly, not sure whether he appreciated Doc's words.

"He was very nice. I know why you're so fond of him, Logan. He's a fine man, and I can't help but feel sorry for him."

"It's been rough on him these past few weeks, but he's a tough old guy. Did he actually tell you I was going back into intelligence work?"

"I think he was hoping I could influence you."

"Is that what you want? For me to return to the Agency?" He leaned back and looked at her expectantly.

"Only if it's what you want. I could be happy passing out life jackets on the glass-bottom boat."

"What about raising corn in Kansas?"

"You want to return to the farm?"

He shook his head. "Despite my father's wildest dreams, I'll never be a farmer...or a tractor salesman. I have had a few job offers, but none of them in Florida, I'm afraid."

"I thought you knew by now that we're portable," she teased.

"You wouldn't mind leaving your job?" he asked, surprised by her easy acquiescence.

"After everything that's happened, it's probably simpler if I do. Melbourne is a relatively small community, and I'm not sure how people are going to respond when school resumes. There have to be other teaching positions—even in Kansas.

Wherever you are is where I want to be,'' she said, then punctuated her declaration with a kiss.

"Why is it that whenever you're beside me I feel as though all I need is the air that I breathe and to be with you?'' he whispered huskily.

"Because that's all that really does matter. Whether we're on a beach in Florida, a farm in Kansas or wherever. We're going to be happy, Logan,'' she said with a smile, then added softly, "trust me.''